PRAISE F
T

MW00809566

"This book will grab you and won't let go until you've reached the final page. And then it will leave you wanting more. You've been warned."

— *YA BOOKS CENTRAL*

"A rollicking and gripping romantic adventure that's a delightful read from beginning to end...an enjoyable fantasy tale readers will instantly love!"

— *IND'TALE MAGAZINE*

"Rich with raw emotion and timeless ideals of sacrifice and loyalty...more than just another tearjerker, this is a tale of hardship, second chances, and the power to change."

— *FOREWORD REVIEWS*

"A swashbuckling, romantic adventure story about a love that spans four centuries, Emmie and the Tudor King is an absolute pleasure."

— *CJ FLOOD, AWARD-WINNING AUTHOR*

"A fabulous, immersive love story...I loved this book and highly, highly recommend it when you have an entire day to devote to reading because you won't want to put it down."

— *JENNY HICKMAN, AUTHOR OF THE MYTHS OF AIRREN SERIES*

Emmie and the Tudor King, The Complete Trilogy, New Adult Special Edition Omnibus

Midnight Tide Publishing

www.midnighttidepublishing.com

For more information, please contact midnighttidepublishing@gmail.com

Published by Midnight Tide Publishing 2022.

Cover design: Deranged Doctor Design

ISBN for Paperback: 978-1-953238-99-3

ISBN for Hardcover: 978-1-953238-98-6

Contact the author at natalie@nataliemurrayauthor.com

For updates, sign up to Natalie Murray's newsletter at www.nataliemurrayauthor.com

AUTHOR NOTE

This special edition omnibus contains the New Adult editions of all three books in the Emmie and the Tudor King series: Emmie and the Tudor King, Emmie and the Tudor Queen, and Emmie and the Tudor Throne. Each book contains mature themes and adult content and may not be suitable for all audiences. Reader discretion is advised.

EMMIE AND THE TUDOR KING

THE COMPLETE TRILOGY

NEW ADULT SPECIAL EDITION OMNIBUS

Natalie Murray

Midnight Tide
PUBLISHING

EMMIE
AND THE
TUDOR KING

BOOK ONE

HISTORICAL TIMELINE

THE HOUSE OF TUDOR

England

1485 Henry Tudor defeats King Richard III at the Battle of Bosworth to end the Wars of the Roses. He founds the Tudor dynasty and becomes King Henry VII, before dying of tuberculosis at age fifty-two.

1509 Henry VII's second son is crowned King Henry VIII. He marries six times and executes two of his wives. During his reign, Henry VIII breaks from the Catholic Church and declares England Protestant so he can marry Anne Boleyn.

1547 Henry VIII's longed-for son becomes King Edward VI at age nine and rules England for six years. Aged just sixteen, he dies of disputed causes.

1553 In a Protestant plot to prevent the throne passing to Edward's Catholic sister Mary Tudor, Henry VIII's distant relative

Lady Jane Grey is proclaimed queen for nine days and is never crowned. She is executed along with her conspirators.

1553 Mary Tudor wins succession to become Queen Mary I. Her persecution of English Protestants earns her the nickname 'Bloody Mary'. She dies childless, aged forty-two.

1558 Mary's half-sister Elizabeth fights off succession claims by her Catholic cousin Mary, Queen of Scots and is crowned Queen Elizabeth I. She cements Protestantism in England and rules the nation for forty-five years. Elizabeth dies unmarried with no heirs, despite a suspected romance with the Earl of Leicester, Robert Dudley.

Or not.

What if Queen Elizabeth I married her beloved Robert Dudley and gave birth to a son in 1560? A son that would become the last, and most notorious, Tudor monarch of all…

Nicholas the Ironheart.

I have both wagered love and land
Your love and good-will for to have.

Lady Greensleeves,
author unknown

1

HE HAD ONE OF THOSE NAMES THAT SPELLED TERROR. *NICHOLAS THE Ironheart.* Like Jack the Ripper or Vlad the Impaler. Cue chills and my groan when my history teacher, Mrs. Campbell, handed out papers about him a month before high school was due to finish forever. Couldn't we just watch *The Other Boleyn Girl* for some Tudor history?

Mrs. Campbell slapped a sheet onto my design sketchbook, her floral sleeve reeking of cigarettes. "Is the nickname 'Nicholas the Ironheart' justified for King Nicholas the First?" she announced, like none of us could read.

Ugh. All I knew about the sixteenth-century Tudor king was that he was a prized ass and the grandson of the infamous head-chopper, Henry the Eighth. In fact, I was pretty sure the Tudors were all a bunch of psychos.

Mrs. Campbell leaned against her cluttered desk, eyeballing me the way most Americans did whenever there was a British topic. Because I'd spent the first half of my life living in England and couldn't shake the accent, it was supposed to make me an expert on things like tea, cricket, and British monarchs. Never mind that I'd called America home for nine years now. Campbell should've read the memo by now. History was *not* my thing.

"Work in pairs with whomever you like," the teacher added.

Cheers erupted, a celebratory pen flying from Logan Hunter's fingers. I swapped a smirk with my best friend Mia, who happened to be the smartest girl in the class.

On our way to the lunch cafeteria, Mia pitched ideas to me about why King Nicholas the First wasn't really a heartless savage. We slid into our usual corner beside the vending machines.

"I think you're confusing him with that other king, Nicholas the Wonderful," I mocked, trying not to lose control of a slippery slice of pizza. "I'm pretty sure this guy killed a whole bunch of people."

"We'll get a better mark if we prove an unexpected angle," Mia argued like it was non-negotiable, and it pretty much was. Mia did everything better than me, starting with her ridiculously perfect eyebrows and silky black hair, gifts from her mother. My mom had given me hair that didn't know whether it wanted to be blonde or brown, curly or straight, and my grandpa once said my eyes looked like ripening olives, which is a weird thing to compare eyes to.

"Happy Pizza Day, queens."

Josh Street dropped a plate of pepperoni beside Mia's homemade tofu noodles. He sneaked in a quick kiss on Mia's lips, and I pretended to gag. Before they'd hooked up at Avery Pearce's Christmas party, the three of us had been best mates. Now Mia and Josh were a cringe-worthy rom-com. Despite that, I'd long forgiven them for making me the third wheel.

"Happy day of birth," I said through a smile, sliding Josh a crumpled packet. He pressed the gift lovingly to his *Labyrinth* movie T-shirt before tearing it open. A bracelet made from odd-sized hex nuts fell into his palm.

"A man-bangle. A mangle! Thanks, English." He clipped the bracelet over his pine tree tattoo.

"It's kind of weird," I admitted.

"I think it's your best design yet," said Mia, straightening her designer watch. "You should've used it for your application."

I scrunched my face. I was already late in applying to Central Saint Martins in London—one of the best design colleges in the world. For them to even consider me for their jewelry course, I needed to design something beyond epic. Something way better than a bunch of hex nuts strung together. I pushed away my pizza.

Mia was huffing to Josh about our unexpected Nicholas the Iron-heart assignment. It meant they had to shelve their weekend plans for his birthday, which was kind of a drag, given his mom was in rehab.

Josh's thick brows pointed downward. "But I dropped my recording session, even though I'm, like, minutes from finishing my EP."

"So un-cancel it."

"Right, because the studio's sitting around waiting for my call?" He pretended to put a phone to his ear. "Hey, this is Josh Street. I'll be there in seven minutes, and I'd like the room cleared of pink tortilla chips. Oh, and I expect shower shoes made from unicorn tears."

Mia whacked his arm and spun to me. "Come over after school? Mom's making *xiaolongbao* for dinner. We can work on the essay."

"Those dumplings with the hot soup inside? I'm already on my way." If we worked on the essay tonight, I'd have the weekend free to scan thrift stores for old jewelry pieces I could rework for the Central Saint Martins application.

After school, I strolled home via the local rest home to pick up my pay slip and tell Mom I was having dinner at Mia's. She was glad, having just started her night shift. I helped her clean Mrs. Horne's bedsore and hurried home to change.

Our house was a two-story clapboard with a decaying wraparound verandah and no dishwasher, but it was the biggest place we'd rented anywhere. I filled the dog bowl with fresh kibble and scooped up Ruby for a quick cuddle before changing into my favorite white sundress. I scanned the jewelry hanger I'd built from hooks and pegboard and chose a synthetic jade pendant I made when I was fifteen.

It took seven months of living in Hatfield, Massachusetts (other-wise known as the back-end-of-nowhere), before I discovered I could get to Mia's faster by crossing the field behind our house. I clicked my tongue at the dusty old horses that inhabited the field, but they didn't flinch. They were nothing like Bonnie, the friendly mare Dad let me ride back when we lived by the English seaside in Essex. "*Easy, Emme-line!*" he'd shout as my nine-year-old legs squeezed the horse to a canter. When Mom and I moved to Hatfield, I waited for years for Dad to visit so I could show him the horses behind our house.

My naive faith in him still made me cringe.

As I neared Bayberry Street, the chaotic grass shortened to uniform blades. Nurtured white roses sprouted along the curb. Across the road, my classmate Avery Pearce's mom was wiping down her bay windows that faced Jane Stuart's junkyard. Mrs. Pearce liked to remind everyone that Jane's junkyard was the sole reason Bayberry Street wasn't featured in any magazine spreads.

But today, Jane Stuart's broken furniture, wheel-less bicycles, rusted appliances, and tangled cables were sorted into ordered piles. A folding table full of trinkets stood beside a cardboard sign stating *YARD SALE: Must Sell Today!*

"There's plenty left; we close at sundown!" called a woman with spiky red hair. The words *Community Cleanup Care* stretched across her tight T-shirt.

I hurried to the table and dug through cheap synthetic pearls and vintage watches, but I found nothing suitable to rework into an application piece for Central Saint Martins in London. My chest sank, and I hoped the thrift stores would have something. Otherwise, I was never getting accepted or ever getting out of Hatfield.

The woman fished a ring from the pile. "It's a touch flashy for me, but you young girls love these sorts of things, don't you?"

I took the ring from her palm, feeling my breath catch. A giant synthetic blue table-cut diamond sat centered on a band of gold, haloed by imitation rosette rubies. The ring was so brilliant I actually thought it could be real. I didn't have a loupe to magnify it, but when I blew on the stones, they didn't fog. I rubbed the edge against the table, but it didn't scratch.

"How about ten bucks?" The lady gripped her hips.

"But this is…I mean, is Mrs. Stuart okay to sell this?"

"The Council ordered Jane Stuart to ditch everything that doesn't sell today. If you're feeling kind, you can give me five dollars, or I'll have the ring back. My niece might like it for her dress-up box." She held out her hand.

My fingers closed around the heavy gold band. There were a

thousand ways I could rework it into a piece so worthy of Central Saint Martins that they'd roll out a red carpet for me.

I pressed a five-dollar bill into the lady's palm and slipped the ring onto my thumb.

When I looked up, Jane Stuart was watching me from behind her screen door. Her wild white hair and pale skin made her look like a ghost.

Guilt pinched my chest as I quickly strode away toward Mia's iron gate. There was no way the old hoarder Jane Stuart could have a ring worth millions of dollars. It had to be a fake, in spite of my breath and scratch tests saying otherwise.

I always felt I should tiptoe up the curved staircase and along the corridor of Chinese silk paintings that led to Mia's bedroom. She emptied a mound of books about Nicholas the Ironheart onto her bed, which smelled like the spa in Springfield she took me to for my eighteenth birthday a few months ago. I groaned at the thought of studying on a Friday night and kicked off my sandals, hearing the patter of rain against the balcony door. Mrs. Fairbanks's restaurant-worthy Shanghai dumplings and salted duck warmed my stomach.

"Play *Say You'll Stay* again," said Mia. "It makes me miss falling in love."

"Yikes, that was fast. You and Josh just got together."

"You know what I mean," she sighed. "Those first days when you can't sleep or eat."

I opened my laptop and clicked on Atomic's mesmerizing new track. Truthfully, I had no idea what Mia was going on about. I'd had a few dates, kissed a few frogs, fooled around with a couple of guys, but I'd never experienced anything close to love, at least the way Mia described it. I twisted the ring on my thumb. When I'd graduated design college and had an internship with a top jewelry designer… that's when I'd think about a boyfriend.

Mia scooted onto her knees. "I forgot to tell you. I saw Logan and

Avery last night buying Garden Party tickets. They were totally butting heads over whether to get one- or two-day passes."

Garden Party was an annual music festival in Northampton, and this year Atomic was headlining.

"Sounds epic," I said sarcastically.

"Shut *up*, it was one of those fights you have right before you break up. When you're totally over the other person's shit."

I just chuckled, choosing not to read much into this. It had taken me a year to get over my missed chance with Logan Hunter, but if he really was breaking up with Avery Pearce, it was way too late for me to care. If I didn't get into Central Saint Martins, I intended to make use of my British passport and move to London anyway. There was something about that city that made me feel like I belonged there, probably because I'd lived there for a while when I was a kid. I couldn't think of any other reason to explain it.

Mia snorted at her phone. "Uncle Pete's making Josh play backgammon."

Her fingers flew over the keyboard, her eyes doing that 'Josh thing' they did nowadays.

I exhaled and grabbed a library book titled *History's Monsters: Nicholas the Ironheart*.

Yawning, I scanned the introduction.

Nicholas I of England (1 June 1560—18 November 1599) was the son of Queen Elizabeth I and Robert Dudley, Earl of Leicester. When Queen Elizabeth died at the age of 39 while giving birth to her daughter Catherine, Nicholas was crowned King of England at the age of 12. The early years of his reign were peaceful, until his eight-year-old sister was murdered in 1580 under mysterious circumstances. The 20-year-old king's reprisal was harsh. King Nicholas slayed thousands of suspected Catholics, believed to be in retribution for Catherine's death. The reign of terror continued for nearly two decades, earning the Tudor king his famous epithet 'Nicholas the Ironheart'.

I flipped to the pictures, pausing on a portrait I'd seen before. The date had the king at nineteen years of age, but he looked twice that. He was flabby and dour-faced, with a feathered flat cap and navy coat draped with a thick gold chain. His mouth was a thin straight line through his dark beard, his eyes as cold and blue as an Alaskan lake.

Mia's phone hit the cushion. "Josh is getting boring. We should start."

After a monotonous hour of reading, Mia pushed *play* on a documentary she'd downloaded about Nicholas the Ironheart while I snuggled under her alpaca bedspread. Her earlier argument that the young king was more misunderstood than merciless had just started to make sense when the images turned darker. Paintings of decomposing bodies in London streets dissolved into drawings of Catholics being hanged. The narrator described a ravage of the nation that plunged England into poverty and civil war.

I leaned into Mia, who snored in my ear.

"Mia!" I whispered. Typical. She'd never once made the New Year's Eve countdown. The screen filled with the same famous portrait from the book. The camera close-up traveled along the king's grim face and down his wide velvet sleeve to his right hand clutching a gold-tipped sword. My stomach hit the floor as I focused on the ring flashing from his third finger.

The center stone was a deep-blue table-cut diamond, circled with rosette rubies.

When the image changed, I grabbed the book I'd had earlier and thumbed back to the portrait. I compared the ring on my thumb with the one on Nicholas the Ironheart's finger. Every detail was identical.

"Mia!" I hissed, but she didn't stir.

I switched off the documentary, my heart pounding, and clicked on a romantic comedy from Mia's movie library. But I barely looked at the screen, my eyes firmly glued to the ring on my hand. How could I have bought a replica of some mad king's ring on the same day we landed an essay about him? It was too creepy. I pulled the bedspread over my legs, the window shuddering with rain.

Just as the movie couple was about to kiss, my eyelids filled with lead. Blackness drifted into my vision, intense images appearing like flashcards...heads on stakes, glittering rings, and deep, sea-blue eyes.

The pain was indescribable. It slapped me awake, shooting from my thigh and right up my back. I rolled sideways, my teeth clenching. Something thin and hard was sticking out of my leg.

"By Christ, it is a lady," said an approaching male voice.

When I tried to speak, a moan came out, dirt crumbling off my lips. Leaves fluttered across a cloudy sky above me.

"Who in the devil's name are you?" The man's accent was English, and he had the rasp of a smoker.

"Please, help." I strained to sit up but something sharp jabbed my chest. I blinked to focus on the gleaming tip of an impossibly long sword. The man holding it was straddling a smoky-black horse, his lace-up ginger coat right out of a storybook. A long bow hung from his broad shoulder.

I touched the stem of a wooden arrow skewering the edge of my thigh. *Oh my God. This medieval-obsessed nutcase has hit me with his bow and arrow!*

"You shot me," I said angrily.

The man leapt off his horse and brought a muddy heel down onto the arrow. My full-bodied scream echoed in the trees.

"I said *who are you*, whore?" he barked. "How did you get in here?"

"Stop, barbarian!" cried a second Englishman, galloping on horse-back through the dense trees. He was small and skinny, but his voice was deep, like a radio announcer's. "You shot a lady?" he asked the first man, his eyes widening at me.

"Shut your gob! Does she look like a lady to you in that scant nightgown? And who says it was my arrow? Sober as a pike, you still cannot shoot for snails."

The two of them began arguing over me about shots, arrows, and who'd find us first. I tried to speak, but I was incoherent, my legs beginning to shake. Where was I? Where was my mom?

"Please...an ambulance," I murmured, pins and needles spiking up my leg. My cheeks felt wet, but I didn't remember crying. *Stay with it, Emmie. What would Mom say to do? To stabilize the wound and get help. Don't even think about pulling the arrow out yourself.*

I fumbled the scratchy ground, but the only cloth I had was my white dress. My feet were bare, the blades of grass like ice between my toes. My hair was matted with sweat, and I couldn't feel my throat.

The petite guy dismounted and squatted beside me, pointing a birdlike finger at the sparkling ring on my thumb. "Where did you get this, mistress?"

"Is that?" grunted the meaner one.

"I believe so."

They started on about the details of Jane Stuart's ring like a pair of fashion critics.

Jane Stuart's ring. Mia's house. Studying. Nicholas the Ironheart. What the hell is going on?

My vision dimmed. I could just make out a small lake about fifteen feet away as a bug whizzed past my eye.

The bigger guy hunched over me, his hair shockingly red. "Who gave you this, girl?"

"Brother, if she is known to him, we are in a storm of trouble."

"How could she be, pigeon? Look at her!"

A leathery hand gripped my thumb and yanked the ring right off.

"Patience, brother. It would be expected of us to handle this with care."

"Fool! She is a trespasser and a thief! He would want her arrested, not paraded in like an honored guest."

Scuffling broke out beside me before they both froze. "By Christ, they are catching up."

Fingers dug into my arms and hauled me upward. I collapsed over a man's lap, groaning with pain. A horse grunted and jolted to life beneath us. My heart pounded against the snarling redhead's thigh, and I started to moan.

He thrust his boot into the animal's gut. "I will take her to the Tower myself. Inform Warwick," he grumbled.

"You cannot arrest her to get out of shooting her!"

We quickly accelerated to a gallop, whipping wind drowning out the elfin man's shrieks behind us.

Through the agonizing bounces and sickening nausea, all I could make out around me was a giant sandy-colored wall with towering turrets that bobbed in my vision. Thunder ignited the sky as we galloped past white buildings crossed with black beams, horses and carts, and whirring bodies in hats and coats. I turned my nose away from the horse's musty hip, sickened by its smell. When the skies burst open above us, I couldn't see anything anymore except splashing mud.

I might've passed out until my eyes opened to the sound of grating metal. A man in a black cloak and stiff cap hovered nearby, waiting under a portcullis. My teeth chattered like a snare drum. This was the worst, most real dream I'd ever had.

My kidnapper dragged me off the horse, covering my mouth when I cried out in pain. Everything hurt—my chest, my throat, my thigh. He slung me over his muscular shoulder, the pebbled ground swinging in my vision.

"Caught trespassing at the Parkside and in possession of crown property," he announced to the man. "I trust you can handle the injury."

"Certainly, my lord."

I whimpered as I was swapped to a smaller shoulder that smelled like herbs. I strained to see how high the whitewashed stone wall reached before the second man carried me through a doorway and into a passage faintly lit with torchlights. We headed down the narrow corridor and up two spiral staircases before he spiled me onto a table that reeked of blood.

There was just enough light to make out a creepy-faced man with monkey ears and a black hood gaping at me. The room felt like it had no air.

"Please," I whispered, gasping through sobs. "Don't hurt me."

I didn't realize he was touching my wound until I heard my own screams. He shoved a vinegary cloth into my mouth that made me gag. The last thing I felt was the arrow ripping through my flesh before a black wall smashed me in the face.

A distant shriek shook me awake. I was sitting slumped against a stone wall in a different room to the one I'd passed out in earlier. Above me, light streamed thinly from a single arched window with intersecting iron bars. The stone floor was brushed with hay, the only furniture a narrow wooden bed and a table splattered with candle wax. My white dress was gone, and I'd been changed into a stained linen smock.

I roared for help but heard only my echo. *Why is this nightmare still going on? Have I gone insane?*

I struggled to stand, unbearable pain tearing down my leg. There were two small holes in my skin that had been cleaned, but without any dressing or stitches. Thank God the arrow hadn't had a barb on its end.

Squeezing my thigh to apply pressure to hopefully keep the bleeding from starting again, I limped to the locked wooden door. A faint scream rebounded from the other side.

I hobbled back to the window and climbed onto a stool. What awaited me beyond the iron bars could've turned my hair white. A jumbled mass of short timber buildings punctuated with sharp spires and smoky chimneys gathered on both sides of a wide river. Ships from a maritime museum swerved their cream sails on the choppy water.

It took me several minutes to figure out it was London, but the London from an olden-day painting or history book about knights and castles. Nausea crept into my face, and my legs wobbled.

I climbed off the chair and inhaled slowly and deeply to settle my asthma, retching into the stench of sewage drifting from a hole in the floor. I had an open wound in a room littered with rat poop and soiled hay. It was a fast track to gangrene and death.

A thump came from the door, my breath stilling. The iron handle grated as it turned, sending my back shivering against the freezing stone wall inscribed with Latin graffiti. My arms shook all the way down to my fingers.

A young man stepped in, barely visible in the waning light. His coat was the color of blackberry jam and patterned with bright red ovals. A heavy gold chain hung across his shoulders, dark chocolate curls spiraling elegantly around his neck. He dropped a silver plate of cherries onto the table, unsettling the dust.

"Where am I?" I stammered.

"In a considerable amount of trouble." A severe black goatee spoiled his otherwise not-ugly face.

"Who are you?" I asked.

His brows slanted downward. "I am Francis Beaumont, the Earl of Warwick. And you are in the Tower of London, accused of threatening the King's Majesty."

I could've laughed. Mom and Dad had paraded me around the Tower of London the day before we moved back to America. It was a tourist destination.

"This amuses you." His glove brushed the gold handle of his sword. "How did you get inside the park, wench?"

The word sent me back a step. "It's Emmie. I mean...which park?"

He launched himself toward me with a slow stride.

"Your mode of speech, your dress, your manner are curious and common. But your hair, your teeth, your skin suggest you are of means. The only conceivable explanation is you are a spy. Which harebrain are you working for? Is it the Spanish?" His pitch-black eyes were accusing.

"Please," I said, my heart beating into my throat. I inhaled deeply, trying to speak clearly. "The truth is, you've mixed me up with someone else. I was in a forest when a guy shot me with an arrow. There were two of them. They said they were brothers, but they didn't look anything alike, and then one of them brought me here. I have no idea why. Please—my wound, it needs proper treatment!"

He shook with laughter, his breath scented with wine.

"The entertainment is tawdry, but appreciated. Now I strongly suggest you confess to your crimes, or you will be punished without delay. His Majesty does not take well to traitors or spies."

"I couldn't care less about your king!"

An arm snapped out, black leather crushing my throat. He smelled of cherries and horses.

"Do not believe I have ruled out torture. Shall we begin with the Cat's Paw or the Scavenger's Daughter?"

Fireworks burst inside my eyes as footsteps charged through the door. The man released his grip so fast that I hit the floor, coughing into the stench of urine.

The jailer's tone was gruff. "Milord, I 'ave not received the proper authority—"

"Get out," Francis snarled at him.

The silver plate clashed like a cymbal inches from my ear, sending cherries scampering across the stone ground. The earl crushed them with his charcoal leather boots.

"You are hereby charged with trespassing and high treason," he spat over me. "You will be sentenced to death by the axe or the rope at His Majesty's pleasure. I do look forward to seeing your face again. At the bottom of a bucket."

The door banged shut, closing in my pleas for him to help me. I doubled over, almost convulsing as I sobbed. I hadn't cried like this since we left London. Mr. Whitecotton, my English teacher, would've called that ironic.

My leg jolted, my eyes springing open. The jailer was leaning over me, grinning in the moonlight through a wiry beard and four teeth.

"Get away!" I cried.

When I thrashed my arms, he squeezed my wounded thigh until I screamed. "We do not get many like you in 'ere. You some manner of strumpet?"

He crawled right on top of me, the straw mattress prickling my back beneath his weight. When he held my arms down and pushed his beer-soaked tongue into my mouth, I bit down as hard as I could. He screeched, blood spilling into his beard.

In one movement, he tore me from the bed and shoved me against the wall. "You fink you the first beast we seen in 'ere?"

He whipped the rope from his belt and tied me to an iron hook in the floor, knotting the rope around my bleeding thigh. The pain was too paralyzing for me to fight back.

"It need not be our weddin' night," he slurred as he barged out, locking the door behind him. I clasped my aching jaw, tears and blood mingling in my mouth. I lay there shaking, sinking in and out of consciousness to the bizarre sound of a distant lion's roar, until another clang shocked my eyes open.

The cell was bathed in the auburn glow of morning. A rat surfaced from the hay and darted into a hole in the wall.

A gentle cough drew my eyes to the doorway and the person I hadn't heard come in.

A young man stood there, his light eyes pinned to mine. His outfit was so grand that it belonged on someone older, but he owned every inch of the navy coat geometrically woven with sky-blue ribbon. A brilliant sapphire shone from the center of his stark-white collar. As attractive as the outfit was, it didn't hold a candle to his face. He was beyond handsome, his chestnut hair sitting up with the perfect mix of rockiness and curl. I wanted to look away, but his magnetic gaze had mine locked.

He walked toward me and crouched, black leather boots rising to his knees. When he reached for my smock, I scrambled backward.

He held a hand out to reassure me, his middle finger circled with a cabochon emerald the size of a lime. "Be calm." His voice was a soft command.

For some reason, I let him slowly tug up my smock, uncovering my bare legs, until he paused at my trembling thigh. His warm fingers met my skin and tilted the bloodstained rope into the light. A line formed across his brow before he gently guided my chin upward, scanning my injured mouth. Up close, his eyes were a clear bluish-green, like the color of aquamarines. Then they narrowed and flared with anger.

He rose back up and marched to the door, flinging it open like he was royally pissed off. Two men in crimson coats stiffened as the young man passed by them, returning quickly. He had the jailer by the collar and kicked him toward me with his boot.

"She attacked me," the jailer stuttered to him.

When I tried to protest, the jailer thrust his swollen tongue out as proof. The men in the red coats drew their swords, but the young man flung his palm out to stop them.

"Release her, before I slice off what is left of that tongue," he commanded to the jailer, resting his hand on the gold tip of his sword.

The jailer's hands shook like jelly in an earthquake as he crouched before me and tore the rope off my wound. I cried out, seeing stars.

"Gently!" added my rescuer through clenched teeth. The jailer's forehead glistened as he slowed his wobbly movements until the bloodied rope dropped to the floor. Sweat slid down my cheeks as the young man turned to face the red-coated men.

"Hold him. And bring her something to eat, for Christ's sake. Tell Master Carey I will speak with him." He sighed heavily.

The jailer backed out of the cell, chased by the two attendants.

The handsome young man and I were alone.

2

HE LEANED AGAINST THE WOODEN TABLE, LOOKING LIKE AN IMAGE from a historical-themed photoshoot.

"You do not look much like a stag," he said, one corner of his mouth quirking up ever so slightly.

I just stared at him like an idiot.

He coughed and stepped forward. "Forgive me, that was indecent of me. Can you rise?"

It hit me that I was free to move. I braced my palms against the icy stone and tried to stand, but every limb felt locked with pain. When I glanced up, the young man was crouching beside me.

"Get away," I snapped. I'd graduated from terrified to anger beyond all reason. There were laws against false imprisonment!

He took a swift step back and frowned. "You have clearly been mishandled. Some food and wine should clear your mind. Be assured that my presence is no cause for alarm. I was merely calling upon Master Carey when I received word of your circumstance. At first, I did not believe what I was hearing."

"That I was shot with an arrow, locked up for no reason, nearly raped by a guard, and left with a festering wound?" If Mom had heard my tone, she'd have said I was back to my usual self. My head felt like an exploding furnace.

He huffed and dropped in front of me again, his breath like fresh mint.

"The jailer will be handled. I detest to say the entire incident smacks of the idiocy I'm surrounded with at present." He raked his fingers through his hair, only encouraging its hot ruggedness. "You plainly deserve proper investigation, which I will supply. You need not despair."

No matter what baffling, adult words came from his pretty mouth, he could've sold wood to a forest. My jaw loosened a little.

A knock at the door brought his hand to his sword. One of the attendants entered and quickly placed a tray of pewter serving platters onto the grimy table.

"Leave us," the young man said to him. He stood up and blinked down at me. "Breakfast?"

My starvation sent me to my feet, pain pulsing down my thigh and sending a hiss through my teeth. Before I knew what was happening, the guy's strong arm had slipped through mine to steady me, our shoulders nearly touching.

"Forgive me," he said to the floor.

He helped me to the table, smelling of something sweet and familiar I couldn't put my finger on. Something tugged inside me when he stepped away.

He lifted a gray lid, releasing a waft of Thanksgiving, and loaded me up a plate of roasted chicken, bread with cheese, and what might've been stewed cabbage. It took proper effort to sit without stumbling.

"What's for lunch then, a blue whale?" I said awkwardly, hunting for a fork, but there weren't any.

His face caught between a smile and a frown as he poured liquid from a flask. "It seems that merely the sight of food is enough to return your strength. That pleases me. You say you are from Hertfordshire?"

I picked up a greasy chicken leg. "Hatfield. For a few more months, anyway."

But he just looked at me like we'd said the same thing as he handed me a cold pewter goblet.

Hang on, I've heard of Hertfordshire.

My mind took a second to pin down the memory. When we lived in England, Mom, Dad, and I had visited an old town north of London called Hatfield, which was in Hertfordshire. Dad did research near there for his history doctorate.

And then I got it. These lunatics had me figured as a girl from Hatfield, Hertfordshire, *England.* Confirmed by the accent I was suddenly lucky to still have.

"That's right," I stumbled through vinegary lips. "I'm from Hatfield in Hertfordshire."

As he crossed the light streaming from the window, I noticed a light scar running down his cheek, which was partly obscured by a light layering of scruff.

He shifted back into the shadow, crossing those bulky arms of his that I was doing my level best not to stare at.

"Your name?" he asked.

"Emmie. Well, technically, Emmeline Eleanor Grace. *Emmie Ellie,* I know…if you call me that, I might have to lock *you* up in here."

A cough burst from his mouth so suddenly, I thought he was choking. But his intense eyes sparkled, studying me.

"You speak rashly. And your name is not familiar. You are not of distinguished birth, I presume?"

I stared at him blankly.

"Are you of the nobility or the gentry, Mistress Grace?"

"My father is a very distinguished doctor in Hatfield."

Emmie. Stop saying things.

He nodded, looking out the window and affording me a longer look at his lovely profile. "I admire physicians," he said. "What is his name?"

"Martin Grace…*Doctor* Martin Grace."

Okay, so technically my dad had a history doctorate rather than a medical one, but this was turning out much better than the truth I'd tried with that psychotic earl, Francis Beaumont. I took a sip from the goblet and nearly choked on warm wine. For the first time since this nightmare began, I could breathe without wanting to puke.

He continued to probe me with blunt, solemn-faced questions, my energy returning with every bite. He asked me how I got into the park grounds and why I had no luggage or "horse", as he put it. I made up a vague story about being in London to visit my uncle and finding my way into the park by mistake. He actually seemed to believe everything that came from my mouth, promising to punish the "dimwitted" guards who'd missed my unintended entry. My performance would've even impressed Mia, especially given the audience. "Get it, girl," she'd have said with a wink. Give Mia a life-threatening situation and she'd still find the romance.

He stood up, tidying his magnificent coat. "You will come to court."

"You mean like a trial?" I dropped my wine cup, which was just as well. I was getting woozy.

"I am beginning to feel you have not stepped out of Hertfordshire too many times, Mistress Grace. Court at Whitehall. I will issue a conditional pardon until we receive corroboration from your uncle. Where may he be reached?"

"Actually, he left London yesterday." My throat stuck like glue. "He had to go to France."

"He knows not where you are?" Lines crossed his brow. "I suppose I could send word to Hatfield. In the meantime, I will inform the court that you are visiting Whitehall with permission from your father. Once your identity is verified, you will be free to go."

I nodded before I could think, my stomach tying itself in knots. There were so many ways this could go wrong. But if time wouldn't wake me from this hellish dream, maybe a sharp blow to the neck would. I shivered.

The young man's eyes swept across my bare legs, his throat bobbing, before he headed for the door. "You will wait here for appropriate dress and transportation. Master Carey will be well informed. Good morrow to you, Mistress Grace."

Panic swiped at me. "You're leaving me here?"

He stopped mid-stride, his lips falling open a little. "If you are asking if I will be personally accompanying you to Whitehall, then perhaps you are in need of rest before you are fit to travel." He glanced at the sagging mattress in the corner. "I shall have a new bed brought in at once."

He looked at me like he was waiting for something before he frowned and gave the door a single tap with his knuckle. It opened immediately, revealing an attendant standing at attention.

The young man's angelic face steeled. "No further harm is to come to the girl. On pain of death." The attendant swallowed so hard I could hear it from where I sat.

The door shut with a bang, sending a draft barreling through the cell. I draped the blanket over my shoulders, finally figuring out the scent that followed this guy everywhere. A smell that took me right back to Bayberry Street in the spring.

It was roses.

It was impossible to tell how much time passed while I counted the forty-seven sailboats crossing the Thames like a superhighway, my forehead resting against the iron bars.

I couldn't help but think the words...*time travel.*

The idea was so bonkers, like something out of a kids' movie, yet I couldn't explain how else I was here. I'd thought it was a dream, but I'd already fallen asleep several times and woken up in the same place. Plus, I'd never known a dream to last so long or to feel so real.

But...TIME TRAVEL, Emmie? Really?

Two boys in breeches burst through the door, breaking my thoughts. They hastily carried out the bed, replacing it with a spotless wooden frame and a mattress that smelled like freshly cut hay.

After they left, I perched on the edge to rest my throbbing thigh, my brain feeling like mashed potatoes. If I'd legitimately time traveled —I still wanted to slap myself for even thinking it—how did it happen? In all the stories I'd heard, there was a tool that made the person pass through time: a portal, a magic door, a sacred poem. I hadn't done or said anything strange at Mia's; even the movie I'd put on was banal. The only connection I had between this place and my own was…the blue-diamond ring.

My whole body trembled, my legs like water. I squeezed my bare thumb, worrying where the ring could be, when the door swung open with a creak.

The impish guy from the park stepped in, his small hand clutching a canvas sack. I stumbled upright, fear swooping through me as I looked for his brother, but the hostile redhead wasn't with him.

The man offered me a small bow. "Mistress Grace, I beg your pardon for this misunderstanding. My brother, Lord Lansbury, was already reprimanded for his impulsive actions. Take your time to change." He handed me the bag and closed the door behind him, his protruding ears as red as his cheeks.

Inside the sack was a thick velvet dress the color of pale-pink ballet slippers and edged with fraying champagne lace. I brought it to my nose, inhaling its lavender scent. The bottom of the sack held a pair of satin shoes, a white square of fabric, and a billowy clover-green cloak. I hadn't been to a fancy-dress party since my friend Gemma's fifteenth birthday in San Diego—two days before Mom moved us to Western Massachusetts.

This dress came in pieces and didn't fit that well, but I was finally warm, fiddling with the ribbon at the front until I figured out how to lace it up. The skirt was long and full, the sleeves tight to the elbow where they fanned outward. I laced up the shoes, which were also a size too big but wearable, with a short heel. As I combed the tangles from my hair with my fingers, I had the weirdest wish that the hot guy with the amazing eyes would come back and catch me dressed like a cut-price Cinderella.

But when I rapped on the door, the elfin man stepped back in, frowning. "Do you require assistance with your coif, mistress?"

"My coif? Always."

He gently tied the white fabric over my hair like a bandana, hiding my ponytail.

"Thanks," I said sheepishly.

He held the cloak open for me. "Your barge is waiting."

I stepped into the cloak and followed him into a slim corridor, burying my nose in the fabric to block the smell of beer and urine. I kept my head low as we passed several whiskered guards, my stomach curling, but none were the rapist jailer.

After descending two circular staircases, we stepped outside into blinding sunlight. I covered my eyes and climbed down onto a dock sloshing with pungent seawater. Bobbing below a raised portcullis was a wooden rowboat with two oarsmen, one whacking pigeons away with his feathered cap.

"This barge will take you to Whitehall," said my sonorous-voiced minder. "The tide is now favorable."

"You're not coming?" I heard the fear in my voice as I stepped onto the rotting deck. The man took a shaky step backward.

"I have king's business to attend to in London." His voice lowered. "You are known to His Majesty, mistress?"

"No way." I hadn't forgotten Francis's threats of torture just because I'd offended his great king.

"I assure you, I offer my hand in friendship. I have known the king since I was a babe." His sight line shifted to my bare thumb. "If there is anything I may assist you with at court, know I am at hand. Sir Mathew Fox."

"Emmie Grace." I gave him a small smile.

Mathew dipped his head. "Good morrow to you, mistress." He signaled to the boatmen, and we glided from the shore, waves tossing themselves at the bow. I sat and gripped the bench like a life raft before spinning to face the land.

The Tower of London loomed in a farewell wave, its onion-shaped turrets higher and whiter than I remembered. Seagulls swooped overhead and foul-smelling saltwater sprayed my shoes. We were on some kind of liquid interstate, sailboats crossing between wharfs leading to muddles of black-and-white buildings with slanted red roofs. The howling wind muffled the oarsmen's chatter as I sat higher in my seat, trying to work out whether the spiked turret in the distance was the old St. Paul's Cathedral. I spotted a tangle of pikes topped with balls jutting from the southern end of a Gothic bridge like olives on cocktail sticks. When I squinted, I realized each ball was a decapitated human head.

I dropped and breathed into my thighs, gulping air infected with fish and sewage. *What is happening to me?*

When I looked up again, an enormous high brick wall was heading right for us, flags of red, blue, and gold whipping in the wind. The castle seemed to stretch on forever as we sailed toward the wharf, boys in flat caps grasping ropes in readiness.

Three figures in billowy dresses stood gathered at the end of a raised dock. I hopped off the boat and slowly climbed the stairs to approach them, the ground still swimming beneath me.

A woman in a high-necked gown stepped forward, an ebony hood framing three neat rows of gray curls above her ears. A diamond centipede necklace with rubies for eyes circled her collar.

"Mistress Emmeline Grace?" Her voice was croaky; her accent right out of a posh costume drama.

"Actually, it's just Emmie," I replied with a nervous wobble.

Her white-powdered cheeks barely moved. "Good morrow to you. I am Margaret Beaumont, the Countess of Warwick. I have been requested to welcome you to court."

"*Dowager* Countess," breathed a girl behind her with olive skin and dark wavy hair that flowed to her waist.

The countess didn't seem to hear her, presenting me with a weathered hand that smelled like potpourri. Her bumpy gold ring nipped my finger as she squeezed. "Henceforth, you will call me Madam. May I present my daughter, the Lady Isobel Beaumont." She gestured to a stony-faced girl with wheaten hair beautifully plaited under a pearled hood. "And this is Mistress Alice Grey."

"Good morrow," I said with a small wave. *Holy shit, I'm speaking Shakespearean.*

Alice was the one who'd said 'dowager countess'. Her face was plain but pretty, with warm eyes the color of gingerbread.

They walked fast down a passageway decorated with rich cloth, their long skirts making them look like they were gliding. My dowdy cloak was a total cringe-fest beside their pearl-lined gowns, but at least it hid my limp. We stepped outside again into a courtyard buzzing with carts and wagons, men with swords swinging from their waists swirling past like the pages of a history book.

"Your father did not bring you to court to announce you?" the Dowager Countess of Warwick croaked at me as we approached a huge building with a gabled roof.

"Uh, not likely."

Alice giggled, jeweled hearts dangling from her ears. She pulled a pouch of sugared almonds from her purse and offered me one. I took it, my hollow stomach grateful.

A man strolled by with a hawk on his shoulder, nodding to the countess in greeting.

"I understand your father is a physician from Hatfield," the countess said to me, sounding progressively more irritated.

"Right. Doctor Martin Grace." *News travels fast in the old world. Take that, internet.*

"Where did your father study?" asked Isobel in a girlish voice. She walked like she was on a catwalk, her ocean-blue dress embroidered with a peacock tail in full display.

I scrambled for the names of England's oldest universities. "Oxford."

"Oh, my cousin is a professor there," she replied. "Charles Beaumont."

My face ignited. "Oxford is where he wanted to go, but he ended up at Cambridge."

Isobel scoffed. "Cambridge men hold nothing against Oxford."

"Well, my father is a Cambridge alumnus, and he is a shameful failure," said Alice with notable sarcasm. "Which college was yours in?" she asked me.

"I always forget." I tapped my skull. "It's temperamental."

She frowned and laughed at the same time. I knew I was acting slightly idiotic, but after the terrifying Tower of London, it felt like I'd wandered into a fairytale.

I could hear Mia's capable voice in my head, instructing me to become a quick study on the University of Cambridge, not to mention formal pleasantries and how to twist my hair into a halo braid…whatever it took to survive here while I hunted down that blue-diamond ring that could hopefully get me back home.

We passed under a sprawling archway painted with a sun garnished with a gold crown and the letters *NR*, entering the grandest building on the lot. My eyes took a moment to adjust to the dark corridor, which smelled like old herbs. Men wearing feathered caps huddled in hushed conversation, while others strode solo with an urgent pace. We crossed through several rooms with paneled walls and painted floors laid with rushes before reaching a gigantic hall lit with hundreds of candles. Practically every wall was adorned with shimmering gold hangings and vibrant tapestries of battle scenes, biblical stories, and mythological creatures. Sunlight seeped through stained glass windows curtained with crimson satin, warming the floor of black-and-white squares. The hammerbeam ceiling was an art masterpiece in itself, its gleaming golden beams intersected with cobalt blue arches.

Alice leaned into me, cinnamon finding my nose. "The first time I saw it, I must have soaked my skirts. But, then again, I was four." She giggled.

The roaring flames inside the cavernous fireplace didn't cut through the cold air. I crossed my arms inside my cloak.

"His Majesty the King!" cried a voice.

Trumpets blasted from the minstrels' gallery, bodies all around us spiraling into bows. Alice folded elegantly forward, her arms outstretched like a ballerina's.

And then all the air escaped my body like a popped balloon.

The beautiful guy from the Tower of London stood in the archway, bounded by a sea of bending bodies. A line of guards behind him scanned the crowd like the secret service. His eyes found mine and locked me in his gaze, one of his brows lifting. Alice tugged my dress hard.

I dropped into a clumsy curtsy, my heart hammering. He was too young to be a king—too gorgeous. Kings were old and obese or had mean faces like Nicholas the Ironheart. Mia would call this guy the King of Pants-Dropping Hotness.

When I stood back up, he was sauntering right to us and Isobel was shuffling from one foot to another. The king walked with a confident elegance, all long legs and muscular shoulders. The Dowager

Countess of Warwick kissed his jeweled fingers as gentle chatter resumed around us. Every eye was on the king.

"I trust you have had a fine morning, my lady countess," he said in that velvety voice that sucked strength from my legs.

"Delightful, Majesty, thank you. The lutenist performed a lovely tune in the south garden." She smiled, exposing three black teeth.

The king tipped his head slightly in greeting. "Lady Isobel... Mistress Grey." There couldn't be a girl at court who wasn't in love with him. His eyes moved to mine. "And this is?"

I felt the surprise overcome my face.

"Oh, this is Mistress Emmeline Grace," the countess rasped. The way the king blinked at me blankly made me understand how quickly I'd been forgotten. "Doctor Martin Grace's daughter, visiting from Hatfield," she added. "I cannot say his work is familiar."

"I was not aware you are an authority on physicians," he said coolly.

"Certainly not." She curtsied, blushing through her white face paint. "That is a gentleman's position."

A pair of men approached the king with feathered caps in their hands, but a bald-headed guard rebuffed them. The king never moved his eyes from mine.

"I trust you will enjoy my court, Mistress Grace. You are in fine and gracious company."

My voice barely registered. "Thank you." The king held his hand out to me in invitation. I dropped into a shallow bow until my thigh wound pinched and took his fingers, nervously pressing my lips to the back of his hand that smelled like a bouquet of roses. His warm fingers curled into mine, and something shifted in my chest, until a shock of cold metal brushed my bottom lip. My eyes flashed open, meeting the blue-diamond ring glistening from the king's third finger. The room started to spin. When I let go of his hand and rose back up, his eyes held me steady, entrancing and curious.

The Dowager Countess of Warwick pushed Isobel forward. "The Lady Isobel and I are greatly anticipating your blessed companionship this evening," spluttered the countess.

"I do hope we may share a dance," Isobel added in a strange, stilted tone.

"I regret your late husband cannot join us himself," the king said to the countess. "He would be immensely proud of this occasion."

"Indeed." She dropped into another curtsy.

He continued past us as hurriedly as he'd arrived, not so much as glancing back in our direction. I turned to watch him stride right out of the hall, my stomach as tight as a fist.

Great, I have to steal a ring from a king. A ring that's probably some major family heirloom. He's likely one of the grandsons of Nicholas the Ironheart. Are they all time travelers? Dating back to freaking Edward the Confessor?

"Mother, we should reconsider the jewelry," Isobel said, looking ashen. "Something less tiresome than diamonds. He is wearing none himself this day."

"What His Majesty is tired of is your impertinent behavior! Fancy asking the king to dance with you in *public*." The Dowager Countess of Warwick shook her head, rattling her tight gray curls. "We must practice again. In haste." She shot me an icy look before hurrying Isobel away.

Alice grinned and took my arm in a way that reminded me so much of Mia it hurt. We continued down the center of the hall, where servants lugged in trestle tables while men pored over card games and papers.

"This is the Great Hall," Alice explained proudly. "Where we dine, where His Majesty's most esteemed guests are received, and where the celebratory feast is happening this night. My father was the one who proposed the new peace treaty with France on behalf of the king." Her voice danced with excitement. "You should absolutely attend this evening; the king encourages maidens of the court to join the feastings."

But I was only half listening as I gazed up at the colossal painting eclipsing the far wall. The portrait was of a grim, bearded man wearing a flat cap and navy coat, a blue-diamond ring shimmering from his third finger. It was the exact painting from Mia's book.

"Who is that?" I asked, my chest seizing.

"Our beloved King Nick, of course," Alice replied. "He does not look at all like his portrait, does he? Although no one dares point that out to him; I think he likes it."

I clutched my stomach, stopping it from crashing to the floor. That gentle, breathtaking guy who'd saved my life in the Tower wasn't a descendent of Nicholas the Ironheart. He *was* Nicholas the Ironheart. One of the cruelest, most fearsome kings in history.

And I'd lied to his face about everything.

3

"There's no scar." The face in the portrait had two perfectly smooth cheekbones. Maybe it wasn't him.

Alice gawked at me like I'd just said I was from the twenty-first century.

"Never speak of the scar, especially when you are near the king's person." She glanced around, her voice hardly above a breath. "And best not stare too long. Until His Majesty takes a wife, every maiden at court is at risk of slander." She glanced at the servers placing steaming platters of whole fish onto lines of trestle tables. "Oh curse it; it's Fish Friday."

A trio of musicians played a lute, violin, and oboe in the minstrels' gallery, the merry tune right out of a Shakespeare play.

"So the king is still single, huh?" I said as Alice and I settled onto opposite benches. Her brows snapped up like rubber bands.

"Just joking," I added with a smile. But on the inside, I struggled to breathe. Nicholas the Ironheart was going to burn me alive.

The spicy wine Alice poured from a pewter flask burned my throat.

"Many believed His Majesty would ask the Lady Isobel Beaumont for her hand in marriage last year," she said, clearly enjoying the chat about the king's love life. "Nevertheless, at Christmastide, the French king proposed his sister Princess Henriette as a match, and my father has made three trips to Paris since. Henriette is said to be very beautiful...they call her the 'Pearl of France'. Father refuses to speak of it with me, but I know an alliance with France is critical if we're to war with Spain. Not even a Beaumont can compete with a blood royal."

"But didn't you just say there's a new treaty with France? Isn't that what the feast tonight is about?"

Alice stabbed a steaming whole fish with a two-pronged fork. "Treaties break. Marriage is forever. Unless one is widowed, of course."

Fishes of all types and smells laid out on the table turned my stomach. Typical that the first boy I'd looked twice at since Logan Hunter was a murderous, medieval, and practically engaged king.

"His Majesty doesn't eat here?" I asked, picking at my boiled white fish with a tangy green sauce. I surveyed the room. There was no sign of the black-toothed Countess of Warwick either or any of the men I'd met at the Tower. I hoped Mathew Fox could help lead me to the ring somehow.

Alice snorted. "The important people at court eat upstairs. Maidens are encouraged to dine in our rooms, which is monstrously dull." She took tiny bites, chewing silently. I was swamped with a sudden ache to share a plate of hot wings with Mia and Josh at Grill 'n Chill.

A scream erupted from several tables away. A man with curly white hair was slumped forward, a young guy whacking his back with violent blows.

"Heaven help him, he is choking!" cried the man opposite them.

I was already on my feet. I'd never forget the time Mrs. Horne crashed to the floor at the rest home, her eyes bulging as Mom skillfully applied the Heimlich maneuver, dislodging a butter cookie from the old girl's windpipe.

"Don't hit his back!" I cried, but the guy with bobbed sandy hair was going at him like a boxer. A wall of ogling ladies in stupidly big dresses blocked my path. I hitched up my skirt and climbed onto the trestle table, treading over platters and flasks, grease spattering my shoes.

The whole palace was a freaking fire hazard.

"Don't hit him!" I repeated, jumping between them and pulling back the choking man's shoulders. I hugged him from behind, jabbing my fist hard into his abdomen. On the third push, a chunk of carrot fired from his throat. He tumbled backward, drinking air. Every eye in the place was on me, and Alice's hand was clamped across her mouth in what looked like shock.

"You saved his life…God bless you!" said the man facing the baron. He plucked the carrot from his bouffant hair.

"No problem." I hurried back to my seat, avoiding the stunned army.

"Did your father teach you that?" asked Alice, a little breathless.

"My mother, actually."

"What an extraordinary lady."

She took a big drink of wine while I gulped fresh milk from one of the smaller flasks, my fingers still quivering.

"I beg your pardon." The blonde back-hitter was standing over us. His dark blue eyes matched the sapphire pinned to his collar. "I cannot thank you enough for your gallantry. Lord Ashley is my uncle."

"I'm glad he's okay," I said. Three men were leading Lord Ashley out of the hall, a King Charles Spaniel yapping at their heels.

The man made a small bow of greeting. "Viscount Hereford. I believe I have not seen you at court before."

"Well, that makes sense, because I just got here. I'm Emmie." I could've offered him a handshake, but it didn't feel right.

"Mistress Emmeline Grace," Alice quickly corrected. Every new introduction felt like a trial that could land me back in the Tower, but they were getting easier. I even made it through the exchange about Hatfield and my fake family without sweating.

"Would you be so kind as to accompany me to His Majesty's celebratory feast this evening?" Hereford's angular jaw stained red. "Presuming you are not already spoken for. It is a dash presumptuous, but I should very much like to learn more about you."

Alice nodded her head vigorously behind his shoulder.

"I guess…thanks."

I instantly regretted the words. I needed a way out of this extravagant prison, not to attend a swanky dinner with some nobleman who looked at me like I was cookie dough ice cream. But going to the feast could put me in front of the king and his blue-diamond ring. I needed it back before he discovered I'd lied through my teeth to him.

Hereford bowed, firing instructions about where and when to meet, before darting after the baron.

"His wife died last year of the sweat," explained Alice. She held her wine cup with both hands like it was a mug of coffee. "Perhaps he is finally ready to share his unspeakable wealth again." She smiled at me. "Marvelous entrance to Whitehall, Mistress Grace."

Alice walked me to my room, which was through a jumbled warren of winding passages, across an inner courtyard, and inside a thin building that smelled like horse manure. My cramped room sat at the end of a musty corridor, and I got the impression that this wasn't the five-star accommodation part of court. But keeping out of other people's way until I figured out how to get out of this place suited me just fine.

I'd taken note of which way we'd come in case I needed a quick escape route. I still had no idea how I could steal a ring from a king— or even if it had any powers at all—but I had to try. The thought of being stuck in this place forever was inconceivable.

"It is a little basic, but we can work on Francis," Alice observed, taking in the single bed and tiny lattice window with its view of a high brick wall.

"You're not talking about the 'Earl of Warwick' Francis, are you?"

She rolled her eyes. "He has not had that title long. Francis is Francis. He is head of the household, unfortunately. He allocates the lodgings."

I swallowed the rock in my throat. Awesome. The guy who'd threatened to torture me for speaking against the king was also in charge of my accommodation. No wonder the room smelled like the window hadn't been opened since the dark ages. Literally.

Alice swept two fingers across the hearth. "At least the fireplace is nice and sooty. I use it to clean my teeth when the mint runs low. Besides, any room at court is an honor these days. Last year, the Venetians went on strike when they learned they would have to lodge in the city." She leaned against the desk. "Is your father a wonderful physician then? He should come to court. The king is quite fascinated with the remedies. Francis would steal the apothecaries' pouches for us all to poke through when we were children." She laughed.

I sat on the edge of the mattress, feeling like a truck had collided with my head. Plus, now I was the one about to soak my skirts.

"Is there a bathroom close by?" I asked, trying not to turn red.

"We passed a wash room coming in," Alice replied. "Although, being the horsemen's quarters, I fear it will be in constant use, and not by any maidens. If you mean relieving yourself, use the chamber pot. The necessary woman will empty it." She glanced at the gold clock on the mantel. "Mercy, I must run. Father will be back and perilously vexed. I will see you at the feast." There was a touch of mischief in her smile. "On the morrow, I can take you to see the entrance to the Presence Chamber where King Nick gives his audiences. We might even see a scandal unfold. Oh, and you should know where the kitchens are. Go early if you want the French macarons. They are miraculous."

She left me alone to stare at the small painting of a young boy in a feathered cap, his eyes two bluish crystals. I'd barely met Nicholas the Ironheart, but he didn't seem like the murderous type at all. He'd been the opposite…gentle and kind. But he'd also forgotten me like an Alzheimer's patient. Was that an early sign of madness?

After making use of the chamber pot, I poked through the space, finding a pile of canvas-bound prayer books under the bed. On the desk was a half-melted candle and a small box filled with metal, charcoal, and paper. The top drawer was crammed with blank scrolls and cool quill pens with ink jars. In another drawer sat a hand mirror, four wooden combs, a tin of creamy white powder, some smudgy black stuff, and bright-red paste. I rubbed a dab of the paste between my fingertips.

The wooden chest beside the bed was packed with stunning dresses in colors like buttermilk, crepe pink, sage green, and lavender. There were three hooped petticoats and a comically large fur coat. Five pairs of satin shoes lined the bottom alongside worn leather boots, a wooden box of tasseled silk scarves, and a container of pins.

A hard rap on the door sent me out of my skin. It had to be the king's messenger, back from Hatfield. I was going right to the bottom of Francis Beaumont's bucket. My eyes darted around the room, hunting for escape routes.

A man in a black hood marched in, squinting with age. He let in a draft from the corridor.

"Lay on the bed, if you please," he ordered curtly, dropping a leather bag onto the table.

My heart shot to my mouth. "What for?"

"I am Doctor Norris. I'm here to inspect your wound."

His weathered hands guided me onto the mattress before gathering my dress to my thigh.

"Why was this not sutured?" He made an unimpressed tsk sound as he opened his bag, retrieving a ball of sponge and a tied bundle of cloth. He opened the tin box on the desk and struck the papery stuff with the metal. It released a shower of sparks, which he caught on the charcoal. He blew to light a flame and heated the cloth bundle.

"We will let the humors drain," he said with his back to me. "A poultice will help the healing after I pack the wound. There will be some pain."

I clenched my teeth, reminding myself that I was lucky to get any wound dressing at all.

Doctor Norris pushed the sponge deep inside the holes. I cried out, my fingers clawing the mattress. Norris didn't flinch, sopping up the blood and placing the warmed bundle over the top before applying pressure. Sweat and tears skated down my cheeks.

"No bathing for several days," he said with kind but weary eyes. "I shall be back with a new poultice in a time."

I wanted to ask who'd sent him to me, but he packed up and left before I got the nerve.

I gripped my aching thigh, dizzy with exhaustion. I needed a four-hour shower and a hundred years of sleep, but my heart was beating faster than a marathon runner's. I limped along the dark corridor, finding a steamy bathing room.

"Bath or wash, mistress?" asked a girl folding linen towels. I hadn't even seen her in the darkness.

"Wash, please."

She handed me a sloshing bucket of water and a cloth tinged with lavender. Behind her was a small room with a burning fire and wooden benches lining the walls like a sauna. I dipped the cloth into the water and quickly wiped myself before I had any horsemen for company. I also speedily washed my underwear.

Back in my room, I changed into a fresh smock and hung my pink koala undies across the window. They may as well have been embroidered with: *Look at me, I'm from the twenty-first century; why don't you burn this koala undies-wearing witch at the stake? Do you even know what a koala is?*

I yanked them back down and stuffed them under the mattress. There was nothing resembling fresh underwear in the clothes' chest, so I tied a clean coif around my legs like an infant.

The clock from the mantel made a dim chime. I was supposed to meet Viscount Hereford in half an hour. Time to get that ring back and get the hell out of Nicholas the Ironheart's house.

I flipped the chest back open, drawn to the sage-green gown with sliced open sleeves. Decorative stitching swirled across the cream bodice and into the petticoat below. The top fit all right, but the bottom hung like a sad balloon deprived of air. I shimmied into a hoop skirt, the dress opening like a flower over it.

I barely recognized myself in the cloudy hand mirror, brushing my face with white powder and lining my eyes with the black cream. I dabbed the red paste onto my lips and cheeks and braided the top half of my hair on both sides before fastening it at the back with a peony-pink ribbon. I'd looked worse at parties.

Hoping Alice wasn't having a laugh, I crouched in front of the fireplace and rubbed soot over my teeth. It tasted surprisingly mild, like charred food, and it did leave my mouth feeling strangely clean.

I kept my head low as I passed through the court that reminded me of a walled city, ornately dressed folk pacing in all directions like they were late for their next meeting. For every one woman, there were at least ten men.

As I cut into the corridor leading to the Great Hall, I nearly collided with Isobel Beaumont. She looked stunning in a black dress crisscrossed with white satin, her pale hair twisted under a white hood.

"You are attending the king's feast?" she asked me, clearly taken aback.

"I'm as surprised as you are," I replied with a chuckle. "You look nice."

She gaped at my dress before her pink lips opened into an unnerving snigger. I thought I smelled wine on her breath. The Dowager Countess of Warwick appeared behind her, fiddling with a diamond spiderweb necklace woven over her jet-black gown. When she saw me, she made a throaty snicker like I was a punch line. "Come, Isobel. His Majesty has already arrived."

They left, giggling and leaving behind a whiff of lemon cake as I hung back from the hall's entrance, my eyes burning. Was there a century on Earth where I wasn't the weird new kid who no one liked?

"I'm pleased I am not the only one who cannot read a sodding clock," said Alice as she practically skidded in beside me, a satin purse wedged under her arm. Her face popped with makeup that complemented her black satin gown, her hair loose beneath a halo-shaped hood.

She took my wrist. "Heavens, your frock!"

"What's with everyone and this dress? Is it on backwards?"

As the shuffling crowd carried us into the Great Hall, I finally got the joke. Hundreds of guests stood chattering over the lively music—every single one of them wearing black or white.

My face burned brighter than the chandeliers. "Why didn't you say there was a theme?"

"Forgive me, I thought you knew," said Alice, clapping a hand to her forehead. She unpinned the black hood from her hair and fixed it on mine. "Here. Only one feature in black or white. Hoods make me itch, anyway." She jiggled her loose waves with her fingers.

I spotted the king in the far corner, touching a man's shoulder as he laughed. He was so hot it was criminal, his black leather coat slashed diagonally with a thick white stripe. When he caught my eye, I tried to look away, but his eyes drew mine back. He gave me a slight nod—like a greeting—and I tilted my head while clutching my dress in an awkward curtsy. When he turned around, I stretched my neck to see if he was wearing the ring, but Alice led me away.

We wandered deeper into the hall, guests greeting Alice like she was royalty. "I could eat a swine," she said, scrutinizing the servers with a hand on her stomach.

The beefy red-haired guy from the park stepped into my vision—the one who'd shot me with his arrow and then taken me to the Tower of London.

"Who is that?" I asked tightly.

"That is Robert Fox, the Earl of Lansbury, with the daughter of Baron Wharton," Alice explained. "Lord Lansbury is a gentleman of the Privy Chamber and one of the king's closest friends. Nevertheless, stay clear of him. He drinks a great deal too much ale for breakfast and likes to take the maidenheads of young girls."

Lord Lansbury leaned closely against a skeletal girl in a low-cut gown. I scanned faces for his pint-sized brother who'd released me from the Tower, but the more cordial Mathew Fox was nowhere to be seen.

Alice pointed out a silver-haired man speaking with a bearded guy in a black cloak. "That is my wonderfully accomplished father, Sir Thomas Grey, with Rodrigo Montoya, the ambassador of Spain. Father is likely doing his best to appease him. Spain may be the most powerful country in Christendom, but it is still no match for England and France united."

Alice then shrieked as a pair of miniscule hands clasped around her skirt. A little girl appeared through the folds in a white V-shaped gown. Her fire-engine-red hair was intricately plaited with matching ribbon.

"Kit," laughed Alice, crouching. "You plum."

The child's startlingly blue eyes met mine. Her face was as serene as an olden-day painting.

"This is my new friend, Mistress Emmeline Grace," Alice explained.

"Oh please, it's Emmie," I said, my cheeks warm.

Kit gazed up at me. "May we be the closest of friends, too?"

I smiled at her. "Sure."

A figure stepped between us, coal black eyes attacking mine like assault rifles. They belonged to the Earl of Warwick, Francis Beaumont.

"I am pleased you arrived safely, Mistress Grace," he said with far more courtesy than he'd shown me in the Tower. "I trust your ride from Hatfield was pleasant." He emphasized the town's name, and I got the message. My stint in the Tower of London was not public knowledge.

My mouth turned to sand again. "It was fine, thanks."

"May we go hunting again on the morrow?" Kit said to Francis. She grinned at me through a missing front tooth. "I shot a boar today."

"Truly? I thought it was a deer," he replied, looking right at me.

Alice glared at Francis. "You took an eight-year-old hunting?"

"I took a young girl out for some amusement. Is there a problem?"

"When you are involved? Habitually."

"Did you wake on the wrong side of the sun today?" he snapped at her. "Come, Kit. We must present you to Philippe Renard, the new French ambassador."

Alice snatched a cup from a passing server as Francis led Kit away. "Pillock," she muttered.

"I pray you do not mean me," said a crisp voice.

We spun to face the triangular chin of Viscount Hereford. He was a touch dashing in a white coat with black pants, James Bond–style, his hair combed straight back.

Alice excused herself with perfect poise and threw me a subtle thumbs-up behind his back. *Holy shit, the thumbs-up is as old as heads on pikes.*

Hereford kissed my hand, his lips icicles. "Mistress Grace, you are an enchantment. You arrived without me, wicked girl, and in the wrong color."

"I just went with one feature in black. Thought I'd switch things up a bit." I touched my hood.

He smiled at me like I was a kitten he wanted to play with. "Tell me. Are you as daring on the dance floor?"

"Depends on who's playing. Got any Atomic?" I couldn't resist.

Emmie, speak normally. Sixteenth-century normal.

A blast of trumpets sent guests hunting for their place settings. It was clear that no one was allowed to sit until the king had settled into his royal chair atop a platform draped with a black-and-white canopy displaying his coat of arms. As the king leisurely took his seat, his golden crown reflected a glimmer from his third finger. I was too far away to tell if it was the blue-diamond ring, but that wasn't the only reason I couldn't seem to drag my gaze away from him. His eyes flashed in my direction and he caught me staring. My cheeks flushed hot as I looked down.

Hereford guided me into my spot beside him, which I was disappointed to find was miles from where Alice was seated.

"I have an estate near Hatfield," Hereford said, offering me a plate of salted anchovies. "Where is your manor?"

I coughed. "Just outside town." *Just keep the conversation focused on him.* "So, were you involved with this treaty?" I asked.

"Naturally." He grabbed a handful of almonds and tossed them at his mouth, a few missing the target and bouncing across the checkered floor. "King Nick lodged at my estate near Dover when he made the terms. His Majesty was quite a fan of my hawks, commandeering two of my best. His Grace swore to replace them with more favorable young, but has not yet obliged, which is scarcely a surprise."

"I guess he's pretty busy. Negotiating world peace and everything."

He sneered. "Actually, if it were not for me forgoing countless jugs of my finest wines, I believe the French king would have been not so agreeable."

As Hereford's Ode to Himself continued, I took my chance to look the king's way again. He was gracefully accepting a parade of dishes presented before him—roasted whole turkeys, pigeons and pigs, enough breads and cheeses to feed a village, vegetable towers assembled like desserts, and a baked swan redressed in its own feathers.

When two servants carefully carried the final platter to the king's table chased by a sweaty chef, Hereford's breath moved to my ear. "Watch closely."

"For what?"

"Magic."

The chef slowly lifted the lid, uncovering a gigantic roasted partridge. When he brought the knife to the bird's chest, I felt my eyes pulled upward. Nicholas the Ironheart was looking right at me, sending a bolt of electricity down my arms and legs. He held the eye contact until my cheeks flushed and my heart tripped over itself, his lips curling up slightly. A second later, five pigeons flapped out of the partridge's open cavity and across our line of sight, breaking the moment.

When the king returned his gaze to the dish and laughed politely, the room exploded with claps. The partridge was switched with a freshly cooked alternative, and swiftly divvied up between each table. I barely tasted it, my brain scrutinizing what had just happened. Why would the king look at me like that? I was a high-school student from the twenty-first century who hated history. And why hadn't he looked back my way since? Was it my scrappy hair?

Hereford was chewing my ear off about his estate in Northumberland as I dug into a block of cheese. I'd barely got a word in by the time dessert arrived, which was giant jellies filled with fresh berries, custard tarts garnished with violets, and freshly baked macarons sprinkled with sugar and chopped almonds. As full as I was, I downed the macarons in two bites and took another serving. Alice was right; they were miraculous.

Hereford rose, dusting sugar from his narrow lips. "A marvelous feast. Now, we work it off." He presented his hand to me. Couples sashayed to the center of the hall as the music lifted in volume and pace.

"I'm not really a dancer," I stammered. "Too much coordination required."

He pulled me to my feet. "It is the most elementary dance in the realm."

It was beyond lucky that the ache in my leg had diminished a little and the steps were easy enough—step toward your partner, hold your right arm up, and circle around them. Repeat the other way. Still, my chest began to constrict with unease. I needed to find that ring, not get my groove on.

My eyes hunted again for Nicholas the Ironheart, seemingly known here as King Nick, when Hereford spun me into the scowl of Francis Beaumont. He took Hereford's place, who circled away with a burly woman wearing a hood of midnight-blue opals.

Francis's black curls smelled like soap. "Less than a day at White-hall and you have already forgotten where you spent the night," he said under his breath as we danced. "And I see you have made a new friend."

"You mean Alice?" She was over at her father's table, straight-ening his velvet coat.

"I mean Lord Hereford. An utter harebrain, but far above you in station. And you would be wise to steer clear of Mistress Grey. Her mind is as sharp as a pike. She will soon catch on that you are nothing more than a spy, especially when I acquire proof."

"You clearly have no idea that it was the king himself who brought me here," I said shakily. "And I'm thinking that even you have to do what he says."

Francis's shoulders tensed. "I take pleasure in anything His Majesty desires, but it is my position to protect him. I will not resign myself to any degree of trust."

"It's okay. The king is a kind person and you're not. I get it."

He laughed lightly, revealing a gap between his center teeth. "You believe the king is merciful? That jailer who attacked you in the Tower? He is already dead. I prepared the warrant myself at His Majesty's command."

The aftertaste of macarons gurgled in my throat as the king's angelic face came into view, speaking intensely with one of the ambas-sadors. *Did he really kill that guard because of me?*

The song ending was an act of mercy. I hightailed it away from

Francis, spotting Hereford taking a seat at the card table with a bunch of bearded noblemen. I crossed a drunken cluster to find Alice, and in doing so, weaved my way into the mesmeric stare of King Nick.

"Mistress Grace," he said with soft surprise. Flecks of diamonds glittered from his mussed-up hair, his strong legs wrapped snugly in black leather. Before I could locate my tongue, a stout man glided between us, speaking French. The king replied fluently, gesturing to me.

The Frenchman kissed my hand. "*C'est un plaisir de faire votre connaissance, mademoiselle.*"

"Sorry, I don't understand French," I replied with a stammer.

The king thanked the man before stepping into my space, nearly tipping me backward.

"Let us dance," he said closely. "An escape from this endless fanfare."

The two dancers beside us circled around one another with their palms facing each other's but not quite touching.

The king rotated around me with his hand held up the same way and I followed, our palms so close together that I could feel the heat of his skin. My heart skipped a beat as my eyes zeroed in on the blue-diamond ring gleaming from his third finger. Panic gripped my chest and squeezed it like a vice.

King Nick's gaze roamed down my sage-green dress that didn't fit the party theme. "You enjoy somewhat unusual attire, Mistress Grace."

"Fashion's pretty forward in Hatfield," I replied, my lips turning dry. "Black and white is so last season."

I wasn't prepared for his heart-melting smile at close range, his cheeks dotted with dimples. His aquamarine eyes focused on me so intensely I had to look away. Behind him, the Dowager Countess of Warwick literally pushed Isobel toward us. Isobel stumbled and nearly face-planted. The king's bald-headed guard led her into a dance as if to rescue her from embarrassment.

Nick's mouth moved close to my ear. "I was not aware you are courting Lord Hereford."

His breath tickled my skin, short-circuiting my heart. "Neither was I," was all I could think of to say.

Thomas Grey cut in, his pale eyes boring into mine as the king took a step backward. Thomas bowed to the king. "Your Grace, may I present the French ambassador, His Excellency Philippe Renard, with a gesture from Princess Henriette of France in celebration of this wondrous occasion."

"Another one?" quipped Nick.

The French ambassador glided forward, clutching a gargantuan bouquet of yellow flowers fastened with diamond-lined ribbon. "The chrysanthemums represent optimism, loyalty, and love between England and France," he said nervously, tipping his coiffed curls.

The king politely inhaled their scent before waving the bouquet away.

He then caught something over my shoulder, his smile lighting up his face. "I fear that I am in a dream. My companion for this evening has finally agreed to dance with me."

I spun to meet Isobel Beaumont's dainty face as she paced toward the king, her eyes glassy from all the wine I'd seen her drink. My chest hit the floor.

But then a tiny figure brushed past Isobel's skirts and reached for the king's hand. He squeezed Kit's little fingers, turning her to face me. "Mistress Grace, may I present my delightful and deeply-afraid-of-dancing sister, Her Royal Highness the Princess Catherine."

I dropped into a curtsy as Kit tapped his arm. "Mistress Grace and I are already close friends."

"You are?"

She lifted her shoulders at me. "I enjoy dancing. But not with my brother. His feet are too quick."

Nick scoffed and tugged her into a turn while I fought to catch my breath.

Kit was Princess Catherine. The same one who was brutally murdered at the age of eight—the exact age Alice said she was now. The murder that would destroy England and turn its king into a merciless tyrant.

Kit squealed with every spin, Nick's face brightening with laughter. He was beaming, his demeanor totally different with her. No one dared cut between them.

If I wasn't gaping at them like a freak, I wouldn't have noticed the king's steps begin to slow, his forehead lining with strain. He stopped and made an abrupt turn, coughing into his fist. He then wavered in his boots and reached for his neck with both hands, his eyes wide.

"Majesty?" said one voice and then another.

Kit's glove flew to her mouth as hundreds of feet stilled, a crowd of spectators quickly taking shape. The music fell to silence, the players leaning over the minstrels' gallery to watch what was going on.

Coughing uncontrollably, the king tumbled backward into the clutches of Francis Beaumont, Lord Lansbury, and three other men with panicked faces. They hoisted him up and carried him away, Thomas Grey chasing them with a handkerchief pressed to his own brow.

"God save the king!" cried the Dowager Countess of Warwick. Isobel burst into tears.

I wasn't sure God could save him. But maybe I could.

4

THE COURT WAS A DIFFERENT PLACE WHEN THE KING WAS IN DANGER: women crying like babies, pale-faced men meandering the drafty halls, everyone whispering. I didn't wait to ask Alice if what I was doing was totally insane, because I already knew that didn't even cover it. Still, my feet steered me upstairs toward the Presence Chamber as if I had every right to be there.

It was the only option I had. Not only was I almost sure I knew what was wrong with King Nick, but I *had* to get that ring, especially if he was on his way to the royal crypt ahead of schedule.

The spiral staircase opened into a waiting room with three sets of double doors crossed with pikes. I folded my arms over myself to keep warm and bounded toward the nearest guard with the bushy beard, summoning all the courage I had.

"May I help you, mistress?" he said, frowning.

"Is it possible to see the king?"

He looked at me like I'd grown seven heads. "His Majesty is indisposed and not giving audiences."

I spotted Francis Beaumont glaring at me through the gap in the pikes. He pushed through the guards and pulled me aside.

"What in the devil are you doing here?"

"I saw what happened. I think I can help."

"Half the country's noblemen saw what happened. Why do you insist on making such a spectacle of yourself? Are you that impatient to meet the scaffold?"

"Is the king okay?" The moment I asked the question, I craved the answer.

Francis exhaled heavily. "By God's grace, His Majesty appears to have recovered again. The deep breathing usually helps, as does the harpist."

"This has happened before?" I dropped my voice. "I think it was the chrysanthemums. I think he's allergic to them. I'm obviously no expert on asthma, but you should look into that, especially if this has happened before."

Francis grunted with amusement. "You accuse the Princess Henriette of France of poisoning the King of England with *flowers?*"

"Not intentionally. But you should get rid of all the flowers in the court to be safe, as well as dust and pets—especially cats. Things that can make his airways swell up until he can't breathe." I held my neck, remembering the feeling. Springtime always made me wheezy.

Francis crossed his arms. "Your father is a specialist in the breath?"

I hesitated. "Yes."

Oh God, I think I just invented the word 'asthma' as well as Dr. Martin Grace, the pulmonologist.

Francis shook his head, his brow lining. "Sir Thomas Grey has had over ten years to fix this dreaded affliction, and yet it plagues His Majesty more than ever. Now before the courtiers, no less. What will it be next? A meeting of Parliament?" He slapped his forehead. "Come. You will share your father's theories with the king yourself."

My face paled, even though this was exactly what I'd wanted.

Francis made a face at me. "Look not so alarmed, Mistress Grace. You are hardly the first maiden to be brought to the king's chambers at nightfall."

I felt a bizarre sting in my chest at that comment as Francis led me through a lavish throne room and into some sort of sixteenth-century office. An elongated meeting table plastered with books and papers drew a line down the center of the room. At the far end, an immense stained-glass curtained window overlooked the Thames, the moon-light illuminating tapestries of eagles in flight and roaring lions.

We approached a door that stood ajar. Francis halted beside a platter of oranges and pressed his finger to his lips, instructing me to stay quiet. I froze, all the air trapped in my lungs.

"—the opportunity, Majesty," said a man's voice through the gap. "You may demonstrate your strength in person, as well as your support of this historic treaty of friendship."

"Is that what you are calling it now?"

My breath snagged at the unexpected sound of Nick's voice. It was a little gravelly, but he sounded okay. Francis was listening intently.

The other man continued. "If I may persist in my most unworthy speech, Majesty, visiting France would be most opportune now. The ink on the alliance is not yet dry."

When his volume dropped, Francis slanted forward to listen closer, accidentally knocking the door shut. A second later, it swung open again in his face.

Alice's father, Thomas Grey, lurched through the gap. "Are you so devoid of your own opinions that you must resort to spying on others?" He glowered at me. "Who is this?"

"Mistress Grace," said King Nick, stepping into the arched door-way, his lips parted with surprise. He was painfully cute in a white linen shirt unbuttoned at the neck, his black leather pants gripping his legs in all the right places. He didn't look at all like he was dying from asthma.

More like he needs to be kissed senseless all over his mouth and neck. Maybe that'll sort out his breathing issues.

Jesus, Emmie. What is wrong with you?

"The lady requests an urgent audience," Francis sputtered, clearly horrified at being sprung eavesdropping.

The king barely blinked at him. "Sir Thomas, prepare a notice to the court that I am in fine health and was simply a touch fatigued this evening after brokering this historic agreement with France. Francis, go to Kit's rooms at once and share the news that I am feeling better. I will break fast with her in the morning." He stepped aside in invitation for me to enter his room. "Mistress Grace."

My feet obliged, knowing I had no choice. Nick made no effort to move as I brushed past him through the small gap in the doorway, my stomach coming into contact with his for a moment. My cheeks heated as he closed the door on Francis and Thomas arguing.

"Christ, since I was but five, they have fought worse than father and son," he said to me, holding up a jug of wine in offer, but I shook my head. "Surely you'll take a macaron then? Provided you did not finish them off at my feast. I am astonished we have any left in the palace." He lifted the lid on a plate that smelled like a French bakery.

I helped myself to two, surveying the tower of beige meringues. "You don't have any other colors?" I said, attempting to meet his sarcasm. Nick frowned and closed the lid.

It was hard not to gape, not just at him but at everything in sight. We were in some sort of opulent living room, the walls lined with crimson and gold satin, purple velvet chairs tilted toward a grand fireplace embossed with a crowned Tudor rose. A table right out of a museum presented fanned-out playing cards and a chessboard. The rose-tinged air was the perfect temperature.

"Is something amiss?" Nick pressed his hands to his thighs, the blue-diamond ring still circling his finger.

"Every room here is so…beautiful."

The firelight glinted in his eyes as he smiled. "You should see Hampton Court."

"You have another one of these?"

He laughed. "I have more than fifty manors. Some are smaller." For a moment we just stood there watching each other, butterflies taking flight in my stomach.

King Nicholas the First, is it okay if I borrow that priceless diamond ring for a few hours? So I can see if it takes me back to the twenty-first century? That'd be awesome, cheers.

He cleared his throat. "What is it that could not wait, Mistress Grace?"

"Oh. Well, I was there when you collapsed tonight," I stammered. "At the party."

"I remember."

"And I thought I might be able to help, but you seem fine now, so I'm really sorry to have bothered you."

A knock cut between us.

"Come," Nick said firmly.

The gentleman who'd danced with Isobel Beaumont stepped into the room with a bow, his bare scalp slick with sweat. "Doctor Norris is still occupied with the apothecaries, Majesty, but insisted I bring you fresh remedies."

"Leave them. Oh, and Mark, bring some more macarons. Do we have any other colors?"

The gentleman's copper brows puckered. "Colors, Majesty?"

"I'm certain you have heard of them. Blue, green, purple, that sort of thing." Nick sent him away with a flick of his hand.

The steaming cups of medicine smelled like Mia's boiled Chinese herbs when she had unexplained dizzy spells. I tried not to swallow the foul stench.

"Norris and his hideous concoctions," Nick said to the bay window, as if he'd heard my thoughts.

"Do they help?" I asked gently.

"Likely not. I have had this condition since I was a child. I have lost count of how many occurrences."

"Do you know what it is?"

He paused, inhaling deeply. "Norris claims it is something called *anxiety*. A condition not of the body, but of the mind. He believes it is a suppressed call for my mother, God rest her soul." He brushed his forehead. "Christ, why am I telling you this? I may have to lock you in the Tower still."

"So you do remember me."

He turned to me, a line forming in his brow. "You doubt it?"

"I didn't seem very memorable this morning when you were chatting with that pompous woman in the Great Hall."

He walked slowly toward me. "If the pompous woman you speak of is the Dowager Countess of Warwick, she is the last person you would want discovering you spent a night in the Tower of London on suspicion of treason. That lady has a small mind and a large voice and will stop at nothing to bring down anyone lovelier than she. You should thank me."

He stopped so close to me that I could smell the rose oil on his skin.

"Thank you," I said, a little winded.

His gaze traveled down the length of my body, sucking all the air from the room, before his eyes lifted again to mine. He moved a step closer, my breath catching. "Tell me why you really came here," he asked softly. "Because, Mistress Grace, it may come as a surprise that I have not met quite so forward a lady—"

"I don't think you have anxiety." My sweaty fingers fisted my skirt. "Unless you get panic attacks or something, but it looks more like asthma to me. That's what I came here to say."

I mean, if he kissed me right now, I can't imagine myself stopping him, but I don't want him thinking I came here to offer my body to him.

His face creased with confusion. "Come again?"

"Asthma is an allergic condition. Certain triggers like flowers, exercise, dust—even grass—can make the airways in your lungs close up so you can't breathe. If you stay away from those things for a while, you could see if it makes a difference."

His brows lifted. "You are proposing I stay away from grass?"

"If that's what it takes. It would only be certain types of grass, I think; I'd have to check." I pointed at a vase of orange flowers shaped like crab claws. "And you should really take those out. Mom said flowers can be the worst."

Emmie, these people are going to lock you up…and for spectacular reasons.

Nick hadn't moved. "But those are from the Canary Isles."

"Exactly. Where the canaries are surely missing them."

Chuckling like he wasn't sure he should, he stepped past me and picked up an exquisitely carved lute. He settled into a chair, holding it like a guitar. "Did your father also teach you that trick you performed today on the Lord Ashley?"

"How did you know about that?"

He plucked a few strings. "Perhaps I shall call upon Hatfield on my next progress, which is sure to have come and gone by the time you sit down. You may keep me company a while."

My stomach trembled as I balanced on the edge of the opposite chair, still working out how to maneuver the dress. Sixteenth-century England needed jeans. *Man, his ass would look good in jeans.*

"Do you enjoy the lute?" he asked, strumming lightly.

I refrained from saying it looked like a smashed guitar. "Sure."

The gentle tune was beautiful, and I could tell from years of watching Josh that Nick played well. As he concentrated on his fingers, I was free to gaze at his beautiful features one by one, before his scar tipped into my sight line. He stumbled over a note.

"Pretty song," I said gently, clueing in that he didn't like his scar stared at.

"It is merely an original composition I've been experimenting with. Although I feel it may work better on the harp."

"You play the harp as well?" I helped myself to another macaron.

"Of course, alongside the lute, the flute, the viol, and the virginals. And which do you play?"

I tried not to laugh. "I'm musically challenged."

He rested the lute between his legs. "You cannot play music, you know not even basic French, your dancing is mediocre at best, and yet you speak in a way that is so..." He searched for the right word. "Worldly." My laugh escaped before I could stop it. His eyes glimmered. "You agree not?"

"Oh, I completely agree about the dancing."

"You should study more. I believe women of decent breeding should be educated in all the classics, as well as music and dance. At age eight, my sister Kit is nearly fluent in four languages and is an extraordinary painter."

His face lit up like a Christmas tree just as mine fell.

Shouldn't I warn him that his adored little sister is about to be murdered?

Dimples deepened in his cheeks as he smirked at me. "Now come on, there must be something you can do. I'll wager that you are a fiend for embroidery."

His playful smile was making it hard to think, but I was determined to prove I wasn't totally useless. My eyes dropped to the tanned fingers grazing his thigh.

"There is one thing, I suppose."

I crouched in front of him, fumbling to untie the pink ribbon from my hair. When I reached for his hand and gently opened his fingers, the air between us sparked like a struck match. I wrapped the ribbon twice around his middle finger, crushing the urge to slide the blue-diamond ring right off his hand before returning my mouth to the skin I'd kissed earlier. *Focus, Emmie.* Holding the ribbon there with my thumb, I pulled each side down and across, before folding the silky fabric to make two loops. My heart thumped so loudly they could surely hear it in Morocco. I tugged the knot to tighten it, and fed the loose ends through the ring.

"Ta-dah," I said shakily, reluctantly letting go of his hand. "It's a knot ring. It looks a lot better when it's done with wire."

When I glanced up at him, those killer eyes entangled with mine.

"Jewelry is what captivates you," he said, his voice a little rough.

"Making it, mostly. And don't forget macarons."

His laugh was too cute. He stood up. "I want to show you something."

I followed him through another small space filled with plush chairs and mirrors, what looked to be a dining chamber beyond that, and into a far room, my cheeks flooding with heat. A four poster bed stood in my path, its wooden pillars twisting like vines in assorted shades of wood. But Nick walked right past the bed and stopped at a stunning cabinet made of layered bone and decorated with gemstones. He cocked his finger for me to join him.

I zigzagged past a tall sculpture of an eagle in flight and peered inside the cabinet. The array of jewels would've put any Fifth Avenue window to shame. Strings of perfectly round pearls shared space with rubies, sapphires, emeralds, and diamonds—some as large as golf balls. One pendant necklace displayed an emerald the size of a postage stamp.

"The ancient people believed jewels were tears cried by their gods," Nick said near my shoulder.

"What a sad day for the gods."

He opened a tray, my eyes drawn to the muscles bunching in his forearm. Resting on purple velvet was a magnificent necklace of glittering blue diamonds delicately positioned beside a pair of matching earrings. I brushed their cold surfaces with my fingers.

"A little ladylike for you, don't you think?" I said.

He laughed, but stiffly. "These are the official jewels of the Queens of England. To be presented to my bride upon our betrothal." He twisted the blue-diamond ring right off his finger and placed it beside them. "Designed as a match to my coronation ring. A ring that you were found wearing yesterday."

Every bone in my body snapped as Nick turned to me, his expression changing to something darker.

"And now you will tell me, Mistress Grace. Why did you have a ring stolen from my court many years ago? And what does it have to do with you compromising your character to come to my chambers at midnight hour?"

I fought to speak, when a thump at the door made us both jump.

"What is it now?" Nick said sharply.

The second I saw his tall shoulders turn for the door, I snatched the ring and dropped it down my bodice. It felt like a block of ice in my cleavage. I nudged the drawer closed with my butt, taking a second to recognize Mathew Fox bowing in the doorway.

He gripped a pair of black leather gloves, his face as shocked as mine.

"What news from Hatfield?" said Nick, pacing toward him. "You may speak it in front of Mistress Grace."

The king's words bounced between my ears like an echo. *Nick sent Mathew to Hatfield to contact my family. I'm too late. I've been smoked out as a liar, and Nicholas the Ironheart is going to slice off my head or possibly burn me alive.*

I'd forgotten the smooth resonance of Mathew's voice. He sounded nervous. "Doctor Grace was not at hand during my visit, Your Majesty. However, I assure you, he is well known in Hatfield and of a respectful name. I assured his family that his daughter Mistress Grace is safe and well. In fact, they would be most honored for her to remain at court as long as the king is gracious. She may write to them at once. Also, Majesty, I corroborated Mistress Grace's account that she purchased a blue-diamond ring from a market seller not three weeks past. She had no knowledge of it being crown property. Naturally, I am following up with the merchants as to how your coronation ring arrived there in the first place."

I'd stopped breathing entirely. In a day of unbelievable shocks, this took the grand prize.

Nick squeezed Mathew's thin shoulder to thank him, before waving him away. The king took a moment to speak, his back to me. "You must think me a monster."

"It's fine." My voice wasn't my own.

He turned to face me, his eyes returning to mine. "I must prepare to greet the court in the morning. You will be seen to your room."

"Of course…sorry." I backed toward the door the way the others had, my heart leaping out of my chest. But the ring felt stuck in my cleavage, and Nick didn't so much as glance at the cabinet. He looked only at me.

"So will you?" he asked, the slight nervousness in his voice stopping my feet. "Stay?"

My heart crawled into my mouth. "Here? In your room?"

His cheeks were like burning tinder and something gleamed in his eyes for a moment before he replied. "At court," he clarified. "Will you stay for the summer? If your father consents?"

When I struggled to reply, his face pinched. "I understand. You have a family to return to." He took a step back from me. "You have my permission to leave court, if it pleases you. Be certain that your family will be granted compensation without delay."

He called for Mark, the gentleman of the bedchamber, who hastily escorted me back downstairs past incoming platters of macarons in various shades of beige. I rushed back to my room and tried to lock the door behind me, but there wasn't one. *Has no one here thought of locks yet?*

I tore off the itchy sage gown, my palms a sweat factory. My fingers fumbled to slide the ring onto my thumb. The king's guards could burst in with swords pointed at any moment.

After throwing on a linen nightgown trimmed with lace, I climbed into the vanilla-scented sheets. I tossed back and forth on the scratchy mattress like the bed was a nest of insects. *Is this going to work? Am I really going home?* My hand pressed a sickly feeling in my stomach.

There was a light tap at the door. I froze, the sound repeating.

"Mistress Emmeline Grace?" said a female voice.

"Yes?" I could barely breathe, my thumb sliding deeper under the blanket.

A young maid entered and dropped a navy velvet pouch on the desk. She curtsied and left.

I scrambled out of the bed, untying the string. Inside was a fresh sprig of rosemary and a note. The writing was beautiful and cursive.

For beneath your pillow, for the sweetest of dreams in this place of unfamiliarity.
Thank you for your kind-hearted care for my health.
I will be mindful of grass.
Goodnight,
NR.
* You are right. Whitehall is very beautiful tonight.

My heart galloped as I reread the words, trying to decipher the last line. I slid the rosemary under my pillow and twisted in the sheets, struggling to get comfortable. All I could see was the glimmer in Nick's eyes as they'd stared into mine. It was like being watched by an angel.

I thought back to the image of Kit's heart-shaped face and Nick's loving gaze as he'd danced with her. She was so tiny and sweet. Why would anyone want to kill her? And why on earth did Mathew Fox lie to his king for me?

The last image I glimpsed before tumbling into oblivion was the Tower of London jailer. He glared at me with ochre eyes, blood splattering across his beard as his head was struck clean off his shoulders.

Just because he'd hurt me.

5

FINGERNAILS PIERCED MY SKIN LIKE NEEDLES. I COULD SMELL FISH sauce, and someone was shaking my forearm. Ebony eyes with smudged liner met my blurred vision.

"Emmie, what are you doing here? Where have you been?" Mia's usually calm voice was shrill, her lean legs bare under a vintage Metallica T-shirt. She lurched off the bed, her eyes glued to me as she shouted for her mom.

I sprang up, lavender walls and marble furniture attacking me from all directions. *You're back. You did it. You're here.*

"Where *were* you?" said Mia, her eyes threatening tears. "And you just show up in my bed? What the f—"

"Stop," I said, holding my palm out. The blue-diamond ring glittered from my thumb. I shivered like I was freezing, but sweat beaded on my neck.

Mrs. Fairbanks barged through the door, calling for her husband. A second later, all four of them were gawking at me—Mia, her mom, her dad, and her brother Tristan. Mr. Fairbanks held his shaking cell phone to his ear.

"Carol, she's here," he said, his voice sped up. He handed me his latest-issue smartphone. I pressed the cold aluminum casing to my ear, my mouth like sandpaper.

"Emmie? Emmie?" Mom was saying frantically.

"I'm here," I said, my voice scratchy from sleep. The Fairbanks still stood there like I was some kind of variety show. "I'm okay."

Mom was sobbing, barely able to speak. When she asked where I'd been, I gripped my lead forehead.

"I'm going to come home now." My cheeks crushed the urge to cry. "I'll talk to you then."

"I'll drive you," said Mrs. Fairbanks. Her husband put his arm around her. Mia wiped silent tears from her puffy eyes.

I hung up on Mom's sniffles and handed the phone back to Mr. Fairbanks, whose face was a firestorm. None of them moved an inch as I scrambled to find my sandals, totally lost as to what to say.

Okay, yes, I disappeared. I didn't mean to, but this ring sent me back to the freaking sixteenth century. To the court of Nicholas the Ironheart, who wasn't the frightening old tyrant in the books, by the way. He was young, and kind, and unbearably cute. And he and his sister are in grave danger, and I could have helped them.

The panic surged without warning, sending me to my feet.

"I'm really sorry," I mumbled. "How long was I gone?"

Mia's voice wavered. "A whole day. Half the town's been looking for you."

"Really?" *I don't even know half the town.*

"Where were you, Emmie?" asked Mrs. Fairbanks.

"And what are you wearing?" Mia cut in. "Is that some kind of costume?"

I glanced down at the thick linen nightie. "Yeah, actually. It's…it's from a play."

"You're in a play?"

I picked up my bag, pinning my gaze to the floor. "At one of those community theaters in Southbridge. That's where I was. Sorry I didn't tell you. I was…I was embarrassed. But I'd forgotten my stuff here, so my friend dropped me off."

"We thought you were dead and you were on *stage?*" Mia cried. "And which friend?"

"It was just one day," I said, biting my lip so hard it nearly bled. "I'll explain it all later, but I just want to go home."

Mr. Fairbanks nodded. "Come on."

Mia didn't even look at me as I climbed into her parents' chilly Cadillac SUV, let alone come along for the drive. The rain had stopped, but the roads were foggy, the street lamps a string of fuzzy halos.

Mom ran down the path as the car pulled up outside. I stepped out and hugged her tightly, breathing in her dollar-store shampoo. She wouldn't take her eyes off me, walking me inside like I was an invalid.

"Where were you?" she said, her chest rising and falling like an old lady's.

I'd forgotten how stale our house smelled, how it didn't feel like home, even after three years. I scooped up our miniature schnauzer, Ruby, and flopped onto the stained mocha couch.

"I was fine," I said shakily. I repeated my vague story about being in Southbridge for a play and my friend driving me to Mia's to get my laptop.

"A *play?* Do you know I had to call your father? And that woman answered?"

If there was a button to switch off my hearing, I would've pressed it right then.

Mom's voice shot up ten decibels. "And then I called the police! But they can't do anything until the person's gone more than twenty-four hours."

"I know," I muttered. "I've seen it on TV."

"Emmie!" she slammed her fist onto her jeans. "How can you take off like that? Even Mia didn't know where you were."

My hands flew to my ears. "Please, Mom, stop! I'm sorry, okay?"

She pinched the bridge of her nose, her fingers shuddering. "Has this got something to do with a boy?"

I kneaded my eyes. "Can't I just go to bed? We can talk about it tomorrow."

"No, you may not. I am your mother, and I was worried sick about you. I have no idea what to even do with you right now."

I stood up and hitched my bag over my shoulder. "Mom, I'm eighteen. I'm really sorry I scared you, but you can't make me do anything. I'm going to bed."

"Is it that Logan boy again? Is that who you were with?" Her broken voice shattered me with guilt. "Because this really isn't like you at all."

I turned back at her, blurting the words. "His name is Nick. And don't worry, I'm not going to go running off chasing some guy like an idiot." I had to press my lips closed to avoid finishing the thought out loud.

Unlike you moving us twenty minutes away from Dad's college in case he decided to love us again.

I tore off the ring that reminded me too much of Nick's perfect hands and dropped it onto my dresser. In my world, girls like me didn't hang out with guys like Nicholas Tudor.

Ruby shadowed me more than usual as I spun the shower tap to hot, wanting the heavy feeling washed away. I caught my reflection in the glass, gasping at the sight of the two small holes bulging from my outer thigh that were packed with bloodied sponge—physical evidence that I hadn't imagined my visit to Tudor England. I gripped the surrounding skin and squeezed, tears I couldn't fight slipping into the shower stream.

I sat on the toilet seat and carefully pulled out the sponge with Mom's tweezers. There was a bruise, but no pus or angry redness, so I wrapped the wound with a clean bandage. I could hear Mom on the phone downstairs.

I threw on my favorite thrift-store T-shirt that said *Will Design For Money* and sat at my desk, pushing aside my tackle box. I flipped open my laptop, Ruby settling at my feet. Typing his name into the search engine sent a ripple of nervous excitement through me.

Nicholas the Ironheart

The image search flooded with various sizes of that same menacing portrait in the books, until a painting I'd never seen loaded at the bottom. My chest caved, emptied of air.

The face was young and handsome, the eyes translucent blue, the dark auburn hair thick and tousled. A light scar drew a thin line down his cheek. It was unmistakably the guy I'd met. Clicking on the picture opened a biography page. I scanned the text, breathless at the fifth paragraph.

The king's closest friend, Francis Beaumont, the Earl of Warwick, married the queen's maid-of-honour Alice Grey in 1580 and was executed for treason in 1582.

Alice married *Francis?* That shocked me more than the fact that he'd had his head lopped off. Almost everyone I'd met at the Palace of Whitehall showed up in an internet search, even Viscount Hereford. There were thousands of entries about Thomas Grey, chief advisor to one of England's most notorious kings, some mentioning his two daughters, Violet and Alice. Their mother, Susanna Grey, Thomas Grey's wife, went missing in 1576 and was never found.

I continued searching. Isobel Beaumont fell off the radar at a young age, while her croaky-voiced mom, the Dowager Countess of Warwick, became one of the richest and most powerful women in England—ugh.

I read about Kit's death until my eyes stung, every article saying the same thing: Princess Catherine was murdered in June of 1580 and her killer was never found. She was taken from her bed without a struggle and strangled with a set of wooden Catholic rosary beads, her neck broken. England was fiercely Protestant at that time and practicing Catholicism was punishable by death. The rosary beads were seen as a symbolic attack on King Nick's Protestant faith.

I rubbed my eyes and typed one more search, my cheeks tingling.

Nicholas the Ironheart wife

Hundreds of portraits of a pretty girl with inky black ringlets and dark eyes sent me sinking into the chair. She was Princess Henriette of France, who the king married in 1580. Henriette died of consumption several years later, leaving the King of England without an heir. He never remarried and died at the age of thirty-nine on the battlefield, but not from war wounds. Witnesses said he choked on his own breath, England rejoicing at the death of their brutal king. The crown passed unchallenged to the Scottish King James the Sixth (the First of England), launching the reign of the House of Stuart and unifying England, Ireland, and Scotland.

So it looked like asthma got him in the end after all.

I didn't know if it was possible to feel any worse as I collapsed onto the mattress, Ruby licking her paws beside me. My mind turned cartwheels, but I was asleep in minutes, kicking the sheets through fitful dreams of Nick collapsing on a bloody field. The image morphed into his corpse burning on a stake as blackened teeth around him cheered.

At first, I didn't know where I was. But then my eyes began to recognize the thin line of light around my alphabet blinds—a relic from the toddler who'd had the bedroom before me. Ruby was barking her head off downstairs: a signal that Mom was leaving for work.

I rolled onto my side, struck with the memory of King Nick and his amazing court. Had it actually happened? Had I survived *time travel*, like an alien abduction, my face nearly ending up on every news channel in America?

I kicked off the comforter and lifted my thigh, the bandage corroborating the story. The idea of it—that something so spectacular had happened to me, of all people—almost sent me catatonic. The hardest part to grasp was: why me? And why did the ring travel between Tudor England and Hatfield, Massachusetts? Was there a connection between them?

I dug my phone from my bag and switched it on. A message from Mom appeared instantly.

I had to leave for work. Please call me when you get up.

There were two from Josh saying he was glad I was home safe, and one from Mia, her tone way terser than usual.

Come over today if you're not out of town. We have to do the essay.

Nothing from Dad, of course. I flopped onto the pillow and dialed Mom's number, tight with guilt over my callous thoughts about her and Dad. Mom's devotion to the man was borderline humiliating, starting with her chasing him to England uninvited when they'd first met, but she'd always looked after me.

Mom was driving, so our conversation was mercifully brief, but she told me she had to work a double shift and if I thought about disappearing again, she'd change the locks.

After a quick shower, I tied on my scuffed shoes and jogged to Mia's house, clouds huddling overhead. How the hell was I going to write an essay about Nicholas the Ironheart? The thought made my stomach curl over itself.

Mia's house had morphed into the rock-music bar we snuck into in Southbridge once, Atomic's sophomore album blasting from speakers she'd set up on her mom's Qing-dynasty cabinet. I'd loved the album when it first dropped, but after the gentle Tudor violins, it sounded exhausting and loud.

"Your folks are out?" I asked, the marble countertop a mess of bacon slices, fried eggs, and piles of grated cheese.

"There's an issue at the hydroponics farm. Something to do with a pump." Mia handed me a breakfast wrap. I hoped it was a peace offering.

"Thanks," I said with a smile, but she didn't reciprocate.

We took our wraps outside to the pool and made a picnic on our towels. Mia had already laid out two new notepads with blue, green, and red pens, and a pile of books about Nicholas the Ironheart.

"We should start," she said, without looking at me.

I lowered my wrap, jitters blowing through my stomach. "You don't want to talk about yesterday?"

"What's there to talk about? You said you were in a play in South-bridge, and I thought you were dead."

My hand flew to her bronzed thigh. "Mia. I'm so sorry."

She angled her cheek away. "I just don't get why you wouldn't tell me about any of this. It's so unlike you. Who's this friend you were with anyway? Do I know her?"

I watched Mia's brother Tristan flap open a towel at the waterfall end of the pool. His size made him look twenty instead of fifteen.

"Actually, it's a *he*," I stammered. "A guy I met in Southbridge. He's a director and asked if I wanted to be in one of his plays. I didn't say anything, because...I don't know, it's not the play I'm interested in —it's him—but he's all wrong for me." I almost wanted to give myself a round of applause. The lies had poured out like water to my best friend in the world.

Mia gaped at me. "Oh my God, Emmie, you have a boyfriend?"

"No! Not a boyfriend."

"And what do you mean he's wrong for you? Is he married?"

"God, no."

"He's a druggie?"

He's a Tudor king.

"He's older than me," I blurted, tossing my pen onto my notebook.

Mia sat up on her knees, her voice speeding up, her hands twitchy. "I had no idea this was why you were acting so nuts. Oh my gosh, you've caught yourself a *silver fox*. Okay, I forgive you."

"Ugh, he's not that old. He's around twenty. I think."

"That's not old! It's actually perfect for you." She licked mayo off her fingers. "I wish you'd just told me this, you stinker. You need to fill me in on *everything.* When am I meeting him?"

I could've laughed if I didn't feel so flat. "Honestly Mia, this one's not going to work out, so maybe we should just get stuck into the essay." My chest constricted. Like dating Nicholas the Ironheart was even an option. Plus, my priority was Central Saint Martins. *Careers before crushes*, I reminded myself. There was no way I was ending up like my mom.

Mia gave me a hard look, sighing deeply. "Em, I've been waiting for you to get *that look* on your face for three years. Not even Logan gave you that face. Don't push this guy away because you're scared."

"Mia, please. The essay." The crack in my voice surprised us both.

She crossed her long legs. "Fine, but we're going to talk about this later." She looked over her notebook. "So I've done some reading. Forget what I said before. Nicholas the Ironheart was unquestionably a psycho. So we should say his nickname is deserved, but argue it better than Avery and brown-nose-Ambrose to get the top mark."

"Wait, didn't we already determine that his eight-year-old sister was brutally murdered?"

"So what are you saying?"

"I'm saying I don't think 'Ironheart' is the right word to describe him. His sister was his only living family. If you really think about his reaction to her death, it's the opposite of cold-hearted. Her loss clearly screwed him up on a massive scale, and he became totally paranoid about who would hurt him in that way."

"So which word do you think is better?"

"I don't know…misunderstood? Paranoid?"

"Nicholas the Misunderstood?" Her eyebrows were doing that thing they did when she felt sorry for me. "Em, I've seriously read about this."

"Well, I actually know a bit about this topic too."

"How? You were in Southbridge with the silver fox."

"You're not the only one who knows about Nicholas the Ironheart!" I could barely look at her. Before yesterday I'd only had one fight with Mia, when she'd wanted to tattoo our names on each other's ankles and I'd refused.

My book snapped shut, the bang louder than I intended. "I think I'm going to work on it on my own for a bit."

Her pen hit her lap. "Emmie!"

"You said you did a lot of reading already. Just let me catch up to you. It's fine."

It took rain droplets sprinkling into our water glasses for her to agree to let me go, promising to call me later. I knew she'd grill me about my mysterious Southbridge guy, and I had no idea what to say. I needed to get over my stupid obsession with a king who was long dead. Why was I even talking like he was someone I was dating? I needed therapy.

I trudged home through the soggy field. My shoes were caked in mud, so I yanked them off and tossed them onto the back deck. I didn't feel like working on the essay or being alone, and I didn't have a car to get anywhere. I didn't even feel like taking Ruby for a run, which wasn't like me.

All I felt like was going back there.

The thought sliced my chest like a guillotine. Mia was right. Even though I'd hardly been in Nick's company, I'd never felt so fluttery about a guy, especially so quickly. Thinking about him made my face heat up and my stomach twist, but in a really good way.

Through the window, I watched the elm tree rustle its leaves, my mind racing. Mom wouldn't be home until the morning. *What if I went back, just for a few hours?* As long as I didn't lose the ring, I could come home if things went south.

For this to be an option, though, I'd have to fall asleep as quickly as possible.

I bolted into Mom's bathroom, tearing folded toothpaste tubes and empty containers off the shelves until I found her sleeping pills. My stomach was flipping every which way. I dropped a tiny blue tablet onto my tongue and gulped water from the faucet.

Sitting on the edge of my bed, I typed a text to Mom, every word carefully thought out.

I'm catching the bus to Hadley to shop. I need a new phone charger, so I'll get one there, but you probably won't be able to call me until I get back tonight. DO NOT WORRY. Your daughter is a grown woman (just) and totally fine.

I slid the blue-diamond ring onto my thumb and climbed into my bed beside Ruby, questions swooping at me like starving hawks.

What if this really works and I never get home again?

Or worse—what if it doesn't and my life is just this after all?

My skin trembled against Ruby's silvery fur as I held her close. As shattered as I was, without a pill, it would've taken me hours to fall asleep through the adrenalin storm of pure fear.

But the sleep came quickly.

6

I couldn't see through the blackness. But where my eyes failed, my skin and nose held the answer. There was no way I was in my own bed. The blanket was too thick, too scratchy, and too scented with vanilla and rosemary to be mine.

The darkness lifted, oak panels materializing on the ceiling. On the opposite wall hung a portrait of a blue-eyed boy in a feathered cap, chilly air drifting through the lattice window.

I'm back at Whitehall!

I rolled over and examined the blue-diamond ring like I might see magic infused within it, every cell in my body somersaulting. For a second, I thought maybe I was dreaming, but I still had on my mint-green wrap top, and curved nails were scratching at the door.

"Ruby?"

She hopped up onto the mattress. Her shuddering body was warm, her anxious eyes two black plates. How had she come with me?

She sprang off the bed and swiped at the door, her "I have to pee" signal. My toes froze against the stone floor, my legs bare under jean shorts. I tugged them off and bundled them into a petticoat with the rest of my modern clothes, Ruby's collar, and the bandage, before pushing the mass under the bed. I considered stuffing the ring inside my bodice again, but it was safer buried under the mattress. I couldn't risk the king's time-traveling ring falling out of my dress and getting lost somewhere.

Awesome. Now you've got koala undies and the king's favorite ring, that's also a time portal, *hidden under your bed.*

Why was King Nick's ring a time portal? Did he know? Was he a time traveler too?

A tingle fluttered across my skin as it hit me that Nick Tudor was in the next building. The gold clock on the mantel revealed it was early afternoon.

Ruby whimpered, circling my feet before pawing at the door again.

I hurriedly tied on a simple buttermilk-colored dress with cut sleeves, kicked my feet into a pair of satin slippers, and stepped into the dim corridor. I fixed my hair into a rough braid, following Ruby into the courtyard. She squatted beside a wooden barrel that reeked of beer, whimpering at me as she peed. A freezing gust of wind lashed the courtyard, sending an empty barrel bouncing on its side. My eyes followed it, my head twisting in all directions at every sound. Two men in black coats ambled past and dipped their heads at me, but no one else glanced our way.

When light rain began sprinkling from the sky, Ruby scampered ahead into the main building. I chased her past the heat radiating from the kitchens. My thigh was still too sore for this.

"Ruby, stop!" I hissed.

I snatched her beneath the portrait of Queen Elizabeth the First, the palace bustling with chatter and music, the courtiers' faces bright. The grief-fest over the king's collapse at the feast was clearly over. My eyes hunted for him with a will of their own, but there were no guards with crossed pikes, no trumpets, no announcements. As long as I could just clap my eyes on Nick—maybe drop some info about Kit's murder that might help them in some way—it wouldn't be a wasted trip.

We followed a moving mass of courtiers across the upper gallery to the entertainment side of court, reaching an outdoor arena. Rain drizzled as men gulped beer and chanted from the tiered seating while girls younger than me, dressed in low-cut gowns, eyed them flirta-tiously. I spotted Alice Grey waving me over from the second row.

"Good God, you are here!" she said, making space beside her. "I thought you had left back for Hatfield." She leaned in. "Lord Here-ford cornered me like a lecher, insisting to know where you were. Were you ill?" Her eyes colored with concern.

"I went to see my uncle in the city," I said in a rush. "And to get this little lass." I scratched Ruby's ears.

"My stars, she is darling. What pedigree is she?"

"Schnauzer. A little German girl." I winced at myself. When did Germany officially become a thing? I should've listened more in history class.

Alice introduced me to the Earl of Shrewsbury and his wife Lady Ascot, who were sitting below us. Their front-row seats overlooked a muddy pit that imprisoned an emaciated-looking brown bear strapped to a wooden pole.

"What are we watching?" I asked, dread inching its way into me.

"Bear-baiting," Alice replied, like I should know, tossing her unpinned hair that still smelled like cinnamon.

I wasn't sure what bear-baiting was, but I didn't dare ask. Instead, I turned away from the chained-up bear and surveyed the crowd, spotting prestigious spectators like Alice's father Thomas Grey, the French and Spanish ambassadors, and Viscount Hereford over on the other side. There was no sign of Nick Tudor's breathtaking face.

Two enormous mastiffs burst into the pit, the bear snarling as two men jabbed its fur with spears. I considered escaping the unfolding horror show, but just then, the Earl of Shrewsbury and Lady Ascot spun in their seats to gape at something behind me, followed by all the spectators in the front row. I turned to see what they were all staring at, my heart pummeling my chest.

Four king's guards were pushing their way along the row behind me, crying, "Make way!"

I scanned every inch of space for Nick, but the guards were alone. They stopped before the Dowager Countess of Warwick and Isobel Beaumont. Mark Macaulay, the king's bald gentleman, bowed to Isobel before grabbing the man beside her and hauling him to his feet. He dug into the man's cloak, retrieving a small scroll. The countess slanted away from the man like he'd been diagnosed with leprosy.

"You are arrested by order of the king and charged with high treason," Mark proclaimed at the top of his voice. "You will be taken to the Tower of London to await trial."

After they shoved the man off the scaffolding, I grabbed Alice's arm. "Who was that?"

"The Bishop of Rochester," she said grimly. "That was probably a papal bull. I have long suspected him to be a clandestine Catholic. I suppose the Dowager Countess of Warwick would know," she added, watching Isobel press a tiny bottle to her mother's nose. When she caught me looking at her, Isobel shot me a look so vicious it could take down a unit of Navy SEALs.

The mastiffs barked like savages at the cowering bear. I nudged Alice. "What did you mean the Countess of Warwick would know?"

She leaned closer, speaking so low I could barely hear her. "The Dowager Lady Warwick is from a devotedly Catholic family, although she pretends otherwise. Her brother was racked and executed by Queen Elizabeth for his involvement in a papist plot to seize the throne."

"Seriously?"

Alice opened a pouch of warm gingerbread and passed me a square. "The lady countess's great-uncle was a distant cousin of King Henry the Eighth. Some still believe Francis, as her firstborn son, should be next in the line of succession after Kit—or even the lady countess herself. Be that as it may, I believe it is why Francis distances himself from the countess and his sister Isobel. He wishes not to be caught up in an intrigue."

Alice's eyes flickered past me, the conversation instantly shut down. Francis Beaumont was climbing over legs and skirts toward us, Kit's tiny hand clasped at his back. Every person she passed bowed at her and whispered like she was a celebrity.

Kit beamed at Alice and me. "I wanted to watch with you and Mistress Grace."

Alice smiled warmly, bunching her teal skirts so Kit could sit between us. I tried not to picture her frail neck snapping in two or her head hanging limp and lifeless.

"Good morrow," she said to me with a warm smile.

"Hello, friend." It was probably totally inappropriate for Tudor times, but I couldn't resist lightly running my hand down her tangerine hair that flowed from a headdress made entirely of pearls. Luckily, Kit didn't seem to mind.

Alice leaned out to Francis. "Is His Majesty aware you brought the princess to such a spectacle?"

"Her governess has taken ill, so we await the next one," he replied lazily, squeezing in beside me. Silver thread was stitched down his black coat in thin lines—the original pinstripe suit.

"Do not make me go back," Kit begged Francis.

"Of course not, kitten, we had a deal."

The mastiffs had their teeth locked to the bear's chin, dragging it to the ground. I held my chest as the bear screamed, biting and swiping, but its claws had been ripped out so it couldn't fight, its mouth a toothless black hole.

"How long do you give the bear, Kit?" said Francis, hunching forward to smile at her.

"Oh, I would not guess," she said with a blush. "I feel dreadfully sorry for it."

"Pretend it is Alice," he replied. Kit giggled.

It was so hard to imagine Alice and Francis tying the knot.

"Do you not have some manner of work to do?" Alice snapped at him.

"Entertaining the court *is* my work and precisely why His Majesty left me in charge of it while he is abroad."

"And why be in charge of the realm, like my father, when you can be in charge of court entertainment?"

"And what are you in charge of? Headaches?"

"The king's left court?" I murmured, the shock clear in my voice.

"Indeed. To France maybe," said Alice. "Last time, he was gone fourteen weeks. He abhorred the stench at Whitehall that summer, but they never discovered what it was."

I couldn't speak. *I'd traveled through freaking time* for a chance to see

Nick again, and he'd already busted out of Whitehall—and possibly the country—with zero thought about me. I was officially the most delusional stalker in centuries. It really was a Grace family trait.

Alice offered me more gingerbread, but I shook my head, biting away my disappointment.

When the bear dropped to its stomach and wailed, Kit squealed, leaning into me like I might protect her. I shrouded my face with my hands, and when I opened them again, she giggled at me. I did it again, and she laughed harder, the game distracting both her and me from the bear being torn to pieces.

She squeezed my wrist. "Will you sew with me this night? I'm making clothes for the poor." Her sky-blue eyes blinked with hope.

"Sure." The word popped out before I could stop it. Mom would still be gone for at least twelve more hours. If I had no hope of seeing Nick, maybe I could use my time to help Kit. Perhaps gather some evidence about who might be out to hurt her. That was more important than some dumb crush that was clearly one-sided.

With a final howl, the bear tumbled forward, literally dinner for the dogs. The spectators clapped, some exchanging coins.

Francis stood over Kit. "We best get you back."

Alice asked if I wanted to walk back through the gardens, which was perfect, because Ruby was getting restless. As much as the bear torture sickened me, it was hard not to pinch myself. I really was back in this magical place!

All around us, women in puffed sleeves and hoop skirts wandered along flowery paths divided by short brick walls and lined with trees manicured into flawless ovals. We strolled down the broadest avenue and stopped at an herb garden beside a green-and-white column topped with a dragon sculpture. Alice broke off a stem of mint and split it into two, handing me half.

"You can steep it in the wine in your room," she said. "Then rub the leaves on your teeth." Her voice softened as we passed the swan pond. Ruby chased sparrows around the rim. "I've been wanting to speak with you." Alice's cheeks flushed pink as she collected her words. "Is something taking place between you and His Majesty?"

"What?" It took physical effort to keep my expression blank.

"Most kings dance with maidens, especially the French one. Even so, ours never dances in public with single ladies, not even Isobel. He is too clever for that. Yet he danced with you at the feast."

"He asked me, so I said yes. That was all."

The gravity in Alice's face frightened me. "I know how handsome he is, Emmie. How warm, like the sun on the most glorious of days. To not notice him would be like passing blindly through a flower garden. But you are new here, so I must tell you. You want not to become another Lucinda Parker. I couldn't bear it. England needs an heir, and His Majesty will take a wife soon. If the queen found out you had known the king behind closed doors, you could be banished from court forever."

"Who's Lucinda Parker?" My stomach tightened.

"She was lodging at court, waiting to be chosen as a maid of honour. Very pretty and accomplished enough. Last year, there were rumors about a dalliance between her and the king. And then, all of a sudden, she disappeared."

I nearly choked on my breath. "Murdered?"

Alice chortled. "No, silly. *With child.* She was sent to a nunnery. Where unmarried girls go to have their bastards. That is the very point, Emmie. A lady in our position can become one of two things at court: a wife or a whore."

My entire body caved in on itself. Had Nick really gotten a girl pregnant and then shipped her off like trash? Was he *that* kind of guy?

Alice's soft fingers took mine. "You promise that all you say is true, and you have no dalliance with the king? Because I'll not tell a soul if you do. You can speak your conscience, I will never judge you."

The opportunity to share my secret with my closest friend at court was agonizingly tempting. I wanted to tell Alice that I'd spent time alone with Nick in his chambers where he'd played his lute for me and ask what she thought of that, but my throat locked up.

"I promise, nothing's going on," I said stiffly. "The king asked me to dance because he was trying to get away from some Frenchman… that's all."

Alice exhaled and hugged me, my chest collapsing. Despite what she'd said about Lucinda Parker, and as much as I knew I shouldn't want this, everything inside me squeezed at the thought of even having a chance with him.

After submerging my mint sprig in my daily portion of wine, it was time to meet Kit. Following Alice's directions, I passed the Presence Chamber and into another guarded wing, my stomach buzzing with nerves.

Kit's rooms were the size of my entire house. Flurrying maids dusted wooden animal sets and embroidered carpets, and the air was gently scented with flowers. Kit proudly talked me through every toy and musical instrument, and the happiness that gave me caught me a little by surprise. I'd begged my parents for a sister up until the day Dad moved us from England to America for a history professorship at Amherst College…that was five months before he left Mom for his twenty-two-year-old associate, and Mom and I ended up in San Diego for two years before moving to Hatfield— twenty minutes from Amherst—in case Dad changed his mind (he didn't).

Kit and I settled by the fire, and she handed me an embroidery hoop with a half-finished rose motif. I kept pricking my thumb and then sucking the blood that pushed out. Evenings at court were so silent without blaring televisions…so peaceful. And, as far as I knew, divorce was outlawed. Another win.

Kit sat forward as if inviting me into a secret. "Guess why I do this before bed? Because it is so dull it makes me fall asleep." I laughed, but her shoulders wilted. "I wish you could do this with me every night. May I show you something?"

Beside a collection of wooden horses was the easel Kit had deliberately overlooked during her tour. When she lifted the sheet concealing the canvas, I nearly lost my balance. It was the young portrait of King Nick that I'd seen on the internet—the one that looked just like him.

"You painted this?" I said. The work was too advanced for any eight-year-old I knew in my world.

"I took lessons from Signor Lucchetto when he was at Hampton Court. It is for His Majesty's birthday." She scrunched her nose. "Do you think it is foolish? Because he already has a painter?"

"Are you kidding? Kit, this is incredible."

She beamed. "Thank you. I want to please him so." Her glowing face was a punch to the gut. It wasn't just knowing she would die soon that made my chest burn. It was the knowing that I could stop it. I could warn them.

My voice thickened. "Do you happen to know the date today?"

She blanched. "I shouldn't think so. Francis said the king's birthday is in two weeks, thus I suppose it is nearly June."

I counted. That meant there were only a few weeks until Kit's murder and the beginnings of Nicholas the Ironheart. If I was going to try to find out who was responsible, I had to work fast.

Minty wine swished around my teeth like mouthwash as I dipped a quill into ink, my shoulders wrapped in a wool blanket. Once I'd worked out how to stop the ink from bleeding onto the page, I began sketching the cabochon emerald Kit wore on her middle finger. It was the only way I could relax myself enough to fall asleep, wishing I'd thought to bring one of Mom's pills.

How can I make Kit's ring more contemporary and cool? Maybe a simple, thin gold band—sleek and stylish beneath the old stone. Central Saint Martins might love that.

Feeling the tightness in my chest beginning to loosen, I drew more sharp lines over the smooth emerald like a modern cage, the contrast between old and new kind of poetic. My mind swirled, chasing my fingers across the parchment. The quill's tip turned the cage bars into thick waves, like strands of hair.

My mind kept returning to Kit. With all her guards and no sign of a struggle, the person who took her had to have known her. Why would someone who knew Kit want to steal her life away? Aside from being a miserable Catholic in a Protestant court? Perhaps because they wanted to clear a path to the throne, one Tudor at a time.

I sketched shadows into the emerald until it looked like a face, the eyes two smoky ovals, the mouth slightly turned down at the ends. A black goatee materialized around the strong chin.

Francis Beaumont was glaring back at me.

According to Alice, Francis had already put Kit in danger by taking her hunting and to the bear-baiting, and if anything happened to her, he'd be a serious contender for the throne. Plus, I already knew that Nick would execute him in a couple of years, so he was clearly a traitor of some kind, despite what Alice said about him not wanting to be caught up in an intrigue. Francis also hailed from a staunchly Catholic family, and Kit was strangled with a set of wooden Catholic rosary beads. It was far from enough to be sure, but it was a start. I had to get closer to Francis Beaumont to find out whether he was capable of murder. I knew I wasn't supposed to mess with history, but I wasn't technically messing yet. Once I found out more about him, I could choose whether to warn Nick or not.

Feeling my eyelids beginning to droop, I checked the ring was securely on my thumb and waited for sleep, keeping Ruby firmly wedged beneath my arm.

I had to return to Whitehall the first moment I could. Plus, I still hadn't seen Nicholas Tudor again. Which meant there was no way I wasn't coming back.

Mom pushed through the front door early on Sunday morning, her slate eyes puffy from her graveyard nursing shift. She demolished the scrambled eggs I'd made her and raised her arms in a star-shaped stretch.

"What's that?" She frowned and reached for the bandage I'd re-wrapped around my thigh.

I stepped back. "It's just for compression. I hurt my hamstring running."

"Want me to take a look?"

"It's fine."

She yawned and dumped her dirty plate in the sink. "Suit yourself. I'm going to bed."

Was that *it?* I could go back right away? The thought made butter-flies dip and dive in my stomach. As Mom dragged her nursing clogs up the stairs, I called out that I was going to Mia's to study and to not wait up for me.

"Don't be late," she said. "School tomorrow. Oh, and Emmie?" She poked her head around the top of the stairs. "Let's have dinner next week. We can try the new Chinese place."

"Aren't you working every night?"

She rubbed her eye socket with her knuckle. "Oh, true. Sunday then." She usually had Sunday evenings off.

"Okay," I said, pinched with guilt about lying to her about so many things. "Goodnight. Love you."

She grunted. "I think you mean good morning, cookie."

I stepped onto the back verandah and called Mia twice, but she didn't pick up. I quickly typed her a message.

Hey babe, Need a favor. I'm going to see the silver fox today, but I don't want Mom to know. Not worth the drama. Ur right, I like him. But pls don't get wound up ;). I told Mom I'm at yours studying for all of today. Don't call my house!! Owe you one. Love, E. xx

As soon as I could hear Mom's soft snore through the door, I was in the bathroom, raiding her sleeping pill collection again. I swallowed one and pocketed another inside my denim shorts.

After locking Ruby out of my room, I crawled back into bed and pulled the comforter to my chin, waiting for the pill to slink through my system. I couldn't remember ever feeling so exhilarated or so alive.

7

A SHORT WHILE LATER, I WAS STANDING BENEATH THE FORMIDABLE King's Gate at the Palace of Whitehall, its high brick walls washed pink from the dawn light. Roosters crowed from the cockpit over the wall. Alice helped me into a waiting coach with burgundy velvet seats and cushions threaded with gold. *Man, the Tudor folk start their days criminally early.*

"Do I look terribly plain?" Kit asked me from the opposite seat, tying a cream scarf over her hair.

"Of course not," I replied politely, although her honey gown was modest.

Her shoulders drooped. "This is the plainest cloth I have."

"You look like a common girl from London," said Francis Beaumont, stretched beside her in oatmeal breeches and a white shirt with a ruffled collar. "Kit cannot go out in public and be recognized," he said to me, like I was dumb not to know that. "She is a child, and the heir presumptive to the throne. It is much too dangerous."

"You look *very* plain," I reassured Kit with a smile and she beamed at me.

We whipped away from the gatehouse, Alice twisting back to watch the disappearing Tudor rose emblems entwined with the king's initials. "Tell me again why you dragged us from breakfast for this foolish exercise?" she scowled at Francis.

"I dragged *you* from breakfast," he replied. "Emmie ran into us in the hall. Feeling deficient today?"

"I meant taking Kit on an outing—to London of all places!"

"No one knows what I look like," Kit said in a small voice. "There has never been a portrait issued. Thus, if I do not look or act like a princess—"

"No one will know," finished Francis. "I promised her," he said to Alice.

"And *I* promised myself to not let her out of my sight," she retorted.

"You seem to not want to let me out of your sight," he said under his breath, but loudly enough to make Alice expel air through her lips like she was fed up.

I squeezed the trinket Alice had draped around my neck at the gate. It was a little brass ball with pin-sized holes that smelled like Mrs. Fairbanks's spices cabinet, which Alice said would ward off bad air in the city. She'd also assured me we'd be back before lunch, or I wouldn't have encouraged us to go. I needed the face-to-face time with Francis.

He played with the string on his shirt, espresso curls hiding his face. *Did you murder Catherine Tudor?* I asked him silently.

"We're outside the castle!" Kit cried, half hanging out the open window. Francis wrenched her back in.

My skin prickled at the familiar sight of the black-and-white timber houses with red roofs, our coach swerving past wagons and rickshaws. Even though the sun had just risen, the streets bustled with women in aprons shouting at men wearing hats and belted coats. I pressed my knees together under my clover-green cloak, my palms sweating. Roaming the public streets of sixteenth-century England was surely a fast track to the plague or worse. But at least I had Francis in my sights.

We were soon within the city walls, bumping through dark, twisting alleys cluttered with overhanging buildings before Francis directed the driver to stop near a place called Leadenhall. We stepped out onto a gravel street near a wagon crawling with leashed monkeys. Francis tweaked Kit's scarf to cover every strand of red and hoisted her onto his shoulders. Alice and I trailed them down a narrow lane swept with sewage, where live peacocks lined up for sale beside squawking chickens in iron cages. When the street opened into a wide avenue, Kit asked Francis to let her down and darted into a grand building with a ceiling as high as the Great Hall's at Whitehall. Bells were ringing, and a stuttering vendor yelled out different flavors of pies, while others handed out packages of oysters, bread, oranges, and cheese.

My stomach was tied in a knot, but I forced myself to breathe, focusing on what I'd learned twice now: Francis had no issue putting Kit in genuine danger. He wandered ahead into the flower section, watching Alice inspect the tulips.

Kit's fingers folded into mine, her excited eyes shining like moonstones. I listened to her point out everything in sight as we strolled past kaleidoscopic carnations and buttery daffodils.

"You and Francis spend a lot of time together," I said to her. "Were you always close?"

"He is like my brother. Oh look, that man has blood on his face." A guy stumbled past us with a cloth wrapped around his head, his cheek smeared with fresh blood.

"Don't look at him." I pulled her toward the bluebells. "Is Francis always so…short-tempered?" I smiled.

"He is funny and sweet. He is the only person His Majesty favors me with when I am at court. Even over the governesses." She nudged a dropped cluster of bluebells with her shoe. "I plan to wed him one day."

I swallowed my surprise. "But isn't he from a Catholic family?"

"Francis is not a papist! At least I think not. It would not please the king."

"What would not?" said Francis.

I spun around.

"That," I said quickly, pointing at a gray-haired woman lying in the corner with an iron cage encasing her head like a helmet. She moaned through a strip of metal gagging her mouth.

"The branks," Francis explained. "Made especially for women who talk too much." His eyes settled on me.

Kit rubbed her stomach. "I'm hungry. We missed breakfast."

"May we go to the inn?" chimed Alice, clutching a bouquet of mauve tulips she'd purchased. "The one where the knights go." She shot me the same look Mia did when there were hot guys around.

Francis creased his brow at her. "We will be recognized at the inn. There is a tavern nearby."

The tavern was dark and stuffy, and our legs crowded each other's as we gathered around a thin barrel. The men beside us belly-laughed over pints of beer. A woman in a tatty dress and heavy makeup hung off one of the barfly's arms. A guy with no chin plucked at a dented lute in the corner.

Breakfast was rye-bread rolls with bacon, lettuce, and tomato. Kit scarfed hers with giant bites, like enjoying it was an act of defiance.

"You know what they call these back home?" I said to her. "BLTs."

"And what does that stand for? Bloody Lousy Thief?" said Francis.

Alice shot him a look. "How about Brainless Little Toad?"

Kit burst out laughing, sending Francis's brows together. "Are you trying to get us robbed with those damn flowers?" he snapped at Alice. She glowered at him, slipping the tulips inside her coat folds.

Kit's grin was so bright I didn't want to point out the lettuce in her teeth and dampen it.

"Is this not more enjoyable than sewing?" she said to me.

"Emptying chamber pots is more enjoyable than sewing," I replied. She giggled.

A man with a ponytail and three daggers roped to his waist plopped a mug of beer on the barrel opposite ours. He squinted at Kit through bushy brows.

Francis glided a hand toward Alice. "Time to go."

On our way back to the coach, Alice and Kit ran ahead to where puppeteers were staging a street show. I stopped at a jewelry stand, inspecting a signet ring embossed with a Tudor rose. Francis loitered beside me, watching a dirty pig sniff the sidewalk as he picked at the membrane of an orange.

"Feeling more at home in the city?" he asked me, and I sensed a put-down in his question.

"You mean among the prostitutes and beggars?"

"I meant more the blacksmiths, the butchers…those who've risen through the ranks, but are still lowborn commoners. Like theologians and *physicians*. Your father is a physician, correct?"

I angled my head at him. "Do you rehearse your insults?"

He popped an orange wedge into his mouth. "You merely seem uncomfortable at court, so I thought you might be enjoying this return to routine."

A nearby seller hacked a live fish with a meat cleaver, spraying blood across my shoe.

My voice rose. "I may not be a member of your fancy club, but I'm not stupid. I know when someone's having a dig at me. The thing is, I don't care."

I headed for Alice and Kit, Francis pursuing me. "And there it is."

"There *what* is?"

"What His Majesty sees in you."

I stopped, blown back a little by his words.

But Francis's eyes were accusing. "You are not afraid to speak your mind, even when it risks your head, but that is all His Majesty sees. Whereas I see it as nothing more than a fleeting amusement, like touching the right girl in a game of blind man's bluff. However, touching the *wrong* girl can cause much calamity to a king on a fragile throne. A lesson he has already learned too well."

I took my chance. "And that's convenient for you, isn't it, that *fragile* throne? If only you could get to it, past whomever was in your way." My eyes moved to Kit. Francis grabbed my wrists so hard he dropped his orange, sending it spattering along the dusty ground.

"You dare speak such high treason! A commoner who was caught with stolen crown property and then used her good teeth and pretty eyes to not only get away with it, but to crawl into the king's bedchamber like a snake? And now you cling to his sister in his absence? You may be intent on climbing that ladder to heaven, Mistress Grace, but be careful you do not fall."

I twisted my arms free. "Why don't you just leave me alone?"

"Because I would follow King Nick and Princess Catherine into a fire if I had to. I will do whatever I must to keep them from danger."

"You think I'm a threat to them?" *I'm the only one who knows what's about to happen!*

Alice met us at the corner, Kit at her heels. "Is there a festivity today?" asked Alice, confused. Masses of people were flowing up the street like a river of lava.

Francis grabbed the arm of a boy in a waistcoat and breeches. "Where's everybody going?" he demanded.

"There's about to be a beheading at Tower Hill, milord."

Francis's face jolted with confusion. "Whose?"

The boy shook his head like he didn't know.

"Come on," Francis said to us, pulling Kit into the horde.

Alice threw me a look like he was being impossible again, but we jogged after them.

By the time we reached the top of the street, I was breathless. We were right outside the wall to the Tower of London, where a swarm of spectators gathered at the base of a wooden scaffold, others gawking from rooftops and balconies. The copper smell of blood lingered, and fear cut through me like a blade. *I can't be back here.*

"We should go," I said to Alice.

"Why did you not tell us!" she shouted at Francis over the noise.

He blocked the sun from his bewildered eyes. "I do not understand."

A stocky man in a leather mask was pacing the scaffold, a giant axe hanging from his hand like a scene from a horror movie. I went to plead with Francis to leave, but the Spanish ambassador, Rodrigo Montoya, shoved his way through the crowd to us, his twisted face bright red.

"How could you do this to such a pious man?" Montoya growled at Francis. "This is shameful behavior for England."

Francis looked as lost as I was, but steadied himself. "If you consider my country such a burden, Your Excellency, you might request another posting. The New World perhaps?"

The congregation swerved as two king's guards led a tall man in a smock onto the scaffold, spectators chanting, "Heretic! Burn him, the traitor!"

Montoya kissed his gold cross and elbowed his way to the front of the pack.

"His Majesty did not tell me," said Francis grimly, a trace of hurt in his voice.

The prisoner was the Bishop of Rochester, who'd been arrested at the bear-baiting. His head was shaved and bruised, his bare feet dragging manacles. I tried to cover Kit's eyes, but she wriggled to see, shaking off her scarf.

"Heavens, my father's here!" said Alice, hiding her face.

Francis darted sideways until he had Thomas Grey's velvet coat in his fists. I stepped in front of Kit, masking her from view.

Francis was snarling at Thomas. "His Majesty leaves you in charge and, suddenly, you are making your own commands?"

Thomas whacked him away, bystanders stumbling onto their heels as Francis crashed into them. "If it were up to me, Rochester would be boiled alive and fed to his dogs for his heresy," Thomas spat. "I received the command from the king last night. He insisted on the merciful axe."

"And you did not think to tell *me?*" Francis snapped.

"His Majesty's tennis playmate? Not especially."

"How dare you speak of the king in such a contemptuous manner!"

Their faces were so close that they exchanged spit. Kit clutched my legs through my cloak, and Alice stayed behind us so her father wouldn't see her.

The executioner swung the blade over his head, making a few practice runs. Thomas Grey pushed ahead as if Francis was making him miss his daughter's wedding.

"We should get out of here," I urged Francis. "Kit's scared."

"Oh please, she is a Tudor girl," he hissed at me.

A guard guided the Bishop of Rochester's quivering neck into the block's cleft, the condemned man's arms opening into a T shape. The bishop chanted about the gates to heaven as the executioner raised his axe to the cloudless sky before letting it plummet.

The dull crack was nauseating. The bishop's skull smacked onto the wood and rolled off it like a boulder, cheers exploding all around us. Kit screamed, her scarf falling to her satin shoes.

The executioner held the severed head to the sky. "Behold the head of a traitor! So die all traitors!" he cried. The crowd howled.

"Is that the king's sister?" cried a woman in a felt hat barely containing her frizzy hair. She directed a grimy finger at Kit. A hundred eyes pointed at us. "And that is one of the king's councilors," the woman added. "I was at court last year, appealing for my innocent 'usband, God rest his soul." Her voice rose like a symphony. "Princess Catherine is 'ere!"

Francis, Alice, and I formed a perimeter around Kit, muddy boots crushing my toes.

"Bless Your Grace," said dirty faces with rotting teeth, while others hid and whispered, "Damn your heretic king! Long live Queen Mary!"

Francis pressed gold coins into as many grasping palms as he could, but it only produced more. When a hand swiped for Kit, he drew his sword and guards pressed closer, red coats flashing all around us. My cries echoed as I pulled Kit into me. Alice yanked my arm until we spilled into a cluster of king's guards. Francis hurried us all into a waiting coach as Alice's tulips burst around us in a purple shower.

"By God's grace, man, drive!" Francis shouted, shoving hands away from the open windows. I slid across the velvet seat as we tore through the square.

Kit's shaking arms hugged a cushion. "Did that really happen? I think it was the best day of my life."

"Never speak that way about your life!" Francis said sharply. Her eyes watered.

"We have made a dog's dinner of this," said Alice gravely.

"Does your daftness have no end?" he snapped. "If your father or

Montoya had noticed Kit, they would have already thrown it in my face. His Majesty need not know of any of this."

"And what about the guards?" I said.

"They are not even permitted to speak to the king."

Francis's head fell to his palms, black curls sprouting through shaking fingers.

He was absolutely terrified.

I listened to the candle pop and sizzle at the foot of the bed, massaging my drilling headache. All I'd uncovered was that Francis was fiercely protective of the king and didn't give a toss about an executed Catholic—only that he wasn't told about it. I was the worst private eye in history. Mia would've had the case stitched up already like Sherlock Homes, but at least I was back within two feet of the blue-diamond ring and my sleeping pill.

I exhaled, deliberating. The honeyed smell of roasting duck floated through the open window, and my stomach replied with a hollow twist. I closed the shutters, pulled a lace shawl over my lavender dress, and hurried toward the Great Hall. There was still time before I had to go home.

Viscount Hereford hovered so closely that I could smell the lemon juice in his limp hair.

"You have neglected me," he said curtly. "At the feast, you promised me a walk in the garden, but then you evaporated like smoke from a chimney."

Alice nearly choked on her hazelnut wafer.

"Sorry. I've been kind of busy," I said, gulping milk.

"A lady?" He laughed, clutching my wrist. It felt like an alligator had latched its mouth around me. "Well, it is a beautiful afternoon. And I care not much for waiting."

Alice raised a brow at me, her molten brown pupils flashing.

I chewed the last bite of my macaron. "I guess this dress isn't getting any looser."

Five minutes later, we were strolling toward the south garden, Hereford's dagger eyes making strikes at the toy spaniel chasing sparrows across the pebbles. He nodded at a patch of bright-purple flowers. "The violets are exquisite in bloom."

"Gorgeous," I agreed. "And yummy with custard."

"They are pasque flowers." Hereford stopped in front of me, blocking the path. "Native to Hertfordshire. Your home county."

My face tightened, my eyes feigning recollection. "Really? I'm not much of a flower person."

"A high-born lady with no interest in flowers?"

I decided not to correct him that I wasn't part of the English gentry.

He bowed at two ladies in feathered bonnets who paused to admire the flower beds. My shoulders stiffened as Hereford guided me under a trellis enveloped with vines and onto a bench painted with a Tudor rose. He stayed on his feet, pacing and breathing like a pug with emphysema.

"Mistress Grace, I am not out to alarm you. However, I am a red-blooded man who has traveled all over this country, farther than the king himself. I know you are more common than you claim. Nevertheless, you are still as fair a lady as I have ever seen, and I have seen a few." I tensed at the unexpected declaration. "No man should live without a lady's servitude. Your complications are plain, so I may regret this, but I would very much like to propose a formal courtship. Of course, I shall need to meet your father. I wish to see the gratitude in his face when he learns that Viscount Hereford has taken an interest in his daughter."

My throat closed, unable to swallow.

"I intend not to startle you," he added, moving behind me to begin rubbing my shoulders like a Swedish masseuse. "But surely you cannot deny what is plainly between us."

As I fumbled for how to respond, he sat beside me and steered me to face him, his threadlike lips inching forward. *He's not actually going to—*

Hereford touched his lips to mine. I tasted a flash of wine and anchovies and lifted my hand in preparation to gently pry his persistent mouth off me.

"You will forgive the intrusion," uttered a commanding voice behind us. Hereford tore his mouth away, his torso snapping straight. I spun around, the smell of fresh roses seizing my every sense.

King Nick stood with his hands braced against two pillars, his eyes glittering brightly through the shadow of the vines. Then they found mine.

"Mistress Grace," he said with surprise, their spark fading. "And Lord Hereford."

8

"Majesty." Hereford's arms were outstretched in a deep bow.

Nick's eyes hadn't moved from mine. "You are back."

"Me?" I said. *Did you forget your vacation to wherever-the-hell-were-you?*

He didn't reply, returning his sharp gaze to Hereford. "I see you are not handling the tax reports for Kent as I instructed."

"I was accompanying Mistress Grace through your exquisite gardens," Hereford stammered. "She has never seen pasque flowers."

Nick held him in a steely stare. "I am curious to learn that pasque flowers are of more importance to you than people's wages."

"Forgive me, Majesty, but you usually allow me suitable time to handle the tax reports."

"You will take as much time as I command!" The king's eyes flamed like blue bonfires.

Sweat beaded on Hereford's dropped brow. "Certainly, Your Majesty. Forgive me."

A bird chirped as it swooped, everyone jumping except the king. Lord Lansbury stood guard behind him, exhaling like we were keeping him from something. Mathew Fox hung at the rear, a foot shorter than his brother and with kinder eyes.

Nick straightened his coat: this one the color of distressed denim with a hint of silver thread meandering through it. "You will present the reports at the Council meeting on the morrow," he ordered Hereford. "Be sure to allow time for the tournament."

"Tournament, Your Grace?"

"I have devised a jousting session for this afternoon. The weather is ideal. I trust you brought your armor with you, unless it is impaired from our bout at Christmastide?"

"I assure you, Majesty, any minor damage caused then is now mended. The prospect of a joust with my sovereign lord is one of the reasons I have remained at court."

"One of the reasons?" Nick's eyes drifted back to mine. "Mistress Grace, I also look forward to your company at the tournament."

A gust of wind cooled my reddening cheeks. I still had an hour or two before I was cutting it too fine. "Of course," I spurted before I could think.

Emmie. Twenty-first century. Pronto.

"I'm pleased you admire my gardens," the king said to me. "Regrettably, I was cautioned to eschew flowers for a while. Lovely things they are." Sunlight ignited the green flecks in his eyes as they held mine, sending a blush to my cheeks.

And then he turned and paced away toward the chapel, chased by the Fox brothers, pebbles crunching beneath his heavy boots. I had to drag my eyes away from his tall, elegant stride that embodied confidence in a way I'd never seen.

Hereford made a pretend sword strike at the pillar.

"Counting over a thousand dockets before sunrise?" he snapped. "I'll scar his other damn cheek."

My mouth fell open. "Isn't it a crime to talk about the king like that?"

"And who is to tell him? A silly girl?" he scoffed.

Instead of acknowledging the treasonous rant, I watched King Nick greet the curtsying women in bonnets, wishing he'd glance back my way for just one telling moment.

But only Mathew Fox turned to look back at us.

When I went back inside, it was like someone had flipped a switch at Whitehall. Sweaty servants tore through corridors, hauling everything from rolled-up banners to giant jugs of ale. The musicians banged out cheery tunes on loop, and every courtier in the castle surfaced in their finest clothing. This time, though, there were no fresh flowers anywhere.

He came back.

An eagle swooped in my stomach, churning everything up, as Alice and I crossed the upper gallery on our way to the tournament. I'd barely had one conversation with the king, and now I was acting like we were going on some medieval jousting date. Not that I even deserved one, after failing to uncover anything useful about Kit.

I'd seen tiltyards in movies, but Whitehall's was smaller and grubbier than those I'd imagined. A long wooden fence dissected the battered sand, overlooked by towers dressed with chivalric emblems. Alice and I settled into the front row of the tiered bench seating, directly opposite a canopied platform housing the VIPs. Thomas Grey poured wine for the affable French ambassador, Philippe Renard. Mathew Fox caught my eye from the rear shadows and nodded a hello. I lifted my chin and smiled. I still had no idea why he'd lied for me, but there was something calming about him. There was no sign of Kit anywhere.

"Good God," said Alice, her palm to her face.

The Dowager Countess of Warwick was shuffling down our aisle from my end, Isobel hovering a tasseled parasol over her gabled hood. The countess didn't hide her revulsion when she realized the last empty spot was beside me.

"A very good afternoon," she said, putting as much space between me and her sickly potpourri scent as she could. Isobel's greeting was more of a death stare.

The king's bald gentleman, Mark Macaulay, stopped to flip his feather cap at Isobel from the pitch below. She made a face like a serial killer had just smirked at her.

"Isobel, you must never shun those close to the king's person," said the countess.

"He has an unsettling face," Isobel whined.

"You mean Mark? Don't worry, he's really nice," I said with a smile. Knowing I had the power to leave this place at any time had charged my confidence.

The countess twisted the diamond fox gripping her pasty wrist, her breath a sardine storm. "First, you publicly paw at the king in front of esteemed ambassadors and noblemen at the feast. It was a humiliation. Now, you speak of his gentlemen by their forenames? Well I do hope you enjoyed your brush with royalty, Mistress Grace, because His Majesty will soon be occupied with a gentlewoman of infinitely superior stature."

"Oh, I know. Princess Henriette of France."

Isobel's glare could've turned Medusa to stone, her fists clutching her slate dress garnished with abstract gold shells.

"Never mind," sneered the countess. "You shall not be here long, considering the information I learned this afternoon from my friend Lady Russell. Her son is a guard at Tower Hill."

"Thanks for the biography," I said to her silent sneer, but my heart hit the back of my throat. Tower Hill was where the king's sister was nearly mobbed under our supervision.

Trumpets halted my panic as a parade of horses cantered into the tiltyard, their hooves kicking up the humid smell of dirt. Francis rode around the arena, dark-chocolate curls protruding from his helmet.

"I pray Francis is speared with a lance after his outlandish idea to bring us to London," Alice hissed at me. "I cannot bear to see his face again."

"His Majesty the King has entered the list!" cried the herald.

The audience rose and clapped wildly, my stomach flipping like pancakes. King Nick circled the mud on horseback like a superstar, voices roaring as he touched his silver chest plate painted with the royal arms.

The riders positioned themselves in front of the clapping specta-tors, the king's mocha stallion pointed right at me. When I smiled shyly at him, he turned his head and rode off the pitch, everyone trailing him except for two knights. *He's not interested, Emmie. Get a clue.*

I bit my lip and refocused on the remaining knights that faced each other at opposite ends of the tiltyard. When the trumpets blasted, their horses flew toward each other like cannonballs. Splintering wood cracked the air as their lances came together. The rules weren't hard to figure out: each rider got a point for every hit, and if they unseated their opponent, they won the game. It was nail-bitingly terrifying, and by the time Francis had warmed up on the sidelines, I was cheering like a fangirl.

"The Earl of Warwick will now joust with the Earl of Lansbury!" the herald announced.

Lord Lansbury tore onto the field so fast that his charcoal horse stumbled. He galloped toward a cluster of girls at one end of the arena and asked the one with the lowest neckline for her favor. They all giggled as the pink-faced girl tied her pink ribbon to the tip of his lance. Alice chewed her fingernail, her eyes locked to Francis as he galloped to the other end of the list while Lansbury trotted into position.

The flags dropped and hooves thundered in a spray of mud. Lansbury's brutish moves faltered at the smooth speed of Francis. During the second round, Francis's lance just missed Lansbury's head, and the crowd gasped. Francis was declared the winner, and Lansbury bowed to the jubilant audience before trotting his horse back to his tent.

"His Majesty the King now challenges the Earl of Warwick!"

Voices whirred with excitement as Nick and Francis circled each other on horseback in a playful show.

"The king and Francis have been jousting rivals since they were children," Alice said with a smile. "This is the fight everyone comes to see."

"It must be hard to decide who to cheer for in this one," I said to the Dowager Countess of Warwick, lifted by the excitement. A battle between her king and her son.

She drew back like my comment was abhorrent. "My heart is always with His Majesty, who is a blessing to all things. Clearly your loyalties remain uncertain."

I just shook my head as exploding trumpets sent the horses into motion. The king scored the first point against Francis with a sickening crack. Nick's skill and strength made my stomach and chest twist tightly together. The thought of going back to guys who wanted to play video games all weekend after this—after him—made me wilt.

The tense match was over quickly, Nick unseating Francis in the third round. As Francis rode away uninjured, they reached out and brushed knuckles like a fist-bump.

Viscount Hereford was the final competitor, his black armor enlarged at the crotch, his chest plate decorated with a roaring bear.

Alice's eyes twinkled at me. "Ready your favor. Everyone will soon know of your courtship with Lord Hereford."

The Dowager Countess of Warwick made a croaky grunt. "Hereford would sooner pay court to a necessary woman."

"I'm necessary," I said with a straight face.

But Hereford was already riding toward me, hugging his helmet under his arm. *Oh shit.*

"Would you allow me to carry your favor, Mistress Grace?" he called loudly enough for the twenty-first century to hear. He aimed the tip of his thick wooden spear at my face.

I didn't know if it was because every eye on the planet was looking at me or the countess's incredulous puffing, but I loosened the porcelain ribbon from my braid and shakily tied it to Hereford's lance. Hands applauded from every row.

Nick scratched his neck beneath his helmet before kicking his horse so hard that it bolted forward like a missile launching. He rode over to me and dismounted with effortless skill. I tried to swallow, but it was as if my throat was glued shut. Time slowed as the king approached my seat, ripping off his helmet with one hand, perfectly ruffled hair springing out. But when he extended his iron-tipped lance, it was directed at Isobel Beaumont.

"Your favor, my lady," he said smoothly, his eyes sunlit jewels.

My stomach sank as the Dowager Countess of Warwick hurriedly freed a scarf from Isobel's slender neck. Nick watched Isobel tie the yellow strip of silk to his lance before scaling his horse again to claps and cheers.

"Heavens, I thought their courtship was over," whispered Alice.

My chest was too tight to speak. The Dowager Countess of Warwick and Isobel gripped each other's hands, their faces as white as their knuckles. I bit the inside of my cheek, reminding myself that I didn't even belong in this century, so why should I care so much who the king offered his favor to?

The riders burst into a dust cloud, Hereford's horse moving fast. Nick's lance struck him hard in the chest plate, and Hereford swung sideways to maintain his balance. When the horses circled back around, Nick said something to Hereford that made the viscount raise his lance higher. On the second run, Nick dropped his lance, and Hereford struck him in the shoulder, sending the king flipping backward like a rag doll. He rolled sideways and smashed to the ground, clutching his side as his horse bolted off the pitch. *No!*

My hand flew to my chest as squires sprinted onto the field to help Nick sit up, the crowd holding a collective breath. When he pulled off his helmet with no trace of blood and rose back up, hundreds of feet stamped in a thunder of relief. Francis led Nick's horse back in, demanding a rematch from the marshals because the king had dropped his lance. The game restarted, Nick's lance aimed at Hereford like a rifle. He rode so fast that Hereford's horse slid sideways to avoid the contact. When Hereford tumbled into the dirt, the spectators roared over the blasting trumpets.

"His Majesty wins the day!"

I dropped onto the bed, gazing at the paneled ceiling.

You have to stop this, Emmie. You have a sick, stupid crush on the most stupid person ever. You have school and work and a college application to finish. You're going to be a world-famous jewelry designer, and guys will chase you, *not the other way around.*

I reluctantly slid to the floor and crouched to dig out my clothes and ring from under the mattress. Thank God I'd brought a sleeping pill this time. I was so wound up over this utterly mesmerizing king that I didn't know how else I'd fall asleep. *Sick, stupid crush.*

There was a sharp knock at the door, chased by a second.

I was stunned to find Mathew Fox standing on the other side, his face pale in the torchlight. "Forgive me for disturbing you, mistress. His Majesty requests a word with you."

The floor fell from under me. "Why? I–I can't," I said. I still had to factor in time to fall asleep.

"It is His Majesty's pleasure," said Mathew, gesturing to the hallway like it wasn't optional.

I trailed him into the courtyard, butterflies tearing at my insides. I was lucky Mom always turned her phone off at work. She hopefully wouldn't notice me missing just yet.

"You don't joust?" I asked Mathew with a shiver, needing his soothing voice to keep me calm the way he had at the Tower.

He chuckled, his breath a spray of mist. "My brother has the strength in the family."

"And you have the brains?" The question came out before I could think, my cheeks reddening.

Mathew stopped, tipping his head at me. "You are an unexpected woman, mistress."

It was my chance to finally ask him point blank why he'd covered for me about Hatfield, but we were quickly swallowed by the main building, the brothy smell of meats from the jousting feast clinging to the air.

When I turned for the Presence Chamber staircase, Mathew stopped me. "We must take a more private route. The courtiers have not yet retired, and the king does not take well to hearsay."

We passed several doors before reaching a thin circular stairwell beside the entrance to the chapel. At the top sat a short passage leading to a nondescript door shielded by two guards. The door had no handle.

"I wish you luck, Mistress Grace," said Mathew, his small fist tapping on the door.

The comment was strange, but the conversation was over. A guard swung the door open, letting me walk in alone.

It was a different entrance to the king's living room that I'd been in once before. Some of his furniture had been rearranged since last time, and the lute was missing from the gilded chairs that were now over at the card table. A gold crown rested on the cabinet where the macarons had been, rubies, emeralds, and sapphires glittering from its rim. *Holy shit. A Tudor crown.* I carefully picked it up and admired how it sparkled in the candlelight before lifting it and placing it over my head.

"That is treason."

Nick stood in the archway leading to his bedroom, his coat unbuttoned and his linen shirt open at the neck. He stepped forward and tugged the crown off my head, my heart a hurricane. "Punishable by death," he added coolly.

"I'm sorry, Your Majesty," I said with a tremble, remembering to curtsy this time.

"Sit down." He pressed his boot to a velvet chair and slid it toward me, wincing at the movement.

"Are you hurt?" I said.

"I commanded you to sit!"

My lavender skirts crushed into the chair, unease eating away at my stomach.

Nick remained standing, his eyes the color of the sea at midnight. "I trust you understand the great privilege bestowed upon you when I invited you to stay at court. All without expense, and without your father's supervision. Have I not done well by you?"

"Yes…of course."

"Then why would you treat me so ungraciously?" He pulled something from the inside of his coat and tossed it at me. It was Kit's scarf from the London trip, partially torn and still stained with dirt. Relief crashed into me. At least it wasn't my denim shorts, the pink koala undies, or—God forbid—the blue-diamond ring I'd stolen from his cabinet.

Nick was a caged lion, pacing before me. "I will speak plainly. It pleased me to learn you spent time with the Princess Catherine while I was away. She speaks higher of you than many. You were a companion to her, and for that, I am grateful. Nevertheless, what you did is inexcusable."

"What I did?"

"Taking the eight-year-old Princess of England to a public execution," he said furiously. "Where she was recognized by heretic deniers of my supremacy and nearly crushed to death. Yes, Mistress Grace, I know every shameful detail."

"I'm so sorry," I said in one breath. "We just wanted a morning out in the city. To have fun, to shop. Kit, too. We didn't know there'd be an execution—even Francis didn't."

"*Francis?*" He stepped back. "Surely you mean 'Lord Warwick'. Or is he your lover too? Along with that dimwit Hereford, whom I dismissed from my court not a moment ago? Perhaps both of them." He scooped up his wine goblet and chugged.

I rose to my feet. "I don't have *lovers*, not that it's your business. And I'm sorry about Kit, but it wasn't my fault. It was Fran—Lord Warwick's idea. Plus, Kit wanted to come; she was more excited than anyone."

"I did not give you permission to speak!" His voice bounced off the walls, his brilliant, enraged eyes deadly weapons. For the first time, I could see why everyone was so scared of him.

This is not a normal guy, Emmie. This is the sixteenth-century King of England.

He stepped into my space, filling my nose with the scent of mint and roses. "Do you understand the significance of Princess Catherine? If anything had happened to her, there would be claims from here to Savoy about the line of succession. Beaumonts, Seymours...Stuarts." His jaw tightened. "You have no idea what that girl means to me. My mother died giving her life, my father following soon after. Do you fail to understand that she is my sister, my heir, my only family?"

I shook through my words. "Then why did you leave her here when you went wherever-the-hell you went?" *Don't you know what's about to happen?*

Shock wiped his face. "You dare question me!" He clenched his teeth before turning to kick an oak wine stand so hard that it crashed to the floor.

A guard sprang in, but Nick shook his head, his watery eyes sealed to mine.

"Mistress Grace, you are a highly uneducated woman. You are ignorant, impulsive, you come and go as you please, you pay court to my noblemen without my permission, and you are a gross offense to our royal presence. You will leave Whitehall this night. Take any coach you desire." His voice fractured on the words.

"Fine, if that's what you want." Tears veiled my eyes, but I had one more thing to say. "If you want to keep Kit safe, you need to make sure her room is always guarded," I stuttered. "Don't leave her alone. Not even for a minute."

His brow crushed with shock. "My lady, I command you to pack up your goods and leave my court before I send you back to that rat-infested cage I dragged you out of."

He didn't move, his finger aimed at the door. I took a step and stumbled like an idiot. My dress had snagged on the chair leg. Nick stepped forward as if to help me just as I bent down to pull the skirt free. When I stood up, my cheek crashed against his jaw and his palms caught the sides of my shoulders, holding me steady. I froze in his grasp, our mouths so close that I could practically taste him. The heavenly smell of roses and the heat of his breath against mine made the room spin. My feet felt glued to the carpet as I looked up at him, finding something alight in his ocean eyes, his hands still gripping my shoulders.

Emmie, he just ordered you to leave.

"I'm sorry I disappointed you," I mumbled as I brushed beneath the hard curve of his shoulder, rushing through the door to where Mathew was waiting for me.

He slumped at the sight of my tears and silently escorted me back to my room like I was a flight risk, the outside air already a degree cooler.

When we approached my door, he spoke softly. "Princess Catherine is a delicate subject, mistress."

I wiped my nose. "I know."

His lips pointed downward. "You took a foolish step. Accompanying the princess to an execution without His Majesty's blessing was a bold and treacherous move. As was courting that featherbrain Hereford, whom the king has long despised."

"I'm not interested in Hereford. And I didn't plan the London trip; it was Lord Warwick's idea. Alice was there too." The moment I snitched on Alice, I regretted it, but Mathew's face gave away that he already knew.

"Mistress Grey is the daughter of Sir Thomas Grey, the king's most trusted counsel. She will be chided, but unpunished. As for Warwick, the king loves him like a brother. Which means his neck is already on the block, to be sliced or saved, according to His Majesty's mood."

My lips quivered. I could barely speak, yet the question tumbled off my tongue where it had been waiting for days.

"Why did you lie for me? About Hatfield?"

Mathew paused, inhaling. "I am not sure what you mean, mistress. I met with your family and they are decent, honest people. They may befall a terrible accident one day, before the king had a chance to meet them, but they were decent, honest people." His bronze eyes bored into mine, his lavender scent soothing. "It does not worry me where you come from. As far as France, or Scotland even. Do you understand?"

His cheeks were wobbly lines through my tears. "It doesn't matter," I said. "I have to leave tonight, or he'll put me back in the Tower."

The space between Mathew's brows deepened. "A king's fury burns as hot as the midday sun, but it, too, cools in hours. If His Majesty has instructed you to leave court, you must do so in haste. But find a way to return—after the king's mind has calmed—and I promise you, if you follow my counsel, it may surprise you what you can accomplish." A door banged shut down the hall. Mathew jerked and straightened his cap. "I must take my leave. I pray you do not lose heart, Mistress Grace." He gave me a single nod. "*Return.*"

Back in my room, I downed the sleeping pill and flopped onto the mattress, trying to make sense of Mathew's strange words. When I rolled to one side, waiting for the pill to take effect, I spotted the note propped against the candle.

I leapt out of bed so fast. Even after everything Mathew had said, I wanted the note to possess Nick's beautiful handwriting. I wanted it to be an apology for how he'd spoken to me. But the writing was jagged and hurried.

You do not belong here.
Leave this night or I will crush you in your sleep.

The note slid from my fingers and plunged to the floor, leaving behind a whiff of dried, moldy flowers. I could feel the sleep sedative inching its way into my bloodstream, slowing my pounding heart and softening my vision. I crawled back into bed and held the ring steady on my thumb. There was only one person I'd met who smelled like potpourri—the Dowager Countess of Warwick. Could she really be that brutal? Or did the king have the note sent while I was in his room? Wasn't that the sort of thing Nicholas the Ironheart would do as retribution for bringing his sister to an execution? That seemed more likely than an apology at this point.

I was so tense that I had to visualize riding my old horse Bonnie across the lime-green fields of Essex before I finally slipped into sleep.

I woke to Ruby leaping off the edge of my bed and the metallic beats of the Atomic alarm ringtone. My phone flashed with light beside a framed photo of Mia, Josh, and I at last year's Garden Party music festival.

I was home.

9

"I DIDN'T HEAR YOU COME IN LAST NIGHT."

Mom sat hunched over a plate of scrambled eggs and charred bacon, reading a gossip magazine article like it contained war secrets.

"I got enough sleep, don't worry," I said, reaching for a banana. "Where'd you find bacon?" My voice sounded like I'd smoked a hundred cigarettes.

"I borrowed it from Kevin McCoy. I left you some on the stove."

"You know borrowing means you have to give it back, right?"

"I've heard it mentioned. There's also pie in the fridge." She stood up and tipped the rest of her rubbery eggs into the sink. "Did you get your studying done?"

I exhaled in a rush to subdue my nerves. "Most of it."

She twisted to face me. "I feel like we haven't seen each other for a week."

"Mom, we never see each other. You work night shift. Don't be weird." I was tired and deeply uninterested in going to school, so the annoyance in my voice was hard to hide. I pulled my knitted bag over my shoulder and grabbed a slice of bacon to take with me.

"I'm not being weird. I just think I need to keep a closer eye on you. We're still on for Sunday dinner, right?" She rubbed one eye and yawned like a hippo.

"Yes. It's fine. Everything's fine. I have to go."

Everything was definitely *not* fine. For a start, Mom didn't deserve my foul mood after my slew of lies, but my blood was still boiling about that nasty note. It had to be from the Dowager Countess of Warwick. Not only did the paper smell like her, but she was a total bitch to me at the jousting match. Plus, I was sure she was the one who'd blabbed to the king about Kit and the execution.

My scuffed shoes pounded along School Street, images galloping at me through the slouching trees. Nick raising his lance to the crowd, kicking an armored heel into his stallion. His leather boot shattering the wine stand, threats shooting from his tongue like bullets. But, most of all, I couldn't forget his face. While he'd sounded angry with me, his expression had told a different story. He'd looked more…hurt.

The memories charged at me through journalism and fine arts, my eyes burning and my body someone else's. Even the stuff in my locker looked alien. What was the point of a doll of Edvard Munch's *The Scream* that actually screamed when you squeezed it? Was the entire twenty-first century high?

I waited for Mia at lunch near the quad, searching the web on my phone.

Nicholas the Ironheart

No change that I could see. Tyranny, torture, death. Wonderful.

Catherine Tudor

Still murdered; still unsolved. Great.

Emmeline Grace 1580

No search results. *Idiot!*

It wasn't until I typed in Alice Grey 1580 that my skin tingled. There wasn't much about Alice, but every entry now said she married a rich baron and died giving birth to their son.

My phone hit my lap, my foot tapping madly.

Alice Grey was meant to marry Francis Beaumont. I'd read it after my first trip back, before I'd returned and started hanging out with them more. Before I'd encouraged our day trip to London that got Alice so mad at Francis that she wanted to see him skewered with a jousting lance. Before my presence in the sixteenth century. And now I'd quite possibly—and probably—altered history. *Shit, what did I do?*

Mia dropped her bag onto the bench. "So guess what Josh told me this morning," she said, licking sauce off her thumb. "His mom's finished rehab and is coming home, so he has to move back to Dwight Street."

"Really? That's good, isn't it?" I stretched my legs out to warm them, but my foot wouldn't stop tapping.

Mia looked over her shoulder to make sure Josh hadn't finished band practice early. "I don't know why he has to be there. He's much happier at Uncle Pete's."

"I guess they didn't want to let his mom out without some kind of supervision."

Her arched brows slanted at me. "So her eighteen-year-old son's meant to be in charge of her? And what will she do next year when he's in Cambridge?"

"Josh is going to MIT with you?"

Mia scoffed. "He's like you; he doesn't care about college."

"When did I say that?"

"Aren't you going to sell jewelry?"

I stopped chewing my mystery-meat sandwich. "You mean at the Sunday market?"

"No, I just meant…you didn't even apply to college. Ugh, forget it. Sorry, Josh's mom just makes me crazy. She's a grown woman, and he's doing all the parenting."

"It's okay."

I watched Avery Pearce cross the inside of the cafeteria. Logan Hunter sat by the window, looking at me. He quickly turned away.

"So how's it going with silver fox?" Mia smiled at me, sipping sparkling water.

I rolled my eyes, but my lips curled upward. "Please stop calling him that."

She kicked me with her leather sneaker. "You started it! In your text."

"No, I continued it, and now I'm finishing it."

She sat forward, black sheets of hair falling past her open mouth. "You mean the relationship?"

"There is no relationship. I'm single, okay? Permanently. And I don't want to talk about it."

"Come on, you can tell me anything." Her lashes were blinking at twice their usual speed.

I shrugged, my voice strange and high-pitched. "He doesn't like me."

Mia's hand flew to my wrist. "No! What happened?"

And just like that, I unloaded to Mia about Nicholas the Ironheart —the grandson of Henry the Eighth. Not that I told her who he really was. If it wasn't so freaking pathetic, it'd be side-splittingly funny. Of course, I didn't tell her any of the batshit stuff about time travel or murders that hadn't happened yet. I just told her the truth… that I'd fallen for a guy I scarcely knew so hard that it felt like an embarrassing cliché. Like Cupid had literally shot me with his heart-shaped arrow before I'd had a chance to blink. But then Nick had gotten pissed at me for something that wasn't even my fault, before telling me to get lost. And now I felt like utter crap.

"Asshole!" cried Mia.

"You might want to try a bit louder, I don't think they heard you in Tajikistan."

"He *is*," she affirmed, snapping her bento box closed. "You deserve way better than that…someone who'll at least listen to you. To be honest, he sounds a bit arrogant and dominating."

I sighed. "Yeah." *A sixteenth-century king? I'd definitely go with arrogant and dominating.*

When I got home, I flipped on the fashion channel, but the choppy editing and electronic soundtrack only raised my anxiety levels. I switched the television off and washed up Mom's breakfast dishes before vacuuming and dusting all three rooms downstairs. When there wasn't anything left to clean, I traipsed upstairs.

My fingers laced together, my thumbs circling.

You cannot go back yet. You know that head you're carrying around? It will end up on a pike. You cannot live without a head.

Trying to ignore the blue-diamond ring burning a hole in my back from where it sat on the dresser, I dug out a pair of spiky earrings I'd bought at the Southbridge craft show and angled my lamp. Using my piercing saw, I carefully sliced the spikes off the earrings and glued them all over a neon pink heart cut from an old keychain. By the time my wrists ached, I wanted to toss it at the wall. The tacky pendant belonged around the neck of a girl with a nose piercing about ten years ago, not on the desk of the jewelry admissions office at Central Saint Martins college. They'd probably crack a rib laughing at it.

I kneaded my eyes with my palms, trying to remember the sketches I'd made at Whitehall…the cabochon emerald encased with a wire cage, a delicate pearl necklace wrapped tightly with wire frames. Beautiful old things in modern cages. I tossed the thorny heart into a drawer and lumbered downstairs to eat peanut butter straight from the jar.

The rest of the week moved slower than a snail on Valium. By Sunday afternoon, I'd clocked up an extra four filing shifts at the rest home in an effort to occupy my brain. The sky looked like a fluffy pink bathrobe by the time I jogged home, wanting to squeeze in a shower before dinner with Mom.

I hadn't expected the hoarder Jane Stuart to be clipping a tree near the sidewalk with a pair of garden shears.

My feet slowed. What would I even say?

Hey, Mrs. Stuart. Remember that ring I practically stole from you? Where did you get it? Oh yeah, and just wondering…do you happen to know Nicholas the

Ironheart? You know, the sixteenth-century king with the ridiculously perfect ass and the fiery-as-hell temper?

I managed a tight smile as I passed her. "Afternoon."

"Lottie?" Her tone was gentle, almost musical.

I stopped. "It's Emmie. Emmie Grace. Carol Grace's daughter."

Mom once said hoarding is a compulsive mental disorder that can cause physical degeneration, but up close, Jane looked younger than I'd expected.

"It is not proper, raising you all on her own," she snapped. "Where is the father?"

"*My* father?" Did she know there were tens of millions of single-parent kids in America?

She aimed a finger at me. "What did you do with it?"

Heat poured into me. "You mean the ring? The one from your yard sale?"

"Oh no, I never have yard sales." Her milky eyes squinted.

"You were selling some things a couple of weeks ago." I pointed at her lawn. "There was a table right there with jewelry. Necklaces, watches, some rings. A lady sold me a gold ring with a blue stone with little red roses."

"You stay away from it. It is a devil!" She drew a line across her neck.

I couldn't stop the quivering words. "Mrs. Stuart, where did you get the ring?"

She pointed her shears at me. "Why did you bring it here? Did he send you?"

"Did *who* send me?" My heart thumped through my mouth. "Do you know King Nicholas the First?"

She recoiled, her face paling. "Get away!" she screamed. "Open it and see the face of evil. Of a heretic! Forget the Scots and the boy! She sent me to hell!"

The white gate across the street flung open. Avery Pearce's mom power-walked to us, half her hair curled with a flat iron. "What the heck is going on here?"

"Nothing," I said. Jane was already hurrying up her path.

"Dammit, I wish we could do something," grumbled Mrs. Pearce.

"You could move," I said as Jane Stuart slammed both her doors.

My palms clammed up as I held the phone to my ear. The house was dark, and Mom had tried to call me four times while I ran home. *Tell me someone hasn't died. Tell me someone hasn't died. Tell me someone hasn't—*

"Emmie?" I could hear eighties music blaring. It sounded like she was driving. There was a "shush", followed by giggling. "Sweetheart, I'm so sorry, but can we rain check dinner? I hope you're okay with that."

"Oh, okay…I guess. Is everything alright?"

"I'm with Crystal; we just left for Springfield. Her partner's playing in a show tonight, so she begged me to come with her—"

"Excuse me, pants on fire, you begged me!" I heard Crystal say. They both laughed and I smiled. Mom sounded happy. It had taken a while for her to find a new friend after our neighbor Jackie moved to Vermont to be closer to her grandkids.

"I'm so sorry," Mom said again. "You know I don't get many nights out."

"Be safe," I replied, trying to feel relieved rather than disappointed. So much for keeping a closer eye on me. But at least I'd dodged an interrogation about my new acting career and mystery man.

"We're going to stay the night, but I'll be back tomorrow," Mom promised. "Love you."

When I hung up, my stomach folded with anticipation, my brain already calculating the number of hours she'd be away. If I cut school, I could have two whole days in Tudor England. I'd only been back home a week, though. How long did it take for a king to cool down?

I boosted the volume on the classical music channel, trying to drown out Jane Stuart's words about the blue-diamond ring as I bit into toast smeared with avocado.

Open it and see the face of evil. Of a heretic!

I dumped the toast and ran upstairs. Fingering the ring's edges, I felt a tiny ridge and pressed it. The blue-diamond setting snapped upward. Underneath was a miniature painting of a woman I'd seen before. The reddish-gold hair and porcelain skin belonged to Queen Elizabeth the First, Nick's mother. My stomach knotted. So that's why the ring was so important to him.

But why would Jane Stuart call Queen Elizabeth the First a heretic? And then it clicked as the memory of Nick's pained voice rattled through me.

If anything had happened to her, there would be claims from here to Savoy about the line of succession. Beaumonts, Seymours…Stuarts.

Jane *Stuart*.

I typed the name into the search engine, but all that came up were pages about the famed Mary, Queen of Scots, whose real name was Mary Stuart. As the first cousin of Elizabeth the First and a devout Catholic, many Catholics considered Mary Stuart the rightful ruler of England throughout King Nick's reign. The thought squeezed. At such a young age, he'd had the whole world on his shoulders, yet he'd made time to play his lute for me.

As for Jane Stuart, she definitely had an out-of-town accent. A mix of western New England, maybe French, some English. If she really was from the sixteenth century and related to Mary, Queen of Scots, though, how did she end up in twenty-first-century America?

All the questions came back to the same thing—the blue-diamond ring.

I changed my search to enchanted rings, famous rings of the renaissance, rings and sorcery. I trudged through countless examples before a ring at the bottom of the screen struck my eye. It was plain gold, but peppered with tiny bumps of different sizes. It took a moment to nail down where I'd seen such a ring before. The Dowager Countess of Warwick wore one when she gripped my hand at the dock. I clicked open the article.

It was called a 'rosary ring', the bumps representing the beads on a Catholic rosary chain. In the sixteenth century, only the most die-hard Catholics wore them so they could practice their banned religion without persecution.

Something dislodged inside me, shifting. Alice had said the Beaumonts were historically a Catholic family and that the Dowager

Countess of Warwick's brother was executed for a papist plot against Queen Elizabeth. Then I'd got that nasty note saying I'd get *crushed* in my sleep, like perhaps my neck with a set of rosary beads. I turned off my laptop, meeting my startled reflection in the black screen.

It wasn't Francis Beaumont who was a secret Catholic sympathizer; it was his mother, the Dowager Countess of Warwick. Plus, the countess had another motive for murdering Kit—her brother had been brutally tortured and executed by Kit's mother, Queen Elizabeth.

If I could just go back and find a set of wooden rosary beads in the countess's rooms, it could be enough proof to bring her down. My neck started to sweat. Changing someone's death, and possibly the reign of a king, massively checked the 'things you shouldn't mess with' list. Heck, one visit from me, and Alice had married another man and died birthing his kid. But that also proved my actions could affect history. It was so wrong that Kit's killer was never caught, let alone punished. Why should the countess become a powerful old bag while Kit turned to dust at the age of eight?

A few minutes later, I lay coiled up under my comforter, a sleeping pill slowly disintegrating in my stomach. I knew in the furthest reaches of my soul that I would never have Nick Tudor the way I wanted, but I couldn't help but feel that helping him and his sister was weirdly right. Like it was the only way to channel my insanely impossible feelings.

Of course, this was dangerous. It was majorly playing with fire, and I could already see myself getting burned to a crisp—probably on a sixteenth-century stake. But the ring had come to me for a reason, and I would do what I could to help them both. Even if it risked my head, my heart, and the entire path of history as I knew it.

The scent of oak was instant, the silence sharp. When my eyes fluttered open, a woman in a coif stood gaping at me. I scrambled up on the mattress.

"Forgive me, mistress," the maid stammered. "He said the room was vacant and to make space for the new lodger." Her linen basket got stuck in the door on her way out.

My head swung in all directions, taking in the narrow lattice window, the waxy wooden desk, the painting of the blue-eyed boy in the feathered hat. It was like returning to a dream you wished would never end.

I kicked off the covers and opened the chest, relief pouring into me. The dresses were still in there. I tied on a blush-colored gown with puffed sleeves and added my white shorts, striped tank, and the ring to the pile of danger under the bed. A tap on the door jolted me.

Mathew Fox stood in the corridor, his fine hair dripping wet. A look of surprise tugged at his lips. "Mistress Grace. You returned."

"And you're telepathic."

His broad mouth widened. "And speaking so peculiarly, as usual. Truthfully, I did not expect you so soon. Nevertheless, I am pleased for it."

"How did you know I was here?"

"I was outside instructing the new grooms when a maid approached. She said that she discovered a young lady in the room assigned to the new bishop." He flicked his chin like the topic was unimportant. "We must speak, but not here. Meet me in the basement downstairs. There is a stairwell east of the confectionary. Once you reach the level below, take your second left and keep walking until you find a wall. I will be there in ten minutes."

His expression made a final appeal for me to trust him before he darted away.

I coiled up my hair and kept my head down, hurrying toward the buttery odors of the confectionary. For all I knew, Mathew had information that'd be vital about Kit.

The fanciful court decorations stopped where the basement began. The stone passages were dimly lit and rancid with mildew. I tripped over a wooden barrel, and a rat scampered into a decaying chest. I took what I thought was the second left, hissing with fright when I nearly stepped right off a ledge. A wooden rowboat bobbed in choppy dark water about four feet below me.

"Who goes there?" called a sharp voice.

My heart rate skyrocketed as I spun around.

Mathew stepped forward from the shadows, a candle raised in his hand as a weapon.

"*Shit*," I said under my breath, holding my chest. "Thank goodness it's you."

"You startled me, mistress. I said to take the second left."

"I thought I did. What is this place?" I rubbed my forearms to shield them from the wind.

"An escape route for a siege, but I fear it brings more dangers than it prevents. Legend tells a duke once used it, but the boat was not at hand when he dropped. The duke drowned in the castle moat below." Mathew stretched a quivering arm out, keeping away from the edge. "You should not be here."

"No need to tell me twice."

We helped each other away from the stink of rotting fish. I could feel the bones in Mathew's thin arm through his walnut coat. He guided me into a room piled with dusty carpets and pyramids of candles. "You can see why hardly anyone comes down here," he said.

"You mean because it's cold, dark, and terrifying, just like the rest of Whitehall?"

His chestnut eyes shimmered. "Mistress, there is not one person in this court who is not afraid to be here, but you need not be. The king will be pleased to see you."

My small snort echoed. "A few days ago, he threatened to lock me up if I didn't leave that second."

"A Tudor sign of great affection."

I could only laugh, sending lines to Mathew's brow. He glanced around. "We have but minutes. There is progress with Henriette of France. Plans are underway as we speak to bring her to Whitehall. Now she has agreed to convert to the king's faith. What business does a Catholic princess have marrying a Protestant king?"

"I have no idea, but what does it have to do with me?" The last thing I needed was to get caught having clandestine conversations with Mathew Fox about banned religions.

His cartoonish features twisted. "Why do you believe His Majesty expelled you from court in the first place? While Mistress Grey received no more than a stern word for her role in the same matter?"

"Because he hates me?"

"Because he *desires* you. And he regrets the way he spoke to you; I have seen it in his face." Mathew's expression was as serious as a heart attack. "Mistress, you are our greatest hope against a marriage with France."

My palm hit my chest, my laughter laced with shock. *"Me?"*

"I have little time to explain it all to you now. But why would the French king even consider wedding his sister to King Nick? France has never been weaker. They need us to fight their enemies for them. That idiot Thomas Grey poisons the king's mind with talk that this marriage will prevent a war. Foolishness. It will cause one! Not only war against France's enemies, but instant war with Spain, who will deem the marriage alliance a hostile act. More so, His Majesty cannot love Princess Henriette as long as he yearns for you, and the troubled heart of a Tudor king causes nothing but calamity to a nation."

I gaped at him. "How can you say this? When you know I'm not—"

He flung a childlike hand out. "Stop, I beg you. It is best I am kept unaware of your true family. It will help keep them safe. Even so, once you are in the king's heart, it will matter little where you are from." His eyes turned pleading. "It sounds like a dream, mistress, but believe me when I say this is in your reach. His Majesty has more curiosity for you than any woman I have seen, and I have known him since we were children. Take care to regain his favor. Be interested, but not infatuated. Compliment him, always. Listen to his dreams, his dreads. Never disobey him or question his decisions, and you may yet win his heart."

When I tried to speak, nothing came out. One of the king's closest subjects was telling me to make a play for him ahead of the Pearl of France. It was textbook *insane*, but it made every cell in my body burn like wildfire with wanting to.

Mathew leaned closer. "If I have a message for you from His Majesty, I will blow out the fourth candelabra outside the Great Hall.

If you notice it extinguished, you must come to the king's chambers by way of the private entrance at once. Understand?"

Something shuffled behind us, a flame dying out. The silhouette of Lord Lansbury crossed the passageway, his brawny arms loaded with scrolls and papers.

When I turned back around, Mathew had already vanished.

10

MY FISTS CLENCHED WITH RELIEF WHEN I FOUND THE STAIRWELL AND dashed back upstairs. Chirpy courtiers were bantering over lunch in the Great Hall. My stomach murmured at the aromas of soup and freshly baked bread as I wandered closer.

When I looked around the room, one face stopped me in my tracks. Alice Grey's toffee eyes were staring right at me. I hurried over to her, and she stood up to fold her arms around me. I breathed in her cinnamon scent, relieved to hug her. I hadn't realized how much Alice had come to mean to me.

"Were you in the city again?" she asked, sounding a touch hurt.

I slid into the bench opposite her. "I went to see my mother. I'm sorry I didn't get a chance to tell you."

She poured me a bowl of pea soup. "It is in the past. I've been busy moving into my new lodgings near the pheasant yard. I never thought I would say this, but I miss Francis."

"Oh, really?" Hope sparked in my chest. Perhaps Alice's destiny could still reroute back to its rightful place.

"He is confined to his rooms for the London incident with Kit," she explained. "Lord Lansbury's become head of the household in his stead."

"And what about us?" Spicy soup trembled on my tongue. "I seem to recall being a part of the London incident."

Alice brushed off the question. "The whole thing was Francis's foolish idea. I should have known better than to follow that feather-brain to any place."

I swirled bread in my soup, sensing to change the subject.

"So any other scandals while I was away?" I hadn't realized how much I'd missed Whitehall.

Alice's eyes brightened. "How about a great honor? Some of the maidens were asked to learn a new dance to perform at His Majesty's birthday. The numbers are odd, so it will be perfect with you, Emmie."

"Yikes. That wouldn't be my word choice."

She spread more butter on her bread. "We rehearse every day after dinner in the Dowager Lady Warwick's chambers so there is no chance of the king seeing us and spoiling the surprise."

I felt my shoulders lift. "Where are the dowager countess's chambers?"

She rolled her eyes. "Take a guess. In the queen's rooms upstairs."

The Dowager Countess of Warwick's rooms were sprawling but garish, with a giant bay window fronting the Thames. Headless wooden mannequins in puffy gowns queued beside feathered curtains and standing mirrors. Her maids hauled away a solid wood dining table to make a dance space. There were six of us, including two girls I'd seen at court. I guessed them to be a couple of years younger than me.

Kit skipped in and clung to me like Christmas tinsel. "I'm the surprise at the end, Emmie."

"Saving the best for last," I said. I gave her pint-sized wrist a squeeze.

The countess handed me a white feather mask. "Mistress Grace, you seem to take pleasure in leaving court without a word and returning with no proclamation of any sort. I have never borne witness to such insult to His Majesty." She twisted the rosary ring on her finger.

"I guess that's a pretty uneventful reign then, if my timetable's the worst of it," I replied.

The countess snapped her fingers at the musicians, everyone scurrying into line. "Emmeline, move beside Isobel," she croaked over the players, rotting teeth on full display. "Left arm! Forward and back, and one, two, three…keep up, Mistress Grace! Alice, *forward!*" Even I had to admit she was a good director.

By the end of the rehearsal, I'd forgotten most of the steps, but I'd learned that the Dowager Countess of Warwick had two maids, a rabbit warren of rooms she shared with Isobel, and no guards stationed outside her door.

During the walk back to my room, I formulated a plan. I'd hover near the entrance to the countess's rooms, waiting until her two maids left for errands or dinner. When I was sure the rooms were empty, I'd hunt for the wooden rosary beads.

I'd just reached my lodgings when Mark Macaulay stopped me in the corridor. "A pleasant day to you, Mistress Grace," he said with a bow. "Excellent timing. I have been requested to accompany you to the horse yard."

"Why, what's at the horse yard?"

"You may wish to wear your riding boots," was his only reply.

He waited outside in the courtyard while I dug out a pair of wrinkled leather boots from the clothes I'd been given, struggling to lace them with sweaty fingers. What was all this about—was it another one of Mathew Fox's messages?

Mark escorted me into the nearby horse yard, butterflies swirling my stomach into a familiar churn. Grooms steered saddled horses across the pebbled dirt, one leading a milk-chocolate mare in my direction. As the horse clopped toward me, she neighed, her leather and hay smells sending me back to the decaying stables I'd loved as a child in Essex. I anchored my hand in the groom's leather glove and placed a shaky foot in the stirrup.

"I'm not much of a rider," I mumbled. The groom pushed me upward by my hips, guiding me into a sidesaddle pose, but my legs slipped apart into a straddle. *What are you doing, Emmie?* I castigated myself. *You're supposed to be searching the Dowager Countess of Warwick's rooms!* But how was I supposed to say no to the king's groom? Could Nick have sent him?

Thankfully, the groom showed no displeasure at my unladylike posture. He just slapped the mare's backside and she sprang to life, my body shifting to adjust.

"Where are we going?" I called out as the horse shot forward. She trailed two guards on horseback, who led us right out of the King's Gate and onto the public road outside the palace.

I hadn't ridden for years, but the mare was smooth and easy to control. We trotted past gawking onlookers for a mile or so before making a right down a dusty side street. The reins slipped inside my perspiring palms. Were the guards escorting me to the Tower of London because I'd disobeyed the king and come back to court?

We continued westward with the River Thames behind us. Wind lashed my face as I upgraded my trot to a canter to keep up until the guards finally slowed their horses at the crest of a hill.

Over the grassy curve stood a tall mocha stallion handsomely straddled by Nick Tudor. A brown leather vest skimmed his neck while tan breeches hugged his athletic thighs above his knee-high leather boots. The sight of him struck my chest with warmth.

"You ride as well as you dance," he said as I approached. He didn't look angry like he had the last time I'd seen him. He actually seemed a little nervous.

"Better, actually," I replied.

"You also ride astride." A trace of amusement touched his lips as he ran his gaze down my parted legs, his horse wavering beneath him.

"Well spotted." I cleared my throat. "So what's all this about?"

His eyes lifted back to mine. "Is it not clear, Mistress Grace? I believed the horses might be an indication. We are to ride this day. The sky has fined up."

"Riding?" I blinked at him. "In public?"

"Would you prefer to see me in private?"

He watched me for a moment with glittering eyes that sent the reins slipping inside my sweaty palms.

A laugh rumbled out of his chest and he flicked his hand at the guards. "Leave us," he commanded.

He kicked his steed, and I obediently followed. A mile down the road, our two horses leapt off the cobbled street and onto thick, wild grass. Wind howled in my ears as we galloped across flowering meadows, not a speck of a red-coated guard or groveling courtier in sight. The earthy smells of the lush English countryside hadn't changed in four hundred years. My mind dove backward, remembering Dad's short ponytail bobbing ahead on his spotty horse across grasslands just like these. My chest contracted at the memory.

"A goldie!" Nick tugged his horse's reins and pointed at the sky. A majestic dark-chocolate bird swooped high above us, its wings outstretched like an airplane's. "I had hoped to see her."

My mare neighed for about the sixth time as I pulled up alongside Nick. I rubbed the back of her neck as I searched the sky, my gaze falling into the king's.

"Your encouragement is welcome, Stella," he said, holding a hand up to shade his eyes from the sun.

"Emmie," I corrected, my cheeks ablaze.

He laughed softly. "Stella is the horse. She is a Florentine, and that whinny is her famous signal. She likes you."

My voice was a nervous breath. "Are you going to arrest me because I came back to court? Is that why we're out here all alone?"

He chuckled and frowned at the same time. "Do not be absurd, I would never arrest you." His shoulders straightened. "I have men who do that for me." He clicked his tongue, and Stella immediately launched into a trot behind Nick's stallion like she'd been trained to follow it. We continued to ride across lush meadowlands for what felt like another hour before reaching an overgrown path where Nick slowed his horse to a stop. A little further ahead stood a modest stone house with a thatched roof peeking through a canopy of trees. A tangled mess of wild flowers carpeted the front gate.

Nick dismounted, offering me his hand. His gloved fingers supported me while I jumped off Stella, my grape-colored skirts tumbling over my boots. His fingers held mine for a moment longer than they needed to before he took hold of Stella's reins and tied her to a tree beside his horse. A spell of dizziness washed over me and I gripped my forehead for a moment as Nick slid a bucket of rainwater to the horses' lapping tongues.

He stepped back around, his tone serious. "Mistress Grace, I thought it was plain, but perhaps it is not. I'm pleased you returned to court. Of course I intend not to arrest you. You must think me heartless."

My cheeks burned as I glanced over at the rustic cottage. "Is this Hampton Court Palace?" I asked with a straight face.

His light laugh was adorable. "Robin House. Let us start small and work our way up, shall we?"

We passed through the home's squeaky gate, meeting explosions of pink, white, and yellow roses that blanketed the sides of the narrow path.

"You forgot what I said about flowers already," I said in a teasing, you're-in-trouble tone as we followed the muddled trail around the side of the house.

The slightest of smiles drew a dimple to his cheek. "This is not the Canary Isles, Mistress Grace. Have you not noticed a reduction in fresh flowers at court?"

"Actually, I have."

He halted and twisted a rose stem until it snapped free before turning to face me in the tight line of space between the rose bushes. My breath snagged in my chest as he brushed the rose's fragrant white petals past my nose, his spectacular eyes holding mine.

"It smells like you," I said bravely.

Warmth danced in his eyes as he smiled and dragged the rose down the curve of his own nose. A second later, he coughed into his fist. He rubbed his neck and then turned, expelling another, raspier cough.

I lurched forward, nearly slipping on the dirt. "Are you okay?"

His hands gripped his neck, his eyes flaring as he coughed harder. He gasped and tipped forward for a moment before collapsing backward.

"Nick!" I cried, dropping to my knees beside him, missing the thorny stems of the nearby rose bushes by inches. My stomach felt like it was leaping out of my body.

His eyes snapped open, light with laughter.

"For God's sake!" I resisted the urge to wallop him, scrambling to my feet.

He sat up, his arms hanging over his knees. "If I were averse to roses, Mistress Grace, I would be long departed."

The amusement didn't leave his face as he led me down a slope of wild lavender toward a sturdy tree. He looked so smug and outrageously cute, and all I could think of was kissing him stupid.

Like, stepping in front of him right now and just grabbing his collar with both hands. I'd shut up his proud little giggles with my tongue until the only sounds he made were hot, desperate moans into my mouth.

I shook away the embarrassing impulse as we reached a sloped clearing enclosed with birch trees. A plush carpet had been laid out and was dressed with platters of berries and grapes, a glazed ham, soft cheeses, breads, and macarons.

"What's all this?" I asked, feeling like I was on an episode of The Bachelor with the most perfect bachelor ever.

He tapped his bottom lip. "I recall the word…food?"

"Funny *and* a king."

With a playful scowl, he handed me an embroidered velvet cushion and dropped down onto another. I twisted back toward the trees, looking for observers but finding only rustling leaves. The late afternoon wind had picked up. England felt ten degrees cooler in this time than in my own.

Nick shrugged off his vest. "This will keep you warm."

Before I could reply, the heavy leather was around my shoulders, smelling sublime. I froze, a little uneasy with the king's personality change since last time. Either he really was a two-faced psycho or Mathew was right—he did have some level of desire for me. Hope flared in my chest.

But I couldn't let myself think too much of that. There was zero chance of me ever becoming England's next queen—not only because it was beyond laughable, but because I already knew that Nick married Henriette of France. Heaviness sank over me at that reality.

"So what is this place?" I asked him, reaching for a small macaron. I'd lost my appetite somewhere between panicking that Nick was going to arrest me and his dimpled smile.

"It is where I come when I need to be alone."

I patted myself down, making sure I was really there.

He poured from a glimmering wine flask. "Amusing. Alone from kingly duties, I mean. As alone as a king can be."

I leaned back on my elbows and absorbed the perfection of this hidden picnic spot. "You have a wonderful life," I admitted softly.

He side-eyed me. "That depends on what you find wonderful."

"Riding horses to secret picnics…eating pies with birds flying out. Is that flask solid gold?"

He made a dismissive grunt. "You believe my life is all recreation? Last month I did not sleep for a week while I arranged the Treaty of Armistice, there are rumors Spanish troops are advancing through the Low Countries, and I must soon entertain half the French court."

"Sounds horrific."

He tossed a piece of ham at me, and I fell backward, his cute laugh drawing my own until something hard dug into my side from the inside of his vest. I fished out a small navy-blue locket.

Nick cleared his throat. "Open it."

I flipped the latch. Inside was a miniature painting of a girl with raven curls tumbling past her shoulders in tidy streams. I'd seen the portrait all over the internet. It was Princess Henriette of France.

"She's pretty," I said truthfully, my chest burning.

"Should I marry her?"

I nearly coughed up a clump of sugary cream. "Why are you asking me?"

"I need the opinion of someone without a vested interest. God knows I have enough of those. You may speak plainly."

I thought for a moment. "Do you love her?" I offered.

He grimaced. "What am I, a peasant?" He took the locket from me, his soft fingertips brushing over mine. "But I am troubled the Spanish king will interpret the marriage as an act of war. Which, let us be truthful, it is. Nonetheless, I have already vowed to wed no lady of whom I have not borne witness with mine eyes. I do not trust portrait painters."

"Well, why would you, after yours," I said under my breath.

His brows rose. "You do not admire my portrait?"

"It's okay, I guess. It just doesn't really look like you."

"Truly? I shall have the painter executed at once."

His expression remained grave before he broke into a smile that could've melted the polar ice caps. He stroked his jaw, his thoughts deepening. "It is no secret there are liberties in the image. Princes should have beards, but the real ones vex my skin. I also demanded to appear large and powerful, to help me attract a foreign queen. It displeases me that you care not for it."

"Why do you need a foreign queen?" I asked, genuinely curious. "What about an English queen?"

He chuckled, fingering the crust of his bread as his voice did something strange. "Who, you?"

"Of course not." My cheeks burned hotter than the August sun. "I just meant a foreign queen could bring her own enemies to England. Plus, as you said, Spain might deem the marriage a hostile act." *Cheers, Mathew Fox.*

His face crinkled with surprise. "A girl with such interest in policy. Your points are just, but taking an English queen would also deny England a powerful foreign alliance while giving rise to civil conflicts."

Right. Cheers, Mathew Fox.

Nick sighed, contemplating. "Thomas Grey is adamant about the match, and I do think good of him, he has always handled me well. Even so, I fear he is somewhat charmed by Henriette's promise to convert to the true faith." He picked at the skin of a grape. "Frankly, Mistress Grace, matters of religion have done too much to destroy the realm. My chief cares are peace and stability. Besides, all this talk of war ruins my appetite." He held up the locket, inspecting the painting. "I suppose Henriette is the most ideal match. If she'll have me."

I raised my brows in an 'as if' expression. "She'll have you. She'd be crazy not to."

Nick's mouth closed as he looked back at me, his gaze sucking me in like sticky caramel. After a short silence, he spoke delicately. "You have not yet mentioned my letter."

My heart jumped. "What letter?"

"The one I sent to Hatfield, requesting your return to court." The confusion in his face matched mine as he read my expression. "You did not receive it?"

I probably should have lied and said that I had received the king's permission to come back to Whitehall, but I found myself shaking my head, already desperate to know more about this letter he'd written to me.

He blew through his lips, frowning. "Good God, I must know where that letter is."

"Why? What did it say?"

He swallowed hard, absently playing with the edge of his cushion. "It said that I was sorrowful for the way I spoke to you in my chambers. About Kit."

He stopped there, but the hesitant look on his face suggested there was more.

"And?" I pressed, the air between us thickening.

His fingers brushed his full lips, and his gaze dropped to my mouth, releasing a hot current of electricity that ran from my chest down to the lowest part of my stomach. When his eyes returned to mine, I found a smoldering fire in them wanting to be ignited. But then it died out.

"I only acted that way about Kit because of how important she is to me," he said in a taut voice. "I'm extremely protective of her, as you have seen."

"I know." I rolled onto my opposite thigh, trying not to feel nauseated by his words. *Less than a month now until the bells toll for Kit.*

"After so many years without my mother or father, Kit has become like a daughter to me," he continued, unaware of the torture he was inflicting. "I fear losing her so greatly that it makes me ill at the mere thought of my own children. How I will agonize over their safety."

A bird squawked high in the trees, echoing the sharp cry inside me. I wanted to tell Nick to take Kit far away from court and shield her with guards until her ninth birthday. But then he'd probably burn me for heresy, and the world as I knew it could change forever.

When I looked back at him, his eyes still felt inches away, but they had lost some of their warmth. "Mistress Grace, if you did not receive my letter, why did you return to court without my permission?"

For a moment, I didn't speak, totally lost as to how to answer. I didn't know the rules of court; that I even needed his permission to be here.

He exhaled and rose to his boots, his cheeks turning hollow. "I have a Council meeting this night. We have stayed too long."

A gust of wind rocketed from the trees, sending goose bumps dancing across my skin.

We didn't speak as we walked back to the horses, Nick putting distance between us that I felt in the pit of my stomach. While he untied Stella, I shrugged his vest off my shoulders and handed it to him.

"Are you not cold?" he asked softly.

Four guards appeared on the narrow path as if they had the king on radar.

"I'm fine," I said quickly, feeling a little whiplashed by his mood changes. *I can't read this guy at all.*

I struggled to keep up as we rode back to court, my butt close to falling off from bouncing in the saddle. But Robin House was much closer to Whitehall than I'd thought.

Nick only looked my way once during the ride back, causing a low twist in my belly when our eyes clung together for an endless breath. But when we reached the wide ditch ahead of the city wall, he took off ahead of me, a guard motioning for me to hold back. *I guess that's goodbye then.*

Only when the king was well out of sight was I permitted to ride through the gates of Whitehall. Stella's hooves trampled the flower petals tossed by the crowds who'd waited all day for their king to return.

I intended to spend the evening staking out the Dowager Countess of Warwick's chambers, but instead I hauled my legs to my room like they were tree trunks. My head ached, my limbs were on fire, and the dizziness I'd felt outside Robin House had returned. After a nine-year hiatus, I'd clearly overdone the horse riding.

What I needed was a quick bath, not least of which was because my shins were caked with dirt. I dragged my feet to the washroom, where a maid younger than me poured steaming water into a wooden tub lined with sheets. I closed my eyes while she washed my hair, imagining I was back at the salon in Hadley with Mia.

When the maid left, I sank deeper into the silky water, wishing I could stay there forever. But it cooled quickly, and there were no taps. I tried to lift a leg out of the bath, but my body weighed more than a truck. My head was in pieces.

"Are you well, mistress?" asked a voice from far away.

I sank below the surface, shivering. When I raised my dripping face, I couldn't climb out, my joints locked, my throat an inferno. A moan rang in my ears. Two small hands pulled at my shoulders as blackness swallowed up the world around me.

11

THERE WERE BLEAK VOICES AND DAMP CLOTHS THAT WERE AT FIRST
stifling but then soothing, at least for a while. Then the dreaded aches
would return, piercing me to the bone. My hair matted with sweat
and cold palms pressed my forehead.

"Please," I whispered into the darkness, my lips cracking. "I need
water. Where's Mom?" *My mom's a nurse.*

"Try not to speak." The weathered tone pried my eyes open. I
clutched Mom's hand. Her skin had aged.

"What's wrong with me?" Talking was like pulling the coughing
trigger. I strained to catch my breath, my chest whistling. When my
eyes found light again, Mia was belly laughing, like the time I
pretended that dissecting a rat was against my religion to get out of
biology.

"Shut up," I said weakly, wanting to smile. "It's not funny."

Icy wind wafted from an open window. The only sounds were
occasional voices, downpours of rain, and splashing water. Sometimes
the faces appeared...Alice, Mia, Kit with her gap-toothed smile and
perfumed hair. I'd never had so many visitors, but when I spoke to
them, they didn't reply.

Warm fingertips traced my cheek tenderly, my jaw tilting into the softness. My eyelids dragged open, meeting eyes the color of a shallow sea.

"Mistress Grace?" Nick said huskily, his worried gaze trailing all over my face. As I fought to focus on the perfect mirage of his features, he was already gone.

As what seemed like days came and went, the room grew clearer and warmer. There was always the burning rosemary and the old lady with a veiled hood sewing in the corner. Another time I could've sworn Lord Lansbury was leaning against the wall staring at me, his beefy arms crossed.

When I opened my eyes, someone was spooning hot, pungent liquid through my sandpaper lips. I tried to turn away, but the soup kept coming. The more I blinked, the more of Mathew Fox's face I made out.

"Am I dying?" I mumbled, remembering how trapped his features looked inside his small skull.

"You will be if you shun your remedies."

I licked my lips. "I need water."

"We have had rain. I'll have it fetched for you."

When I lifted my head, the room spun out of control. I flopped back onto the pillow. "Aren't you scared you'll get sick?" I asked him, trying to inch away.

"What does my health matter when England is at stake?" He hunched forward, whispering. "Mistress, I bring words of encouragement. The king is beside himself over your condition."

Memories attacked my mind. Riding in the sweeping countryside, the picnic lunch at Robin House, collapsing in the bath.

"Is the king well?" I said urgently.

"Physically yes, grace be to God. But Sir Thomas Grey already threatened to resign because His Majesty insisted on visiting you in your state. A Spanish warship was sighted near Penzance this morning. Grey is calling for an immediate offer of marriage to the French princess, yet His Majesty has not obliged."

My throat clenched with a painful rasp. "I've been here too long." Mom would have the police out this time. Maybe Dad had actually been to our house.

"It has only been about ten hours," said Mathew, wiping my forehead again. "And take heart—this may yet be a short affliction. There is talk of a one-day fever in the city. Every minute you do not worsen is a sign this suffering will depart as swiftly as it arrived. But if you do not improve before the day is out, Doctor Norris will call for the barber surgeons. Please, mistress, you must fight."

I must've caught whatever dreaded illness this was when I went to London the week before with Francis, Alice, and Kit. I shut my eyes and focused on my breathing. When I opened them again, the woman in the hood was seated beside me, the tug of her sewing thread louder than an airplane. I had to get to the ring—to a hospital with real doctors and a nebulizer. I tried begging the woman, but she showed no signs of hearing me. My heavy eyes sank closed, and when they opened again for just a moment, hot soup was moistening my lips again, soothing the cracks.

"Thanks," I managed to whisper to the lady. "What's your name?"

"Nicholas Henry Edward Tudor. But if you call me that, I might have to lock *you* up."

My eyes sprang open. He was in a baby-blue linen shirt with the sleeves rolled up, his face unshaven, his hair disheveled. I'd seen nothing more beautiful. He was also feeding me soup. I had to be hallucinating again.

"You're not here," I whispered.

"Oh, but how that would please my councilors. There would be a feast with fireworks and cannon."

I tried not to stare at his elegant features as they sharpened into view. "No, you'll get sick!" I drew back in the bed.

"Not if I keep my distance." He dropped the spoon into the bowl. "How can I command God to heal you from twenty-five rooms away? These physicians and apothecaries are about as useful as an arm in a kicking contest."

I shivered beneath the wool blankets.

"Can you sit by the fire?" He hastily slid the bowl onto the side table. "I fear this bed of illness is doing nothing to rouse your spirits."

Still only half believing he was really here, I let him help me out of the bed, my plaited hair tumbling down my back. He hooked his arm around my waist and slowly walked me to the fireplace. If I wasn't so out of sorts, I wouldn't have let myself fall so freely into his rose-tinged skin, my mouth landing near his neck. He stopped and tilted into me for a heart-stopping moment before he helped me into a chair.

He sat close to me, shuffling a deck of cards with the dexterity of a croupier. "I believe in stimulating the mind to heal the body."

"You mean challenge the sick person 'cause you know you'll win," I replied weakly.

One side of his mouth slanted into a smile as he dealt out five cards each. Josh's Uncle Pete had taught us to play poker the weekend his mom was dragged to rehab. Good thing the suits were the same.

Nick rearranged his cards. "How about a wager? If I win, I get to ride with you to Robin House again."

"And if I win?"

"You get to ride with me to Robin House again."

I laughed, triggering another coughing fit. My fingertips massaged my eyes. *Ugh, I must look like the bride of Satan.*

Nick's face creased. "My secretary has written to your father. I expect your family to arrive at court any day. Lord Lansbury has already allocated spacious lodgings. They may stay as long as they wish."

"Oh, you didn't have to, but thank you." Fear quaked though me. I tried not to show it, shakily switching my cards to line up a pair of sevens.

"Christ, I nearly forgot. I made you something." Nick leaned past me to fish out a pendant of wrapped linen from his coat hanging on the chair. "It is a healing remedy. It has wormwood, devil's-bit—fourteen of the most powerful herbs in Christendom. They are from my personal collection."

"Thank you," I said as I hung the talisman around my neck, my chest warming.

"That is not all." He handed me a soft pouch of red velvet. Inside was the emerald necklace I'd practically drooled over in his bedroom. He blushed through his dimples. "It is not quite as charming as a knot ring."

"You're giving me this?" I asked, my voice rising in pitch.

"Does it please you?"

"Of course, but it's…it's too much." The square emerald was the size of a continent in my palm.

"If only it were enough." His worried eyes focused on me, his voice thickening. "You must get better, Emmie, that is all I ask."

I wasn't prepared to hear him say my first name.

I sensed his breathing change, his chest rising and falling deeply beneath his shirt as we sat and watched each other. My cards fell limply from my moist hands. For a moment, neither of us spoke, my cheeks flushing hot.

Nick swallowed hard, his eyes glittering in the firelight. "Do you still want to know what I wrote in that letter to you?"

I nodded slowly, holding in a breath as my heart began to pound.

He licked his lips, blinking fast. "It said that I sent you away from court not only because I was angry, but…because I was tempted." His greenish pupils pulled mine like magnets as his gaze trailed down to my lips, stilling there. "Because, even now, all I see is your face in its countless perfections and I ache to kiss you."

A hot current shot from my cheeks to my heart.

"You must think me mad," he said softly, tugging his bottom lip a little between his thumb and forefinger.

"No…I think you're lovely."

I think you're lovely, I think you're sexy, I think you're the most mesmerizing person I've ever laid eyes on.

He reached forward to brush away a wisp of my hair, his fingertips gliding down the side of my neck. If my heart had beat any faster, it would've exploded out of my chest.

Just as I thought he was going to catch my jaw in his hands and pull my mouth to his, he exhaled sharply, pressing a palm to his brow. "Christ, when somebody this side of London is ill, I usually hide like a child."

"I know, I'm sorry." I turned away.

God, Emmie. Kill the King of England, why don't you.

"It is I who is sorry." He stood up and pulled his coat up over his shoulders. "You need rest and recovery, not to feel compelled to gratify my personal desires."

I blinked up at him through my lashes. "Who says I'm compelled?"

He swallowed hard, his face flushing. "I pray you understand that I would reach as far as the New World for a physician if I believed he could help you. But Doctor Norris is truly the finest I've seen. You must do everything he tells you." He stopped at the door with his back to me. "Because if you die, he will burn."

My lips fell open as he disappeared through the archway.

Doctor Norris returned in minutes and ordered me back to bed. It was then that I noticed the tension in his gait, the lines of worry on his brow. Determined to keep the poor doctor from ending up on a barbecue, I drank and ate every hideous concoction he prescribed for the next few hours until I could hold my head up without seeing stars.

"I believe it is the one-day fever," said Norris with a smile so big it didn't suit his stern face. He kept touching my cheeks and forehead before clapping his hands like his football team had just scored another touchdown.

When the maids came in to light the evening candles, I asked if I could go back to my room. It was amazing how much better I felt already, kind of like an intense but fleeting bout of the stomach flu.

"You must remain confined for at least four to five more days," Norris ordered, massaging the sockets of his exhausted eyes with his knobby fingertips. He yawned and left me unguarded. I made a swift escape to my room with my head down, struck by how much the tiny space with its prickly mattress felt like home.

As I reluctantly lay there with the blue-diamond ring on my thumb, Nick's words played on loop in my mind like lines of a favorite song. All I could see were his lips saying my name in a way that made me want to bring my mouth to his and taste every part of him.

You must get better, Emmie.

All I see is your face in its countless perfections, and I ache to kiss you.

The painfully hot rasp in his voice summoned me into a deep, almost euphoric sleep.

Words of the king wanting me.

12

IT TOOK FOUR LIGHTNING-FAST NIGHTS AND THREE ETERNAL SCHOOL days before I could get back to Whitehall. Worried that Mom would start to notice her dwindling sleeping pill collection, I spent the whole of Saturday hiking with Mia and Josh to drain my energy so I was tired enough to fall asleep as soon as she left for work.

I arrived back in the sixteenth century just in time for the king's birthday party. Thankfully, my Tudor friends thought I'd been in my room on bed rest recovering from the one-day fever, and were relieved to see me back in good health. Alice loaned me a spectacular gown the color of a tropical sea, waves of silver thread shimmering through it.

Francis waited for his "two chaperones" outside the Great Hall, his silver doublet trimmed with red. He kissed my hand, stopping to gape at Alice's amethyst gown.

"You look like an aubergine," he said.

"Do not get too close then," she replied, her eyes flashing. "I hear they are dreadfully poisonous."

Francis smirked at her profile as he escorted us inside the party, clearly thrilled to be finally forgiven for the London incident.

The cavernous Great Hall had been transformed into a magnificent fairytale scene, complete with an artificial lake and stone bridge. The perfumed air rang with music and voices, extravagant gowns and jewels sparkling like Christmas lights. A stout man scampered past, perspiring like a marathon runner.

"Lord Mayberry, Master of the Revels," Francis explained to me. "If tonight does not please the king, it will be his head on the gallows on the morrow."

Alice just laughed, to my relief.

"The Mayor of London," he pointed out to her. "Always makes the finest decisions when he is tippled. You know the Earl of Northampton, the new Lord Chancellor, and—"

"Mr. George Gardiner, the Vice-Chancellor of Cambridge," Alice finished with warm familiarity.

My stomach collapsed like a house of cards. I'd told everyone here that my dad studied medicine at Cambridge. I had no idea how big or small the student body was in those days. What if Mr. Gardiner knew all the med students? The young vice-chancellor threw his head back in laughter, revealing the source of the hilarity. The Dowager Countess of Warwick flapped her hands at him through an elaborate story, her black bell sleeves catching the shoulder of Kit's sparkling butter-yellow gown as Kit walked past them. My throat withered at the sight of her. I still had to find those rosary beads.

"I'm going to say hi to Kit," I said to the others, making a dash away from Mr. Cambridge.

Kit's hug was healing. "It's so good to see you," I said. I didn't know if I cared so much about her because she was a part of *him* or for herself, but I did. "Your hair looks cute."

She touched her crown of braids. "Forgive me for not visiting you when you were ill, but I was forbidden. I'm so pleased it was the one-day fever. I prayed and prayed for it." She fastened her eyes to the corner of the room. "Oh shame, now she is moving my gift!"

A stunning girl in a raspberry gown was placing a parrot sculpture encrusted with gemstones onto a table piled with gleaming objects. I recognized the spiraling black tresses that were gathered with red roses at the nape of her neck. Sickness swelled in my stomach.

"That's not Princess Henriette of France is it?" I asked Kit.

"It certainly is, and the princess is *always* with him," she replied with a scowl. "His Majesty invited Henriette to court for his birthday celebrations, and she has barely left his side. Come, I want to move my gift back."

The charming Philippe Renard swept away Henriette and her entourage of ladies just as we arrived at the table. I watched as he introduced her to a trio of bowing men, her movements as fluid as a ballet dancer's, her waist the size of a thimble. Nick never mentioned anything about Princess Henriette coming to court. The thought of him looking at her the same way he had me stung like a hurricane of bees.

Up close, the king's gift table was a fancy auction catalog, displaying everything from diamond sculptures to silver tankards and plates, wooden tennis racquets, and textiles threaded with gold. Kit moved her painting in front of the parrot sculpture.

When trumpets blasted from beyond the double doors, Henriette straightened her tresses to hang evenly. Four white horses strode into the hall to momentous applause, chased by fire breathers and acrobatic jesters. At the procession's rear was a gilded chariot with Nick standing inside. He was spellbinding in head-to-toe white, his waist strapped with a gold belt that matched his glittering crown.

I sucked in a sharp breath. Four nights had felt like four ice ages now that I saw him again.

"We have been searching for you," hissed Alice, tugging me. "Our welcome dance is now!"

She pulled on my Venetian mask. Its stem poked my ear as we circled the chariot and froze around it like a hold-up. The dance began to delighted cheers from the audience. Alice stumbled the wrong way into Isobel while the Dowager Countess of Warwick counted under her breath. Kit dashed in at the final moment to perform her well-practiced solo, all of us folding to our toes at the end in a sign of reverence. Nick smiled and clapped as he stepped down from his chariot. His eyes moved straight to mine, sending heat to my face.

"Happy birthday, Your Grace," said Kit with trained formality.

"Thank you, sweetheart."

"Happy birthday," I stammered, curtsying.

He nodded at me in thanks, a dimple showing in his cheek. I wanted to be near his warm, scented skin again, his sleeves rolled up and his collar open, away from the fanfare. Despite everything, I still hungered to kiss him so much it hurt.

The Titanic-sized feather in Thomas Grey's beret cut between us, clearing a path for the incoming Henriette. She was even prettier up close, her slender neck encircled with a choker of blood-red rubies.

"Happy birthday, Your Majesty," she said with a thick accent, dropping to kiss his hand. Her fragrance was so strong it nearly made me choke. "It is lovely to see your charming sister again. But who is this?" She straightened, her smoky eyes on mine.

"Mistress Emily Grace, I believe," said Thomas. "From Hatfield, a small township north of London."

"A small township I was born in," said Nick. "My mother was a great admirer of Hatfield."

"Oh, how I wish to have met the Queen Elizabeth," said Henriette. "I hear she was as wise as she was gracious."

"One of the most glorious women of our age," said Thomas. "And also a great admirer of marchpane."

"Truly? How lovely to have so much in common with her. I fear I am going back to France much heavier." She laughed and touched her waistline.

"That is plainly absurd…you look incredible," Nick said to her.

The words sliced into me like machetes. I was about to excuse myself when Isobel glided toward us wearing a voluminous peach gown. Her sallow neck looked even thinner in a stiff white ruff. She curtsied at the king. "Your Majesty, if I may wish you my best wishes, and ask if you may—"

"Excuse me," said Nick quickly, leading Henriette away to an elderly man in a bishop's cloak. Isobel's shoulders slumped. When she caught me watching her I looked away, but maybe I shouldn't have. We were in the same sinking boat…the runners-up. I tried to make eye contact again, but Isobel was now carrying a full goblet of wine over to the king's gentleman, Mark Macaulay.

"Thank heavens," said Alice, seizing two cups from a tray and handing me one. "I was nearly trapped with Lord and Lady Snell, the most tiresome couple in Christendom. Plus, everyone knows Lady Lennox is his mistress." She grinned. "I saw you met our future queen. Promise me you will stay and become a maid of honour? You will have your pick of the noblemen."

"Maybe," I murmured into my cup. Another lie to add to the pile. I'd sooner chew broken glass than become a slave to Nick Tudor's wife.

"She's pretty," I said honestly, gesturing to Henriette.

"The princess is pleasant enough, although a touch severe," said Alice. "She has been exploring the castle and gardens, receiving guests and concerts, but mostly keeping company with the king. Father says they are sharing all their meals. A pronouncement of their betrothal is sure to come at any moment."

My eyes flickered over to where Nick stood with Henriette, my heart feeling like it'd been kicked with a steel-capped boot. So that's what he'd been doing while I'd been in class this week, a dumb grin plastered on my face while fantasizing that he missed me as much as I did him. *And you thought you had a shot, Emmie? A twenty-first century wannabe jewelry designer and a Tudor king? Get a grip.*

Francis spun a young girl out of his arms on the dance floor, letting Lord Lansbury catch her before making his way over to us. He offered his hand, flirtatiously shifting it back and forth between us, before finally stopping at Alice.

Her hand stayed at her side. "That is how you ask a lady to dance?" she said. "I'm surprised you get any partners at all."

Francis tugged her toward him. "Do you ever stop complaining, Alice Grey?"

The music changed to the volta, their faces a matching shade of crimson as the sexy routine began. It was hard not to smile at them, but I put down my cup, reminding myself that I had a greater purpose than ensuring Alice and Francis got their predestined marriage *and* obsessing about a king fated to marry someone else. I needed to find a way into the Dowager Countess of Warwick's rooms and search for those damn rosary beads. The countess was busy brownnosing the nobles, but I hadn't seen either of her maids, which meant her rooms probably weren't empty at this moment.

I turned into Mathew Fox's petite outstretched hand. His cinnamon coat with gold stitching was the most bling I'd seen him in.

"You look beautiful," he said, leading me into a turn.

"You're not so scruffy yourself," I replied with a smile.

He steered me closer, gripping my hip with his glove.

"Mistress, I have been waiting to speak with you for several days, but I could not locate you." The smile slid off my face as he continued, whispering against my ear. "It is more important than ever to remain determined. The French princess has moved closer, undoubtedly, but you are also becoming close with the king. It is time to draw His Majesty nearer, but discreetly. Our plan risks ruin if the princess notices him favoring you."

"*Our* plan?"

He stopped, confused. "You no longer wish to win the affections of His Majesty?" Right now, his question just felt painful. Mathew's face hardened. "Mistress, so we're clear, this is not about foolish desire. This is about your countrymen. About England."

Wispy curls irritated my cheeks as I looked away. I wanted to tell him that I wasn't here to play war games, but a pair of guards abruptly swept us off the dance area.

Nick and Henriette sauntered into the empty space like a wedding couple, courtiers watching on with thrilled faces. The king stood still and smirked like the prize he was while Henriette snaked around him in some kind of weird Renaissance tease, her cheeks rosy, her smile setting her eyes alight. So much for their setup being just an alliance. She liked him as much as I did.

Thomas Grey's velvet shoulder nudged me. "You are playing a dangerous game, my dear."

I looked at him and then over my shoulder. "Are you talking to me?"

His eyes remained fixed on the king. "Trust me when I say you are forbidden fruit, no more. Certainly not the first His Majesty has tasted."

It took me a second to speak. "He hasn't *tasted* anything."

Thomas's chuckle was cutting. "You carry on with the king and his sister like you belong among them, not realizing that, all the while, you are putting their lives at stake."

Great. Another person who believes I'm the king's biggest threat instead of the only one who knows what's truly coming for him. I wanted to shake Thomas Grey.

Alice cut in to take his hand. "Will you share a dance with me, Papa?" She smiled at us like we were her two favorite people, clearly not hearing what he'd just said. Thomas tossed me a look of contempt over her shoulder.

Thankfully the Master of the Revels announced supper; a respite from the dancing flirt-fest between Nick and Henriette. But I could barely stomach anything from the bottomless platters of roasted meats as I watched Nick sit sandwiched between Henriette and Kit—a life-sized royal Christmas card. Henriette didn't stop talking the entire meal, her cherry lips practically glued to the king's ear. He listened and smiled.

When the torture-show was over, the Master of the Revels lifted his voice. "Gentlemen and ladies of the court, His Majesty has prepared a very special performance for your ears only. May I present our great sovereign lord, His Majesty Nicholas the First, King of England, playing an *original* composition."

"Heavens," whispered Alice beside me. "The king never plays openly, and certainly not an original."

A young page handed Nick his lute. The space echoed with deafening applause, which silenced as soon as he began his gentle strum. Pride curled up inside me like burning paper as I watched him. The melody he was playing was beautiful, haunting, and unmistakably familiar. As the pretty tune tumbled out of his fingertips, my greedy eyes roamed across the ruffled tufts of his chestnut hair, down the slight curve of his nose to his damaged cheek, and hovered on his full lips that were slightly parted with concentration.

It was then that I knew, with absolute clarity and certainty, that I didn't just like him…I loved him. I knew it was ridiculous. How could I love someone I'd never even kissed? But the feeling of longing was so full that I nearly choked on it. There was nothing else to explain the sickening devastation of knowing he'd never be mine and that he'd marry Henriette.

Nick rested his lute across his thighs and blushed as the cheers began. My hands pounded together until his gaze found mine in the crowd of spectators. But within seconds, courtiers had him surrounded and blocked my view, including Henriette, who was fighting her way through to him.

"And now, we invite you outside to our enchanted garden for dessert and more dancing!" the Master of the Revels cried after a blast of trumpets. Isobel's lavish skirts swished past me, shadowed by the Dowager Countess of Warwick's two maids in their usual heart-shaped hoods.

My heart quickened its pace. If the countess's maids were with Isobel right now, then her rooms had to be empty. I told Alice I was going to the lavatory and plowed through servers grappling with a gigantic sugar sculpture of a rising phoenix.

I was out of breath by the time I reached the Dowager Countess of Warwick's chambers upstairs. The silent air was musty. I ran to her vanity chest and hurriedly sorted through drawers without upsetting the contents, rummaging through mounds of pearls and jewels that could've bought her an airplane in my time, but there was no sign of any wooden rosary beads. Other drawers were stuffed with old hoods and colored scarves, the bottom one plugged with dusty books. When I searched through them, a piece of decaying paper fluttered to the ground, scratched with what looked like scriptures in a scrawl I instantly recognized. It was the same handwriting from the vicious note that had been left in my room.

"What in Lucifer's name are you doing?"

The Dowager Countess of Warwick stood in the doorway, her eyes slanted with shock.

I held up the page. "It was you. You threatened me!"

"I did *what?*" She rushed at me. "How dare you invade my rooms like this? I have had more than enough, you parasite."

"Afraid I'll find more disgusting notes?" I tossed the paper at her.

"What notes? Mistress Grace, what in the devil is wrong with you?"

"You really have no clue who I am," I said, blood rushing to my cheeks. "But you should be careful, because I'm onto you. I know *exactly* what you're up to. So before you do anything you'll regret, think twice. Because you can bet your ass you won't get away with it as long as I'm around."

It was hard to tell who was shaking more. The countess practically spat venom. "I am a Beaumont, dear girl, descendent of kings. My only crime is believing your falsehood about being an accomplished physician's daughter. Who is your father really? A farmer? A fishmonger?"

The air in my throat locked. "I have no idea what you're talking about."

She bared her teeth like a charging monkey. "I met an enchanting gentleman this evening: Mr. Gardiner, the Vice-Chancellor of Cambridge. He has not once heard of a Doctor Grace from Hatfield. Which seems sensible, after my friend called into Hertfordshire on her way to Buckingham and made inquiries on my behalf. I am certain that you can guess what she found. Or, rather, what she did not. No Doctor Grace, no Mrs. Grace, no Master Grace, no Mistress Grace, not so much as a dog named Grace. Not one person of significance in Hatfield has ever heard of the Grace family."

"Why do you care so much?" I nearly shouted. "Do you have any idea what goes on around here? Murders and kidnappings, and all you give a toss about is what town I was born in?"

I knew I was saying too much, but I was too scared for Kit—and too annoyed about Henriette—to think straight. My heart thrashed against my chest.

The countess's nostrils flared. "I have been at this court longer than the king has lived! So while you try to devise your next falsehood to justify why you lied about your stock, rest assured, there will be a place for you to go when you are banished for treason. I hear the Tower of London is lovely at this time of year. It is the perfect season for the rats." She reached past me, wrenching a fur shawl off a mannequin. "Now, if you'll excuse me, they are having bonfires outside."

"And why didn't you send your maid to get that?" I said accusingly, nodding at the shawl. "You were following me? Worried what I'd find?"

The countess spun back to me, her expression glacial. "One day you will learn this was never about you. When my daughter no longer requires the presence of my maids to ensure she does not drink herself to oblivion, His Majesty will be reminded of what the Lady Isobel can offer him. And, in the meantime, what you cannot."

She left me in the dark, rigid with fear that she'd tell Nick what she'd discovered about my Hatfield family, or lack thereof. I wiped escaping tears and hurried back down the staircase, the corridor echoing with voices. Nick was standing at the bottom, talking to a guard, and the sight sent me back a step.

"Mistress Grace is here," the king called out, releasing a breath. "I have been searching for you," he said to me, stepping up to meet me.

"Why? What's wrong?"

He guided me to the base of the stairs and around the back until we were in some sort of wine cellar. Towering oak barrels obscured us from view and it hit me that we were alone in here. I blew through my lips as if that might expel the butterflies in my stomach that Nick always roused.

"How are you feeling?" he said, his greenish eyes shining with concern. "I have wanted to ask you for days, but there's all this damn fanfare. You then fled so fast this night that I thought the palace was on fire."

"I'm feeling much better. Thank you."

He reached out to gently cup my face in his palms, weakening my knees. "I cannot tell you my relief. Look at you. A portrait of strength and beauty. Mine eyes can barely believe it."

"Don't you mean *incredible?*" I said, repeating what Nick had called Henriette when she'd joked about looking anything other than perfect. I took a step back from him, slipping from his grasp. "You should get back to the princess."

"Do not be jealous." His eyes gleamed. "You need not be. Entertaining a visiting royal is my duty. Make no more of it."

"Then why didn't you tell me that Princess Henriette was coming here? When you came to see me when I was sick and you said all that stuff about…about perfection and kissing?"

His brow pinched. "I believed you might be dying. It could as easily have been the deadly sweat as it was the one-day fever. I was hardly going to waste time on trivial matters."

You marry her, Nick. I'd say that passes the 'trivial' test.

He closed the space between us again, nearing my trembling skin. "I cannot bear you being angry with me. Not after what you have been through. Did my gift not please you?"

"The herbal necklace? I wore it every day until it smelled like socks."

An adorable chuckle slipped from his mouth. "The song I performed tonight. I wanted to tell you beforehand, but there was no opportunity. I composed it for you while you were ill. I named it Lady Green Sleeves." He traced the edges of my cut sleeves, the brush of his fingertips setting my skin alight. "Because of the way my silks touch your skin. The effect these things have on me." His lips pressed together as if he was fighting something.

I stared at him with my jaw slack. "You wrote *Greensleeves?* For me?" I'd heard the song a hundred times. It couldn't have been written about me. Out of everything that had happened, it was the most impossible.

An explosion from over the palace roof made me jump. The second was even louder.

Nick smirked down at me. "Fireworks. Captivating things. I regret that I have kept you from seeing their beauty."

"Oh, I see beauty," I said softly, looking right at him. His cheeks flushed with warmth. "And it might shock you to know I've seen fireworks before."

"Actually, it does not," he replied, his eyes sparkling.

"I'd rather be right here."

The way he was looking at me made me feel like I'd fall through the floor and land on a cloud. He shifted a step closer until there was hardly any space left separating us.

"Emmie, I must thank you."

"For what?" I didn't know if the thumping heart I could hear was his or mine.

His fingers brushed his neck. "I've done all you ask. My rooms were cleared of dust and the flowers removed. I have been careful not to ride too hard. I have felt lighter since then. No breathing attacks."

My cheeks broke into a smile. "That's good."

"But what if being near you is what makes it hard for me to breathe?"

He reached out to hold my cheek again, softly stroking it with his thumb. I turned my face into his hand, the sweet scent of his skin flooding me with syrupy warmth as I lost all control of myself and pressed my lips to the soft tip of his thumb. A sigh rippled through him before he cupped my cheeks in his palms and lifted my face. And for a moment, we just stayed there, his hypnotic eyes staring deeply into mine before he lowered his mouth and pressed his lips to my own. An astonishing feeling of connection poured into me as he just held me there, every part of my body immobilized by the press of his soft, warm lips to mine.

A man cleared his throat, and we snapped away from each other. Thomas Grey stood clutching his feathered beret in the shadows.

"For God's sake man, speak!" Nick said sharply.

Thomas dabbed his forehead with a cloth. "Forgive me, my benevolent Majesty. The guards informed me of your location. I come with urgent news that should be delivered discreetly." Thomas's pale eyes flickered to mine.

Nick caught my hand in his and squeezed my fingers. "Do not leave," he said to me with a look of longing that squeezed my chest.

He yanked Thomas outside by his hat. I heard a door close and heated talking.

My back fell into the brick wall, a feeling of hot liquid rushing through me and pooling in the deepest part of my abdomen. All I could taste was the soft sweetness of Nick's lips. I wanted to deepen the kiss. I wanted to taste his tongue and swirl it with mine…to fist his hair in my hands and drag him closer. The thought of it made my thighs press tightly together.

Nick burst back into the wine cellar. The change in his demeanor struck me with the speed of a devastating car smash.

"Who are you?" he spat at me, his eyes ablaze. "An ingenious spy or a careless thief?"

"What?" My stomach hit my feet.

"Majesty, may I suggest a more secluded location," urged Thomas. Voices passed by in the hall.

Nick grabbed him by the collar and shoved him up against the wall before releasing him. "Bring her to my chambers. Now."

Before I could speak, I was inside a funnel of guards who escorted me up the stairs leading to the Presence Chamber and into the king's office.

Nick stood facing the moonlit Thames, gripping his forehead.

The door clanged shut behind me as the guards left us alone.

"Who are you?" he asked with his back to me, his strangled voice not his own.

It was hard to speak through my trembling mouth. "You know who I am."

"Enough lies!" He spun around, pain lining his face. "I have had enough deceit in this court to last me a lifetime. The Dowager Countess of Warwick approached Sir Thomas Grey tonight with not one but two sources of evidence that there is no such man as a Doctor Martin Grace from Hatfield. Hence your rooms were searched without delay, and look what they found."

He opened his hand, the blue-diamond ring catching the candle-light. I brought my palms to my cheeks.

Nick approached me slowly, his face washed of color. "When my coronation ring was misplaced again, I decided it could not have been you. I believed one of my manservants was a thief or perhaps the ring was cursed. But you had it all along." His voice caught on his words. "You know nothing of French, Spanish, or Latin. You cannot ride a horse well or even dance the pavan. Furthermore, when I wrote to your family of your infirmity and invited them to court, I received no visitor and no reply. Thus, I am commanding you now as your anointed king to confess who you really are."

The distress in his face made my heart splinter. My gaze fell to his lips, remembering how they felt against mine.

Nick jerked away from me. "You are nothing but a cheap, deceiving temptress. You should burn for it."

"Cheap?" My voice broke. "If only you knew, Nicholas Tudor, what I have done for you. What I've risked for you…for your family. And I don't even know why." Tears flooded my eyes.

His jaw clenched. "Do you crave the Tower rats that badly? Because, so help me, if you cannot explain yourself this instant, I will have you arrested."

The weight of his words crashed into me with the force of a tsunami. I *could* explain myself. I had to, or this sixteenth-century king might actually kill me.

I was shaking down to my feet. "You're right. I'm not who you think I am."

His face fell. "You are a spy. My God, how could I not have seen it?"

"Please let me finish, because this is the hardest thing I'm ever going to say to anyone." I fought the urge to bolt, my words tumbling out choppy and strained. "My name really is Emmeline Grace, but no, I'm not from Hertfordshire, and I'm not a doctor's daughter. In fact, I hardly ever see my father. But I'm not a spy either." My throat closed on the impossible words. "What I am is from a different time. Over four hundred years in the future…from a place called America that I'm pretty sure you call the New World."

He pressed his hands to his hair. "Stop!"

"I know this sounds totally insane, and I don't get it myself at *all,* but it's true. Unless I've gone completely mad, I've passed through time. More than once—"

"Enough! Stop!" He gripped a chair so tightly I thought it would break. "I barely know you, and yet you cannot comprehend the warmth you have brought to my heart these past weeks and the utter despair of learning it was all a lie. Now you preach this heresy? This is worse than a devil! Do you want me to put you on a stake and set you on fire?"

"Just let me show you. Because I'm telling you the truth, I swear. I can prove it!"

Nick looked like I felt…like he was struggling for air in a room that had none. In the face of his chilling silence, I kept going, my voice shaking.

"Your ring," I said. "It's the key to traveling through time. There's something magical about it. And I don't know how it came to be in my time or why it brought me here; all I know is it's sending me back and forth through time. Over and over."

He shook his head, taking fast breaths.

"How do you think I ended up in your fortress of a park wearing your coronation ring that was missing for years?" I snapped. "Why was I dressed so differently? Why do I never say or do any of the right things? I'm not from your time!"

He scrunched his face. "You are performing. A hideous plot to drive me mad." His hands were fists. "I've had enough of these damned plots!"

I was full-blown crying…begging, even. "But I can show you. I can take you with me and prove it. I'll bring you right back. Please, if you care about me half as much as I do you, you will give me this one chance to show you I'm not lying. You have to believe me. *Please*, Nick, please." Tears washed down my cheeks.

He stared at me for an agonizingly long moment, his face finally breaking with defeat. "I have given you so many chances, Emmie, so many reprieves. This is undoubtedly the worst and the last. On my life, if you are lying, you will burn."

"Deal," I uttered.

The crackling fire nipped at the air as I hesitatingly took his hand and unlocked his fingers. The blue-diamond ring glittered from his shaking palm.

"For this to work, one of us has to wear this, and we have to fall asleep together," I said. "With our bodies touching."

He drew in a sharp breath, his gaze flickering down the length of me before returning to my face. "If this is another part of a vicious plan to undo me, you will find yourself upon the rack before midnight hour."

"It's not."

We stood in stunned silence before he exhaled, slipping the ring onto his third finger. "Very well. We'll do it right now."

I swallowed a ball of nausea in my gut and followed him into his bedroom. He sat on the edge of his bed and began untying his boots.

"It's better if you leave those on," I said. I wasn't planning on taking him shoe shopping as our first activity. Was I really doing this? *He's Nicholas the freaking Ironheart!*

When I stepped out of my giant hoop skirt, he looked at me like I was from another planet.

"Those things are ridiculous," I said through burning cheeks. I untied my shoes and crawled onto the navy silk sheets that smelled like roses and pine. It was the softest, loveliest bed I'd ever touched.

He climbed onto the feather mattress beside me, fully clothed. We lay side by side on our backs, his hand resting face down beside mine. I inhaled a breath and placed my palm over his hand. He didn't move.

A midnight-blue canopy stretched above us, painted with electrifying constellations. I focused on it, trying to ease the knots in my stomach.

"Now we go to sleep," I said to Nick's staggered breathing.

But I'd never been more awake. We lay like stones for what felt like hours, my body crawling toward the heaviness of relaxation. I didn't realize I was still awake until Nick's hand slowly turned in the darkness, his soft palm meeting mine. A sigh escaped my mouth as our fingers immediately laced together. He squeezed, and I let the heat of our connecting skin surge through me.

"Don't let go," I whispered.

It was a miracle neither of us moved again, our hands tightly entwined.

13

MY LOPSIDED FAN SQUEAKED FROM THE CEILING. NICK LAY IN MY BED beside me, breathing deeply and rhythmically, his strong arm imprisoning mine. Something inside me broke and screamed. *Holy shit, it worked!*

I carefully unhooked my arm and snuck into the bathroom to brush my teeth with one hand and finger-comb my hair with the other. My reflection gaped back at me. *Emmie, you stole a fucking king. Minty fresh breath is your priority right now?*

I pressed an ear to Mom's door. Her fluttery snores mingled with laughs from the talk show channel. Nerves tightened my stomach. Mom could sleep all day after night shift, but if she woke up and found a twenty-year-old Tudor king in my bedroom, there'd be serious questions.

When I dashed back in, Nick was sitting up, as still as a Roman statue and practically as white.

"Morning, and welcome to twenty-first century America," I blurted, keeping my voice low. "Home of freedom, fast food, and more importantly, famous people." His eyes veered to mine, but looked right through me.

"I told you it was real," I said shakily. "We're in my bedroom."

His diamond-stitched doublet was laughingly misplaced inside the paint-chipped walls. With unsteady movements, he slowly got up and peered out the window. *Nicholas the Ironheart is in my bedroom. What is air?*

"Mom could sleep through a tornado," I said, watching him suck in the view of the tree-lined street. At least I didn't live in Manhattan. My words followed his wide, wandering eyes. "A lamp. My radio that doesn't work. Books that cost ninety cents for a reason."

He walked to me, reaching out. For a second, I thought he was going to embrace me, but he picked up the photo of Mom and I at Disneyland.

"This is...you." His eyes shifted between me and the frame, blinking fast.

"It's a photograph. It captures something that happens and preserves it in a picture. Like a painting, but...real."

There was so much he didn't know, and I was so unqualified to explain. I gently took his arm, my fingers closing around his bicep. "Try to stay calm. Why don't I get you a slice of pie? Pie's still a thing. Yay for pie. And England, which is also still a thing, by the way."

"What is happening to me?" When he caught himself against the wall, it hit me that traveling forward in time was infinitely more intense than going backward. I reminded myself that it was this or the executioner's block. "I fear God is displeased with me," Nick said into his quivering wrist.

I tried to steady him. "It's okay, I promise. Maybe we should go back now. Before they see you're missing."

He glanced over my laptop, which was definitely staying off after his reaction to the photo. "No," he said, setting his jaw. "Show me more."

I expelled a jittery breath and slowly guided him downstairs. Ruby bounded through the screen door flap to meet us and smothered Nick with licks.

"It's how I worked out two beings could travel together," I said, tugging her away by her collar. "Ruby's done the Whitehall tour too. She also likes you, so you must be okay."

Nick crouched to ruffle the back of the schnauzer's neck as his eyes moved from the small wooden dining table to the threadbare couch. "This is your home? I suppose it is not so different."

"About the same size as yours, right?" I joked.

He frowned at the black television screen and the flickering lights of the Wi-Fi box. I steered him toward the couch and helped him undo his bulky belt and thick coat. It had to feel like eighty-five degrees to him after Tudor England's lower temperatures.

"I'll be less than a minute," I said, heading into the kitchen. "Please don't touch anything, okay? Or move. Or freak out. Trust me, you're safe here. This isn't hell. Well, it may be if Mom hears us."

I slid two slices of pie onto plates and carried them in cold, finding the living room empty. "Nick?" I practically screamed.

He was in the downstairs bathroom, staring at the toilet bowl.

"It's like a chamber pot," I explained. "But it's connected to a drainage system, so it takes, uh, things away when you pull that lever thing."

"I have one, Emmie, but it is…different."

We stood there a moment before he gave me an awkward glance. I shut the door and waited for the flush, followed by a "Good God".

When he came back in, I gently guided him down onto the couch and handed him a plate. "Is this Chinese porcelain?" he asked, his brows high.

"If that's the cheapest kind, then yes."

He scanned the room again, his face a blanket of confusion.

My legs were sweating beneath three layers of skirts.

"I should change," I said. "Do you think you can sit here without touching anything or having a heart attack?" Nick nodded, braving a small bite of pie.

I ran upstairs and threw on a light denim dress with the speed of an Olympian, before clipping on a necklace of a flying bird I'd shaped from wire. I swiped my lashes with mascara and quietly bolted back downstairs in my strappy sandals.

Nick's plate slipped, his eyes skimming my bare legs. "This is your traditional attire?"

"You're lucky I'm not from the nineties. Hammer pants were a thing."

"It is quite humid here, I suppose." He untied the top of his shirt and waved the glistening patch of skin, his eyes flashing past my legs a few more times, even though it was obvious he was trying not to stare.

We both jumped when my cell phone blasted from the coffee table with the theme song from *Doctor Who*. I quickly answered it.

"Do you have any idea how bad this is?" Mia's voice was shrill. "Josh can't come today!"

"Come to what?"

"Garden Party! Jeez, what's wrong with you lately?"

Nick was back up and inspecting the phone at my ear. I waved him away. "That's today? I don't think I can go anymore."

"Hell no, not you too," said Mia. "Josh's mom is supposed to come home today, so he's refusing to leave. I want to smack his head! I'll pick you up in ten minutes."

I tried to protest, but she'd already hung up.

"*Shit!*" I hissed under my breath, throwing the handset at the couch.

"Were you speaking with someone?" When Nick reached for the phone, I grabbed his hand. "Forget that. My best friend is coming over! You're lucky you look nothing like your horrible portraits."

"Horrible?"

I marched him back upstairs. "Now you've seen I'm not lying, I can take you back. Mom's got pills." When he insisted I tell him what was going on with that exasperating princely command, I quickly explained everything about Garden Party.

"Could I not accompany you?" he offered.

"You want me to take you to a music festival? With actual people?" It was worth howling over, but I was too busy trying not to yell.

"You have seen more than enough of my time. Now I should get to see yours."

"Are you high? You could get lost. Or arrested. Plus, you need to get back before anyone notices the King of England has vanished. Last seen with Mistress Emmeline Grace, I might add."

He pressed his lips together, clearly alarmed at the thought. But then he grabbed my hand, the warmth of his fingers enveloping my skin. "When we left, I was in my chambers with a beautiful girl," he said. "No one will disturb me until I call for it, even if it takes the entire night. I beseech you: do not take me back right away. I must see more, to learn more. Things that can help my people."

"It's just Garden Party."

"Please, Emmie, this is my chance to take." His fingers squeezed mine. What he was saying was off the deep end, but that's not what got me. It was the sight of this all-powerful king begging *me* for something, his face ripe with need.

I let out a long sigh. "I guess if Mom finds you here I've got more to explain than time travel, especially in that outfit. So if you want to stay for a bit, we've got to get out of here."

I texted Mia to bring Josh's festival ticket and some spare clothes from Tristan's wardrobe. She replied with a '*WTF?*' and about twenty excited winks.

I insisted she wait in the car while Nick changed in the bathroom, his bewildered mutters audible from the living room. But when he opened the door, my smile dissolved. Mia's younger brother had always had good taste—and he was huge, so the clothes fit—but Nick had turned the faded jeans and black T-shirt into a catalog shoot. One that was evidently advertising perfectly toned arms and thighs.

"You speak French here," he said, pointing at the word '*homme*' on the T-shirt like it was a source of comfort.

"*Oui*," I replied. "Nick, you look…amazing."

He looked nothing like a Renaissance king and everything like a regular guy, except a thousand times hotter and with infinitely better hair. I told him he could wear his own boots, which only made the look cooler. He brushed the denim pockets with his fingertips, dazed and apprehensive. I smiled and moved to touch him, but he jerked away like I had leprosy, his face darkening.

He didn't look at me as we left the house and strolled up the driveway to Mia's waiting sports car, not even when I feebly tried to explain what a car was in less than fifty words. I couldn't tell if it was the clothes that had upset him, the fact that I hadn't wanted him to stay, or my world altogether, but it left a bad feeling in my stomach.

I wedged beside him into the car's tiny backseat, worried he might try to open the door or something. But he just stared out the window, his breath short, his mouth open. Mia gawked at him through the rearview mirror.

"This is what I meant when I said a 'car'," I whispered to Nick, relieved that Mia liked her music louder than a heavy metal club. "It's like a coach, but without the horses. I'll explain more later, but if you act like you've never seen one, you could get locked up."

"So you're the director?" said Mia with her trademark bluntness. She turned down the music. "Em, you never said he was a Brit."

Before Nick could even look confused, I jumped in, speaking slowly so he could catch on. "Nick directs theater sometimes, but he also...he works in politics."

"Really?" Mia's mouth gaped excitedly like I'd hooked a marlin fish.

"British politics," I added quickly. "And he's not allowed to talk about it because there's sensitive information involved, right?" I pinched Nick's thigh. He nodded.

"Sounds like he's not allowed to talk at all when you're around," said Mia with a wry smile.

The rest of the way there, she grilled Nick about growing up in England. I hijacked most of the answers, but was impressed at how smoothly Nick spoke and how he didn't flinch at Mia's American accent. It's like he was in diplomatic king mode, charming and educated beyond his age.

After we passed through the festival's compulsory bag check, he faced the main stage and recoiled. "What is happening there?" he asked.

Mia winced. "Death metal. My boyfriend says it's for people who are more pissed off than actually interested in music. Want to grab drinks, and we'll get a spot on the lawn? I'll have a green juice...any kind. It's all on me." She handed him a twenty-dollar bill.

Nick glanced at me with that deer-in-headlights look again as Mia started texting.

I pointed at the organic fruit juice bar. "Over there," I whispered to him. "See the guy in the orange hat? Ask him for three green juices, and if he says 'what kind', say 'whatever's popular'." Nick strolled off, scratching his tanned neck. I tried not to grimace.

Mia's fingernails dug into my arm, her eyes bright. "You never said you were back with silver fox or that he's pants-dropping *hot!* And he had no clothes, huh?"

"He got wet by accident. It's a long story and not what you think."

Her brows danced up like she wasn't sure whether to believe me. "Bummer."

She flapped open her tartan picnic blanket while I peeked into her mom's food containers, so hungry I was about ready to eat the plastic. There was a spiced duck and greens salad, hoisin chicken wings, and vegetarian rice paper rolls with peanut dipping sauce.

"So are you guys like properly together now or what?" she pressed. "This is happening so fast, I love it. Tell me you're going to have his babies." I shot her a look. "I mean, Josh is my honey," she said, "but Nick is like the eye-candy *boss*. Although he's a bit posh, isn't he."

"He's just English."

"Right! You guys sound so cute together. Think of your kids' accents."

I shook my head at her logic, biting into a chicken wing. "Quite the spread, mama-Mia," I said. "Fit for a king." When I couldn't stop giggling, she looked at me like I needed a checkup.

"What's the joke?" said an annoying voice.

I held my hand to my eyes to shield them from the light. Avery Pearce burst through the sun's rays like she was the Virgin Mary, except in white hot pants. Nick towered over her, clutching three plastic cups spilling with green sludge.

"I met your friend at the juice bar," said Avery, touching the crook of his forearm. The way she looked at him took me right back to Princess Henriette's candy-eyes while she whispered in Nick's ear at the birthday feast. I swallowed the instant lump of jealousy in my throat.

"Is Logan out racing boats on public waterways again?" Mia asked Avery in a judgy tone.

"Oh please, he stopped that crap ages ago." Her fake-tan cheeks tightened. "But, if you must know, we broke up last night."

"Shit, you're kidding. Sorry," said Mia sincerely.

"Being single has its benefits." Avery chewed her straw and blinked up at Nick, my cue to jump up. I didn't tell Nick the truth about me and risk a beheading just for Avery Pearce to get her claws into him.

"I was just going to show Nick the rides," I blurted.

"Yes, I'm eager to understand more about that," he said awkwardly.

Avery gripped her hip, looking confused. "They don't have rides in England?"

"We won't be long," I said. I made an apologetic face to Mia and tugged Nick toward the carnival zone.

"It must be all the rain," Avery said to Mia as we walked away.

"Your friends are agreeable," Nick said to me, wincing at his drink. Mine tasted like mowed grass.

"Mia's nice. Avery sucks. Which means 'not nice', by the way."

"She was kind to me. She helped me choose between spinach and something called kale."

"Look, if you'd sooner hang out with Avery, then we can go back."

"Emmie." He reached for my wrist and pulled me to a halt, heat pulsing into my skin at the point of contact.

I looked up into his eyes before a group of college guys with bare chests shoved past us in a drunken mob, whacking the cup out of Nick's hand. They continued down the hill without even apologizing.

"Morons!" I called out.

Nick wiped green goo from his elbow. "So all this is what it is like to be a peasant?"

I half-smirked, half-glowered at him. "Did you just call me a peasant?"

A dimple surfaced in his cheek. "I am more wondering whether those cod's heads have not the means for shirts."

I laughed. "And have no one worship them? Speaking of worshipping, it must be weird having no one recognize you."

He watched the partygoers stumble past us like we were invisible. "I cannot say it is an entirely unpleasant experience."

He must've been adjusting to the constant strangeness, because the carnival section didn't freak him out as much as I thought it would. I even talked him into going on the Ferris wheel, though the blood evacuated his face as the carriage swung to the sky. A giant carpet of stages, tents, rides, a miniature golf course, and a campground stretched beneath our legs.

When we stabilized, Nick shot me a sideways smirk through the breeze. "You have a wonderful life," he said.

His memory of the exact words I'd said to him at Robin House stirred a sleeping butterfly in my stomach.

"You believe my life is all recreation?" I replied with flushed cheeks, repeating the answer he'd given me. "We also go to school, you know. Or work. Both, in my case."

His eyes widened. "You work?"

"Just part-time. I'm still in school for another few weeks, I think. I'm losing track." I pinched the bridge of my nose.

"Why not marry?" he asked, glancing away. "Surely you have your choice of suitors."

"Putting aside that I'm eighteen, women fought for equality with men. We want to work. You should see how smart Mia is when she's not sex-crazed." His brow creased with confusion. "Making love," I explained quickly, my cheeks a furnace.

A shy chuckle fled his mouth, his fingers playing with the entry band on his wrist. "Making love is perfectly acceptable, and even strongly recommended, provided it does not encumber your duty."

Strongly recommended...gah.

The sides of our arms were rubbing together, but he hadn't moved his. "And what duty is that?" I asked. "Let me guess. To be a mother?"

"To serve and obey man. Whether it is through the provision of children or other household duties."

I nearly cracked up.

"I'm amusing you," he said, resting on his elbow and smiling at me.

"You just have some catching up to do."

He nodded at the blanket of trees bordering the campground. "So what else is out there? More *machines* like these?"

I sucked in a deep inhale. "Houses, mainly…and more towns. Some farms with horses. Life really isn't *that* different." I didn't mention Boston, with its millions of people and glass skyscrapers.

"Merely less refined." His jaw tensed again.

I raised a brow at him. "You mean compared with your time? When people get beheaded for having a different point of view?"

He frowned. "Of whom do you speak?"

"Forget it, it's not a competition," I said, gnawing on my lip. "I should probably tell you that my plan for *out there* is to become a world-famous jewelry designer. So there's a bit more future for you to chew on."

I expected him to smile, but his face pulled tight as he looked away. "Jewelry is what captivates you…I remember."

"Don't forget macarons," I added lightly, laying my hand over his.

The speed with which he pulled away was a punch to the heart as our rickety carriage swerved to the ground. Nick didn't say anything as we climbed off, nor did he look in my direction. Half a day in my time and he'd clearly lost all interest in me. Was it because I'd told him I wanted to design jewelry instead of being an obedient wife and servant?

I bought us meatball subs for the walk back, wanting to ask what had upset him, but Nick chewed his in silence a step behind me, his beautiful face a brewing storm.

14

MIA WAVED US OVER FROM BEHIND THE MOSH PIT WHERE ATOMIC WAS blasting last year's biggest rock hit, *Undone.*

"They just started!" she cried, her hair now piled on her head in a loose bun. Thank goodness she wasn't pissed off with us for taking so long at the rides. Music was Mia's favorite fetish when she wasn't fixating on Josh Street or studying.

Nick's face furrowed at the stage.

"Different to the harp, huh?" I said.

"I'm not certain if I love or despise it."

"Welcome to modern music."

A part of me wished Atomic would play something less heavy and loud. *Undone* sounded ironically primitive next to Nick's textured Tudor hymns. But when the band broke into their new ballad, *Say You'll Stay*, he stiffened behind me, listening intently. The melodic track was breathtakingly beautiful, the lyrics perfectly expressing the feeling of wanting someone so much that you could actually burst. We both stood like statues through the first chorus, before two hands gently glided around my waist from behind, sending bolts of electricity charging through me. I sighed and leaned into the euphoria, but when

I twisted my face to look at Nick, it was Logan Hunter's rust-colored eyes that were inches from mine. I jerked backward.

"Isn't this our song?" he asked clumsily, his breath tinged with beer.

I pried his persistent fingers off me. "This song just came out. And I'm not Avery."

Nick moved right beside us, his body rigid. "Nick, this is Logan," I said.

"How do you do, fellow," said one of the most feared kings in history.

Logan stepped back with exaggerated surprise. "Is this your cousin from England or something?"

"He's a friend," I said. I was sure that every inch of my skin was bright red.

Logan clasped my waist again with both hands. "C'mon, don't waste our song, boo. I've been looking for you all day." When I tried to wriggle away, he tightened his grip.

"I am quite certain the lady declined," said Nick, pulling Logan's hands off me.

Logan pushed him backward. "And who are you, God's greatest achievement?"

Mia's brows flew up. A group of guys in sweaty muscle shirts made space for the confrontation.

Nick shoved Logan back even harder, his eyes two firestorms. Logan brought his nose so close to Nick's that he could've kissed him. "Dude, I've never seen you before in my life, but if you think you've got dibs on her 'cause you're some pretty-boy limey or whatever, just know she's already had her tongue so far in my mouth you'd think hers was cold."

Nick's fist was a bullet that smashed into Logan's cheek, sending him flying backward.

Logan swore, clutching his jaw, and then threw his arms around Nick's legs, hauling him into the dirt.

"Stop it, please!" I cried, my stomach collapsing. Their T-shirts became a whir of black and gray, fists flying and landing with hideous smacks.

Within seconds, three security guards had violently separated them. They were shoved into separate first-aid tents, and I caught a glimpse of blood trickling down Logan's cheek. Mia and I waited outside near the portable toilets, trying not to inhale the stench, which was worse than a chamber pot.

"Quite the bodyguard you've got there," said Mia, brushing dirt off her tank.

"Do you think they'll kick us out?" I said.

"Probably."

My hands slid into my hair. "I'm so sorry." I felt like all I'd done lately was apologize to people.

She thumbed through her phone. "It's fine. Josh's mom didn't even show up…idiot."

"Mia."

"What? Even after rehab, she's still screwing up his life."

"Josh's mom adores him. There must be a reason she's not there yet."

"God, Emmie, you're so naive."

I felt anger surge in me. *I brought Nicholas the freaking Ironheart today as my date. I've survived a crossbow attack, the Tower of London, and some mind-altering medieval virus. So don't talk to me about naive.*

When had Mia become such a brat?

"Sorry," she said, knocking my foot with hers. "You know Josh's mom makes me insane."

I sighed, unable to take any more drama. "Forget it. Hey, just remember it's a good thing for Josh."

"As long as she can stay sober and support herself, then yes. And as long as she doesn't expect him to babysit her when he's done school."

I shrugged. "I guess he'll do what he wants."

"You mean if he decides to stay here rather than come to Cambridge, you'll support him over me?"

"Mia, were you drinking when we were at the rides? I'm just saying Josh has got stuff going on like you have, and you guys might have to work out what's best for everyone. He said he doesn't have a plan yet." What was her problem lately? Didn't she know how easy she had it? *At least he's not from another century!*

Nick resurfaced through the canary-yellow tent flaps, a gauze square taped to his jaw. He rubbed the back of his neck, looking more than sheepish. "I should have those guards working for me."

A bouncer seized his arm. "Time to go, pal."

None of us spoke on the drive back, Mia's blasting stereo filling the uncomfortable silence. I tried not to let it get to me that Nick wouldn't even look in my direction. Was he seriously blaming me for the fight he started? Or was this part of what had been eating him before that?

When we swung by Josh's uncle's place, Josh came out to the car to say hi, his bubbly energy infectious. Even Nick stepped onto the pavement to tentatively accept Josh's handshake, giving me the vibe that those weren't a thing yet in Tudor England. Josh cracked a joke about us not being able to last a day without him.

"So sorry you missed it," said Mia, climbing out of the car and shaking out her hair.

Josh caught her with a one-armed hug. "It's cool, babe; I finished the final edits on my EP. You guys wanna hear?" He spiraled his wrist like a butler. "Club Josh is open for drinks."

"We have to get back," I said. It was time the King of England returned to the sixteenth century.

But Nick strode up the decaying wooden steps without even consulting me. "Some cold ale would be superb, thank you."

Josh handed out drinks and snacks in the tiny lounge room that stank like his chain-smoking uncle, a blue sheet pinned across the window. But Nick didn't seem bothered. He was explaining the fight to Josh, who pretended to hide behind Mia for protection from Nick while we all laughed.

Josh aimed a remote at the vintage stereo with brand-new speakers, a Frank Zappa track kicking in. Nick lifted a little, nodding along.

"You dig this stuff?" said Josh, fishing through his shelf of vinyls.

They pored over albums while Mia and I flicked through a guitar magazine together. The sight of Nick looking so relaxed as he glanced over the cover of Tool's *Ænima* leaked sadness into my bones. Why did he have to be who he was? Why couldn't he just be a normal guy from my time? He picked up a Jeff Beck album and inspected the guitar on the cover.

"A Les Paul man," said Josh, jumping up. He grabbed the shiny black guitar in the corner that had cost him two summers at the tire shop. When Nick touched the fretboard like it was an alien warship, Josh laughed. "Dude, is music like your fourth language?"

It was a clear diss from Josh, and I felt weirdly responsible. Nick was borderline musical genius, just from a totally different era.

"Hey Josh, do you know how to play Greensleeves?" I blurted defensively.

"Isn't that a fiddler tune?" said Mia.

"Just play it," I urged. "If you know it."

"'Course I know it," said Josh, swapping the Les Paul for his Fender acoustic. "I learned it when I was, like, nine."

He strummed a few chords, wrinkling his brow to remember the right progression. His black fingernails then kicked into a version of Greensleeves that was rockier than Nick's, but note-for-note the same track. When he finished, Nick was hunched forward, his face drained of color.

I could've kicked myself for being so reckless, putting Nick's pride over the whole time-traveling king thing. What if he introduced rock music to the freaking sixteenth century? What would happen to The Beatles?

Josh offered the guitar to him. "You play, man?"

"That song," Nick stumbled. "Where did you say you learned it?"

"We should go," I said, grabbing my purse. "Mom will kick my butt if I'm not back for Sunday dinner."

"Since when?" Mia raised a brow.

"Since now."

Nick and I walked home in silence, his brow set with a frown. After two blocks, he finally spoke. "My composition, Emmie. How did your friend know it?"

I couldn't look at him. "I shouldn't have done that, it was stupid. I guess I just wanted you to know how amazing it is. That the song you wrote is one of the most famous songs in history. I wasn't thinking."

Nick shook his head, visibly bewildered. He waited before he spoke. "Did you know it was about you?"

My chest squeezed so tightly that I thought it could crush me.

"Of course not. I don't think anyone knows who Greensleeves is about. I still can't get my head around that."

When we neared the church, he spoke again, his boot scuffing the ground. "Emmie, am I a…a noted king?"

"What do you mean?"

"There have been a great number of kings before me, but I have only read of the ones who won wars, conquered lands, reformed the word of God. Am I another worthless prince, or do you know of me in your time? Of my accomplishments?" He looked like he might puke all over my sandals.

I didn't know what to say. That he was famous for becoming a savage tyrant because his baby sister had her neck snapped in two?

"Please don't ask me about your future, okay?" I said shakily. "It's one thing to go back in time, but to go forward and see things that haven't happened yet…it's not right."

He took my wrists, but not affectionately. "I need to know, Emmie," he choked out. "What happens to me? To Kit? Do I marry? How many sons do I have? Does England war with Spain? Do we win?"

I twisted out of his grip. "Please stop asking me these questions! Is this why you've been acting like you're mad at me?"

"I am on the brink of war! And days from becoming betrothed to a lady I am barely acquainted with." Nick didn't even look at the car that zoomed past us. "And you have it in your power to say what is coming, so I may prepare."

"Life doesn't work that way! We don't get to know what's coming. That's just the deal. I'm sorry, but I…I'm not going to tell you anything."

The look he threw me made my stomach twist as we headed up my stone path.

I made him wait in the back garden while I grabbed his clothes, but Mom's door was still closed. I quickly changed into the sparkling gown I'd borrowed from Alice, which was infinitely easier to walk in without the hoop skirt.

"You'll have to get changed in the field," I said to Nick, tossing him his sixteenth-century suit. "Mom will be up soon, and I still have to take you back, then get back here again and change my clothes. Ugh, it's going to be tight."

"You mean to simply forget all this." He didn't look at me.

"Everything but the busted face," I replied, trying to brighten the mood. "You have to admit, it's a pretty cool souvenir. But you better not take the gauze…it smacks of the New World." I gently peeled the dressing off his jaw. The cut underneath looked small and clean. It took physical effort not to lean into his gorgeous scent that was seemingly immune to time travel.

"I should not have struck that man," Nick said, guilt coloring his cheeks.

"You went a tad medieval on me," I replied lightly. "But it's cool. He was being an idiot."

"Yet you kissed him?"

My breath caught on the unexpected question. I lifted my face to find Nick looking at me like he was hanging to hear my answer.

"He kissed *me*," I admitted. "Once, years ago, and not like how he described. Actually, it sucked. So there's an exclusive for you to take home…kissing sucks in the New World."

Something touched his clear eyes, making them hard to look at.

"C'mon," I said, stepping under his arm to open the back gate leading to the field. "We need to go to sleep super-fast."

I turned to face the decaying fence, giving him privacy while he changed his clothes. Goosebumps danced up my neck as I imagined him bare chested, having noticed the stacks of muscles beneath his thin Tudor shirts on more than one occasion. But when I spun back around, he was already back in his kingly doublet trimmed with gold. The contrast from trendy jeans to handsome white suit confused my heart. He fit so perfectly in either era.

Ruby whined from the gate as we traipsed across the grass, stopping near a patch of trees that led to the river. Nick twisted to face me, the tips of his hair dyed pink from the dwindling sunlight. My whole body warmed at the sight of him.

"You need not come back with me, Emmie," he said gravely.

I was so surprised at the seriousness of his tone that it took me a moment to reply.

"Yeah, but I brought you here, so I should get you home."

His lips stayed closed, but his bleak expression spoke volumes.

"You mean you don't want me to come back with you," I said.

His voice thickened as he looked away. "I fail to see the point."

Hurt hammered a thousand nails into my chest. After everything, he wanted to just disappear right now and never see me again. *Sayonara, freaky future girl. Thanks for the tour.*

My voice wobbled on the words. "But if you go without me, how would I get the ring back off you?"

His eyes locked me back in his gaze. "Well, the ring is mine. So you would not."

"What makes you so sure it's yours? It could be a copy."

He chuckled, but there was no pleasure in his face. "This is the way things operate in the New World? Any common woman may keep the king's property as she sees fit?"

My lips parted. "I'm not a *common* woman, and you're not the king here. In fact, we don't even have a king. We have a president, chosen by the people. Which can be a man or a woman, by the way." Nick looked mortified. I heard Ruby barking from the house. "Crap, I wanted us gone before Mom got up."

He held his palm out. "Give me the ring, Emmie."

"No!"

"Is this because of its value?" Concern shadowed his face. "This ring can rescue you from poverty? Because...I—I could leave you my cloth."

When he started pulling off his luxurious doublet, I tossed the ring at him. It bounced off his chest and hit the grass. "Just do whatever you want, like you always do," I said sharply as he crouched to pick up the ring, looking stunned. "Even here, you think you get to decide everything," I added. "Well, you may have been a living god four hundred years ago, but guess what? The world's moved on. You're nothing here. You are literally ancient history."

He rose back up to his imposing height, his mouth curving downward. "Mistress Grace, I am merely trying to—"

"Oh, so we're back to 'Mistress Grace' again?" I shook away tears, which was pointless because they kept spilling. "I'm not trying to be a jerk, Nick. But you can't come here and dismiss my world, tell me it's unrefined—which is a massive joke—and then take off back to head-chopping land without so much as a *thank you* and expect me to be happy about it."

His mouth fell open. "You want me to thank you. For deceiving me, stealing my property, fooling every nobleman and gentlewoman in my court, and then bringing me here to demonstrate your superior land in comparison to which my kingdom pales. Am I wrong?"

"Are you even serious right now?" His handsome face blurred through my accelerating tears. When he reached for me, I jerked backward.

"No, it's okay, I get it. I'm just a poor, unsophisticated, common girl from the future, who did nothing but cause you trouble. And, clearly, I don't mean anything to you."

His eyes widened with dismay. "You believe that sincerely?"

"I believe it sincerely."

He exhaled heavily, a hand on his hip. For several moments, we just stood in silence, drawing breaths but not speaking.

I saw myself standing there, the spitting image of my mother, trying to convince a guy to want me who clearly didn't. I'd never felt so pathetic. It made me want to scream and throw up at the same time.

"Aren't you going to go then?" I eventually muttered, hearing the anguish in my voice. "If that's what you want."

Nick barked a humorless laugh. "You speak as if I am permitted to have wants and act on them." He shook his head, his face pained.

"Oh, don't be ridiculous; you're the King of England, for crying out loud."

He stepped closer to me, his hands shaking as much as his voice.

"You truly believe my every desire is granted? That I know not the agony of yearning for what I cannot have?"

His skin flushed pink, his hands clenched at his sides. Our faces were inches apart.

"Like what, Nick? You've got jewels beyond belief, a palace out of a fairytale, the most perfect princess I've ever seen, enough gourmet food to feed an entire country, people waiting on you hand and foot… what on earth could you possibly want that you can't have!"

He grabbed my collar and tugged my mouth up to his, our lips connecting like burning magnets. White-hot need surged through me as he parted my lips with his and sank his tongue into my mouth, capturing me with the most delicious, captivating sensation I'd ever experienced. His hands gripped my face, holding me in place, as my fingers clawed at his collar, my mouth desperate for more of him. When my knees buckled, we fell to the ground with our mouths locked together and our tongues swirling, the incredible taste of him making my head spin as we kissed with a depth of hunger that made me cry out. Each glide of his tongue drew more moans from my lips, his fingers gripping my jaw and angling my mouth up so he could kiss me deeper.

When we finally broke for air, he wrapped both his arms around my waist, dragging me into his chest. "I want *you*, you beautiful, stubborn fool," he breathed into my neck as I hugged him tightly. Every cell in my body was an exploding firework that showered glitter from the sky. I'd never felt so consumed, so besotted.

He buried his mouth in my neck, the heat of his breath leaving sparks of electricity on my skin. "You know not what you have done to me…my miracle girl." He lifted his forehead and pressed it to mine. "You are the most divine, the most dear—"

"Emmie?" cried a voice from far away.

I sprang up. Mom swung open our gate, her head leaning toward Bayberry Street.

"What's she doing?" I hissed. Something gleamed from her hand.

Nick grabbed his waist. "My belt."

"We have to run…now. We'll find another spot."

"The diamonds in it belonged to my mother, God rest her soul."

He pressed his palm to his forehead, his hair a mess of curls from our frenzied kiss.

I couldn't resist pressing my lips to his again, tasting the sweetest kind of honey. He cupped my cheeks with both hands and pulled me closer, but the thought of my mom catching us and having to explain all this to her had me in a panic. I broke apart from him, the reluctance in his face matching mine. "I'll get the belt," I said. "You wait here…stay behind the trees." He nodded at me through glassy, just-kissed eyes, and I just about melted into the grass.

By the time I got to the house, Mom was halfway back inside. Her palm flew to her chest when she saw me. Tristan's jeans and T-shirt were draped over a dining chair.

"Emmie, what were you doing out there? Ruby's barking woke me up."

"Sorry, I was just getting some air." My lips were still tingling.

"It's fine, I was oversleeping." She blinked rapidly at my shimmering sea-colored dress. "What on God's green earth are you wearing? It's…stunning."

I seized the belt from her. "My drama costume. I need to redesign it, and I can't work out how, hence the walk. But I think I've got it, so I'm…I'm going to go to Mia's for a bit to show her. I'll be back before dinner."

"Do you know what these clothes are? They were near our gate." Mom lifted a corner of the black T-shirt.

"They're Tristan's. Here, I'll take them back to him." I reached past Mom to grab the clothes, trying to ignore the spider's web of confused lines on her forehead.

"Tristan Fairbanks? Isn't he fifteen?"

"I'm not dating him," I said with an exasperated whine. "He lent them to us for the show."

"The school show, or the one in Southbridge?"

"Mom, please!"

I gave her a quick kiss and waited for her to stop gawking at me like I was the creature from the black lagoon. I waved at her through the kitchen window and latched the gate behind me. The field was a black hole now that the sun had set.

"Nick?" I whispered, running back to the trees, the belt swinging from my hand. But the spot we'd just been in was empty. I thought I had the wrong place, so I jogged in and out of clearings all the way along the river. I called his name with rising volume until the Rottweilers in the corner house on Bayberry Street began barking like hell beasts.

It took nearly two hours of tramping through the leafy mud banks in a sixteenth century ball gown for the truth to shatter me into a million pieces.

Nick was gone.

15

THERE WAS NO TRACE OF HIM ANYWHERE. NO TALL SHADOWS wandering the streets, no strange-talking men on the news with striking eyes, no twenty-year-old John Does in the hospitals. I'd called them all before school on Monday, pretending to be nurse Carol Grace. I knew it was wrong, but I didn't care. Showers of knives were falling from the sky, slashing me with loss that felt twofold.

The blue-diamond ring was gone…something too incredible, too priceless to even fathom.

But the most inconceivable loss of all was Nick. The guy I'd risked everything for—even my life—had left me without a second thought when he'd found out who I really was. Plain, poverty-stricken, unrefined Emmie Grace. But not before stealing the best kiss of my life. It lived on my mouth like a wound that wouldn't heal.

Mom was trained to spot heartache like a fractured limb. At first, she kept out of my way in the few hours we were both awake—her usual strategy when I was in a mood. Then she began huffing every time I slammed a drawer closed or turned my nose up at dinner, without actually asking me what was wrong. But in the early hours of Thursday morning, my door quietly opened, and I heard Mom's feet shuffling across my floor, trying not to wake me. I kept my eyes shut as she placed a hand on my forehead, stroking her thumb across my hair. When she left the room, I turned into the pillow, the storm of tears unleashing its violent deluge.

Josh's rock music tracks kept me distracted on the walk to school all week, but on Friday morning, I kept my phone in my bag and tuned my ears to the birds and gusty breeze. A longing crushed my chest when I imagined I was back in the sixteenth century, where the streets smelled like death, people ate with their fingers, and heads on pikes garnished the London Bridge. Yet the people's downtime was spent reading poetry, learning languages, and listening to astonishing melodies. In a way, Nick was right. They were the most refined people I'd ever met.

After work, I furiously typed notes about that time period into my research document until Mia showed up. I'd insisted she come to me this time, past the point of giving a toss what she thought of my house. The King of England had stayed with me, for crying out loud.

"Hungry?" I said, hoping we had something in the cupboard other than tea.

Mia reached into her bag and tossed me sweet-potato chips and chocolate-covered almonds. She nodded at my laptop. "Got some background tunes on there?"

When I opened my music folder, *Music from the Tudor Court* kicked in as my last-played album.

Mia grimaced. "What's this oddness?"

I tried to switch off the lively, Shakespearean-style track, but my touchpad was sticky. "I thought it might get us in the mood."

"Good joke, hon." She took over the touchpad, choosing an elec-trorock album Josh had downloaded, which sounded like a robot having a seizure. "Okay, let's motor up." She flipped open her sleek new laptop.

"I've done tons of research," I said, amazed I hadn't crumpled like a soda can yet from grief. But Mrs. Campbell was hardly going to take my failed romance with Nicholas the Ironheart as an excuse for no paper about him.

I spun my computer to show Mia my document and read it again over her shoulder. The argument was impressive, even for me, and made a real case for why King Nicholas the First was pushed into paranoia and vengeance as a young orphaned monarch whose only living family was murdered by a trusted subject.

Mia's brows knitted. "I thought we were arguing he was a vicious barbarian who started a holy war because his religion was under threat."

"Huh? He only killed those Catholics because he figured it had something to do with his sister's murder. He didn't even care that much about religious divisions. For a sixteenth-century king, anyway."

"Have you been reading a book I haven't? Because I've been through everything and I didn't come up with that at all."

I slid into the chair opposite her. "How can you just assume he's a vicious barbarian? He wasn't much older than us when it started. He may have done those things, *if* the books are accurate, but that's because his grief drove him crazy."

Mia. You wanted me to have his babies.

"He's a nutcase who killed innocent people!" She pressed her forehead. "Why are you being so stubborn about this?"

"Because I don't think you're seeing the forest for the trees. He saw the good in people, he forgave the ones he shouldn't, he trusted those he barely knew. Imagine how he would've felt when he discovered one of his trusted subjects killed his sister, whom he loved more than anything. Plus, the death penalty was the norm back then; it was the punishment for a lot of crimes. People actually loved it; executions were like a big party."

Mia gaped at me like I had twelve heads. "Where did you get all this? Because we have to cite everything with actual evidence. You can't make up your own story."

"I'm not!"

She angled a high cheekbone at me, our snacks sitting untouched on the table. "Come on, when have you ever taken a school subject seriously?"

"All the time?"

"Em, you're always off with the pixies or making some jewelry thing. You don't study hard, and you know it."

"You mean like that friendship bracelet I made for your birthday? Is that *some jewelry thing?*"

"Oh come on, I love that." She slid her bare wrist toward me, but I moved mine away. Her face hardened. "I'm just saying that I've always had higher marks in history. If we disagree, don't you think I'm more qualified to decide?"

"Not at all." I sounded equally as bullheaded, but if there was one expert on Nicholas Tudor in the room, it wasn't Mia Fairbanks.

"I don't get why you're making such a big deal of this," she moaned. "But we should probably just double-submit because I'm not risking anything less than an *A*. Mom hasn't paid my tuition yet for next year."

"Fine." I pursed my lips. Double-submitting was when two people who couldn't work together submitted individual assignments instead. No one ever actually chose it. "I guess we don't need to study anymore then," I added, my cheeks hot. I clicked the music back to the Tudor harps while Mia returned her laptop to her leather bag.

She stopped at the door, her gaze steady. "I'm only saying this because I care. If you screw up this essay, you could fail history. If you fail another subject, can you still even apply to college?"

"I don't know, I don't have every minute of my future mapped out like you. As well as every second of my boyfriend's future, whether he likes it or not," I added before I could stop myself.

A line creased her forehead.

"Sorry," I said quickly. "I'm just…I'm tired."

"You're eighteen, Em. If you're this tired now, how will you feel when you're eighty?" She sighed, flicking a black sheet of hair over her shoulder. "Forget it…I'm going to go. I'll message you later or something. Got a whole essay to write by myself now."

"Same here," I said.

When the door closed, my chin hit my palms. Gut-wrenching memories of Nick's hips pressing against mine as we twisted in the grass attacked my mind.

Freaking arrogant king who kisses me like he's the world authority on the subject, grinds himself against me like the world's biggest tease, and then takes off to Neverland.

I slammed my laptop shut and threw some frozen ravioli on the stove.

After wolfing down the pasta in front of the fashion channel, I trudged upstairs and unlocked the box in my nightstand. I snipped off a large piece of turquoise from an old bracelet and held it under my desk lamp. Three attempts to shape the wire cage was killing my fingers, so I dug out some old cocktail sticks and taped them into an abstract pyramid over the turquoise. When the shape was just right, I disassembled the sticks and cut a section of wire to match each one, before attaching them with jump rings. I didn't have a butane torch for soldering, so I closed the wire with pliers and wrapped the frame around a plain silver band, hoping it would hold. In case the cage busted over the Atlantic, I sketched the concept for my online portfolio, drawing a solid gold cage over a cabochon emerald ring. I felt a small smile hijack my face. *Beautiful old things in modern cages.*

All that was left was the personal statement. When I opened the file for my Central Saint Martins application, the few words I'd attempted for my Nicholas the Ironheart essay popped up on the screen, slicing into my chest. I began typing into that document instead, gushing words about the king whose parents died when he was a child, leaving him with power-hungry advisors with their own agendas. The words then turned to his sole sibling, Princess Catherine, who was violently murdered by someone he trusted, the king never able to discover who was responsible. Grief spiraled him into suspicion and vengeance during a time when a king's chief weapon was the death penalty, which was also the punishment for crimes like blasphemy, practicing magic, and spying. As the conclusion flowed, so did my tears, until relief settled in my bones. While I couldn't do anything to help Kit, maybe I could convince one person—even if it was my history teacher—that King Nicholas the First wasn't a savage monster without a conscience. He was the opposite...sensitive and alone, and broken by loss and betrayal.

When I was done, I ran a bath and buried myself in the water until it turned cold. And, for the first night in days, I might've actually slept more than four hours.

Mia left for a family weekend in Boston without us speaking again, which only made me feel more knocked around. I worked in the rest-home kitchen on Saturday and strolled home via the takeout pizza shop. The solitude was becoming embarrassing. *Why don't you have crowds of friends like those girls on social media? What's wrong with you?*

My heavy sigh was cut short by the sight of Josh's 1974 van parked outside my house.

"Got a flat?" I said through the window, nearly choking on the dank smell. He kicked his feet off the steering wheel and rubbed his eyes.

"Fell asleep. I spent most of last night chatting with Mom."

"She's back?"

"Since Friday. She looks good."

"That's awesome; I had no idea. Explains why I didn't see you at school. You okay?"

"Yeah." Josh didn't like to dump his problems on anyone, so I was used to him not talking about his mom's issues.

"So are you stalking my house because you're a big lonely-heart this weekend and need pizza?" I asked him.

"Is it Hawaiian?"

I scrunched my nose. "Pineapple does not belong on pizza. Do you put grapes in your tacos?"

"Every day. Actually, I hoped you'd come with me to Avery's party."

I tipped my shoulders, weighing the scales. "Pizza…Avery…how will I ever choose?"

He flung open the passenger door, nearly knocking me over. "Don't be lame. She's bragged all week about her cousin staying with her who works for Lynx Records. I hope he hasn't died from boredom already."

A wave of guilt swept through me. Ever since he'd hooked up with Mia, I'd thought of Josh less as a friend and more as my best friend's boyfriend. I hadn't joined the dots on how Avery's cousin could help his music.

"Give me a few minutes," I said, ducking inside to change.

Avery's home was a saccharine wash of coral curtains, lemon walls, and turquoise throw cushions. Most of the kids from our year were already tipsy, Riley Cole shooting his arms and legs out like a starfish as a dance track kicked in.

I was checking out framed photos of Avery with her older sisters in New York when Josh returned from the kitchen carrying two red cups.

"So, how've you been?" I asked him. "Feels like we haven't chatted in ages."

"Yeah, you know. Studying, so I don't end up entombed in Uncle Pete's tire shop. Convincing shitty radio stations that my music doesn't suck. The usual."

I pouted. "Have you decided yet about going to Cambridge with Mia?"

He shook his head. "Hotshot producer guy might fly me to L.A. first class and put me up at the Playboy Mansion." He grinned, but it didn't reach his gray eyes.

"Well, as I say, life is what happens when you're busy making other plans."

"As *you* say? Rule number seven: Never rip off Lennon to a musician."

"Hey, he ripped it off me. As well as *Imagine;* I stayed up all night writing that damn song."

A scrawny girl from junior year ran past us in a polka-dot bikini, guys whistling after her.

Josh took a swig from his cup. "So why the long face, English?"

"You know I'd sooner stick pins in my eyes than hang with these people. Can we go yet?"

"I meant lately. I dunno if it's got something to do with that Nick dude leaving or whatever, but you've been acting weird, and we just want to make sure you're cool."

"*We?*" I pretended to look over my shoulder. "I'm fine." I returned his gaze with a frown. "You really are trying to get me to drink, aren't you? I'm fine, honestly."

He smirked at me, but concern lingered in his eyes. "You've always been a dud liar."

"Actually, I'm a pretty good liar, as it turns out."

"Oh yeah? Whatcha been fibbing about now? Apart from pretending to be American?"

I whacked his arm. When Josh's caring eyes met mine again, the words gathered in my throat, begging to be released. Nick was gone for good, and so was the ring. Did it even matter anymore?

"You know Jane Stuart who lives on Bayberry?" I stumbled.

"The hoarder? Yeah, I heard she checked out."

"She *died?*"

"No, crack-head, moved outta town."

"Seriously?" I brushed the back of my burning neck, my stomach curling over itself. "Did you know she had a yard sale a few weeks ago?"

Josh looked like he was trying to recall it when Avery sang my name in a halo of perfume, air-kissing my cheek.

"Did you bring that hot friend of yours?" she asked me.

"Obviously." I nudged Josh.

"*Nick,*" Avery corrected, fluttering her fake eyelashes at me. "The British guy. The ten."

"Oh, him. He's gone back to England." Hearing Avery say Nick's name was like being stabbed with a pitchfork.

"You're kidding me. Is he online?" She already had her phone out.

"Actually, he's kind of all over the internet."

Her eyes expanded. "Seriously? Is he famous? What's his last name? We were totally on the same wavelength."

"I'll tell you after you introduce Josh to your cousin, the music guy. His EP's freaking awesome, and he should totally hear it."

"Em!" Josh balked.

"Done," said Avery, her eyes already hunting for her cousin.

"Good luck, man." I fist-bumped Josh's shoulder before looking for the bathroom. I had to squeeze past Noah Percival and Kayla Simmons making out like sex-starved nymphos in the corridor. Some-

thing twisted deep in my gut at the thought of doing that with Nick…
to kiss him for hours and hours until our lips and tongues were raw
and swollen.

That will never, ever happen. My heart sank into the pit of my
stomach.

When I got back, Josh was chatting with a guy with platinum hair
who had his fingers pressed to his mouth, listening intently. I kept my
distance and found a whole new party going on by the pool. Amanda
Bash and Chloe O'Donnelly brushed past me in a waft of coconut oil,
their bare legs lengthened by wedge-heeled sandals.

Totally uninterested in small talk with people who'd teased me
more than been nice, I rolled up my jeans beside the pool and sank
my toes into the glassy water.

"Where's your buddy, the British boxing champion?" Logan
Hunter plunged his feet into the pool beside mine.

"He got kicked out already," I said, after I'd recovered from the
shock of his appearance.

Logan chuckled, wrinkling the fading yellow bruise on his cheek. I
resisted the urge to ask him if he'd just taken a cologne shower.

"I guess I owe you an apology." He swallowed the words like they
were hard to say. "It wasn't cool to hit your boyfriend."

"He's not my boyfriend." I squirmed on the pebbled ground. Nick
Tudor had spent less than a day in my time, and he was all anyone
wanted to talk about.

We sat in award-winning awkward silence, the pool's ripples
echoing the uncomfortable swell in my chest. I wanted to ask Logan
where his rekindled interest in me had come from, but something
about this guy always rendered me a little mute.

"So what are your plans after we break out of prison?" he asked
before draining his beer cup.

"You mean school? It's a mystery. Maybe travel. Build mega
yachts for billionaires…whatever. You going to college?"

"Nah. I dunno, maybe next year. Fishing for a bit." He sniffed.
"So you don't think you'll stay around here then."

I shook my head vigorously, sending him into silence.

"You know I've done some lousy things," Logan said eventually, his eyes fixed to the water. "I guess I just wanted to say that. Before you go on your yacht trip."

"I don't think I have a clue what you just said."

He scratched his carefully styled hair. "I know what I did was an asshole thing to do, and yeah, I still feel lousy about it."

"What you did?"

"Telling everyone you had gonorrhea."

Ambrose Alderson dived into the water in his boxer shorts, the splash making us both jump.

My jaw hung at Logan. "What the hell? You told everyone I had *gonorrhea?*"

He exhaled, muttering as he blushed pink. "I was, like, fifteen. I didn't even know what gonorrhea was. And I was pissed you shot me down. I'm really sorry. If it's any consolation, I did feel like a total dick, and I told everyone a few months later that I made it up."

I avoided his gaze, trying not to remember how horrible I'd felt back then. I'd gone from being the new kid with the cool accent, to the girl everyone whispered about overnight just because I didn't want Logan Hunter to feel me up behind the bleachers. If it weren't for Mia and Josh, I'd have become the school loner.

Logan twisted to face me, regret filling his bronze eyes. "Sorry, Em. You just have this weird ass effect on me. I can't explain it."

"Actually, it explains a lot."

He chewed his lip so aggressively he looked like a chimp. "You see, the thing is…you're so fucking pretty, and when you told me you didn't like me, I was just broken, you know? Like heartbroken. For real." His thigh started to shake beside mine. "I really am sorry. It was seriously uncool and I totally own that."

My heart was racing, but my voice sounded weak. "I never said I didn't like you. But I was only fifteen back then, and I didn't want to do that stuff at school. I guess I just freaked out. To be honest, it hurt like hell when you didn't want to talk to me anymore."

He sat and looked at me for a heart-stopping moment before leaning forward. I gasped with surprise as his lips landed on mine, cold beer bleeding onto my tongue as he clutched the back of my neck and worked his mouth against me. My hand slid up to hold his jaw, and for a few seconds, I tried to lose myself in the kiss, until flash-backs of Nick's sweet, sighing mouth made Logan's taste like dried-out modeling clay. I pulled away.

"Sorry, I've gotta go," I said, jumping up and sliding my dripping feet into my sandals. Logan didn't follow me when I headed back through the stained-glass doors leading to the packed living room. My head was spinning.

"Em, you cool?" Josh grabbed my shoulder, his eyes shining. "Declan's going to listen to my EP!"

"That's awesome," I said, straining to focus. "But I'm not feeling so great, so if you want to stay that's cool, but I need to find a ride home."

"Don't be a boob, I'll drive you. No more beer for Emmie Grace." He removed an imaginary cup from my hand.

"You owe me a name," said a silvery voice.

I spun into the smell of fresh buttercream. Avery Pearce teetered in five-inch wedges, her phone ready. "You said if I introduced Declan to Josh, you'd give me the hot English guy's full name. I'm considering Europe for the summer, and I could seriously bang that hottie like a screen door."

A possessive flash of jealousy tore through me. "He isn't really into stalkers, and he doesn't use social media. He's kind of old-school."

But Avery's dagger eyes made me worry she'd blow Josh's chances with her cousin.

"Fine, Nick's actually his middle name. His real name is John Doe," I said, pushing past her.

"His name is *John Doe?*"

"Not to your taste?"

"Just give me his real name," she demanded over the rising volume of music.

"I'm telling you, it's John Nicholas Doe. Take it up with his folks and their imagination deficiency." I tugged Josh's sleeve and backed out the door, wanting to laugh hysterically, despite my aching heart.

"There are eight-hundred-million search results for John Doe!" Avery cried, still scrolling.

Sunday meant dragging Josh on our pledged hike to Satan's Kingdom, which he moaned about the entire time. Sweat had fused my T-shirt to my back by the time Ruby and I arrived home to the syrupy smell of roast turkey.

"Did I forget Thanksgiving?" I said, shutting out the outside heat.

Mom stood up from the stove and wiped her stained oven glove across her brow. "I thought we could have a nice dinner together to make up for last time."

I gulped ice water from the fridge while she carved into the turkey. "Is this cooked?" she asked, tilting a slice at me.

"Looks perfect."

Her mouth twisted. "It's ready earlier than I wanted. Something went wrong with the timing."

"It's awesome. I'm starving. Although, you'll have to put up with my sweaty stink." Memories of meat-laden dinners at Whitehall in the early afternoons tortured my eyes as we sat down. I pushed the images away.

"Mom, what happened to Jane Stuart?" I asked. "The hoarder on Bayberry."

She licked grease off her thumb. "One of the nurses made a follow-up visit after the cleanup and found Mrs. Stuart unfit to care for herself. They took her to Boston for psychiatric evaluation."

"Seriously? What was she doing?"

"Oh, I don't know the details, but they usually do that when they find the person's become a danger to themself or others. She certainly has dementia. Has had for a while, I suspect."

"What about her family?"

"No one knows who they are. She doesn't even know her first name."

"Huh?" I nearly dropped my fork.

"Jane is a name the state gave her when she was found roaming the streets outside town. She only remembered her family name to be Stuart, and that the house was left to her in the previous owner's will. But all the Stuarts in the area were contacted, and none knew of her."

My face crinkled. *If she's not Jane Stuart, then who is she?*

Mom took a big sip of wine. "Emmie, I wanted to talk to you about the ring you made. The one with the box around it."

"The cage one?"

"I saw it this morning when I was looking for some blank paper. It's fantastic." She put down her glass and reached into her purse on the countertop, her fingers unsteady. "You've been sad lately, cookie, and I don't know if it's because of school ending, or this boy you met, or Mia going away, but it hurts me not to see you happy." She handed me a white envelope. Inside was a wad of hundred-dollar bills.

"Mom!"

"It's for college. Whichever one you choose. The design one, if you like."

"But I haven't even got in. Christ, I haven't even sent the application yet."

"Then use it to travel...or make your own jewelry collection. You'll figure it out." The circles framing her eyes were darker than ever.

"But how can you afford this? It's way too much."

"It's almost all of it, actually. What do I need it for? A trip to the Bahamas?" She chuckled at her plate.

"If that's what you want," I said seriously. "Mom, this is your money."

"It's our money, and right now, you need it more than me. So I won't hear anything except you taking it. Pay me back when you're a famous designer adorning the stars of Hollywood."

I reached over the table and pulled her into a hug, my heart lifting for the first time in weeks. Until it hit me again that leaving Hatfield meant leaving Mom. The thought of her beat-up car driving back and forth between our house and the rest home cut me open. I was always the one to check the oil in her car and put air in the tires. And what if she started trying to contact Dad or something? I clung to her tighter.

"Thank you so much," I said, her wiry hair tickling my shoulder.

She rubbed my back. "Your dad would be proud of you."

After a shower, I sat at my desk with my overdue personal statement for Central Saint Martins, staying on Mission: Distract Myself from All Thoughts of Nicholas Tudor. I didn't look up again until I'd finished the conclusion, convinced myself it was good enough, and clicked 'Submit'. I sealed the practical application packet with the cage ring inside and left it downstairs on Mom's outgoing mail pile.

Back upstairs in bed, I switched the lamp off and turned onto my side, my nose burrowing into the smell of clean sheets. There was still a knot inside me I couldn't untie, but it was getting smaller. I had enough money to go wherever I wanted—this time on my own terms. Plus, maybe Mom would be just fine. She had her work and Crystal. The Fairbanks had no shortage of friends, but they were gracious enough to invite her over for dinner now and then. Everything was going to be okay.

I was almost asleep when soft fingertips stroked a gentle line down the side of my face. A second hand met the other to cradle my cheeks in a nest of warmth.

"Emmie? Do not be afraid," said a deep, velvety voice. "Your garden door was unlatched."

My eyes burst open. Nick's clear-green pupils were inches from mine, glistening with emotion. He smelled incredible.

Tears sprang to my eyes faster than my heart could beat as he dropped his forehead against my own, his breath heavy as he sighed. "My miracle, Emmie. You cannot believe my relief."

"Is this a dream?" I was utterly breathless.

He pulled back, his brow creasing as a desolate look overcame his face.

"Please...I need your help at once." His voice broke open. "Kit has vanished."

16

"Say you know something about this." Tears glazed Nick's red-rimmed eyes. "Kit disappeared from her chambers last night. Emmie, you know things about me that have not yet occurred."

The blood left my face in one big rush.

If you tell him Kit dies, he could turn into Nicholas the Ironheart overnight. This is the event that spurred Nick's descent into darkness. Telling him everything is totally different from trying to figure out whether the countess is guilty and stop her, in her tracks.

I shook my head, guilt ravaging my insides. "I'm sorry, I–I don't know anything."

His devastated gaze fell to his lap. "I know not if she is dead or alive. For the love of God!" His fingertips swept away tears, which only made room for more. "I've tortured all her guards, some of her maids—no one can find her. Christ, Emmie, I am living a nightmare." He took my hand and pressed my palm to his wet cheek. "You must help me. I am begging you."

The option of telling him the truth still crouched behind my teeth and gnawed at my lips, nearly splitting them open. I hated my head and heart for never agreeing on anything. Mostly, though, I hated my heart for wanting something so badly that it could never have. Like the guy who'd kissed me like his life depended on it and then left me without a word. Now that he was sitting here, it felt like even more of a betrayal, and my eyes watered at the memory.

Nick's face fractured as he clutched my hand. It's like he could hear my thoughts. "Heart and soul, the moment I arrived back to Whitehall those weeks ago, I fought everything not to come back here and get you," he said.

"Then why didn't you?" I bit my bottom lip, trying not to cry.

"And bring you there? Someone so precious, so perfect, in a place like that? Where I cannot even..." His forehead dropped, the nearness of his lips making my mouth tingle.

"Cannot even what?" I pressed.

I let him stroke my hair as my head fought everything my heart wanted to say.

"Cannot even be who I long to be," Nick finished, a yearning look in his eyes as he lifted them back to mine.

When I cast my arms around his back, he exhaled into my neck, the heat of his breath smothering me with goosebumps. My hand glided up the back of his shirt and across the silk ridges in his collar, chestnut curls coiling into my fingers.

"What do you want me to do?" I whispered into him.

He sounded so drained. "Can you find some knowledge about Kit? Do you have libraries here? Books about my time, or have they all been burned?"

The naivety of his words struck me. If only he knew how easy it was to find information in my time. Biting away tears, I pulled back and shook my head. "There's no information here that will help. I'm so sorry." It was true, I'd already looked. There was hardly any detail about Kit's murder.

He swallowed thickly, every inch of him drooping. "Then I must get back. Any minute I'm away, she could be found."

The knot in my stomach grew instantly, matched by the one in my throat. "But maybe I could help back in your time," I blurted. "I could look for her, I could see if anything triggers a memory of something I've read. I could help *you*. Stay sane, I mean. For as long as I can be away from here without all hell breaking loose."

When I looked down, Nick's fingers caught my chin, tilting my face back to his. "You would do that for me?" he said. "Leave this place? Because, now that I am here, I fear I cannot bear this without you."

The aching need in his voice was devastating and irresistible. Every cell in my body burned to be close to him again. Plus, maybe there was a way I could still help Kit without having to tell him the hideous truth.

"Nick, I've left this place for you before, and for far less. I want to help you and Kit." I shrugged, defenseless against my own heart on this. "To be honest, I can't remember wanting anything more."

He cupped my cheeks and brought my face close to his. The minty heat of his breath washed over my lips before he made a tsk sound like he couldn't hold back anymore and pressed his mouth to mine. I didn't realize quite how much I'd been deprived of this feeling until it bolted through my body again like a charge of electricity. I clutched his shirt to draw him closer, a sigh escaping my mouth that he caught with his. Our tongues met and stroked each other's in a delicious glide as I kissed him urgently and heatedly. My fingers bit into his shoulders, gripping solid muscle before sliding down and finding the ass that I'd wanted to touch since the moment I'd laid eyes on it. I cupped his round curves and tugged his hips hard against mine, a groan escaping his lips. He pulled back for a moment and I relished the way his eyes had turned hooded as he looked down to where my legs had parted over his, the movement of my own hands giving him permission to grip my ass in his palms and give it a needy squeeze. I'd never been so easily turned on by a man, and so keen to touch him everywhere without any fear. I could feel the hard length of him pressing against me, and I trailed my hand down the soft fabric covering his chest, fascinated with how he might feel down there, until he caught my wrist.

"Emmie, I cannot," he said in a breathless voice. "God, I want you." He muttered a sound of frustration as he tightened his hands over my ass. "But not now. I must return to court in haste, and I wish for nothing more than for you to come with me."

My heart thundered like a racehorse as I dropped my cheek

against his soft, rose-scented hair, reminding myself of the suffering I'd felt over this guy in the past few weeks. But now that he was here in my arms again, I felt like I was being freed and held hostage all at once by a feeling I couldn't control. It didn't matter that Mom was asleep in the next room or that I'd spent the past two weeks crying buckets over him. I wanted him more than I could remember ever wanting anything. I couldn't bear to see him leave without me again, not knowing if he'd ever return.

"Can we go together in the morning?" I whispered. "So I can think of something to tell my mom?"

His eyes pinched with distress, his head slowly shaking. "Forgive me, Emmie, I must return without delay. If I am discovered to be missing, too, along with my only heir, there could be war."

I nodded, my throat sticky. "I understand. Just give me a few minutes."

He lay back and watched me with his distractingly magnetic gaze as I sat at my desk and scribbled on a notepad, my handwriting chaotic from drowsiness and a severe lack of knowing what to say.

But the words soon flowed, the letter to Mom visual proof of my inability to be honest with anyone anymore—even Nick. I told Mom she was right: that I'd lost the first guy I'd ever loved, and I needed to get away or I'd lose my mind. I'd signed up for a teenagers' health camp in Connecticut that my friend recommended. I wouldn't be contactable for a few weeks, but I'd be safe, and if school wanted to kick me out for missing my final week of classes, I was okay with that. I also underlined that this had nothing to do with my dad.

It was shockingly insufficient, but it was all I had right now. I'd just have to figure out a way to make it up to her later.

I dropped the pen onto the page, a hollow cave opening in my stomach.

My eyes popped open to a dazzling painting of a night sky. The satin sheets were vacant beside me, the air warm and sweet. I peeked through a gap in the pearled netting. A boy in a black cap leapt backward.

"Excuse me, mistress," he said, leaving quickly through a paneled door.

Nick leaned into the opposite doorway from where he sat in a chair, a quill between his fingers. Heat found my cheeks. He tossed the quill aside and stood up, eye-poppingly handsome in a royal-blue coat stitched with gold flowers.

"You need not hide like a dormouse," he said, pulling the curtain wide open and sitting on the edge of the bed. "My gentlemen will say naught to anyone."

"How do you know that?"

"Because I'm the king."

I swallowed the stinging urge to ask him how many girls he'd had in his bed before me. "Is there any news?" I asked softly. "I didn't think I'd sleep so long."

He shook his head, unable to speak. His skin was the color of pale jade, his face drawn.

Catherine was taken from her bed and strangled with a set of wooden Catholic rosary beads, her neck broken.

I wanted to ask where the Dowager Countess of Warwick was when Kit disappeared, but it was like someone had glued my mouth closed and wrapped my heart with barbed wire while they were at it.

Nick reached out to tuck a wisp of hair behind my ear. "I still find it impossible to believe this has occurred."

"I know. How could anyone even think about hurting Kit?"

He traced my knuckles with his fingers before lacing our hands together. "I was speaking of you." His eyes held mine, unblinking. "Why did God send you to me?"

I glanced down at my bare legs beneath my sleep shirt. "You still believe in God? After everything you've seen?"

He touched my chin with his free hand and steered my eyes to his. "Never more."

My heart swelled and I ached to pull him into the bed with me. But before I could, he sluggishly rose back to his feet, his face a study in sadness. "I must take my leave. I am receiving information every hour. Pray for news before I make some of my own. Oh, and Emmie. You must tell no one about Kit. Only my privy councilors have knowledge of the situation. To everyone else, the Princess Catherine has traveled to Windsor."

I nodded, gripping the sheet tightly.

"Rest assured, you are entirely safe at court now. The Dowager Countess of Warwick, or no other fool, will give you any more trouble."

"You told her I'm from the future, huh? How'd she take it?"

His finger flew down to my lips, a line deepening in his brow. "Never speak those words. For if anyone were to hear you, not even I could save you."

"I thought you just said I was safe."

"From your falsehood about Hatfield, not from accusations of heresy. Listen carefully. You are indeed a physician's daughter, but your family lives in Worthing, although they were originally from Hatfield, which is where the confusion arose. Most importantly, you are the distant niece of the Duke of Norfolk."

"But I don't even know who Norfolk is," I said, my stomach clenching. "And I've never been to Worthing." *I can't go through this again.*

"You will meet Norfolk when he returns to court."

"And the duke agreed to this? Was he high?" I could feel my incredulous expression.

"Men do not get rich by acting foolishly, Emmie, or by denying their king's request. Do you not see what this means? You are a gentlewoman now. No one will ever question you being here again. Now, wait here for a maidservant. I will have cloth brought in, and you will be shown to your new chambers."

He bent down to kiss my cheek and I sighed, reaching up to pull him closer, but he just drove a reluctant look into my eyes that said: *I want to, but I can't right now.* A moment later, he left the room like a president going to war, a parade of gentlemen and attendants scampering after him.

I puffed an exhale and ran my hand down the twisted pillar at the foot of the bed. I really was back at Whitehall with Nick. My insides warmed like a fire. But then I thought of Kit, and I was swept into a snowstorm, fighting to breathe.

As Nick promised, a maid turned up and helped me into a rose-colored dress with ribbon crisscrossed down the bodice. While she tightened the straps, I plaited my hair on both sides and connected it at the center.

I knew that getting my old room back was too much to ask, but I'd hoped for at least the same wing. I liked hearing the faint chatter of passersby on the public street over the wall. But the maid escorted me into the fancier section of court and lugged open a set of wooden double doors.

My chin dropped at the ornate four-poster bed and the red velvet chairs facing a fireplace bigger than Mia's bathroom. I'd been upgraded from a closet to a mansion—one that smelled more heavenly than a perfume store.

I opened the jewelry coffer on the mirrored dresser, my breath stalling at the expensive display of gemstones and goldwork. The emerald necklace Nick gave me when I was sick lay on top. I fastened it around my neck, the square stone cooling my skin.

I was contemplating silencing my rumbling stomach with a trip to the kitchens when there was a loud rap at the door.

Waiting on the other side was Francis Beaumont's dim smile, his face as drained as the king's. I hadn't realized until then that I'd missed him too.

"I am pleased to see you have returned, Mistress Grace," he said with a cautious smile. "I trust your rooms are agreeable." He stepped inside, taking a look for himself.

"They're ridiculous. In a good way." I refrained from telling him that I actually preferred my pokey end room near the horse yard.

"His gracious Majesty has requested I accompany you on a recreational activity this day as he is well occupied. I propose hunting. The rain has cleared, but the grounds remain damp."

"Hunting? Thanks, but that's not necessary." My mission was to find the Dowager Countess of Warwick and find out if she was involved in Kit's vanishing.

Francis's jaw hardened. "I am afraid the king has insisted upon it.

Mistress Grey may join us. In fact, she will be delighted to see you after your unexpected journey to Worthing. We shall see you at the stable yard in an hour. Breakfast will be brought to you in the meantime."

Argh. It was just enough time to change into a looser dress and wolf down the selection of hard cheeses and stewed fruits that arrived. The thought of shooting animals with crossbows made my stomach coil. Not that I had any idea how to hunt, despite being a famous duke's niece. Plus, Kit could already be dead—or worse—killed while we were out on a "recreational activity". Had Nick's madness already started?

As I walked into the cobblestoned horse yard, Alice immediately crossed it to hug me. "Heavens, Emmie, why not say you are Norfolk's niece? We could have dined upstairs forevermore." Her arms were thinner than I remembered, but her cinnamon scent hadn't changed.

"I guess I don't like talking about myself the whole time.'"

I meant it as a light joke, but Alice didn't even crack a smile, her cheeks as ashen as Francis's. When a groom steered my favorite horse, Stella, to me, my uneasiness loosened a little. I hoisted myself into the saddle, finding my comfort spot.

We trailed the hunting dogs across the moat bridge and deep into the Parkside through pristine oak trees before halting at a flowering meadow that edged a small mossy lake. My eyes darted around, familiarity bleeding into my vision. This was the exact spot where I'd arrived in Tudor England the first time, where Lord Lansbury had shot me with his arrow. For a moment, I couldn't feel my face.

A second later, a run of arrows tore past my ears and a deer collapsed beside the lake. Francis cheered and guided his chestnut stallion over to it.

Alice hung back, fiddling with her crossbow. "You do not shoot?" she asked me.

I shook my head. "I feel bad for the deer."

She just looked at me like I'd just said *I love eating mice for breakfast.* But then she sighed. "It is hideous doing this while worrying where Kit is, or even if…" She cut herself off, fighting tears.

I steered Stella around to face Alice, my lips parting with surprise.

"You know about Kit?"

She nodded. "Francis told me. He also said that you know too." She watched him dismount near the writhing stag. "It has been so difficult for Francis; he is utterly distraught. His mood is more than sour, especially given he has taken on all of Lord Lansbury's tasks. Lansbury's been scarcely sober since his brother Mathew Fox was put in the Tower. Oh my, Emmie, I'm surely pleased you are back."

The words blurred, like I didn't hear them right. "Mathew Fox is in the Tower of London?"

"He was arrested after you left for Worthing, but I'm uncertain why. Certainly nothing to do with Kit, that happened long since." We watched Francis trying to slash the wiggling deer's neck with his dagger. "Oh, I pray the princess is found alive and at once," Alice added. "I have not felt this dreadful since my mother vanished."

I guided my horse a little closer to her. "I was so sorry to hear about that."

Her face paled. "She left for the market about three miles from here and never returned."

My voice tightened. "Did she...did she ever call herself Stuart? Jane Stuart?" My head whirred. *Jane Stuart, whose name wasn't really Jane.*

Alice frowned. "Surely not, why?"

"Shall we ride on?" called Francis, trotting back to us with the deer sprawled across his thighs. The hunting dogs followed obediently.

"I should get back," I said, taking my chance. "I'm still pretty tired from my trip." The blood pouring from the stag's wound made me want to puke.

"Fine, we'll return," Francis huffed. He spun his horse toward the court. "I am to play tennis this afternoon with the Duke of Savoy in the king's stead. The man has the worst timing in history."

Alice shoved an arrow into her leather quiver. "So what am I? A cat's behind?" She kicked her horse and galloped through the mud back to court.

My whole body sagged with relief, watching Alice go. There was only one way to explain why she was so mad at Francis for not offering to stay and hunt with her alone.

Alice Grey was utterly besotted with the roguish Earl of Warwick.

It was quite an achievement how visibly tense the exchange had made Alice as we carried our dessert plates to the bench by the swan pond.

"Why do you dislike Francis so much?" I probed cheekily, biting into my ginger cheesecake.

"You mean apart from his unsightly face?" She grimaced at the feeding swans.

I laughed, accidentally spitting crumbs out.

Alice flashed her amber eyes at me. "You think Francis is handsome?"

"No, I think he's hideous," I said sarcastically.

"He has decent hair. But that is beside the point. Francis is trouble, in spite of his eyes or hair. He nearly ruined my sister's life."

"How so?" I asked, hoping I hadn't overstepped. There was clearly more to the discord between them.

She fingered the linen folds of her skirts. "My sister Violet and I grew up with Francis here at court, but he and Violet were especially close. They were the best of friends from when they were almost babies, but you know friendships between men and women become thorny after a certain age. Francis soon offered marriage, and I never saw Violet happier. But on Midsummer's Eve a year past, he confessed he did not want to wed her after all. Because everyone already considered Violet the future wife of the king's favorite, no other man would go near her for fear of offending His Majesty. Violet had to leave and go back to Northamptionshire, or risk becoming an old maid."

I rested my plate on my lap. "Yikes, poor thing."

"She met a northerner of modest means last year, and he agreed to wed her. She moved to Lancashire and is now Mrs. James Fisher. Even so, Emmie, I fear she is unhappy. She adored Francis."

I circled my plate with my finger, trying to imagine them all at that age.

"The king is coming," said Alice, her mouth full. "And my father."

Nick was striding up the path, leading a string of councilors fronted by Sir Thomas Grey.

"All rise for the king; all rise for His Grace!" ordered the guards. Everyone stood and parted like the sea for Moses.

When Nick passed by, his weary eyes flickered to mine. They softened at the edges as he held my gaze for a long moment. I sank into a delayed curtsy, a nervous flutter chasing through me. When I looked back up, the group had stopped at the lion fountain.

That was when I saw her.

Princess Henriette of France emerged from behind the wall of vines, her pearled hood matching her indigo gown garnished with black feathers. When she greeted Nick, he lifted her dainty hand to his mouth and kissed it. I almost lost my lunch. The Dowager Countess of Warwick was next to arrive with her band of ladies. Isobel Beaumont was almost unrecognizable in a doublet-inspired coat over an emerald-green gown, stringy strands of her hair hanging loose.

Thoughts swiped across my mind like fighter jets. Kit had disappeared and the countess was taking a garden stroll. Did that mean the countess was innocent or psychopathic? And *Henriette* was still at court. Which Nick had failed to mention—especially when his tongue had been busy deep inside my mouth.

"You should have a frock made for the betrothal feast," Alice said as I watched them with a throb in my chest. "Something pale. It seems the princess prefers the deeper shades."

"Sorry…what are you talking about?"

"His Majesty and Princess Henriette are to be married," she replied, like she thought I knew. "She is already lodging in the queens' chambers. The Dowager Countess of Warwick and the Lady Isobel have moved beside me, beside the pheasant yard." She stifled a giggle.

I couldn't take my eyes off them.

Nick was engaged. More than that: parading his beautiful, regal fiancée around right in front of me. But he'd brought me back to this place because he *couldn't bear this without me*. Not to forget the breathless make-out session in my bed. When Henriette tripped on Isobel's dress, Nick caught the small of her back with his palm. My heart felt like it was exploding into my lungs. I was ready to march over to him, regardless of what it cost me, when a passing man nearly knocked me to my butt.

"Pardon me, mistress," said Lord Lansbury, smelling like a brewery. His blaze of red hair rushed toward the king, chased by three guards.

Alice and I shared a silent question. *Has Kit been found?*

But Nick just leisurely turned his back as the men seized Thomas Grey and wrapped his wrists with rope.

"What are you doing!" cried Alice, racing over to them. I jogged after her.

"Sir Thomas Grey, you are under arrest on suspicion of high treason," slurred Lansbury. "You are charged with conspiring with Ambassador Rodrigo Montoya to deprive the King's Majesty of his royal state and holiness and to procure his death and destruction."

"What? That is preposterous!" sputtered Thomas as Alice burst into tears. "Your Majesty, I pray you, you are sorely mistaken; I serve only you; I live only for you—I beg you!"

Nick didn't flinch as the guards pushed Thomas toward a stone staircase leading inside the castle. Henriette turned away and caught my eye, her face startled.

"Why? How?" sobbed Alice.

"I don't know, but I'm going to find out," I promised shakily.

"I must write to my sister at once," she wept, hitching up her dress and running for the pheasant yard.

Henriette's gang hastened toward the court, as if to escape the tainted air of the arrest. When Nick turned toward the stone stairs, I sprang forward, my heart thundering in my chest.

"Nick!" I called across the pond. He spun back around, halting his guards. As I hurried toward him, he met my onrush, grabbing my wrist and tugging me behind the wall of vines.

"What is wrong with you?" he hissed, stealing a look around in case someone had seen us.

"What is wrong with *me?*" I was already breathless. "You brought me back here with you, leaving my home, my mom, after I'd spent two weeks crying myself dry over you. But all you've done is send me off on some hunting trip while you take a stroll with the *fiancée* you conveniently never told me about."

His brow puckered like I was speaking Swahili.

"Your bride-to-be! The girl you're going to marry…whatever."

I didn't want him to see me cry, but it was impossible to stop my tears from spilling.

Nick's face fell. He gripped his hip and stood there a moment before he spoke, his voice heavy. "I wanted to tell you about Henriette, but I feared you would not come back with me."

"Well, you were dead right about that." I waved the tears away, trying in vain to stop him from seeing.

"What do you expect of me?" he pleaded angrily. "She is the sister of the King of France. Would you have me put her on the street?"

"Oh, c'mon, you didn't give her a bed and a blanket. You asked her to marry you."

"A matter of state! You do not understand…you are without a king. This is not personal feelings; you are that ignorant to believe I get to *love* my wife?"

My heart twisted like a wrung-out dishcloth. "So you've no interest whatsoever in that beautiful, elegant princess. Are girls like me dumber in your time?"

"Christ, Emmie, stop questioning my every action!"

My chest crushed with the most painful thought I could imagine. I was convinced that Nick wouldn't have slept with the French king's daughter before marriage in an era like this one, but the thought of him kissing her the way he had me, of allowing her hands and lips on his body, burned a hole through my heart.

"Well then, you haven't even kissed her, right?" I asked, my voice wavering. "If it's just about the alliance?"

When his gaze dropped to his boots, I froze. "Don't even think about lying, Nick. You and I are way past that."

He shifted on his feet, unable to look at me. "Emmie, when a man asks for a lady's hand in marriage, he must demonstrate suitable feelings."

A guttural sob exploded from my lips, spurring me to turn away. He caught my wrists and forced me to face him.

"Whether he feels them or not," he finished, nearly collapsing into me. "Do you understand the roar inside me at the moment? I have Spanish troops breathing down my neck, waiting to strike, and I'd be a fool if I believed we could fight them without France. And France's princess, their *pearl*, wants to marry me. So, there it is—decision made —however I feel about it. Meanwhile, here I have a girl before me who I desperately want to know…to hold…to love. But I cannot. I feel like the only man in Christendom who cannot have that. Yet, here she stands in front of me, like an act of torture." His eyes were wet, shining jewels. "Among all this, my sister—my Kit—has been snatched by a person so sinister, so evil, I will not sleep until I see their bones charred like tinder."

"Nick—"

"I am not even finished, Emmie. Together with all this, I just learned that the only father I have ever known has betrayed me. All in one miserable day."

"What do you mean?"

Lines strained his brow. "The palace is being searched thrice daily. This morning, Francis found letters between Thomas Grey and the Spanish ambassador concealed inside pomegranates. Rodrigo Montoya promised that the Spanish king would give assistance if the English Catholics took up arms against their king, and Grey was in support."

Thomas Grey in bed with the *Spanish?* "But why would he do that?" I said. "I've heard him push harder than anyone for your marriage to Henriette. He's all about the French alliance. Why would he conspire with Spain now?"

"I hardly know. Nevertheless, if he is behind Kit's disappearance, every bone and tendon in his body will break while I watch."

My mind sped to the rosary beads twisted around Kit's neck. Whoever took her was a diehard Catholic. Thomas Grey had wanted Bishop Rochester boiled alive for being one. He despised Catholics.

"But isn't Thomas Grey a Protestant?" I said, still confused. "Like a hardcore one?"

"What does that have to do with it?" Nick stared at me, his skin slowly whitening. "Emmie, what does Thomas Grey being Protestant have to do with Kit's passing from sight?"

My lungs emptied of air.

He grabbed my shoulders, crushing them in his fingers. "Is there something you are not saying? Christ, Emmie, tell me what you know!"

The words spilled out in a gush beyond my control. "I'm so sorry. I wanted to tell you, but I couldn't."

He was losing his voice. "Is she dead? Tell me! Tell me this is nothing. Say she will be well!"

I bit away tears, but they were too strong.

"Dear God." Nick fell to his knees. A moment later, his face flew back up, his eyes flaming aquamarines. "Will I ever see her again?"

"I'm so sorry." My nose was congesting from tears. "She dies, Nick. I worried about what you might do if I told you."

"What I might do?" He scrambled back to his feet, his boots smashing the pebbles as his voice rose. "You mean save her life?"

"I mean turn totally insane!" I sobbed. "Because history says you do not react well to this sort of thing, which I can see already. I mean…charred bones and broken tendons? Torturing maids?!"

"What are you talking about?"

"I'm talking about Nicholas the Ironheart! You once asked me if you're a noted king in my time. Well, there's not a person on Earth who doesn't know your name. But they don't know you for the war you won, or the lands you conquered, or the song you wrote. You're famous because of how you reacted when you lost Kit. You became a monster, Nick, almost overnight. You started executing your councilors, one by one, in case they had something to do with it. Then you picked off people in the city too. You burned crops, houses, even churches. And when the streets of London were choked with the burning bodies from your vengeance war, you were given a new name: Nicholas the Ironheart. That's what the world knows you as. One of the cruelest, bloodiest kings in history. That's why I couldn't tell you."

He fell into the wall, pain bleeding into his eyes. "You are saying Kit is murdered? And I never discover the men to blame?"

Saltwater dribbled down my cheeks. "I've read it all, over and over, and there's nothing else. History is more vague than you think. But you heard what I said, right? You have to keep your head through this. I've just given you what no one in the world has…a chance to change. To stop that madness before it happens. And I don't even know if I should have. I can't see this happen to you, I *can't.*"

"That wild-eyed guard, Cavendish," he mumbled to himself. "Or, Christ, even Francis. He has always taken such an interest in Kit. Why?"

"Please stop," I wept, trying to take his hands. He shook me away.

"Emmie, I have always felt there was something black inside me. Now I understand what it is. You said it: you have given me what no one else in the world has. I know the man I'll become. Why waste any more time?"

"Because this isn't you," I begged, falling to my knees, my peach dress crushing into the dirt. "You're a merciful and kind person. You're not a killer." I wanted to reach out and touch his face. "You're beautiful. You're sunlight. Please, Nick. I...I love you."

But he wasn't listening. He sounded like a dead person would if they could speak. "You will tell me everything you know about the plot against my sister. And, like a true and faithful subject, you will help me stop it."

Tears slipped off my face into the dirt. "I–I've already told you everything I know."

He gripped my arm and yanked me to my feet. "I believe you not! You already kept this from me; how can I know you are not with-holding more? Knowledge that will keep my sister alive?"

"Nick, you're hurting me."

"You will address me as Your Majesty! And you will yield to your lord's command, or God help me, Mistress Grace, you will get out of my sight."

It was a gunshot right to the heart. "Fine, if that's what you want," I spat at him. "Give me the stupid ring then." I shook my palm at the blue diamond on his finger.

Nick shoved his hand behind his back, his face paling. "You will remain at Whitehall until I decide what to do with you. Now, obey my order and get away from me without delay. Guards!"

But before they drew their swords, I tore away from him, hardly able to see through the tears streaming down my face.

17

Before the sun had consumed the morning fog, my coach crossed the drawbridge to the Tower of London. I was yawning on loop despite the pulsing energy in my veins. I'd spent the night in Alice's room, comforting her, which had at least kept my own grief-fest at bay. I should never have shown Nick what the ring was capable of. I should have known a sixteenth-century king wouldn't give up power without a fight.

I pulled my hood over my hair to barricade the wind and followed the guard past the menagerie housing the lion I'd heard that first night in the Tower, and into the stone fortress. The streets of London smelled like a pinewood forest compared with the Tower's dank corridors. I dropped my face as we climbed the staircase to a run of cells, stepping into the fourth.

Mathew Fox stood in the corner, the whites of his alarmed eyes like two glow sticks through the shadows. "Why are you here?" he said to me.

"I came to ask you the same question."

He smelled like a homeless guy and looked the part too. "I lied to the king about you," he replied matter-of-factly.

"Me?" After a few seconds, my hands flew to my cheeks. "Because you said you had met my family in Hatfield. That's why you're in here? I had no idea. I'm so sorry." Another thing Nick neglected to tell me.

"Mistress, if I hadn't deceived the king, it would be you hiding from the rats in here. Which was precisely why I did it. You are not to blame for this."

My cheeks felt tight and hot. "I'm going to get you out of here."

His sigh was bleak. "For a lady with such a lion's heart, how easily you misjudge. I made the king look a fool. There will be no mercy."

"But he pardoned me when I showed up at the Parkside, remember? He forgave Francis for taking Kit to an execution."

"I am not loved by the king."

The words sent a blade to my throat. "He doesn't love me either."

Mathew raised his brows, skeptical.

"He told me," I assured, the memory still painfully raw. "Well, rather, I said I loved him, and he said to go away. Dreamy, huh?"

Mathew exhaled, rubbing his peg-like fingers together. "Something has gone awry. There has been too much tantalizing...or too little. Perhaps it is because you have come and gone from court like a queen, though you are quite the opposite. It is time to strike. Have you given him your maidenhead?"

"My what? No."

He lunged forward, his deep voice taut. "Then you must offer it. Before the marriage to Princess Henriette comes to pass."

"Mathew, I..." My voice trailed off, lost for what to say. I'd barely had my dad in my life for the past ten years. I wasn't up for a chat about my virginity with any man, let alone Mathew Fox.

"Come back when it is done," he said after a while, his back to me. The conversation was so awkward, so unexpected, that I didn't protest when he asked me to leave.

On the way out, a man screamed from a floor below, startling me so much I nearly skidded down the moldy staircase. The guard responded with about as much zing as a corpse.

"Would it also be possible to see Sir Thomas Grey?" I stammered. "I'm a friend of his daughter Alice. I'd like to visit on her behalf."

At least that got a reaction. He grunted with annoyance and shuffled back up the stairs, unlocking a single door on the top floor with his huge, cartoon-sized key.

"You 'ave a visitor," he grumbled, pushing me in like I was the prisoner.

Thomas Grey looked up, his bare legs stretched beneath a canvas smock. His knees were bloodied, his cheeks badly bruised. "The king's whore," he muttered. "What in the devil do you want?"

"Not to be called a whore would be a good start." I stayed at the wall, already shaking. The room smelled worse than a toilet.

"Did my daughter send you? Or was it the king?"

"I actually made a decision on my own on this one."

Thomas tried to get up, but gnashed his teeth, clutching his thigh. "What do you want, Mistress Grace?"

"I guess I wanted to see if you're really capable of it."

"Of plotting against the king?"

And his sister.

His eyes scrunched shut, tears trickling from the corners. "I cannot even consider the loss of His Majesty. Since he was a babe, I have protected him with my every breath, given my life to him."

"But the letters—"

"Speak not of such treachery! Those letters were forgeries to slander me. Yes, I communicated with the Spanish emperor through Montoya, but in appeal for a treaty, not a holy war against His Majesty. The notion is preposterous. Now the idiocy of this state of affairs has ruined any likelihood of peace with Spain." He reached out, chains jangling. "Tell me. Does His Majesty have good counsel? Has the betrothal with Henriette progressed? France is the only answer now."

"He's pretty preoccupied with finding Kit," I replied, scanning his face. "He's beside himself."

But Thomas didn't even flinch. "Get Norfolk involved. I beseech you: do whatever you can to restore the king's mind to clarity. His enemies have never been more cunning, and they will not stop until the great Tudor name has descended into ruin. I will not see that come to pass. Not while I still breathe."

His forehead met his gnarled knees, his shoulders quivering. It took me back to Mrs. Shaw, a rest home resident with dementia who was trapped in an endless panic spiral. I staggered forward to place a gentle kiss on Thomas's head, tasting sweat. His eyes flicked open with comfort and confusion—just like Mrs. Shaw's.

"That was from Alice," I said, before hurrying to the door and banging on it. I was glad the guard let me out quickly.

Back at court, I wandered through rooms like a forlorn ghost, searching for the Dowager Countess of Warwick and any evidence I could find about Kit. When a sudden energy swelled behind me, I spun into the razor-sharp glare of Princess Henriette.

"You," she accused from under her silk bathrobe. "This is why you came back, no? You will not get away with this." She tossed a piece of paper at me. Her maids guided her away as she spat at me in French, a black snake of braided hair curling down her back.

I picked up the crumpled paper, ignoring the prying eyes of passersby. It held the same choppy handwriting as had the threatening note left for me.

If you do not go back to France today,
I will crush the king's sister like a grape.

I darted through a clump of men violently arguing and dashed up Nick's private stairwell. Two guards chased me, declaring the king wouldn't be disturbed. Before they could stop me, I banged hard on the door.

The soft timbre of Nick's voice made me freeze. He had to be inches from the other side. There was a splash of water, followed by a scraping sound.

"That will be all, Charles," I heard him say. "Come in, Mistress Grace," he called without a trace of surprise. The guards released me and opened the door.

The king's secretary was wedging scrolls under his arms, clearing them from the room. Nick was freshly shaven, his white doublet gleaming with rubies.

"Were you not advised about this?" he said tightly, looking anywhere but at me. "You will not come to me directly if you need something. You may speak with Lord Warwick or my secretary, Charles Talbot."

"I'm not here for advice." I ignored the knife he'd just plunged into my heart. "There's something I need to say about Kit."

Nick dismissed a boy who'd been strumming a lute in the corner. He finally looked at me, his face torn with pain. "I thought you wanted Kit thrown to the dogs. Because, in hundreds of years' time, it is what your countrymen say happened."

"Do you want to know or not?" I handed him the note Henriette accused me of writing, explaining the similar one I'd got before. Nick's fingers quivered, his cheeks colorless.

"I left out something about Kit's death," I stumbled. "According to records, she was strangled with a set of wooden Catholic rosary beads." It was almost impossible to continue while looking at his shattered face, so I studied the ground. "I'm so sorry to have to tell you that. But this note proves Kit is still alive! And whoever has her also wrote these notes. It's someone who hates any girl who gets near you, *and* they're a Catholic. That's why it can't be Sir Thomas Grey."

"Speak plainly, Emmie! Whom do you believe it is?"

My tone dropped to a barely audible level. "I've long suspected the Dowager Countess of Warwick. She's from a Catholic family, right?"

His brows jammed together. "But the Dowager Lady Warwick left for Derbyshire yesterday. She said something about a poorly cousin."

Charles Talbot burst in, bowing in apology. "Majesty, the Princess of France is making her way to see you with some urgency." He glanced at me.

Nick gripped his forehead, sapphires glinting from his fingers. "Boy!" he shouted, and a pink-faced pageboy appeared. Nick swept his hand at me, a gesture to have me removed.

"I'm not done," I said evenly, starting to seethe.

Nick opened his mouth to speak, but I got in first. "You could've told me you put Mathew Fox in the Tower because of me."

He strode toward the page, who got the message and ran away. The king slammed the door and spun back to face me, his cheeks flaming.

"What in heaven's name is between you and Mathew Fox?"

"Nothing! You know who I am and that he couldn't have had anything to do with that. It might've been stupid to say he found my family in Hatfield, but he also knew I was harmless and in over my head." I left out the part about Mathew's matchmaking plans.

"I would not go with harmless. Trouble, yes."

"Mathew lives to serve you, to be in this court. While your buddy Lord Lansbury is getting drunk off his face and chasing virgins, Mathew is worrying about foreign alliances, and who might invade, and what's best for the country."

His jaw clenched. "Enough! I need not hear every detail about your fondness for Mathew Fox!"

"Well, I saw him today, and he doesn't look good. Neither does Thomas Grey, who I think is innocent of everything, not just Kit. He swears those letters were forged, and I believe him. He was crying because of how much he loves you. Did anyone even see him write the letters? Do you have any proof?"

Nick gaped at me. "Emmeline Grace, I command you to stop this! Going to the Tower to question my prisoners—what in God's name are you thinking?"

"Alice has already lost a mother. So if you're going to take her father, too, you better be sure he's guilty."

He stepped closer, his irresistible gaze and scent nearly knocking me over. "Listen here. No one else at court understands who you really are. I have no excuse to treat you any differently. I may be God's chosen king, but everything I do and say is questioned, so you must be more than careful. Hence I am instructing you, as the king of the realm in which you presently breathe, to stop urging the release of my prisoners. That is a command!"

"No," I cried, our bodies so close that we were sharing the same breath of air. "No more commands; I've had enough! No more telling me when to come, and when to go, and who to be friends with, and what to say, and when to hunt. I might be your prisoner here, but I am not your subject and I never will be. And I am *not* afraid of you."

I tore myself away from him and charged for the door, my chest aching so badly I thought it might break. But something compelled me to stop and turn around.

"The first time I came here was a total accident," I said shakily, unable to meet Nick's eyes. "But then I worked out I could come back at any time. I was thrilled. I thought maybe I'd be happier here, maybe this was my place…with you. Above everything else I've ever wanted in my life." My teeth nearly bit through my bottom lip as he stared back at me with a pained look on his face. "But now I know it's not," I continued. "And I've never felt so stupid, so mistaken, or so far from home."

I left through the Presence Chamber, trying to outrun my tears. The world had become so blurry that I nearly missed Henriette striding past me, her face a thunderstorm. But I did notice she'd changed into a silk ball gown before deciding to tell the king about the note that proved his sister was still alive.

It wasn't hard to get my mind off what Nick and Henriette were up to in his private chambers, given what he'd just revealed to me about the Dowager Countess of Warwick. If she had left for Derbyshire, how could she have got that note to Henriette?

At bedtime, I was as awake as a prisoner on death row. I wrapped myself in a wool coat and strolled through the flame-lit gardens along my old route, wishing Ruby was at my feet again chasing the sparrows. So much had happened since then.

I expected the halls to be a ghost town by the time I stepped back inside, but a trio of musicians was warring their oboes, flutes, and viols in a far corner of the Great Hall. Two councilors were busting a move, Tudor-style, on a table.

Francis strode toward me through the fray, holding a cup of ale. He was glowing.

"What's with the dance contest?" I sounded like I hadn't slept in a hundred years.

Francis spoke quietly, but it was evident the privy councilors already knew. "Kit was found alive. She is safe!" He gave me a brief hug, enveloping me in his scent of musk. "And it is all due to you. Praise God for you, Emmie."

My head burst open like a stepped-on ant's nest. Kit was safe. Kit was alive. Kit hadn't been murdered.

"How?" I breathed. "Where?"

He gritted his teeth. "She was rescued from a lodging in Holborn that belongs to Mark Macaulay, one of the king's gentlemen. Did you know Isobel had a dalliance with Macaulay? Her new maid Clemence is a wicked telltale. Remind me never to employ her."

When I looked like I might shout, Francis returned to the more critical topic. "It is a miracle Kit was unharmed, but she was frightened beyond her wits. Macaulay claimed it was Isobel who forced him to capture Kit. She wanted to scare Princess Henriette away. Isobel then disappeared, leaving him without a thought as to what to do with the princess. Now, we cannot find Isobel." He gripped his stomach. "Heaven knows what would have happened had you not told the king about those ghastly notes and your suspicions. For Isobel to believe she could win the king's heart by harming his sister. She is not only the worst of the harebrains, she is worse than a devil. My faithless family has shamed me for too long."

The bile in my throat nearly spilled over onto Francis's shiny boots. Of course Nick had been smart enough to figure it out. Isobel was also a Catholic who shared a room with the Dowager Countess of Warwick, and she hated Henriette's guts—and mine—for being near the king. Isobel Beaumont and Mark Macaulay should've killed Kit, except I'd indirectly stopped it from happening. What I'd revealed to Nick had changed the course of history on a potentially massive scale. I looked around me, waiting for the universe to start collapsing.

"We'll catch her," Francis assured darkly, like he was talking about trapping a spider instead of his own sister. "My mother is our first stop. The king banished her from court until it is confirmed she had nothing to do with the plot."

"Where's Kit now?"

"With the king. Christ, I'm so relieved. I feared how he might have responded to a different result."

Yikes, you're telling me.

"Now can you help Sir Thomas Grey?" I whispered, my throat locking.

Francis tossed back a shot of ale, horrified. "Why would I help a traitor?"

"Because you have no real proof he wrote those letters to the Spanish, and it makes zero sense that he would have. You know the work he's put into the French alliance and how much he hates Catholics. Plus, you owe it to Alice."

"What do I owe Alice?"

"You split her family apart once before." It was a low blow, but it was all I had.

"Now hang on a minute." Francis took my arm and guided me into the corridor to a more private area, stopping below the portrait of King Edward the Sixth. "If you speak of Alice's sister Violet, I should have you know I never loved her. If Alice had not encouraged the match with such fervor, I would never have asked for Violet's hand. Would you have had me marry a girl I did not want? And, make no mistake, it shredded my heart to wound Alice that way."

"So you did it for Alice."

His brow pinched. "I do not follow."

"You said it shredded your heart to do that to *Alice*. Not Violet." Francis looked even more confused. "We all know Alice can be a prickly person sometimes," I said slowly. "But sometimes I think she pricks those she likes the most. She's a bit of a sadist in that way."

"What are you saying?" Francis looked frozen solid.

"I'm saying that I think you didn't marry Violet because you were crazy about someone else. And I think Alice feels the same way about you."

His face turned redder than the surface of Mars. "But that is…it is utter folly."

I could only smile. "Are you sure about that?"

He fingered a groove in his cup. "But Alice's father despises me, who also happens to be the king's hand."

"Then help him," I urged. "Just go and talk to Sir Thomas. To Montoya, if you can. Do the interrogating yourself. Aren't you the 'cat's claws' torture guy? Actually, forget I said that. Torture will be a stain on history one day."

Francis's shoulders fell with a frustrated breath. Behind him, I spotted one of Princess Henriette's maids leaving the kitchens. She glided up the stairs that led to the king's chambers, carrying three plates of marchpane. One for Henriette, one for Nick, and one for Kit, I quickly figured out. Pain swelled in my chest and I pushed it back down, turning toward my room.

I spent most of the next day sleeping, even though I had zero excuse to feel sorry for myself. I'd gotten stuck in Nicholas the Ironheart's world, I'd laid it all bare about Kit, and I'd indirectly saved her life. Now I could be stuck in the sixteenth century forever, destined to star on *America's Unsolved Mysteries*. I felt like crawling into a hole and never coming out.

After a long bath, I dragged my listless feet to dinner. The entrance to the Great Hall looked darker than usual, which I quickly figured out was because the fourth candelabra had been snuffed out. I strode right past it before my mind hurtled back to Mathew Fox in the basement a few weeks earlier.

"If I have a message for you from His Majesty, I will blow out the fourth candelabra outside the Great Hall. If you notice it extinguished, you must come to the king's chambers by way of the private entrance at once."

I turned back. It was definitely the fourth candelabra. I questioned what sanity I had left as I changed direction to Nick's secret stairwell, the guards stepping aside like they were expecting me. Mathew stood in the head of the passage, kicking a loose rush on the floor with the heel of his boot. I ran up and hugged him.

His smile was audible. "Lord Warwick arrived at dawn to pardon

Sir Thomas Grey and said the king had added me to the list at the final hour."

"You *and* Sir Thomas are free?"

His dusty eyes clouded. "Rodrigo Montoya was put upon the rack last night. Only after passing out twice did he admit that Grey had no connection to the plot and the letters were forgeries. Although he insists he was not the one to plant them."

Typical Francis. He'd got his torture-fest after all, but he'd also got what he needed. I couldn't wait to see Alice.

"What perplexed me further was that the king promoted me closer to his person," Mathew continued, straightening the gold chain decorating his narrow chest. "Not only am I returned to His Majesty's good graces, I am now his chief gentleman. And my present task is to see you to a private supper."

"Supper with him?" I pointed at the door, my stomach already a mess. "I'd rather not."

"But it is His Majesty's pleasure."

"And you can tell His Majesty I said 'no, thank you'."

"Mistress, if I do not bring you to the king, he may throw me back into the Tower."

I moaned. "Ugh, fine."

But instead of opening the door, Mathew guided me back through the shield gallery and took me outside to a concealed stone staircase leading to Nick's private wharf. Frigid wind blustered from the River Thames, and crying seagulls signaled the onset of dusk. But it was the giant sailing ship painted with candy-cane stripes that I couldn't tear my eyes from. Flags bearing the king's crest whipped in the wind.

One of Nick's manservants climbed down a rope ladder and offered me a thick velvet coat. I turned to Mathew, my insides shooting up to my throat.

"Go," he called over the salty wind. "There is nothing up there to fear. His Majesty's mood is good today."

"Will you come?"

He smiled, blushing. "On a ship? Not unless we are at war, mistress. Now, because of you, we may not be. Time alone will tell."

He withdrew to the palace, disappearing into the shadows. The manservant patiently helped me up the ladder to the top deck, my body stiff with nerves.

Nick stood leaning against a dining table, all wrapped up like a Christmas present in purple and gold, his hair unsettled by the wind. Seeing him gutted me like a fish again. I should've insisted on not coming. Despite everything, my feelings for Nick wouldn't switch off that fast, and I didn't know how much longer I could take being this close to him without actually having him.

The table was draped with glimmering gold cloth and sprinkled with red and white rose petals. There were two chairs and two place settings.

"What's all this?" I asked flatly.

He stepped toward me, swallowing thickly. "My actions toward you these past days have been unforgiveable. I need you to know I am sorry."

"You're sorry."

His eyes traveled all over my face. "Yesterday, I received the best news of my life. Kit was safe. Yet I have never known such sorrow." His voice split on the words. "Emmie, I bid you to come back here with me, to leave your home—your family—and then I...I pushed you away so unforgivably. I am so sorry, I am begging you to forgive me."

You did exactly what Nicholas the Ironheart would do.

But I couldn't say those words to him. Instead, my eyes swept the expansive deck and the giant gold cross adorning the doorway to the cabin. "So you bought me a ship or something?" I muttered.

The corner of his mouth quirked up. "I do not buy ships, I commission them. You are standing upon the first English vessel to sail around the world. I could not think of a more fitting place for supper with my miracle."

I pulled out a chair, my chest stinging. "Please don't use that word."

He sat down opposite me, watching a flurry of servants flicking open cloth napkins and pouring wine. "If you do not believe you being here is a miracle, then—"

"I meant the word *my*. I'm not yours."

Lines crossed his brow as I slid into my chair. But it wasn't the same expression he'd had when Kit was missing. There was life in him again, albeit ravaged by war wounds. I hoped the Nicholas the Iron-heart darkness never returned to his precious face.

A trumpet blasted beside my ear. A procession of spotty-faced servers began carrying out plates of macarons in every color of the rainbow. The cheese and meat platters that followed barely fit on the table.

"How many of us are eating?" I said, biting away a smile that I couldn't help.

"Did you expect the King's College Choir?"

"No, but I think you did." I picked up a candy-pink macaron. "How did you work out the coloring?"

"My cooks came up with marvelous ideas. Blueberries, carrots, a curious herb named turmeric…beetroot, spinach, to name a few."

"Oh, so they're healthy now." I bit into a mint-green one.

He laughed into the lip of his cup. "I should have known you are an impossible girl to impress."

I felt my frown. I didn't need galleons or multicolored macarons to be impressed. Give me a picnic at Robin House or a turn on the Ferris wheel at Garden Party. Just Nick and me, away from the pomp and the privilege…from the frightening monarch he was here.

We chewed without speaking, but the silence that stretched between us was undeniably comfortable. It was always comfortable with him, even when we were fighting.

"Thanks for letting Mathew Fox out of the Tower," I said finally, dabbing my mouth with a silk cloth.

"You need not thank me. You were right. That man is of more use to me out here."

"Is that why you made him your chief gentleman? Because of what I said?"

"Yes and no." He brushed sugar off his lips. "I advanced his station to keep him close. To keep an eye on what is between you. I do not like that you shared secrets with him and kept them from me."

Heat trickled into my chest at the thought of Nick being threatened by my unusual friendship with Mathew Fox. "Better the devil you know than the devil you don't, hey?" I said lightly. "Don't worry, it's just a saying from my time."

"Ah, you do not get to take that one," he replied through a smirk. "My father used the phrase regularly."

"Seriously?" Our eyes locked together. It was so hard to look away.

"You saved Kit's life," Nick said suddenly. He cleared his wobbly throat. "Which means you saved mine. I'm truly lost for how to thank you."

"You're the one who rescued her."

The tightness in his face mirrored mine. Nick also knew that Kit was meant to die. We were partners in crime…world changers.

"To imagine someone like Isobel Beaumont is made of such depravity," he added darkly, stabbing his cheese with a two-pronged fork. "Not to mention that monster Mark Macaulay, whom I'd permitted to take leave the very moment he was capturing my sister. Good God, what is the world coming to?"

"Cars and photographs, remember?"

He chuckled, but he looked battle-worn.

"What will you do to him?" I asked nervously.

He gulped half a cup of wine. "Macaulay? Best you do not ask."

I ignored the unease inside me, watching the sailboats glowing with lit torches as they crossed the Thames.

"And how's Kit?" I said softly.

"Shaken but miraculously unharmed. She is lodging in my chambers and has already turned my new French cabinet into a playhouse. She removed all the drawers and turned them into a table."

I giggled, and he blushed a smile in response.

When we'd finished our meals, he reached for my hand, a grape-sized emerald bulging from his finger. "The sun is nearly set."

We moved to the front deck, where a carving of a lion's head roared over the sloshing Thames. I halted three feet from the edge, my legs turning numb. It was a long way down. Nick pressed his hands to my shoulders and turned me around, smelling almost as good as he looked from this close a distance.

"Emmie, I have something to give you."

He took my hand, the other one digging into his coat. He produced a small ring pouch, and I tried not to gasp. For an insane second, I thought he was going to propose, but then the blue-diamond ring tumbled into my palm.

"You are not my prisoner," Nick said, his face bleeding with apology.

I shuddered, closing the ring in my fist. Tears threatened my eyes.

My reaction drew him closer, his voice thick with remorse. "When you said those things about my future, I fell to pieces. At first, it was mostly over Kit. I defy any man to keep his mind when he is told a child who is like a daughter to him is about to die." He swallowed hard. "But I also fell to pieces over you. About what you knew of me, what you thought of me. What you still think of me." His eyes glimmered with a film of tears. "I know I am a beast to you. A primitive, savage beast from a dark, lowly place."

"No, I—"

"But it is not right to force you here. You were right…you are not my subject. I am not your king. And you are in no way obligated to serve me purely because I love you."

My tears finally spilled over. "But you don't love me."

His eyes clouded with emotion. "Do not say what you know is not true."

I just shook my head, tears sliding down my cheeks.

"Stop that, Emmie, I love you," he rasped, stepping closer to me. "You know I love you out of my mind. I have nothing to gain, no reason at all to stand here and declare it, apart from the fact that I cannot seem to change it." He laced our fingers together and squeezed. "You told me that you thought this could be your place… with me. And now I am asking you, Emmie, please. Stay here, in my world, and become my royal mistress. You would be respected and served, and I would keep you safe. You may take any manor you wish as your own. You will never feel like an outcast here again."

The words almost blew me backward. "What does that even mean? Royal mistress?"

"It means you would be my companion…my lover. Officially."

"And Henriette would be your wife?"

He took a moment to answer. "Yes."

My gaze dropped to the pitted floorboards. "So she'd be the Princess of France and the Queen of England, and I'd be the king's whore."

His brows collected in the middle. "Do not speak such words. Kings have had mistresses for centuries. Henriette would be my wife, the mother of my sons. You would be my *love*."

His breath streamed into the chilly air as I fought the urge to cry. I kept my eyes locked to his leather boots, trying not to let his ridiculously beautiful face unhinge me.

His fingers touched my chin and tilted it upward. "Emmie, God chose me as his king. I cannot only reign, I have to rule. If I deny Henriette after what I have promised, France will turn their back on me and may even side with Spain. England would be annihilated. But, together, we can destroy Spain."

With my eyes still spilling sadness, he dragged me close and wrapped himself around me.

My voice was a throbbing whisper against the heat of his skin. "But…I don't want to just be your mistress. I want more."

He clutched my face and lifted it to look at him, emotion swimming in his eyes. "Every kiss I give Henriette out of duty, I will give you a thousand more out of love. That is the most I can offer you, Emmie. It is everything I have."

My stomach was hollow and clenched, my head declaring war on my heart. I didn't just love Nick, I loved this place. I loved the history, the wonderment, the dangers, the people. I searched my soul for the right answer.

"If I stay," I breathed, gazing up at him. "Could I keep the blue-diamond ring at all times and use it whenever I want?"

He expelled a heavy breath, clearly not liking my question. "Can I not merely command you to stay?"

"I'm an American citizen. We have rights." He frowned and poked me in the ribs, drawing a chuckle from my throat. "I can't imagine not seeing my home again," I added seriously. "My mom. Maybe I could try to do both, as insane as that sounds. I could stay here and visit there. But I'd never leave here and vanish into thin air without telling you." I reaffirmed the promise with pleading eyes.

He brought my fingers to his lips and kissed them one by one, a hot flush creeping across my face. "If that is the only way I can have you."

When I folded my arms around his neck, he lifted me upward, and my lips melted into his waiting mouth, absorbing the staggering enormity of what I'd agreed to. The feelings I'd tried to drown so many times were back at the surface, like a shameful truth that wouldn't sink.

I loved him. Right or wrong, I didn't want to let him go. And whether it was God's plan or plain old chemistry, I was done trying.

18

I STOOD IN FRONT OF KIT'S DOOR, MY FIST FROZEN, TRYING TO DECIDE whether I should make my presence known or not. A glower from one of her new guards decided for me, and I quickly knocked.

Kit was sitting on her knees beside her wooden animal sculptures, playing with them like nothing had happened. I cried a little as we hugged, her tiny arms clinging to mine. Afterward, she sat me down to read a poem she'd translated from Latin. That was so Kit. At eight years old, she had the nerves of a queen. She was thinner, though, if that were possible, and her eyes looked stitched open, like she was constantly watching for something.

"May I read to you every night?" she asked, her voice giving away nothing of her ordeal.

"I think it's the big person's job to read to the little person. But I guess since I won't see you for a bit…sure."

She tensed. "I wish not to go to Kenilworth. Can I not stay here with you and Francis and everyone?"

I smoothed down her hair. "After what happened, can you blame the king for wanting you as far from here as possible?"

"They did not hurt me. They gave me playthings…a quilt. Even cherries."

My voice was taut. "I'm glad."

Her eyes grew wider. "But His Majesty promised I may stay until after the Midsummer's Eve feast. Right?"

"Why ask me?" I said with a chuckle, fingering the lace on her sleeve.

"Are you not his mistress?"

The air thickened as I paused. "Kit, I'm not sure you should be using that word."

"Oh, forgive me." She looked alarmed. "I overheard Lady Ascot talking in the garden. Emmie, do you love my brother? Like in the tale we read about Lancelot and Guinevere?"

"Kit." I covered my eyes.

"It is not to be feared. We all pray for the king's love and happiness."

I was scared to look back at her, but when I did, she was beaming at me.

"Yes, we do, sweetie," I said, leaning forward to kiss her forehead. "We all pray for the king's love."

Seeing Kit every afternoon for the next three days stopped me from pacing the Great Hall entrance every five seconds, my eyes pinned to the fourth candelabra. Sometimes Mathew Fox's signal was there before breakfast, sometimes long after lunch, and once when I was on my way to bed.

Since our conversation, Nick and I had spent as many hours together in his private chambers as we could. I didn't know if it was normal to kiss someone so much that your lips swelled and all your breath disappeared, but I'd never felt so alive. The sounds coming from his mouth made me crazy as our lips and tongues twisted in deep, almost wild kisses, the taste of him making my back arch and my breath ragged.

The third day we were alone together, Nick's mouth was in the middle of devouring mine when his hand shifted to my shoulder and slid a trail down the front of my kirtle. A sigh fled my mouth as he cupped my breast through the thick fabric, a crease of desire deep-ening in his brow. He squeezed, stroked, and rolled his palm over the firm swell before moving to the other one and paying it just as close attention. A sound of frustration left his lips as he brushed his thumbs over my nipples, trying to draw them out through the fabric, but the embroidered satin was expensive and thick. Making a decision that made my pulse race, I sank back down onto the mattress as my fingers moved to the sides of my kirtle, my breath shallow as I began unlacing the strings.

"Emmie," Nick breathed as he looked down at me with hooded eyes, and I wasn't sure if he wanted me to stop or continue.

"I want you to touch me," I whispered through a tremble, working the strings free on both sides of my dress before tugging the kirtle down past my shoulders. My aching breasts bulged through my linen smock, and Nick made a small groan as he brushed his knuckles back and forth across my nipples over the fabric before making firmer circles with his thumbs. I breathed a moan, and before I knew what was happening, he lowered his mouth to my breast and circled his tongue around it over the fabric of my smock, my knees drawing up as I arched with desire.

"*Nick,*" I begged as he dragged his tongue along my other nipple over the linen, shifting over me until I felt his thick arousal pressing against my thigh.

"I ought to stop," he said in a hot whisper as he guided me back up by my shoulders and sat facing me, his fingers playing with the base of my smock that gathered around my thighs. "Do you wish for me to stop?" he asked as he paused his hands and blinked at me, his pupils dilated and his hair a mess of curls.

I shook my head and raised my arms. Nick's gaze burned with desire as he swept my smock up over my head and then pressed me back down onto the mattress. He murmured a sound of need before his mouth closed over one of my bare breasts, my head tipping back as I moaned at the sensation. He made his own sounds of desire as he licked and sucked on my sensitive peaks, swirling wet circles over them before making broad, firm strokes with the pad of his tongue.

"My God, woman, you are torturing me," he said as he sat back up on his thighs to look down at my swollen nipples as he continued to tease and tug them with his fingers.

With a tentative look in his eyes, he lowered his hands to where my kirtle gathered around my thighs and pressed his palms to my skin there, guiding my knees apart. While this wasn't my first time doing this, I should've been more nervous, yet something about Nick made me desperate for more of this…more of him.

"What is this?" he asked, breathing a light laugh as he frowned at the coif I'd tied over myself like a pair of panties.

A hot blush flashed across my cheeks. "There was no underwear in my room."

I pressed my hand to my mouth with embarrassment and nearly laughed as I realized how weird this invented fashion item must look to him.

"Underwear?" he repeated with a brow raised, but it was pretty clear what the word meant.

"Just in case the King of England tries to get into my pants," I deadpanned, and an adorable chuckle rumbled off his lips as he ran his palms up the inside of my thighs.

"Are you sure you wish not for the king to *get into your pants?*" he asked with a playful glint in his eye, smirking at me with that ridiculously sexy face of his. I just breathed a nervous laugh as he sat back on his knees between my legs and gazed down at me, making a needy tsk sound as my legs lay open. "Emmie, you have been put upon this earth to ruin me."

I blinked up at him with my heart pounding as he continued stroking my inner thighs, moving higher and higher until his fingertips skimmed the inner edges of the coif.

"I truly ought to stop," he said breathlessly as his fingers dipped beneath the line of fabric, brushing along my slick flesh. "You must tell me if you wish for me to stop."

"Don't stop," I said with a deep longing that inspired him to push my legs wider apart and press his thumb to my most sensitive spot over the coif, which was growing damper by the minute.

I moaned as he began making circles with his thumb, his pupils turning dark as he switched between watching my face and the spot where his hand lay. Keeping his thumb where it was, he tilted the base of his palm down and pressed the heel of his hand hard against my center, a groan bursting out of me as he rubbed it.

"Christ, Emmie, I need to touch you so sorely, but I must stop," he panted, suddenly pulling his hand away as my brows met in the middle.

"No, don't stop," I said, but a resolute look bled into the king's expression that I'd seen before, and there was no talking him out of anything once he'd made up his mind.

"I may be a king, but I am also a man of honor," he replied by way of explanation before turning away from me to rearrange his obvious arousal inside his pants.

I'd already agreed to be Nick's mistress, and I wasn't exactly sure what he was holding out for, but the last thing I wanted was to try to force him to touch me bare. Now that I'd decided to stay in Tudor England, I had all the time in the world to get closer to him, and I couldn't deny that there was some appeal to taking things slow. Plus, I hadn't yet told Nick that I was a virgin, and I wasn't quite sure what he'd think of it. I'd been doing my best to not think about the fact that he'd already slept with other unmarried women, like the mysterious Lucinda Parker that Alice had told me about. The idea of him with that girl made me jealous enough—there was no way I'd let my imagination spend any time on thoughts of what he was getting up to with Princess Henriette behind closed doors.

For the few days that followed, Nick and I returned to kissing like our lips were on fire and we needed each other's mouths to smother the flames away, but he didn't let his hands roam down my body again.

On day five, however, he was looking particularly gorgeous and entirely edible, and when I ran my tongue up the length of his neck and he groaned against me, I climbed up onto his thighs and straddled his body.

"My lady," he said breathlessly as his palms caught my waist and squeezed. "You ought not to do that."

"No?" I said as I rocked my hips against him, fisting my hands in my skirts and bunching them up until my coif-underwear was grinding against the thick ridge in his breeches.

"Emmie, stop," he said hotly as one of his hands snapped around my wrist.

But instead of pulling me off him, he pressed his length harder into me and rubbed himself against my core, making me cry out at the friction I'd never felt before. I followed my instincts and dragged my center up and down his swollen shaft, drawing a deep groan from the back of his throat as his fingers bit into my thighs.

My breath snagged in my chest as he wrapped his fingers in my hair and used it to tug my mouth down to his, stamping a hot and hungry kiss on my lips. Feeling him grinding against my throbbing core through the fabric of our clothes was unexplored territory for me, and yet my body responded by matching his movements with my own, drawing delicious, desperate moans from his mouth as ripples of heat washed through me.

I wanted more—to feel him bare—but when I dropped my hand and ran my palm up the length of him over the velvet before gripping him tightly, he gasped and caught my wrist again, this time stopping me.

"My lady, you are determined to bring my resolve to its limits, but we must stop." When my brow pinched, he brushed a soft fingertip down my cheek. "You must know I want you to the point of agony, but we need not act in haste. You mean so much to me that I must feel in my heart that I am not coercing you."

My palm met my forehead as I groaned through a smile. "You're not coercing me, believe me. If anything, you're making me extremely frustrated."

The look in his eyes made clear he didn't know what that word meant, but I just leaned forward to fold my arms around his neck and kissed him sweetly. If my Tudor king wanted to take things slow, then that's what was going to happen.

"I must cool myself down," he said as he buried his mouth in my neck, sweeping his lips over my skin before jerking his head back with a growl of frustration.

He climbed off the bed and held his hand down to me. "How

about I teach you how to play chess in an effort to return my mind to clarity? You did say that you were eager to learn."

My fingers slid into his palm. "Sure. If I can't undress you with my teeth right now, then I may as well learn how to beat you at your own game."

Heat flared in his eyes as he looked down at me through a blush, but he made no move to return to the bed.

With a contented sigh, I got up and trailed him into the drawing-room while straightening my kirtle with my other hand.

How many days had I been here now? I knew Mom would surely come looking for my mysterious health retreat if I stayed much longer, but I couldn't bring myself to go home just yet. In eighteen years, I couldn't remember being this happy.

Then came Nick's bombshell, halfway through our chess game.

"Emmie, I have decided not to make our union known until after Henriette is with child, which I pray is soon. Forgive me." His bishop captured my knight.

Pain ricocheted through my chest at the thought of him getting Henriette pregnant. "I'm sorry. Do you mean forgive you for making babies with the Pearl of France, or forgive you for taking my knight?"

"Again?"

"Let me get this straight." I slid my rook sideways with trembling fingers. "You can get married and impregnate your wife, but I'm not even allowed to tell my friends about us until you say so—especially Alice Grey, apparently."

He made a face at the board. "Emmie, your queen could have had my king in the check position."

I stood up and grabbed my shoes. "She's all yours."

19

I COULDN'T GET WARM IN MY ROOM THAT NIGHT, CHILLED TO THE bone at the thought of Nick and Henriette together and what might be happening between them. But I had to trust Nick's promise to me that Henriette was little more to him than the other half of a marriage alliance that would give England the power it needed over Spain.

I also hated acting like those jealous girls who ranted on social media. I never thought I'd become one. It didn't help that I missed hot showers, and peanut butter, and the friends who knew my secrets. Except this one, of course. Nick was the one secret I couldn't share with anyone except Mathew Fox. But in the short chats Mathew and I had had outside the king's quarters lately, all he talked about were religious alliances that confused me.

I filled the next morning watching a hideous cockfight with Alice that I wished I could un-see. We'd planned a walk after lunch, but the king summoned me again, so I had no choice but to tell her I wasn't feeling well.

I waited for Nick in his bedroom, my legs crossed over the woven rush matting with my back against the bed. I felt like an idiot for storming out during our chess game. I'd already accepted Nick's terms about Henriette, and then I'd lost my shit over it.

But I knew I'd feel a lot better if I could just go home for a day. Tell Mom I was moving to London sooner than expected, which wasn't exactly untrue. Becoming Nick's mistress meant staying here most of the time, but there was no way I was giving up my home forever. He'd already agreed to me trying to manage both. It was crazy to think I could be a twenty-first-century jewelry designer *and* a Tudor king's mistress, but sanity had left the station a long time ago.

"Christ, what has happened now?" Nick said from the doorway. A manservant gently removed his hat and Nick raked a hand through his disheveled hair, his eyes on me.

"Nothing, I was cogitating," I replied. "I've always wanted to use that word. I had no idea it was this old; I heard the Earl of Shrewsbury say it this morning."

I drank in the sight of him dressed in black leather, a white shirt with silver thread peeking from the collar. I still couldn't believe he was mine.

And Henriette's.

"Your displeasure is remedied," he observed, relief creeping into his solemn expression.

"If that means I'm not mad anymore then you'd be correct," I said, suddenly unable to meet his eyes. "I'm going to try harder."

He just looked at me, his face softening.

"How was the slaughter-fest?" I asked, lightening the mood.

Two servants peeled off his thigh-length coat. "Lord Russell was mauled by a bloodhound."

"Yikes."

"Norris says he'll be fine."

He waved the servants away. When they shut the oaken doors behind them, he crawled down onto his knees and stamped his lips to mine. I responded immediately, my fingers digging into his hair and tugging him closer.

But, now that we were alone, I needed to confess everything that'd been on my mind or it would chew up my insides.

My words poured out in a rush as I cupped his jaw in my hands. "I think I want to go home tonight. Just for a day or two. To see Mom...Ruby. A warm shower would be nice. I think that's why I flew off the handle yesterday; I need to get back. Just for a bit."

For a moment, he looked stunned. Then he sat back on his knees and dragged me into his lap until I was straddling him. "I've neglected you today," he said, hooking a loose strand of my hair behind my ear. "Forgive me, I was anxious that you needed solitude." Our faces were so close that our lips drew together again like magnets in a short, soft kiss that left my mouth tingling. It was hard not to take more, especially while my thighs were parted over his hips like this. But Nick had more on his mind.

"I hoped you would come to Robin House with me this night," he said, blinking nervously. "We can dine there, sleep, and return in the morning. I have already asked Mathew Fox to make the preparations. Unless you would rather go home."

My eyes popped. "You're serious?"

The tenderness in his face sent a rush of heat to my cheeks as he leaned forward to kiss me. "Never more," he said against my lips.

The worn house with the pitched roof was even more modest on the inside, but Nick's shoulders relaxed the moment his boots hit the floorboards. When he draped his coat over the chair and leaned his sword against the circular dining table, it hit me. Apart from the guards patrolling outside, we were totally alone, which had to be a pretty massive step for him.

He took my hand, the pinkish sky through the leaded window making his eyes appear greener. He pulled, but I was already moving. His lips were warm and soft, his palms cupping my cheeks. He moved his tongue against mine and my fingers rushed to his face, caressing him, before landing on the grooves of his scar. Our lips detached as he pulled away.

"Was it jousting?" I asked softly.

He faced the fire with a hand on his hip, taking a moment to answer. "It was Clinton Radcliffe. My tutor when my father died."

He fiddled with a tinderbox and crouched to light the charred logs. "I was not yet a man, but I can remember as clear as yesterday the first time he struck me when he asked me a question in French and I responded in English."

I moved closer to him, but he wouldn't look at me. "But you were the king," I said. "How could he get away with that?"

"I was also a child, a frightened one, and Radcliffe was no fool. He struck me in places that would not leave a mark and poisoned my ears about my illegitimate mother and loutish father. When I turned thirteen, he instructed me to translate a passage from Latin to Spanish and I struggled. He whipped me so hard that my cheek split open."

"Nick."

I'd imagined the source of the scar so differently. I wanted to punch Clinton Radcliffe in the face.

He strode to the table, pouring wine from a flask. "He told the Council I had tripped on the staircase and was fortunate to be alive. They praised him. Only when I came of age did I understand I did not have to listen to him anymore. I never had to. It was the first thing Thomas Grey taught me. When he learned the truth, he counseled me to have Radcliffe hung, drawn, and quartered, which he was, but not before I'd had him tortured for hours. He couldn't even walk onto the scaffold, his legs were so broken."

Nick downed the entire cup of wine in one go. "See, Emmie?" he said bleakly. "I have a monster in me."

I caught his wrist, stopping him from pouring more. "No," I said. "You lost your parents when you were a child, only to be surrounded by people you barely knew who wanted to control you. You had too much love from people who didn't matter and not enough from those who did." I tenderly stroked his face, pulling him closer to press my lips to his scar. "But not anymore."

234

After dinner, I sat on the edge of the small four-poster bed, untying my shoes while Nick closed the window shutters. I squeezed my stomach muscles to quell the butterfly storm brewing at the thought of spending an entire night with him in the same bed. It wasn't like we hadn't done some fooling around already, but how far would he want to take things tonight while we were alone?

"So you don't mind if I go home?" I blurted, filling the nervousness in the air and wondering if I should untie my bodice. "Not right now, obviously."

He spun to face me and cleared his throat, tossing his shirt over a chair and giving me a clear view of his muscled chest. "You should go whenever you please. I will be torn to pieces until you return, but I will wait, for the rest of my days if that is what it takes."

I stood up, bringing my hand to his bare shoulder. "Nick."

He pressed his palm over my fingers, his forehead lining. "Something has changed in me. I have never known such uncertainty, such fear. I should not have told you that about Radcliffe. About the torture."

"You know that's not why I want to go home."

He dropped onto the bed and sighed as I sat beside him. "I missed you this day while I was hunting," he said, looking away from me. "I missed you last night when we parted. I missed you every time before that and every time since. The thought of you going so far away is agony for me." He ran a hand down his face. "I am cursed with loss, Emmie. It is a shadow over my soul that is always with me. If I lose you, too, I—"

My mouth silenced his anguish, my lips parting in invitation. Our kiss caught fire immediately as my tongue glided against his, eliciting a sigh from him that made me clutch his face and draw him closer. I melted into his sweet taste as we fell onto the bed, our mouths uniting with equal parts ferociousness and adoration. He separated his lips from mine and began kissing me all over my face like he couldn't get enough of me, his fingers threading through my hair and his tongue devouring my neck.

"Nick," I breathed, fisting the back of his hair before he clamped his mouth to mine again and sucked on my tongue until I moaned.

"God, Emmie, I want you so much," he gasped, pulling me up to a seated position and twisting me around to face the headboard while his fingers worked frantically on my bodice. My heart was thumping against my ribs, but as nervous as I was, the last thing I wanted was for him to stop.

When he'd unlaced me, he peeled the embroidered fabric down off my shoulders and skimmed his fingers beneath the loose collar of my smock before replacing them with his mouth. I sighed as he ran his tongue across my neck before he guided my arms upward and tugged the smock over my head, my exposed nipples hardening in the cool air. He wrapped his arms around me from behind, enveloping me in warmth, before he caught my chin in his hand and turned my face back to his, his lips landing on mine.

After a deep and hungry kiss, he kept his chest pressed to my back and nuzzled the curve of my neck, sending shivers of electricity through me. He curled his arms around me to stroke and tug the peaks of my breasts, my needy moans encouraging him to keep going as he glided his tongue over my neck again.

I needed more—to touch him—so I shifted around to face my body to his, finding his eyes foggy with desire as his gaze slid down to my bare chest. He took my breasts in his hands and squeezed, his lips parting as his eyes flicked back up to mine. For a moment, we just stared at each other, a rush of affection coloring his cheeks. When he smiled at me with a glowy look in his eyes, my chest felt like it could burst open, and I rushed forward to press my mouth to his, kissing him like it was the last time I ever would.

After I pulled back for air, his lips began a trail of kisses down my neck and chest until he captured one of my nipples in his mouth. He resettled himself on the bed so he could get comfortable while he licked and sucked both sides of me while I ran my fingers through his rose-scented hair, held captive by the sensation of his mouth on my skin.

I want to touch you," I whispered, and he looked up at me with his lips still closed over my nipple, the heated look in his eyes making me wish I had a camera to photograph this moment.

He released my breast from his mouth but replaced it with his hands, giving me room to slide my palms down his bare chest, feeling every hard curve before I ran my fingers across the ripples of his toned abs. His hands had also traveled further down my body, but before he could touch me where I needed him most, I wanted my own turn.

My gaze slipped down to the thick swell pressing against his breeches, and something about that sight wet my mouth as I shifted closer to him and ran my palm up his hard length. He inhaled sharply as I stroked him harder over the fabric, clutching his thick shape and finding the tip with my fingers. I fumbled with the strings at his waist, and he breathed a chuckle and helped me untie them until there was enough of a gap for me to slide my hand inside. Nick groaned as I gripped him bare, my eyes drooping with lust as I savored the feeling of his skin that was satiny-soft yet hard as stone. I ran my fingers over his tip, loving how vulnerable this Tudor king looked as he bit down on his bottom lip and hissed through his teeth as I rubbed him. I yanked at his breeches until he got the hint and slid them down his legs, kicking them off as my hand returned to his length. I closed my fingers around him and ran my fist up and down his solid thickness, his breathless moans like music to my ears. I could've done this all night long, my hand sliding tightly up and down, but when I increased my speed, Nick gripped my wrist to still my movements.

"Emmie, stop, or I will come," he said in a rough voice.

My lips fell open. "You know that word?" I asked with genuine surprise.

He just smirked and nodded before catching my face in his palms and lifting my mouth to his. We kissed hotly until he broke free to slide his hand beneath the skirts piling around my thighs.

"May I touch you?" he breathed, the neediness in his face making me even more desperate for him.

"Yes," I replied in an aching voice, bunching up my skirts to expose my coif-underwear. Nick caressed his fingers up my inner thigh, his other hand pushing my legs apart so I was wider open for him. A shy blush heated my cheeks, but I stayed in that position, watching Nick's eyes flare with heat as he dragged his fingers up the seam of my flesh over my underwear. I groaned and let my legs fall further apart as he began circling my most sensitive spot through the wet fabric.

"Do you like that?" he asked thickly, and my reply was another breathless moan. I was dying for him to touch me bare, and when he sank two fingers beneath the coif and brushed them against my slick folds, I clawed at the sheets beneath me.

"How may I remove this damned coif?" he said, tugging at it, and a laugh tumbled from my lips as I sat up to untie the cloth diaper I'd created for myself. When I peeled it off my soaking skin, Nick murmured a sound of pleasure as he pushed my thighs apart to open me up in his gaze. "God, Emmie, you are more beautiful than can be said."

He grazed two fingers up the length of my core before pressing his thumb to that perfect spot between my thighs. My hand returned to his cock as he began rubbing me with the perfect amount of pressure. He was so hard in my fingers that I felt like he could burst, and I squeezed and stroked him until he sank a finger deep inside me, stealing all the attention I had to give. My hips bucked off the bed, my body adjusting to the feeling.

"You are so tight," Nick whispered hotly, his brow creasing.

An initial tinge of pain was quickly replaced with a swell of breathtaking pleasure as he moved his finger inside me, stretching my core. Watching my expression to make sure I was okay, he added a second finger, and I lost my grip on him as my head lolled back beneath the weight of ecstasy. He twisted two fingers up inside me to the base of his knuckles, rubbing a spot deep inside me that made me feel like I could explode into a million pieces. When I moaned hard and my hips lifted off the mattress, he gripped my ass with his other hand, driving it down to push his fingers deeper into me.

He was panting as much as I was, enjoying this as much as I, and he leaned back and watched my expression as he began pumping his fingers in and out of me, letting go of my ass so he could stroke my clit with his other hand.

"I want you to come on me," he said in a raspy voice as both his hands worked me until my cries of pleasure filled the air, bringing me closer and closer to release. A hot, bubbling wave of liquid grew inside me with gradual force until it suddenly crested and crashed over me in a torrent of euphoria, washing pleasure through every cell in my body while Nick brought his mouth to mine and kissed me through my climax.

He seemed reluctant to stop touching me and continued gliding his fingers over my tingling flesh while murmuring sounds of satisfaction. But I was so sensitive after that mind-blowing finish that I had to catch his hand and gently shift it away. A playful chuckle tumbled off his lips into mine, and I kissed him silent, still wanting to pinch myself that I was in bed with this incredible man.

I was aware that Nick was still hard, and when I went to grip him in my hand, he moved to crawl over me instead. A seductive, suggestive look flickered in his eyes as he grinded his hips against mine, evidently past the point now of wanting to take things slow. *Ohmygod. He wants to have sex. Right now.*

Panic tore through me, and I froze beneath him, my eyes blinking fast. He caught the look on my face and suddenly stopped, rolling onto his back.

"Forgive me," he said, doing that 'I need to cool down' exhale again. "I presume you have never…"

"No. I'm late for everything." I was redder than a fire engine, but he looked relieved at that answer.

"How old were you?" I mumbled as I twisted to face him, my stomach as hard as a rock. "The first time."

He dropped his lips to my shoulder. "Too young. Women seem to throw themselves at kings, and young men lack the restraint to resist."

A question caught in my throat that I was desperate to ask but was equally terrified of the answer. Yet, the question flew off my lips. "Have you with Princess Henriette?"

He sighed as his gaze dropped down. "Certainly not. We are not yet wedded."

But it's okay to sleep with me out of wedlock?

Instead of saying those words aloud that pinched my heart, I asked the question in a different way. "But you weren't wedded to Lucinda Parker when you were with her."

He pulled back a little, his brows meeting in the middle. "Where did you learn that name?" When I didn't answer, he brushed his fingertips back and forth over a freckle on my arm. "You need not worry about Mistress Parker."

"But you got her pregnant, right?" The words were coming too fast for me to stop them.

Nick's brow pinched with confusion.

"*With child?*" I explained.

A flash of annoyance crossed his face. I didn't want to ruin the moment, but as I watched his fingers nervously playing with my arm, I knew why I couldn't let this go. What made me any different from Lucinda Parker? If I got pregnant with Nick's child…I shifted uneasily, and a moment of gladness rippled through me that I hadn't let him have his way with me just now. Especially given the lack of contraception in this time period.

After releasing a long breath, he spoke quietly. "After I learned that Mistress Parker was with child, I discovered I was not the only man to enter her bed. Furthermore, the time was not exact. Thus, I did not believe the child was mine, and I chose not to pursue it."

"But you did sleep with her, even though you weren't wedded. Then she was going to have a baby, and you sent her away."

He tilted my chin up, his eyes drilling into mine. "This is not the same thing."

"Why not?"

"You know why not." The softness in his eyes echoed his voice. "Because I love you."

I reached up to touch his hand that stroked my face. "For now."

The insecure comment was beyond embarrassing, but it infected the air like a virus anyway.

Nick expelled a heavy sigh and gently rubbed my back. "Let us go to sleep."

A crease formed on my brow as I glanced down. "But you haven't…"

"Oh, Emmie, worry not about that." With a blush, he grabbed his nightshirt and tugged it over his head, his dimpled smile sending a clear message that we were all good here.

I tossed my loose smock back over my shoulders and climbed into his arms. He blew out the candle, washing the room in the soft glow of the dying fire. Rain pattered gently on the window, lulling me to unconsciousness. Despite the uncomfortable conversation about Lucinda Parker that had dumped a bucket of iced water over our heated make-out session, lying beside Nick gave me the warmest, deepest sleep I'd ever had.

In the morning, I woke up alone and pressed my forehead to the foggy window. Nick was down in the garden, tearing leaves off rose bushes and hacking away dead branches with his dagger. I watched him until he looked up as if he'd heard me there. The happiness in his eyes as he smiled made me melt.

We ate breakfast on the grass, starlings pecking at our bread-crumbs. Nick tossed them more, his hair still messed up, his cream shirt open at the neck. My whole body hummed with bliss.

"Can we stay here today?" I asked, thinking back to that bedchamber upstairs and how Nick had felt beneath my fingers.

He finished off his boiled egg. "I'm afraid I cannot, my lady. There are problems with the new draperies' passage to the East. I should really have attended to it last night."

Within an hour, we were in a coach back to Whitehall, both his arms locked around me and our fingers intertwined like we couldn't get close enough to each other.

When we approached the King's Gate portcullis, he drew the curtain closed and turned to me, a nervous look brimming in his eyes. "You are not going away?" he asked, clearly referring to the twenty-first century.

I smiled. "Not today."

He pressed a kiss to my lips that was soft and lingering before bringing his mouth to my ear. "I already miss you," he whispered, lowering his hand to rub small circles into my lower back. My heart burned with the heat of a thousand suns.

As soon as Nick's heels hit the dust, he was surrounded by a huddle of attendants and guards. Thomas Grey spoke in his ear, pulling him far from the coach swathed in royal-blue velvet and up into the Gothic arches of the Palace of Whitehall.

Out of nowhere, the truth slammed into me like a gut-punch. Nick Tudor had everything he wanted: his kingdom, his sister safe and well, his royal fiancée, and me…his dirty little secret who'd literally given up the whole world for him.

20

It wasn't until I was back inside the castle that I heard the gossip. Isobel Beaumont had been arrested near the border of Scotland. With Kit's kidnapping still under wraps, Lady Ascot and her friends were having too much fun guessing why. They were way off the mark, accusing Isobel of everything from terminating a pregnancy to witchcraft. While I strolled down the long gallery toward the pheasant yard, I shuddered at what might happen to her. Maybe Alice would have more info.

I'd almost reached the north wing when Princess Henriette sauntered past me with her graceful gait. My silk slippers met her embroidered pumps beneath the wall of maps.

"Your Grace," I mumbled politely, my cheeks on fire.

She stopped, her spicy perfume irritating my throat. "I have not seen you in here before. I walk here every day. To see how England interprets the world." Her onyx eyes landed on the painting of Henry the Eighth at the Field of the Cloth of Gold.

"They're incredible paintings," I acknowledged uneasily.

"Oh, we have many like these at my homes," she replied. "Rooms of them." She snapped at her ladies in French. They curtsied and left us. "Come, you may take this walk with me."

Uh, okay.

We strolled back the way I'd already come while she commented on each artwork. My stomach tangled. Was this her attempt at an apology?

My question slipped out. "You know I didn't write that horrible note, right? I'd never do that."

"I know. It was that devil Isobel Beaumont." Henriette paused at a painting of a fleet of warships atop a whirling sea. She fingered the diamond galleon brooch pinned to her midnight-blue gown. "I admire this painting. It makes me think of His Majesty." Her finger moved to the square emerald sitting in the small cleft of my cleavage. "Tell me, did you receive this from His Majesty also?"

My throat clanged shut, my cheeks filling with heat.

"I know you keep friendship with him," Henriette said steadily. "I know he was away from Whitehall last night and so were you. I have more eyes in this court than in my own." Her scarlet lips moved to my ear, hissing. "I see what you do. But I tell you, I will not leave."

I stepped backward. "I don't know what you're talking about."

"Did he tell you he give me this letter?" She pulled a folded piece of paper from her bodice.

"You live in the same building, and he wrote you a letter?" I quipped, my chest burning.

She held it out to me. Both her commanding presence and a sickening curiosity made me take it and start reading.

Henriette, my queen of hearts.
Your gracious companionship during these difficult days has kept me afloat. In a time of such heartache, you have healed mine. You are a flower in bloom, which I long to nurture to all its beauty.
Thank you for staying and warming my court with your smile of pure sunshine. I will think of you when we are apart, and gaze upon you with affection when we are together. When we cannot be, let this ship be a symbol of our union. A safe passage between our two worlds.
Your most loving,
Nicholas R.

I handed the paper back to her like it was on fire, my eyes clinging to the glittering brooch on her bust. A symbol of their two worlds. Because clearly France was more of a freaking obstacle to overcome than twenty-first century America.

"I cannot blame you for loving him," said Henriette, and a bizarre moment of understanding passed between us. But then her icy tone grabbed me by the throat. "When I am queen, however, you understand why I will not choose you as a maid of honour. Therefore, there is no reason for you to stay here at court."

"It's okay," I said coolly, hiding the throb in my heart. "I have a reason."

She moved like lightning, and her nail tore my neck, sending a hiss through my teeth. I grabbed my burning skin, blood wetting my fingertips. Henriette was clutching my emerald necklace, her black eyes venomous spiders as she tossed the priceless stone to the ground and stormed past me.

I slid down the paneled wall at the end of the gallery, holding my chest as if that might protect it from the hideous, twisting pain.

My queen of hearts.

Your smile of pure sunshine.

Your most loving.

"Mistress Grace?" Thomas Grey's black cloak swished down the last few stairs behind me.

Shit. What does he want? I stood up, sniffling.

A flash of sympathy crossed his face before he offered me a handkerchief that smelled like plums. "I was about to take dinner in my library. Would you care to accompany me?"

"Me? Thanks, but I'm…I'm not hungry." *What's with everyone today?*

"I must insist," he said with the authority of a school principal. "I was planning on calling upon you this afternoon. This way, if you please."

He gestured toward the stairwell and I dragged my feet after him, my stomach tightening with thoughts over what this could be about.

Thomas's upstairs study was surprisingly meager, most of the space consumed by an oak dining table wedged beside a desk littered with scrolls, quills, ink pots, and cups. Even though I felt like I'd swallowed a flock of seagulls, the modest spread of cured meats, cheeses, bread, and meatballs looked appetizing.

He flipped a cloth over his lap. "I have not yet had the opportunity to thank you for your part in my acquittal."

I must've looked confused.

"His Majesty listens to you because of his lust for you," Thomas explained. "Pass the cheese, if you please?"

I held the plate out, trying to keep it steady. "I'm not sure I had much of a hand in anything, but I'm glad you're back," I replied honestly. "For Alice's sake."

He bit into a meatball, his pale eyes fixed to me. "You have become close with His Majesty in a short time, but I have known our gallant king since he was a babe. I was the first of Queen Elizabeth's councilors to meet him. I still recall much of those days...he was always the sweetest child." Thomas's face warmed as he chewed, but my body remained stiff. While the thought of baby Nick made my stomach flutter, the reminiscing from Thomas Grey, of all people, was unnerving.

He continued, a glob of cheese jammed in the corner of his mouth. "Shortly before the king's father went to God, he gave him a rather modest gift. It was a cup with a string attached and a ball on the end. You had to swing the handle and catch the ball in the cup. It was more difficult than it sounds, and we all had turns. It took His Majesty a week to conquer it, and when he did, you could not get that thing off him. Until the day he received his first chessboard and he dumped that silly cup, never to pick it up again."

Thomas took a large swig of wine, letting me digest the story until it clicked.

"You're saying I'm the cup," I said.

He tilted backward and blinked at me as if I'd impressed him. Then he began rooting around in his desk behind him, digging out a black pouch. It dragged with weight when he slid it to me. There were more gold coins inside than I could count.

"I understand your family is not without means, but I pray you consider this compensation," he said not unkindly.

"For what?"

When he didn't answer, I stared at the pouch, my heart slicing. "You mean for leaving."

Thomas stopped chewing. "You are nobody's fool, Mistress Grace." He placed his worn fingers on the table, reaching out. "I know you care for him as a wife cares for a husband. But, my dear, he is not a man, he is a king. He has been married since he was twelve… to England. And because England must have an indisputable heir, he will soon marry the Princess of France, and you will remain nothing more than——"

"The king's whore," I finished, my vision blurring with tears. "So you've said."

He sighed heavily. "Are you not troubled that Spain is on our doorstep?"

"Of course I am." I shrugged helplessly. "I love him."

"You both demonstrate your devotion," he said gently. "And it is a very real love, only a fool could not see it. But His Majesty is not writing a sonnet, he is ruling a kingdom. Any mistake he makes is another arrow in the bows of his enemies. If the Tudor dynasty tumbles, the Catholics will return in numbers you cannot imagine. The reformation will be utterly destroyed."

"But I've already told him he can marry Princess Henriette. I won't stand in his way."

Thomas tapped the table, the ruby on his finger like a swollen raspberry. "Have you seen what is happening in the inner courtyard?"

When I shook my head, he rose. "Let us go."

My once-quiet courtyard near the horse yard had become a hive of shouting and swinging planks as men hoisted timber frames, laying the foundations for a new building. Thomas and I hung back under the archway.

"His Majesty is building a new pleasure house for Princess Henriette's favorite recreations," Thomas explained. "Billiard tables, a French theater, a ballet stage…did he tell you this?" When my fingers rubbed my quivering lips, he changed his question. "And what will he give you, Mistress Grace? The people's scorn?"

"Please stop," I said, my voice choked.

Thomas turned to me, compassion clouding his eyes. "I say this not to wound you, but to convince you. Forgive me for speaking plainly. Do you comprehend how quickly the king will tire of you? When his sons are born to Henriette, you will fade into their shadows. You have seen how he feels about family. He will send you away to a manor far from here, to be summoned only when he pleases. Is that what you want at such a ripe age? You will never be permitted to marry another, nor to have children of your own. If the king should grant you children himself, they will spend their lives running from death. They may not succeed. Besides, let us not forget his bountiful allure, of which he has a great deal too much for a king. He could have any woman in Christendom in his bed, and many will try. Most of your own ladies, you can be sure of that. Do you believe he will be able to resist them as you become older and they younger?" Thomas's expression was grave. "My dear, the only woman in the world unhappier than the wife of a king is the mistress of a king."

Tears spilled from my eyes. "Please stop," I said. "I get it."

He returned the pouch to my hand, closing my fingers around the worn velvet. "Allow me to feel I have offered you something in return for your loss, however insufficient. I do hope you will believe me when I say that I am truly sorry for your loss."

Thomas's eyes held mine, the despair over his missing wife reflected in his face before he went to leave.

"Will you tell Alice about us?" I asked, my question halting his red slippers.

"That is not my business, Mistress Grace. England is."

I tossed and turned all night, Thomas's words exploding in my ears like gunshots.

Do you comprehend how quickly the king will tire of you?

He could have any woman in Christendom in his bed, and many will try.

The only woman in the world unhappier than the wife of a king is the mistress of a king.

It was long past breakfast when I lugged myself out of bed. My knotted hair hung loose as I wandered toward the kitchens, needing water. I didn't want to see anyone in my state, but Alice spotted me near the court's entrance.

She sidestepped a swarm of aristocrats rushing to the courtyard. "There you are," she said to me.

"What's happening?" I asked, keeping my face tilted down to hide my puffy eyes.

"The French marriage commissioners have arrived. The king's betrothal is becoming official!" She grabbed my hand and tugged me outside, weaving through the horde of nobles to the front of the pack where Lord Lansbury was handling crowd control.

Coaches draped in velvet and satin were lined up in the courtyard. Ladies in jeweled caps and men with mustaches stepped out of them in orchestrated sequence.

"Who are they?" I asked.

"Ladies and gentlemen of the French court, cooks, servants, hand-maidens, anyone you can think of," Alice replied. "Father said there will be a celebration during the Midsummer's Eve feast on Sunday. I do hope you arranged that frock!"

Henriette emerged from the final coach to thunderous applause. She did a little circle, waving her ruby-red gloves, every part the serene queen and nothing like the girl who'd drawn blood from my neck with her fingernails.

When she dropped into a deep curtsy, I knew the king would appear at any moment. The crowds separated around us as Nick strode right past Alice and I, stunningly dressed in gleaming gold and black, before bending at the knee to kiss Henriette's hand. He didn't so much as glance at me.

Instead, he raised Henriette's arm to the sky. "May I present Her Royal Highness, Henriette of France, your next Queen of England!"

he cried. Palms pounded together, and Nick's heart-stopping smile made Henriette blush like a doting schoolgirl.

I pictured Kit standing between them with her red Elizabethan hair and wise eyes, completing the new dynasty of Western Europe. The jealousy that spread through my body felt malignant. Without thinking, I pushed past puffed sleeves and hooped skirts to get back inside. When I reached a quiet corridor, Alice—who had followed me —spun me around, gaping at my tears. "What is it?" she breathed.

I could only shake my head, wishing my fairytale gown would fall right through the stone floor. What stupid fantasy was I living? Why had I ever thought I could be happy just being the mistress of the man I loved?

Alice walked me to the corner where the violinists often played. "You are not pleased," she said with a confused frown. Her warm eyes were so alarmed, so disarming, I could feel my resilience cracking. I gritted my teeth. "Emmie, you are frightening me," Alice pressed.

Nick entered down the hall with Henriette and her entourage of officials while Francis halted the outside crowd.

"Francis Beaumont is in love with you," I announced to Alice, wanting to slap myself. "He's being stubborn as a mule, but I'm telling you, he's mad about you."

Her face puckered. "What in the high heavens?"

The words raced out. "I shouldn't be the one to say it, but I think it's why he didn't marry Violet."

She looked like she'd doused herself in Isobel's white face powder. "But I do not understand. You are weeping."

"It's because I…I like him," I said, the bald-faced lie a final nail in my coffin. I'd lied so much to Alice Grey that I didn't deserve the time she'd given me. "But I'll get over it, I swear." My eyes moved to Nick as he shared a laugh with Henriette, his hand pressed to the small of her back. I looked back at Alice, biting away tears. She was glaring at Francis.

I clutched her hands. "Alice, no…don't blame him. I promise you, none of it is his fault. He proposed to Violet because he thought it would make *you* happy. And he's never led me on here; he's always had eyes for you. You just can't see it."

Alice tipped back on her heels, like she might faint.

I squeezed her fingers to reinforce my words. "Francis is a good guy, and he's still a free man. If any part of you feels the same way, you have to go for it before it's too late. If it's really what you want."

Her mouth widened. "But *Francis?* He is like my brother. Everything he does vexes me." But her eyes were bright, searching. "And Father would never approve, he despises Francis."

I took her hands. "Trust me on this. There will be a day when girls don't need their father's permission to marry, and if anyone deserves to kick off the women's movement, it's Alice freaking Grey."

I stole one more glance at Nick. He was looking right at me, the smile slipping off his face.

I quickly turned back to Alice. "I have to go," I said, my aching heart ripping at the sides. I flung my arms around her, squeezing. "I love you. More than you know. Please think about what I said."

When I arrived at the horse yard, a groom fetched Stella at my request. The despair in my bones made it hard to mount her without slipping. Mathew Fox ran out from the stable yard, clasping a leather horsewhip.

"You are riding out alone?" He looked at the sky.

"Just for some air." I rubbed Stella's neck as she neighed. "There's big stuff happening inside. Don't you need to be there?"

He waved his whip at the stable. "The French coach horses are arriving. I'm to greet them all with great dignity."

He stepped closer and a sad smile touched his face. "Oh, Mistress Grace, all is not lost. We knew this would happen. Being the king's mistress is, in some ways, a more favorable position. I hadn't really considered it until now. Do not believe this to be the end of the road."

"I think it is." Hot tears stung my eyes. "I know you care so much about your country—your king—and that's amazing and noble. But this is my heart, Mathew, my life… and he's taking it from me. He's turning me into something I don't want to be."

Saying the words out loud made me realize how true they were. It crushed me to my core.

Mathew's elfish face was etched with worry, a leather bridle twisting in his fingers.

"I've told the king how brilliant you are," I said to him, patting Stella to steady her. "How much you care. If he's half as clever as you, he'll see you as I do."

"You are a gracious woman, mistress." Mathew bowed at me.

"Just promise me one thing," I added shakily. "Please look out for Princess Catherine. I've never seen Nick so protective of anyone or anything. Keep Kit safe, or I guarantee that your gracious king will totally fall apart, and it will be far worse than you know." My knuckles brushed my eyes, catching tears. "Say goodbye for me? Please...I can't."

Mathew squared his fragile shoulders, his face brooding. I kicked my boot into Stella's gut, riding her across the moat bridge and deep into the Parkside.

It took a few wrong turns to find the correct spot by the overgrown lake. I hopped off Stella's back, noticing that the scattered flowers crawling with ladybugs had grown taller. There was no trace left of my blood from when I'd been skewered by the arrow. This time, I was hemorrhaging on the inside.

"Never change, you beautiful thing," I whispered into Stella's side, my tears darkening her coarse coat.

I slipped the blue-diamond ring onto my thumb and lay down on the nest of green blades. The sun warmed my seeping eyes as I pressed them shut.

And with my heart bleeding out onto the lush English earth that I was four hundred years too late for, I waited for sleep.

21

I woke in Nick's bed. The silhouette of his chestnut curls crossed the candlelight, his face flushed with affection as he hovered over me, his palms pressed to the mattress...

Light sliced the image, my sluggish eyes drawn to the source. Lines of moonlight materialized around the edges of my alphabet blinds. Ruby lay slouched over my feet.

Not Nick's bed. Mine.

My lungs collapsed, my hands balling into tight fists. After frantically swapping my crushed cinnamon gown for a T-shirt, I crawled back into bed and waited, knees to chest, for the grief hurtling toward my heart. It took only seconds to arrive.

I was still crying convulsively into my pillow when the front door banged shut just after 7 A.M. I met Mom at the top of the stairs. She grabbed the railing to stop herself from tumbling backward, before she ran up and hugged me. I cried into her shoulder, my tears soaking her shirt that smelled like disinfectant.

"Oh Emmie," she said, running her hand up and down my back. Her voice was hoarse. "You're making me sick from worry."

"I'm okay, Mom. I'm home. I'm so sorry." I squeezed tighter.

For a while she just held me, stroking my back as I wept, the saltwater flushing some of the swollen grief that had clogged my insides like mud.

"You need to tell me what's going on," said Mom, pulling away to rest her hands on my shoulders. "Why you took off… Who this boy is that has you so upset you missed graduation?" She pressed her eyes like she was in pain.

My stomach tightened with dread. "Did they kick me out?"

She sighed, stepping past me and undoing her top button. "No. I already spoke to the school. Thankfully, you were a good student until now."

"I was never a good student."

I followed her into her bedroom and flopped onto her jersey comforter. "But thank you for doing that. I'm glad I graduated."

She sat beside me to slip off her shoes. "Do you know how many health centers I called in Connecticut? I never knew you were into all that. Where in heaven's name did you go?"

I swallowed, my throat raw. "In the end, I was further away than that."

She slid her hand down my back. "Were you with that boy? Nick, is that his name?"

My voice caught in my throat. "Yes."

She sighed at her thighs. "I can't believe I haven't even met him. Is this what it's like to have an adult daughter? I'm never going to know where on earth you are or who you're with?" She looked at me, her brow crumpling. "And can I gather from the look on your face that you and this Nick person are no longer together?"

I could barely say the words. "We're not. I broke up with him."

Is it really a breakup if you abandon him without warning after you'd promised you wouldn't?

Mom's fingers took mine. "I want to be angry with you, but I can't. Cookie, you look so sad. You've got to snap out of this, okay? Disappearing to chase some boy before you've even finished high school?" She squeezed my hand tightly. "I gave you that money so you could start your future. Not to waste it on someone you won't even remember in a year."

I looked at her, feeling the words slap me across the face. "Spot on, Mom. That's exactly what I'm going to do."

When she stood up, I called after her. "Did you tell Dad?"

She stopped in the doorway, her voice low. "No. Quite frankly, Emmie, if your father wants to know where you are, all he has to do is ask."

I nodded, glad to finally hear her say that, but despair crawled back into my stomach like nausea.

I missed Nick Tudor so much.

The river was tranquil early in the evening, when the kayakers and boaters had stopped ruffling its skin. I squeezed the blue-diamond ring so tightly it nearly pierced my palm. With Jane Stuart gone, there was nowhere else to put it without risking using it again.

And I couldn't. I could never face Nick again, not that he'd ever forgive me.

What had he done when he'd realized I'd left? Was he wild with anger? Choked with heartbreak or even...relieved?

My heart buckled with my knees, and I hit the ground.

After thinking about it so many times, the way it happened was a stunning anticlimax. I inched toward the sloped foreshore, stretched my trembling arm over the midnight-blue ripples, and let go. The silky blackness ate the ring in seconds.

And then my tears burst past the seams of my eyelids as I fell forward and sobbed into my knees.

Despite Mia's heroic efforts to cheer me up with feel-good playlists and clips of baby animals taking baths, every morning I woke up feeling like a monster was pinned to my back. Mia joked that I was banned from the post-graduation school fair so I wouldn't feel bad if I chose to stay away, but truthfully, I wanted to go. I didn't want to be alone any more than I had to be.

When we got there, Josh waved us over from the soccer field. He'd dyed the green tips of his hair blue, and there was a new tattoo on his hand: a flock of flying birds.

"Glad you're back, English," he said to me, echoing his text messages. He gave Mia a brisk kiss on the cheek.

The exhaustion of heartbreak had made my voice huskier. "Thanks, Mr. Street."

Mia grabbed his tattooed hand. "When did you get that?"

"Last night," he said dismissively. "C'mon, let's get on the Gravitron before brown-nose-Ambrose pukes on it." He took off ahead of us.

When we stepped off the ride, Mia and Josh were butting heads over the tattoo he hadn't told her about, and I was about to christen the ground with half-digested egg sandwich.

I jogged to the portable toilet with a line-up longer than tickets to the Stones. I bent over, inhaling deep breaths through the porta-potty stink, which was totally counterproductive.

Logan Hunter's white shoes with navy laces stepped into my view. "I thought you'd left town," he said.

I lifted my head, my hands on my knees. "Wish I had. I just went on the Gravitron."

"Whoa, a masochist. I'll hold your hair if you like." He winked. "So were you sick or what? Didn't see you at school."

"Something like that. Sorry I missed our last biology class. All that mitosis and meiosis psychosis." The line wasn't moving. "So I guess we finally joined the land of the free," I added, filling the awkward silence.

"Yeah, now you can build those mega yachts of yours. I'll take a gym and a swim-up bar please." His muddy eyes sparkled. Logan was definitely cute, and funny at times, and probably a solid guy deep down. He'd make a decent boyfriend to someone. But at that moment, I knew with every part of my being that it wouldn't be me. Not anymore.

"I think I'm okay now," I said. "I should find my crew. So, hey, I really hope you have a happy life." I stuck my hand out, as if I couldn't get any more embarrassing.

"That sounds permanent." He shook my hand with clammy fingers.

I smiled at him, pulling away. "Well, this is our last unofficial school day, right? So I may not see you."

He nodded. "See ya."

I walked away, feeling hollow.

Mia was over by the selfie booth. Mascara-filled tears streamed down her face.

"Josh and I just broke up," she said.

"What? You're kidding me."

"He won't come to MIT with me." She dabbed her eyes with shaking fingertips. "He wants to go to L.A. and get a record deal. I mean, who even does that?"

"Lots of people," I said gently. "Maybe you guys can still work something out. What about the colleges in L.A.?"

She made a dismissive grunt. "I honestly don't think I can date someone who wants to be a musician anyway. Like, how will he ever support a family? I love music as much as anyone, but it's not a proper job."

There were so many things I thought of to say but didn't… That some of the most successful people in the world were musicians. Or that Josh had his own dreams too. Mostly, though, that I knew exactly how Mia felt.

"Want to come over tonight?" I said. "We can watch a war movie. No romance."

"Yes, please; one with no hot actors. Where are my freaking tissues?" She rummaged through her tote and pulled out a wad of paper.

"Oh shit, your history essay. Sorry, I forgot to give it to you. You were right, by the way. Stupid Campbell gave me a *B*."

It was my essay about Nicholas the Ironheart, blue pen scrawled across the top.

91/100 A. Well done. R. Campbell.

It was my first ever *A* in anything. Mrs. Campbell had pinned another document to the essay, introduced with a note:

Incidentally, you are the only student to have argued this angle in my five years of teaching at this school. Your research is solid but, had it been more thorough, you would have received closer to 100. Check out the book 'The Murder of Catherine Tudor' by Gabriela Dunsborough. It was the inspiration for one of my research papers during my history master's. I have attached the short summary, in case you are interested.

I quickly skimmed sections of Mrs. Campbell's paper while Mia continued digging through her tote.

Dunsborough (2006) suggests Princess Catherine was found in the basement of the Palace of Whitehall, fatally strangled with a chain of wooden Catholic rosary beads…
The Earl of Lansbury was a close confidant of the king's, and later revealed to be a member of a secret Catholic family (Dunsborough, 2006)…
Given the slight but compelling evidence, it is my belief that Robert Fox, the Earl of Lansbury, murdered Princess Catherine Tudor on the night of the Midsummer's Eve feast in 1580…

"I have to go." I shoved the paper into my bag, my heart thrashing in my chest.

Mia's cheeks were still wet. "Hello, war movie, no romance?"

"Can we do it tomorrow?" I squeezed her lean forearm. "I'm so sorry. I totally forgot I promised Mom I'd help out at the rest home tonight. She's got a double shift. I've really gotta run. I'm sorry. I love you."

Before she could protest, I weaved through the fair, scouring for Logan's blonde spikes of hair. When I was about to give up, I spotted him sitting inside his idling black Chevy. I bolted to the window and banged on it.

The glass dropped a few inches. "Thought you never wanted to see me again."

"I need your help. I lost something really important in the river… a—a family heirloom."

"You want me to get the boat out?" He winced at the angry sky.

"I don't think you need a boat. It's a ring I dropped near the river-bank behind my place…where the water indents."

"How long ago did you lose it?"

I counted again. "Six days."

He shook his head. "Long gone."

"Logan, please. You live in the water. I barely go in baby pools. You've got goggles, right? A wetsuit? The ring's got a big blue stone with little red ones around it shaped like roses. I can't begin to tell you how important it is." My teeth were chattering like I'd spent the morning on Mount Everest.

He tapped the steering wheel, biting his bottom lip. "Actually, I'm heading to meet Avery for pizza. This fair's lame." His eyes met mine. "But, hey, I hope you have a really happy life."

His tires screeched so fast they nearly ran over my feet. I stood there in shock before my legs sprang to life, sprinting to the river through sheets of rain. The water was choppy and rising, branches fighting to stay afloat.

I held my breath and leapt into nothingness. Half a second later, I was flooded with bone-shattering cold, my legs kicking until I found air. My mouth hung open, icy water pouring down my hair. Grunting and quivering, I lined myself up with the rock I'd crouched on when I tossed the ring and dived forward. I couldn't see a freaking thing, probably because my eyeballs had frozen. I sank to the muddy ground, sweeping my hands through slime and branches. It was like combing the surface of Mars for a single red hair. Two of my fingers were bleeding.

After nearly twenty minutes, I heaved myself onto the bank, shivering into slushy soil. I was so drenched by the time I got home that I couldn't distinguish between tears and water on my cheeks.

A hot shower scarcely stopped the shaking. I sat on the couch, my hair twisted in a towel, my mind lost. It wasn't Isobel Beaumont who murdered Kit. It was Lord Lansbury on the night of the Midsummer's Eve feast—days after I'd left Tudor England. *Emmie, what have you done?*

The doorbell rang three times before I moved. I expected Mia to be standing on my front step, not Logan. Damp hair was pasted to his brow.

"Is this it?" he asked, opening his hand. The blue-diamond ring was caked with dirt.

My mouth fell open.

"Sorry I took so long. I had to see Avery first. Lucky it's a ring, or it wouldn't have got jammed on one of the branches right where you dropped it. Still wouldn't have found it without my mask, though. The ring's not real, is it? Like the stones, I mean?"

I glided the ring to the base of my thumb. "I honestly can't believe it. It's like it wanted to be found."

"Man, you even pull off the turban look."

I yanked the towel from my hair and folded my arms around Logan's broad back. His cologne actually smelled pretty good.

"Thank you so much," I said, squeezing. "You have no idea what this means."

His uneven breath tickled my neck. "You want to go get a pizza?"

I separated us. "I'm sorry, I can't hang out right now. It's…it's not a good time. But I'm *so* thankful for this, Logan. I owe you big time."

He paused, idly kicking the step. "I'm not back together with Avery. Just so you know."

I couldn't help but smile. "Thanks for the clarification."

He pursed his lips into a smirk, and it lingered. "Guess I'd better let you go then. I'll see you, Emmie Grace."

"You will when I'm looking at you."

I closed the door on his chuckle, checking the clock on my phone. If I fell asleep within the next hour, I could be back at Whitehall in time for the Midsummer's Eve feast.

I threw on the cinnamon-colored gown and braided my hair before downing our last two bananas and a tall glass of water. I hunted through the bathroom cabinet, but Mom's sleeping pill bottles were empty. *Shit!*

When I lay on my bed and shut my eyes, they kept opening. I

changed positions, closed the window, opened it again, and hung a fleece blanket over the blinds. I was still awake. When Ruby barked to be let out, I screamed into my pillow.

After she'd peed, I went straight back to bed, refusing to move for anything other than an alien invasion. My mind emptied with the pace of a snail, my breath gradually becoming more rhythmic.

When my eyes opened again, I stared into a black curtain of a thousand stars.

Gusts of wind carried voices and violins from within Whitehall's sandy-colored walls, which blushed with torchlights. I crept toward the glowing courtyard, grateful for the cloak of nighttime.

I wandered into a haze of music and lights, where countless members of the English nobility were dancing like drunkards around the wine fountain. Keeping my head low, I passed beneath a series of rose arches that progressed through the middle courtyard into the Great Hall. Its walls were living flowerbeds bursting with vivid red roses in full bloom, thousands of glittering candles hanging from the eaves. Every inch of me felt broken, never to be put back together the same way again.

Lady Ascot met my sight line, her brows flinging upward. She elbowed her husband. I zigzagged past them, surveying the crowd. There was no sign of Nick, Kit, or Lord Lansbury.

My stomach dropped. Alice Grey was in the dance area, circling around a courtier with cropped gray hair. When she turned, I caught the side of her smile. Francis watched them from across the room, his lips pressed to a wine cup. But it was okay. I'd already googled their names; Alice and Francis would be wed within a year, a couple of years before his execution for treason. I shivered.

Emmie, you don't have time for this. These people aren't your friends. This is not your century.

I turned back and walked to Kit's rooms as fast as I could without arousing suspicion. Passing the corridor leading to Nick's rooms was almost unendurable.

I suppressed the anguish in my chest, readying my story for Kit's guards. But the corridor was vacant, except for six upturned ale jugs in the corner. Her door was ajar.

When my knocks on Kit's door went unanswered, I pushed it open.

"Hello?" I said into pitch-black silence. The fire had gone out, cooling the air. I took a few steps forward, my hip slamming into a table.

"Your Grace? Princess Catherine?" I shout-whispered, rubbing the sore spot and wincing. I couldn't see more than a foot in front of me. My hands searched the hard surface, bumping a tinderbox. I fumbled with it until the flame flared and dimmed, exposing a shape on Kit's bed. I hurriedly lit a candle and moved closer.

A scream erupted from my throat. Kit's favorite maid Lucy was face down, her arms folded strangely beneath her. I flipped her over, spilling candle wax onto her pale hand. She didn't flinch, and her mouth and eyelids were blue.

"Kit!" I cried, digging through the disordered sheets. The bed was empty.

I ran to find some guards, pausing outside Kit's door. How would I explain all this to Nick? What would he even do if he saw me?

Think! Princess Catherine was found in the basement of the Palace of Whitehall.

Male voices were heading up the stairs. I hid behind Kit's door. After they passed, I ran down to the confectionary where servers entered in a steady stream, carrying towers of dirty plates. I passed whiffs of baking pastry and crept down the grimy, winding steps.

When I reached the basement, I unhooked a burning candle from the wall, struggling to remember where I'd seen Lord Lansbury last time. After two dead ends, I found the room crammed with dusty candles and carpets, some rolled into cylinders, others unfurled across the stone floor. I held my candle out, scouring for a hiding place.

"Kit!" I hissed into the stale air.

Thick dust coated all the carpets except for one. Its ends curved up like it'd just been unrolled. One of the frayed corners moved.

My heart was a bass drum going full pelt. I crept toward the carpet and slowly lifted the edge. A rat bolted across my forearm. I shrieked, falling backward. The answer was a faint banging beneath my feet.

"Hello?" I called out. More banging.

I clenched my teeth and flipped the carpet over, coughing into the dust. There were floorboards underneath and a latch so tiny I almost missed it. I hooked my finger and pulled. The latch resisted and then flung open.

"Kit?" I said, whipping the torch across the black hole.

A high-pitched voice tried to talk. I spun the light to the other side, illuminating Kit's terror-stricken face. She was gagged and bound with rope in a pit about five-feet deep. My heart pounded frantically as I pointed downward, silently asking if anyone else was there. She shook her head and whimpered, her eyes like prey.

"I'm coming," I mouthed.

Oh my God, what Kit's gone through. Screw life as a royal in the sixteenth century.

I rested the candle on the edge of the pit and flipped my legs over.

Just as I was about to jump down, a boot rammed into my side, knocking me away from the hole. I slid along the carpet and onto my knees, winded.

"You never stop," said an even voice. It took me a second to identify it and another to believe it.

"No," I said, clutching my burning side.

Mrs. Campbell had been so close to figuring it out. But she was slightly off.

22

Mathew Fox stood several feet away, swinging a spiked iron mace like a pendulum.

"You didn't do this," I stuttered. "You couldn't." I gripped my throbbing side, terrified he'd use the mace on me next.

"This constant conspiracy to misjudge me is astounding. I live in a world of fools." His voice was higher pitched than I'd known it. Angrier.

"But you love the king." I was shaking.

"I love England. And I despise its bastard, heretic king."

"*Bastard?* He's the son of Queen Elizabeth the First, the grandson of Henry the Eighth!"

"God strike me down, I believed you were smarter than this," Mathew spat. He pointed the mace at me, stepping sideways to balance its weight. "Elizabeth was the daughter of a whore and no queen. To think I once believed that Queen Mary sent you here. It is *I* who is the fool."

"Queen Mary?" I stammered, taking a minuscule step toward the pit, hoping he wouldn't notice it if I kept him talking. "You mean Mary, Queen of Scots?"

"The Queen of the Scots, the lawful Queen of England, and the true servant of Catholicism." He came toward me in a burst of speed, and my hand flew out.

"Mathew, this is *me*. I'm your friend. How could you do this? How could you believe a Scottish woman is more fit to rule England than Queen Elizabeth's son?"

His voice dripped foulness. "Elizabeth and her children are enemies to England and to God."

It was like I'd left Tudor England for the twilight zone. "Then what was all that about you wanting me to *marry* Nick?"

He laughed out loud, smacking his palm with the mace handle. "Ah, yes. When you were discovered in the Parkside wearing the king's coronation ring, I believed that Mary, Queen of Scots had sent you to me as a messenger. Finally, a substitute for the ingenious spy Susanna Grey. However, it did not take long to learn you were merely another helpless girl in love with our sinful king. Except that this time, he loved you back." Mathew crept closer as my heels teetered on the rim of the hole. "But I had him there. All I needed was to put another idiot commoner on the throne, another *Anne Boleyn*, and the people would have rebelled. I should have wagered you were no match for the bewitching Pearl of France."

When he stepped sideways, I followed, a barrier between him and Kit.

"Okay, I get it," I said shakily. "You haven't accepted the new religion and you want a Catholic queen. Mary, Queen of Scots, to be specific. Good luck with that. But why hurt Kit? What's she got to do with this? If you hate King Nick so much, why not just go for him?" My heart leapt from my chest. "Is it because she's more your size?"

He snarled at me. "Be not so swift to deny your entanglement in this, Mistress Grace. I have not yet finished my story. After my plans for you had failed, you came to me with an idea even more shrewd than my own. Catherine is the king's heart. He has never been '*so protective of anyone or anything*,' just as you said to me. Cut off a king's head and another grows in its place. Have *him* cut it off, however, and every person in Christendom turns against him. Yes, mistress, your plot was perfect. Not only would eliminating Princess Catherine destroy King Nick's only heir, but it would make him lose his mind. I merely had to kill Catherine."

His doll-like eyes gleamed, and I felt like an invisible hand was choking me.

"Yes, Mistress Grace, *you* did this," Mathew said steadily. "What is the trouble? Not such a good idea after all?"

He lunged at me, but I'd had enough and leaped toward him. I grabbed the handle of the mace, clawing at it until we tumbled sideways. Mathew roared as my nails dug into his bony fingers. A moment later, the mace was in my hand. I hopped to my feet, hearing Kit's muffled moan from the pit below. Mathew thrust himself toward her on all fours like a lizard.

"Get away from her!" I screamed, aiming the mace at him. "Help! Someone, help!" Fear ripped through my voice, but only my echo replied.

He jumped up and ran for me. I swung the mace, sending him stumbling backward through an archway. A wintry gust hit us both in the face. We were on the small wharf beneath the castle, the rowboat swaying four feet below.

"Please, Mathew, you wouldn't hurt a child." He backed away from me like a pirate walking the plank and tripped over a pair of oars, his wild eyes locked to the mace. I tried not to breathe in the stench of sewage. "You could've killed Kit right away, but you didn't. Why don't you work with the king instead of against him? He trusts you now. He's also tolerant of Catholics. That's one reason he's marrying Henriette: to stop these holy wars. A Catholic-born queen for England...isn't that what you want?"

"I would sooner burn than see a Catholic queen convert to the devil's faith. Elizabeth's filthy changeling Catherine will be dead by morning. As will you, the king's other heart. Every skillful falconer knows a bird in the hand is worth two in the bush. But in this case, two in the hand."

He pounced on me, knocking me off the wharf's edge into a short but breathless free fall. I grabbed Mathew's shirt like a lifeline and pulled him with me. Half a breath later, my cheek smashed against the wooden rowboat. Mathew scrambled to his feet in front of me.

When the boat rocked beneath us, he shrieked a piercing cry. That's when I remembered. *He's afraid of water!*

I seized him from behind and tried to drag him into the black water. He spun and clawed at my face with crazed slashes until I had to let go. The boat tilted again.

"Not another step!" Mathew screamed, sweat dripping from his jaw. His eyes bulged with fear, his scrawny body motionless.

I threw myself to one side, the boat leaning with me. He clutched an oar with both hands like a terrified cat. *If I could get him in the water, he'd probably drown, Kit would be saved, and I'd be a murderer.*

I looked up at the wharf's ragged edge, calculating. If I jumped high enough, I could make it. Sucking in a deep breath, I charged forward, ready to leap, when I was wrenched backward by my neck. I scraped at the tiny balls suffocating my windpipe, my mouth making silent screams. My head pulsed with indescribable pressure, and my legs kicked wildly. Stars formed and burst in front of my eyes.

A moment later, air spurted back into my lungs and I fell to my butt, coughing. Mathew had let me go. When I looked up, he was pointing at the blue-diamond ring on my thumb, his face aghast.

"You still have that ring," he spat accusingly. I crawled away from him. He stepped forward. "If you are not plotting with Mary, Queen of Scots, then how did you get that?"

My voice rattled like a chain smoker's. "What does this ring have to do with Mary, Queen of Scots?"

He smirked with pride, looking more than a touch psychotic. "I began plotting with Mary Stuart when I was fourteen. Five years ago, she sent a messenger to me who asked for a possession of the king's to curse. I snatched that very ring from his chambers and had it secretly delivered to her. It was Susanna Grey who rode to the market to collect the ring back from Mary's soothsayer. We were to return the ring to the king so its curse would overcome him. However, Lady Grey never made it home. That was the last anyone saw of her or the blasted ring. Until you arrived at court with it four years after. Do you know how long I have waited for Mary to come forth again?"

He took a step closer. I flung my hand behind my back. "You want this ring?" I snapped. "Come and get it. But there's one thing you should know. I have no idea what you expected from Mary's curse—fire and brimstone? A heart attack? Well, that was one seriously powerful soothsayer. This ring makes people *travel through time*. To more than four hundred years in the future, where I'm from. That's right, I've been zipping back and forth like weekend trips to Paris. Can you get your head around that? Oh, and I know what happens to your Mary, Queen of Scots, by the way…she gets beheaded. Apparently, it took a few blows to get it off."

Mathew shrieked and threw himself at me. The stone ceiling became a whizzing tumble dryer before I crashed into freezing liquid. I was fully submerged, kicking through my sinking dress. When the water became darker, I spiraled and swam the other way, my lungs ready to burst. And then the thrashing stopped. The entire world turned silent and black, except for a glistening ball of gold. I reached for it, trying to dig the ring out of the mud, before I realized it was still on my thumb.

I kicked and kicked until I swallowed air, blasted with biting cold. All I could taste was saltwater. The boat bobbed upside down several feet away. I flattened my body and crawled my arms the way my swim teacher showed me until my fingers hit decaying wood. There was no sign of Mathew, just a floating set of carved wooden rosary beads. I threw them over my head, sickened at what could be happening to Kit.

It took all the strength I had to climb up the side of the boat. Hovering my bare feet on the edge, I cried out like an animal to help propel me upward. After four thrusts, I felt the boat flip under me, but my hands clung to the edge of the wharf. I elbowed my way onto dry wood and caught my breath through chattering teeth. My toes were icicles, the mace lying beside them.

I grabbed the handle and shot to my feet, breaking into a run. The candle was still burning beside the hollow. Checking over my shoulder every second, I held the candle down to Kit. She was in the corner, her head in her knees. When the light found her, she glanced up. Her shivering cheeks were wet.

I waved my hand to tell her to stay back and positioned the candle closer. Watching for a shape inside the archway, I pushed one of the rolled carpets over until it teetered on the edge of the pit and crashed into it. One end poked toward the ceiling. I squeezed the mace between my knees and slid down the carpet into the hole. Kit tried to throw herself at me, but her arms were pinned with rope.

"We have to hurry," I said, sweat or seawater sliding down my neck. "Don't move."

I raised the mace, and Kit whimpered.

If my visiting the past caused Kit's death in the first place, doesn't that mean I can undo it?

I struck, the rope splitting into threads. I tugged it off, checking Kit's skin for blood. When something clanked a few rooms away, she cowered in the corner. I frantically undid her mouth gag and held my hand out.

"C'mon. We have to climb up."

She shook her head, unblinking.

"Listen," I said in Mom's tone when I used to ask about Dad. "If you die here, not only will it change Nick forever, but everyone around him will suffer, because I guarantee you he'll never, ever get over it, and the effects of that will be worse than you can ever imagine."

She blinked and offered me a quivering palm. I folded her legs around my waist like a baby's and clambered up the carpet, dropping her onto the floorboards. I fell forward, wheezing into straw. Kit tugged at my shoulders.

"We must go," she said in a shrill voice.

I pulled her close, whispering calming words as we found our way back through the dark, jumping together at every sound. I wanted to bolt up the stairs, but I didn't have the strength, my feet dragging like lead blocks. I finally spilled Kit into the flame-lit corridor beside the confectionary. Footsteps thundered in and out of the kitchens, the air rich with voices and music. I panted with relief, still looking over my shoulder.

"Are you hurt?" I asked, rifling through Kit's dress. She grimaced at my face. I felt my cheeks, sticky with blood where Mathew had scratched them.

"It's okay," I whispered, shivering. "It's going to be okay."

Kit started weeping, clutching me like a baby monkey. For an imperceptible amount of time, we sat in the shadow of the stairwell, holding each other while violins and flutes played on the other side like a bizarre funeral march.

"Is he dead?" Kit finally breathed as she wiped her eyes.

"Mathew Fox? I don't know."

Her voice burst. "I want my brother."

It took me a moment to orientate myself. I hugged her into my dress and hurried us toward the private stairwell leading to Nick's chambers, keeping my head bowed. The ground was rough and cold beneath my bare feet.

There were two guards at the end of the corridor, one sitting on the floor with outstretched legs. He jumped up, his face whitening with shock.

"Mathew Fox attacked the princess and killed her maid," I said clearly and slowly so there'd be no mistake. Kit clutched me tightly. I handed the rosary beads to the guard. "These are his. He was keeping Princess Catherine in the basement. But I think you'll find him in the river beneath the castle." The guard snapped his fingers. The other bolted down the stairs and shouted for reinforcements.

The unmistakable sound of Nick's voice floated from the other side of the door, chased by a second voice that was low, female, and French. Everything inside me twisted in a gut-wrenching tug.

The guard raised his fist to alert the king, but I stopped him. "One second, *please*."

Tears trickled down my cheeks as I crouched to face Kit, speaking fast into her matted hair. "Nick loves you so much. You need to look out for him, not just as a subject, but as a sister. Do whatever you can to be safe. Trust no one, do you hear me?" The guard shuffled impatiently, and my hands fisted at my sides. "Tell your brother that Emmie said it was like a dream," I whispered to Kit, my eyes dripping. "The most beautiful and impossible dream. But it was real. You tell him it was the realest thing I ever knew."

When the guard banged on the door, I was already running, leaping down the stairs and into the courtyard, past too many ogling onlookers to count. I bunched my dress in my fists so my feet were free to run deep into the Parkside. My cut cheeks stung from the saltwater dribbling down them. When the thick trees obscured me from view, I collapsed onto the soggy grass and held the ring to my forehead, shuddering through sobs. But the blackness came almost immediately, like I was passing out. And, whether it was in my mind or real, I swore I heard Nick calling my name.

The next morning, I filled the sink with cold water and submerged my bloodied pillowcase, pressing an ice pack to my cheek with my other hand. I felt like roadkill on the outside and even worse on the inside. The shivering hadn't stopped.

I also struggled to process that Alice Grey's missing mother had been a traitor working with Mathew Fox and Mary, Queen of Scots, to bring King Nick down. *Poor Alice.* I wondered if it was nuts to think her mom, Susanna Grey, could possibly be the hoarder Jane Stuart. After all, Jane was a name given to her by the state—like Jane Doe—and she'd apparently babbled the name Stuart. What if that was because she could only remember her devotion to *Mary* Stuart, the Queen of the Scots?

Something crawled in my hair, breaking the thought. My fingers flew up. A ladybug scuttled onto my skin, the ice pack hitting the tiles. I watched the tiny creature with utter disbelief before it jumped to the basin.

"No!" I snatched one of Mom's empty pill containers and flipped it over the ladybug, trapping it. I carried the container downstairs and hunted for an empty glass jar. I carefully poured the ladybug into it, sealing it with plastic wrap and a rubber band. The critter could be carrying a sixteenth-century parasite with the power to wipe out insects across America.

"Hey there, bud," I said, bringing my nose to the glass. An ache ricocheted through me. Keeping the jar pressed to my hip, I sat on my bed in cotton pajamas, my eyes as heavy as my heart as I typed into my laptop.

Catherine Tudor

When a short biography page came up, I scanned to the end.

Catherine died on 9 January 1644 at the age of 72, leaving behind four daughters.

I must've read the words fifty times, pressing my wet eyes with my knuckles. Then it hit me. My house looked exactly the same. The elm tree's branches were clawing the window like they always had. The broken-down blue Corolla was still parked across the street. I typed in a news page. Britain's monarchy was identical, the world fighting and turning as I knew it. Saving Kit's life hadn't changed a thing.

My fingers raced over the keyboard.

Nicholas Tudor

There were nearly eighteen-million search results about the notorious English king, the information the same on every page: King Nicholas the First died at the age of thirty-nine on the battlefield, childless to his deceased wife Henriette. A brutal ruler whose rage propelled his nation into civil war, he became known as Nicholas the Ironheart, one of the most feared kings in history.

I kicked the laptop, sending it crashing to the floor. Ruby barked and scampered from the room. When the doorbell rang, I covered my eyes. Then my cell phone started ringing from the charge dock.

"Mia," I said into the receiver. I was panting, even though I hadn't moved.

"Sorry, I got stuck helping Tristan with a geometry thing for his summer school. But I swiped some of Mom's mango sago. I'm outside."

I peered out my window. Mia had her phone to her ear. I'd forgotten that she was coming over to watch a movie. I carefully placed the glass jar on my dresser and headed downstairs.

Even after countless sleepovers, it was the first time I'd seen Mia without any makeup on. Still, it was my face she reached for. "What happened?"

I turned away. "It's a…a cat thing. I saw one stuck in a fence yesterday, and I tried to get it out. It wasn't grateful."

"Holy shit. We're a pair of awesome right now, aren't we."

I tried to smile, but my cheeks wouldn't lift. Neither did Mia's.

"Is that the sago?" I nodded at her recycled shopping bag.

"It better be." She dumped the bag on the countertop and rummaged for spoons.

But it was Mia's hunched shoulders, the listlessness in her movements, her vacant stare that made my lip tremble. "Mia, I just lost someone I really loved too. Actually, a few people." My palms pressed my throbbing chest. "And I feel like I can't breathe."

She looked up, dropping her spoon to catch me as I burst into tears.

23

A RELIGIOUS PERSON WOULD'VE THANKED GOD FOR THE THINGS THAT got me through the next five weeks. Sleeping past noon every day erased a good chunk of sulking time. Then there were the extra shifts at the rest home, the long swims with Ruby at the river beach, frantic shopping runs with Mia for MIT, and two trips to Amherst to watch Josh play before he left for L.A.—not that I told Mia about those. I hadn't lost my head in the sixteenth century, and I planned on keeping it in the twenty-first. I'd spent eighteen years hemorrhaging friends as we moved from town to town. I was going to make an effort to keep some this time.

A smashed computer and limited Wi-Fi on my phone also meant I couldn't search the internet, which was exactly what I needed. I didn't want to think about the past anymore, or the future, or anything other than how to not die from heartache (which is a real thing—Mom explained it to me when a rest home resident passed away a day after his wife).

But the letter came ten days later, sent by international courier. The Head of College from Central Saint Martins congratulated me on my offer of a place in their undergraduate degree in jewelry design. Someone must've pulled out at the eleventh hour. I had seven days to decide.

"Emmie, you *must*," cried Mom, hugging me in her blue bathrobe. "Gosh, you didn't spend that money already, did you?"

"Are you kidding? I've been a bigger tightwad than that guy who snaps off the broccoli stalks at the grocery store before paying."

Watching Mom chuckle in her tattered slippers made it hard to jump with joy. "What about you?" I said, dropping my peanut butter toast onto the plate. "Will you stay here?"

"Why wouldn't I?" She blew on her instant coffee.

"Well, you don't exactly utilize the nature around here, the rest home screws up your back, and your best friend is in Springfield half the time." *Dad is never going to ring the doorbell and beg you to take him back.* "Why don't you come with me? We could get a little flat in London."

"We've already had a little flat in London," she said with a smile. Her eyes glinted, looking away. "Too many memories for me there, I think."

"You still miss him," I said, an ache in my throat.

Her voice wavered, her brows slanting. "You know I don't want to talk about that. He doesn't deserve it."

"Of course he doesn't."

Mom gripped the back of a chair like she'd fall to her death if she let go. She waited and then sighed. "Someone needs to stay with Ruby and the ladybug." She rolled her drowsy eyes. But at least Mom had stopped trying to talk me into setting the sixteenth-century insect free. She'd even made an urgent trip to the store to buy raisins for it.

I slid two slices of bread into the toaster for her and trudged upstairs to get dressed, wishing that talking about Dad didn't still make me feel so heavy.

As I painted mascara on my lashes, noticing the red emptiness in my eyes, I let the urge claim me. I pulled the phone out of my pocket and dialed Dad's number. He answered quickly.

"Emmeline?"

"Hey." I already wanted to hang up.

"Is everything okay?" He sounded stiff. We both did.

"Yeah. I just wanted to call to say hello and let you know I got into a jewelry college in London."

His phone crackled like he was gesticulating, and I heard a door close. "Well, that's fantastic news. Which one?"

"Central Saint Martins. It's part of the London University of the Arts."

"I know it. It's a great school."

A moment of uncomfortable silence stretched between us.

"I wasn't aware you were still on this jewelry craze," Dad said eventually.

"It's not a craze——"

"I know. You were always good at it. I still remember that stall you made on my street, selling those necklaces. The grocer took seven!"

"For her grandkids." I smiled. A point for Dad. "How are things with you?"

He sighed. "Oh, fine. We've had record-low applications for history majors this year. All the kids want to do now is make apps and get rich. Never mind understanding the nature of mankind and how the past explains the perspectives of society today."

I climbed on my bed and curled onto my side, listening to Dad gush about his work, his two pet birds, a foray into painting on the weekends—everything except the woman he'd left my mom for. Six minutes in, and I was actually laughing at his stories. Before we hung up, Dad promised to call me when I settled into London, and I promised myself I wouldn't get my hopes up.

After her nap, Mom used her work laptop to help me book a flight. I decided not to tell her about the chat with Dad; she might start googling him again like a stalker. Together, we replied to an ad from a Finnish anthropology student looking for a roommate near Central Saint Martins.

"You'll be able to see some amazing things now you're old enough to remember," said Mom, running her hand down my ponytail. "The British Museum...the Tower of London," she added in a dramatic voice.

"I remember the Tower of London."

"Really? Me too, I loved it." She slapped her thigh. "Want to watch a movie with it today? There's that one about Henry the Eighth or lots of Nicholas the Ironheart ones."

"Sorry, I can't," I blurted. "I have to sort through more of my stuff."

I barreled upstairs and shut my door, pressing my forehead against the peeling paint.

I was officially moving to London. Where I'd fought with Francis Beaumont on a cobblestone street, watched a priest get his head hacked off, survived a mob attack with the Princess of England. I wanted to be back in Nick's city so much it made everything throb. But the thought of it being so different now was equally unbearable.

The blue-diamond ring was back on my thumb in seconds, cooling my skin. My hunger to use it—despite everything that'd happened—was staggering. I'd thrown the ring into a four-hundred-mile river, and there it was, still sitting on my hand. I couldn't seem to unlock myself from it...from him.

I fell onto the bed, overcome by a crushing need to just go to sleep. To wake up four hundred years in the past, where Nick would be wait-ing, his seawater eyes glowing with love. Right before leaving me to make heirs with his precious wife Henriette. Pain splintered through my chest. *Is this feeling ever going to go away?*

Ruby climbed on top of me, as if she knew what I was consider-ing. I pulled her to my cheek and stroked her wiry beard. She was the only one in the world who understood where I'd been. She'd also loved Whitehall, with its sprawling flower gardens and flocks of spar-rows to chase. For a second, I actually thought of looping the ring through Ruby's collar and sending her back there. Returning the ring to where it belonged.

I lurched onto my elbows, staring at the jar on my dresser. The ladybug was nesting on a raisin under its leaf. Maybe there was a way to send the ring back for good, to remove the intolerable temptation forever. Even if the ring somehow made its way back to Nick, he'd never find me once I'd left Hatfield. Not that he'd even try. It was me who couldn't seem to let go.

I used my eyebrow tweezers to lower the ring into the jar. The ladybug crawled deeper into its leaf cave and stayed hidden while I stuffed piles of school notes into trash bags. The ladybug was still giving the ring the royal brush-off. When I tipped the jar, she flew to the opposite side. I lifted the ring out with my tweezers, considering a smaller jar. A moment later, it clicked. I didn't need a jar at all. I needed wire, a flush cutter, and snipe-nosed pliers.

It took more than an hour to construct a wire cage over the blue diamond, leaving a small gap at one end. I tipped the ladybug onto the stem of the leaf and used it to guide her inside the wire cage. I blocked the opening with my fingers, her wings whirring madly.

"I'm so sorry," I said, using my pliers to quickly cinch the cage closed. I left a tiny space so she could eventually crawl out.

Feeling like a lunatic at a full-moon party, I shut my blinds and lay on my bed. I wedged the ring between two pillows so gravity made sure the ladybug stayed parked on the stone.

"Go home," I whispered to her, my voice cracking beneath the heaviness in my chest. "Go back. *Please* go back, please. I can't do this anymore."

I closed my sore eyes and listened to Mom's footsteps downstairs, followed by the sound of an old movie starting. A lawnmower revved up in the McCoys' front yard. When it switched off again, my body tipped to one side. Drool tickled my chin. I flew up, nearly hitting the headboard. I'd nodded off. My fingers fumbled through the pillows.

The ring was gone.

I searched the floor, my heart pounding like a jackhammer. I hadn't seen the ring fade to nothing like a fantasy film. It was just…gone.

Sensing the intolerable call of grief that I already knew too well, I tied on my shoes and told Mom I was going for a run, not stopping until I was at the outskirts of town. Everything reminded me of him: the streets we'd driven through squeezed into the back of Mia's car, the houses on Main Street he'd gawked at like circus acts, the rusted Corolla that was the same shade of his eyes when he wore sky-blue.

I couldn't get away from him. Maybe I never would.

But at least this time I wouldn't have a choice.

I held back the floodgates of tears by slamming myself with jobs for the next few days, focusing on packing, finishing all the laundry, sorting out the trash, scrubbing the bathrooms, vacuuming, and mowing the lawn. Mom even helped with some of it, but I suspected it was because she knew she'd miss me more than she'd admit.

Mia invited me for a sleepover the night before my flight. We watched the latest superhero movie in her basement theater while Mrs. Fairbanks made her special Peking duck with homemade hoisin sauce. Over dinner, she served sparkling soda and made us all cheers to "two clever girls going off to college". "Do you see that Tristan?" she'd added to Mia's younger brother.

The sky was still pink when Mia dropped me home, her lips turned down at the sides.

"Why can't you stay for the summer?" she asked me again.

"There's so much I have to do over there. And I think I just need a new start. Like yesterday, actually."

"I hear you." She nodded like she really did. "Can't wait to visit."

"I'll be waiting," I said, smiling. "With toad in the hole, bubble and squeak, and maybe some spotted dick."

She broke up laughing. "The food is so weird over there." She pulled me into a hug. "I love you."

Her satin hair tickled my cheek. "Don't stop hustling until you're president, Madame Mia Fairbanks," I said through tears.

When we pulled back, I held onto her arms, memorizing her face. Being best friends with Mia was kind of like being a cast member of *The Mia Show*, but she'd befriended me when no one else would. I'd never forget it.

Mom and I had already agreed to no teary goodbyes, not that I wanted her driving me to the airport in her twenty-year-old car with dodgy brakes anyway. Instead, I'd talked her into going to Springfield with Crystal for the night so she wouldn't have to watch me leave and booked an airport shuttle to pick me up. I was secretly glad for the alone time. Being around Mom with all her London reminiscing only made me more anxious.

The shuttle was due early, so I swung my arm around my bedroom door to grab my suitcase, giving those hideous alphabet blinds a farewell wave. I was halfway out the door when a flash of peony pink caught my eye from across the room. Weird, I'd forgotten a piece of jewelry in the pegboard.

But then my suitcase plunged to the carpet.

I dived forward and detached the knot ring woven out of luxurious sixteenth-century pink satin, gasping for air. My eyes hunted everywhere, landing on the disheveled comforter. I was sure that I'd already made the bed. I ran and pushed the window open, unseasonably cool July air rattling through my hair.

"Nick?" I called out, feeling certifiable.

Then I heard a distant neigh. And another one, from a hundred or so yards away. A third. I knew that sound.

My heart thundered in my chest as I glided down the stairs and through the back gate like I was walking on air, picking up speed to jog into the center of the field. A chocolate-brown horse chewing grass over near Bayberry Street stopped my heart. But it was just one of the old geldings.

When I spun back to where the trees veiled the river, a shape crossed my view, silhouetted by the dawning sun. I held my palm to my eyes, the tall figure on horseback moving closer. It, too, was gliding...galloping...until Nick slowed Stella and jumped off her back, striding toward me.

Tears slipped down my cheeks as his arms slammed around me, his rose scent like medicine flooding my veins. He said my name over and over into my neck, squeezing me until I almost couldn't breathe, my tears wetting his shoulder.

I could barely make words. "I don't...I can't...this isn't real."

His lips turned into my hair. "Dear God, Emmie, mine eyes can barely believe it. You are here."

I pulled back, his face as stunned as mine. His doublet was double-breasted, military style, and unfastened with a white shirt underneath. He was an angel...an angel too beautiful, too impossible, to be real.

He took me by the shoulders, his grip gentle but firm. "Why did you leave me? Only to come back and save Kit's life and then disappear again?" His face twisted like he was in pain. "Did it bring you pleasure to rip out my heart not once but twice?"

It was impossible not to cry. "After I came home, I found out that Kit was still in danger," I choked out. "I felt awful I hadn't seen it coming. Isobel Beaumont wasn't the real threat; she left before Kit was even rescued. It was Mathew Fox."

"I know. Kit told me everything, including that he attacked you." He searched my skin for injuries. "That you saved her life."

I swept tears from my eyes. "Did you find Mathew?"

Fire roared in his eyes. "In the channel beneath the castle. His soul is already damned to hell." But then his voice softened. "You did not answer me. Why did you leave, Emmie?"

A car horn honked on Bayberry Street, reminding me. "I have a car coming."

He stepped back a little. "A car."

"I'm supposed to be going. I have a flight. I mean…" I looked back at the house. "I can't stay."

His face fell. Then he turned away and reached for Stella's reins.

"No!" I said, gripping his arm. "I don't mean for you to go." My mind was racing. "I just need to think of what to do. Maybe I can call the airline, or…" Nick looked at me like I was speaking Swahili again. "I need a second to think, okay!"

My heart splintered at the distressed face gazing back at me. I grabbed Stella's saddle and climbed onto her back, wriggling backward to make room. "Get on."

Nick gaped at me for a second before mounting Stella in one movement. I slid forward and folded my arms around his waist, my mouth a breath away from his neck. "Get us away from here," I said. "Just keep going until we find somewhere we can talk."

His warm hand slid over mine, our fingers weaving together. I rested my nose on his shoulder, breathing in the heady mix of fresh roses and worn leather.

We rode past the trees lining the river and dismounted in the clearing where I'd thrown in the ring. Watching Nick lace Stella's bridle around a low-hanging tree branch was a head-trip. *Am I dreaming this?*

"We don't have long," I said, beginning to shiver from shock. "How did you find the ring?"

He stepped closer to me, wiping his hands on his thighs. "I found it not. One of my courtiers spied it while hunting in the park."

"Did you think I had come back to your time with it?"

"Of course I did, or I would have come here in greater haste." He swallowed tightly. "The entire Royal Guard searched the palace, and the city, for you for days. After they failed to find you, I decided that maybe you had found a way to return the ring to me. Thus, I chose to come back here and look for you." His cheeks flushed. "I did not wish to cause alarm for your mother, so when I wakened in your bed, I left the knot ring as a symbol that I hoped you would understand. That you would remember. I am pleased I thought to bring it."

My heart grew. I didn't know he'd kept that silly knot ring. "I could never forget making that," I said softly.

The affection in his face made my knees weak. "How did you get the ring back there if you did not return with it?" he asked.

I almost snorted a laugh. "I'm not sure you'd believe me if I told you. Let's just say a tiny insect of yours hijacked a trip to modern America, so I sent the little time-traveler back to where she belonged."

His face washed with realization. "The cage attached to the ring. Good God, Emmie, you are marvelous."

"I guess the bug escaped then. I even considered sending Ruby at one point."

He just nodded. And then hurt seeped into his face as he looked away.

"Why did you bring Stella with you?" I asked softly.

He pressed a hand to his hip and sighed. "I needed a strong nose familiar with your scent and the means to travel…I was uncertain where you would be. I convinced Francis to steal me into the horse yard, where I slipped into Stella's stable and rested with her until we fell asleep."

"Holy crap. What's Francis doing now?"

"Standing guard outside the horse yard, most likely anguishing about his king's sanity. Which is why I also have little time." His pained expression leveled with me. "I pray you speak the truth to me, Emmie. Why did you leave my world and then send the ring back so you could never return?"

My throat constricted on the words. "Isn't it obvious? I can't do it, Nick. I tried, but I—I can't be your mistress while you marry Princess Henriette." My cheeks squeezed, resisting tears. "She showed me a letter you wrote to her. It was so...*loving.*"

He collected my hands in his, stroking my fingers. "I swear to you, I wrote Henriette letters merely to guide her away from her suspicions that my heart was not true." A sheen of tears coated his eyes. "I have not told you this yet, but I sent Henriette back to France. The same night Kit told me what happened and what you did; what you said to her. I could barely contain my grief, and Henriette knew." His face pinched at the memory. "I could not eat nor sleep. I began believing I had imagined you from the very beginning. But now I see...you would rather be here." He scanned our surroundings with a frown, like the dense willow trees and muted burble of the river weren't good enough.

"Here is my home."

But as soon as I'd said the words, I knew they weren't true.

"Not Hatfield, but this time period," I corrected. "This world. I'm meant to be driving to the airport right now to catch a plane to London. The jewelry school that I told you about accepted me."

He nodded, trying to smile. But all I saw was my own heartache reflected back at me. The strange thing was, now that Nick was here, the thought of Central Saint Martins made me feel completely hollow, like all my insides had been sucked out.

"Why don't you stay here with me?" I pleaded. "Kit's safe now. There's so much about this world that would amaze you. Airplanes... medicine...democracy. Well, maybe not democracy. But we could go to London together. The *new* London. Don't you want to see it? No more responsibilities, no more wars. Just us, like when we were together at Robin House."

Pain deepened in Nick's eyes. "I would love to," he said finally.

"But you can't." My face dropped to my faded white tennis shoes.

"Emmie, you are free. I'm not. When Henriette left for France, Sir Thomas Grey quit. A demonstration of his displeasure at my actions. Now I'm without a secretary of state, my councilors are fighting like dogs, I have disgraced the King of France, and Spanish troops are ready to strike. If I stay here now, I will have abandoned the realm in that state. Their own king! Leaving Kit, my only heir, to more vicious plots than you can imagine. She is not yet nine. The privy councilors will battle over lord protectorship, and who knows what will happen to her…to England. I beseech you to not ask that of me."

"Then why did you come here then?" I snapped. "Just to torture me a little longer and make me miss my flight?" The shuttle had to be there by now. Maybe I could still go.

He bit his bottom lip, blinking nervously. "I came here to ask you a question. The one I should have asked you that night on the ship." He fumbled in his pocket, pulling out something so sparkly it caught the morning light and nearly blinded me.

He sank to one knee and looked up at me, a string of blue diamonds glittering from his palm.

"Emmeline Eleanor Grace, I am here to formally offer you the jewels of the Queens of England." My hands flew to my mouth. Nick's heartfelt eyes stayed pinned to mine. "When I first discovered who you were, I believed that God never meant for us to be together. Now I know it is just the opposite. I have never felt more myself than when I'm with you. I know this is not the heart of a king speaking, it is the heart of a man, but that is what beats in my chest. And it is telling me—it is begging me—to be with you. To show you, and all of Christendom, that my heart is with you alone."

Tears dripped down my cheeks. "But you've always said you need to marry for an alliance."

"It is too late for that now. The fact is, my marriage is mine alone, and I have allowed my subjects to interfere too much in it. I am their anointed king, and they *will* accept my wishes. England will fight its own battles, as she always does, with great courage and dignity."

He rose back up and pressed the priceless jewels into my trembling hands. His skin burned hot over the cold diamonds.

"You know I cannot offer you coaches that move without horses, and structures turning through the sky," he said. "I cannot give you the New World or the new London, but I can give you me. My whole heart. There will never be another again, and forgive me for ever asking that of you." My eyes watered as he pulled my fingers to his chest, laying my hand over his pounding heart. "Emmie, I will build you the most wonderful jewelry workshop you have ever seen. Finer than any you could have here, I swear it. You will have ropes of pearls and pails of diamonds, and as many tools and goldsmiths as you wish." He shifted on his feet, the most mesmerizing eyes I'd ever seen fixed to mine. "You once told me I want for nothing. That I have magnificent castles and cloth and horse, and all manner of princely pleasures. And you were right. I demonstrate my power as God's chosen servant, and for that I complain not. But, my lady, you mistake need for want. What I yearn for in all hours of night, what I crave, what I hope for—when my kingdom is shrouded in the dark threat of war—is you." He squeezed my fingers with both hands, a sheen of tears glimmering in his eyes. "The truth is I have everything I need, but nothing I want without you. If you will only marry me, Emmeline, please. I beg you."

My heart filled to the point of bursting, every cell in my body shouting from the rooftops.

"Yes."

"*Yes?*"

"Yes."

He cried out with surprise, lifting me with both arms into a dizzying spin, the jewels dropping to the ground. I grabbed his cheeks, his fingers losing themselves in my hair as he brought our mouths together, kissing me like I was the most precious, desirable thing in the world. My lips parted for him, our tongues connecting and moving as one as his fingers dug into my arms. For the longest time, we just stood there kissing deeply and hungrily, his aching moans nearly sending me to my knees.

When we were both out of breath, he pulled away, pressing his soft lips to the back of my hand before leading me toward Stella, his eyes dazed.

Cold fear shot through my stomach. "I have to tell my mom," I said, grabbing the jewels and sliding them safely back into his pocket.

Nick stopped and looked at me, blinking fast.

"I can't...I can't just disappear," I explained.

"I know. I wish not to ask that of you." He took my other hand to show his support, but his fingers quivered.

"So what do we do?" I asked.

For a moment we stood there staring at each other, his skin beginning to pale.

When I spoke again, my voice was calm. "I'll come back with you now. I know you need to get back before they find you gone. But, before long, you have to let me come back here and tell my mom something."

His face fell. "Only to leave me again, intending never to return."

"I promise I would never do that."

He sighed heavily, his expression torn. "How am I to believe you, Emmie? You have done so, not once, but twice."

Lines creased his brow as he turned away, but I stopped him with a reassuring squeeze. "Then come with me when I do that. Meet my mom. Heck, maybe we should just tell her the truth." I reached up to lace my arms around his back. "Look, we'll figure it out. I won't leave you without warning, okay? I promise I'll never leave you like that again." My voice was almost a whisper. "You know I love you."

He brought our foreheads together, resting his there for a moment. When I looked up again, he touched his lips to mine. My entire body tingled as our mouths connected again with need.

Panting, we reluctantly broke apart and led Stella to the river's edge, weaving between willows until we found a secluded nook. Nick and I lay down on the soggy sand. I pulled off my shoes, and he folded an arm around me. He tried to keep one hand locked on Stella's leg, but she kept kicking it off. When I had a go, she neighed and relaxed.

"Last one to fall asleep explains all this to Francis Beaumont," I said.

Nick laughed, but quietly. After a few beats, his voice turned grave. "There is something else you should know, Emmie." He cleared his throat. "In the time you were gone, I felt myself growing...*dark* again." My whole body tightened. "Here, at least you were able to understand that my time had already passed," he said. "But, back there, you never even existed. I could not bear it." He twisted to face me, his cheeks flushed with shame. "Do you not see? It was not losing Kit that turned me into a monster. Not in the end. It was losing you."

I shifted to face the glistening surface of the river through the drooping curtain of branches, trying to process what he'd just said. Did *I* cause Nicholas the Ironheart? That would explain why the history books still called him that after I'd left, despite Kit's life being saved.

My mind whirred with a zillion thoughts, battling to block out one most of all. I'd read everything about that time, and there was no such person as Queen Emmeline of England. If I did marry Nicholas Tudor, would the history books change like they did with Kit and Alice? Or would it all go hideously wrong?

Before I spiraled into panic, Nick tilted into me, dropping his lips to mine until I was consumed by the most captivating feeling in the world.

And, in an instant, I knew.

Right or wrong, I wanted Nick Tudor more than anything else I'd ever known. And he'd just risked everything—his marriage alliance, even his kingdom—to get me back. Now it was my turn to show him what he meant to me.

"Let's go to sleep," I said into the perfect bow of his lips.

He cupped my face with both hands, my chest tightening with love as he looked deep into my eyes.

"Do not let go," he said, pulling me into his arms.

EMMIE
AND THE
TUDOR QUEEN

BOOK TWO

Seas have their source, and so have shallow springs;
And love is love, in beggars as in kings.

A Modest Love,
Sir Edward Dyer (1543–1607)

1

EVERYTHING BEFORE ME LOOKED BACKWARD, LIKE SEEING A FRACTURED limb snapped into a surreal angle. After waking up from a heavy sleep, I'd expected to find myself lying on the grubby stones of a sixteenth-century English horse stable. Instead, I sat shivering on the bank of the Connecticut River, its surface a sheet of inky-black glass through the drooping branches of a willow tree.

A few hours ago, I'd dozed off on the sandy river's edge in the arms of my dream boyfriend, Nick Tudor (make that dream *fiancé*), one of my arms awkwardly locked around his horse's bony hoof. So long as our three bodies stayed connected and we all fell asleep— including the horse—the enchanted ring on my thumb should've sent us four hundred years back in time, to where I'd decided to live and marry Nicholas the First, the King of England. *Gulp, no biggie.* But instead of rising and shining in King Nick's court in the year 1580, I'd awakened right where we'd fallen asleep: in Hatfield, Massachusetts, in the present day.

Nick lurched up beside me, his voice raspy with sleep. "Good God, we are still in your time."

"I know; I don't get it, the ring's still on." My fingertips brushed the blue diamond's rock-hard ridges again to make sure.

He yawned, moonlight drawing a silver line down the slight curve of his nose. "One of us plainly had not yet fallen to sleep. We must begin again." He clicked his tongue, guiding his horse Stella closer and hooking his broad arm around her leg.

I lay back down on the cold slope of mushy sand. Nick cradled me from behind with his other arm, my quickening pulse like whitewater rapids in my ears. It wasn't me who'd kept us awake: I could tell by my gunky eyes and sticky throat. Nick looked just as groggy, so it must've been the horse who'd failed to fall asleep and kept us all from traveling through time. It was the only explanation.

Nick's soft lips grazed the skin beneath my hairline, stealing my thoughts. I sighed and turned to face him, catching his mouth with mine. The sighs of pleasure he made as we kissed made my thighs hook around his leg and squeeze, but when my tongue left his mouth to begin sweeping across his delicious neck, he pulled away with a frustrated groan.

"I fear that falling to sleep beside you shall never be a simple business," he said through a drowsy smile. "But sleep we must. Lord Warwick is likely awaiting my return and may have already raised the alarm. Christ, what if the men see us appear before their eyes? You must feel favored at court, not mistrusted from the first moment." His beautiful eyes brightened with visible alarm.

I whispered a calming hush into his scarred cheek. "Don't stress. We've got this."

Rolling onto my side again, I shifted to get comfortable.

Got what exactly? How on earth was I going to convince four-hundred-year-old English aristocrats to trust me when I had literally no idea how to be a Tudor queen? It had all happened so fast—Nick's 'now or never' marriage proposal and my heartfelt acceptance. I wasn't sure I could really pull off being queen, or even if I wanted to, but I'd lost Nick before, and I had no intention of doing it again. *Ever.*

He tightened his arm around me like I might disappear if he didn't.

The next time I opened my eyes, my body felt like a bag of cement. Had we finally arrived at the Palace of Whitehall?

The world took shape and color around me. A golden blush of

sunrise painted the mirrored surface of the Connecticut River, its steady burble like a nature soundtrack. Stella lay motionless on her side while Nick breathed rhythmically into my shoulder, his eyelids fluttering with a dream.

Oh my God, the time-traveling ring isn't working! Which means…

I rolled over to face him, my eyes devouring the dimple that appeared in his cheek when he moved his mouth a certain way, the eyelashes cute enough to kiss, the delicate curve of his lips. Could my treasured King of Pants-Dropping Hotness really be stuck in my time?

I clamped my eyes shut, rising excitement burning away months of chronic anxiety. If the enchanted ring had stopped working and Nick had to stay here forever, I could have my Tudor king *and* my college degree *and* my mom *and* my friends *and* things like flushing toilets, television, and peanut butter! I could also keep Nick without having to follow through on all the scary queen stuff! I shut my eyes and lay still, immobilized with relief so intense that it felt nauseating, when something squeezed my shoulder.

"Hmm?" I muttered, my throat clogged. Nick's handsome face sharpened into view. The air tasted like smoke and straw.

"You must rise in haste," he whispered. "Francis is asleep."

I used both hands to sit up. My eyelids felt glued together. As they came unstuck, objects materialized through the darkness. A pair of misshapen candles burning from iron mounts in a brick wall. Tattered ropes dangling from a low-hanging beam. A flagstone floor brushed with hay.

We're back in the sixteenth century.

My stomach twisted into knots. *I guess Nick Tudor and my mom are going to remain mutually exclusive and I'm going to have to figure out how to be a Tudor queen. Yikes.*

Nick draped an auburn cloak over my T-shirt and jeans and whispered for me to change in the corner of the horse stable. He handed me a smock and kirtle combo that was simple enough for me to tie on myself. I guessed he'd hidden them earlier in the hope that I'd accept his marriage proposal and come back to Tudor England with him.

I slipped my bare feet into a pair of satin slippers and gasped as

Nick bundled up my modern clothes and tossed them into the fireplace. Sleepy and disoriented, we silently watched the fabric curl into flames, crackling and sputtering, before he gently guided me through the stable gate. I tightened my cloak to keep warm, my head spinning with the fact that this was really happening—I was back in the Tudor world and engaged to its king! *Mind-blown.* But at least I had Nick by my side, the thought coating me with a giddy warmth.

The sleeping Earl of Warwick, Francis Beaumont, sat crookedly on an upturned log. Stella whinnied behind us, kicking her legs for momentum before pushing herself up onto her hooves.

"Harebrain!" cried Francis, his ebony eyes flashing open. He jumped to his feet with one hand on his sword.

"Be calm," Nick hissed at him. "Has anyone come? I feared you raised the guards."

Francis shook his head, squinting at me. "But mine eyes heed someone is with you, Your Grace. So all is well then." He exhaled, sliding his hands down his midnight-blue doublet.

"Mistress Grace is in need of rest," Nick said evenly. It was a command to make no further comment about my arrival, and Francis knew better than to disobey. The smells of hay and horse sweat chased us beneath a tall stone archway and out onto a cobblestone road flanked by statuesque trees with sturdy branches. None of this looked familiar.

"You were gone for many weeks, Emmie," Nick explained. "The court is no longer at Whitehall. I have since taken up lodgings at Hampton Court Palace."

I had a zillion questions like, "*Should I act like I've seen Hampton Court Palace before?*" but I kept my mouth shut in front of Francis as the three of us climbed into a waiting coach. With the crack of a whip, the carriage jerked forward, and I avoided the earl's curious stare as I watched the peach haze of dawn illuminate the narrow road through the curtained window. Up ahead, a smattering of smoking chimneys skewered the sky, and a high gatehouse topped with onion-shaped domes emerged. Nick squeezed my hand, his palms a touch clammy. I wasn't the only one who was nervous about this new arrangement.

We bumped across a bridge decorated with Roman busts and

passed through the towering gatehouse into a stony courtyard enclosed with redbrick walls patterned with black diamonds. As we stepped out of the coach, my eyes trailed a diving flock of birds to a servant in breeches washing the ground with a broom. He bowed to the king and scampered away with his sloshing bucket. The wall lanterns still glowed with fire, but the rising sun was brightening the courtyard by the minute.

Nick didn't hesitate to make a beeline for the next gatehouse with Francis following a few paces behind us. I hugged myself beneath my cloak. I'd forgotten that sixteenth-century England was cooler than my time.

"You cannot begin to imagine how heartened I am to have you here," Nick said to me as we passed a stone fountain. He nudged my shoulder affectionately.

I tilted into him but sensed Francis's eyes on my back. "How much did you tell Lord Warwick?" I whispered. "Does he know about time travel?" The thought of someone else here knowing the real me would've actually been a relief.

"Heavens, no," said Nick. "I simply informed Lord Warwick of my desire to bring you back to court and that I planned to do it alone, commanding him to wait in the stable for my return." He leaned into me. "*Our* return."

My heart squeezed. Being back in Tudor England, this time by Nick's side, had to be worth all the unnerving parts, like convincing the locals I was queen material.

An imposing building with a gabled roof dominated the next, smaller courtyard. My gaze traced the battlement ridges, searching for archers, although Hampton Court's tall windows made it clear this was a pleasure palace rather than a fortress castle. Behind us, a gigantic gilded clock reflected a ribbon of early morning sunlight. It was bizarre to think that I should've been arriving at college in twenty-first-century London at that same moment. I pushed that thought away.

Nick's face tightened as he turned to Francis. "Lord Warwick, you will see Mistress Grace to her chambers. She may lodge in Princess Catherine's rooms until her own apartments are constructed, for which I favor the south side. You will also nominate a lady's maid until appropriate ladies of the bedchamber are appointed. Inform the Lord Chamberlain."

Francis bowed. "Forgive me, Majesty. You are constructing new apartments? For Mistress Grace." I tried not to take offense at his stunned tone.

"Mistress Grace is to become your queen," Nick replied coolly.

Francis's eyes widened, every inch of him stiffening. The opinionated earl wasn't exactly raising the roof with excitement over our decision to get hitched—quite the opposite. A dart of alarm struck my stomach.

Nick's steely voice carried a warning. "You will arrange a feast for this night to present our promised queen to the nobles. I have no patience for any slander about Mistress Grace's attendance at court. I expect the utmost heights of magnificence, of which our lady is worthy in every measure."

"A feast *tonight*?" I said, but my voice didn't cut through the growing tension between the two best friends.

Francis's narrowed eyes met the king's daunting stare. "Your Majesty, may I enquire after Mistress Grace's kin for her presentation at the feast? I will wager her father has not yet visited court."

"Mistress Grace's father has gone to God."

Nick draped a protective arm around me and kicked off an elaborate lie to Francis about how my entire family had just died of consumption in my hometown of Worthing. He explained that it was the reason I'd been called away from court for the past few weeks, and why the Duke of Norfolk—who everyone at court thought was my distant uncle—would formally present me to the nobles on my family's behalf.

My stomach tensed. The Duke of Norfolk was the most powerful man in England, second only to the king. We'd never even met, but Nick clearly trusted the duke to perpetuate the lie about me being his niece.

Francis bowed, but his voice stayed taut. "I am honored to fulfill my king's every command as his most humble servant."

Nick snapped something in French that sent the earl stumbling back a few paces. When Francis was out of earshot, the king cupped my elbows and slid me closer, stilling the quiver in my belly. He was so different here: stressed and almost scary. But when he gazed at me with those devoted eyes the color of a shallow sea, I was liquid caramel all over again.

He pressed his forehead to mine. "It will not be like last time," he breathed, smelling more like a rose garden than a riverbank. "I will build you the finest chambers you have ever seen with a chapel, rooms for music and dancing, libraries—any such thing you desire. With all my heart, I wish for your happiness here."

I ran my fingertips down the knobby gold stitching in his doublet. It was so weird to think that the dirt on his elbows came from the banks of the Connecticut River.

"I love you," I said, the words lighting up Nick's eyes. "Even though you just killed off my entire family," I added with a cheeky smile. "I guess that having them move to a tropical island would've been too much?"

His brow crumpled. "Forgive me, I intend only to make less trouble for you. Forget not that your true family has not yet been born."

"Well, by that logic, neither have I."

He chuckled and sighed simultaneously. "I slept but a few hours by a river. Do not make my head sorer than it already is." He pulled me into him, my hips brushing against his strong thighs. "You must know that my heart is full to bursting."

My palms gripped his lower back, and I wished I could track my hands lower and give his perfect ass a hard squeeze, but early-bird courtiers were beginning to surface on the edges of the courtyard. Nick unlocked himself from me with visible reluctance and stepped backward.

"I give you leave," he called, a cue for Francis to draw nearer again. "Please sleep a while," Nick said to me. The boyish smile decorating his face as he backed away liquefied my legs.

Francis called for guards, and a flurry of red coats appeared like a magic trick. They chased after the king through a Gothic stone archway at the next gatehouse.

Francis seemed irritated, and we barely said a word to each other on the way to my new chambers, but it wasn't for lack of trying on my part. The earl and I had locked horns before, and this time I wanted us to get along. But all I could get out of him was that he was now the king's chief counsel after the retirement of Sir Thomas Grey. I swallowed an urge to laugh and fist-bump him at the same time. I wasn't sure Francis had the temperament to help run a country, but his new position as the king's right-hand man was all the more reason to get him back on my side.

The chambers that were usually reserved for Nick's little sister Kit were at the rear of the palace, behind the main chapel. We crossed a quiet, square-shaped courtyard to a three-story building, where Francis used a monster-sized master key to unlock a pair of arched doors.

Stepping inside was like leaving a monochrome world for the Land of Oz. Francis hunted through a drawer for a tinderbox and lit a candle, its glow dancing up the walls draped with vibrant tapestries that disappeared into a ceiling gilded with geometric shapes. After staggering over uneven cobblestones, the woven rush matting felt like clouds.

Francis muttered to himself as he tipped the flickering candle to light the remaining wicks. "Damn orders. Leaves me to sleep on a damn stump while he rides into the damn night. Pay no heed to thieves and assassins, mind."

"All good, Lord Warwick?" I said.

He ignored the question and threw open a cupboard, checking over the pewter plates and cups. "You should have ample provisions. The chambers are regularly made ready for the Princess Catherine."

"How is Kit?" I asked, a flicker of fear in my gut. The last time I'd seen Nick's eight-year-old sister, the traitor Mathew Fox had nearly murdered both of us.

"By all accounts, the princess is well. Lodged at Kenilworth Castle and quite safe, grace be to God." Francis stood watching me for several moments while rubbing his trimmed goatee. When he spoke again, his tone was brusque.

"It may be the king's pleasure to seek holy matrimony with your person, Mistress Grace, and I yield myself to the will of our good and gracious king. However, I speak for the Privy Council, and indeed all the peers of the realm, when I say that this union does not come without surprise."

Heat flooded my face. "I think we're all a bit surprised," I said in a small voice.

I instantly regretted the missed opportunity to sound more confident, but Francis was already making his escape.

He offered a small bow before he passed through the oaken doors. "I shall have a lady's maid sent in haste to prepare your person for the feast. We cannot delay in announcing to the noblemen that their new queen is to be the daughter of a departed physician whom they have not had the pleasure of meeting."

His suspicious eyes didn't break from mine as he backed away, leaving my palms sweaty. I was getting the impression that my old mate Francis would've preferred Nick to marry the frosty French princess, Henriette.

But thinking about Nick's loving words kept me from falling into panic as I explored the drawing-room, warmed by the signs of Kit's previous stay here. A collection of carved horses, lions, crocodiles, and a spiky porcupine was piled inside a toy cart. A play castle stood guard beside it, dressed with wooden figurines of knights and ladies. I made a mental note to ask Nick if his sister could come to Hampton Court Palace so we could hang out again and she could read me poems that she'd translated from Latin.

Smiling at the thought, I meandered through the series of chambers, finding a dining chamber, another drawing-room with pallet beds for servants, a small garderobe with a medieval-style toilet, a dressing room, and a bedchamber with a hand-painted map of England on the wall. It was all a serious step up from my pokey old room at the Palace of Whitehall.

After placing the blue-diamond ring safely inside a jewelry coffer, I stripped down to my smock and climbed into the four-poster bed hung with embroidered textiles. The silk bed sheets smelled like orange blossom.

My heavy eyelids closed without effort, sparking an image of

Mom watching me. She stood smiling with her back against the laminate kitchen counter, a mug of milky tea in her hand. I'd never have moved so far away from her had it not literally come down to her or the man I loved. My chest pinched, and I turned over, sinking my cheek into the feather pillow.

I refocused my mind on Nick, remembering the way he'd flirtatiously kissed my palm on the rocky sand beside the river, and how his mouth had then moved to my fingers, his soft lips skimming them one by one, making me lose my breath. The memory of his mouth near the blue-diamond ring sent my stomach into free fall. Through all the anxiety about being back in Tudor England, I'd forgotten that the enchanted ring was acting super weird last night! It had never taken more than one try to carry us through time like that before.

I rolled onto my back and gazed at the wooden beams intersecting above the bed. What if something was wrong with the ring? I still knew hardly anything about it, and why it even traveled to my time. What if its magic had finally conked out and I was here for good?

You are *here for good, Emmie. You agreed to marry a Tudor king and become a sixteenth-century queen, even though you're an eighteen-year-old from the twenty-first century who has no idea how to do those things. And you've been here for what feels like three minutes, and he's already left you alone.*

The thoughts kept coming, and it was a miracle I fell asleep at all.

Firm fingers jiggled my arm, stirring me from a restless sleep. My eyes opened to meet a ruddy-faced girl with a tangle of red curls escaping her lopsided hood. She curtsied, silky beige skirts fluffing around her.

"My lady, I am Mistress Bridget Nightingale, here to assist you. With your permission, it will honor me to serve you as a true and faithful subject." Her squeaky voice was cute. She could've been a cartoon voice-over artist.

"Oh, hi, good morning," I mumbled through sticky lips.

"Forgive the correction, but it is afternoon, my lady. It is time to make ready for the feast where His Majesty will present you to his most favored noblemen." She heaved me out of bed with the grip of a gorilla before handing me a silk robe.

"Thanks," I said, throwing the robe over my shoulders and trailing her through to the drawing-room, even though the idea of being presented to the aristocrats made me want to hightail it back into the bed.

"I am still to make ready your chambers," said Bridget. "Forgive me; there was no forewarning of your arrival." Her cherry lips offered a nervous smile.

"Oh, it's fine, don't worry." *It's not like you knew a time traveler from the New World was heading your way. It's cool, Bridge.*

She brushed her hands on her skirts and shoved open the oak doors, nearly toppling over. I hurried to help her, and together we struggled to hoist a wooden pushcart strapped with a humungous chest down the stone steps and roll it inside. Bridget didn't want me to trouble myself, but I insisted. Anything to feel like less of a queen-to-be and more of a normal person.

"Would you care for some water?" she asked, sounding breathless. "Lord Warwick said that you favor it." She grimaced, accenting the peach rouge on her round cheeks.

"Water sounds perfect, thank you."

Sweeping a ginger curl off her neck, Bridget reached into a shelf at the base of the pushcart to retrieve a pewter jug. After pouring me some water, she guided me into a fringed chair. Next to appear from her bottomless pushcart was a cheese tart, a bowl of sugared strawberries, and a plate of freshly baked macarons. The sight sent butterflies to my stomach. Nick had remembered my weakness for macarons. My skin flushed hot at the thought of seeing him. How many hours had it been?

I sat and chewed the crisp meringues, feeling utterly useless as Bridget guided the pushcart into the dressing room. She soon reappeared, clutching a shimmering silver-colored gown embroidered with falling feathers. Artful slashes in the silver satin revealed blush-pink silk fabric underneath.

"You may choose any cloth you desire for the feast, but I much prefer this one," she said, grinning through crooked teeth. All at once,

I loved Bridget and could tell she would be a great help to me in navigating this court.

"It's stunning," I said, jumping to my feet. The perks of becoming a queen were beginning to show themselves.

I ate three macarons in a row while she dressed me piece-by-piece, beginning with several petticoats and one of those ridiculous hoop skirts. The fabric had been warmed by the fire and smelled faintly of lavender.

"How long have you been at court?" I said a little timidly. My instinct to make conversation with Bridget was matched by my fear that she'd ask questions about my life that I wouldn't know how to answer.

"I was blessed to join His Majesty's service in the year last." She tied on my skirts with the speed of an expert. "My father is the king's Master of the Horse."

Her brow pinched with concentration as she set to work attaching the sleeves of my dress, which felt heavy and expensive. It was a relief to have the company of someone fluent in all things sixteenth century.

"Thanks for helping me," I said. "It's good to have a friend here."

Her whiskey-colored eyes widened. "My lady, it pleased me to no end to learn of your arrival. To speak plainly, when the Princess Henriette of France was in the king's heart and lodged at Whitehall, she had little interest in English ladies for her household. Furthermore, Princess Henriette's French maids were rumored to have desires of the most carnal nature. I wish to become a queen's maid of honour." She blushed. "I may then find a husband of mine own."

"You're looking for a hubby?" I said through a smirk.

She giggled. "Most heartily. Is it just I, or are the noblemen becoming more handsome by the year? The Earl of Warwick steals my breath away." I tried not to chuckle at her crush on the hot-tempered Francis Beaumont. "As does the Earl of Surrey and the gentlemen company he keeps." A blush crept across her cheeks. "And, my lady, I cannot even speak of the magnificence of His Majesty. The king is the most divine person on which I have ever laid mine eyes. You are wedding pure beauty itself."

Our cheeks blushed in unison. "And that's no lie," I said.

She tugged the silk kirtle over my head, lacing it so tightly that I gasped.

"So are there any courtships on the horizon for you?" I teased, trying to breathe.

"Heavens, no, for I am tainted. I fear I will never marry at all." She sucked in a breath. "My cousin, Agnes Nightingale, is a known practitioner of the dark arts. It does not please the king, which is why my cousin was not granted permission to come to court and remains in Buckinghamshire."

"Wow. I'm sorry to hear that." In my time, magic was more of a party joke than a capital offense.

She reached for a velvet box, recovering her smile. "His Majesty had these sent while you were at rest." She lifted the lid, unveiling a necklace of sapphires set in white diamonds with dangling earrings to match. Making jewelry had gotten me through plenty of hard times in my life, and I could've hyperventilated with excitement at the sight of the precious gems.

"Fortunately, our beloved king has never been enamored of ruffs," Bridget said, fastening the cold gemstones around my bare neck. "I find that all ruffs do is hide the jewels."

"And make people look like frilled-necked lizards," I added.

She laughed politely at the joke she couldn't have understood. I was pretty sure that Australia and its creepy animals were still blissfully unaware of European existence in this time.

I stood before a cloudy mirror. As cumbersome as the outfit was, the cushiony swarm of layers felt comforting…like the real me was buried so deep within the dress that I could hide from the nobles while presenting the facade of a Tudor queen. I'd seen how Princess Henriette of France had charmed the English courtiers with her stately Renaissance dances and fluent English, Spanish, and Latin—what would they think of Emmie Grace from Hatfield, Massachusetts? How would Nick feel about me if I failed to win over the peers of the realm?

These people are going to eat you alive.

Bridget tore an ivory comb through my hair. "Forgive me," she said, frowning at my knotted curls. Once she'd separated the strands, she wove my hair into a waterfall braid and draped it with a delicate web of diamond flecks. The final touch was a sprinkling of perfumed oil over my head.

"My lady," she said, spinning me to face her. "I am unable to accompany you to the feast, but I must speak my conscience and caution you." Her expression sobered. "There has been much despair at court since Princess Henriette returned to France. While the gentlewomen could hardly bear the princess, the men adored her—a common tale. But mostly because of what Henriette represented...*hope*. For an alliance with France, but more so for an undisputed heir. A royal prince for the people to love." Her kind eyes turned grave. "I admit that I know little of your kin, but I know you are not a blood royal. That puts you in danger of dislike by the noblemen. Do not let them frighten you, and *never* trust them. One alone may seem harmless, but together, they could make you vanish like smoke. Do you understand?"

When my mouth fell open, Bridget sank to her knees. "Oh, I beg your forgiveness, my lady. I have said too much. It is my greatest fault."

I guided her back up. "No, Mistress Nightingale, thank you," I whispered, already trembling.

2

THE LAST TIME A PERIMETER OF GUARDS ESCORTED ME TO THE KING'S quarters inside a Tudor palace, I'd been suspected of treason. Today, I felt like a popstar being ushered to the stage. I caught glimpses of passing courtiers gawking at me in my glittering gown as we ascended a staircase into the more secure areas of court. I swallowed a balloon of nerves. *You got this, Emmie.*

My layered dress swished noisily along an L-shaped gallery before we crossed the Great Watching Chamber and entered the Presence Chamber. A gilded throne with a crimson cushion sat on a dais beneath a golden canopy embroidered with the king's royal arms. It might've looked cartoonish had Nick been perched on the throne holding a scepter, but instead he stood casually beside the smoldering fireplace, inspecting a crease in his palm.

He glanced up and lurched toward me, cupping my cheeks. "I missed you without end," he said, pulling me close. The palace smoke was sitting heavy in my throat, and I gladly breathed in his scent of springtime and roses.

I could barely look at him without blushing. His claret-colored doublet and coat were slashed to reveal contrasting streaks of cobalt blue lined with gold. From the shimmering crown that circled his chestnut hair all the way down to his shining boots, he was a polished jewel in itself.

See, Emmie? Everything's going to be fine…this is why you're here.

His gaze slid down my body like he also liked the way I looked before his sparkling eyes lifted back to mine. "Ready to greet the finest nobles in the realm?"

I inhaled deeply. "Being the new girl is kind of my thing."

Our hands brushed and our fingers clung together as we passed back through the Great Watching Chamber, pausing at a set of double doors crossed with pikes. Guards in red liveries stood stiffly in all corners of the room. Nick released my hand to straighten his cuffs.

"His Majesty the King, and Mistress Emmeline Grace!" cried a herald, followed by a blast of trumpets.

"We will soon bestow upon you a worthy title," Nick said under his breath.

"I didn't know I needed one," I whispered.

The pikes separated, and we stepped onto a platform at the eastern tip of the Great Hall, which would put any grand city cathedral to shame. Its hammerbeam ceiling had to be more than fifty feet high and was stunningly decorated with royal badges and fantastical creatures in vibrant shades of sapphire blue, ruby red, and metallic gold. Hundreds of lit candles crossed the space on wires, illuminating the gold thread in the sparkling wall tapestries and turning the cavernous chamber into a magical valley of light. Gentle music drifted down from the minstrels' gallery as if sent from heaven itself. The country's highest-born aristocrats were like extras in the theatrical scene, bowing to us from beneath the platform in their pearl-encrusted Tudor fashions.

"Okay, Hampton Court officially steals the show," I said in a low tone.

Nick's voice exposed a quiver of nervous pride. "Before long, all my palaces will be ours to share."

I squeezed his fingers, but what I wanted to say was: *I only want you.*

The king spoke calmly but held the room's attention. "My dearest lords, it is with every pleasure that we proclaim Mistress Emmeline

Grace our most dear betrothed. God willing, this precious lady has agreed to marry your true and faithful king and will make a most blessed queen."

The lively music cut to a desolate silence as the sea of faces gaped up at us. The reaction was so arctic that I'm surprised I didn't freeze solid on the spot. One guy with a pointed beard even glowered at me like he'd caught me double-dipping the ketchup and fries. *What the...?* When Nick's forehead tipped regally forward, however, the nobles clapped politely and bowed. The crisp harmonies of lutes, violins, and oboes again floated from the balcony, and my shoulders loosened as the room's chatter resumed. Had I imagined the icy reaction?

Nick and I crossed the tiled dais strewn with perfumed rushes to take our seats at an ornate table crowned with a green-and-white canopy. Servants washed our hands with rose water while guests hurried into their assigned seats at trestle tables positioned around the hall's edges. Nerves had dried out my mouth, so I threw back a shot of sweetened wine.

After the king said a prayer of thanks, the servers began their parade of dishes, offering slices of roasted eel, porpoise, lamb, turkey, pheasant, and swan. I hunted for vegetables but found only sliced citrus fruits artistically displayed like Chinese fans. A sweaty chef carved the turkey in front of the king and used a two-pronged fork to distribute it smoothly onto our gold plates. Nick grabbed a dark slice of meat with two fingers and slid it into his mouth.

Everything he did was adorable, but I raised my brows at him. "You saw that guy use a fork to pick up the meat to put it on the plate, right?" I whispered.

He licked his fingers. "I believe so."

I leaned closer. "So you haven't joined the dots on what else a fork might be good for?"

He reached for his wine, considering my question. I nearly disclosed the answer to my riddle when it hit me that I might bring the fork's prevalence in England forward by a century or two. I'd changed more than enough history merely by being here. To divert Nick's mind from my reckless question, I dug into the turkey with my fingers and probed him about our audience of stony-faced guests.

He leaned close to me and whispered funny stories about some of the men sitting below us, thawing some of my unease. When his fingers began discreetly caressing mine in my lap beneath the table, I turned to look up at him through my lashes, his gaze traveling all over my face as the air between us thickened. *Focus, Emmie.*

When Nick began speaking in French with one of the passing chefs, I directed my mind to surveying more of the crowd, nearly choking on my turkey. My old court bestie, Alice Grey, was watching me from the far end of the hall. Beside her sat a courtier with trimmed gray hair—the man I'd seen her dancing with at the Midsummer's Eve feast. I tried to nod hello to her, but she didn't look my way again through four more pungent meat buffets and an onslaught of sugary desserts. A chill blew through the drafty hall. I'd expected at least a smile from Alice.

Nick's warm hand cupped mine. "I will present you to my most favored nobles, and we may then retire. You must be wearied."

I swallowed alarm as the king stood up, guests scrambling to their feet in response. Servants carried away plates of half-eaten marzipan treasure chests as the courtiers left the tables and huddled into groups like a networking event.

Showtime.

The first man brave enough to approach us was the Earl of Dorset, who was the same height as me and shaped like an upside-down egg. He bowed to the king and kissed our hands.

"I have had the pleasure of seeing you at Whitehall, madam," he said to me, subtly tugging at the sash stretched too tightly around his waist. "It grieved me to hear of your family's demise."

"Thank you," I said softly. "It's been a difficult time."

It was a necessary lie, but it still made my jaw clench with guilt. I reminded myself that lying to people in this place was going to become my full-time job.

The conversation had barely begun, but it was immediately exchanged for introductions with the Lords Chancellor, Chamberlain, and Privy Seal; a tipsy mayor of London; and several earls and barons, including Lord Ashley, who I'd once saved from choking. It was all so different from the days of the Palace of Whitehall. Rather than secret trysts with the king behind closed doors, I was now openly by his side, presented to the most important men in the country as his chosen bride. My nervous panic was beginning to feel like motion sickness.

"The woman who has bewitched the King's Majesty," called the baron Lord Wharton in an insulting tone as he approached me with Alice Grey behind him. Beneath a pearled hood, her wavy hair was woven into a cluster of braids pinned with fresh flowers. Alice hated wearing her hair up.

Despite my efforts, she wouldn't meet my gaze and angled her neck past my shoulder like she was more interested in whatever was happening behind me.

The baron's face held a sinister smirk beneath his walrus-style beard trimmed into two points. "Mistress Grace, do I recall your person from Whitehall, when the king proclaimed his betrothal to Henriette of France?" he asked. Bringing up Nick's former fiancée was a clear strike at me.

"I can't say; you're not familiar to me," I couldn't help but reply. My eyes flashed to Nick, but he'd stepped away with the new French ambassador.

Wharton pursed his lips. "I understand that your late father was a physician?"

"That's right. Doctor Martin Grace from Sussex. Worthing, to be specific."

I knew I was sounding like a dingbat, but the baron was already edging his way into the king's conversation as if I'd bored him, rudely angling his back to me.

Alice and I were left alone. "Welcome to Hampton Court, madam," she said to me, curtsying stiffly in her prune-colored gown. "It greatly pleased me to receive the happy news of your betrothal to the king."

"Thank you. It's *so* good to see you." I smiled nervously, breathing in the cinnamon scent that was an Alice Grey hallmark.

Her expression stayed cool. "It seems the circumstances of loved ones may change substantially without any caution at all," she said. "As you are quite aware, I have come to suffer this knowledge on more than one occasion."

The smile slid off my face. I'd never seen Alice angry with me before. Her mom once vanished from court without a word—just like I did several weeks ago. Was she pissed at me for putting her through the same thing again?

A pair of arms pierced the tension between us, offering two cups of wine. It was Francis Beaumont in a stark-white coat strikingly draped over a doublet of emerald green. He looked as suave as always, but Alice scarcely glanced at him as she strode back to the baron.

I accepted one of Francis's cups. "Are Alice Grey and Lord Wharton a couple now?" I asked him, taking a large sip of wine. I already knew from Google searches that Alice was destined to marry Francis, at least until I first arrived in the sixteenth century and began influencing their relationship. If she married the snide Lord Wharton instead, she'd die in childbirth. A lump grew in my throat.

Francis huffed into the lip of his cup. "Ask me not about the fancies of Mistress Grey. The lady has refused to speak with me since your disappearance from court." My tight grip on the cup slackened. At least Francis was still crushing hard on Alice. There was hope for them yet.

We watched the king swallowed up by a cluster of fawning men.

"I must rescue His Majesty from this weariness," said Francis, dumping his cup onto a server's tray.

"Are you upset about Nick and me?" I cut in before he could step away. "About our betrothal?"

His coal eyes pinched at the corners. "I take pleasure in anything His Majesty desires."

"*Francis,*" I pleaded. Maybe it was too much wine making me so insistent, but I didn't care about the formalities or protocols of the court; I cared about Nick, Alice, and Francis. They were my people here, in a place where I had no family. I needed at least one of them to be real with me. "You said earlier that this was all a surprise," I added, a little shakily. "But I'm starting to get the feeling that none of it is a *good* surprise."

His lips pressed together. "Mistress Grace, it pleases me without end to see His Majesty merry, and the affection between you is plainly genuine." Once he'd rattled off the expected statement of loyalty, he dropped his voice. "A marriage, however? That will come at a cost higher than you can imagine. England is closer to peace than she has ever been, and our good king does not hunger for war. I wish not to see our realm come to ruin."

"To *ruin?*" It was hard not to let my offense show. "That's the last thing I want."

Nick knocked past Francis to gently hook my arm in his, drawing the room's attention with his natural magnetism. Was Francis right to be concerned? Had Nick really made a terrible mistake in choosing me over Henriette of France?

"My dear love," the king called loudly. The eyes of nearby gentlemen nearly popped from their sockets. "It will please you to see your *uncle*, the Duke of Norfolk, has presently arrived from his duties in Sussex for this most joyous occasion. His Grace received word only this morning."

A colossal man stepped through the throng in a navy coat trimmed with black ribbons and dotted with seed pearls. His sausage-sized fingers clutched a hat sprouting an ostrich feather.

The duke dropped into a bow and kissed my hand. "My dear lady and precious niece. It pleasures me beyond measure to look upon you again."

I felt like I'd walked into a Shakespeare play, except I'd forgotten all my lines. When had Nick had the time to convince the Duke of Norfolk to continue this fabrication about being my uncle? But if Norfolk was as thrown about the sudden engagement as everyone else, he didn't let it show. Courtiers tipped their heads at the duke like he was the King of England himself, and he was legitimizing me to every one of them. I could've freaking hugged the old upper cruster. When the duke rose back to his imposing height, a thick gold chain swung from his chest.

"Will you lodge at court awhile, my lord?" Nick said to him.

"Naturally, with His Majesty's permission."

"On condition that you wash in haste; you smell like a horse's chamber pot," Nick quipped.

Laughter echoed through the hall like it was the funniest joke ever told, Norfolk's loudest of all.

The duke offered me a gloved hand. "A stroll in the courtyard, madam? All these haughty gentlemen…you must be in need of some air."

Nick winked at me, sending a flock of butterflies to my stomach, before turning into a circle of waiting courtiers that I knew bored him to tears.

I smiled shyly at Norfolk, mentally latching onto him after his endorsement of me. He boldly took my hand, steering me out of the Great Hall and down a stone staircase that led to a drafty gatehouse. A sword swung from his hip as we strolled outside into the clock court-yard, where a smattering of drunken courtiers lay slumped on benches. I paced away from the stomach-churning stench of barf at the base of the wall.

The evening air felt slightly warmer with Norfolk around, like he really was my only family here. His face was attractive for an older man and sharply angled like it was carved from marble. I hadn't seen my dad in months, but the thought of him still pierced my chest.

"I appreciate you riding all this way to meet me, Lord Norfolk," I said, hoping that was the right way to address him.

"I bid you to call me Uncle Harry."

I knew that Norfolk's real name was Henry Howard and that most Henrys here were called 'Harry' for short. He gazed up at the astro-nomical clock that presided over the courtyard. My eyes followed his, blown away by the giant disc of gold that was tinted cherry-pink by the last hour of daylight.

"I have no true niece, you know," Norfolk said to me. "Well, until now, I suppose. I will speak plainly; I had not supposed that King Nicholas would marry for pleasure. After the despair it brought to King Harry…to the Queens Mary and Elizabeth. However, I suppose that foolish desire is in the king's blood."

My fingers curled, starting to feel the cold. "It's not foolish desire,"

I said in a small voice. "Nick and I have already been through a lot together, and this is the right thing."

Norfolk grunted. "How would a girl know any measure of what is right for a king?"

The temperature in the air seemed to plummet as we stood facing the clock, the evening shadows masking the crease of disappointment that crept onto my brow. *Please, no. Not you too, Norfolk.*

"I don't pretend to be anything I'm not," I finally said, the hypocrisy of that statement shaming me in my period gown. "But I love the king, and I know he loves me. We just want to be together and make each other happy."

A bark of laughter burst from Norfolk's throat.

Before I could form a response to that rude reaction, he took a lofty step inside the gatehouse beneath the clock tower. "Have you yet laid your eyes upon this?" he called, aiming a thick finger at the stone ceiling.

I steadied myself and gathered my skirts to follow him, gazing up. Among the intricate stone carvings in the vaulting was the image of a crowned falcon.

"The falcon was the royal badge of Queen Anne Boleyn," Norfolk explained, like he was narrating a documentary for the history channel. "When King Henry had Queen Anne executed for treason and adultery, he neglected to have the badge removed."

I'd read up on the Tudors lately. Anne Boleyn wasn't a royal princess like Henry's first wife, Katherine of Aragon, but Henry the Eighth had married her out of genuine, passionate love. When he tired of her and met Jane Seymour, however, he had Anne's head hacked off with a sword.

A burning torch in the wall morphed Norfolk's striking face into that of a monster's.

"The necks of foolish girls in love are highly desirable, Mistress Grace. You would be wise to take good care of yours."

He made a small bow and left me there, frozen solid beneath the relic of a besotted young queen who'd gambled her life on the heart of a Tudor king…and lost her head for it.

3

I HURRIED BACK UPSTAIRS AND INTO THE WARMTH OF THE GREAT Hall, but Nick's calming face was absent from the thinning crowd of courtiers. There was also no sign of Alice Grey, who must've called it a night. I asked after the king, and a guard ushered me into the Presence Chamber. Aside from the guards, Nick and Francis were the only men in the room, and were speaking intently beside the canopy of estate.

My instinct was to back away, forever out of my depth on important Tudor matters, but Nick spotted me and ushered me over. Francis had been addressing the king, but when I approached, the earl's mouth clamped shut.

"You may speak freely in front of your promised queen," Nick ordered him. "Inform Mistress Grace what you did me. There will be no secrets between us."

Francis's throat bulged in a tight swallow. "Madam, I have it on good authority that a squadron of Spanish warships was sighted this night in the English Channel."

I felt the blood leave my skin. "Warships?"

My reaction sent Nick stammering like he was embarrassed. "Four ships, which is hardly a fleet. King Philip seeks peace more than I, given the mess he has made of the Low Countries. It is no more than a pretense."

Francis gripped his hat so tightly that his knuckles whitened. "Sending warships as a mere performance? Majesty, Spain has more than a hundred ships like it…the strongest navy in Christendom."

"You need not remind me of King Philip's admiration for his glorious self," Nick said with sarcasm.

Francis gnawed at his lip, unable to conceal his annoyance that I was privy to this discussion. I was more than happy to leave them alone, but I didn't dare move. First the nobles disliking me, and now the threat of war with Spain. What had it been—less than a day since I arrived? Tudor England needed to take the intensity down a notch.

Nick's eyes flashed with anger. "My patience with King Phillip is at an end. That idiot seeks to increase my troubles while we are preparing for a new queen. We shall remain idle no more."

Francis stuttered through his nervous suggestion. "Majesty, before such a glorious occasion as the crowning of your chosen queen, I counsel you to propose a meeting with the King of France. If you sail to Calais in haste, you may yet save the peace treaty between France and England. When King Henry beholds the magnificence of the King of England in person, he will be persuaded. A visit of your sacred person is a pledge of commitment…an apology for what transpired with his sister, Princess Henriette."

Henriette's name felt like a shard of glass in my throat, and Francis probably meant it to have that effect. She was the French princess to whom Nick had once proposed but then ditched for me. Now Spain was taking advantage of the severed marriage alliance between England and France by taking a swing at England. I wanted to disappear for my part in this unfolding disaster, but instead, I stood there, coiling my fingers into tight fists. Was Nick already regretting his decision to leave Henriette and marry me?

The king drew a deep breath and then expelled it. "I will think on it. Inform the Lord High Admiral to examine the forts and make ready the beacons and warships." Francis made a gracious nod as if he was accepting a gift. "My Lord Warwick," Nick added, "I am trusting you to see to it that the Spanish withdraw their provocation, or you will answer for it."

Francis bowed as he backed away, sweaty curls pasted to his neck. A flame of sympathy sparked in my chest for his thankless position as the king's right hand, which had eclipsed the cheerful friendship they'd shared until now. Alice's father, Thomas Grey, had the job before Francis and had been only too glad to throw in the towel.

Nick scooped up my hand into his soft fingers. I was well acquainted with how my fiancé could flip from Jekyll to Hyde—the drawback to dating a Tudor king.

"My love, we must part," he said. "I must think on this issue of Spain."

His palm skated up my cheek, and I tilted into his touch. I brought my lips to his fingers and kissed them one by one like they were strips of candy. A fluttery sigh escaped his mouth, and he turned into me. "Baby," I whispered, wishing we could just be alone.

A moment later, feet thudded, pikes detached, and members of the Privy Council began filing in, headed by the formidable Duke of Norfolk.

Nick drew away from me and ordered the gentlemen to follow him into his council chamber. They disappeared through the Great Watching Chamber like a consortium of high-powered CEOs, leaving me standing beside a candelabrum of polished gold.

A pair of polite guards offered to escort me back to my chambers, and I accepted with relief. I'd had more than enough excitement for one day. The opulent palace corridors and gemstones swinging from my earlobes would never get old, but as we headed downstairs to my rooms, I felt only the terror of Nick facing a medieval-style war. Having him hacked to bits by a Spanish sword was so *not* my idea of wedded bliss.

Eager for sleep, I avoided chatter with Bridget Nightingale about the night's events as she undressed me. I climbed into the warmed blankets and breathed in their orange scent, the oppressive silence clawing at me. At my home in modern-day Hatfield, my mom often left her television on, even when she was at work. Cars sped up and down our street at all hours. Dogs barked at annoying times. Here, the only background noise was a deathlike silence. I blew out the candle and rolled onto my side in the empty bed, my fingertips tracing the pattern of entwined vines embroidered into the curtains. A gentle pattering crept through the window, and I closed my eyes, relieved for the sound of falling rain. Just any sound at all.

At the first blackbird's cry, Bridget heaved open the window shutters like a boarding school mistress, leaving me to eat breakfast in bed and say my morning prayers. I sat up on the mattress and massaged the back of my neck while chewing crispy white bread and pondering the timeline of coffee.

Bridget poured me a bath at my request, and I sank into the water strewn with fragrant herbs and rose petals. My fingers swirled through the cloudy liquid, circling the small scar from the old arrow wound on my thigh, which had healed nicely.

My head exploded with thoughts about how I might help Nick with his war pressures. I wanted to be more than an obedient Tudor queen who decorated the king's court as a silent symbol of piety. That was definitely—and hilariously—not me, but I was kidding myself if I believed I had any advice to offer about sixteenth-century European conflicts. Sir Thomas Grey's earlier plan of a marriage alliance between King Nicholas of England and Princess Henriette of France was sounding more ideal for England by the minute. Now I'd woken up freaking out that Nick would regret his decision and send me on a one-way ticket back to the twenty-first century, where I'd never see him again.

My toes squished the cloth lining the bathtub as I climbed over the wooden edge, landing on a linen sheet. After I'd dried off and slipped on my smock, I dunked the ewer into the bathwater and carried it out to Bridget.

"Where can I put the water?" I asked. "Is this the best way to empty the bath?"

She swerved away from her sewing. "Oh, my lady, I will attend to it."

"It's okay; I want to help."

She wrestled the ewer from my hands. "Forgive me. I must complete my tasks, or I may be relieved of my duties."

With a sigh, I relinquished the ewer, reminding myself that Tudor folk were comfortable with their rigid master-servant roles. I didn't need to call extra attention to myself by challenging the system.

After Bridget had rubbed my teeth with mint water and a tooth cloth, she dressed me in a pretty ivory gown embroidered with hundreds of tiny botanicals. She fixed my hair into a plaited bun and pinned a pearled hood over the top before handing me an embroidery hoop, a silver thimble, a pincushion, and a monster-sized needle. I barely restrained a sigh of annoyance. Had I seriously just spent an hour getting dolled up for a spot of sewing in my private chambers?

Good morrow, obedient Tudor lady of the house. Prithee, would thee sew with me?

There were some upsides to the tedium: more than an hour spent stitching the tentacles of a giant caterpillar distracted me from fears about Nick facing the Spanish Armada. I was glad for the company of the chambermaids who flittered between the rooms, changing the sheets and brushing down the outer pieces of my gowns. A French tailor turned up to take measurements for my new wardrobe, nattering to himself while making notches in a long strip of parchment. As the morning progressed, I soaked in as many tips as I could about the protocols of the Tudor court.

Nonetheless, I was ready to toss my mindless needlework into the fireplace when one of Nick's gentlemen of the chamber arrived to request my presence for dinner with the king.

Oh my God, finally. Presence freaking granted.

We carefully crossed the cobblestones that were still slick with rain and headed upstairs to the heated splendor of the king's Privy Chambers. The gentleman instructed me to wait in the Presence Chamber, so I hung out beside the stone fireplace that smoldered with chalky logs. So much for a normal relationship…things felt even more formal than before.

The king appeared within minutes, sending away a flock of councilors with a flick of his wrist.

He strode toward me with his confident gait, his hypnotic eyes sending searing heat to my stomach.

"Forgive me," he said, taking my hands. "The feast last night brought many distractions." He wrapped himself around me like we hadn't seen each other in months, smelling as amazing as ever. *Gah.*

Guards parted in smooth succession as we clung together and strolled through Nick's withdrawing chamber, study, and library before reaching his private dining room. The walls gleamed with cloth of gold, absorbing the rich smells of the roasted meats and pies drowning in tangy sauces—every dish presented with the fanfare of trumpets. There were so many servers fussing over us that I couldn't ask Nick if there'd been any developments with the Spanish conflict. As I forced myself to eat beef pie with my fingers, I imagined fixing him a tuna melt sandwich in my Hatfield kitchen, which inspired a pang of longing that surprised me. I was also too aware that I'd barely touched him since we arrived back in Tudor England. Memories of his hands and mouth on me at Whitehall and Robin House throbbed through me, but now that I was on public display, we hadn't been alone for even a minute.

Nick distracted my thoughts with our usual effortless chatter, and by the time we finished dinner, we were canoodling our way into his drawing-room. *Finally.* I was desperate to peel off some of his luxurious layers of clothing and get to the real splendor beneath.

I balked at the sight of six people in the tight space. There were two pages stoking the fire, a long-haired boy blowing into a flute, guards policing each doorway, and a servant holding out a fruit platter that must've given him carpal tunnel syndrome. This was the least private living room on Earth. I turned to face Nick with frustrated eyes.

"Now that you are my betrothed, we should be watched when we are alone to make certain there is no question that you are pure," he explained, folding his arms around my waist and locking me against him. "There is to be no uncertainty about our son's legitimacy."

The thought of falling pregnant at my age tightened my stomach even more than the idea of having to keep my hands off my fiancé. A son? *Yikes.*

"What if we have a girl?" I couldn't help but dangle. "We can call her Nicky."

He made a strained smile. "If we are blessed with a daughter, we will make her a suitable match." His knuckle stroked my cheek. "The son of a great king."

"So now our baby is getting married? Holy smokes, I'd like to have at least met the guy first." My gaze flashed across the room, but none of the attendants showed any signs of listening.

"Do not torment me with talk of our babies," Nick said, relaxing into a chair beside the fireplace. "I can imagine nothing sweeter." He hooked his boot around the leg of another seat and dragged it closer, cocking his finger for me to sit with him. "Besides, as much as I yearn for the day you take to your childbed, I also fear it in great measure."

He swallowed tightly and didn't elaborate, but I knew what he meant. Postpartum deaths were common in Tudor England, and pregnancy could steal a woman from the world at any moment—and the baby. There were no medical hospitals, antibiotics, or nurses like my mom.

With both of us happy to change the subject, we played cards and teased each other with delicious kisses that I wanted so badly to escalate to something more, but Nick was in self-control mode and kept rerouting my wandering hands back up to his smirking face. I groaned under my breath, and he lowered his head, bringing his lips to my ear.

"When we are wed, my girl so fair, you may be doing your utmost to keep this king's hands *off* your sweet body that my mouth thirsts to taste to sorely."

My heated face flew up as a gentleman strode in and bowed, clutching Nick's traveling cloak.

"Already?" the king said to him with dismay.

"The congregation has gathered at the royal barge, Your Majesty," the coat holder replied, his chapped lips trembling. "Forgive me; Your Grace wished to be informed without delay. The tides are now favorable." Another attendant fluffed the king's feathered hat.

Nick chugged the remnants of his wine and took my fingers in his. His dimpled cheeks had reddened. "Emmie, I have come to a decision to sail to Calais. I shall meet with the King of France at first light on the morrow."

"Oh?" A chill spiraled up my neck.

"Spain is acting in a most provocative manner, and God willing, I must save the alliance, or we risk many men. You know I desire only peace and stability, but if there is to be war, we must have France side with us. We cannot allow Spain and France to unite their faith and mount an offensive."

"Of course." My stomach roiled at the thought of him leaving Hampton Court practically five minutes after I'd moved here. I still had so much to learn about court etiquette, and now I'd be alone. "Can I go with you?" I asked.

He ran his palm over the back of my hand. "You must know I desire nothing more. I just won you back, and to part again feels intolerable. But there is no way for you to come; we have not the time to make ready your presentation ceremony. Besides, I must make peace with King Henry about what came to pass with his sister Henriette."

Hearing Nick say his former fiancée's name scorched my chest. He tilted into my line of sight, reassuring eyes of translucent blue holding mine. "You need not feel troubled about Henriette. You know that I love you with all my heart."

I nodded, fingering the silk ridges of his embroidered sleeve. I didn't say it aloud, but I feared that one look at Henriette's royal family would be all it would take to remind Nick how much more suited she was to him than me.

He stood up, cueing the men to drape his traveling cloak over his broad shoulders.

An idea struck me with sudden clarity. "Should I go back home while you're away?" I suggested, hopping to my feet. "I mean to Worthing," I added for the benefit of all the ears in the room.

The shock in Nick's face was startling. He knew precisely which home I was talking about: Hatfield in modern-day Massachusetts, not Worthing in sixteenth-century Sussex.

His brow pinched with alarm. "My palace does not please you?"

"Of course it does, it's just...I thought it might be a good opportunity."

His eyes clouded with the sort of anxious fear I'd seen before—twice. It was the same expression he'd had after I'd disappeared back to my world without intending to ever return to Tudor England. A few days earlier, I'd promised Nick that I would never do that to him again.

"Don't worry, we can talk about it later," I said, reaching for his fingers.

His gaze searched mine while the gentlemen fluffed up the feather in his hat. "Enough," the king snapped, and they scurried away.

"With all this Spain business, I have been careless in reporting news of your household," Nick said to me, his voice a little shaky. "Suitable ladies and attendants are being appointed as we speak. Construction of your apartments is already afoot. I have instructed the Master of the Revels to keep your person and your ladies merry in our absence. I pray you will come to feel at home here."

My shoulders felt rigid as he wrapped his arms around me. "By God's grace, be safe," he said, nestling his soft lips into my neck. "My heart remains here in your hands."

Tears sprang to my eyes without warning. Nick Tudor was about to leave for France on a primitive sailing ship that could sink at the first sign of a storm. What if he came home with a renewed marriage alliance with France—or worse—never came home at all? Before I could gather my words, he was already striding away from me, the blue-diamond ring glinting from his third finger.

The next day, I woke to the rich smells of roasted meats that reached my bed from my dining chamber, more lunchtime aromas than breakfast. I must've slept late. My toes disturbed the creaky floorboards, and Bridget burst into my room to dress me, explaining that one of my new lady attendants was waiting in the next chamber.

"Oh, you should've woken me."

"I was commanded to leave you at rest," she said, tying on my sleeves. Her tight coral-colored gown accentuated her generous curves.

"Next time, you can wake me," I insisted, a little frustrated that Nick now wanted to control my sleeping schedule. I would've liked to have at least been up before dinner, which—to be fair—was at ten o'clock in the morning in this place.

The dining chamber greeted me with fragrant wafts of cooked rosemary and lemon. My lips fell open as Alice Grey glanced up from the circular mother-of-pearl table. She rose to curtsy at me.

"My lady, may I present your new lady of the bedchamber, Mistress Alice Grey," said Bridget. "She is the daughter of the—"

"I know Alice," I cut in with a chuckle. But the woman who had been my closest friend at court refused to meet my eyes.

We all sat down, and I appraised the spread of roasted chicken and lamb, a tower of meatballs, at least twenty white bread rolls, and a platter of carrots carved into Tudor roses. The perfect breakfast for a lion, or perhaps a Neanderthal man.

Alice washed my hands in a bowl of rosewater, a nervous tremble between our fingers. "It is rather strange," she said evenly. "Queens usually choose from their own relations for their households. But, then again, Mistress Grace is not yet the queen."

The words hit with the punch of an insult, which wasn't like Alice at all. I dropped a chicken leg onto my plate that I couldn't imagine eating, and not because I'd just woken up.

Bridget's painted eyebrows fluttered with excitement. "According to the Lord Chamberlain, a third maiden has been called to court to attend to your household but has not yet arrived."

"Have mercy on us if the Sackville ladies should be forced upon us," Alice replied, scratching beneath her hood.

Bridget giggled. "Did you hear what occurred this winter last between the Sackvilles and the Lennards?"

Alice nodded with a grimace.

I bit into a peppery meatball, working hard to keep a smile on my face. It was hard to watch Alice and Bridget chat about the upper-class connections they had in common, reminding me how lowborn I was and out of place here.

"I do wonder who the new maiden shall be," said Bridget. "Perhaps somebody with a devilishly handsome brother?" She spun to me.

"My lady, may I ask when you came into favor with his most gracious Majesty?" She blinked with what looked like pure envy.

I instinctively glanced at Alice for help, but she just rested her chin on her palms, watching me.

"The king and I got together this summer," I replied, my face a furnace. "We kept it under wraps for a bit. I mean...we kept it a secret."

Alice finally chimed in, but it was far from a rescue effort. "You may recall that Mistress Grace purported to be visiting Whitehall on behalf of her father in the summer," she said to Bridget. "Mistress Grace took pleasure in flirtations with several noblemen—Viscount Hereford was the first, if I remember—before climbing the tallest tower in all of Christendom and snatching the king from the arms of the Princess of France. It is truly a tale for the theatre."

Bridget smiled politely through fuchsia cheeks. My gaze fell to my plate until the browned chicken skin and carrot chunks began wobbling through my swelling tears.

"Excuse me, I just need some air," I said, sliding my chair back and making a beeline for the drawing-room. I shook open my folded coat, wrapped it around my shoulders, and headed outside to the courtyard.

A war with Spain, threats from the Duke of Norfolk, the expectations of becoming an accomplished Tudor queen, and now my best friend Alice Grey turning against me. Coming back to 1580 was starting to feel like a mistake.

4

I KEPT GLANCING OVER MY SHOULDER TO SEE IF ALICE HAD FOLLOWED me, but only a pair of brooding guards trailed me through the stone corridors bordering the clock courtyard. Most of the courtiers had vanished upstairs for dinner, so I grabbed my chance to explore more of the palace without the constant stares and scrutiny.

Strolling along twisting galleries, I paused to admire paintings of Nick's achievements and magnificent biblical tapestries threaded with gold. I passed a gallery of canaries in ornamental birdcages to reach a library with leather-bound books stacked horizontally. Two men who were evidently late for dinner sat arguing on a bench beneath a stained-glass window. Their troubled eyes deflected to me—probably thinking I was a poor exchange for Princess Henriette of France—and I escaped back outside. Carpenters and bricklayers milled about the courtyard, swinging planks of wooden scaffolding into place. Was this where my new apartments were being built? I shivered. It was too weird to think about Hampton Court Palace being redesigned because of me. How would that change the future?

I breathed through my tense stomach, becoming irritated by the guards who wouldn't get off my back. They lingered in my peripheral vision like goons from a mafia movie.

Nick! No one's going to attack me in broad daylight.

Ducking into a windowed corridor near the palace entrance shook the guards off my tail—at least until they located me again. Relieved to be free of them for now, I stepped into a smaller courtyard crowded with wagons, pack horses, and servants clothed in cheap leather doublets. The sour stink of rotting vegetables attacked my nose. Horses' hooves clopped along the cobblestones while servants unloaded sacks of sugar and barrels of cabbages and cauliflower. The trademark Tudor opulence was gone, and I'd clearly crossed into an area of court where I didn't belong.

With the main passage obstructed by an enormous cart carrying a mountain of firewood, I proceeded down a thin, doglegged passage that opened into a sunless corridor. Now it was the stench of fish that sent my palm to my mouth. I lurched toward the more bearable smells of roasting meats in the next building.

I felt the intense heat of the raging fires before I saw their furious flames snapping the air, practically searing my skin. A sweaty servant fanned smoke toward the windows as I registered the sequence of blazing fireplaces, each one gigantic enough for me to stand inside. Perspiring cooks in sooty aprons sat beside the open hearths, turning massive spits threaded with chunks of meat.

A man whose pleated coat failed to cover his ample belly slid sideways through the trestle tables to reach me. "Good morrow to you, my lady. May I be of help?" he said, wiping his hands on the frayed ribbon supporting his hose.

"I'm a bit lost," I replied, salty sweat dripping onto my lips.

"If you are unaccompanied, may I call for one of the lords?" he said with a frown. "This is no place for a lady."

"It's okay. I'm just leaving."

Escaping into the next corridor, I tripped over a cluster of men lying on sacks who were either asleep or three sheets to the wind. I knew that Nick wouldn't like me being here. I stumbled my way back into the burning-hot roasting kitchens, slamming into the master cook's burly chest.

Emmie Grace: making a spectacle of herself since the day she was born!

"The lady is here, Your Grace," the chef stuttered with the sort of servitude that made my eyes search for the king. But when the chef stepped aside, it was the Duke of Norfolk who appeared behind him. Wanting to shake myself for losing my bearings, I had to follow the duke's forest-green cape like a naughty schoolgirl back through the stinky warren of kitchen corridors. When I recognized the windowed passage leading back to the western courtyard near the palace entrance, I thanked the duke and glided past him.

"I have more important tasks than chasing after a featherbrained girl," he uttered behind me.

"I was just going for a walk and lost track of where I was," I said over my shoulder. "Is that a crime in your neck of the woods?"

Norfolk cut in front of me, blocking my path. He smelled almost as good as Nick: like sandalwood and vanilla.

"His Majesty has traveled to Calais," he said to me.

"I'm aware."

His prominent lips pursed. "The truth is that I desire war with the cod's-headed Spanish, but our king desires peace, and it may be too late. The French may never forgive His Majesty for disgracing their princess—the daughter of a king—for no more than a common upstart from Worthing. Make no mistake, they are mocking King Nicholas in France as we speak."

Norfolk's glare declared that I was to blame for England's latest troubles, and even though I'd never admit it to him, he wasn't exactly wrong. Yet I had no intention of ever leaving Nick, and my chest crushed with a burning need to win over the duke. He was supposed to be the one to help me. Would he address me this brazenly if the king were still here?

"I trust that the king knows what he's doing," I said, trying not to stammer. "I'm not here to cause any trouble, and I'll do whatever I can to help keep the peace."

"How about serving as the king's mistress?" Norfolk offered like it was a simple solution.

My teeth gnawed my lip. It was a fair question in Tudor times, but I'd genuinely tried to be Nick's mistress before while he had a romantic relationship with Henriette. "I wish I could do that," I replied honestly. "But I love him too much. It would break me."

Norfolk's cool eyes narrowed. "Madam, what right do you have to place your needs before a king's? What dowry do you even offer? No family, no treaty, no land. You say you love His Majesty, but you willingly demean him."

I maintained my stare. "I don't *demean* anyone," I said through my teeth. "For your information, the king was the one who chased me— begging me to marry him." Norfolk scoffed at the concept. "And you have no idea what I've had to give up to be with him," I added. "So unless you want me to update him on all the unpleasant things you've said about us in the five minutes you've known me, I suggest you cool the hell down and find a way to get over it."

I was sure that would scare him off, but he squatted to meet my eye level, wine and rosemary on his breath. "You are incapable of ruining me," he said. "I am the Duke of Norfolk; I speak my conscience. Furthermore, I have known His Majesty since he was a babe. Our dear king has a known weakness for pretty girls. You may be the only pretty girl in England with a mouth and mind dumber than a pail of rocks, but you are not the only pretty girl in England."

His sharp stare delivered a warning before he shoved past me and continued on his way.

Tears blurred my vision as I wandered back into the western courtyard in a daze, the whir of carts and horses seeming even more foreign than before. I considered the quiet safety of my chambers, but the thought of again facing angry Alice made me want to scream.

Instead, I left the palace proper altogether, crossing the west gatehouse bridge to find a patch of wildflowers sloping its way down to the olive-colored curve of the River Thames. Slippery mud gripped the heels of my satin pumps as I hitched up my skirts and climbed down to the riverbank. White daisies peppered the grass like snowflakes, and I sat among them and hugged my knees. I was still reeling from my intense chat with Norfolk.

For a few minutes, I watched servants offloading bags of grain from barges onto a wooden landing platform. Aside from the wind delivering an occasional odor of sewage, the soothing gurgles and horn-like calls of ducks could have come from the Connecticut River.

No wonder Nick liked it here at Hampton Court Palace; it was peaceful.

Thinking about him aroused a twisting heat in my stomach. When entitled jerks like Norfolk weren't trying to intimidate me, I loved being here with Nick. Having him feel the same way about me as I did him was a literal dream come true. But I had to find a way to be happy here when he wasn't around. Aside from learning the customs of the court, I needed a freaking *life* in Tudor England.

I swatted away a bee so that I could snap off the stems of a few daisies. After slicing open their stalks with my fingernail, I wove each flower through the split ends, fastening the daisies into a garland bracelet. When Nick proposed to me, he also promised me a jewelry workshop. Once that was ready, I'd learn how to make the most striking bracelets, necklaces, earrings, and rings that Tudor England had ever seen. Emmie Grace: Tudor queen and jewelry designer. I smirked and slipped the garland over my wrist.

My chest felt lighter as I made my way back to my chambers, surprised to find them empty. After untying the ribbons of my muddy shoes, I sat on a velvet chair and curled my legs up in my silk stockings. I helped myself to a macaron from a silver bowl on the table, already conceptualizing the first showpiece I'd create in my jewelry workshop. I'd seen a noblewoman at the feast wearing a cool chain of pearls tied into knots, and it spawned an idea for a corsage-like bracelet of knotted pearls and gemstones.

While hunting for a quill to sketch the idea, I spotted the black box on my pillow. It was tied with a bow made from peony-pink ribbon—the same color of the knot ring I'd once made for Nick.

Butterflies crowded my stomach as I untied the bow and lifted the lid. On a bed of navy velvet sat the enchanted blue-diamond ring and a folded note. All the air in my lungs escaped in a rush of relief. I brought the ring to my nose as if I could smell the future through its cold surface...my mom, my friend Mia, my schnauzer Ruby...even those hideous alphabet blinds in my bedroom.

I slipped it onto my thumb and split open the king's seal to read Nick's note.

Dearest Emmie, my miracle girl.
My heart is so sore to take leave of you.
However, it is made worse by the thought that you feel a prisoner here.
You are not. You never will be. Therefore, I commit this ring to your care.
Please know that, no matter where your person shall lie, there is a king, and a man,
who desires to be with you, then and now, and every day for all eternity.
You have not—in any time or place—a more loving or loyal servant.
Your most true,

NR

I flopped back onto the bed, my heart a racehorse flying at top speed. My season ticket back to my homeland sat on my thumb, ready for boarding. But Nick had trusted my promise not to use the time-traveling ring without him, and I had to be worthy of that. Plus, the ring had taken a few attempts to work correctly last time. What if I used it to pop home and then I couldn't get back here again? It was unthinkable.

What I needed was to find out more about the enchanted ring... like why it sends people through time when they fall asleep and its reasons for acting so strangely the other night. There was so little I knew about it, apart from the fact that it had been cursed by a sooth-sayer hired by Mary, Queen of Scots. Bridget Nightingale had told me her cousin was a renowned soothsayer in Buckinghamshire—perhaps she could help; maybe she was even the same soothsayer! Feeling the dangers of witchy business in Tudor England creep up my spine, I turned to the map of England on the paneled wall, but I was terrible at English geography. My fingers traced the parchment, searching.

The front doors to my chambers banged shut, making me jump. I slid off the ring and locked it inside my jewelry coffer.

In the drawing-room, Alice was helping Bridget out of her cloak. Bridget fell into a curtsy. "Oh, my lady, Mistress Grey and I searched for you."

Alice tugged off her fringed gloves with her teeth. "We found you not, but Mistress Nightingale did discover the Earl of Surrey making his way to a tennis match."

"His silk shirt was so fine that one could see his flesh right through it," Bridget added, her bronze eyes glinting. "Surrey must have felt the chill. It was no wonder that his handsome tennis partner closed his arm around him as if to keep him warm."

"Never mind that," Alice replied. "It is the king's pleasure to begin your lessons this day, Mistress Grace. The pavan, the almain, and the volta."

Lines of confusion touched Bridget's brow, and I flushed hot. These were basic sixteenth-century dances, and a queen-to-be should have learned this stuff years ago, if I'd been of this time. Now, if I had a hope of convincing people like the Duke of Norfolk that I wasn't an appalling substitute for a French princess, I needed to become a total badass at all things Tudor, starting with the weird dancing.

"I'm ready," I said. "I'll get up to speed with all the moves, and the three of us can put on a show that'll bring the house down."

Alice laughed, drawing my smile to hers. Her icy expression had thawed a little.

Bridget had to finish her embroidery, so she stayed behind while Alice led the way to the rehearsal room. I fumbled for something to say as we strolled in awkward silence, but it was Alice who spoke first, sounding surprisingly choked.

"I pray you forgive me for my earlier words about your closeness with the king," she said. "I meant not to upset you. My damn tongue."

I nearly tripped at the apology, my pulse soaring. "It's okay," I said. "Your summary about us wasn't exactly off the mark."

As we turned into the clock courtyard, I gathered the courage to ask Alice the question that'd been on my mind since the feast. "Are you mad at me because I disappeared from Whitehall a few weeks ago without telling you?"

Her lips turned downward. "Well, it was not the first time you vanished from court, and I understand if you are unhappy here; sometimes, I miss Northamptonshire in great measure. But you did not even speak a word of farewell, yet you know what I have suffered with my mother's passing from sight."

"I know." We reached the gatehouse bustling with courtiers

queuing to ascend the staircase to the Great Hall. "I'm so sorry, Alice. Please believe me that I've never wanted to hurt you."

She pulled me outside to a streak of graffiti chipped into the brick wall, lowering her voice. "Then why must you lie? I once asked you if you had a dalliance with the king, and you assured me you did not. We spent every day together, yet you never mentioned your pursuit of His Majesty's hand. Now you return from Sussex as our promised queen?" Her tanned forehead rumpled. "For how long had you been plotting this?"

I'd started to tremble. "I never wanted to keep this from you. There was no plot. I only became close with the king after I caught the one-day fever, but he was still pursuing Princess Henriette...he asked me not to tell anyone. I didn't know what to do."

She exhaled, shaking her head and staring at her feet. I'd never known life at Tudor court without the friendship and support of Alice Grey. I wasn't sure I could pull it off.

"Why does it bother you so much that he and I love each other?" I said, a little exasperated at the constant disapproval.

"It bothers me not!" She spoke quietly but vehemently. "I can think of no one I desire to see His Majesty with more than you. But the last time I saw you, you told me you loved *Lord Warwick*. You were weeping over him. And then you left court without a word—was it not Lord Warwick who drove you away?"

Shock overcame my face. One of my countless lies to Alice Grey was that I was in love with Francis Beaumont, the Earl of Warwick. I'd forgotten all about it. No wonder she was so angry with me!

"Alice, *no*," I said. "I made the Lord Warwick thing up as part of my cover for being with the king. God, I'm so sorry. I don't love Francis; I never did. The person I'm in love with—the one I was weeping over—is Nick."

There had been so many lies that I didn't know how to untangle them. When tears threatened my eyes, Alice pulled me into a hug, her fern-colored gown silky beneath my fingers. "I have been furious with Francis for driving you away like he did Violet," she said into my hair. "I have not spoken a word to him since."

I pulled back, gutted at my role in this. "Are you serious? I already told you: I think that Francis Beaumont loves *you*. In fact, I know he does. Please don't push him away because of me."

She blanched at my endorsement of Francis as her potential boyfriend, keeping her focus on me. "Emmie, I am happy for you, truly. I am happy for King Nick…for the realm. While the advantages of marriage alliances are plain, I do feel our glorious king is deserving of a love match of the greatest measure."

I squeezed Alice's small hands, the return of her favor lifting a boulder off my chest.

Inside the dance chambers, a stout man with a beard clipped into a triangular point greeted us with a bow. I recognized him from Whitehall as Lord Mayberry, the Master of the Revels. He invited us to sit on the window seat while he barked in French at the quartet of musicians who were warming up their instruments.

We sat down, and I begged Alice to catch me up on any gossip. She beamed, seemingly only too happy to do so, intense relief loosening my shoulders. We fell back into our old routine as easily as slipping on a cloak. She told me that the Dowager Countess of Warwick was still under house arrest for her suspected role in her daughter Isobel Beaumont's plot against the king, and that Robert Fox, the twin brother of the traitor Mathew Fox, had been exiled because of the disgraced family name.

"Yikes. How's your old man, Sir Thomas?" I asked. I kind of missed Alice's cantankerous dad, even if he did once try to bribe me to break up with the king.

She smiled. "I am greatly pleased that my father has retired. His mind is calmer now. He has taken to caring for hawks and raising bloodhounds for hunting. It was not a simple decision for me to remain at court without him, but I fear that if I return to Northamptonshire, I may miss word of my vanished mother. Such news would likely reach the king first."

I swallowed the beginnings of a lump in my throat. Alice had no idea that her mom had been a traitor conspiring with Mathew Fox and Mary, Queen of Scots to bring down King Nick. Another Titanic-sized lie between Alice and me.

She twisted toward Lord Mayberry and huffed. "Shall we begin, my lord?"

He glided across the squeaky floorboards like that was a dance move in itself, his slender fingers pressed together. "My ladies, I bid you forgive me for the delay. Mine instruction partner will surely arrive here at any moment."

"*I* am to serve as an instruction partner," Alice corrected.

"You may assist," Mayberry replied with an anxious smile. "A lord of the Privy Council has advised that Mistress Grace's new lady of the bedchamber has presently arrived at court and is accomplished in all the dances…one of the finest ladies in the realm."

Alice's brow puckered. "What does a member of the king's council care about dancing?"

We jolted at the thump of the oak doors swinging open, a tall, feminine figure striding toward us. I thought I'd seen beautiful with Princess Henriette of France, but this was another level.

"Heavens," whispered Alice.

The Victoria's Secret model curtsied at me, her honey-colored skirts rippling with silk cleverly embroidered to catch the light. Her hairstyle belonged in an art museum: the wheat-colored curls styled diagonally across her scalp and topped with a stylish French hood.

"Hi, I'm Emmie Grace," I blurted, my supremely un-elegant voice echoing off the paneled walls.

She dipped her heart-shaped face at me, the letters 'LP' swinging from her pearl choker. "Good morrow to you, madam. I am—"

"Mistress Lucinda Parker," Alice finished, her voice barely above a breath.

Their eyes met in a steely stare, and my mind tore backward. I'd heard the name Lucinda Parker before. She was Nick's former mistress before I came along…the one who'd been in his bed in ways I hadn't. Rumored to have had a child with him. Pain shot through me like a lightning bolt.

"Shall we begin with the volta?" Lucinda offered, smiling playfully at the mention of the seductive dance. "His Majesty always took such pleasure in it."

My head swarmed like a shaken beehive. When Norfolk said I

wasn't the only pretty girl in England like it was a threat, this must have been his plan. He wanted Nick to fall back into the arms of his former girlfriend, Lucinda Parker, who was elegance and beauty on steroids.

It wasn't just Spain that the Duke of Norfolk wanted a war with, it was also me. And he'd just fired the first shot.

5

Did Nick know that Lucinda Parker was at Hampton Court? Did he want her here? The questions pecked at me like pigeons as I watched Lucinda frolic through dances like a gazelle while I did my best to copy her with my trademark clumsiness. When the torture-fest ended, Alice suggested the three of us return to my chambers so Lucinda could become acquainted with "all manner of our promised queen's needs and wishes." It was a pointed remark to drum into Lucinda that I was the king's girlfriend now.

I slipped Alice a look of appreciation as we wandered back to my chambers, but Lucinda's statuesque shadow trailing us left me a little flat. It'd never been in my nature to be catty or to make a girl feel unwelcome. I'd been a new girl out of my depth enough times to know how lonely it felt. But that didn't mean it was easy to watch Lucinda flooding my drawing-room with her perfume and intimate knowledge of Nick's body. The thought of her claiming him, of her feeling him come undone for her, hollowed my stomach. Especially when I wasn't even allowed to be in the same room as him without the watchful eyes of guards and attendants.

We introduced Bridget to Lucinda, and the four of us chatted with tedious politeness over mini cheesecakes before Lucinda excused herself to use the privy.

"Mistress Parker is *so* pretty," Bridget gushed to Alice and me. "I do wonder if she has a handsome brother. For no other man shall look twice at any other maiden as long as Mistress Parker is present."

Alice shot Bridget a look.

Our dear king has a known weakness for pretty girls.

Norfolk's cruel words crashed back into me. Before Lucinda returned from the washroom, I filled Alice and Bridget in on my uncomfortable conversation with him.

"Should I tell the king?" I asked them. I shuddered to think what Nick might do to him in retaliation, and I didn't fancy antagonizing the duke any further, but Alice and Bridget were quick to school me on the power of Norfolk. Even the king had to be careful about offending the most influential duke in the land. It wasn't exactly music to my ears.

Alice pressed a slender hand over mine. "Norfolk is a pillock and has always been. However, I caution you to trouble the king not with the matters of women. His Majesty is likely to think ill of such things, and we should handle this with discretion."

I nodded through my disappointment, but I knew that Alice was right. Nick wasn't the boy next door. He was a sixteenth-century King of England. He had bigger issues to deal with than any insecurity I might feel over his ex.

"I pray you are not vexed, my lady," Bridget said to me. Her rust-colored eyes radiated awe. "For it is *you* His Majesty has chosen to marry, and you are quite extraordinary." Her gaze brushed over my tweezed eyebrows, my teeth that had been straightened by metal braces, my hair recently softened by a sample from Walgreens.

I squared my shoulders at them both. *Damn straight.* Lucinda Parker may have the demeanor of a Tudor princess, but I had four hundred years of human evolution on my side. I could take her.

Alice smirked at me, reading me like a book the way only Alice Grey could.

It was a relief to discover that Lucinda Parker was easy to get along with and a decent lady of the bedchamber. What bothered me was that she was so freaking *good* at everything. Her accomplished presence judged me through my attempts at memorizing the strait-laced almain dance, the bumbling beginnings of my French lessons, and my first wobbly tune on the virginals. She embroidered better than me, danced me under the table, played the lute like the Tudor version of Eric Clapton, and never once looked at me like she was jealous of my relationship with the king. My imagination wasn't nearly as restrained. Without effort, I could see Nick kissing her, whispering in her ear, gripping her tiny waist with his perfect hands as he pushed himself into her. The thought of it hardened my stomach to rock, chased by an urge to barf. When he returned, surely he would see that she was a thousand times better suited to a queen's role than I was.

At least Lord Mayberry had arranged countless amusements to keep us all distracted, and my ladies and I were treated to dance concerts, masques, plays, acrobatic displays, and a four-hour organ recital that was more sleep-inducing than any opiate.

One Saturday after dinner, the choristers of the chapel royal staged a special performance for the peers of the court. The Duke of Norfolk stood at the back, rudely chattering to Lord Wharton through a breathtaking solo sung by a nine-year-old boy. It hit me that Alice Grey hadn't spent much time with Lord Wharton since my arrival feast. I didn't know if it was what I'd said about Francis Beaumont crushing on her, but I didn't dare bring it up. The last thing I wanted was to encourage her back into Wharton's arms, who was about as affable as Norfolk.

After the concert finale, the duke hung out near the Great Hall's exit like a security guard, bowing to my ladies and me as we passed.

"Mistress Grace, it must please you to have a maiden so accomplished as Mistress Parker join your household," he said, his sky-blue eyes giving away none of his dislike for me.

Fortunately, I'd had a few acting lessons in my day. "Oh, I haven't thanked you yet for bringing Mistress Parker to court," I said to him, offering Lucinda my sweetest smile. Hers was so freaking gorgeous that it nearly blinded me. "I'm delighted to have her in my service."

Lucinda fidgeted with her jeweled belt, blushing at me. She dipped her head at Norfolk. "My lord, I am most thankful for your petition to bring me here. I owe you my gratitude for allowing me to provide for my dear daughter."

My forehead pinched. I hadn't been aware that Lucinda's employment at Hampton Court was helpful to her baby.

"I am certain you shall find a most worthy husband," said Norfolk, ignoring the mention of the bastard child. "You are so fine a lady that there is no man in England who would not desire to court you."

No man in England who would not desire you—including its king. Another strike aimed at me. I made sure that Norfolk heard my bored exhale as I swept the girls away without so much as a polite farewell.

As the days dragged on, I tried not to think about Nick at sea—or in the vicinity of the polished Princess Henriette—while my ladies and I strolled through the privy gardens, continued my lessons, sewed in my chambers, read poems, and attended performances.

"So many merriments even without the king's presence," Alice commented during yet another masque. She smirked at me. "His Majesty is showing the court how important you are."

The sparkle in her eye caught me. I'd never considered Alice much of a romantic, but she was becoming more flushed by the day over my courtship with King Nick. It was reassuring to have her blessing, even though she still had no idea who I really was or where I came from.

The masque concluded with a ceremonial dance, before the Great Hall transformed into a feast of pepper eel, honeyed pigeon, and roasted swan devoured to the bones. While the courtiers danced up a storm, I kept an eye on the arched entrance to the Great Watching Chamber. Alice skillfully averted Lord Wharton's advances, her eyes also glancing toward the king's doorway every so often. It struck me that I wasn't the only one waiting for a cute boy with blue blood to stride through the archway. Francis Beaumont had also been away from court for an awfully long time.

That night I lay awake, cursing myself for eating rich foods to the point of bursting, when images of my mom's kitchen drifted into my restless vision. I'd been so distracted by improving my Tudor skills that

I'd stopped thinking about my life in the modern world. It reminded me of when my dad left and I'd started to forget about him—almost like he'd died. I could see that happening to my other life now: having it slip into nothingness like it never even existed. I swallowed the heavy thought and focused on counting how many days Nick had been away: seventeen.

It felt like seventeen years.

Seventeen long nights turned into thirty-four—feeling like thirty-four *years* of waiting—until a blast of trumpets on an otherwise routine Wednesday morning declared that the King of England was finally home.

I escaped the chair where Bridget had been pinning my hood and dashed to the window, pressing my face to the grimy pane between the lattice frames. Alice appeared beside me, but all our looking was pointless because we couldn't see the river from here.

"I think he's back," I said.

"Which means Francis, too," she added, biting away a smile. We fell back from the window and grinned at each other, nearly laughing. "I knew I should have washed my hair this day last," Alice said with a moan.

"Goodness, and I," called Bridget, still in her nightcap. Beyond the windows, distant murmurs of activity reached us from the adjacent servants' section of court.

"Shall I have a maidservant pour a bath?" asked Lucinda as she glanced up from her pallet bed. "There is certainly much time until His Majesty will wish to see the ladies of the court. He may not call for us until supper."

I didn't think she meant any offense, but Alice stepped forward. "The queen's ladies are capable of running our baths, Mistress Parker. We need not trouble the maidservants. Furthermore, His Majesty *will* wish to see his betrothed in haste, and Mistress Grace must be made ready for the king. Two attendants should suffice." Alice grabbed Bridget's arm and yanked her toward my dressing room.

"Thanks, Alice," I said quickly. "But I could use Lucinda's help too."

I'd never called Lucinda by her first name before. Her eyes softened with gratitude. I appreciated Alice's militant protection of me, but I was determined not to freeze out Lucinda Parker because she'd once dated Nick. Even if she had slept with him.

The atmosphere relaxed over a fashion parade of gown options and a bowl of fresh strawberries soaked in sweet wine. By the time we were appropriately blinged up, the three of us were in fits of giggles over one of Bridget's gossipy stories involving an earl and a pair of slippers. The temperature was above average for late summer, and I lugged open the oak doors to let in some fresh air.

I gasped, nearly falling backward. Nick Tudor stood on the front step, taller than I remembered, more tanned—and more beautiful, if that was even possible. For a moment, we both froze with shock before his lips curled into a half-smile. I just about lost my legs. We were being watched, so I sank into a quivery bow.

"Dear God, Emmie." The emotional words escaped his breath as he pulled me up and into him, a stunning whiff of roses enveloping me through his tight hug. A sheathed sword swinging from his waist knocked against my thigh.

"You're back," I said into his freshly washed hair. I could see the claret-colored shoulder of one of the guards behind him, hear the shuffle of Alice's footsteps beside me, but everything drew me to Nick, and I clung tightly.

The muscles in his back slid out of my grip as he pulled away, his eyes locked on something behind me. "Good God, it is Lucy," he said, a little breathless.

Lucy?

I swiveled, my heart rising to choke my throat as Nick strode past me to offer Lucinda Parker his hand. She fell to one knee and kissed his bronzed skin. When she rose again, her eyes shone, her body language mimicking his. It was as if I could feel the tight braid that tethered Nick and I snap free and begin frantically unraveling.

"May I inquire after your daughter?" Nick said to her, his voice like ripples of silk.

She beamed. "Elinor is well, Your Grace. We call her Ellie. She is presently lodging with her grandmother, undoubtedly already learning her way around a card table."

Nick chuckled. "Your mother is a dear lady. I miss her on occasion."

The ground felt like it shook beneath me, and I jerked backward, colliding with Alice's bundle of skirts. Regardless of etiquette—or even sanity—I couldn't be in the room one more second. *Lucy? Really?*

"I'm finding it warm in here, so I'm going to head out for a bit," I blurted in a hollow tone. "The lavender is so pretty at the moment, especially with those white butterflies. You guys have seen them, right?" *Shut up, Emmie, you mumbling fool!*

I lurched past Nick, but his fingers caught my arm. "My lady, you may first accompany me to dinner," he said smoothly. "I am quite famished after such a journey."

"The king flatters our lady with his personal visit and invitation," Alice said behind me, subtly reminding me that rejecting the king's direct invitation would be unthinkable.

Nick dipped his ruffled hair at my curtsying ladies and led me out the doors.

Our arms rubbed together through our silks as we crossed the small courtyard. "So how did it go in Calais?" I asked without looking at him.

He sighed. "The alliance is presently secure, and the Spanish appear to have retreated from the channel."

"That's great." Relief loosened the knot in my stomach. "I knew you'd pull it off."

I wanted to reach for his hand—to play with his fingers again—but there was the whole 'Lucy' thing; plus, there was something so formal about striding through court with the king. The guards announced his presence at every turn, and courtiers would bow like their lives depended on it, never meeting Nick's eyes or turning their backs on him. I gathered my skirts so I wouldn't trip as we ascended the stone staircase leading to the king's apartments. Sometimes he wasn't my boyfriend, he was just a monarch—so frustratingly untouchable.

"What was the French king like?" I asked him, genuinely curious about the omnipotent sovereigns of sixteenth-century Europe.

"I must say that Henry was rather ordinary," he replied. "Shorter than I remember and quite gaunt. He refused my invitation for a cheerful wrestling match. I suspect because he feared he would lose." I could tell that this pleased Nick. He didn't bring up Henriette, and I felt a touch looser in my shoulders.

The Great Watching Chamber had been reorganized into a dining room for the most important men at court, with competing aromas of savory and sweet dishes. The nobles bowed at Nick from their chairs ordered by rank, with the Duke of Norfolk in prime position. His staring eyes were a pair of daggers in my back as we passed through to the king's private dining chamber.

"Is something amiss, my lady?" Nick said to me as we sat down at opposite ends of the long table. He ran his fingers through his dark auburn hair.

"What do you mean?" I replied, my cheeks hot. After so many weeks of craving Nick's return, something felt uncomfortable between us. His reaction to Lucinda Parker had thrown me; I'd felt the chemistry between them, not to mention that I couldn't forget how accomplished she was compared to me. *Another puke.*

He brought a gleaming wine cup to his lips. "You seem not at ease."

"Oh no, I'm fine," I said, the reply an obvious lie.

He cleared his throat, helping himself to a bread roll. "Well. You may wish to hear that, as part of the treaty terms, King Henry has proposed a marriage alliance between his brother and the Princess Catherine."

"You mean Kit?" I blanched. "But she's eight."

"It is a betrothal, Emmie, not a marriage until my sister comes of age." I couldn't believe how delighted he looked. While the idea of French royalty didn't stink, it was still an arranged marriage for an eight-year-old.

"How old is this French guy?"

He dipped his bread roll into a saucer of melted butter. "The Duke of Anjou is twenty and five."

I nearly dropped my slice of mustard chicken. "Twenty-five? That's a massive age difference. Don't you want Kit to marry someone she loves?"

Eyes of glistening sea-green flashed at mine. "I must protect England against Spain. A marriage alliance with France is more important than ever. It will bring peace to the realm."

My stomach sank. The political marriage alliance was supposed to be between Nick and Henriette until I came along and refused to play the role of mistress. Was poor Kit to be the trade-off? Marrying an old French duke that she'd never even met?

We sat there chewing in restless silence while servants and gentleman milled about, trumpets blasting beside my ear at the arrival of every deluxe dish. Memories of our private picnics on the grass at Robin House stirred my chest. Maybe being the king's secret mistress hadn't been such a terrible option after all. At least it meant some privacy and no arranged marriage for Kit.

Nick's knife clinked as it dropped to his plate. "For the love of God, Mistress Grace. I beseech you to tell me what vexes you." Lines of concern crossed his brow.

It took me a moment to clarify my thoughts. "This is all so amazing," I said honestly, my eyes circling the overdone extravagance. "I've never seen anything like it. But I haven't seen you for more than a month, and I guess I want some time with my boyfriend Nick, not King Nicholas, if that makes sense. It's just...there's always so much pomp. And a heck of a lot of people."

I knew my words sounded foolish. In this world, Nick was a divine creature, appointed to rule by God's hand. How does one even separate man and king?

The perceptiveness of his reply stunned me. "You wish for less formality and more seclusion." He flicked his silk napkin over his plate. "I understand. I have missed four and thirty dinners with you, and I could hardly bear it."

Thirty-four days. He'd also counted.

"Mister George," the king said without raising his voice. One of his gentlemen appeared through a tapestry that'd been sliced up to hide a secret door. "Pack up some of this. Make certain to include wine, and water for Mistress Grace."

"Pack it up, Your Grace?"

"In some manner of pouch," Nick said with annoyance. He gave an order in French to one of the gentlemen, who dashed off ahead of us.

"What's going on?" I said as we both rose to leave the table.

Nick gestured toward the Great Watching Chamber. "This way, my lady."

The visibly confused nobles rose again over half-eaten platters of meat as we passed back through the chamber and descended the king's staircase to the clock courtyard. A discreet series of twisting corridors spilled us out into the majestic gatehouse that guarded the road entrance to Hampton Court. We crossed the stone bridge to where two saddled horses stood snorting and stamping their hoofs. A groom whose skin was overrun with zits was tying leather pouches to the saddle of Nick's mocha stallion. Another boy gripped a pair of my riding boots.

"You're kidding," I said through a breath, rushing to my favorite horse, Stella, and running my palm across her furry side. "We're going riding?" I beamed at Nick like an idiot.

"Riding and dinner. And, dear God, I have dreamed of that smile." He looked at me in a way that roused a butterfly swarm in my stomach as I tied on my riding boots.

The king mounted his horse in a single, swift motion while I fumbled with two grooms to clamber atop my neighing mare. Nick clicked his tongue, and our horses lurched into a trot past the iron-tinged stench of the slaughterhouses and into the grassy hunting park. The guards who accompanied us kept their distance as we accelerated to canter across miles of wooded fields and swampy meadows, eventually stopping at a thin stream that gurgled contentedly through the wild landscape. A stone wall peeked through the gnarled trees. We must've reached the perimeter of the palace grounds.

Nick helped me climb off Stella, sweat slipping down his brow. He offered me a leather pouch of water before pouring some for the horses. I finally had him all to myself in this secluded space. I was so giddy with happiness that I could've turned cartwheels.

"This is perfect—thank you," I said. "But no picnic blanket, velvet cushions, and golden flasks this time?" I added cheekily.

His lips curled into his dimples. "I thought that surely there would be less mockery if we did this the Emmie Grace way—without the fanfare. Of course, however, mockery *is* the Emmie Grace way."

I bit through my smile as he untied a leather satchel from his horse, whipping out leftovers from our fancy-pants lunch that were wrapped in linen. He unrolled the strips of cloth and laid the portions of bread, chicken, lamb, and beef out on the grass, swatting away a hovering bee. It was like watching the president of the United States make his own coffee.

I forced away an aching desire to have things with Nick this simple all of the time.

But here, alone with him, seeing him behaving so informally, I couldn't restrain myself. I reached for his shoulders, turned him around, and tugged him into me with both hands.

He sighed as our lips connected like magnets. Our tongues met and tangled in a hot, needy kiss, the king tumbling backward as I practically tackled him. I climbed up onto his thighs and returned my mouth to his, and for several glorious minutes, I let myself fall into the gooey sweetness of Nick Tudor again, swallowing every delicious moan he made and tasting sweet wine, mint, and berries. The perfect Nick-flavored cocktail.

Then the lovestruck eyes of Lucinda Parker flashed in my mind. I fell off him, panting as I hit the wiry grass.

"Are you well?" Nick said, sitting up. His lips were red and swollen.

I wasn't sure if I'd ever get used to the feeling of loving someone so much that the thought of them being with anyone else was like gutting out your own heart with a hook knife. I thought this time would be different. That I wouldn't have to compete with anyone for his attention, even in my mind. But it seemed I'd moved on from paranoia about Princess Henriette's sixteenth-century poise and accomplishments to worrying about Lucinda's instead.

"Should we have a chat about Lucinda Parker?" My words came out strained. "I know that you didn't invite her to court...it was the Duke of Norfolk because he hates my guts for marrying you."

I expected shock and fury, but Nick just breathed a light laugh.

"Norfolk is plainly dramatic. You will come to know his impetuous nature."

I opened my mouth to protest, but he continued speaking in that maddeningly authoritative tone. "Your suspicions that Norfolk invited Mistress Parker to court are likely true—she is a cousin of his of some sort, and I can think of no other councilor who would undertake such a deed without my permission. That said, I do understand why you are not roused by Mistress Parker's presence; however, I made a vow to you that I would keep no mistress, and you must trust me."

"I know," I said, discomfort seeping into the pit of my stomach. "I don't want this to be a *thing*; I really don't. For a start, that'd make Norfolk far too smug for my liking. But while the thought of Lucinda being here freaks me out a bit, I also think that her having a position at court is good for her baby daughter, right? These aren't exactly the golden years of single motherhood. So I think she should stay. I'm officially okay with it."

He kissed the back of my hand like he was proud of me. I was also proud of myself. Nick had all the power in the world, and if he wanted to hook up with Lucinda Parker, there'd be jack squat I could do about it. But there was no way I was letting Norfolk win. He'd brought Lucinda here to torment me, so I was determined to be okay with it.

Nick tugged me toward him, his breath washing over my lips as he looked into my eyes. "If only you could see inside my heart," he said softly. "You would know how mine eyes desire you above all things. You would know this to be true, and it would release you from the burden of your fears."

"Well, either that, or I'd see a bunch of blood, muscle, and some of those ventricle things if I could see inside your heart," I said through a straight face.

Rolling his eyes at another wisecrack that we both knew he wouldn't understand, he climbed to his feet, indicating for me to stay put. "I have something for you, you troublesome little thing. Well, two somethings." He untied another satchel from his horse and retrieved flashes of purple and cream, hiding the mystery articles behind his back. After dropping to his knees and shuffling toward me, he smirked and nodded at his arms, a mute invitation for me to choose a hand.

I grinned and pointed at his left arm. He produced a petite velvet pouch that drooped with something heavy. I fished out a heart-shaped locket dangling from a delicate silver chain. Clicking the pendant open revealed a miniature painting of Nick that was unlike his usual portraits. There was no crown, no pretend beard, no added weight, scepter, or flat cap. It was simply Nick Tudor wearing a white linen shirt and a chocolate-brown leather jerkin, with his hair unkempt and a slight smirk on his face. Every part of the portrait was the man I loved.

"Will you wear it close to your heart?" he asked a little shyly.

I threw my arms around him. He toppled backward, crying out.

"What's wrong?" I said, scrambling off him as he smoothed out a crushed scroll. "Oh, yikes—sorry."

Nick unrolled the now creased page he held in his right hand. "This is a royal decree proclaiming that you are to be granted lands and the title of the Marquess of Pembroke."

I covered my mouth with one hand, the humid smell of dirt reaching my nose from where my fingers had hit the earth.

When Nick grinned with flushed pride, I hugged him again, thanking him repeatedly. An alarming thought pierced my swelling excitement: Norfolk and the nobles already thought I wasn't worthy of Nick's attention, and with good reason. What would they think of my free pass into the English peerage? I reminded myself for the millionth time that I was here for Nick and that was all that mattered.

We stretched out on the grass and lay there for as many blissful minutes as I could steal, chatting and laughing, but mostly kissing. *God, is there a man on earth who tastes this good?* My tongue swept across his, my hands clutching his face and his fingers knotting in my hair. He grunted sighs into my mouth like he was starving for this, and when I climbed on top of him and straddled my legs over his thighs with my skirts billowing out, he gazed up at me with hooded eyes like a prisoner I was holding captive. He'd swollen thickly in his breeches, and I pressed my pelvis down onto his solid length, rolling my hips.

"Christ in heaven," he gritted out, his hands snapping to my waist.

"I can see that it will take much to satiate you, my girl, and I wish you to feel entirely assured that I am up to the task."

The rasp in his voice sent a ripple of heat through me, but when I brought my lips to his neck, he tightened his grip on my waist and lifted me off him with a groan of frustration.

"But not now, my love," he added, his darkened eyes and panting breaths making clear that he didn't want to stop this any more than I did.

"But there's no one around," I moaned.

"Emmie, you understand not a man's lack of restraint." His forehead dropped against my own, his seawater eyes blinking into mine. "If you continue to ride me like a steed, I will lose all manner of control, and I cannot have that in the palace park. I am the king of this realm."

My shoulders lifted and fell with a relenting sigh. "I know."

His gaze raked over my face, affection burning in his eyes. "But if you do not kiss me at this very moment, Emmie, I fear that my heart will burst out of my chest."

I grabbed his collar and yanked his mouth to mine, kissing him desperately as I wrapped my arms around his neck and pulled him back down onto the grass.

It had to have been early afternoon when Nick finally declared that he had to return to court to deal with a new trade bill. He was straightening his saddle when I spotted his bare finger and remembered that the blue-diamond ring was still in the coffer in my room.

I slid between him and the saddle, the closeness of our hips making his brows rise.

"Hello," he said, looking right into my eyes as he kept tying the leather.

"I forgot to thank you for leaving the ring with me when you went to Calais." The seriousness of the subject tightened my voice. "I didn't use it behind your back, just so you know. I'd never do that."

He swallowed hard. "I am relieved to hear it."

"I've been meaning to talk to you about something, and it's good that we're alone. This won't take long." My fingers drew circles on his muscular forearm. "One of my ladies, Bridget

Nightingale, has a cousin who's a soothsayer. She lives in Buckinghamshire."

His hands paused on the leather. "Agnes Nightingale."

"You know her?"

"Certainly not. She is a known heretic and ought to be burned. You must stay away from her."

The harsh words sent me back a step. "Actually, I was hoping we'd go and see her." Nick's brows shot up, and I barreled on, my breath short. "Rather than *burning* her, she could help us with the blue-diamond ring. Maybe this Nightingale girl could tell us why a ring that was supposed to curse you sends people forward in time instead...to twenty-first-century America, of all places. And why didn't the ring work properly the last time we used it? Maybe she can tell us." I scanned Nick's expression for evidence that he was also concerned about the ring acting oddly.

His body stiffened like a statue, before resuming his tying. "I admit that this alarms me."

Relief expelled hot air from my lungs. "I know. What if the ring has stopped working altogether and we're stuck here?"

His face twisted. "I mean to say that your *words* alarm me...your preoccupation with this ring and the dark arts. If the people even suspect that their queen is a heretic, they will petition to have you burned." He tugged the leather to tighten the knot, unsettling his grunting horse. "Furthermore, what you say of being 'stuck'...is that not the purpose of you being here? To stay?" He scraped a hand through his mussed hair, looking frustrated.

"Of course it is!" I replied, trying not to lose my cool. "But you promised me that I could go back home and tell my mom why her only child has disappeared for the *third* time. When you asked me to marry you, you said that we had to come back to Tudor England immediately, which gave me hardly any chance to think and no time to talk to my mom." I emphasized every word like Nick was a two-year-old.

He brought a hand to his brow, holding it there for a moment.

When he finally looked at me, he could hardly meet my eyes. "Forgive me...you speak the truth. I gave you my word, and I have been too occupied with all manner of headaches since we arrived to think of it." His teeth grazed his bottom lip. "There remains much to prepare for your coronation, but you must see your mother."

He found my fingers. "We will go to your home this night," he said matter-of-factly, like he was suggesting tacos for dinner.

The floor slipped out from under me. "Tonight? *We?*"

"I fear that I will survive not if you return to your time without me. When there is talk of war, a prince does well to remain secure in his chambers. Amid this Spain business, I can make preparations to be confined to my rooms without being disturbed, and we shall take leave to see your mother. God willing, I could get us a day at best. I pray you say it is enough."

"It's enough, it's enough," I cried, folding my arms around him and squeezing with relief so intense that it pinned a smile to my face.

An uncomfortable shiver jerked through me, wiping away the grin. I'd planted myself in Tudor England for nearly two months. How had my presence here affected the path of history? Not to mention my poor mom. Guilt thickened my throat at the thought of what my disappearance had done to her. At least now I could finally tell her the truth about where I went and end all the mystery.

It was time for my mom to meet Nicholas the Ironheart.

6

It was past midnight when Nick summoned me to his chambers, a portrait of cute kingliness as he pored over a scroll in a navy-blue jerkin with teal herringbone stitching. He must've commanded we be given our privacy because the gentlemen and pages swiftly evaporated from sight. Guarding my chastity was evidently no longer priority number one now that time travel was on the agenda.

I crawled right on top of him in the chair, its wooden legs protesting with a creak. He was chewing a mint sprig that smelled like toothpaste, and a gilded wine cup sat on the hand-painted table beside him.

"Sleepy?" he said, planting a gentle kiss on my nose.

"That's me," I replied, drawing my knees up and snuggling into his chest. The room always felt lighter when we were alone.

He dropped his papers onto the side table and shifted to get comfortable beneath me.

It was the first time we'd cuddled this closely without kissing each other senseless, the heaviness of the situation overpowering the intense attraction that burned between us. Plus, all I could think about was whether the ring would fail to work and if I'd never get back to my time again. I shut out the depressing thought. After Nick pressed his lips to mine in a lingering goodnight kiss, we stayed locked together on a sixteenth-century chair, waiting for sleep to carry us to an uncertain future.

The first time I awakened, Nick was deep in slumberland. The candle beside us flickered lower, and the silk bed sheets were still folded open, prepared for the king's rest.

Please, no. We're still at Hampton Court…I'm never getting home again!

I twisted to relieve my stiff muscles, and Nick stirred. "The ring's not working again," I hissed in the darkness.

"Fear not," he said drowsily. "Let us move to the bed. Perhaps it is not restful enough here."

Hoping with every fiber of my being that he was right, I followed him onto the raised four-poster bed and crawled into the silk sheets. Maybe that's what went wrong on the uncomfortable riverbank when the ring failed to transport us through time on the first try—perhaps we hadn't fallen into a deep enough sleep for it to work correctly. Nick wrapped himself around me from behind, and I nestled into the cradle of his arms, waiting for the tiredness to overcome my body again. Every hour it took for us to get to my world was one less hour I could spend there.

If we get back there at all.

My body had begun to sink into the mattress when I rolled over onto a jagged rock, the humid odor of moist sand overwhelming my nose. My sticky eyelids broke open.

The creamy edges of Nick's linen shirt fluttered in the wind from a few feet away. He stood facing the lapping shoreline of the Connecticut River—right where we'd left the last time. I could've cried out with relief. The sun's position suggested it was mid-morning.

"Good morning," I called, my voice hoarse with sleep. He spun to me and smiled, but his cheeks were drained of color. Still, the sight of him in my time made my chest twist with an ache I felt keenly. He was a Tudor king, yet he somehow suited this place. If only this world could be enough for him…if I alone could be enough for him.

Goosebumps speckled my neck. Temperatures had cooled since we were last here.

Nick climbed back up the bank and took my hand. His shook a

little. "What of your cloth…and mine?" He gestured to my white satin stomacher and lush gown the color of red wine.

"If anything, they'll help explain where we've been," I said, realizing how idiotic that sounded. *Emmie. You haven't just been in Maine for the summer.*

We scaled the tangle of muddy roots until the field behind my house emerged through the slouching willow trees. It felt like I hadn't been here in ten years. Something was comforting about the quiet meadow dotted with the tired old horses. If you squinted to shut out the power lines and the glimpses of white fencing from Bayberry Street, we could've been in Tudor England. I hoped that Nick took solace in that as we inched closer to my fence, one petrified step at a time. Were we really doing this?

As the chipped tiles from our roof came into view, my palms dampened with sweat. My fingers slipped on the latch of our fence, and Nick pressed a hand to the small of my back to steady me.

"Are you okay?" I asked him, swinging the gate open. He nodded stiffly, and we pushed through to my yard. The silence made clear that our schnauzer Ruby wasn't home: she'd bark at any sound. Mercifully, the spare key was still wedged beneath the untrimmed hedge.

I unlocked the back-porch doors and took a hesitant step inside. "Mom?" I called out, my stomach in knots. Nick must've been sweating bullets as we entered the weathered clapboard house. To him, Carol Grace was more than his future mother-in-law—she was practically an alien from an unknown world.

Silence greeted us. Perhaps Mom was upstairs asleep after one of her overnight nursing shifts. Dishes clogged the kitchen sink, and a trace of coffee circled the bottom of a cup on the counter. A pile of unfolded laundry sat on the living room floor beside a fresh spaghetti-sauce stain on the carpet.

I left Nick on the couch and hopped up the stairs, two at a time. Mom's unmade bed was empty, but her toothbrush felt damp. Prescription pill bottles sat opened on the counter, but I didn't know what they were for. Remorse wrenched my insides apart. Had my disappearance made my mom sick?

Opening my bedroom door revealed the modest space mostly as

I'd left it. The only thing different was my suitcase: it sat open on the bed with the contents unsettled. My old jewelry tackle box looked pitiful beside the neighboring trio of new sweatshirts I'd bought for London. All those hopes and plans that never happened. The book Mom bought me, *A Student's Guide to Living and Learning in London*, had been searched through. She must've looked for signs for why I never caught that plane.

Feeling heavy with guilt, I untied the pieces of my Tudor gown and changed into jeans and a pale-pink sweatshirt. After tying on my sneakers, I wrapped my arms around myself, savoring the comfort of cotton.

"Mom's not here," I said, trotting back downstairs. "But she was home recently."

Nick nodded, more color escaping his cheeks at the sight of my modern outfit. "We will wait."

I spent the next half an hour tidying up while Nick tapped his thighs with his fingers, surveying the living room he'd seen once before. I could tell he was trying not to flip out, which I appreciated. His nervous gaze scanned the faded wooden dining table…the thread-bare cushions on the couch…the paint-chipped walls…my masculine outfit. He must've thought my time was so drab compared with Hampton Court and his twelve thousand other palaces. Thank the stars he didn't ask me about the black rectangle in the corner; he was so not ready for daytime television.

After washing up the dishes, I made us some tea and buttered toast. Nick inspected the neatly sliced bread before risking a bite.

When he glanced at me, it was clear that honey-wheat bread wasn't the heaviest thing on his mind. "Tell me, Emmie; I must know. Is the King of England a Tudor?"

I choked on my crust. Last time we were here, I'd refused to tell Nick anything about the future. My presence in the sixteenth century was bad enough; we didn't need its king editing his decisions to accommodate my version of what was to come. But we were getting married now, and he deserved something. So I explained the current state of the British monarchy and the added role of prime minister. Nick didn't have a conniption or start foaming at the mouth, which was a relief. He then asked me about France and Spain, but all I shared was that Europe was mostly at peace. When I reminded him that America had no monarch but a president who was accountable to the people, his brows practically hit his hairline. "That is madness."

"Actually, a democratic government is infinitely more equitable and fair than an absolute monarchy." When I realized what I'd said, I rolled my eyes at myself. I was talking like him, even while back in my world. All those lessons with my ladies were starting to pay off.

"It defies the will of God Himself," said Nick. "I am pleased that England remains dutiful of its princes." He shook his head, glaring into his teacup, genuinely miffed.

I swallowed an urge to quote some of the Declaration of Independence—especially the part about all men and women being created equal. It wasn't like I had no regard for the royals, but we'd come a long way since the divine right of kings.

Our shared silence was an agreement to disagree, and we finished our snacks with no sign of my mom. I considered calling her, but if she was driving, it might shock her into a car accident.

A distant vibration drummed a ripple across the sky through the screen door.

I stood up and grabbed Nick's arm. "I know what we can do for a few minutes that won't require a car. Come with me."

We headed back to the field where two horses stood flicking their tails and crossed the field to Bayberry Street. Nick gaped at everything in sight, asking me what more things were, and I did my best to explain without freaking him out. We cut away from the street and onto a rustic path behind my friend Mia's farm. It led to an abandoned fire lookout tower on the crest of a small hill.

"It's over here," I said, leading him to the tower. I climbed the first few rungs of the ladder, brushing the orangey rust residue off my fingers. "I hope you're not afraid of heights."

"Not nearly as afraid as I am of your coaches bereft of horses," he said behind me. He scampered up the ladder with ease. We paused at the top, my feet hovering a few rungs above his. "I never go onto the balcony," I explained. "It's old wood up there, so I'm scared it'll collapse." I dropped down a few rungs until we were eye level and carefully snuggled close to him without disturbing our footing.

Nick's neck twisted in all directions. "Good God. Is this what you wish to show me? This gray matter?"

I chuckled. "The gray rectangles are roofs. The big ones are probably farms or warehouses. But that's not what I wanted to show you." I pointed to an overgrown strip of runway in the distance. "There's a small airport there…mostly for recreational flying."

"Flying?" His face crushed with a frown.

I grinned. "Just wait. It's a beautiful day, and there's a family with a huge farm out that way, bigger than Mia's. I'm pretty sure I heard their plane already."

I was supposed to be watching for the Cronin family's light aircraft, but the sunlit flecks of green in Nick's confused eyes were hard to look away from. The wind blew a wisp of hair across my face, and he brushed it away, my heart picking up speed. His fingertips drew a slow line down my cheek, his gaze becoming soft and intent. He tugged me forward without losing our balance on the ladder, and our lips met and melted into one, tasting of heat and love. Despite our precarious position, my arms curled around his lower back, my palms gripping his ass that I hadn't stopped thinking about, when the sky growled. Our mouths parted, and our heads jerked up as the canary-yellow plane swooped past the tower with its wings outstretched.

"Forget cars; this is how the well-to-do travel," I said over the wind and distant propeller, a smile of pride in my voice.

Nick blinked at me, his eyes enlarging. "*Flight?*"

"Aye, Captain." I felt my chin lift. "It's another form of travel in my time. In a big passenger plane, we could get to England from here in less than ten hours."

His gaping face wouldn't look away from the sky.

Even while clinging to a dodgy fire tower in rural Massachusetts, it was impossible to deny how much more advanced the world was in my time. It was hard not to look at Nick and feel like I'd beaten him in the Olympics…again. Why was he so sure that he couldn't live here? It was infinitely less tense, and the terrifying nobles were hundreds of years away. Plus, I could be so much more impressive in this place—I knew how to take the twenty-first century by storm, but in the Tudor world, I felt mousy and untalented. Did Nick really want that side of me?

Regardless, his deer-in-headlights expression over the airplane was priceless. I was still giggling about it after we'd crawled back down the ladder, our calves cramping with stiffness.

"It was like you were a kid with every single ice cream flavor on one giant cone," I recalled, pausing to bend over and laugh again.

"What is ice cream?" said Nick, and I howled so loudly that I couldn't breathe.

I knew I was acting batshit—losing composure over something that wasn't even that funny—but the months of unbelievable fear and stress had finally caught up with me. The sincerity in Nick's dimpled smirk as we strolled back to my house reminded me of how I'd felt the last time he was here. I'd have given anything for him to feel this unburdened in his own time.

It turned out that ice cream was already a thing in early Renaissance Europe, except it wasn't called that yet. The spotlight shifted as Nick shared more stories about his world, including the impressive names of people he'd crossed paths with like Nostradamus and Catherine de' Medici. It wasn't until we reached my gate that I understood we were engaged in some sort of competition over whose time was more impressive. Surely it was a no-brainer who took the title on that one. How could Nick root for a world that was outdated by more than four hundred years?

He was halfway through a story about Sir Francis Drake's voyage around the world when I grabbed his arm. Our back gate was open, but I was sure I'd shut it. As we watched, Mom's back appeared through the gap, a phone pressed to her ear.

My instinct was to push my Tudor boyfriend out of sight and into the elm trees flanking the fence.

"Can I just talk to her first?" I said with a breathless pounding in my chest. "Please. But you *have* to stay here. Don't you dare leave without me." We'd been in this situation once before: when I left Nick alone in the field after our first real kiss, and he'd dumped me for Tudor England without a word.

He took my hands, squeezing my fingers. "Of course, you must. I will wait here. Besides, you have the ring, Emmie." He gave me a nod of encouragement. I'd broken out in a cold sweat.

My sneakers crunched the grass as I pushed through the back gate. Mom spun to look at me, blood leaving her face. She said something into the phone and hung up before shakily sliding the handset into her pocket without moving her eyes from mine.

The next few moments happened in slow motion: Mom pressing her forehead with both palms, turning away and then back to me, before crumbling to her feet and hitting the grass. I dashed over and helped her up while she mumbled that she was okay through pallid lips. Ruby was running in circles nearby, snapping the air with frantic barks.

"Mom, it's okay…I'm here," I repeatedly said as I guided her through the screen door and onto the couch. Ruby was now licking my ankles like they were carved from peanut butter.

Mom squeezed my forearm so tightly that I winced. "Emmie, you're okay." She stared at me with a face I hardly recognized. Had she aged that much over the weeks I'd been away—had I stressed her out that much? Or had I already forgotten the spidery lines sprouting from her eyes, the crooked front tooth that people found so attractive, or the fact that she'd given up using makeup? I wasn't sure I wanted to know the answer.

She was muttering again. "I saw you were here already, but I was —I was taking Ruby to the vet and, I…well, I always knew if you came back, it would be when I wasn't here; it's just my luck, you know? I was saying that to Kevin…Kevin what's-his-name the other day."

"Is Ruby okay?" I asked, sitting beside Mom.

"She's fine. Just her shots for the year."

Guilt grabbed my chest and shook it hard. I usually took care of Ruby's medicine.

The mumbling had stopped, and Mom was now gaping at me. *Man, she looks tired.*

"I'm *so* sorry," I said, the words inexcusably deficient. "I know you must've been so worried."

Her eyes flared wide like they could shoot lasers. "*Worried?* I called the police! There's a case file…they searched for you for days. Mostly at the river." Her voice broke, unlocking a trickle of tears.

"I'm sorry," I said again, this apology no more forgivable than the first. "Should we call them?"

"Of course I will," she snapped like I'd overstepped on something. "As it turns out, missing adults who have taken off before are not considered a critical emergency." She brushed both eyes with her knuckles. "So, where on God's green earth have you been? I truly can't believe this."

The question wrapped a taut rope around my neck and squeezed.

I was in Tudor England, with Nicholas the Ironheart. He's actually a good guy, by the way, and we're getting married. I'm going to be a Tudor queen. Surprise!

When I didn't answer—not sure how to—Mom shrugged. "I know you never caught the plane to London…never arrived at college. Your bag is still here. What were you planning?" She was starting to hyperventilate.

"Nothing. I *was* going to go to London, and college, and to do everything we talked about. But something happened with someone, and I had to go somewhere else for a while. I wish I could explain it all to you, but it's…it's a lot."

Her face distorted with disgust. "Something…someone…somewhere. You sound like your dad when he left."

My jaw fell open. My first memories of my dad were of laughter and adventure when the three of us drove through England for his history doctorate. But after we moved back to America when I was ten, he traded Mom—and me—for his coworker within five months. Since then, I'd barely seen him. I wasn't even sure I could call him *Dad* anymore.

"Please don't compare me to him," I said gently, but inside that shot had hit home, like she knew it would.

"*Don't?*" She threw a cushion at me. "You're doing just what he did, except worse—giving up all your dreams to chase some selfish person who is clearly more important to you than your own family! Don't treat me like an idiot, Emmie. The second you walked through that gate, I knew you'd been off with that boy from the summer. I can't believe you would be so stupid!"

I slunk away from her. "I'm not treating you like an idiot. I came back here for you!"

"You've been gone *without a trace* for weeks and weeks! Have you not heard of a damn phone!" Her shoulders shook with tears, a wet tissue balled up in her fist.

"I'm so sorry, Mom," I said through a sob as I reached out to her, but she shoved my hands away. "Believe me, I would've called you if I could have, but there was no phone."

Every part of her face twisted before she cried into her palms, greasy clumps of her unwashed hair falling in front of her face.

"Please, I'm sorry," I begged, forcing her to let me hug her. "I love you, okay? There's a really good reason why I couldn't call." Her arms finally accepted the embrace, and I relaxed a little. "There's so much to explain. I know I haven't been myself."

She pulled away, dabbing her eyes with her soggy tissue. "Then it's time to start because, God help me, I've hit the last straw. You need to tell me everything right now. All the someones and somethings."

My stomach folded over itself. I should've rehearsed this conversation. There weren't many ways you could explain the reality of time travel to someone. But Mom leaned back into a cushion and crossed her arms at me, ready for the truth.

I blew through my lips, my sweaty palms rubbing my jeans. "It all started when I found a ring. Actually, I bought it from that old hoarder, Jane Stuart." I wiggled my thumb at her. "This one."

She leaned closer. "I remember it. Very dazzling."

It was hard to speak through my thick throat. "The first time I went missing for a day—when I was at Mia's—I'd fallen asleep at her house wearing the ring. Then I…I woke up in a different time."

Mom barely blinked.

"I was in the sixteenth century," I spurted. "I'm not kidding. This ring is, like, *magic.*" As the words left my lips, I heard how side-splittingly ridiculous they sounded. "It makes people travel through time when they fall asleep wearing it…back to sixteenth-century England.

Can you believe that? I've been hanging out with the freaking Tudors!" I barked a jittery laugh.

Mom's brow furrowed, and she began rubbing her thumb and forefinger together like a nervous tick. When she finally spoke, her voice was hardly louder than a breath.

"Emmie, what's going on? Are you on drugs?"

"Of course not. Ew."

"What is wrong with you then?" she cried. She slid away from me. "Why would you tell such a stupid and *weird* story?"

"It's not a story. I know it sounds crazy—believe me—but it's the truth." Mom looked like she might barf all over my new sweater. "I can prove it to you," I pleaded, instantly regretting the idea. I couldn't keep shipping people back and forth between worlds like time-traveling tourists. But Mom looked like she didn't even register the offer… she was too busy trying to breathe, her hand clutching her stomach.

I grappled for something convincing to say when I remembered that I had another way to prove my insane story.

"Just wait here," I said, before rushing back outside to the field behind our house.

Nick rested against the fence between the weathered roots of an elm tree, his athletic legs outstretched. The strong winds had brought the fishy smells of the river closer.

"Come with me," I said, wrenching him up by his arm. "I told Mom the truth about the blue-diamond ring, and she's freaking out. You need to help me prove it's true."

"What?" Nick exclaimed as he chased me through the back yard. "Christ, to what end? Do not trouble your mother with this; I beseech you!"

I halted at the steps leading to the porch, gasping with tension. "Look, my mom has no idea who I am right now, and she is my only family, okay? You have your people and your kingdom. I have my mom. *She* is my people. Apart from you, she's all I have. I have to make her understand what's going on."

He pressed his lips together, squaring his shoulders. There was a shiver of movement at the screen door. Mom was gaping at Nick through the mesh.

"Mom, this is Nick," I blurted. "He's from the sixteenth century." After grabbing his clammy palms, I walked us into the house where he towered over Mom's petite frame. Her cheeks were colorless, but her eyes expanded with awe as she took in his features. I made a snap decision that the whole Nicholas the Ironheart thing would be a step too far. It would be like bringing home King Henry the Eighth or Queen Victoria.

I threw Nick a look, silently instructing him to listen carefully. "Nick and I met during my first visit back to the sixteenth century. He's a courtier in the court of Queen Elizabeth the First. He can tell you anything you want to know about that time." I reached for his hand, but our sweaty fingers struggled to lock. "He's also the reason I've disappeared a few times—*without a trace,* Mom. I was with Nick, in Tudor England, where they don't exactly have cell phones. And if you don't believe us, well, you'll have to come back and see it for yourself."

And how exactly will you do that, Emmie? Will the three of you fall asleep creepily holding each other's hands? Or will you leave Nicholas the Ironheart alone in modern America while you take your mom for a little jaunt back in time? Moron!

Mom gawked up at him, her voice thin. "Go on then, prove to me that you're a friend of Queen Elizabeth the First." She spat a humorless laugh.

Nick frowned and fidgeted with his sleeves. I couldn't blame him for being lost for words. How do you prove your identity to an alien from the future? I had to jump in—to get Nick out of this position I'd put him in—but when he found his voice, it was clear that he didn't need my help.

"Madam, it is my sincerest pleasure to be presented to you, the beloved mother of my dearest betrothed. May I humbly prostrate myself at your feet."

He dropped to one knee and kissed Mom's hand before returning to his imposing height. "Most precious lady, what Mistress Grace claims is indeed true. The moment I laid mine eyes upon her—within the Palace of Whitehall—my heart knew two truths. The first: that our lady, most adored, was not of my realm. Her speech, her manner, her inclination was most certainly of another time." His eyes moved to mine. "The second was that Mistress Grace owned every piece of my heart, and I knew that I would love her until my dying breath."

It was dizzying and dreamlike. In my dowdy living room, one of the most famous kings in history was speaking sweet nothings to me. Not to mention bowing to my commoner mom in her sweatpants.

Mom tilted her head at me, a trace of a smile on her lips. "Is this one of those prank TV shows?"

"Sometimes I wish it was," I replied. Nick blinked at us, obviously lost.

She groaned and pressed a palm to her hip. "Whatever. I'm going to figure this out. But for now, my daughter is home, and you, young man, are nothing if not well-spoken." She sidestepped us to enter the kitchen. "Is anyone hungry?" she called weakly.

"We had some toast, but I'm still pretty hungry," I replied.

"Sorry, but I think it's going to have to be sandwiches." She was digging through the fridge. "There's not much else."

"That's fine," I sang out.

For the first time since Nick and I had arrived back in the present, I could exhale without effort.

Nick gobbled up Mom's overcooked grilled-cheese sandwiches dipped in ketchup, and his hands had finally stopped shaking. However, any hope that Mom believed my story about time travel was dashed when she asked if Nick and I had been living in the forest. She'd moved on from the reality television show idea and now thought we'd joined one of those historical fan groups that camped out in medieval costumes.

The weird thing was that Nick and Mom seemed to get along. They chatted at the table for a while: all superficial stuff like preferred styles of cheese and the weather. Anything that Nick didn't understand, he changed the subject to something else. When he said anything loopy, Mom looked at me and laughed, her eyes lighting up in the way only Nick Tudor could inspire. The whole time he sat with his fingers loosely clasped in his lap, breathing easily with a relaxed smile.

Nicholas the freaking Ironheart is sitting at my ketchup-stained dining table, sweeping my mom off her feet. Yeah, nothing to see here, folks.

Amazingly, Mom hadn't picked up on the earlier 'betrothed' comment. Instead, the bigger issue was her evident belief that I was back home to stay. Nick had been away from his kingdom for hours, and we didn't have much time left.

"Where do you live, Nick?" Mom asked. "Do you need to sleep on the couch?" She side-eyed me like I better not consider having him in my bedroom.

"Actually, we were just going to go upstairs and have a chat about that, weren't we Nick," I said, passing him a look.

"Indeed." He rose to his feet, tipping his head at my mom in a Tudor-style farewell. "This has been a pleasure beyond words, madam."

"It was good to meet you." She turned to the window with a dazed expression, and we headed upstairs.

"Your mother is dear," said Nick as he took a tentative seat in my desk chair. It swiveled, and his legs shot out to steady himself.

I chuckled. "And you make one heck of a twenty-first-century boy." I slid into his lap and folded my arms around him. He murmured his delight and nuzzled his lips into my neck. A flash of yearning heated my spine. "You and my mom seem to get along," I ventured nervously. "Why don't we just stay here? There's no war with Spain to fight; no scary dukes, or stressful council meetings. Just you and me. And ketchup."

His laugh was more like a breath, but it cut nonetheless. Why was he so sure the question was a joke? Was the idea of staying in my time that ludicrous? Couldn't he tell how anxious I was about becoming a sixteenth-century Queen of England without making a muppet of myself—or worse?

For a few seconds, neither of us said anything. Awkwardness chewed up the air, and the chair squeaked beneath us.

Nick fingered a lock of my loose hair. "Is there any more you wish to do before we take our leave? I fear you may suffer when we part from this place."

His eyes couldn't meet mine, and I could tell he was picking up on my reluctance to leave my time so quickly. He didn't need to worry: despite how badly I felt for my mom, I wasn't about to let Nick jet off to the sixteenth century without me. *Been there, done that. And it sucked.*

I thought about his question. "There is one thing I'd like to do," I said, fear crawling across my skin like spider's legs. I didn't have a laptop anymore, but Mom's phone had internet.

I led him back downstairs, finding Mom still staring vacantly through the window. She said I could use her phone, and I opened an internet search window. Nick had seen a cell phone before, but his eyes still boggled. He slid nervously into the couch.

My fingers locked up in protest as I typed the words that I knew I shouldn't.

"Queen Emmeline Tudor". *Click.*

No results found for "Queen Emmeline Tudor".

I frowned and typed a less specific search.

Emmeline Tudor, 16th century. *Click.*

No results found. Showing results for *Elizabeth* Tudor, 16th century.

The phone hit the table, my stomach splitting. Why wasn't I there? Was this proof that things didn't work out between Nick and me? I couldn't bring myself to type in 'Nicholas the Ironheart's wife'. I'd already learned that it was too much of a head-trip to try and live in two different centuries. My decision had already been made, and my home was with Nick in Tudor England. If I kept coming back here and googling myself, I was legitimately going to end up in a psychiatric hospital.

Nick sat tapping his feet, twiddling his thumbs madly. He kept glancing at the clock on the wall.

"Mom, Nick and I have to go now," I said, trying to sound calm. "You know I love you, and if there was any other way…"

Her face fell. "Where are you going?"

"Tudor England," I explained again, trying not to sound impatient.

She huffed with exasperation. "Enough of this… Emmie!" she cried. "I'm going to have to call your father again. I just can't deal with you on my own anymore."

"No, don't call him," I said, aghast. Mom blatantly still held a candle for the guy and didn't need much of an excuse to contact him. I did not want to be that excuse.

I held my forehead with my trembling fingers. I had no idea what to do. Telling Mom the truth had been a mistake, but Nick had to get home.

"I don't know what to do," I said to him. "Should we take her back with us?" In the corner of my eye, Mom's head was in her hands.

"Christ, no," he whispered. "I have enough ladies from the future running around my court. It is not so easy, Emmie." An apology flooded his face, but he was right. I wasn't sure my mom could convincingly play the role of Tudor lady, which could put her in real danger back there. Norfolk would sniff her out like a bloodhound.

Another idea struck me. "Mom, can you come upstairs? Nick, do you mind waiting outside my bedroom for a minute?"

Mom sighed but didn't resist as I ushered her up the stairs with Nick following behind. While he waited outside the bedroom door, I lugged my suitcase off the bed.

"What are you doing?" Mom said in a sharp tone.

"Proving that Nick and I aren't total nutjobs. But first, you have to help me with these clothes."

"Oh my," she breathed as sixteenth-century silk rippled through my fingers. I explained each step so she could help me dress, sparking a sweet memory of her fastening the intricate straps of my prom gown—only a few weeks before I met Nick Tudor.

"You look incredible," she said, pacing backward to take in the full sight of me. "I can see why you like this English history stuff." She flopped into my desk chair and crossed her arms.

I yanked Nick into my room, despite his visible reluctance. When I guided him onto the bed and lay down beside him, Mom hopped to her feet.

"If you think I am going to sit here and watch you two—"

"Ew!" I said. "What you're going to watch is Nick and I going to sleep. And because I'm wearing this enchanted ring that I told you about, we're going to disappear before your very eyes." *Ugh, I sound like a wannabe magician with her own YouTube channel.*

Mom burst out laughing. When Nick and I didn't join in, she sighed. "Fine…okay."

Nick lay as stiff as a board beside me. I willed myself to relax.

It was a moment I knew I wouldn't forget, and not only because it was certifiably insane. The room was silent save for the breathing of the two people in the world I cared for the most. Two people who had nothing in common—apart from me—and who'd probably never see each other again. As I lay with my eyes pressed shut, I imagined the wedding Nick and I could have had here in my time. Something casual and intimate, with Mom and Nick shooting the breeze about cheese and my maddening stubbornness. Mia would be there, and our friend Josh, and gawd, maybe even Dad. They'd all think I was on crack for getting married at the age of eighteen.

And while my mom watched my boyfriend and I fall asleep together, her face revealing how uncomfortable she was with this, the soothing vision of a modern life with Nick Tudor lolled me to a peaceful sleep.

7

THE MOMENT I OPENED MY EYES, THE SPELL BROKE. NICK WAS OUT cold with our fingers still tightly fastened. Mom sat drooped in the chair, gently snoring like one of the elderly ladies at the rest home.

"Mom!" I hissed. "You have to look at us."

"Hmm? I know," she grunted, shifting to straighten her back. "I worked last night."

Luckily, I'd become a world-renowned guru at falling asleep on cue. The blackness returned within minutes.

The next time my eyes peeled open, Mom was watching us closely. Both Nick and I had fallen asleep, yet we were still in my Hatfield bedroom. I tried to explain to Mom that the ring had recently began acting strange, and might take a few attempts to make us disappear, but she was already in the doorway.

"I think it's time we get some help," she grumbled. "I can't deal with this anymore."

"No!" I pleaded. Nick stirred and rolled onto his back beside me.

"I won't tell your dad about this," Mom said as if to reassure me. "But, I am going to call a psychiatrist in Boston." She returned to the bedside for a quick feel of my forehead before clomping down the stairs.

I swore at the ceiling, and Nick shifted to face me, cuddling me with both arms. "We must sleep, Emmie," he said groggily. "I am out of time."

I lay there, examining his dozing face. He'd done his best to help me, and my mom wasn't his biggest problem. A Tudor king couldn't melt into thin air without all hell breaking loose, so there were two possible scenarios here: Nick and I could fall asleep and disappear together, leaving things unfinished with my mom—but at least she now knew I wasn't at the bottom of the Connecticut River. Or, I could let Nick travel back to his time alone, and remain here to sort things out with Mom. Before returning to get me later, he'd have to explain the abrupt absence of his bride-to-be to the likes of Norfolk, and potentially be consoled by Lucinda 'Lucy' Parker. *Hell no.*

The choice was clear. I wasn't going back to two-timing the different centuries. I'd already made my choice, and being with Nick was still the right decision for me.

"We need to fall asleep again as fast as possible," I said, burrowing into the heavy warmth of Nick's arms. "Carol Grace on the rampage can be a dangerous thing." I was still dopey with tiredness, and the protective cocoon of his embrace soothed me back to sleep.

Hours later, an earthy sweetness tickled my nose. I turned my face away from the rose-scented sheets and onto my back, sighting billowy mounds of black velvet punctuated with red and white Tudor roses. Nick lay beside me, staring at the canopy.

We were back at Hampton Court Palace.

Nick's concerned eyes moved to mine, his fingers slipping into my hand. "Are you well?" he asked softly. Leaving Mom behind in that state had clearly freaked out the both of us.

I tucked my free arm behind my head, letting my jumbled thoughts crystallize. *I guess I'm not going to see my mom again for a good while.* What would happen to her?

"Emmie?" Nick pressed gently.

"I'm a bit sad to have left my mom that way," I admitted, my chest pulling.

He lay still, aside from the fingertips circling my palm. "I share your sorrow. You are fortunate to have a mother who cares for you so."

I twisted to look at him. Nick's capable maturity made it easy to forget that he'd lost a mother of his own. His mom, Queen Elizabeth the First, had died soon after giving birth to her daughter, Nick's little sister Kit. My finger traced his facial features, many of them gifts from his handsome father, Robert Dudley, the Earl of Leicester. "I bet your mom would give anything to be here with you," I said.

He shrugged. "My mother would yearn for her throne, but to see me not."

"That's not true."

He smiled bleakly. "Elizabeth was born to be a glorious prince. Despite her many troubles—her mother's beheading, betrayment by her father, imprisonment by her sister—Elizabeth yet won the throne with pride and might."

"She was amazing. Just like her *son*."

His voice drooped with sadness. "A son who snatched his mother's fortune and promise. Elizabeth wedded my father only because she was with child, Emmie…with me. If my birth had not come to pass, my mother would never have married beneath her station. If she had not then sought a second heir—my sister—then God would not have called Elizabeth away. When all is said and done, it is I who caused Queen Elizabeth's untimely death."

I cupped his trembling face. "No. Your mother loved you and Kit more than anything; I know it. You've had so much to deal with for someone so young. Too much."

He dropped his chin to my shoulder. "We have both felt loss, have we not? But we have one another now, and that remedies my heart in great measure."

"Mine too."

I relaxed a little as his long fingers played with the blue diamond on my thumb. "You spoke the truth when you said that this ring has become strange," he said. "Once again, we awakened no fewer than two times before it carried us back here."

"I'm glad you agree." I inspected the diamond for any signs of change. "I still think a soothsayer could help us out with some answers. Maybe someone like Agnes Nightingale?" I made a pleading grin. Last time we'd spoken about this, Nick had spurned the idea of paying the soothsayer a visit. "If it's too risky for you, we could start with an astrologer," I suggested, remembering what I'd been reading about the more accepted sciences in the sixteenth century.

His teeth pressed his bottom lip. "To speak plainly, Emmie, I bid you consider that we destroy the ring."

For a second, I couldn't process the words, like they were in a foreign language. "Destroy it? Why?" That'd mean never going home again. Never seeing my mom again. *Ever.*

Peach sunlight cast diamond-shaped shadows across Nick's strained face through the leaded window. "If the claims are true, this ring was enchanted to ruin me. Now it has plainly become impaired. We have no knowledge of what its sorcery may yet do. Must we wager our lives on it?"

I could barely speak. "There's no evidence to suggest the ring could harm us in any way."

"But do you not agree that the ring has become fickle?"

"If by that, you mean 'acting a little weird', then yes. Of course."

He leaned away from me. "Then what is to say that the next occasion we travel to your time, we will not become trapped there forevermore?"

It was apparent that the thought of having to stay with me in my time frightened Nick to death, which was impossible not to take personally. "Why would that be so hideous?" I said sharply. Had Nick already forgotten the incredible invention of human flight? How about the peace of anonymity and of being out of this Tudor pressure cooker?

His face read mine and then crumpled. "Emmie. We have suffered through this puzzle enough. I am a king, and one bereft of an heir. If I were to quit my kingdom, there would be unthinkable bloodshed. That vile woman Mary Stuart would come for my sister and the Tudor throne. If mine actions were to surrender England to a Catholic heretic, it would mean the damnation of my soul. Must we even speak of this again?" His voice rose with frustration.

"It's okay, I get it," I said. "You want to destroy the enchanted ring, meaning I can never visit my mom or my home again, because those things don't matter as much as your kingdom and throne."

He made an exasperated huff. "You must know that I do not ask this lightly. This ring has proven itself unstable and may cease to take effect at any moment. Therefore, if we were to journey to your time again, I would have to stake my kingdom on it, for the ring may never bring me back here. If you were to journey to your time without me, then I would stake losing you to all eternity if you could not return."

I didn't know what to say. Nick was so used to getting his way, and it showed.

He slid out of the bed. "What is certain is that you made a choice to be my bride, Emmie, so the question is: what are you prepared to give up? When my grandfather wed Katherine of Aragon, that woman never set foot in Spain again. There are many stories of English princes marrying foreigners who were content to live out their lives in their new kingdom. If you choose me, I want you to choose *me*. But if I am not enough—if all of England is not enough—then perhaps you have made the wrong choice." He turned his face away from me.

"Nick, I did choose you, but it was a fast decision, and I didn't think it meant I'd never be able to see my mom again," I called after him, but he'd already tapped once on the paneled wood. The doors opened immediately to the scurrying of boots and a voice crying, "His Majesty the King!" Nick disappeared into the frazzle, leaving me blinking away tears.

It felt like I'd been away from court for a week, but the ease with which I slipped into my old routine reminded me that it'd only been a day. Bridget quizzed me with cheeky questions about why I'd been locked away with the king overnight, but Alice shushed her. Lucinda kept her focus on her sewing like she didn't want to know.

I didn't catch sight of Nick for several days, and he was evidently avoiding me. Our conversation about the enchanted ring festered in the pit of my stomach, and I wanted to clear the air. I was nowhere near ready to destroy the ring without at least trying to learn more about it. Surely he could agree with me on that.

I distracted myself with my snore-fest lessons, took leisurely strolls in the gardens before the weather changed, and sank into the ease of some girl time.

At first light on Sunday morning, one of Nick's gentlemen delivered a message that I'd been requested to join the king at chapel. I still wasn't used to being summoned without notice like the family pet. *He's a Tudor king*, I reminded myself as I waited in the processional gallery upstairs, smoothing my hair and fidgeting with my dress.

Nick arrived swiftly, draped in a velvet coat of forest-green that stunningly contrasted with his blush-pink doublet. Courtiers and attendants kissed his hand at every turn, and what I thought would be us catching up became a public performance as he formally led me through to his royal pew.

We'd barely spoken to each other before I was ushered into a separate balcony beside his. A thick curtain of crimson velvet separated us. I couldn't even *see* Nick, let alone talk to him.

Tudor king, Tudor king, Tudor king.

I focused on snapping mental photographs of the Chapel Royal ceiling, which I'd never seen from this vantage point. Lifted from the pages of a fairytale, it shone in a cobalt blue constellation of golden arches, stars, and royal emblems. Its majestic beauty was enough to entertain me through the liturgy that was difficult for me to understand. When a choir of boys in white ruffs began singing, their euphonic voices like angels, I gripped the balcony handrail, fully absorbed. *Okay, so maybe airplanes and ketchup aren't all the world has to offer.*

When the service ended, the curtain between Nick and I glided open, and I swept toward him before he could disappear. As soon as we reached the processional gallery, courtiers rushed at the king with scrolls and petitions in their hands. Francis Beaumont had arrived on the scene to field them off, allowing Nick and I to duck into the concealment of one of his private stairwells and have a moment alone. Perhaps Francis was warming to our relationship, which served as a timely boost of encouragement.

"Was the service to your satisfaction?" Nick asked me, his expression hard to read.

"The choir was incredible," I replied, my voice bouncing off the stone walls. "It was probably the most beautiful thing I've ever heard."

His shoulders relaxed a little. "I am pleased to hear it."

He couldn't look me in the eye, clarifying that he was still as uncomfortable with things as I was. He offered me his hand. "I wish to show you something."

My palm slid into his, mini fireworks bursting between our skin as his fingers laced with mine. Our argument had done nothing to weaken the dizzying electricity that had brought us together in the first place.

We reached the drafty downstairs corridor and continued toward the construction site on the south side of the palace. A supersized canvas tent had been erected to protect the works from the rain. My new apartments were still haphazard muddles of building sites, but Nick led us right beneath the wooden scaffolding. The King of England was clearly endangering himself by marching through an active worksite, but no one dared stop him. Workers bowed in deference before fleeing like scurrying roaches. We climbed a dusty stairwell that smelled recently laid and passed through two unfinished chambers. The third room shone in stark distinction to the others, because it was already complete—a dazzling masterpiece among the uncut timber and grimy bricks.

"Wow," I murmured as I spun in all directions, taking in the magnificent jewelry workshop. Wooden trestle tables filled the space, neatly arranged with gilded files, iron pincer-like scissors and smaller cutters, brass blocks and molds, crucibles for heating metals, and other archaic tools I didn't recognize.

"Is this all for me?" I breathed, turning to Nick. He'd remembered his promise to build me a jewelry workshop, and he'd evidently made it a priority.

He nodded, a shy flush overcoming his face. "The gold and jewels are being kept safe, but you shall have as many as you need. Does it please you?"

I exaggerated my pretend grimace. "I guess it'll do."

He was accustomed to my sarcasm and finally smiled, closing the space between us. I had to stand on my tiptoes to wrap my arms around his neck.

"Any such thing you desire, tell me, and you shall have it," he said as we rocked together in a standing hug. "I have summoned a fine jewelry craftsman to teach you anything you wish. His name is Mister Andrea Bon Compagni. Call upon him any time you please; he is presently at court. Your maidens will assist you."

"I don't know what to say, which, as you know, is unheard of." I squeezed him tighter, my mouth falling into his neck. "Thank you so much."

"The pleasure is mine," he said into my skin, tightening his embrace.

His efforts had subdued some of the growing pressure between us, but we still hadn't agreed on what to do with the blue-diamond ring. He hadn't asked for it back, and for now, it was living inside my locked jewelry coffer. As the king, Nick could have the ring snatched from my bedchamber and destroyed with a single command, and I tried not to think too much about that possibility.

"I must take my leave," he said, breaking away from me and straightening his collar. "I have made time this day to prepare for your investiture ceremony."

I rested against the edge of a wooden table, already missing the touch of his body against mine. "Anytime you need me, I'll be here. And if I'm not…nah, I'll be here."

His sparkling eyes held my gaze as he backed through the doorway, looking so kissable with his naturally ruffled hair that it made my stomach twist.

"Your new cloth should also be at hand this day," he added, before rolling around the doorframe to disappear.

"My new cloth?" I called after him.

"For the harvest feast of Michelmas," he replied. "This year, I much desire a masquerade. We must also honor your new title."

His voice faded, and I sat there, processing the news. I had to appear at another royal ball with the Duke of Norfolk, Lord Wharton, and the rest of the sullen aristocrats—this time as a new member of their exclusive nobility club. But perhaps this is what it'd take for them to finally accept me. I was going to become the Marquess of Pembroke, followed by Queen Emmeline Tudor…*yikes!* Do or die, this was happening.

Deep in my gut, questions still wriggled about the blue-diamond ring and Nick's desire to destroy it. King Henry the Eighth's first wife, Katherine of Aragon, may have chosen not to sail back to Spain, but she presumably had the option. I was willfully marrying a Tudor king who I adored with every bone in my body, but I was still a twenty-first-century American girl. Freedom was the one thing I wasn't prepared to give up without a fight.

Mercifully, only a handful of Privy Council members attended my investiture ceremony in the Presence Chamber the following morning. My plush ceremonial robes sank into the woven matting as I knelt before the king, and a sacred coronet as freezing as an ice sculpture was placed over my head. As the letters patent were read out, and King Nick formally granted me the title of Marquess of Pembroke, a tremor quaked through me. I could barely look at Nick in this state without feeling like I was making eyes with a living angel. The jewels in his crown splashed prismatic colors across the candlelit wall, and despite my modern viewpoints, I couldn't deny that every inch of him radiated power and glory from within his scarlet robes.

When Alice was washing my hair in the bath afterward, she told me that all the Privy Council members usually attended the investiture ceremonies. There should've been plenty more people there. I swallowed the discomfort that brought. If I continued freaking out about every little thing—needing every person in the realm to like me—my life here would be a misery. I was trying the best I could.

You're the Marquess of freaking Pembroke! I reminded myself as I began dressing for the masquerade feast. Truthfully, I had little idea what a female marquess even was, how she ranked, or what she was supposed to do. I knew I could ask Alice, but I'd have to be careful about sounding like I'd barely heard of the title. At least it would be swallowed up by 'Queen of England' before long, and it was pretty clear how that one stacked.

My anxiety over the Michelmas feast was borderline paralyzing, but the dress that arrived for me from the Royal Wardrobe sweetened the deal a little. The sleeves and gown of scarlet-red satin were draped open to reveal a white kirtle threaded with triangular patterns of white diamonds centered with rose-shaped ruby brooches. Behind me, Bridget and Lucinda chatted at length about the eligible men who'd be at the feast while weaving my hair into elaborate braids. It was a shame that their efforts were entirely concealed by a magnificent ruby-encrusted hood. I usually hated having all my hair covered, but Alice's makeup had turned me into a magazine ad for glowing skin, and she'd accented my lips with the perfect shade of creamy red.

I swiveled from left to right in the mirror, glittering like I was tangled in fairy lights. The ensemble was comically swanky for Emmie Grace from Hampshire County, but at least I looked the part of my new title. I could nod and wave like a real queen-to-be and not have to say much to anyone. I wished I had useful contributions to make, but I'd have to rely on a dignified silence to get me through until I learned enough in this century to be able to offer something worthwhile…if my position even allowed that.

I repressed another pang of longing for my time period.

Alice and I were unhooking our masquerade masks from their storage pouches when a messenger arrived with a letter for Lucinda Parker.

"It is from my mother," she said, hurriedly snapping open the wax seal. "She brings news of my daughter, Ellie." She read a few words before slumping into the table. "Dear God."

Bridget finished clipping on her jeweled belt and dashed to her. "What is it?"

We all gathered around Lucinda. "Ellie has taken ill," she breathed. "My mother believes it to be consumption."

My chest leaped. "You should go to her." I was pretty sure that consumption was what the Tudors called tuberculosis.

"Mistress Parker cannot travel alone," said Bridget. "I will go with her." She threw me a nervous glance.

"Of course," I agreed. "Alice and I will look after each other, won't we, Alice?"

Alice nodded, giving Lucinda's arm a compassionate rub. Lucinda's pendant necklace tinkled as she fell into a chair, finishing the letter. "Mother complains here of the costs," she said. "The king has raised taxes, and now she cannot afford to buy remedies for Ellie."

"For what has His Majesty raised taxes?" Alice griped, like Nick was her frustrating older brother.

Lucinda folded the letter in her lap. "It says here that taxes have been raised to pay for the coronation of the new queen."

I felt my jaw hang. "I can't believe that—I'd never agree to that; I'm so sorry."

Lucinda's silvery-blue eyes were free of judgment as she looked at me. "I shall remain at court. I must petition the king for some course of aid for my household."

"But I can do that," I said. "You should be with Ellie."

Lucinda rose to smooth her skirts. "You are most kind, my lady. However, I would not ask you to do my bidding. In any case, I fear that His Majesty will be less favorable if I do not make mine own case for my daughter."

"The king may not like Mistress Parker leaving court without his permission," Alice explained to me as though she knew I was confused. "She is to become a lady to the queen."

I took Lucinda's clammy hands. "Ask the king tonight then. Apart from the fact that time is clearly of the freaking essence, it's usually when he's in his best mood. And if he doesn't help you, I will." I had income from my lands now, even though I had no idea where my lands were.

Lucinda didn't want to write to her mom until she'd spoken to the king, so we tied on each other's shimmery, feathered masks and left for the king's Privy Garden. It was a chilly evening for an outdoor shindig, but that's what the king wanted, so it was happening.

Masked noblemen voiced their admiration and tried to guess our identities as we strode past the avenue of clipped yew trees and into the pre-party zone. Guests hovered in clusters around the low hedges of the knot gardens, drinking wine, nibbling hors d'oeuvres, and dancing merrily in the open spaces. Green-and-white poles topped with heraldic beasts overlooked fragrant beds of primroses, violets, and cherries that masked the river smells. Each square-shaped garden was bordered with an impeccably manicured hedge.

A tall guy with thick, windswept hair sprouting from an ivory mask took my fingers and led me into the volta. I pretended I had no idea it was King Nick, to keep up his charade, and the guests paced backward to give us space. After so many tedious hours of dance practice, I actually didn't make a total idiot of myself and kept pace with the king's smooth movements. Cheers sounded as Nick gripped my waist and lifted me to the sky—practically dirty dancing for Tudor times—before concluding the display by dropping to one knee and kissing my hand. A collective gasp at the kneeling king rippled through the crowd, but within seconds, Nick was back on his feet. *Holy shit, I just pulled off the volta.*

"Do you know me?" he said in a theatrical voice, and I tried not to laugh. Dorky Nick was adorable.

"Are you the Earl of Warwick?" I replied loudly. Alice cracked up —always the first to react over a Francis Beaumont joke.

"Only if I have shrunk by a head," Nick replied, tearing off his mask.

The nobles roared with laughter like it was the funniest joke ever told. Nick beamed down at me, affection pouring from his sea-colored eyes. He slid a hand inside his coat that was the Tudor colors of green and white, extracting a sliver of gold.

"For my lady, most dear, and your promised Queen of England!" he cried, draping the glistening chain over my head. I'd expected more cheers, but there was mostly gentle clapping as my fingers clutched the heart-shaped ruby that pressed against my neck. My mind shot back to Nick sitting beside my mom, dipping sliced bread with orange cheese into ketchup. He must've thought my home—my life—was so unimpressive and beggarly compared to this. Enough rubies were hanging off my body to buy a planet. Had he really raised the people's taxes to pay for all this?

The frazzled Master of the Revels hurriedly cleared a larger space. Two armchairs were carried in for Nick and me, and the rest of the guests gathered behind us on foot. A masque unfolded before us—an iridescent spectacle of actors playing unicorns, nymphs, knights, and damsels, accompanied by lively music and primitive fireworks that could've blown us to smithereens. When the performance finished with a lady rescuing the archangel St. Michael from danger, Nick threw me a covert smirk. He'd arranged the surprise feminist ending to impress me. If it hadn't been the sixteenth century, I'd have kissed him right here.

After our chairs were removed, a mob of waiting nobles and diplomats sucked the king inside their huddle like a whirlpool. I waited on the perimeter, peering around for Lucinda. She had to have her chance to speak with the king, and single mothers didn't exactly enjoy priority access in this place.

Alice arrived beside me with two cups of wine.

"You're a good girl," I said, accepting one. It was sweetened with warmed berries.

I winced at the sight of Bridget trying to engage the visibly uninterested Earl of Surrey in conversation. While it wasn't my business who the cute earl hooked up with, I suspected that pretty maidens weren't exactly on his radar. I'd noticed the way he looked at other dashing gentlemen of the court with shining eyes, and his intimacy with his male tennis partner. Not that I'd ever mention my theory to Bridget, or even Alice—this was a dangerously different world to the one I knew.

Just beyond Bridget and Surrey stood Francis Beaumont among a throng of lords.

"How do you think Lord Warwick is going as the king's right-hand man?" I asked Alice, genuinely curious.

She considered her answer. "It appears that Francis has been a good servant to the king, and he has fairly handled the Spanish threat. However, he has become as single-minded as my father: sparing no end in his efforts to please the king and the lords. I suppose his sense of duty is to be commended, but I fear he will end up like my Papa...wedded to his work." The longing in Alice's voice spoke volumes. I'd never have pushed this hard if I wasn't sure that Alice and Francis secretly fancied the pants off each other.

"Okay, enough," I ordered, the effects of the wine relaxing my inhibitions. "You and Francis need to get together, like yesterday."

"What in the high heavens?" she said through a chortle.

"Stop it," I said like she was a naughty schoolgirl. "You and Francis have had more misunderstandings than Romeo and Juliet, but they're all cleared up now. Let's go through this again: Francis was once betrothed to your older sister Violet, but then he called off the wedding, not because he was a jerk, but because he is actually in love with *you*. The second issue was that you thought Francis had driven *me* away from court for similar reasons, but that also turned out to be false. Does that cover everything?"

Alice gaped at me, before spinning to face Francis again, her slate-colored skirts rustling against the gravel. Together, we watched Francis brush sweaty black curls from his temples while he listened to a nobleman speaking with wild gesticulations. Francis patted the man's shoulder before turning to another man who appeared equally as distressed.

Francis's gaze moved to catch Alice's stare. Neither of them looked away for several seconds. When the irritated noblemen turned his back to Francis, the earl swayed on his feet, clearly deciding whether to approach us or not. I took Alice's arm and walked quickly over to him.

"Good evening, and God save you, my ladies," he greeted us with a bow like we were two strangers. Alice dipped into a polite curtsy.

Oh, for goodness' sake, you two.

"I am grateful for your timely rescue," he said, guiding us into a quieter space. "Every harebrain in this palace finds it his duty to make petty complaints without end." The scent of musk drifted off his skin as he brought his wine cup to his lips.

"Much has changed since you were merely in charge of court entertainment," Alice said to him with a wry smile.

A torch flame flickered in Francis's dark eyes. "Make no mistake, my lady, pacifying the nobility is a performance indeed."

She laughed. "Perhaps if this is all to fall short, you may join the theatre. You would make a fine Narcissus."

Ha, typical quick-witted Alice. In Greek mythology, I remembered Narcissus to be the hunter who was physically beautiful but utterly self-absorbed.

"I feel I would be more suited to Achilles," Francis quipped. "And you, my lady, would make a finer Helen of Troy."

Her cheeks tinted the color of cherries, but she held his gaze. "A lady in a playhouse? I have heard there is much kissing to be observed."

Francis smiled. "Well, if there is to be kissing, I would then wish to change my part to Prince Paris."

The love match to Helen of Troy, I remembered. Biting down on a smirk, I backed away from them. "I'm just going to find the king," I said. "Sometimes he drinks too much wine before he eats."

The truth was that no one could stop Nick from drinking or eating whatever the hell he wanted—not even me. But Alice and Francis were finally flirting like they'd been suppressing it for years and I wasn't going to get in the way.

It was past sunset, but supper couldn't begin without the king's command. I weaved through clusters of guests, searching for Nick, most of the courtiers morphing into horror-movie characters through their strange masks in the dim light.

Looping back around, I ambled past the musicians until I spotted flashes of green and white fabric through the torchlights. I slipped between the flaming lamps, careful to avoid their heat. I curled around to see Nick with Lucinda Parker standing beside a stone dragon fountain, both their masks removed. She must've finally been asking him for money to help with her daughter. Good. *Nick…be nice.*

I leaned closer. Neither of them was saying anything. Was he being difficult? Nick was just gazing down at Lucinda, whose tilted face was a few inches from his. They looked like two models shooting the cover for a historical bridal magazine.

The gesture was so unexpected—so shocking—that, at first, I thought I imagined it. But no, Lucinda took Nick's hand in hers and tugged him toward her, catching his lowering lips with hers.

8

I DIDN'T KNOW IF—OR FOR HOW LONG—NICK KISSED LUCINDA BACK. The unfolding scene was too blurry behind the stinging fog of my tears. I tore away from the streak of torchlights and onto an avenue leading back to the privacy of my chambers. I couldn't be here—four hundred years away from home, doing my best to convince myself and others I was Tudor queen material—if Nick was cheating on me. I had to get away...to escape...to be out of this stifling outfit. Its sleeves were so tight that they pinched my skin as I reached up to wipe my eyes.

It was just my luck that the moronic Duke of Norfolk was tucked away on a bench within a coterie of standing councilors, like he was the king holding court. Beneath the cloak of nightfall, the men didn't appear to see me as I scaled a short hedge and landed within a tangle of rosemary in a strip of greenery that ran alongside the pathway. I felt bad for the well-tended garden, but I'd sooner bash my way through rose thorns than have those jerks question why I was fleeing the feast.

The memory of Nick's lips touching Lucinda's plunged a stake into my heart and twisted it. Had she been playing me this entire time? God, had *he?* I squashed the unbearable thought and continued silently along the shadowy garden bed, attempting to sneak past the men without being noticed.

"…His Majesty's private inclinations," one of them said.

"The king's marriage is no matter of privacy," snapped the Duke of Norfolk. My satin heels stilled in the dirt, every inch of me listening. "King Nicholas's decision to marry this featherbrained girl instead of a blood royal will lose him the affections of the people and give cause for civil war."

"I suspect the people may come to love her," argued the first man. "She does have some quality of allure."

Baron Wharton grunted. "This marriage is no more than a laughingstock. It does naught to further the realm and may even bring England's standing to ruin." Lord Wharton spoke robustly, and the others shushed him.

"But to petition against your niece," the first man said to Norfolk. "Surely you desire such a match?"

The duke scoffed. "Half the silly girls in England may lay claim to be my niece. My brother was quite the ladies' man."

Rambunctious laughter exploded, chased by more shushing.

"Mistress Grace is no more than a nobleman's daughter," said Norfolk. "You can be certain that she is of little value to me."

Not even a nobleman's daughter, idiot. Plus, it's Lady Pembroke to you. I still wanted to snort at that name.

"The girl has plainly poisoned His Majesty's mind," Wharton said. "He has a foolish devotion to her. She can have any pillock in England; she need not have our king."

Norfolk's voice dropped. "Are we all in agreement that this marriage cannot move forward? We have need for swift action."

I expected some contention—especially from the guy who defended me at the start—but there were only murmurs of acceptance.

A blast of trumpets nearly jolted me into a hedge. Sheathed swords swung from the men's leather belts as they scampered away to the riverside banqueting house to guzzle the king's expensive delicacies.

Backstabbers. I huffed quietly to myself.

We have need for swift action. What did that even mean?

Surely nobody would dream of attacking the king, but it'd only take a single blow from one of those mighty swords to my heart—or Nick's—to end our relationship for good. We couldn't exactly marry if one of us was in the ground.

I'd put the King of England in danger again by being here.

Shit, and all the bad words.

I climbed back over the hedge and trudged up the path leading to the banqueting house, feeling the torchlights cast me back into the limelight. A guard buckled almost to his knees at the sight of me and called off his mini search party. It was obvious that Nick had already realized I was missing from the feast and had ordered the guards to find me or suffer the king's wrath. The guard looked so relieved to see me that he made the sign of the cross. Jeez, I'd only been gone for ten minutes.

The banqueting house smelled like a country fair, with rustic parcels of peaches, oranges, radishes, parsnips, carrots, and onions hanging from the candlelit eaves. The king sat on his throne beneath a canopy of odorless deep-purple daisies that wouldn't bother his asthma, with Francis whispering into his ear. Nick's hand gripped the back of my empty chair to his left, his body angled toward it. I untied my mask and braced myself as I approached the dais.

"For the love of God," Nick cried as I slid into my seat. Francis slumped forward with visible relief. He'd probably had to handle Nick's panic over my disappearance.

"To where did you vanish?" Nick huffed as Bridget scrambled onto the platform to help me with my dress like it was my bridal gown. There were too many faces in the stately chamber to find Lucinda Parker's. "Why do you smell of rosemary?" Nick added, studying me.

"I'm fine," I snapped at the fussing Bridget, shame sending heat to my face. She bowed and returned to a table beside the angel's wings sculpted from wheat fronds. There sat Alice and Lucinda, murmuring at each other through cheerful grins. My cheeks felt like they had turned to stone.

"I just went for a walk," I said to Nick, looking at the decorative floral crusts of the blackberry pies on a nearby table. Anywhere but at him.

"Yes?" he prodded.

"I saw…" My voice trembled. Nick's hand had curled into a fist over the purple-and-gold table runner. A cook was shucking oysters before the king, each sticky clack unsettling my nerves.

I saw Lucinda Parker kiss you.

"I saw the Duke of Norfolk with some of the privy councilors, including Lord Wharton," I said under my breath. "They were talking about our marriage, and Norfolk encouraged them to try to stop it."

Nick's face twisted with disbelief as Francis hunched forward, also listening.

"They said they were going to take *swift action*," I continued. "There were five of them, and they're all sitting with Norfolk now." I subtly gestured toward the treasonous gang.

Nick lurched forward and snatched the knife right out of the oyster chef's hand.

"Majesty," Francis hissed, slamming his palm over Nick's wrist. The cook scurried away to safety.

"You are certain?" Nick asked me, his eyes flaming jewels of aquamarine.

"One hundred percent."

"Majesty, it would do well to remain calm," Francis cautioned, carefully sliding the knife away from the king.

Nick's hands were now tight fists of white skin. "No man may question the pleasure of their sovereign king," he said through his teeth. "*All* are bound by God to obey me."

Francis's curls tipped in a gesture of submission. "My gracious lord, I caution you to consider the cause of such plotting between Norfolk and the councilmen before they increase in numbers." He shot me an uneasy glance. "A king's marriage should bring greater power and esteem to the realm. What case have you made for Lady Pembroke, who offers no such benefit?"

Nick slammed his fist down so hard that the table shook. The musicians were trained to play loudly enough so guests couldn't hear the king's conversations, but nervous faces peeked at the evidently furious monarch.

"Any man who does not have his king's welfare at heart will be summoned before me to explain himself—no matter his station," he warned Francis in a steely tone.

The earl returned an obedient nod. "You shall continue to find me your most true and faithful servant, Your Grace."

Humiliation scorched my cheeks over hearing Francis still overtly questioning our relationship, especially given how I'd just gone in to bat for him with Alice. No matter how Nick and I felt about each other, it would never be enough for Francis, who wanted his king to be politically secure above all things. But I truly believed that he genuinely loved Nick too much to ever cross a line the way Norfolk had and conspire to stop the marriage.

Nick sat stewing over his wine cup before he smacked it across the table, sending red droplets flying like blood splatter. "I cannot even look at these faithless cod's heads," he snapped at Francis. "You will arrest every member of the Privy Council on the grounds of sedition. Interrogate them all and make ready a warrant of execution for those found guilty."

Francis's face mirrored my own horror. "Majesty, the entire council? I beseech you—"

"You dare question me!" The king grabbed him by his ruffled collar and yanked him to his feet.

"Nick!" I chastised, and he squeezed the fabric with barely contained fury before releasing Francis.

"No man shall ever speak on matters of my marriage!" Nick bellowed to the chamber of nobles, every face a white sheet. "Those who offend the will of their anointed king will find themselves on trial for high treason." He thrust both hands beneath the dining table and shoved it forward, sending gold platters and cups clanging across the tiled floor.

A moment of chilling silence followed before Nick grabbed my arm and marched me out beneath a procession of arches woven from wheat fronds.

"Let go of me!" I cried when we were safely out of earshot. I was hot with rage at how Nick had treated me in public, not to mention the violent outburst that had Nicholas the Ironheart written all over it.

He was already calmer and halted on the path, but I was just getting started. I continued my brisk pace toward the palace.

"Lady Pembroke, I command you to stop," he called after me. I didn't break my stride. One of the guards stayed close to me, awkwardly passing by the king. I couldn't care less what they thought of us.

"Vexatious girl," Nick huffed before he briskly caught up again. He dashed in front of me, pacing backward while I charged forward. "Christ, Emmie, I bid you to speak your ill feeling!"

At that moment, I just couldn't. Lucinda…Norfolk…Nick's scary eruption and talk of executions…the relentless pressure to become a convincing Tudor queen overnight. *Where do I even freaking start!*

"Blessed girl, I love you," said Nick. He stopped still at my onrush, and I banged right into his sternum. I spun away to face the sundial, my stomach a hollow cave.

I could hardly get the words out. "If you love me, then why did you sneak off into a private part of the garden with Lucinda Parker and let her kiss you?"

Nick gasped. "Who said such things to you?"

"I *saw* you!" I clenched away the urge to shove him with both hands. "To be honest, you both looked pretty cozy." His silhouette wobbled through the tears threatening my eyes.

He dismissed the comment with a shake of his head. "It was nothing of the sort. Mistress Parker's daughter has taken ill—a private matter—and she bid me aside to ask for my assistance. As she is your lady, I granted it. Mistress Parker's kiss was no more than a gesture of gratitude."

"A gesture of gratitude?" The words ripped through my bewildered laugh as I turned away again.

He took my shoulders and swirled me to face him. "Do not make more of this than it is. Do you know that it is considered polite in this realm to kiss another man's wife before first entering his home? You stake too much in a chaste kiss. Mistress Parker brought her lips to mine for scarcely a moment, did you not see?"

"Just…please!" I waved my hands to shut him up. I didn't want to imagine any more lip-locking than I'd already seen.

Nick's palms kneaded his forehead. "Christ, I would sooner see Mistress Parker banished from court than have you doubt my devotion to you."

"No." My jaw hardened. "You know that she's got a sick baby, and she needs the money." The memory of Lucinda's plight roused another thought. "She also said that you raised the people's taxes to pay for my coronation…people now can't afford medicine for their babies."

Nick crossed his arms. "And by what means do you expect me to pay for the crowning of your person, my lady? Have you found coin growing upon trees in this realm?"

"Haven't you got something like *sixty* palaces?" I countered, vindictively repeating what he'd once shared with me with such pride.

He paced away from me before circling back with frustration. "I fear that you understand nothing. Not me, not mine intentions, not my wishes, not my kingdom, nor my decisions."

"That's not true," I said, seizing the chance to air what'd been plaguing my mind most of all. "But there is one thing I don't get: why you would ask me to destroy a ring that's literally the only way I could ever see my family again. I'd never ask that of you."

He expelled a heavy breath. "Emmie, it is not so much the ring as that I feel you have one foot in this thing and one foot out. This night alone proves this marriage to be a battle hard won, it is true. I cannot turn any which way in this place without meeting a lord who believes he has the right to interfere in the subject of my marriage. But I am the king, and I will choose mine own wife. That choice is *you*, in spite of the falseness of my subjects and the losses I must endure. Is it not fair that I wish not to lose you too?"

My throat sealed shut. All this time, Nick had been sensing my trepidation about becoming queen and assuming that it was him that I was unsure about.

"You won't lose me," I said, stepping closer to him. "*You* are the only reason I'm here. But if you need me to destroy the ring to prove it, then I'm not ready for that yet. So I'm sorry, but the answer to that is a hard 'no'."

The grind of boots on gravel severed the cord of tension between us. Francis Beaumont bowed to the king from the shadows. "Your Grace, the members of the Privy Council have been seized, as you wish, and are being taken to the Tower."

Nick squared his shoulders. "You have pleased your king. Now, I instruct you not to draw Lady Pembroke into this matter any further. My lady has been burdened enough. You will lead the interrogation of the councilors and determine who is to be charged."

Francis offered a stiff, reluctant bow before leaving us alone. Nick shrugged off his velvety coat that smelled like freshly cut roses and draped it over me.

"I don't want those men to be killed because of me," I said to him. "I've never been a fan of the death penalty."

His bottom lip disappeared between his teeth. "A king cannot appear weak, Emmie."

"No one heard their seditious words but me," I argued. "If they're found guilty, can't you keep them locked up instead? You can't behead them just because they don't like me. It'll sicken me with guilt. It's *not* the way things are done where I'm from."

He caught my chin between his thumb and forefinger and brought his lips close to mine. "How any man can think ill of you, I will never know," he said, the heat of his breath tickling my skin. His other hand slid down to rest on my shoulder. "If it shall please your heart, then I will pursue imprisonment for those convicted of speaking out against our marriage and forgo the scaffold. However, I cannot make the same pledge for those who are found to have plotted against your life or mine."

"That's fair." He took my hand in his and I held tight. "My only worry is what Norfolk knows about me. He could tell people that you asked him to lie about being my uncle." I hushed my voice so the guards couldn't hear, not that they'd ever speak out.

Nick's eyes shone brighter than the cabochon emeralds sewn into his doublet. "If that dimwit Norfolk would be so foolish as to make that claim, I will heartily refute it. You would have the word of a king to support you, my lady. There is none stronger than that."

The next week that passed was eerily quiet at court. Only six members of the king's council had been cleared by Francis to return to work; the rest were embroiled in a trial that I wasn't allowed to witness. Nick assured me that any punishments resulting from the matter would be imprisonment and not execution, but Alice thought that was a fairy story. While she painted on my makeup one morning after breakfast, we debated over how merciful King Nick really was. For every example Alice had of a violent beheading ordered by the king, I had zero rebuttal. My only choice was to trust that my boyfriend wouldn't lie to my face—including about getting snuggly with his ex.

At least Lucinda Parker had taken leave from court to visit her daughter, assuming that poor Ellie was still alive. While the thought of seeing Lucinda still turned my stomach, I'd simmered a little on the whole kiss thing. Alice assured me she'd given plenty of men a peck on the lips without any hint of flirtation, and even Bridget thought it was common practice, despite her obsessions with romantic passion.

For now, my wedding and coronation were proceeding like nothing had happened with Norfolk and his treasonous tribe. Nick was full steam ahead on the marriage mission, and I sensed he was trying to prove his affection for me more than ever after the Lucinda incident.

The week after the Michelmas train wreck, the painter George Gower rode into court on the king's orders to compose my formal portrait.

I was never gifted at sitting still for long periods, but posing for a taciturn artist was the break I needed from the pressures of my lessons. I didn't have to pretend to speak Shakespearean to anyone, perform an oddball Renaissance dance, or play an instrument I'd never even heard of. Gower only needed me to sit deathly still, and it took all the mental space I had to keep my feet from falling asleep. I focused on a pretty fringed cushion in the chair behind him, my fingers clasping a single red rose. Nick had sent in a harpist to keep me entertained, and the glittery tune lulled me into a blissful meditation.

Just before supper, the oak doors swung open, shocking me from my trance. "His Majesty the King!" cried a guard.

"Your Grace, the portrait is not yet complete," spluttered Gower in a deep bow.

"I wish to see it not," Nick replied, covering his eyes as he side-stepped the canvas to approach me.

I blushed at him through a tangle of butterflies at the rare sight of him in casual black leather. He glided a scented hand down my cheek, turning my legs so weak that I could've sunk right into the woven matting.

"My love, I come to share news, and I plainly could not wait," he said, the playfulness in his voice divulging that the news was good. "I have made formal the preparations for our marriage rites. Before this, we shall leave Hampton Court on progress. The castle must be cleaned and replenished to make welcome the many men who will wish to behold the wedding of our most blessed queen."

"Progress…isn't that like a king's tour of the country?"

He nodded, pressing his lips to the back of my hand. "Occurrences remain of the one-day fever on the roads to Sussex, so we shall travel west, and perhaps north. First to Windsor, then over to Oxford, and God willing, to Kenilworth to meet the Princess Catherine."

"Oh please, yes—can we visit Kit?" Nick's little sister was one of the only people here who felt like family. I ached to see her.

His dimpled smile lit up his eyes. "Kenilworth it is. Kit will be enamored to see you. We shall depart on the morrow." Nick spun to address the painter. "You will finish the portrait this day. Our Lady Pembroke will inform you when she is weary and in need of rest."

Gower's oil-stained fingers flew to his goatee as he watched the king leave.

"It's okay," I reassured him. "I'll stay as long as you need."

The painter tipped his head at me in gratitude, before his fingers began dashing across the canvas with panicky scrapes. I became a sitting statue again, processing the good news: I was about to travel through sixteenth-century English villages and meet some of the common folk...those who were surely more like me than anyone in this posh court. It would be an escape from the constant unease I felt from not being able to perfect the Tudor protocols quickly enough. A smile tugged at my lips, inducing a tsk-tsk from Gower. My cheeks slumped back into somber Tudor portrait mode.

I climbed into bed after midnight, making a stop at the map on the wall in my bedchamber. The route we'd take on progress was northwest, passing right through Buckinghamshire, where Bridget Nightingale's family was from.

My eyes flickered to the jewelry coffer still protecting the blue-diamond ring. This was my chance to show the enchanted ring to Bridget's cousin—the soothsayer Agnes Nightingale—and find out what it was meant for and why it'd been acting strangely. If I could just prove that the ring wasn't going to conk out on one of its journeys to the twenty-first century—erroneously trapping us there—Nick would stop freaking out, and we could even visit there now and then. I wouldn't have to choose between the man I loved and my mom.

I tugged the sheets to my chin, making a firm promise to myself: before Nick had a chance to destroy the enchanted ring that clearly terrified him, I was going to stop at nothing to get some answers about it—with his blessing or without.

9

SPLINTERS OF SUNRISE THROUGH THE CRACKS IN THE SHUTTERS roused me out of bed without my usual sleepy protests. I was fully charged and springy with excitement for my first road trip across sixteenth-century England.

But when I got outside, the number of people lined up to join us was a shock to the system. It was never going to be a couple's escape, but I hadn't expected literally a thousand people to come along for the ride. From the west gatehouse of Hampton Court Palace, hundreds of carts, wagons, and horses queued noisily outside the slaughterhouses and stables before disappearing into the hunting park. Half the court's residents stood in their traveling cloaks, hastily tying last-minute pieces of furniture, bedding, and wall hangings to their horses and wagons.

I clung to the last corner of warmth inside the gatehouse with my three ladies. Lucinda Parker had arrived back at court the night before, giddily sharing news of Ellie's improvement. I was genuinely relieved that Ellie was okay, and nothing was going to dull my perky mood—not even the memory of Lucinda's lips on my boyfriend's. At this point, I was taking everyone's word for it that lip-locking in an age of widespread disease was inexplicably commonplace.

Bridget was bouncing from heel to heel. "My first royal progress," she sang, already on the lookout for rich hotties.

Alice groaned, separating the tangled chains of the brass pendants she'd made for us to ward off bad air outside the palace. "You may come to loathe the progress, with lodging conditions of every which way and no manner of receiving letters." I felt a pang of guilt over my careless excitement—for Alice, our trip away also meant potentially missing news about her mom's disappearance.

"We shall sleep in great comfort," Lucinda argued cheerfully. "We are so fortunate and blessed to be traveling with our promised queen." She tipped her pearled hood at me, finally acknowledging my station over her. I couldn't decide whether or not her kindness was genuine, but I gave her the benefit of the doubt and returned a cautious smile.

"Come then," said Alice, draping the talismans over our heads. "The king will not wish us to ride on horseback so late in the year. We must find our coach."

The four of us edged through whirs of servants securing rolled-up mattresses and trapped hunting dogs yipping from carts but could see no sign of our carriage. Nick emerged through the chaos, a superstar strutting the red carpet toward us as infatuated courtiers bid him good morning from every angle.

"Good morrow, my lady," he said to me, dropping into an elegant bow.

I'd never acclimatize to the sight of Nicholas the Ironheart bowing to me, nor the impact of Nick Tudor in full finery. He liked the comfort of long pants, but today he'd chosen breeches to impress the nobles with his muscular legs. The silk cloth encasing his hips and chest shone with swirls of pearled white, coconut cream, and pale ivory. A thick cloak of jet-black blanketed one shoulder, the bottom half embroidered with snow-colored seashells. The tongue-in-cheek frown I'd attempted was eaten away by an embarrassingly doting smile. Nevertheless, I fired a teasing shot.

"No one seems to know where we're supposed to be," I said to him, indicating my ladies. "The dogs and puffin birds have carts, but we don't. Should we walk to Windsor?"

Nick chuckled with his unflappable coolness. "You are to travel with my person, Lady Pembroke."

Bridget gasped and fluffed out her skirts. "My glorious lord, will Lady Pembroke's ladies be blessed to join His Majesty's coach?"

Nick's eyes didn't move from mine. "I am afraid not, madam. There is not room in my coach for so many beautiful maidens." They all blushed, and I forced my mind away from Lucinda. "I have appointed the Earl of Warwick as your companion."

Alice's cheeks flushed scarlet at the news that she'd be traveling with Francis Beaumont. She was so obviously smitten with the fiery earl that it made me want to squeal, but she'd made clear nothing had happened between them at the feast. Something was still holding Alice back, and I intended to find out what.

What snagged my attention the most, however, was that Nick not only avoided Lucinda Parker's gaze, but he turned his back to her, offering me an elbow. "Come, my lady," he said.

"Make way for the king!" cried the guards. My shoulder brushed Nick's bicep as we walked, and he tilted into me.

He led me up the stairs of his coach, which was swathed in blue velvet braided with ropes of gold. Before I could take in the lush interiors, we were already kissing. He reached behind me to tug the curtain closed without separating his mouth from mine, his movements heated and urgent. It was a ridiculously inappropriate time to launch into a make-out session, but common sense and Nick Tudor had become an oxymoron. After our recent rough patch, it felt like he hadn't kissed me in weeks, and he feverishly hooked an arm around my waist and tugged me into his lap until my legs parted over his thighs. I clutched his face between my palms and kissed him like I was doing it to save my own life, his hands pushing beneath my skirts until he found my ass and gripped it in his palms.

My eyes flashed open, looking into his flushed gaze as he rolled his hips against me. I breathed a moan against his lips at the heat of his arousal, wondering if he'd consider delaying our departure.

Nick cursed under his breath as he rubbed his thickening length against me, the ache in his expression mirroring mine. One of his hands let go of my ass, and he slid it to my front and dragged one of his knuckles up and down the seam of my core over my underwear, his lips parting as I moaned.

The shout of a commander right outside the curtain was the wake-up call we both needed. I slipped off Nick and onto the cushioned bench beside him, breathing like I'd just run cross-country.

"Forgive me," he said breathlessly, adjusting himself in his breeches. "I grow weary of all this fanfare and never being able to see you without the company of others."

The comment caught me by surprise. I'd thought it was just me who craved for it to be only the two of us.

"The king is ready to depart," Nick called hoarsely before I could shamelessly ask him if there was any way to continue what we'd just started. Seconds after his command, our coach shook to life.

The king sat back with his hands on his knees, as accustomed to riding in golden coaches as he was to drinking from fountains of wine. I peeked through the gap in the curtain, watching the stables and kennels shrink away in our trail of dust. The graveled road soon melted into dirt tracks as we rumbled along the river dotted with white swans, the crisp taste of the breeze reminding me how stuffy the palace walls had become. Children in tattered shirts and dresses were jogging alongside us, waving with gap-toothed grins.

"God save the king!" their musical voices shouted. "Long live the king!" A bunch of boys had gathered a short distance ahead, their woolen caps pressed to their chests. I reached through the curtains to wave at them, hearing their delighted shrieks as the coach rolled on.

"Can I open the curtains a bit?" I asked Nick.

"If it pleases you." He unrolled a scroll containing trade updates. We'd been out of Hampton Court less than five minutes, and he already seemed more at ease.

I tugged the curtain apart two inches, aware that any more might put the king at risk on the open roads. Our coachman skillfully negotiated the deeply rutted paths as we bumped through acres of dense forest, harvested meadows sprinkled with grazing cattle, rustic cottages bandaged with vines, and colorful constellations of wildflowers grasping the last weeks of spring. When the road made a sharp curve at the tip of a small hill, I twisted to check out the hundreds of carts trailing us like an ant colony on the move—visual proof that the King of England would never have a private life. He would always be surrounded by his court, his nobles, or his guards.

I shut the curtain and curled into the crook of Nick's arm. The rhythmic bounce of hooves coupled with the security of him holding me rocked me to sleep within minutes.

I woke to the clanging of church bells and the icy touch of Nick's sparkling rings on my skin as he stroked my chin.

"We have arrived at the castle of Windsor," he said gently.

I sat up with a yawn. "What time is it?"

"Time for dinner, I should expect." He helped me climb down the coach steps into the windy and overcast chill. Dinner was Tudor speak for lunch, so I guessed it was before midday.

"Wow," I said, taking in the sight of the fortress castle with its cylindrical battlement towers that dwarfed us. The damp air warned that rain was imminent. Carts, wagons, and horses formed an impatient line down to the river like a medieval traffic jam, waiting for the king to make his exit.

"My lady," he said, finding my fingers beneath the silky ruffles of his sleeve.

We crossed the drawbridge over the castle ditch and stepped inside the windy stone fortress where honking trumpeters broadcast our arrival.

The arched palace entrances were inscribed with royal emblems and the polished initials *NR*, every servant and courtier greeting the king as if he were an angel arriving from heaven. Noble families trailed us into the palace in order of their rank, hunting for their chambers like a flurry of guests boarding a cruise ship.

Nick and I had lunch alone in his royal apartments before he suggested the two of us take a ride through the village before the rain set in.

"It is time my people set eyes upon the lady who has stolen my heart," he said with a smug smile as we mounted our horses.

After everything that had happened with Norfolk and Wharton, I wasn't holding my breath that the villagers would find me as endearing as Nick did. Still, perhaps they'd appreciate my ordinariness more than the nobles. We set out with only the guards accompanying us, clip-clopping down the dirty hill past wild pigs and rabid-looking dogs that smelled like they were already dead. I covered my nose with my scarf, but Nick turned and shook his head at me, and I let the fabric slip back through my fingers—he didn't want us to offend anyone. Market sellers and butchers scurried out of white stores that were framed with wonky planks of black timber, waving and tossing flowers at us. They couldn't have known that the most fragrant varieties aggravated their king's asthma.

"Lady Pembroke! My lady!" cried boys and girls from the roadside, their mothers protectively holding their grimy hands and beaming at me. The people here already knew who I was—even my name.

"We most heartily thank you," Nick called ahead of me.

"Thank you!" I said to my bizarre new fan base. "Bless you all."

If only they knew you're a teenager from Hampshire County who sucked at history at school—yep, smile and wave, Lady Pembroke.

As we guided our horses over a narrow wooden bridge connecting Windsor to Eton, it hit me why I was on a ticker-tape parade through one of the most populated villages in England. Going on progress wasn't just about making space to prepare for the wedding and coronation—this was a national sales pitch. After Norfolk and Wharton's rejection of me, Nick wanted to ensure my success as his chosen bride by parading me directly before the masses. It seemed he'd listened to Francis.

A cold lash of wind from the river echoed the shiver in my chest. I trusted that Nick had all this handled, but the fact that this 'Emmie exhibition' was necessary left me uneasy.

After a week of late-night parties and hunting expeditions in which I refused to participate, our dog-and-pony show carried on through the bustling villages of Brakenhale, Wokingham, and Reading, where lush, warmed manors were always waiting for us. Every night, I curled up in a strange bed alone wishing Nick was with me, but the constant eyes around meant we needed to keep our distance to ensure my virtue remained intact.

The farther we got from London, the grungier and more rustic the townships became. Potholes riddled the slushy roads between towns, and our lengthy procession had to grind to a sluggish halt more than once: usually when vagabonds were sighted up ahead.

Rain or shine, Nick insisted on parading me on horseback through every village to the unrelenting clanging of church bells. The commoners clearly idolized their brilliant jewel of a king, but my growing discomfort was becoming harder to hide. Not only did it weigh on me that it was apparently necessary to promote me to the people, but showing off our riches like pompous peacocks before the most impoverished people I'd ever seen made my throat thicken with embarrassment.

"What troubles you?" Nick asked me when our coach neared our next resting place, the village of Ewelme. The coachman skillfully steered our carriage through webs of vines and branches that crowded the narrow road.

"Nothing," I replied, absently playing with the tangled strings on my traveling cloak.

"Speak not falsely," he said calmly, reaching over to free the laces with his deft fingers. "I fear you are suffering a temper. Is it the journey? You are wearied?"

"No, I like being away," I said quickly. I was in no hurry to be locked back at Hampton Court. "It's just that…"

"Yes?" Alarm eclipsed his features.

"Everyone here is so poor. Of course, I know that things are different in this century, and it's well known that kings in your time had insane wealth, but…it's a different thing to see it in person. Some of the people out here look like they have nothing."

To his credit, genuine compassion stirred in Nick's face. "The plague spared no mercy in its destruction. Grace be to God, no cases have been reported in many months, or we would not be here."

I nodded, but the emptiness remained. Surely it wasn't just the plague to blame for the decrepit streets, the ramshackle sheep farms falling apart, and the bony children. What responsibility did the Tudor dynasty—did *Nick*—take? I then reminded myself that this was how the world worked back then, and I'd have to get used to it like I had chamber pots and beheadings.

We arrived at Ewelme Manor to greetings from a bumbling Lord and Lady Clifford, each as stout as the other. The manor occupants were evidently terrified of their royal visitors, which I found strangely comforting. For once, I wasn't the only one a bit dazed and confused over the constant, jaw-dropping Tudor splendor and the expectations they carried to behave in a certain way.

The king's chef whipped up a lavish feast, which this time didn't include the welcome company of my ladies. By the eighth course, I was fighting to stay awake, until Nick brought the gentle touch of his lips to my ear.

"Can I come to you this night?" he asked me.

I glanced up at the heated plea in eyes, warmth streaking up my spine. He was asking to come and lie with me in my bedchamber, possibly for the entire night. Our uncomfortable chat in the coach had clearly left him nervous, and it wouldn't hurt to reconnect and remind ourselves why we two polar opposites were choosing to make a life together. I didn't dare question him on whether it was a good idea to be seen together in private after everything he'd said for fear of scaring him away.

"Sure, you can come to my room," I replied softly. The lowest part of my stomach began twisting with yearning flutters.

His heavy thigh leaned against mine, and I sensed he was about to call it a night when Lord and Lady Clifford began a sweet but dithery presentation of gifts. There were pearl buttons and fur-lined hawking gloves that didn't quite fit for Nick, and a painted comfit box and feathered hat for me.

The king thanked them, rising from his royal seat that had—ridiculously—traveled with us from Hampton Court. I was the next one on my feet, fixated on the image of being wrapped around Nick Tudor's body in a dark room.

Lord Clifford bowed, snapping me out of my thoughts. "Your Majesty and Lady Pembroke, receiving your divine persons at our home is an honor most sacred," he said to Nick and me. "If it pleases you, may we present an entertainment for the king's pleasure: The tragedy of Phaedra by Seneca."

The king's mouth shot open, and I squeezed the plush velvet

encasing his forearm. "Thank you, my lord and my lady," I said. "We would both love to see it."

I steered my bored boyfriend outside to the central courtyard, where a short platform had been erected out of uneven planks of wood with a row of chairs before it. Nick dropped onto one of the only two seats swathed with cloth of gold, passing me a subtle eye roll as I settled in beside him.

The whole play was gobbledygook to me. Some of the roles appeared to be women, but men played them all, and there was something about lust and beasts and topics that made Nick blush. I spent most of the performance's endless hours forcing my eyelids apart.

By the time I slipped into my bedcovers of blue velvet fringed with silver, the sky was as black as the air was silent. When my ladies quietly retreated from the chamber, I knew that Nick was near. A gentle knock sounded from the door, followed by a guard's hushed announcement: "His Majesty, the King."

Nick crossed the candlelight, looking more like a strapping Greek god than an English monarch.

"My lady," said one of the men who followed him, inviting me to leave the bed so he could plunge his sword through the expensive mattress in search of daggers and other dangers. Yikes, poor Lord and Lady Clifford!

I glided into Nick's arms as we waited there, my fingertips brushing his muscles through the cream silk of his featherlight nightshirt. The moment the guards left, he fell into me, our lips fusing with hungry twists as we kissed our way to the bed. His tongue was sweeter than ice cream, and I relished the taste as he crawled over the top of me on the mattress with his mouth still fused to mine.

When we broke for air, he sat up and I dragged his nightshirt over his head, my lips falling open at the sight of him naked before me. His sculpted body tensed in my gaze, his cheeks flushing as he copied my movements and tugged off my smock. Sitting there before him with neither of us having a stitch of clothing on felt like the most intimate thing in the world, and my heart leapt as Nick's heated gaze traveled all over my body.

"My girl, you may very well make a king lose his mind," he said in a rough tone, catching my breasts in his hands and squeezing them. My palms hit the mattress beside me and I arched my back, sighing as he stroked and tweaked me until he replaced the touch of his hands with the heat of his mouth. Hot liquid pooled in my core as he swirled his tongue over my swollen peaks, and my eyes fell closed as I savored the sensation, fearful that, at any moment, Nick might change his mind about being together in private after resisting it for so long.

Be he didn't; he just licked and sucked on my nipples like they were giving him life while his hand glided down to gently guide my legs apart.

"Let me look at you," he said in a throaty whisper, shifting down onto one elbow and dropping his gaze to my glistening core. A flush of embarrassment rushed over my skin, but it disappeared at the sight of the desire burning in Nick's eyes.

"Touch me," I murmured bravely, and his gaze flickered up to mine.

He shifted a little closer and watched my expression change as he touched his thumb to the sensitive spot between my thighs and circled it. "Touch you here?" he asked as a light moan thrummed out of me. "Or here," he said, sinking two fingers all the way inside me, as far as they'd go. My hips bucked as I cried out, the sounds sharpening when he began dragging his fingers out before pushing them in again. Dragging and pushing, dragging and pushing, his gaze locked to mine as his lips parted.

"That feels so good," I said in a pant. Nick's brow creased with desire as he continued curving his fingers up inside me and rubbing the spot that made me see stars.

"I wish so desperately to taste you," he said in an aching voice as his other hand began caressing my clit.

A shiver of apprehension danced up my spine. While I'd been touched by boys before, no one had ever gone down on me. But if it felt even half as good as Nick's fingers did…

"Then why don't you?" I said in a breath.

A look of need overcame his face, but he didn't change his position on the bed.

"If I put my mouth to you," he said, still driving me crazy with his hands, "then I will wish to be inside you the way a husband would his wife. So, it will truly cause me less pain if I do not," he added, breathing a helpless chuckle that was so adorable that I tugged him higher up the bed so I could kiss him.

His tongue glided with mine, making me even wetter than I already was as he continued twisting his fingers in and out of me and stroking me with his other hand as I writhed on the bed.

Just when I thought I might pass out from the fiery pleasure, his breath washed over my lips. "*Come*, my lady," he said hotly, and I moaned as he upped the pace of his hands while his face tipped back to watch mine.

"Look at me when you come," he said like he was begging for it, and my thighs fell further open as I lost myself in the intoxicating ecstasy he was building between my legs. My eyes were heavy with lust, but they held Nick's gaze as he set off an explosion deep inside my core that splashed pleasure down my arms and legs and left me panting.

He made a 'mmm' sound of satisfaction and brought his fingers to his lips, tasting my climax with his darkened eyes on mine.

The sight of that started another fire inside me, and I reached out and gripped his rock-hard length in my palm, loving how his face contorted instantly at my touch. I was more turned on than I'd ever been, and I ran my hand all over him, rubbing the soft tip and fisting the solid length as he made a sharp inhale.

"*Come*, my king," I said, my eyes flaring as I repeated what he'd said to me.

He choked out my name and fell back on his elbows while I pumped his slick cock in my hand. A sudden urge to lower my mouth over him flashed through me—something I'd never even considered with anyone else—but I had no idea how to do that, so the idea withdrew as quickly as it'd arrived.

Instead, I glided my hand tightly up and down his thick length with increasing speed, the raspy moans leaving the back of his throat telling me I was doing this right. The pleasure in his eyes was the sexiest thing I'd ever seen as he groaned deeply and spilled his hot release onto my hand, something shifting inside me that I knew would never be the same.

Still catching his breath, Nick smiled at me in a way that made my heart swell before he rolled over to reach for one of the cloths sitting beside the bed. I watched him wipe the mess off my fingers with careful attention, a rush of warmth spreading through my chest.

"I love you," I said softly, and his gaze flew up to mine.

His brow creased with affection as he reached to cup the back of my neck, pulling my mouth to his.

"I love you so truly," he said against my lips, and the cloth fell to the mattress as we kissed our affection into each other's mouths, Nick's fingers sinking into my hair.

After his relentless, talented hands had made me come twice more, I slept in the cradle of his arms before a crackling fire, paralyzed by a peace I'd never felt before. Nick and I had rarely slept a whole night together without intending to travel through time. It enveloped me with a feeling of being right where I belonged.

Our procession left an undoubtedly relieved Lord and Lady Clifford at Ewelme and rolled on through the emerald blankets of the Oxfordshire farmlands. Wherever we slept, Nick rose early for days packed with hunting, hawking, and feasting, before he'd sneak into my bedchamber after midnight to avoid any whispers about my virtue. We'd kiss and touch each other until the crows of the roosters, and then my boyfriend Nick would become King Nicholas the First again: sought-after, pressured, and somewhere away from my company.

Our relationship had begun in a lightning-fast blaze of secret, stolen moments, but now that I'd been this close with Nick, I loved him more than I thought possible. And even though I'd willingly given up my world for him, I'd come to realize that I'd only ever be a small piece of his. The truth of that cut a wound into me that I wasn't sure would ever heal.

10

I<small>T WAS A GLOOMY</small> T<small>HURSDAY AT DUSK WHEN OUR TRAIN OF CARTS AND</small> wagons rumbled up the lonely hill on which Kenilworth Castle stood. Skirted by a midnight-blue lake known as the Mere, the sandstone fortress cut a romantic, fantasy-like figure from a distance. Our coach rattled across a walled tiltyard over the dam, reaching a small figure waiting within the gaping jaws of the portcullis.

"Christ, she not only stands in a draft but waits openly as if to meet the end of an arrow," said Nick, his eyes flared with disapproval. He climbed down from our coach that'd barely stopped.

He marched toward Kit as if to scold her for hanging about so publicly, and I winced in anticipation. Kit dropped into a regal curtsy, but within seconds the brother and sister were embracing, the sight warming my heart. The medieval monarchs were all pomp and stiffness in the history books, but Nick Tudor was as unreservedly loving as he was hot-blooded…just one of the forty-billion things I loved about him.

"Kit!" I called, as I jumped onto the gravel. I felt the smile light up my face.

"Lady Pembroke, I am so greatly pleased to see you," she said into my side as we hugged informally. Her high-pitched voice gave away her age, though she clearly had Nick's height gene.

The wind off the Mere was bitterly cold, and Kit's new governess, the sour-faced Lady Dormer, hurried us inside. Leaving the rest of the procession queuing down the road to Coventry, we crossed over the castle ditch and paced up the sloping inner courtyard. I'd imagined Kenilworth to be a smaller, cozier place for young Kit's household, but with its gothic web of four-story stone battlement towers, it could've passed for a medieval prison.

Kit led us into the Middle Court, her silk slippers embroidered with Tudor roses pausing at the gateway to the royal apartments. "I beseech you: I wish to come back to court," she blurted to me. Even her voice sounded suffocated. "I miss the king and Francis and everyone." She couldn't get the words out fast enough.

"Oh, Kit, make no burden of our lady most wearied from travel," Nick cut in. "You must remain here to complete your lessons. How is your study of arithmetic coming along?"

"You mean fractions and algebra?" She narrowed her eyes at me, making me giggle. I couldn't stop staring at her. Her adult teeth were finally growing in, maturing her pretty face.

"Kit can bring her tutor to Hampton Court, can't she?" I said, turning to Nick. "Why can't she come and stay there? I'll play with her."

He shot me a look that could cut steel. The message registered beyond any doubt: I was to stay out of it. The way he'd shut me down with a single glance pecked at my mind through our tour of the castle apartments. Kit was about to become my sister-in-law—the only sort-of-sibling I'd ever had. Was I allowed to have no opinion on her, especially when she was unhappy? *Cute Tudor king is starting to become frustrating-as-hell Tudor king.*

After an unsettled sleep, Kit and I caught up over a breakfast of sugared pancakes with apple slices fried in cinnamon and butter. I took my chance to gently grill her about her life at Kenilworth. She said she had plenty of time to paint, and her childish optimism was evidently keeping her spirits buoyed, but I sensed that she was lonely. At least I had more time to spend with her than I thought I would.

Nick disappeared for days at a time, hunting, boating on the Mere, or playing tennis with Francis and his guy squad. He adored his little sister to the point of obsession, but as long as she was safe, he didn't want her interfering with his fun.

Throughout our six-day visit, Kit spent her mornings translating complicated devotional texts for her tutor before joining me and my ladies in an open-air terrace swathed with vines and honeysuckle. We'd sit overlooking the knot gardens and sew to a soundtrack of twittering birds in the aviary. I loved me some girl time, but the endless sewing and embroidery were becoming a snore—even with the added novelty of having Kit nearby.

"What news of Francis?" Kit eventually asked me, stitching gold thread into an emblem of a portcullis. "I have scarcely seen his person since your arrival."

Alice's chin sprung up, sending her pin into her fingertip. "Ouch," she griped.

"You should ask Alice," I replied with feigned innocence. "She's the one spending all her time with him."

Kit's heart-shaped face fell. "Will you be his wife?" she said to Alice. Poor Kit had been crushing on Francis for years.

"Heavens no," Alice said with a flush. "We are friends, nothing more."

Lucinda snorted, and I laughed out loud. While on the road, we'd all noticed Alice and Francis hogging each other on the dance floor during the evening feasts. In spite of that, I was sure that Alice and Francis hadn't yet crossed the line from platonic to romantic. Something had her heart locked up in a cage, and I suspected it to be the mystery over her missing mom.

Kit brought her embroidery hoop to her nose, sulking for a few minutes before she spoke again. "In any case, I am truly pleased you are to marry the king, Lady Pembroke. For I have never seen our good and gracious Majesty more merry than when he is with you…it is a love match most true."

The girls mumbled their agreement—even Lucinda. I hadn't realized until then how much I needed to hear those words. Perhaps it *was* acceptable for kings to marry purely for love in this century.

When I tried to reply, however, nothing came out. I hadn't stopped thinking about Nick's icy reaction when I'd merely suggested that Kit come to Hampton Court with us.

After celebrating St. Crispin's Day at Kenilworth, Nick announced it was time to be on our way. Kit said she couldn't bear to watch us leave, and this time, there was no tiny figure waving at us from the tilt-yard gatehouse. It wasn't until our coach neared Warwick Castle that the tightening coil of my frustration snapped.

"Why does Kit have to stay at Kenilworth Castle?" I said to Nick, stretching my lower back. The bumpy roads were a fast track to a slipped disc.

He didn't remove his hand from mine, but his fingers stiffened. "Must you ask me that sincerely?"

"Did you see her crying when we left? You've always kept her close to you before. Now she's locked up in a glorified cage, a million miles from anywhere. Will she even be allowed to come to our wedding?"

His penetrating eyes focused on me. "You recall not the occurrences of this midsummer last? Of how my sister was snatched from under my nose not once but twice and nearly slain?"

"Of course I do." Both Kit and I nearly ended up six feet under.

"The only way to keep my sister safe is to put her where no devil may harm her again. The princess has her household and all manner of princely pleasures at Kenilworth. There is no reason for her to feel troubled."

"How about the fact that she's lonely? And that she misses you?"

He had no answer for that, returning his gaze to his bottomless mound of work papers. The lack of response dumped more fuel over my burning irritation.

"Is she going to spend the rest of her life in that castle until you marry her off to an old Frenchman?" I pressed. "Did you even tell her about that deal you struck with the French king?"

"Enough!" Nick snapped, both of us lurching as the coach skidded over a pothole.

"Am *I* going to end up locked inside one of your castles when you eventually get bored of me?" I said to his furrowed profile. "You'll throw the blue-diamond ring into a fire like you suggested and then lock me away forevermore?"

He just sat there for a moment, breathing heavily, before suddenly reaching to pull me into him. He didn't want to fight, and I didn't know where to draw the line on Kit. I was out of my depth on royal life, and she was his sister, but if I didn't stand up for her happiness, who would?

"One day, Emmie, you may come to see my home as something other than a cage," he said grimly. "Perhaps it will be the same day that you learn to trust me."

I didn't know how to reply.

Our next major stop was Northamptonshire, where we were to stay with Alice's dad, Sir Thomas Grey, at their family home. The modest Grey manor was across the street from the parish church and overlooked a noisy paddock of bleating sheep and a pen of hunting dogs.

I'd been freaking out about facing Sir Thomas for days. He'd been the king's right hand until he retired in protest over Nick's decision to jilt the princess of France and marry me instead. When Thomas met us in the entrance hall, however, I realized that I'd wasted hours of my life sweating over the reunion. His pale eyes drew me in with kindness, and time away from the pressures of court appeared to have mellowed the old grouch.

"Good morrow and bless you, Lady Pembroke," he said with a bob of his head. He wiped a handkerchief across his brow.

When I replied with a nervous stammer, Thomas patted my hand. His fingers were ridden with arthritis, and he'd slimmed down since I'd last seen him.

His gaze drifted past my shoulder. "My dear daughter," he said, lurching forward to hug Alice. The sight tugged my chest a little. While I'd have given anything to help Alice get her mom back, she was lucky to have a dad who loved her so openly. Everyone in this world believed my dad was dead, and he may as well have been— even if he had been living in the same century.

Another girl stepped into the chamber, a smaller version of Alice, but more mature in the face.

"Violet!" Alice cried before halting at the sight of her older sister's red-rimmed eyes. She put her arm around a sniffling Violet and led her away.

Before I could find out why Alice's sister was in tears, I had to partake in a formal meet-and-greet with a handful of rich, tedious men from the county. Ugh. I itched to get to my room and see if everything was okay. What if Alice's mom had turned up dead? But surely Thomas would've appeared more upset if his wife's body had been found.

When I'd sufficiently impressed the nobles, I was shown to a small chamber adorned with expensive tapestries. My ladies stood gathered around Violet Grey.

Alice spun toward me. "Emmie, may my sister join your household and come to court with us?"

Violet dropped to her knees, her faded satin skirts crushing into the floorboards.

"Dearest Lady Pembroke," she said, her eyes at my feet. "I beseech you to forgive my sorrow on this most merry occasion. It is because I have suffered a great loss. These past weeks, my husband was struck with smallpox and has gone to God. Be assured, I am void of any illness and would be not in your gracious presence if there was any danger of it."

"Oh no," I said, my hand clasped over my stomach in alarm. The mortality rate in Tudor England was enough to send anyone running for the hills. I helped Violet to her feet and guided her to sit on the edge of the bed. "I'm so sorry to hear that. Of course, you can come and join us. Please just ask me if there's anything you need."

Violet cupped my hands with gratitude, blinking fast like she was trying to block tears.

"Bless you, Emmie," said Alice.

Despite the bleak start, the feast that Thomas Grey hosted that night was hands-down the yummiest of the trip—even Violet joined us in her mourning gown. By all accounts, Francis Beaumont was doing fine as the king's new right hand, but when the men launched into a political discussion, Thomas offered nuggets of wisdom that sent impressed murmurs rippling around the table. There was no doubt that Alice's dad was a genius, and when Nick commented that he wished Sir Thomas would return to his side, awkward silence swept the space. I'd been around the king long enough to know that could be taken as a formal command. Thomas's cheeks, strawberry-pink from drinking floods of wine, turned chalk-white.

"My father is most merry in the countryside, Your Majesty," Alice said carefully, capturing every eye in the room. "Who would tend to the village sheep, should he return to court?"

Everyone laughed except Francis, who tossed back his last inch of wine.

When Nick squeezed Thomas's shoulder and suggested they discuss the Spanish threats in private, I glanced at Francis. Jet-black curls hung over his face as he looked away, humiliated by the king who also happened to be his best mate. When Nick and Thomas withdrew to the drawing-room without inviting Francis, the earl blasted his way out the back door before they'd made their exit—a classic Lord Warwick tantrum. I sympathized with Francis; Sir Thomas Grey not only cast a long shadow, but from what I could remember, he also enjoyed criticizing the impulsive earl.

Alice excused herself to follow Francis, but Violet was already slipping through the archway. Alice's surprise gave way to a look of distress. I understood why; When Alice and Violet were kids growing up at court, they'd shared Francis as a best friend. Violet soon fell in love with Francis, and he proposed to Violet before abruptly dumping her. He only did that because he secretly desired Alice, but the three of them had never sorted out this triangle. Now Violet was single again, but in the meantime, Alice had also fallen for the dashing earl.

"Want to go outside?" I said to her. "I'd like to see your dad's gardens before it gets dark."

"The gardens belong to my mother, and Father merely tends to them in the hope for her short return," she said a little faintly, but she led me outside to the inner courtyard. Our square heels clopped along the cobblestones as we cut through an archway leading to the walled garden.

Francis and Violet were sitting on a stone bench several yards away, their legs so close together that her skirts bunched into his breeches.

"Perhaps wasted hope is a Grey family custom," Alice said to me with a sigh.

"You must be thrilled to see Violet," I said, lightly knocking her leg with mine. "I can't even imagine what she's gone through. You're not going to let Francis get in between you two, are you?"

Francis's jaw jerked toward us. He slid away from Violet faster than we could blink.

"We wished to inquire whether you are well, Lord Warwick," Alice said stiffly. "You took leave of my father's feast so rudely, and as his house guest, no less."

"Did your father not take leave of his own banquet so rudely?" Francis replied, crossing his arms. "*No less?*"

Alice huffed. "Why is your every intention to vex me? I pray to God that we return to larger grounds in haste."

He paced toward her. "That is plainly absurd, given you have not wished to leave my side since Windsor!"

Alice made an 'as if' snort. "And yet, here you are, with your lecherous manner toward my sister, who is in mourning. After you shamed her once already!"

Francis stepped so closely to Alice that they shared the same breath. "Who says I am lecherous! Madam, you offend me as if it is a sport. I will suffer it no longer."

"I will pray for it, then," she snapped. Had he leaned forward an inch, his mouth would've met hers.

"I beseech you both!" said Violet, stepping between them with her arms splayed.

As she launched into an appeal for a ceasefire, I caught sight of a mess so unseemly for a Tudor manor that I zoned out. Edging the pristine garden was a chaotic mound of decaying wicker baskets, tattered saddles, broken wagon wheels, and other junk spilling onto the cobblestones. When I moved closer, I realized it was surplus clutter from a barn so stuffed with crap that you couldn't see into the windows.

"Emmie!" Alice called behind me. "I bid you stay away from that unsightly serpent's nest; there are many dangers."

"What is all this?" I said, the haphazard jumble of broken ladders and planks of wood evoking a memory that felt light-years away.

"Our mother's things," Violet replied in a weak voice. "I have bid Father to be rid of them many a time."

Alice moved beside me. "Father fears that our mother may one day return and feel a stranger without them. It troubled her heart to be rid of anything, but this is plainly a burden."

Blood rushed to my face, leaving me lightheaded. Only a classic hoarder could have this much garbage piled up at home. A hoarder like Jane Stuart—the eccentric lady who'd once lived on Bayberry Street in Hatfield, back in my time. Her garden had been a scrapheap of hoarder's junk, which was where I found the time-traveling ring that brought me to this century in the first place. A cursed ring that was created in Tudor England and last seen with Alice's mother, Susanna Grey, before it ended up in my world.

It just had to be.

I spun toward Alice. Her caramel eyes were set with an almost permanent frown—the evidence of too many years of worry and uncertainty. Past her shoulder stood Violet—Susanna's other daughter —who'd lost not only a mother but now a husband.

"Is something amiss, Lady Pembroke?" said Francis, stepping forward.

"I'm okay," I said, short of breath. This family had been through too much suffering.

As I zeroed in on Alice's worn face, I made her a silent promise: I was going to go back to my time to find Jane Stuart and figure out if she really was the missing Susanna Grey.

And if she was, I would bring Alice's mom home.

11

IN THE FEW DAYS WE SPENT IN NORTHAMPTONSHIRE, I GOT TO KNOW Violet a bit better, who was endlessly polite and unassuming. It felt like a mean thought, but I could see why Violet never had a shot with Francis while Alice was around. Alice was as sharp, witty, and charismatic as Violet was naïve, serious, and hard to make compelling conversation with. I felt for Francis, who'd blown up the romantic headway he'd made with Alice by merely sitting beside Violet on a bench.

When I gently reminded Alice that I was sure that Francis had feelings for her instead of her sister, she insisted that she only cared that he didn't hurt Violet again. I hoped that she wasn't sacrificing her own happiness out of some misguided theory that Francis could be the one to restore Violet's heart—that'd be a classic Alice Grey move.

There was no chance to talk to Nick about any of it. He'd spent days locked in council meetings until the early hours and had stopped visiting me late at night. When our procession departed for Buckinghamshire, I was downgraded from the king's coach to the one housing my handmaidens so Nick could sit with Francis and talk shop. At first, I thought the king was pissed with me about the Kit disagreement, but all his councilors sported the same dazed gazes and unshaven edginess. Something grave had happened, and I prayed it wasn't more war threats from the Spanish.

When Nick's coach ahead of ours made a squeaky turn toward the town of Aylesbury, my stomach clenched. Bridget's cousin, the soothsayer Agnes Nightingale, lived in Aylesbury. Now that I wanted to go back to my time and find out if Jane Stuart was really Susanna Grey, I felt more determined than ever to get some answers about the blue-diamond ring that was still carefully locked inside my traveling chest.

Peasants jogged alongside our coach as it lumbered through the gates guarding the township. Guards used their pikes to block beggars from entering as we were eaten up by swarms of spectators scrambling for a rare sighting of their king. Bored babies fussed on the shoulders of men in tattered hats, while mothers gripped the grubby hands of little girls in tiny coifs. I considered unclipping my pearl earrings and tossing them down to a scrawny street urchin who beamed up at me, but I was worried she'd get trampled for them.

Right after we'd checked into our chambers at Aylesbury Manor, my shoulders slumped at the sight of Nick already behind closed doors in another meeting. Not only did I miss his closeness to the point that it ached, but whatever was troubling the king was clearly important. For all I knew, he could tear the lot of us out of Aylesbury by morning to attend to it, so if I was going to try to find Agnes Nightingale, I had no time to lose.

The stifling air in my modest dining chamber was laden with pungent smells from our supper of mutton soup, fried beans, fritters, and aged cheese tarts. Alice, Bridget, Lucinda, and Violet chatted cheerfully while I silently fretted whether to ask them about Agnes or attempt to see the soothsayer on my own. Witchcraft was illegal in Tudor times, and Bridget had spared no mercy when sharing her opinions about her heretic cousin. Even worse—what if involving Alice or Bridget got them into trouble? Before I risked that, I had to at least try on my own. As for Nick, I could think of a million reasons why I needed to leave him out of this...not least of which was because he'd wanted to toss the enchanted ring into a fire.

The incoming winter had brought some luck by steering in an

early nightfall. With the blue-diamond ring securely on my thumb, I told Alice that I was going to see the king, making clear that we weren't to be disturbed. I hated giving her orders, watching her curtsy like a lackey, but I needed to be sure that no one would come and look for me.

In the unlit corner of the corridor outside our chambers, I threw on an unadorned traveling cloak. Draping the hood over my hair and keeping my head low, I waited for the patrolling guards to disappear around the corner and hurried in the opposite direction to the rear staircase that led to the buttery and pantries. The downstairs walls were plain brick instead of expensively paneled with linenfold, confirming that I'd reached the servants' zone.

Getting past the rear door guard was straightforward—none of us were under lock and key, and plenty of nobles came and went from the manor, visiting friends or conducting business in the village. To be safe, however, I kept my head bowed beneath my hood and gave the guard the name "Mistress Grey", mentally apologizing to Alice for stealing her identity for a night. I wasn't planning to get into any trouble, but I didn't need the guard alerting the overprotective king that his fiancée was heading out on the town.

I stepped outside into the frigid night air, my embroidered boots scuffing the gravel as I hurried along the narrow roadside, past wild pigs sloshing in the open drains. I pulled the cloak over my nose to block the stench of sewage and continued down the muddy street, careful not to slip.

When I reached the dim glow of a lantern marking the entrance to an alehouse, I halted, my throat tightening with fear. I considered turning back to the warmth and safety of the manor, but instead, I pushed open the rickety wooden door, my palms slick with sweat.

Inside the dingy alehouse, hard-faced men huddled over flagons of ale. They watched me as I crossed the earthen floor over a sleeping dog, looking for a bar, but there were only self-service barrels of ale. I caught the eye of a skinny man clearing empty mugs.

"Thou a pretty thing to be out late," he said to me, his lean jaw overwhelmed by a thick blonde beard.

I licked my lips, but they stayed bone dry. "I'm looking for a lady that lives in this town. Her name is Agnes Nightingale."

His bushy brows met in the middle. "I want no trouble here, madam."

"No trouble…I just want to see Mistress Nightingale. Do you know who she is?"

"What doth thee accuse me of?" He stepped back, his gaze roaming down my cloak to the embroidered tips of my costly boots. "Thee be here with the king? Raif!" he called, and a gorilla-sized fellow stepped out of the shadows. "This mistress be making trouble. Lookin' for Mistress Nightingale. Best the lady be on her way."

The bouncer took my arm and walked me to the door like a dog on a leash. My cloak slipped off my head, and a drunk guy whooped at my pearled hood. "Please," I said to the doorman, "I need to find Agnes Nightingale tonight!"

"Thou shouldst find her in the market square," he said, shoving me into bitingly cold air. The door banged shut behind me, and I darted away from it like ghosts were chasing me. The few crumbling lanterns that actually worked barely lit the street. I hurried farther from the manor until the tangle of black-and-white buildings widened into an uncluttered space that I assumed was the market square. I'd heard of witches leaving markings outside their residences, and I hastened along a row of small doorways, searching for unusual motifs, hanging talismans, or any other signs of black magic. I leaned in to examine a scribble of graffiti on a door when a mangy dog lurched at me through an open window, barking loudly enough to wake my mom in the twenty-first century.

Spinning to escape the alarm the dog raised, I found myself facing the silhouette of a figure hanging by the neck from a wooden frame. My feet dragged me closer in spite of my hammering chest. A young woman dangled from a noose in the dark, her pale face swelled to distortion, her brassy-red curls the only shade of color left in her lifeless body. A picture of a flower within a circle had been scratched into one of her cheeks, leaving streaks of dried blood. The girl hung there in the cold, broken and brutalized, and no one had cut her down.

I backed away, stumbling into a thin figure in a tawny-brown cape.

I shrieked, but it was a gentle-faced woman who removed her hood, her startled expression mirroring mine. She smelled like moldy herbs and vegetables.

"They took my daughter," she said to me. "My daughter, they… they took her and they…" Her prominent chin pointed toward the hanged woman. "They said it was allowed, that she would not be… you see, they took my daughter."

"I'm so sorry," I stammered. "This is your daughter?" I motioned to the pallid corpse. "Who took her?"

"The king. The King's Majesty. My daughter made her dinner this day, and they…they took her."

"The *king* took her?"

"The king's men…the king's men."

"Why?" I cried. Nick couldn't have done this. "Who's your daughter?" *What did she do to deserve this?*

"Mistress Nightingale," the woman replied, gazing over the girl's body like it was a sculpture she was considering. "They took my daughter."

"*Agnes* Nightingale?"

She nodded. "The king is here, you see…and they took Agnes. They took my daughter."

I should've done something to help the poor mother, but a thousand bricks crushed my chest as I turned back toward Aylesbury Manor, striding toward it with a fury that could've set the whole universe on fire.

He'd *killed* her.

I'd been clear to Nick that I wanted to visit Agnes Nightingale—to find out what I could about the blue-diamond ring—and he'd killed her without even talking to me about it first.

I couldn't get up the manor stairs fast enough. I marched through the king's chambers and into the oak gallery, pushing through a luxurious curtain of purple velvet.

Expecting to find Nick engaged in another meeting, I halted midstride. He was alone, strumming his lute in a straight-backed wooden chair. His linen shirt was loose and untied, his hair unkempt. Moonlight lit up the blue illustrations in the magnificent stained-glass window behind him.

"You come to complain of my distance," he said without looking at me. "Forgive me. I have been well occupied with matters of importance."

"I just went to see Agnes Nightingale," I replied flatly. There would be no sugarcoating this. Nick gaped up at me as I continued speaking. "I wanted to ask her about the cursed ring, as I told you already. I know you didn't want me to, but it's something I needed to know, and I'm a grown woman, so I went. I found Mistress Nightingale hanging from a rope in the market square. Her mother was there, too shocked to speak properly, but she said that the king did it…that the king's guards came and took her daughter away." I stepped forward as if being nearer to Nick would draw out the truth. "Did you have Agnes Nightingale hanged today?"

For a painfully long moment, he just sat there, blinking at me. When he finally spoke, his voice was stiff. "You would do well not to pursue these discussions, Emmie. You will not question my deeds, nor will you speak to me on matters of business. As for you taking leave in the dead of night, in Aylesbury of all places—"

"So you did do it! You executed Agnes Nightingale, just like you probably killed Norfolk, Wharton, and all those councilors that no one has spoken of since!" I turned away, dropping my face into my hands as I crumpled inside. The stark silence of Nick sitting behind me— doing nothing to console me or to tell me I was wrong—swallowed me whole. The thought came so fast and violently that it sliced right through me: *This relationship is never going to work. We're just too different.*

"Emmeline, look at me," he said, but I refused. "Agnes Nightingale was a known heretic who does the work of the devil," he continued evenly. "You may feel otherwise, but in this realm, that is an act of treason against God."

I spun to face him. "Tell me the truth, Nick. You killed Agnes so I could never prove that the enchanted ring is safe to use and that I'd be forced to never leave this place again."

"Speak not for me!" he snapped, before glaring at a guard who popped his head through the curtain. The guard quickly disappeared, and Nick leaned toward me. "Here is the truth you seek: A villager here made a claim that Mistress Nightingale threatened his person. Days after, the man's daughter died of no known cause. The witch was then justly tried, and judgment passed upon her. When she refused to give penance, I had her die by the rope, rather than the fire. That I did for you, knowing how you despise prolonged death. Yet you remain not gladdened."

I shook my head. "For me? God, Nick, who *are* you?"

Frustration rippled across his brow. "If you do not know that by now, then I am not sure you will ever. Christ, nothing is ever enough for you, Emmie—you wish for only a world and a set of rules that I cannot provide."

I didn't reply, and the room turned silent—the sort of unbearable stillness that I'd only known in the Tudor period. I'd expected Nick to shout at me—perhaps kick something like a petulant child—but he just sat there with his head in his hands.

"Are you okay?" I eventually mumbled. Guilt grabbed me by the throat. All this time, I hadn't considered what my brazen, modernistic views might do to this sixteenth-century king; how they might make him question his own worth and place in the world. Part of Nick's job was to execute people convicted of heresy, and I was laying the guilt trip on thick like he was the criminal.

None of it changed the fact that he'd just had a young girl killed—and one that he knew I'd wanted to see.

"I'm going to bed," I said, my voice hoarse with exhaustion. "You better take some deep breaths, so you don't kick off your asthma."

He nodded, wiping an eye with the heel of his hand. I spun away as fast as I could. I couldn't bear to see him cry. I also didn't want to run into the arms of an executioner. With fists at my side, fighting the urge to turn back, I headed to my chamber and crept over my sleeping ladies and into the bed.

Bridget received word of her cousin's death at first light. I gave her the morning off, wanting her to sleep and not have to think about mindless things like my hair and makeup, but she staunchly refused. The last thing Bridget wanted was to be seen grieving over a dissident, but I could tell she was shaken up. Before we could chat about it any further, the king ordered all the courtiers staying at Aylesbury Manor into the Great Hall after breakfast.

Nick emerged in head-to-toe Tudor glamor, and I questioned whether he was making a point to me that he was still brilliant and beautiful. Gemstones glittered from the intertwined serpents stitched into his jade-green doublet as he announced that we were all to head back to Hampton Court as fast as possible. In a clipped voice, he explained that the French king had soured on the alliance, and—fueled by Spanish support—the Catholic Viceroy of Ireland was now raising an army in the north of England.

Gasps rumbled through the hall, including mine. Nick wouldn't look at me, but I studied his drained face. So this was what all the meetings had been about. A Catholic rebellion was looming, with troops already on English soil. I nearly bit through my lip. Was this also because of our marriage?

Not surprisingly, I wasn't invited into the king's coach for the ride home. We made one stop overnight in Hertfordshire, where I didn't even see Nick. By the time we reached the lofty redbrick turrets of Hampton Court Palace, the courtiers were yawning and dragging their feet. Nobles hurried away to the heat of their lodgings, leaving me standing in a windy courtyard, searching for the king. Things felt so unfinished between us. But he never appeared.

With a sting in my chest, I returned to my rooms with the girls, grateful for Violet's infectious enthusiasm at lodging in a royal apartment at one of the king's palaces. After we'd all washed, we sat around nibbling cheesecake and macarons. I collapsed into freshly cleaned sheets and didn't move the entire night.

After a long and dreamless sleep, something soft stirred my arm. My eyes fluttered open, before sinking closed again. A soft pat roused me again, and I sluggishly rolled over to meet the source. Nick's angelic face was watching me from where he sat on the bed.

"A good morrow to you," he said tightly.

I elbowed my way to sit up, too stunned to consider my bed hair. "What are you doing here?" The pinkish light piercing the shutters had me guessing it was nearly sunrise.

He rubbed his neck, releasing a gentle waft of roses. "The hour is early; forgive me. I wished not to depart without bidding you farewell, but I cannot delay any longer."

"What are you talking about?" I registered Nick's traveling cloak and the leather gloves resting in the upturned flat cap beside him.

"I must journey to Lancashire to demonstrate support for my troops and to prevent more idiots giving heed to the Irish savages."

I couldn't move nor breathe. The agitation polluting the air we shared had spread like venom, and now Nick was off to a battle-ground. He might never come back.

"Emmie, I feel this parting may do us good," he said grimly, unable to look at me. "I shall be gone weeks, and it would be a favorable time for you to call upon your conscience and decide whether you trust me…whether you wish to live in a place of war and the necessary protection of princesses…and, perhaps mostly, whether you wish to love a king bound by his duty to punish heretics who refuse their penance."

I waited for my brimming tears to spill onto the sheets. His words were so hard to hear, but he was spot on. I'd been trying so hard to adjust to my new role in this place, but lately I was falling apart, and the Agnes Nightingale incident had been a particularly low point.

"You have to understand that all this has been a massive change for me," I said through a choked voice. "I know that you want me to be happy here, and I *am*—most of the time—but there's a lot to get used to. Frankly, I find the idea of becoming the queen in this place beyond terrifying, and it's not why I wanted to marry you. You have to give me time to adjust to it all. It's not fair to be angry at me when things freak me out—like hanging girls who aren't much older than me."

He slumped forward, looking so tired. "I wish not to beseech you, and I understand the burden of what you have lost, and of what you must now become accustomed. However, Emmie, I must know that I have your hand in marriage most resolutely, for any change of heart—once too late—could bring the Tudor name to ruin."

Tears dripped down my linen nightgown as I tried to unravel my knot of thoughts. While I'd given up my world to be with Nick, he'd also risked his kingdom to marry an unknown like me. I understood why he wanted total reassurance that I could handle it. This was the furthest thing from a normal relationship, and there was more than our hearts at stake.

When I didn't reply, Nick stood up, his eyes glittering with a film of tears he obviously didn't want me to see. "I must take my leave. I am afraid there is no time to spare." He grabbed his hat and gloves.

A robin's piercing cry through the window shook me to sense.

"Nick, I've been meaning to tell you something," I said, chasing after him. He paused near the doors. I quickly filled him in on what I'd discovered at Alice Grey's home…how I believed that her missing mother was living in my time and utterly lost. I left out the fact that Susanna Grey was allegedly once a spy who conspired with Mary, Queen of Scots to destroy King Nick. The Jane Stuart I knew was old, frail, and demented. I could barely imagine her buying a carton of milk, let alone plotting a king's demise. Instead, I reminded Nick that Susanna Grey had a family here and that we both knew what it was like to lose people.

I didn't tell him that a part of me hungered to get back to my home just to give my mind a break from all this.

"What are you saying?" he said, his brow pinched.

"I'm saying that I want to go home for a little bit." Fear seeped into Nick's expression as I continued. "While you head up to the north, I want to go back to my time and find Jane Stuart. If she really is Susanna Grey, I want to bring her back here to where she belongs. Nick, I *will* come back."

Our watery eyes locked together, the conversation silent but clear. We loved each other enough to get this far, but we'd become lost somewhere. We both needed time in our own corners to think, and we had to stop pretending this relationship was working. My chest felt gouged out and torn to pieces.

Bridget Nightingale pushed through the doors holding a fire poker, gasping at the sight of the king. She struggled to lug one of the doors shut, apologizing over and over.

"Leave it," Nick commanded, and Bridget dropped the heavy iron handle, stumbling. Through the archway, I could hear the rest of my ladies frantically shuffling around.

"My lady Pembroke," Nick said loudly, so they would hear. "I heartily wish you a fine journey home to Worthing and look forward to your short return. Release your conscience from your burdens and look to the light of your kin, so desired and loved by you." Alice was peering at us through the gap in the doors. "I pray you to be merry, and bid you farewell, my love most true," the king finished, his voice slipping.

Alice disappeared out of sight, and Nick just stood there for a moment, his gaze holding mine. A breath later, he rushed forward at the same time as I did. His palms caught the back of my neck and he pressed his lips to my own, branding me with a desperate kiss as I melted against him. I needed so much more; to feel his arms wrap tightly around me and to hear him tell me he loved me and that everything was going to be okay. But, with tears in his eyes, he released me and turned to leave.

He escaped through the door before I could stop him, blending into a group of waiting attendants so rapidly that my ladies didn't bother scrambling for their dresses. Through the leaded window, I watched him stride across the courtyard without a backward glance and I wrestled away an urge to weep.

"We are to travel to Sussex, my lady?" asked Lucinda, stepping beside me.

"I do take pleasure in the seaside," added Bridget. After her cousin's execution, she brightened at talk of another getaway.

I could barely speak. "Actually, I'm just going on my own."

"Oh?" said Alice.

"It's been arranged with the king," I added, looking right through her face. Lying to Alice never failed to make me feel hideous. I ached to share the news with her that I may have found her mom, but I gave away nothing. "It'll be a short trip and easier if I go by myself...the guards will keep me safe. You girls have a nice rest. Sleep in, read poems, have parties. But first, I need a bit more sleep."

I offered them a brave smile and backed away, heaving my bedchamber doors closed. I unlocked my jewelry coffer and slid the blue-diamond ring onto my thumb, sickened by how things had ended with Nick. He'd made it clear that I had his blessing to go back home, but I hadn't had a chance to ask him how he felt about it. At the same time, he was heading off to a war zone in the era of swords and cannons.

The image of Agnes Nightingale attacked my vision, her limp body, her dead, bloodshot eyes.

My chest sank. Nick didn't just sanction my trip home so I could potentially help Alice's mom. He wanted me to have another think about where I wanted to be. His heartfelt proposal had happened so fast that only now was he giving me time to decide once and for all if I really wanted all this. If I loved him enough—Tudor king and all—for it to be worth it.

I bid you farewell, my love most true.

Was this the end?

The chilling thought chased me back into bed. I wrapped the covers around me like animal fur. My eyes fell closed, burning for more sleep, but my chest was a raging cyclone. When Alice checked on me a short while later, I pretended to be asleep. She felt my forehead before stoking the fire back to life. A minute later, I heard all the girls departing for chapel.

A vision struck me of Nick's infectious smile and the boyish flush of love that softened his eyes whenever he kissed me. The thought of never seeing him again sent me deeper into the bed until the blanket was right over my head. I shut my eyes inside the cave, fighting tears. I couldn't bear the confusion anymore, the heartache.

Sleep blew in with ease, but I'd forgotten how frustrating the enchanted ring had become—I woke up still in my Hampton Court bedchamber. I tossed and turned, kicked the covers off, pulled them back on, and sat up for a drink of water. I rolled onto my side, meeting a majestic portrait of the king hanging on the wall. It speared my heart, and I flopped over to face the other way.

When the restlessness passed, I snoozed a little more before a raspy, man's snore penetrated the silence. I rolled over, instinctively searching for Nick's dark auburn curls, but the middle-aged body beside mine had silvery hair, pockmarked skin, and a tiny nose with a curved tip.

I kicked my way out of the polyester comforter, stifling a scream.

12

I HAD TO BE DREAMING, HALLUCINATING—ANYTHING. MY *DAD* LAY beside me in my bed in twenty-first-century Hatfield, a man I hadn't set eyes on in the better part of a year. I thanked the stars that I was on top of the covers and he was beneath them.

I pivoted off the bed as Dad rolled over, blinking at me through eyes still hooded with sleep. He looked older then I remembered and thicker in the jaw.

"Emmeline?" he said, his mouth a stunned hole. He elbowed his way upright. "Carol!"

"Mom!" I added, rubbing my eyes again like he might disappear. Through all of my traveling back and forth through time, I'd come to know when something bizarre was really happening and when it was a dream. This was legit.

Feet thundered up the stairs, and Mom appeared in her bathrobe, her wiry blonde hair flying in all directions. Ruby scampered over to me, her wagging tail a whir of silver.

"You're back," Mom said to me. "Did you..." She breathed at Dad. "How did you..."

He slid his bare feet onto the frayed carpet, revealing loose cotton shorts, an old university T-shirt, and a round belly. "I'm confused. You said that Emmeline was missing again."

"She was, I…" Mom couldn't speak right, and I felt responsible.

"I *wasn't* missing," I clarified in my Tudor nightdress. Dad gawked at me, but mostly at my face. "I told you that I was in Tudor England," I said to Mom. "Even though you'll never believe me, it's where I was, and I'm not going to lie about it anymore."

Dad scratched his upper back, the side of his nose, and his forearms. It wasn't bed bugs; he'd just never been comfortable in our family. What was Mom thinking when she invited him to stay over?

"Where is your special friend Nick?" she asked me in an apprehensive voice.

"He's back in his time," I replied like that was normal. "The Catholics are planning a rebellion, so he traveled to the north to deal with it. I thought I'd pop home in the meantime."

I fought the urge to burst into raucous laughter. If I wasn't careful, Mom or Dad could have me locked up. They both stood and gaped at me.

"Do you still have your key?" Mom said. "I didn't hear you come in."

"You know that's not how I got here." I sank into the edge of the creaky bed and yawned. I never slept well during a trip through time. "What are you doing here?" I asked Dad in a small voice.

"I told him you'd disappeared again, so he came over," Mom cut in. "We called Paul and Livvy in England to see if they'd heard from you, given this whole British obsession."

Paul was Dad's cousin from Clacton-on-Sea. We'd stayed with him and his wife Olivia back when we lived in England, which felt like a thousand years ago.

"I'd had a bit too much wine to drive," Dad added quickly, his cheeks tinting pink. We both knew that Mom's stalker tendencies didn't need to be encouraged. Instead of escaping home to his girlfriend, though, Dad asked Mom if she could leave us alone for a few minutes. "I'd like to have a talk with Emmeline."

"Oh, okay. I'll finish making tea," she said, a decades-old infatuation still visible in her eyes.

Ugh, Mom.

When she left, Dad flopped into my squeaky desk chair. "I bet you didn't expect to see me in your bed."

"I don't really expect to see you period."

He slumped lower into the chair and crossed his arms. "Your mother has been worried about you. For her to even call and ask for my help, I knew it had to be serious."

I decided to ignore that one. "Did you expect time travel to Tudor England?" I replied lightly, hugging my knees. I was just so over faking everything.

Dad puffed. "It's because of me, isn't it? We don't see each other enough, so you've concocted an absurd history story because you know I admire history." He wasn't smiling, but his eyes twinkled like he'd guessed the stumper in Jeopardy.

The laughter finally arrived, straight from my mouth to Dad's face. "Are you even serious?" I said. "You think I'd go through all this because of you? Just to entice you the eleven miles it'd take for you to visit me once in a freaking while?"

His whole body stiffened. "How could I visit you at this house? Do you know your mother once sent Nina threatening letters?"

"Oh please, do you think I give a toss what your teenage girlfriend thinks?"

"Do not speak to me like that!" Flecks of green blazed through his hazel eyes, reminding me of Nick when he was fired up.

More stairs thundered before Mom burst in again. "Is everything alright?" she said.

Dad stood up, snatching his jeans and shirt from the back of the chair. "It seems that Emmeline is back and healthy, which is the most important thing, but I need not sit around and listen to abuse."

"*Abuse?*" I countered.

My lips pressed together as if it might stop the pressure of my welling tears. This was so classic Dad...to make it all about him. I felt bad about insulting his girlfriend—who was in her twenties and definitely not a teenager—but he needed to take some responsibility.

"Marty," Mom pleaded as he marched to the bathroom and shut the door.

She shot me a fed-up look like this was all my fault, which was ridiculous. Dad throwing a hissy fit over something selfish…Mom acting like she had any power to soothe him—it was all too familiar. I'd seen the same thing a hundred times before Dad left us.

"Why did you even call him?" I said, striding past her to the stairs. I needed water and something to eat that wasn't a roasted animal drenched in rich sauces.

"I called him because you've been acting like a complete lunatic," she replied, following me downstairs to the kitchen. "All this nonsense about time travel and disappearing tricks…sneaking away while I wasn't looking and pretending you're some magical fairy."

There were two mugs on the counter and an open packet of chocolate cookies. Dad could only drink tea with something sweet in his hand, even if it was early in the morning. I couldn't help but think my 'lunacy' was the excuse Mom had been waiting for to draw him back into her life. She'd even stocked the cupboards with actual food.

She flicked the lever on the electric kettle and watched me pour myself a bowl of cinnamon crunch. I'd forgotten the euphoric taste of sugary cereal. Yet, while it filled the hole in my stomach, it didn't touch the one in my heart. Had Nick arrived in the north yet? Was he in danger? Was he already missing me, too?

"Your college sent a letter," Mom said flatly, reaching to dig out an envelope from a pile of bills. The 'UAL, Central Saint Martins' logo was stamped in the corner.

It had already been opened, and I fished out the letter, my tummy clenching. It was an approval to defer my first year in the Bachelor of Arts in Jewellery Design course. All the letter needed was my signature and it'd be a done deal.

"A deferral?" I said with confusion, scanning the note for more information.

Mom poured steaming water into her chipped mug. "I spoke to them a few weeks ago about the health challenges you've been facing and convinced them to arrange a deferral for one year. If you sign the form, I can send it back to them."

I stared at her and then again at the letter. A tight coil in my chest that I hadn't even realized was there snapped free. Studying jewelry design at Central Saint Martins had been my dream before Nick Tudor popped onto the scene and derailed me with his invitation to become a sixteenth-century queen.

"You're welcome," Mom said as I grabbed a pen and signed the form. I couldn't see myself ending up at Central Saint Martins now, but a deferral felt less depressing than being kicked out altogether.

I thanked her, and we sat in silence for a while. "Have you heard from Mia?" I eventually asked. Mia Fairbanks had been my best friend in Hatfield, but now she lived on campus at MIT in Cambridge.

"Heard from her?" Mom said, her brows lifting. "I must have called her twenty times in the last few months. She's always been polite, but I don't think she's happy with you. Like me, she thought the worst until you came home a few weeks ago. I told her you'd run off with your boyfriend, Nick."

My eyes bulged. "Did you tell her about the Tudor stuff?"

"Don't be ridiculous. I don't think I'd get the words out without laughing. Or crying."

A door opened upstairs, and Mom pressed the boil button on the kettle again before spooning sugar into Dad's mug. I scooped up Ruby for a cuddle and rubbed my cheek against her wriggly fur. It'd be so easy to just stay here for the weekend—to watch television and cuddle Ruby and eat a whole packet of tortilla chips.

But that wasn't why I was here. "Mom, can I borrow your phone?" I said.

"Sure." She sprang up to grab it, obviously glad for my interest in something un-historical.

I took the phone upstairs to my bedroom, passing Dad on the stairs.

"I was just coming down to see you," he said in a tight voice. I could tell he felt guilty about storming out.

"I'll be down in a minute," I replied, offering him a slight, peace-making smile before slipping into my bedroom and shutting the door.

The last I'd heard about the old hoarder Jane Stuart was that she'd been taken to a Boston hospital for psychiatric evaluation. There was more than one hospital in Boston that handled that stuff, but I'd start with the biggest: Massachusetts General Hospital. Nerves tickled my stomach as I dialed the number.

The lady on the phone from the psychiatry unit was rude but helpful. Her fingernails clicked the keyboard as she looked up the name Jane Stuart. There were two in the system, but the last Jane Stuart had been admitted in June and then transferred to the Cedar Lake Rest Home. She hung up before she could tell me anything else, like how likely it was that Jane would still be at Cedar Lake. Still, I was lucky that this was turning out to be pretty straightforward.

The Cedar Lake Rest Home was in Newton in suburban Boston, but when I called them, they refused to give me information about any residents unless I was a family member.

Jane Stuart's family is in the sixteenth century dancing the freaking volta! I wanted to shout. Perhaps I'd have more luck if I showed up in person.

Using Mom's travel app, I worked out that I needed to get a bus from Amherst to Boston, and then another bus to Newton. I changed into the same jeans and sweatshirt that I wore last time I was here with Nick, suppressing the twinge of pain that memory drew. Despite all the drama, I wished he was here with me.

After pocketing my phone and a charger, I sneaked two sleeping pills out of Mom's canister, slipping them into my pocket with the eighty dollars I still had in my wallet. My pockets felt bloated, but I had everything I needed.

"I think I'm just going to go see Mia in Boston," I lied as I hopped back downstairs. "It'll be easier if I explain things to her in person." I had no plans to turn up on feisty Mia's doorstep yet after my months-long disappearance, but it was the perfect excuse to head into Boston. I didn't want Dad or Mom knowing about the Jane Stuart stuff.

"You just got back," Mom said, frowning.

Dad appeared from the kitchen, holding a half-eaten cookie. Mom passed him a cup of tea like an obedient sixties housewife. It was a jarring flashback to a childhood that I'd worked hard to forget.

"Are you sticking around, or can I get a ride to the bus station in Amherst?" I said to him, still finding it hard to meet his eyes. "I need to get to Boston."

He glanced at Mom. "What are you doing in Boston?"

"Visiting a friend at MIT."

Dad's chin lifted like that was impressive…like his daughter could be smart by association instead of a loony who thinks she's a time traveler.

"How long until you can be ready?" he said.

"I'm ready now."

He dropped his mug onto the counter and grabbed his keys. The look on Mom's face broke me. Dad wasn't here for her; he was here for me, and now we were both taking off. But this was the way it had to be, at least for now.

"Thanks for everything, Carol. It was good to see you." Dad dropped an awkward air-kiss onto Mom's cheek and hightailed it outside to his car.

She watched him go from the doorway until I wrapped an arm around her. "Bye, Mom." She smelled like she needed a shower.

"When are you coming back?" she said into my shoulder.

"I don't know. But I promise you that I'm keeping safe." I pulled her tighter, telling myself that our separations were becoming easier—even if I didn't believe it—before heading outside to the car that was already running.

After months of riding in horse-driven coaches, Dad's Toyota Camry felt like a roller coaster, but a cushiony one. He turned the heat up and tuned the stereo to a public radio channel, and for the first ten minutes, neither of us spoke. I'd felt more comfortable with total strangers. We'd just crossed the bridge over the river when he spun the volume dial down.

"Will you still be in Boston next week?" he asked. "I'll be there on…uh, Friday I think it is, and maybe we can have lunch." He gripped the steering wheel so tight that blue veins bulged from his wrist.

It took me a second to find my voice. "Maybe." Next Friday was an epoch away. "But, to be honest, probably not."

He drove toward Amherst in silence, before spinning the wheel to make a right turn.

"What are you doing?" I said, watching the town center shrink in the rearview mirror.

"Driving you to Boston. I don't have classes today, and it will give us a chance to talk."

"Jeez, thanks, if you're sure you don't mind."

The car picked up speed, and for a few painfully awkward minutes, we just listened to the hum of the engine.

"Why did you drop out of college?" he finally asked me, checking his blind spot so he could merge onto the highway.

The question felt so heavy, especially from Dad, who'd taken such little interest in my life in recent years.

"It wasn't an easy decision," I replied honestly. "I still regret it sometimes."

He seemed pleased about that. "Your mother said she deferred you, so you can still go."

"I know." I didn't turn away from the bottle-green blur of passing trees through the window. In my view, Dad didn't deserve to speak to me about Mom or my future.

"Why all the interest in the Tudors?" He glanced at me.

I sighed heavily. "Dad, I don't really want to talk about this. I appreciate you taking me to Boston, but can we save this conversation for later?"

He chewed his lip and nodded. "Alright."

I just wasn't ready to talk to him about something so significant as my relationship with Nick and what I'd given up for it. For years, I'd fantasized about long drives with Dad again, his random talk shows playing on the radio, but now that it was happening, it felt too little, too late. Dad had absolutely no idea who I was, let alone why I'd done this. Plus, what was the point of rebuilding our relationship if I was only going to leave again?

After a radio program about the connections between people's desires and brain activity, we resumed light chatter about Dad's pet birds, my latest jewelry ideas, and how funny Ruby was, until we were deep into the suburbs of Boston. He insisted on driving me all the way to MIT, and I had no reason to protest.

He pulled up outside the main entrance and jumped out of the car, stepping onto the sidewalk to hug me. I let him, breathing in the scent of his shampoo that hadn't changed in ten years.

437

"Bye, Dad," I said. "Thanks so much for the ride."

He squeezed my shoulders, his olive-colored eyes shining. "Let me know when you have a new phone number."

"What do you mean?" I said as he climbed back into his silver Camry. Cars were beginning to queue up behind him.

"I must have tried to call you fifty times in the past few months," he called as an irate driver honked her horn. "I've been emailing too —I wanted to know how you were settling into London. That was before I knew you never turned up, of course."

I waved as he drove away, grappling with his statement. Dad had tried to call me before he even knew I was missing. Sure, it came after years of neglect, but it was something.

I turned to face the imposing columns of MIT, which reminded me of pictures of ancient Greece, the impressive sight flooding me with hot pride for Mia. The temptation to just walk through the doors and find her residence was eaten up by nerves that upset my stomach. But I couldn't. For now, I had to stay focused on my mission: finding Jane Stuart.

At the bus station, I bought a sandwich and a ticket to Newton and parked myself on a bench, plugging my phone into a socket to charge. A few minutes later, I sucked in a deep breath and switched on the phone. The background selfie of Mia and I beside her swimming pool last summer lured a sad smirk to my face.

The messages and voicemails arrived in a flurry of beeps and flashes. Tensing my muscles like I was preparing for battle, I opened the texts from Mia. The last message appeared first.

> Emmie, I don't understand this at all. If I've done something wrong, PLEASE tell me. Please.

Chewing my lip, I scrolled back further.

> You better be dead or I'm going to KILL YOU myself!! Seriously. Where the f are you????

I clicked the icon to reply, but my fingers stiffened over the empty speech bubble. What could I say?

Hey babe, I'm SO sorry for the delay, I was back in Tudor England. They don't have cell phone reception there.

My love! I would've been in touch sooner, but I was planning my wedding to Nicholas the Ironheart. OMG, he's so intense.

How are you?? I'm good. Been missing everyone, but Hampton Court Palace is awesome...apart from the Duke of Norfolk wanting me dead, ugh. How's MIT?

My bus rolled into the stop with a strained squeak, and I slid my phone back into my pocket.

Downtown Tudor London was hardly a perfume store, but the buses of modern-day Boston weren't much of a step up. I sank into my seat, tugging the collar of my sweatshirt up to my nose. The city was neat and impressively developed, but I'd forgotten how much hideous gray concrete had been dumped onto the Earth in my time. If I shut my eyes and ignored the poisonous smell of exhaust fumes, I could still see the broad meadows and smoking chimneys scored by a steady clop of horses' hooves.

I missed Tudor England already. I missed Nick, and the revelation of how far away I was from him felt blisteringly disorienting. This was so much worse than a long-distance relationship: wherever he was, I couldn't even look up at the sky right now and feel comforted that he was sharing it somewhere. He may as well have been on another planet. I didn't think I'd ever truly understand a world in which people were executed purely for their beliefs, and our relationship had issues the size of a continent, but nothing felt right in my time anymore. Coming back home alone hadn't been the respite I thought it would be. The thought of never feeling Nick's protective arms around me again turned my whole body cold.

It was early afternoon when I scaled the cement steps of the Cedar Lake Rest Home. There weren't any cedar trees or lakes in sight, just a brick building scrawled with illegible graffiti. The cheerless foyer smelled like disinfectant, and the reception desk sat vacant beside a locked pair of doors. I peeked through the gap like a creeper, watching for Jane Stuart.

A young guy strode into the foyer from the street door, balancing three jumbo-sized packages of toilet rolls on his chest.

"Hey, can I help you?" he said in a friendly voice. His dark hair was carefully blow-dried into a fifties-style pompadour.

"I'm looking for a resident called Jane Stuart," I stammered. "She came here in July. I'm a really good friend of her daughter's."

"Janie has a daughter?" he said with a squinty grin. "I had no idea."

"Her daughter lives…far away. I just came from Hatfield, where Jane used to live."

He dumped the toilet rolls beside the lavatory door. "Janitor didn't show up this morning," he explained with an eye roll. "Come on, I'll take you through. I'm Ajay, by the way."

He waved his ID card over the panel beside the double doors, and they clicked open. I followed him down a short hallway leading to a recreation room that smelled faintly of urine. At the far end sat Jane Stuart in a tattered armchair, her white, wild hair and vacant stare unchanged since the last time I'd seen her. An elderly lady was seated beside her, brushing her fingertips up and down the arm of her own chair.

"You've a friend here, Janie," said Ajay, crouching in front of Jane with a cheerful smirk. "Her name's Emily."

"Emmie," I corrected, pulling up a wooden chair beside her. Jane didn't look at me, her knobby fingers tightly clutching two plastic forks.

The woman beside her tilted toward me. "Hello, Chris," she said in a frail voice, clip-on crescent moons dangling from her paper-thin earlobes. "Look at your pretty face."

Before I could reply, Ajay guided the lady up onto her worn ballet flats. "How about we find that fashion magazine you like, Molly?" he said, throwing me a sympathetic smile.

"Oh good, Chris," she said to him, stumbling a little as they walked away.

Jane Stuart hadn't moved the entire time.

"Jane, do you remember me?" I asked softly, leaning forward.

She looked right at me but revealed no recognition. I gave her a reassuring smile, scouring her for evidence of an earlier century. Her polyester shirt and checked pants were straight from a discount clothing store rack downtown. Triangles of dry skin peeped from the sides of her slippers.

"I'm Emmeline Grace from Hatfield," I said clearly. "The nurse Carol Grace's daughter." Jane made a flinch of understanding. The blue-diamond ring was safely tucked away in my pocket. When I mentioned the ring to Jane once, she went ballistic and spurted half-nonsense about evil and heretics. The last thing I wanted was to resurrect that side of her.

Yet, I had to find out whether she was Alice's missing mother, Susanna Grey. It wasn't like I had a selfie with Alice from the Tudor world to show her, so there was really no choice except to ask point-blank.

My voice dropped to a whisper. "Lady Grey?" I said. Jane's sallow brow crinkled. "Is your real name Susanna Grey?"

Her milky-brown pupils expanded, revealing copper edges. In a flash, I recognized that her eyes were the same color as Alice's sister, Violet's.

"Madam, it is I, wife to Sir Thomas Grey," she replied without flinching. "May God save you."

13

My chest emptied of breath. Beside me, in a faded floral armchair, sat Alice Grey's mom, Susanna Grey...the wife of the former chief advisor to King Nicholas the First. I could've hugged her, but I didn't want to freak her out—or break her.

Blankness seeped back into Susanna's face and her knobby fingers fumbled with the hem of her shirt as she watched a man with a walking frame shuffle past us.

Hesitant to push her, I silently helped her eat her lunch, which was two scoops of mashed potato topped with ground beef and gravy. She wanted to hang onto the empty bowl, but the kitchen lady gently pried it from her fingers with a knowing smile.

Ajay glided by again and suggested I take Susanna for a stroll outside in the back garden. She didn't say much as we meandered along a short but pretty path that circled the rear of the rest home. I pointed out the fuchsia flowers, and Susanna seemed to understand—even smiled at times—but she never asked why I'd called her by her long-lost name of Susanna Grey. If I brought her back to Tudor England, would it reverse some of her inertia, or was it permanent?

I wasn't exactly pumped to return to the musty recreation room with the florescent lights, and Susanna seemed happy enough to sit on a bench warmed by the sun. A plastic straw was impaled in the flowerpot beside us, and she plucked it out and slid it inside her shirt pocket.

"You are in need of lodging, dear?" she eventually said to me in a withered voice. Her cloudy eyes had fallen back into confusion.

My chest constricted as the words cascaded out. "No, my lady. I am Mistress Emmeline Grace, the Marquess of Pembroke. I'm a friend of your daughters, Mistresses Alice and Violet Grey."

Susanna's face brightened with clarity. "Lottie," she said. I'd heard her say that name before, but only then did I realize it's what she called her daughter Violet.

I set my hand on hers. Her skin was warm and startlingly soft. "Lottie and Alice are at Hampton Court Palace," I said. "They're both well and are in His Majesty's favor."

Oh my God, if Ajay could hear this.

Susanna Grey's fingers froze beneath mine, her eyes glistening with recognition. I decided not to mention anything negative, like Violet losing her husband, or any of that stuff I'd been told about Susanna Grey once plotting against the king.

"Your husband, Sir Thomas Grey, is also well," I said. "He has withdrawn from the king's service and is living in your manor in Northamptonshire. I just visited there a few weeks ago on progress with the king, and everything is as exactly as you left it."

Susanna's eyelashes darkened with tears. I patted her hand and watched for any sign of reproach after mentioning King Nick, but her face disclosed only relief. She wiped her cheeks and hunched forward, her papery eyelids falling closed. I'd exhausted her.

We slowly made our way back to the recreation room. A nurse with braids of black hair wheeled a trolley of medicines from one resident to the next.

A protective instinct triggered me to guide Susanna the other way. She didn't need drugs; she needed her family back. When I asked her if she knew how to get to her bedroom, she nodded at one of the U-shaped corridors. We headed down it, past a series of half-open doors that offered glimpses of colorful patchwork bedspreads and framed family photographs. Susanna's bedroom looked more like a hospital ward, with unadorned walls and stock-standard sheets. The number '23' was pinned to the door.

An unexpected shiver of apprehension scrambled up my spine. Susanna Grey was only in the twenty-first century because she'd fallen asleep wearing an enchanted ring that was supposed to curse my beloved fiancé to die. How was it my right to bring a treasonous conspirator back to Tudor England? God, what would Nick do to her if he found out? I could never tell him about Susanna's past.

She sat on the bed and drew her legs inside the thin sheets that smelled like antiseptic. No matter the cause, Susanna Grey was trapped in the wrong century with zero family here. She'd probably live out her days in this bleak rest home, perhaps paid for by the forced sale of her house in Hatfield. I didn't know how she came upon that house or why the previous owner left it to her in his will, but boy was I glad she'd lived there. Without Susanna, without that ring, I would never have met Nick Tudor. The thought of life without him left me feeling suffocated with loss. Why had I let us push each other away so quickly?

"Lady Grey, would you like to go home?" I asked gently. "Do you want to go back to Northamptonshire, to Sir Thomas, Alice, and Lottie?"

A ghost of a smile touched her lips. "Oh, blessed Alice...my Lottie. I pray that God shall bring me to their grace. Have mercy on me, eternal Father." She closed her eyes.

I took that as a yes.

"Then please wait here a moment and don't go anywhere," I said like she'd suddenly lurch up and dance the Charleston out the door. I slipped into the surprisingly spacious bathroom, psyching myself up to steal a resident from a rest home. I swallowed one of Mom's sleeping pills in my pocket and gulped water from the faucet, slipping the blue-diamond ring back onto my thumb. I poked my head around the door. Susanna lay on her side, drawing slow, steady breaths.

Making a split-second decision, I pulled my phone from my pocket and shut the bathroom door. I sat in the shower chair and pressed Mom's number. She answered right away.

"Hey, Mom," I said, already jittery at the sound of her voice. "I'm in Boston. Dad drove me all the way in."

"Oh, did he? How did it go with Mia?"

"Yeah, all good...thanks." I scrunched my face. Mom would probably give Mia a call and ask her for feedback on my mental state.

No more lies.

"Actually, I didn't see Mia," I added, my voice echoing off the tiles. "I chickened out."

She sighed. "Emmie."

"It's cool. I decided that I didn't want to lie to her anymore, and she can't know about the Tudor stuff. Can you imagine if something like that got out? You can't tell Mia, ever. Or *anyone*, okay? Please."

"I won't." The phone rattled like Mom was scratching her ear. "How did things go with your dad?" Her voice always crept up an octave when she mentioned him.

"Yeah, all good. We didn't trade blows, so I'll take that as a win."

"It was nice of him to drive you. And to stay over so we could look into things more, don't you think?"

I didn't reply.

"Did he mention anything to you about Nina?" Mom dangled.

I wasn't exactly a fan of chitchat about Dad's live-in girlfriend, the one he'd left Mom—and me—for.

"No," I said. "Should he have mentioned something?"

"Of course not. I'm just wondering if something's changed there. He's taking more of an interest, don't you think?" She sounded as naïve as a little girl, and I felt sorry for her. At the same time, snakes writhed in my stomach. I just didn't want to see her hurt again. We'd both come so far.

When I spoke, my voice was soft. "Mom, you're way better than him. Don't waste your time anymore, please. He's not going to come back."

"You don't know that! Why do you always have to say things like that?"

I'd hit a nerve. I slid the phone down my neck, blocking out Mom's rapid switch to an ardent defense of her and Dad's failed marriage. If I went back to Tudor England now and never returned, would she drive herself mad over this?

The thought of being cocooned inside Nick's arms again melted my growing rigidity. I had to get back there. Not knowing whether he was safe on his mission in the north felt like torture.

"Will you be coming home?" Mom said after she'd finished her diatribe about her and Dad.

"Not right now. I was actually calling to say goodbye because I'm going away again for a bit." My teeth pressed my bottom lip.

I could've sung the national anthem in the time it took for Mom to reply. Her voice had flattened. "I don't know what to do anymore, Emmie. I am just so tired of all this."

"You need to do something for yourself," I realized out loud. "You know now that I'm okay, right? I'm not at the bottom of the river or in a ditch somewhere. So instead of wondering where I am every minute, why don't you go out and do something fun, like a dance class or learning an instrument? Sewing is actually quite cool if you can believe that. I *will* come back and see you whenever I can. I think about you all the time."

Mom didn't acknowledge my suggestions, but her tight swallow made clear that she'd understood the message…she had to let me go for a while.

"Will you promise to be safe?" she said a little hoarsely.

"Always." I thought it best to leave out the beheadings, burnings, and smallpox.

"Oh, and Emmie?" she blurted before I could hang up. "You've always got a home to come back to, okay?"

I nodded into the phone, swallowing an urge to cry. "I love you, Mom."

"You too, cookie."

After hanging up, I sat in the shower chair and breathed deeply through the familiar feeling of guilt. Among other wrongs, I'd officially rekindled the firestorm between my parents—something I'd tried for years to avoid. Now I couldn't even be here to help Mom through it.

Wedging my cell phone under my chin, I carefully dragged the vinyl armchair close to Susanna's bed without making noise. A battle erupted in my mind about what to do with the phone. What if I brought it back to the sixteenth century with me? I could take photos and videos of one of the most famous periods of British history and its key characters. I'd be like scoring footage of Henry the Eighth!

Susanna twitched on the bed, jolting me out of my stupor.

Attempting something like that would not only be a betrayal of Nick's trust, but no one would believe the images were real without proof. It would become a conspiracy theory, like Bigfoot or the faking of the Moon landing, and I'd be a laughingstock.

All that mattered was getting back to the sixteenth century in one piece so I could make things right with Nick.

I switched off my phone and opened Susanna's cupboard door, unsettling a mountain of toilet rolls, latex glove packets, dog-eared paperback novels, and a couple of television remotes. The rest home staff were probably unaware of how many missing items their resident hoarder was storing. I slid my phone into the back of the top shelf and shut the cupboard door. Whether someone discovered the phone before I returned was not my biggest issue right now. Susanna Grey could wake up at any minute.

The sleeping pill was beginning to take effect, and I sank into the armchair beside the bed. My breaths eased, and I felt warm and heavy all over. The call of Tudor England tickled the corners of my mind, enveloping me with a crushing urge to be back there in an instant.

I placed my hand lightly over Susanna's, cautious not to wake her. Rhythmic breaths broke through her mouth with popping sounds. She was fast asleep. I inched my fingers beneath hers until our palms touched. Holding my friend's mom's hand was one for the weird book, but I focused on my relaxation, silently begging for the ring to work without a struggle.

After an imperceptible amount of time, my head crashed forward, and I woke to the soft click of my dry lips. Susanna's hand had crept away from mine on the rest home bed, but her eyes were shut. The weight of the sleeping pill coated my bloodstream with lead. If

Susanna Grey finished her afternoon snooze and got up to eat a cookie...*please, please, please.*

I'd done this before...I could do it again. *Come on!* I berated myself like a tennis player losing a match. The pep talk worked. After a yucky dream about my friend Mia calmly watching me fall out of a plane, I rolled into the comfort of silk sheets. I was no longer sleeping upright in a stiff chair, I was...my eyes flashed open.

Four walls of pearled netting surrounded me, carrying a stark silence I'd know anywhere. I clutched the sheets to my chest, the gentle scent of orange blossom clarifying that I was back at Hampton Court Palace. I could've kissed the mattress, the gilded ceiling, the paneled walls.

The next thought flung me upward. I'd brought Susanna Grey with me!

She stood at the leaded window, fingertips pressed to the glass like spider's legs. *Holy shit, she's still in her hideous polyester get-up...and I'm in denim jeans.*

It was evident that no one expected me back this soon—even though it was after lunch, the fireplace hadn't been lit and the room was an icebox. I heaved open the chest stuffed with folded undergarments, hurriedly digging out a smock with a high neck for Susanna, before tearing off my clothes and slipping a plainer smock over my shoulders. I hid my remaining sleeping pill in the tiny compartment within the blue-diamond ring that concealed the miniature portrait of Queen Elizabeth the First.

When I pressed an ear to the crack between the doors, it returned only silence. Thank goodness my girls were out, but they could return at any moment. I had to think quickly.

Susanna Grey's cheeks were paler than milk. "Hi, Lady Grey," I said as I approached her. "You need to get changed right away."

The urgency in my voice clearly frightened her, but she let me help her replace her shirt and trousers with the frilly smock.

I rolled my modern clothes, Susanna's, and that freaking plastic straw into a sheet and tossed the bundle into the hearth, coughing at the chalky cloud of ash it dislodged. That was the end of the seventy-two bucks still left in my pocket.

Susanna watched me as I lugged a fresh log onto the mound and lit it with tinder and flint. The fire kindled quickly, and the heat of the flames thawed some of my tension as I watched the clothes begin to disintegrate.

"We need to go over how you came to be here," I said, guiding Susanna into a wooden chair. If she began mouthing off to people about time travel and the twenty-first century—including me in it all —we could both be burned for heresy. After everything that had happened with Norfolk and his gang, I couldn't withstand another scandal at court.

I sat close to her, speaking slowly. "You are back at Hampton Court Palace. Your daughters are here." Susanna blinked away tears. "You have been missing for more than four years, and what's important is that you are back with your family. Everything else: the blue-diamond ring, the time you spent away...*America*...doesn't matter anymore. If you talk about that stuff to anyone, Lady Grey, you could receive a terrible punishment." I reflexively checked that no one was within earshot. "Let's just say that you wandered back into court and that you have no memory of how you got here or where you've been. Just say you remember nothing of your disappearance and go home to your husband and your garden. Okay? Do you understand?"

Eyes of creamy brown scanned me from head to foot. "Have mercy on me and I shall be saved," she said hoarsely, the smock more at ease over her thin shoulders than any modern clothes I'd seen her in.

There was fresh wine in the drawing-room, and I poured Susanna a cup before escaping to the refuge of my dressing room. I dug through the neatly folded silks, careful not to upset them, and retrieved a simple, iris-colored gown with a square neckline that I managed to tie on myself. Weaving my hair into a braid stirred a memory of my first days at Whitehall Palace. It felt like a lifetime ago.

Back in my bedchamber, Susanna hadn't moved. "Where may I find my daughters?" she said with faint confusion.

"They should come back here soon," I replied as my stomach made a hollow twist. Dinner wouldn't be served for hours.

I kneeled in front of her. "Do you think you can wait here while I get us something to eat? You have to promise that you won't go anywhere, please. I want you to see your daughters first."

She nodded, and I trusted that she wouldn't want to be anywhere other than the safety of my fire-warmed bedchamber at a time like this.

Blocking thoughts about Nick's whereabouts that threatened to send me into a panic spiral, I grabbed a cloak and braved the icy air, racing down empty corridors toward the kitchens.

"Do you know where everybody is?" I asked one of the chefs as he piled a pewter platter with cured meats, rosemary meatballs, soft cheeses, and prune tarts.

"There be a wrestling tournament this day at the tiltyard, my lady," he said.

It was a Nick Tudor trademark to stage court entertainments during his absence to keep his subjects occupied and out of trouble. The deserted corridors now made sense as I weaved my way back to my chambers, carefully balancing my tray. Making sure no one was following me, I slunk back to my rooms and bolted the door behind me.

After the mush that Susanna had been eating at the rest home, I wasn't sure she could handle the rich, fatty flavors of the Tudor court, but she scarfed up the spread like she hadn't eaten in weeks. Coaxing light conversation out of her about court stuff helped ease her a bit, and after another glass of wine, she asked if she could lie down for a while.

"Absolutely...I don't blame you," I replied with a yawn, and helped Susanna into Violet's pallet bed. I tried to give her mine, but she balked and refused to take the bed of someone who was higher up in the peerage. She obviously remembered the way things worked around here, which was promising.

An hour into her snooze, I decided that we could be waiting all afternoon for my ladies to come back and swung my cloak back over my shoulders. Sometimes the chambermaids turned up later in the day, and Alice and Violet deserved to see their mom before anyone else.

Anxious about Susanna Grey going missing again—this time on my watch—I hurried to the northern side of court, past the Privy Orchard, and across to the tiltyard. The redbrick arena had morphed into a gambling pit, with eager punters hanging from balconies in the high towers. After a minute of scanning, I spotted Alice, Violet, Bridget, and Lucinda squashed together within the third tower. They were cheering at the sportsmen in the pit who'd tied themselves into a jumble of biceps, calves, and breeches.

As I climbed over disgruntled nobles to reach my ladies in the fourth row, Alice saw me and clapped a hand over her mouth. I'd been gone for too short a time to make it to Worthing and back, and I told the girls it was because I ran into someone on the roads outside the palace.

"Of whom do you speak?" said Alice, handing Bridget her pouch of sugared almonds.

There was no way I was about to answer that in front of hundreds of drunken courtiers.

"Why don't you come back to my chambers and find out?" I said cryptically.

"Emmie," Alice blurted through a laugh, but lines filled her forehead.

"Who could it possibly be?" said Bridget, already halfway off the bench. She couldn't resist a mystery.

"Sorry to be vague and to interrupt the show, but you're going to want to see this," I said, my stomach crunching with nerves. I could've cringed at myself for making it sound like I'd planned a fun surprise. For all I knew, the shock of reuniting Alice and Violet with their missing mom could send one of them into cardiac arrest.

We headed back toward my chambers while they grilled me about this secret person. Alice's curious smile confirmed that she had zero idea it was her mom. The best guess thrown around was the king's sister Kit, and I swiped two fingers across my lips like a zipper, before remembering that zippers were practically as modern as Wi-Fi.

I was relieved to find that Susanna had woken up from her nap. She was sitting in a chair in the drawing-room, playing with her hair. Her eyes flared wide as Alice followed me inside, shadowed by Violet.

"Mother?" Violet said in a flat tone. I might've thought she was unaffected had it not been for her bewildered expression.

"No, Violet, Mother is…" Alice's usually confident voice drifted off.

"She is here," finished Violet.

"Lottie?" said Susanna.

I clutched my side, where I'd tied my kirtle too tight. "I found this lady near to the palace," I explained, the lie burning my throat. But maybe this reunion would finally atone for all my lies to Alice. "She said her name is Susanna Grey."

Alice pushed past me, all her etiquette gone. "Mother?" she whispered breathlessly.

"Alice…sweet Alice," Susanna replied. "By God's grace, I see now that you are a lady."

Susanna rose from the chair, catching both her daughters' hands as they fell to their knees in tears. "Most blessed daughters, oh, how my heart sings at the sight of you. I know not how this has come to pass, but if you are the subjects of a dream, may I never awaken."

A silent cry punched my chest, and I backed into my bedchamber with Bridget and Lucinda, quietly shutting the doors so the family could reunite in private. A silent decision took shape in my head: if Susanna Grey told Alice and Violet about her time-traveling expedition and my involvement in it, I'd have no choice but to argue for her insanity.

After a brief catch-up with Bridget and Lucinda, I asked if they could watch over things while I took a nap. My eyelids had become sheets of lead.

As Bridget and Lucinda sat in the corner and quietly shared theories about where Susanna Grey could have been all this time, I dozed off. When I woke to the distant blast of trumpets announcing dinner, my bedchamber was empty. The robust flames in the hearth said that the fire had been tended, and there was a jug of water and a cup beside my bed. I opened the double doors leading to the drawing-room, bracing myself for what I might find.

Girlish laughter trilled through the comfy space. Shining faces glanced at me from a cluster of fringed cushions on the floor. Alice, Violet, Lucinda, and Bridget scrambled to rise.

"Stay where you are," I said soothingly, crouching beside Alice on the floor. Lady Grey sat in a chair before us, like a librarian instructing an eager circle of children. In just hours, she looked ten years younger.

"Mother was speaking of Hatfield," Alice said a little breathlessly. "It seems the lady has been there these past years, but she keeps speaking of a moving coach with no horses and then laughs and laughs."

The smile slid off my face. Everyone else, however, looked more amused than concerned, including Susanna. There was color in her cheeks, and life had kindled in her eyes.

"Lady Pembroke, we are most heartily pleased to have our mother returned," Violet said to me. "The lady has no memory of how she came to return to court, but we are truly thankful you brought us to her before informing the Council."

"They will wish to question her," Alice added, her mouth tightening. "However, I fear our dear mother has become frantic."

Susanna just stared at her daughters with her narrow lips curled into a frozen smile. It was the face of someone who didn't have a clue what was going on but felt content.

When a single tap sounded at the doors, Lucinda welcomed a wooden trolley packed with steaming pewter serving platters. We arranged six chairs around the circular table. Over dinner, I filled the girls in on my fabricated tale about how I'd come upon Susanna wandering along the nearby River Thames, not only drumming the story into Susanna's head, but also hopefully blocking her from telling more tales about cars or modern inventions.

It was time to experiment with my growing influence around here, especially now that I felt sure I wanted to stay here with Nick and accept his world for what it was—provided he returned from the north with his head still on his shoulders. I erased that thought as soon as it came.

"Alice and Violet, I'd like you to take Lady Grey home to

Northamptonshire," I said, sinking my knife into a poached pear. "As you say, there will be interest in her whereabouts for the past four years and how she ended up at court with no memory of anything. However, that's an issue that should be discussed with her husband, Sir Thomas." Susanna's fingers curled into a knot as I continued. "Bridget and Lucinda will be here to attend to me in the meantime; just come back when Lady Grey has settled in. We need not trouble the king with this, and who knows when he'll be back. You can take one of the coaches."

Alice and Violet looked at each other, eyes gleaming. "Bless you, Emmie," Alice cried, abandoning her chair to hug me from behind. It was probably an outrageous way to treat an impending queen, but I'd encouraged a relaxed closeness in the privacy of my chambers, and I was thrilled to see it in effect. I was never a fan of being at court without Alice, but as one of the future queen's maids of honour, she wouldn't be allowed to stay away for too long. Besides, getting Susanna home safely was more important than me having my best friend at court.

"I shall write to Father," said Violet, twisting toward the desk.

"Don't bother with that; just go tonight," I said quickly. "While the king is away." I looked at Alice. "While the Earl of Warwick is away." Her toffee eyes met mine for a moment long enough to reveal a flash of regret. She hadn't yet patched things up with Francis.

Both the Grey girls were apprehensive about leaving court without permission or planning, but I insisted. Within a few hours, Alice, Violet, and Lady Grey were bundled up inside a swaying coach bound for Northamptonshire.

I slept deeply that night, waking late and spending a contented few days tucked away in my jewelry workshop. The craftsman that Nick had summoned to court, Andrea Bon Compagni, schooled me on the equipment with cheery patience. I felt instantly comfortable around his gentle face that was pockmarked with smallpox scars.

In the afternoons, Mister Bon Compagni would leave me with the company of neighing horses through the window or the muted crunches of boots crossing the graveled courtyard below. I'd file and pummel the silver until my wrist seized, crafting a simple thumb ring with a hammered pattern for Nick as a thank you present for the studio. It was going to be a total snore-fest beside his blingy Tudor jewels, but I had to start with something I could handle. There weren't exactly online video tutorials on this old-school equipment. Plus, I had years ahead to perfect my craft here, and for the first time, the thought of a long life in Tudor England excited me more than it freaked me out. All I needed now was my boyfriend back, but imagining where he might be—or if he was being skewered with a bloodied sword—sent my lunch into my throat. I forced myself to focus on whatever else I could to intercept my catastrophic thoughts.

With the absence of Alice and Violet, I became closer to Bridget —and even Lucinda, who was a shining example of a queen's lady, making sure my chambers were never short of freshly baked macarons for us all to share. When she received word that her daughter Ellie had fully recovered from her bout of illness, the three of us held a small dessert party.

Two weeks after the Grey girls left court, a letter from Alice arrived. She wrote that her mom was doing okay, but her father, Sir Thomas, had been called away on the king's business. I wanted to kiss the letter. Surely it meant that, somewhere out there, King Nick was alive. I knew that I would've heard about it had he not been, but communication in Tudor England made a snail look supersonic. It was hard to relax without knowing anything for sure. I wrote back to Alice and urged her to stay on in Northamptonshire until Sir Thomas returned home.

With so many letters coming and going from court, every tap on the door sent me flying toward the handle, hankering for one from Nick. Every day brought disappointment and a reminder of how unfinished things were between us. I wanted to tell him how I felt— that I was ready to make things work with him here. Why wouldn't he write? The constant fear that something bad had happened to him left my stomach in pieces.

The calendar had reached mid-November when another knock sounded an hour after supper.

"I'll get it," I cried to Lucinda and Bridget, and threw open the doors to find Francis Beaumont clutching a feathered cap. After greeting me, he ran a nervous palm down his espresso curls that reached his shoulders.

My throat locked, and all the air fled my body.

"His Majesty is well, but not yet at court, my lady," the earl said, reading my fear. He glanced past me.

"Oh, you're here to see Alice?" I blurted through my crushing relief. "She's gone back to Northamptonshire with Violet." Francis's face fell, and I explained. "Their mother is back, can you believe it? Lady Grey was found near here and seems well enough, but she has no idea where she's been for the past four years. Isn't that great news?"

Francis's mouth was agape. "Tell me everything."

I invited him inside the warmth of my chambers, but he politely refused. Any man who hung out behind closed doors with the king's fiancée without His Majesty's permission had a death wish. Instead, I asked Bridget to pass me a shawl and sat on the front step beside Francis, filling him in on everything I could reveal about Alice's mom. Nick's name didn't come up again until Francis mentioned that the uprising near Lancashire had been quelled for now. I'd been too scared to ask, so I was grateful that he'd volunteered the news.

"Where is the king now?" My voice was a nervous puff of smoke in the frosty air.

Francis rose to his feet and knocked a boot against the step. "That is why I am here, my lady. His Majesty received word that you had returned from Sussex in haste. He desires to speak with you on a great matter but wishes to do so in private."

"What great matter?"

He pressed his lips together like he was ill at ease. "The King's Majesty is expecting your person without delay at Robin House."

"Robin House?" I repeated with confusion. The humble manor in the countryside with the thatched roof was the king's most private place that most people didn't even know about. Nick clearly had something to tell me that required secrecy, and anxiety slid into my stomach, churning everything up. Perhaps he'd decided the opposite of what I had these past few weeks: that our engagement was a mistake and the smartest thing for him to do would be to marry

Princess Henriette of France after all. Wouldn't that solve all his problems?

Francis surely knew what the deal was, and I tried to read his face, but it was concealed by winter darkness.

"You will consider this matter not to be delayed and will make ready to leave, my lady," he advised briskly. "You may bring your ladies." He bowed and marched away before I could press him on the topic any further. The earl was clearly keeping any opinions on this mysterious matter to himself—perhaps by order of the king.

I rubbed my clammy palms up and down my thighs, my mouth drying up. Not only was Nick's great matter urgent, but it came after our unspoken agreement to reconsider our engagement.

Bile surged in the back of my throat, and I felt like I might be sick on the damp cobblestones.

After all the troubles we'd already been through—Norfolk, Lucinda, Agnes Nightingale—what did Nick have to say to me that was so important? I wasn't sure I wanted to find out.

14

Heavy rains made the roads dangerous for travel that night, so I slept at Hampton Court Palace with my mind in overdrive. What was Nick's 'great matter' that prevented him from riding to Hampton Court to face me in public? At first light, I yanked the shutters open, gaping with trepidation at the clear sky through the diamond-crossed panes. Was this the day that I would find out he wanted us to go our separate ways after all? The thought stole any appetite I might've had for breakfast.

Bridget gnawed her fingertips for most of the slushy coach ride through the mud to the king's secret hideaway—thrilled for another adventure—while Lucinda gazed silently through the open window. Did she know about Robin House? Had Nick taken her there for a romantic couple's weekend during their fling? I pushed the jagged thoughts away.

The moment our coach swung onto the stone pathway leading to Robin House, I watched for Nick through the window, my stomach a storm of butterflies. I wasn't ready to go through what could be the most heartbreaking day of my life.

The modest manor's front yard looked desolate except for a couple of discreet guards hovering in plain clothes. The main house with the thatched roof was even smaller than I remembered—perhaps because Hampton Court Palace had become the benchmark by which I now measured all royal residences.

A stocky guard with strong hands helped me to the ground. "His Majesty awaits your person inside, my lady," he said as our short procession of carts and horses clopped toward the stables. A gust of wind bit my neck as I approached the house, nerves thundering through me. I inhaled a steadying breath and pushed through the thick wooden door.

The sight was so unexpected that it sent me back a step. Around the modest dining table sat Alice's dad Sir Thomas Grey, the wrinkled Bishop of Winchester, and my fiancé in a doublet of navy velvet, his white peekaboo collar centered with a blood-red ruby. When he glanced up at me and our gazes seared together, the urge to rush toward him was so intense that my thighs clenched, holding me in place.

"Lady Pembroke, I give you good morrow," Nick said formally, his glittering eyes making a quick slide down my body but giving nothing away.

I found myself curtsying, a scorching flutter in my stomach. The other men rose to kiss my hand.

"You may sit with us," Nick added, like I'd just joined a corporate meeting. A touch stung by his cool reaction after our time apart, I reminded myself that we weren't alone and Nick rarely let his guard down in front of his most esteemed lords.

A page slid a chair in for me beside the king. My elbows brushed Nick's as I sat, sparks heating my skin through the fabric. I wanted to lean forward and kiss the sweet-smelling space beneath his ear, but that would've been weird. Being this close to him always offset my balance in a way that I never wanted to end.

"It is time for your king and the Marquess of Pembroke to be united in holy matrimony," Nick stated without looking at me.

I nearly choked on my breath, needles of shock prickling my cheeks. *I'm sorry…what?*

The only sound was the king's commanding voice. "The Bishop

of Winchester will conduct the proceedings, and Sir Thomas Grey will serve as a witness."

Wrinkled skin sagged beneath Thomas Grey's wearied eyes as he took note of Nick's continuing instructions like his life depended on it. So, this was the 'great matter'…Nick had decided to push forward our wedding without even speaking to me about it. I gaped at his frustratingly perfect profile as he continued issuing orders without even looking my way. "Lady Pembroke, you may take your dinner and then dress, and thereupon the service will begin."

"We're getting married *today?*" I sputtered, unsure whether I was more relieved or aghast about the lack of notice. I was getting used to the opinions of women being an afterthought in this place, but surely I got a say in my own wedding day.

The king rose quickly, and the rest of us scrambled to our feet, bowing as he strode out of the chamber without a backward glance. As relieved as I was that he wasn't breaking up with me, I could've throttled him in that handsome doublet. We were going to have words.

I excused myself to Sir Thomas and the bishop and picked up my skirts to dash up the narrow staircase leading to the upstairs bedchamber.

There was no sign of Nick, however—only Bridget standing before the fireplace, warming her fingers. She danced toward me as I entered. "Lady Pembroke, we hear there is to be a wedding—oh, blessed day!"

Lucinda scooted over from the clothes chest and dropped to her knees, pressing her soft lips to my hand. "My lady, if you find the heart to forgive my past actions and permit me to attend to you as Queen of England, you will find me a most loving and loyal servant."

It was the first time she'd openly alluded to the kiss with Nick, but that seemed pretty far down the scale of bombshells right now.

"Why would he want to get married in this small house?" I asked them, genuinely gobsmacked.

"To hide it," Bridget answered plainly.

"Because he loves her," Lucinda argued. "It is the pleasure of the king to keep his more tender inclinations private."

My stomach rolled over itself. I had to find Nick and ask him what planet he was on. The girls looked startled as I rushed back out to check the washroom before clomping down the stairs, where four cooks bustled in the tiny kitchen, bumping hips.

"Do you know where the king is?" I blurted to no one in particular.

A guard with imposing shoulders stepped forward. "Mister Joseph Blackburn, my lady," he introduced with a bow. "I believe His Majesty is in the guest lodgings beyond the garden."

"Guest lodgings?" I didn't know there were any here.

I thanked the guard and headed outside to a grassy courtyard, where Thomas Grey and Bishop Winchester stood chatting in their billowy black cloaks like two stage magicians who'd popped out for a smoke.

"Lady Pembroke," said Thomas, stopping my stride. His pale eyes fixed on mine. "When I once bid you to leave the company of the king, I admit that I had mistook you for little more than a lovesick girl. But, madam, I see now that you are nobody's fool." He tipped his head at me with a short nod.

A hot flush of embarrassment crept across my cheeks as I made a thankful curtsy for the vague apology. Thomas had once offered me money to break up with Nick, and I'd not only done the opposite but ended up becoming the future Queen of England.

"I also understand that it was you who helped return my wife to her home," Thomas added, a peace offering in his eyes.

"Uh, yes, you could say that."

When he made a nod of thanks and turned away again, I knew this was the closest thing I'd ever get to the old man's blessing.

Before he could leave, a nervous question spilled from my lips. "Why Robin House, Sir Thomas? Why would the king choose to marry me here on this small property—away from everybody?"

I'd expected him to warn me about rebellions and what the nobles really thought of me, but his cheeks blushed fondly. "Your dear betrothed may have the heart of a king, my lady, but he also bears the heart of a man."

As I glanced over the stony courtyard that clung to visibility within invading thickets of wildflowers and rose bushes, it came together. A part of Nick—a bigger share then I'd have guessed—envied the simplicity of the quiet farmer's life. It was the reason he enjoyed visiting Robin House so much, where I'd seen him tending the roses and picnicking on the grass. Despite the countless times that I'd butted heads with Thomas Grey, he knew layers of Nick that'd take years for me to peel away. He was the father that Nick had never had, which was why he'd been asked to witness the wedding—even above Francis Beaumont. That gave the old grump a stack of cred in my books.

"I'm really happy your wife is finally home," I said to him with a wary smile. "I hope you can get back to her soon."

A film of tears brightened his eyes. He bowed in gratitude and stepped aside for me to pass.

Wedged into the back corner of the courtyard was a tiny cabin built from hand-sawed planks of wood. The door was so stiff that I had to shove it with my hip to get it open.

Inside, I found Nick sitting on a wooden stool beside a square hole for a window—a jewel swimming in mud inside the ramshackle space.

"Oh, sorry," I said quickly. "You're praying."

He looked up at me, his lips falling open with surprise. "Lady Pembroke. You are to be preparing your person for the ceremony."

I felt my forehead crease, but this time, I promised myself I'd stay calm. Nick would never be a modern guy, and he'd always think like a dictatorial Tudor king, but I still deserved a voice in this relationship. I'd never stop fighting for that.

"What's all this about?" I asked him in a delicate voice. "The last time I saw you, things were weird between us, then I went home for no more than a day, you were away *forever*, and now you announce a sudden wedding without even speaking to me about it?" I shook my head, bewildered. "That's really different to how things are done in my time and definitely not how I imagined our wedding day to be. We haven't even had a chance to say a proper hello to each other."

He twisted back to face the window, sunlight tinting his chestnut hair a lighter shade of caramel as he spoke in a choked voice. "Emmie, I cannot bear the uncertainty of this matter any longer. I

462

love you so truly that it makes me ill to consider that you have had a change of heart about us. But I must know—you may speak your conscience now, I beseech you to."

His words had my heart racing. "When do I ever *not* speak my conscience?"

It was my attempt to lighten the atmosphere, but his cheeks didn't move. I grasped what was happening: despite the show of command in front of Sir Thomas and the bishop, Nick was giving me one more opening to back out of this thing and return to the twenty-first century if that's what I wanted. I sensed that he wouldn't try to stop me this time.

My voice broke on the truthful words that drew me closer to him. "When you were away, I went home to my time and brought back Susanna Grey—as I'm sure you've heard. But the whole time I was there, I couldn't wait to get back here to you. All I've thought about since you left is you being home, and safe, and with me."

He turned to meet my gaze, his tormented eyes softening at the edges.

"Do I always agree with you?" I continued, stepping between his thighs. "No. Will I ever completely understand you? Maybe not. Do you make me insane? One hundred percent. But do I seem to love you more every day, rather than less, for some irritating, inexplicable reason? Completely."

His voice was a nervous tremble. "So you do wish to marry me?"

"Didn't I already say yes?"

His full lips puffed with relief, and my heart swelled. For a moment, we just drank in the sight of each other before his mouth curled up into a teary smile. He lurched up and wrapped his arms around me, pulling me into him, and I fell into his light like a sunflower. After so long apart, our embrace quickly escalated to deep, drugging kisses that made my head spin, before we broke apart, panting and remembering ourselves. Nick dropped back onto the stool and tugged me down into his lap, tightening his arms around me and burying his face in the crook of my neck.

"If you weren't sure that I still wanted to get married," I said, "then why did you go ahead and try to force it? Why plan everything without me?"

"It is the custom in my time for the man to make ready the marriage rites, even though most assuredly I would have stopped it, had I not had your consent." He drew away from my neck to bring his eyes to mine, skimming his fingertips up and down my arms. "I also feared that mine idleness was causing you to drift away. I should have wed you in more haste. I have taken too long…been too consumed with the Spaniards, and the French, and all manner of duty." He caught my cheeks between his palms and gave them an affectionate squeeze. "You mean more to me than aught, and I wish to wait not one moment longer to marry you."

"Who's Aught?" I said with mock horror. "She's not another one of your ex-girlfriends, is she?"

He breathed an adorable laugh, and I tilted into him, kissing the dip in his crinkled brow. "Then let's do this thing, Nicholas Henry Edward. Make me a Tudor too."

Upstairs in the bedchamber, Bridget and Lucinda had laid out a pretty pale-yellow kirtle sprinkled with diamond dust and embroidered with a trail of silver wildflowers that wouldn't irritate Nick's asthma. After dressing me in the gown's myriad pieces, they pinned a medieval circlet of fresh wildflowers over my loose hair and clipped on a necklace of white diamonds. I appraised myself in the hand mirror, my fingers shaking. If only Alice was here to keep me calm with her steadying words. I couldn't believe that she was about to miss my wedding, but I didn't have time to send for her, even if I'd been okay with dragging her back from her mom's side.

Lucinda and Bridget gathered my tissue-soft train and followed me down the narrow staircase and outside, my feet slipping around in my satin pumps that were half a size too big. My heart sank a little as I caught sight of the overcast sky. It hadn't looked that grim when I went upstairs. The next to meet my vision was Thomas Grey, also wincing at the clouds before he spotted me and dropped into a gentlemanly bow.

Nervous excitement hummed low in my belly at the sight of Nick. He stood before the Bishop of Winchester in a coat of marble-colored satin pinned with solid-gold buttons, an affectionate smile adorning his face. Tufts of his tousled hair peeked from beneath his crown of glittering crosses and fleur-de-lis.

Smiling so wide that my cheeks could've touched my eyes, I strolled toward him to a gentle rendition of "Lady Greensleeves" performed by a flutist. I halted beside my fiancé and gazed up into the blue-green stare that possessed every part of my heart. When he winked at me and smiled, a rush of love tightened my chest.

Bishop Winchester delivered most of the service in Latin, and I copied Nick when he knelt on a cushion and read from a prayer book, the somberness of the ceremony surprising me. In my time, weddings were cheerful expressions of love and commitment, but in Tudor England, it was a deadly serious vow before God that I felt could never be undone. That might've freaked me out had I been marrying anyone else, but with Nick, the assurance that he'd always be mine filled my body up with warmth.

We were halfway through the ceremony when the skies made good on their threats and freezing raindrops began spilling from the clouds. At any other time, I'd have shrieked and run for cover, but I just giggled as Nick made an adorable scowl at the sky.

"A most glorious day indeed for the wedding of God's chosen king!" he cried with mock anger, and we all laughed before the ceremony was sped up.

Thomas Grey quickly presented matching gold rings carved with the entwined initials *N&E*. Nick slid mine over my fourth finger, and a taut balloon burst inside me, releasing a euphoric feeling of peace. My fingertips brushed the ridges of an inscription on the inside of the ring, the Latin words *Ne Dimittas*.

Nick smiled at me, reading my thoughts. "It means 'do not let go'," he said under his breath. I beamed, catching his hand in mine and bringing his newly ringed finger to my lips. It was the phrase I'd whispered to him when we first traveled through time together.

Do not let go.

Ne dimittas.

Thunder whipped the sky, and Nick hurried me inside to where the cooks had squeezed a feast of dishes onto the circular dining table. There was just enough space for our small wedding party, and we dug into platters of duck, quail, and swan, enjoying the closeness and chatter that reminded me of Thanksgiving at my friend Mia's house. Between courses, Nick held my hand beneath the table, his thumb caressing my palm in a way that made my thighs press together. In all the excitement, I'd forgotten that tonight was also our wedding night. The moment I remembered what that meant, I could think of nothing else. I was finally going to be able to be with Nick the way my body felt desperate to, but at the same time, I was scared of it hurting...of not being able to do it properly...of whether he would think I was a complete let-down.

My eyes locked on Lucinda Parker as she chatted politely with the bishop between small bites of violet-flavored marzipan. Lucinda knew what to do—she'd been with Nick before. I chugged an entire cup of water, but it didn't cut through the drought in my mouth.

"The hour is late, and our lady is undoubtedly wearied," said Nick, dabbing his lips with a silk napkin. "We are grateful for your service and bid you retire to bed." Everyone rose to bow to the king, and Nick walked me toward the stairwell. He paused there, my heart beating into my throat.

"You may expect my short return, my lady," he said a little huskily, pressing his lips to my hand as his gaze clung to mine, heat building in his eyes.

Despite my nerves, a thrill danced through me, low in my stomach.

15

THE MOMENT NICK LEFT, BRIDGET AND LUCINDA ARRIVED TO TAKE ME upstairs. Bridget couldn't contain her glee at the idea of a wedding night, which only escalated my jitters. They drew me a bath scented with fragrant herbs, washed and combed my hair, and helped me into a silk nightgown that I noticed could be easily slipped over my head. Candles danced light up the walls, my throat sticky with anticipation. Bridget offered me a knowing grin as they left me alone, and Lucinda wouldn't look at me for the first time in weeks. I tried not to let her obvious envy affect me as I climbed into bed and pulled the fur covers to my chin. Despite the fire hissing and cracking in the hearth, I couldn't get warm.

Several minutes later, the distant song of a flute rapidly gained in volume until it was right outside the door. I sat up to a gentle knock and men's voices. Nick strolled into the dim room in his silk nightshirt, followed by Bishop Winchester, Thomas Grey, and three of Nick's gentlemen of the bedchamber.

WTF, has war broken out or the plague arrived on our doorstep?

Winchester launched into a benediction in Latin, blessing Nick, me, and the bed. A gentleman carried in two dining chairs and angled them toward the mattress, and Bishop Winchester and Thomas Grey sat down in them, inches away from me in the tight space. Servants carried in a small buffet table before dressing it with wine and bread.

Nick sat on the mattress beside me, smelling almost as delicious as he looked. A thick fur blanket draped over me still separated us.

"Nick," I said quietly, my cheeks hotter than the flames in the hearth. "What is going on?" The flutist trilled a little louder.

"My queen, this is our wedding night," he said with the same breathy emphasis. "You know not what is required to sanctify our marriage before God?"

"I know what's required, but with an audience? Is this some kind of creepy Tudor joke?" I hissed.

Nick's mouth opened and shut like he was lost for words. I spotted Thomas's jowly face beyond Nick's shoulder and yanked the covers a little higher.

"The men are here to bear witness that the marriage is consummated," Nick explained to me.

"Yeah, I'm catching on to that." The shiver returned to my skin.

Nick's gaze considered me for a moment before he twisted to face the cluster of men. "You may leave us and remain beyond the door."

Mercifully, the lot of them bowed at the king's command and scurried out to the hallway carrying their chairs, shutting the door behind them.

"Did I screw everything up?" I asked Nick, my fingers splayed over my face.

He pulled my hand away to bring his lips to my forehead. "It is plainly not the custom in your time," he said into my skin. "The men may *hear* the consummation of the marriage, which will suffice."

A sigh of relief burst from my lips, and Nick smirked at me like I was cute.

Our fingers were twisting together again, touching and swirling with focused strokes. There was so much excitement churning inside me that I almost felt faint. I brought Nick's irresistible fingers to my mouth and began kissing them, one by one. He watched me closely while combing his other hand through my hair, strong and steady.

"I love the touch of your mouth on me," he said, his voice becoming raspy. His words inspired me to part my lips around the tip of his forefinger and draw it inside my mouth, sucking on it. A heated murmur rumbled out of him as I stroked my tongue over his fingers, one after the other, wrapping my lips tightly around each one and moving my mouth down on them like they were a different part of his body that I wished to taste.

"God, what you do to me," he said through sharp breaths, still watching my mouth and weaving his fingers through my hair. When I sucked harder, his palm dropped to his groin beneath his nightshirt, his face straining. My mouth watered at the thought of touching him —of finally lowering my lips over him and seeing what that solid length felt like in my mouth—but right now, I couldn't peel my gaze away from his face.

He was so ridiculously beautiful like this: his eyes clouded with desire, his cheeks flushed, his lips glistening and slightly parted. I suddenly needed to taste that mouth more than anything, so I knotted my fingers in the back of his hair and yanked his lips to mine.

He hummed a laugh against my mouth and pulled back a little, making me chase the kiss like the cheeky devil he was.

I tightened my hold on his hair and pouted. "If you do not kiss me at this very moment, I fear that my heart will burst out of my chest," I said, repeating his own words from the hunting park at Hampton Court Palace.

The fact that I'd committed that sentence to memory made him look at me like I'd just told him I loved him for the first time.

His eyes gleamed in the flickering candlelight as they held mine, and he caressed a hand down my cheek, catching my jaw and tugging my lips to his.

"My heart *is* bursting out of my chest," he whispered against my mouth, and my heart swelled as he brushed his tongue against mine. The kiss soon escalated to frantic as he gripped my face and twisted our tongues together with deep, hungry strokes, the taste so intoxicating that if we just did this all night long, I would have been more than content. I was gasping into his mouth, kissing his face off to the point of embarrassment, but the sounds Nick was making signaled that he was as lost to this as I was. With our mouths and tongues still grasping for each other's, we fell down onto the mattress together.

I fisted his nightshirt and dragged it up over his shoulders, baring his athletic body to me and inspiring me to run my tongue over the swells of his chest. His palm carved a trail down my back until he cupped my ass hard over my silk nightgown. "With the men near to verify consummation of the marriage rites, Emmie, I cannot promise to be silent."

Something rumbled low in my abdomen at that thought.

Good. I had every intention of making him moan tonight.

I sat up so I could fully appreciate the view of his toned muscles, skating my palms over every ridge and curve, my eyes heavy with desire for him. I gently pushed at his shoulders until he was leaning back on his elbows, his hair mussed, a sexy-as-hell look on his face— basically the most edible meal on the planet.

A low chuckle escaped his throat, and he caught his mouth with the back of his hand.

"What?" I said with an unsure laugh.

The adorable grimace on his face sent a flutter to my stomach. "Imagine if I had not expelled Sir Thomas and Winchester from the chamber. They would be sitting here at this very moment beside us."

I winced. "Out of all the Tudor rituals I've seen since being here, *that* one's the weirdest."

"Your ritual is better," he agreed, the trace of a smile on his lips revealing how much more comfortable he was with this arrangement.

"It's still weird though that they're on the other side of that door," I whispered, brushing my fingertips across the ripples of his abs before wrapping my hand around his thick length.

The moment of surprise on his face quickly transformed into a clench of pleasure as I squeezed his solid ridge, loving how hard and soft he felt—all at once—before I glided my hand up and down. *So gorgeous.*

Nick made a sharp groan as I fisted him tightly, wetness pooling between my thighs at the sight and feel of him, so hot and engorged in my hand. I didn't know if the sounds he was making were for the benefit of the listening ears, or because he couldn't help himself, but they made me ache for him even more, and I sped up my movements, my breaths becoming jagged and needy.

"God, Emmie," he gritted out as he thrust his hips into my hand, pushing himself up and down in my grasp. At that moment, all I could think about was sucking on him. The thought of it pushed my tongue to the front of my mouth, but before I could work up the courage to try it—worried I'd do something wrong or hurt him—Nick lurched upward and snapped his hand over my wrist.

"I will come all over you," he warned, but his words only spurred me to squeeze and pump him harder.

"*Emmie*," he breathed hotly, his eyes sinking closed, but after a few more seconds, he shifted to release my hand from him.

He leaned forward and cupped my face, drilling his sensual eyes into mine. "Fear not, my girl. If I come, that does not mean this night is over. But I feel as if you are paying me a great deal too much attention when the very thought of touching and tasting you makes me hard to the point of bursting." He bunched my nightgown in one hand and tugged it over my head.

His lips parted at the sight of my bare body, my nipples puckering in his heated gaze as he sat back for a moment and just stared at me.

"Hard," I repeated in a throaty voice, and Nick's brows lifted like he didn't know what I meant. "You used the word *hard* like someone in my time would," I explained with a timid smile. "It's another word we have in common."

He bit down on his bottom lip and shifted closer, capturing my thighs in his hands and folding my legs around his hips. His cock brushed against my slick folds like it wanted to bury itself in there, a low groan leaving Nick's throat as I gasped.

"*Very* hard," he said as he rolled his hips up and down, coating his length in my desire for him until his shaft was glistening.

A wave of panic crashed into me at the realization that this was it. I was going to lose my virginity right here, right now. And while Nick's talented fingers had come to feel like they were sent from heaven when they were inside me, his cock was so thick and large and—

"Be calm, my girl," he said softly, catching my face between his palms and pressing his lips to mine. "We have all night long," he reassured me like he'd heard my thoughts. "And there is plenty I still wish to do with you before we consummate our marriage."

He combed his fingers through my hair again like he knew the action soothed me, affection warming his eyes as he studied my expression, making sure I was okay.

"I have a question I wish to ask you," he said before touching his lips to my cheek, the soft kiss making me tighten my legs around him.

"Yes?"

He gently cupped the swells of my breasts in his hands and squeezed them.

"In your time, what is it that you call these?" he asked, pressing his thumbs against my puckered nipples and holding them there. I whimpered at the touch. "Not *these*," he added, spanning his fingers out over my full breasts. "But these." He rubbed the peaks with his thumbs before making little tugs that stole my breath.

"We call them nipples," I said with a slightly embarrassed chuckle as he circled and played with the nubs. "What do you call them?" I asked breathlessly.

Nick's darkened eyes flashed to mine. "Dessert," he replied before lowering his head.

He closed his hot mouth over one of the nipples, a deep sigh falling from my lips as he slid his tongue over me on both sides, sucking on my peaks tightly like they were pieces of candy.

"Look at them, so swollen and begging for my mouth," he said in a gravelly voice as he leaned back with a hungry stare before giving me a few more licks.

"We, too, call them nipples," he then explained with a breath of laughter, his glassy eyes lifting to mine and sending a flush across my cheeks.

He gripped my waist and leaned forward to catch my lips with his again. I melted into the languid, dreamy kiss, forcing out an image of Thomas Grey and the bishop sitting on the other side of the door. My God, what if they were getting off on this?

Nick's hands began a slow journey down my body, pausing to palm the curves of my ass before he unlocked his mouth from mine and sat back a little.

He brought his hand between my thighs and brushed the tips of his fingers through my soft folds.

"Emmie, you are so wet," he rasped, deepening the drags of his fingers until they were coated with my slickness that he used to stroke my clit. His breaths quickened as he touched me with a crease in his brow that made clear he was enjoying this as much as I. When he pushed my thighs apart and sank two fingers inside me as deeply as they could go, I cried out.

Nick watched the expression on my face, his lips wet and parted as he curved his fingers, brushing a spot deep inside me that was like pushing the pleasure button. My head fell back, and I grinded against his hand, a sexy sound of approval leaving his lips.

"You like that," he said, his foggy eyes on mine as he continued rubbing me in that one spot.

I could hardly catch my breath, let alone speak, and I just tipped back on my elbows and angled my hips up as Nick thrust his fingers in and out of my soaking core.

"I need to see you closer," he said huskily, leaving me empty and aching as he pulled his hand away and shifted further down the bed, positioning his face between my open thighs.

My instinct was to clench with embarrassment, but Nick rested a warm hand on my inner thigh and began a trail of kisses there, his soft lips moving higher and higher.

"Do you wish me to stop?" he breathed into my skin, but when his tongue made a long, wet slide up my inner thigh, my legs fell open with a will of their own.

Nick drew his head back a little so he could gaze at my parted core, which was swollen and shining wet for him.

"So sweet," he said in an aching voice as he pressed his fingers to either side of me, spreading me open. He pushed two fingers inside me again, my moans echoing his as he dug deep inside me, his face even prettier when it was washed with pleasure like this.

"May I taste you?" he asked in a needy tone, burying his fingers inside me while his thumb brushed over that perfect spot between my thighs.

"Yes," I gasped, desperate to know what it felt like to have his tongue down there.

Nick shifted even closer, the heat of his breath tickling the most sensitive part of my body. Then he made a long stroke up the length of my core with the full pad of his tongue. *Ohmygod.* He brushed his nose over my clit, breathing me in with a sigh, before he gripped the backs of my thighs and pushed my legs up, opening me wider.

He moaned hungrily as he placed his whole mouth on me, licking me from top to bottom, side to side, swirling and sucking on me like he couldn't get enough of this as his hands stayed plastered to my thighs. The most intense physical pleasure I'd ever experienced fizzed through me, from my toes to my fingertips. *This is...unbelievable.*

"*Nick,*" I whimpered helplessly as I fisted my hands in his hair and shamelessly tilted my hips up into his face.

"I will never tire of this," he said as his tongue licked up my core like it was made of melting ice cream, searching for even more of my taste even though he was already consuming all there was to have. Everything around me sank into blackness, and I was left with nothing but the sensation of Nick's mouth devouring me as I moaned and twisted on the mattress. Just when I thought I couldn't take anymore, he pulled back and looked up at me, his chest panting and his pupils blown.

"I need you," he said like he was in pain, his hand gripping his tight cock. I couldn't resist wrapping my hand over the top of his until we were both stroking up and down his firm length.

"What do you need?" I teased in a husky voice.

One side of his mouth curled up, his eyes gleaming. "What are the words you use in your time?" he asked, clearly referring to the act of sex.

When a moment of shyness heated my cheeks, I redirected. "What do *you* call it?"

He smirked and gently guided my thighs apart with his knees before he crawled up the bed and positioned himself over me.

"Here, we would say...I wish to do you," he said, gazing down at me.

I laughed. "*Do* me?"

His smile widened as he blushed. "It sounds foolish to you."

I skated my palms down his shoulders, stopping to grip his

muscular biceps that tensed as he hovered over me. "No, we actually say that too," I said. "It's just...not as commonly as other words."

His brows lifted. "What is it that is more common?"

I inhaled a sticky breath, still gaining my confidence to say these sorts of things aloud. "Well, I guess the more technical way of saying it would be to *have sex,* but the hotter way of saying it would be..."

I sucked my bottom lip between my teeth, and Nick smiled down at me, nearly laughing. "Go on," he encouraged.

"We would say *fuck,*" I said in a whisper, blood rushing to my cheeks.

"Fuck?" Nick replied, trying out the word. He pinned his hips against mine and rolled his solid ridge up and down my core, seeming to savor the reaction that blew across my features.

"So you would say: Would it please you if I were to fuck you?" he said.

I snorted a laugh, and his face dropped into the curve of my neck, hiding there like he was embarrassed. If there was anything cuter than this all-powerful Tudor king being embarrassed in front of me, I didn't know what it was.

I clasped the back of his neck and gently guided his head back up.

"This is how you would say it," I said, whispering the correct phrasing into his ear.

When I rested my head back on the mattress and blinked up at him, Nick traced his fingertips down the side of my face before grasping my jaw in his fingers.

"Can I fuck you?" he said to me, sending a shiver of heat skittering down my spine until it bloomed deep in my core.

"That's better," I said through a shaky breath, widening my thighs beneath him and arching my back like some sort of wanton porn star. But this was a side of me that Nick Tudor drew out without effort. A thousand ways I wanted to be naked with him flew through my mind, none of them on the wholesome side. And the indecent look in Nick's eyes as they trailed over my body made clear that he wasn't really the innocent type either.

"I want to fuck you," he tried again, gripping his cock and rubbing the velvety tip up and down the swollen skin of my core. I dug my elbows into the mattress on either side of me, bracing myself for impact.

"Before we do this," he said thickly, "there are two matters I wish to discuss."

I just gazed up at him with a puzzled sort of affection, marveling at how this guy could go from sexy young hottie to formal Tudor king in one beat.

He touched his lips to the left side of my cheek. "The first is that, as you have not yet been crowned as queen, it would be the custom to avoid placing a child in your belly," he said carefully, like this might be a sensitive subject. "Would that be agreeable to you?"

If only he knew how much those words loosened my chest. "If you mean that you don't think we should get pregnant right away, then yes, I one hundred percent agree with that." I considered myself way too young to have a baby, but as a future sixteenth-century Queen of England, I knew I'd soon have to make some compromises there. But it evidently wouldn't be tonight, and I was grateful for that.

He seemed pleased with my reaction. "The other," he said, kissing the right side of my cheek this time, "is that you must tell me if you wish me to stop at any moment. If you feel pain, if you feel fear, if you wish to stop, say so, and I will stop. We need not continue at all. Worry naught about our wedding night, or the lords seated outside the door, or my endless love for you—if you wish to stop, we stop. Agreed?"

I lurched up and stamped my lips to his, wrapping my arms around his neck and kissing him fiercely. He clutched my face and returned a hot, possessive kiss that made me drive my hips up like I wanted to be even closer to him. Nick grinded his pelvis back against mine until my juices were coating him and we were both gasping for breath.

One of his hands drifted down, and I steadied my nervous mind by focusing on the muscles that bunched in his arm while he positioned himself at my entrance.

A feeling of soft yet firm pressure pushed against my core, and Nick's glazed-over eyes locked on mine, making sure I was okay.

"There is one more thing yet to say," he said, his breath shallow.

"What is it?" I panted, clutching onto his arms. *Tudor king likes to talk.*

His tropical-sea eyes stared deeply into mine. "I love you more than I will ever love anything," he said, the heat of his breath washing over my lips.

My heart exploded, and I wrapped my arms around his neck and kissed him again, whispering the same words against his lips.

When I lay back down, Nick sucked in a sharp breath as he pushed himself past the entrance of my core, my entire body locking at the abrupt feeling of unfathomable fullness. Pain shot into my center, and I clenched my jaw, making him freeze on the spot.

"Are you well?" he asked, making a move with his hips that indicated an intention to withdraw. But I was determined to go through with this, and I clasped his lower back, holding him there.

"Don't stop," I whispered. "Just go slow."

He held still for a few beats longer before he pressed forward a little more, making my hips buck off the mattress as my body adjusted to his size. He already felt enormous even though he was only partially in. He paused there, and his forehead fell into my neck as he grunted out a low hum of pleasure.

Nothing seemed to turn me on more than seeing Nick turned on, and it inspired me to slide my hands further down his back until I was cupping his ass, using it to push himself deeper into me.

Nick hadn't expected that, and his face flew back up as he sank all the way inside until our pelvises were flush together, my core so tightly stretched that I feared it could tear as Nick fought to catch his breath.

"God, Emmie. You feel like heaven," he said, his features pulled tight.

His teeth clamped down on his lower lip like he was fighting to keep control, and he looked at me with a question in his eyes: *Are you okay?*

"I'm good," I reassured him through a hoarse whisper, my palms running up and down his back as I adjusted to the fullness of him, feeling a jolt of pain every time he moved.

"Let us remain here a moment," he said against my cheek, and the sweet heat of his breath drew my lips to his. There was so much sensation bursting between our legs that, instead of kissing each other senseless like we usually did, we just stayed there with our lips pressed lightly together, breathing in each other's exhales like we were one being and one breath.

Love splashed warmth through every corner of my body as Nick breathed into my mouth while he was so far inside me that I didn't know where I ended and he began. I'd never felt a feeling of connection like this before. It made me feel like my lungs had been bottled up my entire life and were finally being given air.

I knew enough about sex to know that this wasn't really *it* until he began moving, and I was keen to know what that was like, so I dropped my head back onto the mattress and gazed up at him. I made the gentlest tilts forward and back with my hips, encouraging him to take the next step with this.

Nick hissed through his teeth as he dragged his hips back a little, the stab of pain in my center mingling with a shiver of pleasure. My hands clutched his back while he pushed all the way into me again, the sensations repeating. I couldn't deny that it hurt—perhaps even more than I'd expected—but between every flash of pain was an even sharper wave of almost unbearable pleasure that would leave me gasping.

Nick checked in with me again, and I told him to keep going, the look on his face making clear that he was feeling only the pleasure part. I wanted him to enjoy this, to enjoy *me*, so I made a decision I was comfortable with.

"Go faster," I whispered, my fingers still running up and down his back, over his shoulders, and down his arms like I couldn't stop touching him everywhere. "Please, go faster."

Nick exhaled like he'd been holding in the world's biggest breath and drew out of me almost entirely before sinking back in, filling me completely again. He repeated the movements, his gasps of pleasure building as he increased his speed and depth, bracing one of his hands against the mattress while the other grasped my hip.

I'd expected the pain to increase, but it was doing the opposite. Those waves of mind-blowing pleasure were rolling through quicker and stronger between the stings.

"Emmie, you feel so good," Nick choked out as he sat up a little and tilted his hips, the angle deepening his thrusts, and I trained my eyes on this gorgeous man falling apart in front of me because of how I made him feel. It was an aphrodisiac to me like no other, and after several more minutes, I realized I was moaning as hard as he was, my mind empty of everything except this.

I *loved* it.

"Does this feel good?" he asked, his breath short and his eyes hooded.

I just nodded, my head so heavy with lust that I could barely lift it. "I want more," I breathed, and Nick hummed his approval at that and pushed my thighs up and back so I was spread further open.

He held me in place as he began pumping harder and deeper, the sound of wet smacks filling the room from the intense desire soaking my core.

"I want to do this all the time," I moaned, and Nick made a sexy murmur.

"Worry about that not, my girl," he said thickly, his deep thrusts climbing me higher and higher toward a summit I couldn't see. "I am going to fuck you in every room in this manor."

Each slam of his hips elicited another moan from my mouth that I was sure the men outside could hear, but I didn't give a toss. There was only this. There was only him.

"I want you to look at me when you come," Nick said hotly, hooking an arm around one of my legs and lifting it over his shoulder to give him deeper access. "Come all over me, Emmie. That's it. Look at me."

The ache in his voice was all it took to tip me over the edge, and I crashed over that summit and into a swirling whirlpool of liquid heat, every nerve in my body exploding into a spray of fireworks as I throbbed and pulsed around Nick's rock-hard cock. It was the most mind-bending climax of my life, and after the final wave had washed through me, Nick scooped me up into his arms and pressed my panting chest to his, kissing me all over my face while I caught my breath and waited for my heart rate to slow.

When we pulled back, the happiness in his eyes dug into my heart, and I fell forward and kissed him deeply, showing him how thankful I was for making me feel so good. *So astonishingly good.*

God. I was ready to do it all over again.

Nick was still inside me, and I grasped his hips and rocked my body into his, making him grunt out a moan.

"You're still so hard," I said into his cheek, threading my fingers through his messy curls, adoring how vulnerable he looked in this moment—how much this pulled-in-all-directions, publicly owned Tudor king felt like he belonged only to me. Like Mary, Queen of Scots herself could stroll through the door right now, staking a claim for the throne of England, and Nick might turn around and say: *Sorry, I'm fucking my wife right now. Could you come back later?*

I smirked at the ridiculous thought, and Nick gave me a questioning look, but I didn't explain. Right now, I needed to feel him come undone for me the way I had for him.

"What other positions can you show me?" I asked brazenly, already suspecting I knew the more common ones, but I wanted to see what Nick liked.

His brows lifted a little as he rolled his hips against mine again until he was buried inside me to the hilt, exactly where I wanted him to stay. I bit back a moan.

"We did once speak of you riding me like a steed," he said in a breathless voice, "or I admit that I would very much like to see you on your hands and knees."

That last part made his pupils darken, and while I had every intention of climbing over Nick's thighs and bringing him to ruin beneath me, I sensed that the second offer held particular appeal to him right now.

"I *am* going to ride you like a steed," I promised, shifting beneath him until our bodies separated. "But maybe we should save that for another room in the manor."

I edged in front of him and rose up to my knees and elbows, curving my back as Nick's eyes zeroed in on my exposed core. Any embarrassment I might've felt evaporated at the sound he made as he moved close behind me and spread me open. A heartbeat later, his soft tongue sank inside my core as he grunted out a sound of need that vibrated through me.

Oh God, if it's going to be like this all the time, I don't see why I could ever leave this bed.

Nick buried his tongue inside me as far as it would go, humming a murmur of satisfaction before he moved to wash his tongue over my most sensitive spot, sucking and swirling like this was his last meal on earth.

After I came again, this time into his hot mouth, he smacked a hand down on my ass and positioned himself behind me, plunging himself inside and filling me up.

I cried out with pleasure as he began driving himself into me again, lifting one of his knees so he could push deeper in. He took me so hard that the bedframe banged against the wall with each thrust, my throat crying his name while his sexy grunts made me push my ass against him like I couldn't get enough.

When I thought I might collapse from the relentless ecstasy, he stopped to gently guide me around by my shoulders, flipping me back over so I was laying down and gazing up at him, panting.

"I want to see you," he said softly and scooped me up until I was in a seated position with my legs folded around his hips. He pressed all the way into me again, my body becoming boneless as he began more hard thrusts, his face flushed with arousal, his beautiful chest glistening with sweat.

With a sharp groan, he tightened his grip on my hips and then pulled out of me with the world's hottest look on his face, spurting his hot liquid over my lower stomach. It was far from a foolproof way to avoid pregnancy, but it was all we had to go with without the modern inventions of birth control or condoms.

After he'd gently cleaned me up with a cloth from the buffet table, we fell into the mattress together, and he wrapped his arms and legs around me, whispering breathless words of love into my ear that made my heart pound against my ribs.

Now that I'd been this close to Nick, the thought of being parted from him sent a sharp stab to my chest. I clutched him tighter like he might vanish into thin air if I didn't.

And when we both drifted off into an exhausted sleep only to wake several hours later with his arousal digging into me from behind, we were at it again. This time, Nick pinned me to the mattress with his hand braced on the wall behind me, and then I climbed over the top of him and practiced riding him to ruin like I'd promised.

I still couldn't believe I had a lifetime of this ahead of me. I couldn't imagine ever tiring of this feeling…of *him*.

After months of uncertainty in Tudor England, I'd finally come home.

The few times I'd woken up beside Nick in this century, he'd almost always disappeared before dawn. The next morning, however, there was no squawk of the cockerels, and the light filtering through the leaded window held no golden tinge. It was late, and the king still lay beside me, his bare skin tangled up in linen sheets. He stirred at my movements, and I froze so he could sleep longer, but his eyes had already fluttered open.

He folded an arm behind his head and stared at me, a fusion of love and heat flaring in his sleepy eyes.

"Good morrow to you," he said huskily, his smile giving my heart a little tug.

I crawled over the top of him until I had my palms pressed to the mattress on either side of his chest. "Good morning, my sexy husband."

Dimples deepened in his cheeks as he smiled. "*Sexy*," he repeated, practicing another word I'd taught him last night.

His palm began a trail down the curve of my side, his eyes following the path. His fingers paused at my hip, squeezing.

"Yes, that is a word I believe I am going to use on you most often," he said, shifting his weight beneath me until our pelvises aligned. A whimper rumbled out of me as I felt how hard he was already, my body heat rising to a thousand degrees as I rolled my hips up and down his beautiful length.

After he'd made wild and uninhibited love to me again, we helped each other dress in our complicated outfits because I wanted to preserve our time alone, and ate a leisurely breakfast of manchet bread rolls, hard cheeses, and stewed fruits in the privacy of the bedchamber. Thomas Grey, Bishop Winchester, and my ladies had already departed Robin House to give us some space, and, at last, Nick had nowhere more important to be but with me. It felt like heaven.

Given how short the days had become, he suggested a walk outside while the sun was still high. With plain-clothes guards trailing us, we set off past the jumble of rose bushes becoming dormant for the winter and down the slope of wild lavender. Nick had battered me so hard last night and this morning that I had to walk on a slight angle to appease the burning between my legs. When I told him why I was walking funnily and insisted I was perfectly fine, his initial concern morphed into a smug smirk that suggested he was pretty damn pleased with himself.

And I couldn't blame him. As sore as I was, I already ached for more.

We reached the clearing where we'd once shared a picnic and nervous glances during my first days in Tudor England, pausing to take in that memory with our arms entwined. And now we were back here as a married couple, and I was set to become the Queen of England. It was almost too insane to get my head around.

The wind whispered at us through the fruit trees as we strolled farther from the house, coming to the curve of a small hill. We hiked to the top, catching our breath as we took in the bird's eye view of a honey-toned meadow interrupted by a village that was too small to be walled. In the distance, a handful of residents milled about in their veggie gardens like toy figurines. A girl in a white coif tilted her face up toward us.

I instinctively stepped backward. "Do you know that village?" I asked Nick.

He was snapping pink wildflowers off at the stems. "The hamlet? They are all about the place. Hardly more than farms and cottages." He presented me with a bundle of fuchsia blooms. "For my queen, so entirely edible."

I brought the fragrant petals to my nose, feeling my flushed smile stretch my cheeks. *Gah, it's still so long until bedtime.*

"Shall we make our return?" he offered, blinking at me with his bed eyes that I didn't have a hope of resisting. "I am feeling rather in need of rest, my beautiful wife."

I switched the flowers to my opposite hand so I could thread my fingers with his and tug him down the hill. "I'm also beat from all this walking," I said. "I could use a lie down." We headed back toward the house with flutters of anticipation that made my legs weak.

The moment we rounded the rear courtyard garden, Nick grabbed me by the arm and kicked open the door of the small guest cabin, pulling me inside.

"What the—" I barely got out before he pinned me against the door with his hips and slammed his mouth against mine. He sighed into my mouth as he stroked his tongue over my own in a deep, lush kiss that was full of insatiable hunger. While a pair of guards hovered somewhere on the other side of the door, chatting about a troublesome horse, Nick and I stood there making out like wild animals, our fingers fisting each other's hair, our tongues licking, swirling, and sucking like we couldn't get enough.

Through the fabric of our clothes, Nick grinded his solid ridge against my throbbing core before bunching the satin at the back of my kirtle and pulling it tightly until my hardened nipples pressed through the fabric. His heavy eyes locked there as his fingers began circling, tweaking, and rubbing the peaks, getting them to a place where they were so erect through the fabric that I may as well have been naked.

"I want to eat you up," he said roughly, my body already so overcome that my knees nearly gave out.

Nick fumbled with the laces on the sides of my dress until it was loose enough for him to free my breasts, pulling them out into the open air while the rest of me remained covered. I was so aroused that I was nearly seeing double as he drew one of my nipples toward his starved mouth. He wrapped his lips around the tight little bud and sucked it before he moved to the other one and dragged his tongue over it until it glistened wet.

A moan erupted from my lips, and Nick's eyes flashed up to mine, delivering a message that we needed to keep quiet with the guards outside. At this point, I'd have to bite down on my knuckles to stay silent if he kept working his mouth over me like this.

He rose back to his full height while palming my breasts needily, and my gaze dropped to the shape of his thick erection that strained against his pants. I couldn't take my eyes off the outline, remembering how perfect he was; how incredible he felt inside me.

He sealed his lips over mine again, and I cupped his hardness over the leather that was stretched tightly over it. He sucked in a sharp breath as I gripped him. After I rubbed my palm up and down him several times, his impatient hands untied his pants before digging for my skirts and hitching them up.

He kicked my legs apart with his knees and stepped between my legs, pinning my arms against the door over my head.

"You must remain silent, my girl," he ordered, and tugged my coif-underwear to the side with his other hand before burying his thick heat all the way inside me.

I cried out with pleasure, and the murmuring of the guards outside suddenly stopped.

Nick shot me a look that only made me want to kiss the disapproving expression off his face, but before I could take his lips with mine, he pressed his warm palm over my mouth.

"Those sexy sounds you make are for me, not for my guards," he said into my ear as he dragged his hips backward and smacked them harder against me, each deep thrust setting off a fireball inside my core. The white-hot pleasure was indescribable as his movements became wilder, his hand over my mouth covering my moans as he pounded me against the door until my feet were lifting off the floor.

A tightening pressure grew inside me, winding itself into an unbearable knot of tension that would soon snap as he kept hitting that one spot over and over. He was just so hard and deep, but most of all, the reason why I'd fallen into this all-consuming dreamland was because it was *Nick* doing this. It was his electric touch, his shaky breaths, his irresistible scent, his thumping heartbeat that toppled me over the edge.

Within minutes, my whole body clenched and I cried out into the palm of his hand, my walls clamping around him. Soon after, Nick was groaning and spilling his hot release into his hand as his body fell against mine, our hearts exploding into each other's chests.

Later that afternoon, I sat wiping off my makeup with a damp cloth, buzzing with happiness. While Bridget and Lucinda had become my beloved girl crew, I didn't ache to have them back in my company at all times with little privacy. Instead, I imagined Nick and I never returning to the palace at all, just living out our lives at Robin House while I learned how to grow vegetables like the villagers from the hamlet and he tended to his roses. *This* was what I came back for. This was the life I craved with Nick.

He dropped to one knee behind me, swiping my hair to the side. The warm press of his lips to my neck sent a ripple of goosebumps across my skin. "We must soon determine your royal badge," he said. "I propose a swan."

I reached back to bury my fingers in the soft curls of his hair. "A bit graceful for me, don't you think? Do you really see me as a delicate little swan?" I turned my face to his and raised my brows.

"An elephant?" he offered, sliding into a chair beside mine and pulling it so close that my thighs slid between his.

I whacked his arm. I'd actually been thinking about this.

"A phoenix," I replied. "The bird that rises from its ashes to be born again. A bird that begins a new life."

His tender smile fired another love-dart into my chest.

"A phoenix is fitting." The soft tips of his fingers stroked my forearm like he couldn't help but keep touching me. "We must also settle upon your household, your patronages, your council. Do you enjoy your ladies? We will appoint them in greater numbers."

A mild-mannered knock tapped the door.

Nick rose to his full, imposing height. "Come," he said.

A skinny attendant with acne pustules bowed from the doorway. "Your Majesty, a messenger brings urgent news."

Nick's jaw tightened. "What news?"

When the kid glanced at me and hesitated, Nick commanded, "Speak, boy!"

"The Duke of Norfolk has escaped capture by night and is believed to have made for Dover, Your Majesty," he stumbled. "There is word the duke is planning a revolt on the grounds of your betrothal to the Lady Pembroke."

Nick grabbed the boy by his stiff collar. I cried out, scratching at Nick's arm to let go. He obliged, and the kid dropped to the floorboards.

Nick leaned over him, speaking through his teeth. "The Duke of Norfolk has been stripped of such title. On pain of death, you will refer to his person only as Henry Howard, the traitor."

The boy hunched forward and begged for forgiveness, his bony shoulders shaking.

"Make ready the horses and coaches to return to Hampton Court at once," the king snapped at him. The poor kid couldn't get out the door fast enough.

Nick dropped back into the chair, catching his head in his hands.

My voice wavered with both shock and guilt. "You didn't kill him," I said, the memory crystallizing. "I accused you of executing Norfolk and lying to me about it, but you didn't. You did send him away…I'm so sorry."

Nick's chest swelled with tense breaths. "That is true. I killed him not, Emmie, but I should have. For now, that traitor Henry Howard is intending to kill us."

16

NICK AND I RODE BACK TO HAMPTON COURT PALACE AT FIRST LIGHT, leaving the cherished privacy we'd shared at Robin House behind in a cloud of dust. Our honeymoon was officially over now that a disgraced former duke was raising an army to bring us down.

From the moment we returned to court, the king disappeared into secretive council meetings for hours on end. When I did get to see him, I expected the dark moods and outbursts that were his trademark in tough times. Instead, however, he adorned me with jewels and gifts, spoiled me with fancy feasts, staged private performances in my chambers, and issued a wedding announcement across the country. While behind the scenes Nick may have sent soldiers to find Henry Howard —the man formerly known as the Duke of Norfolk—publicly, he was playing every kingly card he had, flaunting his wealth and power to me so I would feel protected rather than afraid. I didn't want to muddle things further by telling him that all I needed to feel safe was to have him close to me.

But instead of privacy and seclusion, the king had put every aspect of our public life on fast-forward. He ordered the commissioners in charge of my coronation to work quickly, and my crowning as queen was scheduled for the first week of December in a flurry of dress fittings, practice ceremonies, and etiquette coaching. I missed Alice even more, who would've kept me calm with her wry jokes and explanations of things I didn't understand. As pleased as we all were for her to be reunited with her mom, it wasn't just me who felt the pinch of her absence. Francis Beaumont didn't dance with anyone at the court feasts, and his usual wayward spirit had simmered, which I suspected was also because Nick had gone ahead with our wedding, despite Francis's misgivings. Fortunately for the both of us, a letter soon arrived from Alice that announced she'd be back at court in time for the coronation. *Yes!*

Whether Kit would join the festivities, however, was another battle between Nick and me.

"She didn't even get to come to our wedding," I pleaded to him while we were wrapped up together in his silky bedsheets, my head nestled against his bare chest.

His pause made it clear that his sister traveling was still a sore point. "The roads are too dangerous for the princess to travel such a distance, especially with that traitor about. You know that I had wished to wait for a summer coronation, but now that Henry Howard intends to turn the people against us and bring my kingdom to bloodshed, we must delay no longer. As it is God's will, I will see my wife become queen, and I will thereafter crush that spawn of the devil and make an example of him."

I made a disappointed face at the paneled wall while Nick ran his fingers through my hair, hating the idea of Kit missing out on the thrills of the coronation that were right up her street. Still, I had to face that Nick was the expert on the safety of princesses who'd once been destined to die. Kit and I would just have to share a private celebration when I could return to Kenilworth. I planned to ask Nick if we could spend the next summer there—just us and Kit. I couldn't think of a better newlywed vacation.

December arrived, bringing fewer sunlight hours and a cloudy coolness that promised snow. Nick's distracted mood made it clear that Norfolk was still at large, yet the king remained defiant about the coronation plans. In keeping with tradition, we were to spend the night before the ceremony at the Tower of London. Our flotilla of barges sailed along the curvy Thames, carrying hundreds of atten-dants, courtiers, ladies, and guards. It took nearly a day for us to reach the Tower's sloshing water gate, where I had to hide my nose in my velvet sleeve to obscure the stench of fish and sewage.

We were to lodge in the medieval tower of St. Thomas that over-looked the river, its stained-glass windows offering glimpses of the slanted red roofs atop London Bridge. I didn't want to leave the safety of the spacious bedchamber with its own chapel, and it dawned on me just how nervous I was about the coronation ceremony. I would've swapped the pomp and splendor for the intimacy of our simple wedding a thousand times over, but Nick's unwavering enthusiasm pacified my bursts of blind panic.

The city's curfew bells clanged at dusk. The blacksmiths and carpenters halted their hammering in the alleyways below, and an eerie, silent, blackness descended over London. I had every intention of getting in a good sleep before the ceremony, but when Nick snug-gled into me from behind, I arched my back and pressed myself against his swelling length, and it was game over. He reached for my jaw and turned my face so he could take my lips with his, and more than an hour later, my hands were braced to the lattice windowpanes while he drove himself into me from behind with his fingers biting into my hips and moans erupting from my mouth. Now that Nick had shown me what married couples could do in Tudor England, I couldn't get enough of him, like I had a permanently desperate need that only he could fulfill.

The few hours of sleep I managed were surprisingly sound despite my rising panic about the coronation, and we both rose early to take morning prayers in our chapel. After a lingering kiss goodbye, Nick slipped away to prepare for the big day in his own chambers, and my heart rate skyrocketed again with nervous jitters.

Lucinda and Bridget arrived after breakfast, sending my squeals of relief bouncing across the brightly colored tile floor.

"Mistress Grey has been caught up on the roads," Bridget said with an apologetic grimace, sending my stomach into free-fall. I'd have to cope with all this pageantry without Alice after all.

But my spirits lifted again as Bridget and Lucinda dressed me for the ceremony in an outfit too beautiful to be believed. My scarlet-red kirtle and stomacher were stitched with sapphires amid golden wing patterns that broadened as they descended to the floor. The gown draped over the top was made entirely of snow-white fur. It made me ill to think about what animals may have been slaughtered to construct the silky cloak, but it would at least keep me warm. My hair hung loose in combed waves, the top of my head left bare in readiness for my crown. The final touches were a sash woven entirely from white diamonds, plus the jewels of the Queens of England which Nick had given me when he proposed to me—a magnificent necklace of glittering blue diamonds with matching earrings.

When I faced the full-length mirror that Nick had installed for the occasion, I appreciated why Bridget and Lucinda were blushing at me like I was some sort of magical creature. I was the living image of a glorious Tudor queen, missing only my crown and scepter. *You go, girl.*

The intense day that ensued was mostly a blur to me. Six of Nick's most loyal courtiers, including Francis Beaumont, led me on foot to Westminster Abbey beneath a mobile canopy of purple velvet fringed with gold. We kept to the broader streets, but the surrounding alley-ways with their narrow timber-framed buildings and overhanging balconies were jammed with chanting spectators. When we reached the gothic arches of Westminster Abbey, I could barely feel my face, but I wasn't sure if it was because of the sharp wind off the river or the nerves attacking my gut. The constant clanging of bells from the city parishes amid the grimy city smells were overwhelming my senses, and I began to feel suffocated and weak at the knees. By the time I stood inside the abbey before the Archbishop of Canterbury, I was ready to puke all over his fancy robes. But one look at Nick when he strode into my view in full Tudor regalia, a proud smile echoing the glimmer in his eyes, and I stabilized.

You can do this, Emmie Tudor.

The ceremony unfolded precisely as we'd practiced, except a thousand times faster. Before the High Altar, the Archbishop of Canterbury bestowed on me a ceremonial crown, an ornamental mace, and a scepter. Hymns were sung, and then it was over in the blink of an eye. I was officially the Queen of England and would go down in history as a member of the Tudor dynasty. *Take that, Henry Howard, and your backstabbing gang of conspirators. You can all bite me.*

The king took my hand, and we emerged from the abbey into blinding light and a full-fledged street party. My protective husband sat beside me in a golden chariot, and the commoners cheered—some even wept—at the sight of him. The coronation parade was to lead us down to Westminster Pier, where a feast would be held aboard the royal barges because there hadn't been enough time to spruce up Westminster Hall.

Our glimmering, sunlit chariot moved slowly to the harmonies of a walking choir, its gentle volume swallowed by the rising chants of the crowds. A gigantic sculpture of a rising phoenix loomed over a moving constellation of fire-breathing dragon puppets, acrobats, and dancers with scarves and bells tied to their limbs. I'd never seen anything more spectacular or more expensive, and I tried to put the impoverished peasants we'd seen on progress out of my mind.

Nick snapped at a string of grimy-faced men standing without caps on their heads—a sign of disrespect to the new queen. As we continued past a classical fountain that poured wine, a tall man with an ostrich feather in his hat appeared in the swarm of spectators, and I stretched my neck to make him out. I could've sworn it was Henry Howard glaring right at me. Another guy with a face like thunder looked just like Viscount Hereford, the stuck-up nobleman who Nick had once expelled from his court. As we passed the men, however, I realized my eyes were playing tricks on me—seeing monsters that weren't there. As our chariot tilted toward the pier, a rush of bodies chased us down the hill. By the time we'd reached a standstill beside the stone water gate, I was clambering to get out of the chariot and away from the stifling crowds. There were too many of them.

Guards jostled with forceful revelers as I stumbled down the carriage steps in my ridiculously oversized farthingale. I stepped forward and jerked to a violent halt. My dress was caught on something. I spun to face a mob of wild-faced spectators, their grubby hands clinging to my skirt folds, preventing me from moving.

"What are you doing? Let go!" I cried in shock, but there was too much noise, too many fingers clawing at me. I couldn't see Nick, but I heard him shouting my name. The more the guards pushed to get through to me, the more the wall of strangers pulled at my skirts until I was crushed into a pit of deafening blackness.

My heart was beating a hole through my chest, and I couldn't breathe through the web of bodies closing in on me. My arms, flailing in panic, were seized and ripped upward, nearly popping from their sockets. My legs and shoulders were being violently tugged in all directions, and I screamed in pain until my throat was raw. I was about to be dragged through the streets of London and torn apart, limb-by-limb! I had to fight, but there were too many grabbing hands, before an incredible source of power gripped me and hoisted me toward the sky. Two beefy guards had got hold of me and were carrying me out of the swarm like a crowd-surfer, a dense blanket of clouds swinging over my head. Nick was still yelling behind me—at whom, I couldn't tell—before I was dropped onto a bundle of plush cushions. In seconds, the clawing fingers had vanished.

"Make haste!" roared the irate voice of Francis Beaumont, and the ground beneath us glided forward with two sturdy arms holding me steady.

"All is well now," Nick whispered soothingly into my ear. I clutched him tightly like a terrified cat, whimpering.

"What happened?" I said, orienting myself so I could sit upright. We were among a pile of silk cushions inside the cabin on the king's royal barge.

"The people set upon you," Nick said grimly. "This is why I shun the city as I would the plague. The people love you so greatly that they could have suffocated you for it." He nuzzled his cheek into mine. "Dear God, if something had happened to you."

Nicholas the Ironheart would split this country apart. That's what would happen.

I gripped my quivering knees, finding a tear in the delicate fabric of my gown. The men and women who'd mobbed me hadn't looked in love with me. I didn't want to break it to Nick that their expressions had held nothing but hatred. Just because I'd come around on the concept of Emmie Grace, Tudor Queen, didn't mean the rest of the country had.

Through the curtains, Francis Beaumont was speaking gravely with the king's security team. I shut my eyes and curled into my new husband, fighting to forget the feeling of a thousand enraged fingers on my skin. We were supposed to enjoy the coronation feast on the river outside Westminster, but our barge continued gliding farther from London. Cannons blasted salutes as we passed with our procession of boats drifting close behind. Nick announced that the coronation feast was to move closer to Hampton Court Palace, which subdued my thumping heart. It'd be safer and quieter there.

The wharves of greater London were soon replaced with fishing villages and lush parklands. The oarsmen swept the murky water as we coasted along the river's edge to the cries of swooping birds finding a home for the night. Trying to forget the nightmare at the water gate, I watched a heron land on a grassy river island, its beak digging into its wing. By the time we made our way around the windy bend to Hampton Court Palace, the sky had blackened.

"We shall feast here," Nick commanded, and our fleet of barges formed a line outside the palace. A crewmember dropped anchor, and a slow barge three times the size of ours drew up beside us, holding feasting tables that were hurriedly being checked and redressed. Sweet herbs were lit to mask the river smells as we climbed on board.

A second boat delivered the senior nobles to the feasting barge, as well as Bridget and Lucinda, who were freaking out about the pandemonium at the pier. Nick left us alone so they could cheer me up, and we sipped wine inside the barge's cabin while a musician gently strummed his lute. Already, I felt the terror of the mob at Westminster withdrawing from my bones.

Through the cabin window, I spotted a girl in a grape-colored gown standing at the Hampton Court Palace water gate, her waist-length, wavy hair making me sit higher on the cushion. She said something to a guard and pointed at our barge.

"That's Alice; she's here!" I cried, jumping to my feet. I leaned out of the open window, waving, but Alice didn't see. When she climbed into a small boat that began rowing to the furthest barge containing the dullest nobles, I cupped my hands around my lips and called out to her.

"What in the devil?" Nick said, pushing through the curtain. When I explained, he ordered his attendants to retrieve Mistress Grey and make her a place setting on the king's feasting barge.

"She'll sit beside me," I instructed, trying out my new authority. Nobody dared argue with me.

Minutes later, Alice climbed aboard, grinning with a healthy glow. She flew toward me but then remembered herself and bowed, praising me as her new queen. Francis Beaumont tipped his tousled curls to her in greeting, and a deep blush coated her cheeks.

"Can you believe it: I left Northamptonshire a week past, but we were stranded in Aylesbury," Alice moaned. "We rode so hard that one of the horses came up lame, and we had to acquire a new one." She gave both Bridget and Lucinda an energetic hug.

Grateful for the heat of the torches in the chilly night air, I caught up with Alice over a sprawling supper of roasted lamb, pheasant, venison, peacock, swan, dolphin, and seal.

As we nibbled on edible marzipan phoenixes with gold wings dressed in rose petals, Alice updated me on her mom. She said that Susanna Grey recognized her former home and appeared happy to be reunited with Sir Thomas, but there was a change in her. Susanna had become frail and unable to look after herself properly. My mind tore back to Massachusetts, where Susanna—as Jane Stuart—had lived in a state of helpless confusion. Alice trembled a little as she asked if her sister Violet could stay in Northamptonshire and care for her mother. Her smile returned when she said there was also a man of three-and-forty years, a Mister William Cornwallis, who had proposed to marry Violet.

"Of course—if Lottie is happy with that, then so am I," I said, licking cream off my spoon. "I'll miss having her around, though. She's a sweetheart."

Alice's knee bounced nervously. "I may also wish to return to Northamptonshire to find a husband so I may be of more help to my household."

I nearly coughed up a coral-colored rose petal. The Alice I knew had mostly shunned the idea of her own marriage. Plus, how would I pull off my new job of Queen of England without her?

She couldn't look at me. "I wish not to leave your household, my lady. However, I remain but a maiden, and if I find not a husband, I fear that I may end up forever dependent on my sister. If any ill should befall her, I could become destitute and as frantic as my mother has become."

"I would never let that happen," I said, sensing the blue diamonds weighing down my earlobes that could probably buy Alice her own house and then some. She had helped me so much already; I would gladly share everything I had with her.

Francis had turned silent beside the king, and I could tell that he was listening. Now if he would just *do* something about it.

A glittering water pageant abruptly commenced in front of our barge, shutting down the conversation. An artificial island that was tied to the wharf erupted in a shower of fireworks, before entertainers dressed as mermaids dived off the island to perform a synchronized swimming dance with coordinated tails flapping. Before they could catch hypothermia, the swimmers returned to shore, and dancers in glittering unicorn costumes began prancing across the island. A breathtaking performance of sung verses followed, before a 'wild man' actor draped with moss and ivy dramatically professed his love to a nymph played by a young man, who suggestively unwrapped his greenery to reveal a suave knight. It was hard to believe that, only a few short hours earlier, a hysterical mob had nearly ripped me to pieces. Now, beneath a blanket of stars and surrounded by people I loved, I was having the best night of my life.

When the pageant ended in a second spray of fireworks, Nick rose to his feet, cueing the courtiers to follow. "Let us dance!" he said. "May I present your queen, Emmeline of England!"

Cheers resounded as Nick took my hand, leading me to a small space in the heart of the barge. Thank goodness for the bit of wine I'd had because he launched me into the volta without a heads-up, stepping and hopping to the lively music. He gripped my waist and lifted me over his hip, and a thrill shook through me that rippled through the audience.

When the song ended, Lord and Lady Ascot were the next couple to dance, followed by Lord and Lady Snell, who were clearly keen to upstage them before the king. Nick and I stood aside with his arm curled around me, politely watching the dances unfold. I glanced over at Alice and Francis. They both sat at the head table like statues, neither looking at the other.

Oh, for fuck's sake.

"The Earl of Warwick and Mistress Alice Grey!" I cried out, enlivened by the wine I'd had. Alice's mouth dropped open, and Francis shot to his feet, his olive skin turning pink.

"Naughty girl," Nick chuckled against my ear as Francis led Alice off the dais and into the dance zone. She shot me a 'you're in trouble' look as they passed by, but she couldn't hide her smile. Francis and Alice laced their fingers and hopped together before he grasped her waist and spun her high in the air. Each time they repeated the move, their bodies pressed closer together, their dark eyes fusing. I leaned closer into Nick, and he rubbed his jaw against my hair. Love was blooming, and it wasn't just ours.

The song ended too soon, and Francis folded into an elegant bow like Alice was the new queen. I adored every second of it. Nick announced a change to a more subdued tune, and the harpist took over. The metallic glitter was the perfect backdrop to gentle chatter as Nick pulled out his pocket watch. I could tell he was getting tired, and after the way he'd exhausted himself last night—and me—over the desk and against the window—I couldn't blame him.

When we all returned to our seats to formally conclude the night, Francis leaned close to Nick. "Majesty, may I share a short speech?" he asked softly. Nick frowned with confusion, and Francis dropped his voice to a level I couldn't hear.

After the king whispered his response, the earl rose and stood before Alice, speaking quietly. "Mistress Grey, may I inquire whether you are in need of the privy at present?"

Privy was the Tudor word for bathroom, and the question was weird. Why would he ask her that in public?

"I beg your pardon?" she replied, her voice taking on an edge.

"The privy...a lesson on how to hunt without every error under the sun...another sudden departure to God-knows-where...I mean to know if I may have your full attention for a moment?"

Alice glanced at me, jaw open. "Lord Warwick, does taking no heed of your tedious questions pass as an activity?"

Francis just breathed a laugh, looking more than handsome as he strutted to the center of the barge, rubbing the heels of his palms together.

"Gentlemen and ladies of the court, the King's Majesty has agreed that I may have your attention on a matter of great importance!"

Nick snorted lightly beside me.

"Good God, what is he doing?" said Alice.

Francis wavered on his feet, tipsy but coherent. "This night, I wish to honor a lady of true eminence." Every guest on the barge glanced over at me. "I believe it makes me more of a man, and not less, to say that there are certain ladies I cannot bear to live without," the earl continued. "This day, we celebrate the Queens of England!" The guests cheered and raised their glasses. I could feel Alice beaming at me. Nick placed his warm hand over mine and squeezed my fingers.

Francis kept going, his natural charisma holding the barge's attention. "For me, the queen of my person—and my heart—may be slow to believe, but I beseech her to understand why my mouth can be so shy to speak when my heart is in such a roar. Our gracious Majesty has awarded me his blessing to speak it now, so I may show mercy on my soul and share what I can no longer burden with the weight of silence."

When Francis approached Alice and dropped to one knee, we all gasped, Alice loudest of all.

He gazed up at her, affection lighting up his eyes. "Mistress Alice Grey, I cannot pleasure in anything anymore without the hope of your love. For you have mine—above all things—you have my love. Dearest lady, would you do me the honor of becoming my wife? I beseech you, for my heart can hide no longer from what is plainly true."

A rush of whispers broke out; it was unthinkable to steal the king's glory at such an event. But Nick looked anything but bent out of shape and threw his best mate a supportive smirk. I wasn't sure I was breathing.

Time slowed as Alice Grey stared down at Francis Beaumont, his eyes blinking up into hers while his chest rose and fell with nervous breaths. The electricity between them could've powered a kingdom.

In one swift step, Alice stood up and came to my side, crouching to whisper in my ear. "Emmie, may I have your permission to accept? It would mean I could remain in your service, which would greatly please me."

I wanted to shake her but in a good way. Silence swept the barge as I replied under my breath. "First of all—*hell yes.* Secondly, you'll never have to ask my permission for anything that makes you happy... ever. That's not how things are going to be between you and me. Got it?"

Her moist eyes gleamed at mine before she hitched her skirts so she could descend the dais to the trembling Francis. Alice pressed a petite hand to the cherry-colored lining of his gray coat—a scandalous but exhilarating move in Tudor England—and slid her palm up to his ruffled collar, sinking her fingers into the black curls of his hair to cup the back of his neck. Francis sighed as Alice pulled him close and kissed him with a conservative sweetness before the king, but one fueled by visible longing.

When their lips separated, Alice whispered in Francis's ear. His smile was teary.

"The lady agrees!" he cried, and the barge roared with cheers. The love scene before me blurred through the tears that skimmed my cheeks. Nick flicked a hand to cue the harpist again, and a hum of contented chatter fell over the barge. The boats behind us glittered with lit candles, none of them allowed to return to shore before the king.

Nick let Francis and Alice share some time alone in the secluded cabin, passing the minutes by slipping his hand beneath my skirts under the table and rubbing gentle but firm circles into my inner thigh with his thumb. When his fingers drifted higher and I was just about keeling over with arousal, he grunted a sexy laugh under his breath and commanded the boatmen to have us returned to the palace.

We climbed aboard the royal barge, which made a sluggish turn toward shore, commencing its glide. I dashed closer to Alice and wrapped my arms around her with a squeal. Francis stood back with the Lord Chancellor, still on duty as the king's right hand, but he couldn't stop smiling despite the chancellor's dull tone. I hoped that maybe the genuine love between Nick and I had inspired Francis in some way, despite his early reservations about us.

Our barge rocked as the tip grazed the water gate. Nick gripped my elbow to keep me steady.

"His Majesty, the King!" cried a guard on the platform. Nick and I took a step forward, and a whiz of wind exploded past my ear.

I grabbed the soft folds of skin there. "What was that?" I said, but was cut off by loud yells.

"Duck! Save the king!"

A sudden force tackled me to the ground. I screamed in shock, my chin banging against planks of wood. Fingers clawed at me to roll me over, and I spun into Nick's shaking arms. Shouts and screams tore through the air above me.

"We are being ambushed," Nick hissed as my eyes searched through the wall of black-leather boots surrounding us.

"Stay back!" a guard shouted above us. "Protect the king!"

Two more whizzes sounded, followed by a thud. A woman shrieked, and a heavy weight dropped onto my leg, nearly crushing it. I cried out, but my calf was pinned.

"Every man down!" another guard cried, and bunches of fabric sank over boots and heels as people crouched all around us. Nick kept my torso pulled tightly against his.

The barge fell silent, amplifying the sloshing of waves against the side as our boat rocked in the water. Male voices bellowed in the distance. Footsteps rushed toward us and then stilled before the thwicks of releasing arrows began in fast sequence. Nick gripped me tighter.

Endless minutes later, boots thundered closer to the wharf and voices shouted, briefing our guards that the assassins had been apprehended. The guards gave the all-clear for the king to rise within a funnel of men that offered a complete circle of protection.

"Is everyone okay?" I said hoarsely as Nick helped me up and shoved away a guard who tried to touch me. My chin stung, and my lower leg ached.

"We must make haste," Nick said, wiping my chin with his sleeve. The damp spot hurt, confirming that I was bleeding. The barrier of guards escorting us off the barge made it impossible to see, but a woman moaned behind me, and a commotion of people tried to help her.

A second later, Francis's unmistakable voice cried out. "No, no, *no!* By God's grace, no—I pray you!"

I spun around with my heart in my mouth. "Where's Alice?" I said to Nick.

"Make haste!" he said again, pulling me close as we climbed onto the landing stage. The king appeared unscathed, but his eyes flamed bright green with a blinding rage that I'd rarely seen.

A coach waited on the road behind the royal water gate. Guards with crossbows sat poised inside each window as Nick and I were speedily ushered onto the coach's opposite bench. Perhaps walking up the slope to the palace would be too dangerous.

"Was someone hurt?" I said through the bile in my throat as I angled to see past the guards. People were still huddled over someone on board the barge.

"Who took the arrow?" Nick snapped at a page standing outside the coach window.

"I believe it was Mistress Alice Grey, Your Majesty," the boy said, his crooked teeth chattering. "I saw the arrow strike the lady in the chest."

The noise that blasted from my lips sounded inhuman. Nick took me in his arms, holding me tightly as I clutched the edge of his cloak and howled into his side.

17

I was trapped inside a nightmare, worsened by the sickening jolts of our coach tearing across boggy ground. I sat up, absorbing the passing blur of tangled woodlands and farming cottages. Hampton Court Palace was long behind us.

"Where are we going?" I said in a choked voice.

"Robin House," Nick replied. "Hampton Court Palace is no fortress."

"But neither is Robin House."

"Few know of the manor's existence," he explained. "You will be more safe there."

I slumped against the window, watching the brave bowmen on horseback riding alongside our carriage, ready to strike at anyone following us.

Alice was shot in the chest with an arrow. Francis was wailing. Alice is dead.

My throat constricted until I couldn't breathe. There was only one reason the king's barge would be ambushed on the eve of his wife's coronation: no matter how well I played the part—no matter how much I tried to fit in—the people didn't want me as their queen. The same way the Duke of Norfolk, Thomas Grey, and even Francis Beaumont hadn't. Would this ever end?

"They are having bonfires in London," Nick said, pointing at a blush of light haloing the horizon. Given the circumstances, I was pretty sure they weren't fires of celebration.

The memory of Alice's face pushed into my mind again—her smitten smirk melting into Francis's—and another sob convulsed from my throat. Nick squeezed me tightly, his breaths deep and heavy.

We held each other until our coach slowed along the mossy pathway leading to Robin House. The guards rushed ahead to check over the manor and light the fires, but Nick and I barely saw them as he ushered me upstairs. We said nothing to each other...the creaking of floorboards as we moved was the only sound to penetrate the unbearable silence.

Not wanting to see anyone, we untied each other's intricate coronation outfits and climbed into the bed, grasping for each other's warmth. Exhaustion sent me to sleep almost immediately, but I soon woke to an inky-black sky through the leaded windowpanes. Nick lay sleeping, a peaceful silhouette of a troubled angel. I knew he loved me —he wouldn't have risked everything to be with me if he didn't. But for Alice to die before she was meant to...just because Nick and I had defied the path of history to be together? The thought tasted like bitter poison.

Emmie, what the hell have you done?

When the thoughts turned so cold that I shivered, I tugged the fur blankets to my chin and took slow, focused breaths so I didn't end up with an asthma attack on top of everything else. I twisted every which way to shake off the despair in my heart, but there was nowhere to hide from it.

By some miracle, I slept a while longer until my eyes twitched open to the relief of daylight and an empty mattress beside me. The memories of the night before resurfaced, and I dodged them by dozing for as long as I could. Before long, however, my mounting concern about my new husband's whereabouts pushed me out of bed.

After sluggishly dressing in the simplest kirtle I could find in the clothes chest, I headed downstairs. Nick was in the dining chamber, huddled over a hand-painted map with four of his privy councilors, but there was no sign of Francis Beaumont. He must've stayed with Alice while she...I swallowed a sob. One of the earls was addressing the king about war taxes, but when Nick saw me, he excused himself, guiding me outside to the courtyard.

"Are you well?" he said, surveying my injured chin. "I wished not to awaken you."

I tumbled into his arms, my stinging eyes locked on the patch of ground where, not long ago, we'd married each other with nothing but hope in our hearts.

As I struggled to speak, Nick pulled me to look at him. "Emmie, my lords brought word from Hampton Court. Mistress Grey is alive."

My hand flew to my heart as tears rushed to my eyes. "Are you serious?"

"The lady was shot in the shoulder, not the chest. Doctor Norris says she will be well." He exhaled like he still couldn't believe it. "Mistress Grey is being tended to at court, and Lord Warwick will remain with her."

The hopeless, heavy mass inside me suddenly exploded into a burning ball of light. I wanted to cry and scream and shout from the rooftops.

"When can we go back?" I said.

Nick cleared his throat. "You shall not return to the palace, my lady. However, I will take my leave from here this day."

I didn't know how to reply. Why would he leave me here? Nick took my stunned silence as an objection, and his worried eyes pleaded with me. "It is much too dangerous for your person to be at court during this time. My council has gathered news throughout the night." His cheeks reddened, his jaw tight. "Fires of high treason are blazing across London in protest of your coronation. Henry Howard's rebellion against you is spreading, and we believe he sent the archers to the coronation feast. Fear not, my lady; when I find that devil, I will see him dragged through the city alive, and then hung, drawn, and quartered, with his innards fed to the street dogs."

My stomach rolled with nausea. Hopefully, Norfolk didn't feed *me* to the dogs first.

"Just tell me what to do," I said, shaking away the terrifying image.

I couldn't believe this was happening—that people actually wanted me dead for marrying the king.

"You will remain at Robin House under close guard," Nick said firmly. "You may keep a maidservant, but no one must know you are here—not even your ladies; do you understand? Few know of this place, and there is nowhere more safe for you to be while I crush Howard and every traitor who seeks to defy his sovereign king."

He began detailing a play-by-play about arrests and burnings and beheadings…the words right out of a textbook about Nicholas the Ironheart. His hands balled into fists so tight that his knuckles whitened. I wanted to calm him down—to talk him out of this merciless spiral—but my lips wouldn't open. Not only did I need Nick to continue being honest with me, but I was no longer sure that kindness and mercy were the best ways to govern a sixteenth-century country. Norfolk's allies had just tried to assassinate me, nearly killing Alice in the process. I had to stop acting like we were living in the twenty-first century. If this fight came down to Henry Howard, the traitor, or Nicholas Tudor, the reigning King of England, I would support my husband, regardless of how much blood was spilled.

"Please be careful," I whispered, my body weak at the thought of losing him. For all I knew, harming the king was part of Henry Howard's plan to get back at me.

Nick caught the fear in my face and tried to hug it away, a tingling heat coursing through our connected bodies. When we parted, he twisted the blue-diamond ring off his finger and slid it onto my thumb.

"What are you doing?" I uttered.

He pressed his lips together, steadying himself. "My dearest love, it is time for you to make me a most important promise."

I froze, hanging on every word that Nick struggled to say.

"Emmie, if your life is in danger—at any moment—you will wear this ring and do everything in your power to use it," he choked out. "Wait not for me. Do you hear me? If your life is at stake, you will go home to your time without hesitation. I must have your word."

I couldn't grasp my whirring thoughts. The enchanted ring had acted strangely for so long now that I wasn't sure how many time travel trips were left in it. What if I did what Nick asked, and then I could never get back here to him? I'd made my choice—it was to stay here with Nick. We were married now, and I wasn't going anywhere.

A sheen of tears glazed his restless eyes as they searched mine.

"I don't want to use the ring any more without you," I said. "When I went back to my time to get Susanna Grey, the ring was struggling to work again. I woke up in Massachusetts, like, four times. Now that we're married...now that we've *been* together...I–I can't be that far away from you. We have to figure something else out."

He stepped forward, threading our hands together. "Let us then make one more vow. Should your life be at stake, you will use this ring to journey home without me. I beseech you to give me your word on that. But for any reason other, we will use this ring only together."

I squeezed his fingers. "Only *together*," I affirmed. "I'm never leaving you again unless it's to literally save my life."

"Only together," he repeated in a strained voice. "We will swear it."

We sealed the vow with a prolonged, distraught kiss, and I cried into his chest, dreading letting go.

Our goodbye was quick and heavy with despair. We couldn't even look at each other for fear of it being the last time we ever would.

Tears streamed down my face while I watched from the upstairs window as the man I loved more than anything in the world climbed aboard his coach. It careened away from the house in a fog of dust.

My back slid down the stone wall until my bottom hit the floorboards. I rested there for a while in a brokenhearted daze, listening to the reassuring sound of the guards' footsteps pacing the manor downstairs. A scary number of people wanted my head on a stick, and I was pretty sure that Robin House didn't have a panic room. I had to come up with a hiding place where I could fall asleep in case the assassins figured out where I was and stormed the house—if the enchanted ring even worked properly. I slid it onto my thumb and curled my fingers over the smooth stone.

So much had changed in a handful of months. I'd gone from arguing with Nick over my right to use the blue-diamond ring whenever I wanted to hating the idea of traveling to my time without him.

Things had become worse here than I could have imagined, but what mattered most to me now was that we stayed together.

Only together.

As long as Henry Howard doesn't jam Nick's head onto a pike and parade it through the city of London.

A descending curtain of dread sent me to my feet. I had to dig myself out of my grisly thoughts before they buried me alive. I moved to the cloudy standing mirror and sized up my appearance, straightening my lacy sleeves. After dragging an ivory comb through my knotted hair, I braided the unruly waves and pinned a hood over the top. Despite being under glorified house arrest, I was still the wife of the King of England.

My young maidservant Clemence entered with a buttery-smelling custard tart and a bowl of winter berries. I wanted her to stay and chat with me, but she didn't dare impose, and I was too slow to request it. The door shut behind her, and I ate in gloomy silence except for the soft slurps of my lips savoring creamed sugar.

Those sounds—alongside the clink of pewter plates, the thud of oak doors closing, and the shuffling boots of guards on patrol— became my life for the next few weeks. I stopped counting how long I'd been at Robin House after seven days because time was moving agonizingly slowly and keeping track only made it worse.

During our breathless farewell, Nick had explained that we couldn't write to each other and risk the letters being intercepted. He kept to his word, and no news came. Knowing nothing about his efforts to capture Henry Howard was like living in purgatory. One minute I'd be dusting the bookcase and imagining the former duke spearing Nick with a ten-foot sword; the next, I'd be perked up by a vision of my king in a parade of victory. Which one was it to be?

To release some of the nervous energy bubbling up inside me, I asked the chief guard, Joseph Blackburn, if I could jog along some of the wild pathways around the house if I took a bodyguard with me. He agreed with visible reluctance, and I set off in my leather boots down the slope to the birch trees and back again, with four plainclothes guards trailing me. On day two, a painful blister had formed where the knot of my garter held up my woolen hose. Without any gym shoes, I was going to have to make do with brisk walks instead of jogging. I fell into a favorite route that ended atop the grassy hill over-looking the hamlet, where chirping birds rollicked in the rustling trees. I'd sit there for a while and watch the villagers tending to their winter gardens, taken by the simplicity of their lives. I ached to go down there, not only to see a sixteenth-century farming settlement up close, but to feel less alone here. Aside from Clemence and the guards, I hadn't seen a human face in weeks.

When I asked Mister Blackburn if I could visit the village, he declined with a physical recoil. Later that night, I overheard him arguing with one of the younger guards. The kid warned Blackburn that blatantly refusing the queen's request could be a shortcut to the Tower of London—or worse—if the king learned of it. The next morning, Mister Blackburn apologized and offered to take me to the hamlet himself *if* I agreed to avoid the villagers, in case any of them had been in the city for my coronation—as unlikely as that was—and recognized me. Shadows circled his bloodshot eyes. The poor guy hadn't slept a wink over this thing.

I borrowed some clothes from a confused Clemence, noting the relief that blew across Mister Blackburn's face. No one would guess that I was the persecuted queen in a tawny woolen kirtle and a plain apron and coif. I wore no jewelry but kept the blue-diamond ring close to me, hiding it on my thumb inside a pair of woolen gloves.

Four guards hid on the hillside as Joseph Blackburn and I approached the village on horseback, disguised as father and daughter out for a ride. The hamlet was no more than a dirt path lined with single-story wattle-and-daub cottages with few windows. We tethered our horses to an iron ring in a wall and strolled down the dusty track on one side, clinging to the last strip of sunlight. A trio of grubby-faced girls in knitted dresses were feeding scraggly lettuce leaves to a goat beside the pigsty. When they saw us approaching, they scampered to hide behind a man tending to a crop of onions with a hoe.

Mister Blackburn's horse grunted from the wall a few feet behind us. The poor steed had trodden into a tangle of sheets hanging from a wooden frame. Joseph paced back to untwist the horse, apologizing to the farmer. The man stopped weeding and rested on the handle of his hoe, giving us a slight nod of greeting that also delivered a message: we were being watched, so we'd better not be here to start trouble.

Mister Blackburn moved us on, and we ambled past a pen of undersized sheep and a healthy bed of spinach and cabbage, before reaching what looked to be a small alehouse.

"Shall we make ready to return?" Blackburn said, chewing the inside of his lip.

The sight of a marking scratched into the wall beside the alehouse interrupted my response. It was the shape of a flower within a circle, which I'd seen before—carved into the cheeks of the witch Agnes Nightingale.

A man stumbled out of the alehouse holding a flagon, and Mister Blackburn stepped between us. I shifted closer to the dwelling, scanning for more mystical signs. A fur that hung over a small, glassless window jerked sideways. A girl's face gazed out at me with ebony braids of hair that were partially covered by a dirty coif. Her wide-set eyes darted to where the blue-diamond ring sat on my thumb inside my woolen glove. She reached an arm through the hole and cupped her fingers, calling me to her.

I stepped back and tripped over a flock of chickens, sending them into flustered squawks. The girl in the window burst out laughing.

"I'm ready to go," I blurted to Mister Blackburn, my cheeks burning.

He was too fixated on the drunkard from the alehouse to notice the girl, and he led me away from the man with obvious relief. Just a few feet behind him, the dirty-faced girl stared at my gloved hand again with a look of recognition. She'd detected my enchanted ring right through the woolen cloth like it was a flashing lightbulb. She had to be some kind of witch.

As she watched me, the girl's lips curled upward into a strange smile before Mister Blackburn hurried me away.

18

THE FIRST SNOWFALL FORBADE ME FROM CONSIDERING GOING TO THE village again, which had its upsides. I was still mad with curiosity about the enchanted ring that the witch had sensed—what it was all about, and if it could be repaired—but I wasn't sure I was ready to face any more dangers. As long as the snow was this heavy, there was no decision to be made.

The first few days hiding inside by the fireplace felt peaceful and cozy, and I managed to make sense of the first few chapters of *The Canterbury Tales* by Geoffrey Chaucer. I also added *The Chronicles of England, Scotlande, and Irelande* to my reading pile, given that the rest of the books on the shelf looked even more tedious and mostly devotional.

However, as the days became shorter, I spent more time lying in bed thinking about that witch. What if I was wasting my only chance to find out more about the mysterious ring? But, unlike Agnes Nightingale, I knew nothing about the girl from the village. What if she was dangerous or tried to steal the ring from me? What if she wasn't a witch at all and reported me for my interest in the dark arts? The questions kept circling, but no clear answers landed.

It was a Thursday afternoon when one of the patrolling guards shouted out from the front yard. Joseph Blackburn had been feeling off-color, so one of his sidekicks thundered through the front door to see what was going on. I sprinted to the window. The guards had apprehended a girl with flowing hair the color of dark chocolate who'd pulled up in an unmarked coach. *Oh my God—it's Alice!*

Fortunately, the guard recognized her, and she hurried inside to where I was waiting.

"What are you doing here?" I cried, throwing my arms around her petite shoulders before remembering her arrow wound. I jolted backward.

"Fear not," she said, reading my thoughts. "My shoulder is healing without trouble." She took my hands in her gloved fingers that were powdered with freezing snowflakes and bowed. "Oh, Emmie, I am surely pleased to see you well! I have waited for news of you for weeks, but I then thought to see if you might be here. Mistress Bridget informed me of this secret place of your marriage."

Every inch of me iced over at the question that I knew I had to ask.

"Any news about the king?"

Nothing in Alice's face suggested catastrophe, but her brows dipped as she led me into the library so we could sit down. I pushed aside the washed linens that were drying before the fire, making space for us.

She clutched my hands with freezing fingers. "I bring no pressing news, my lady, but the latest word I received was that His Majesty is far in the north. Lord Warwick is with him." Alice's lips tightened at the mention of Francis, but she continued steadily. "Henry Howard has raised an army of many hundreds of men. They have horse and armor in great numbers." She played with the lace circling her wrist, unable to look at me. "The heralds bring terrible stories to court. They say the king has not yet found Howard and has burned villages in search of him. Men have been hanged by the rope, and I have heard of many rains of arrows." Her slim palm clasped her forehead. "Oh, Emmie, I suffer many fears. I fear that the king will summon my weakened father to his duty; I fear our countrymen will come to despise our king for his deeds. I fear that Francis will stop at naught to protect His Majesty and that Francis will…" Her voice caught, and I reached out to touch her hand.

"Don't go there," I said. "We can't think that way."

She nodded and pressed the corners of her eyes with her fingertips to wipe away tears while I tried to process her words. Nick was still trying to catch Henry Howard, who'd raised an army with every fighter prepared to go to war and potentially die in protest of our marriage. That wasn't even the hardest part to stomach; the boy I knew to be gentle and loving was nose-diving into a future I'd worked so hard to prevent. In his furious search for Howard, Nick had been burning villages and hanging men, possibly without the time for proper trials. He was becoming Nicholas the Ironheart—violent and vengeful—all because of me.

Alice reached across to rub her injured shoulder, sending guilt to my throat. "Alice, I'm so sorry. That arrow was meant for me."

"Oh, I pray you, Emmie, speak not of it," she said, cupping her ears in protest. "I cannot bear to imagine the loss of your person. I am heartily pleased that we are both well."

Clemence carried in a thrown-together platter of cheeses, manchet bread, and wine. Alice took a grateful sip, and we shared a withered smile. I didn't know how to cope with the news she'd brought. Nick was still in danger, villages had been reduced to ashes, and men were being put to death. I wrapped my arms around myself as if I might fall apart if I didn't physically hold myself together.

"How long can you stay?" I asked weakly. "There's a ton of pie in the pantry."

Alice glanced at the window. "The weather is surely worsening, and my place is with my queen. I wish to remain here as long as it pleases Your Highness. We may pray together."

I beamed, my fatigued body roused by the thought of Alice staying. "Of course, I'd love that," I said. "But you should know that we get no news here…the king didn't want any messengers to know where I am. You'll hear more about Francis if you go back to court." I understood the weight of that as much as anyone.

"Perhaps I could ask my coachman to return with any urgent

news from the north," Alice offered. "He now knows that I am here, so there can be no harm. Fear not; he is most discreet, my lady."

"That's fine by me," I agreed, relieved to have an avenue for some news. Alice and I shared a smile. At least we had each other now.

Winter at Robin House became infinitely more bearable with Alice Grey there. We played card games, embroidered, read poems aloud, and waited for news that never came. On the Twelfth Night, we welcomed in the new year of 1581 with blessings, fruitcake, and sweetened wine. Poor Mister Blackburn was back in bed with a headache, but I had some cake sent up to him in the hope he could enjoy a slice.

The entire household was passed out after the celebrations when a fist banged on the downstairs door in the dead of night. I thought I dreamt it until two more urgent thumps sent the outside hens into confused cackles. I shot upward in bed, finding Alice's silhouette facing our doorway. She turned to me, her moonlit expression sharing my thought: was it news about Nick and Francis?

Alice draped a shawl over me before we dashed down the stairwell. The guards on night duty stood gathered in the entrance hall, where a young girl in a blood-red cape waited on the doorstep. The wind that blew through the open door was shockingly cold.

"What mischief is this?" one of the guards snapped at her.

"Forgive the hour, my lords," she said in a mature voice that didn't suit her childlike face. "I am in search of herbs in great haste. Mandrake, wormwood, chamomile…any such thing thee may 'ave."

I gaped at her thick braids of black hair. It was the witch from the hamlet.

"What do you need the herbs for?" I asked, stepping forward. Had she come looking for me?

"There is a plague of smallpox in the village," she replied without emotion.

"*Smallpox?*" a guard cried with horror.

"I 'ave not enough remedies for everyone," the girl added quickly. I emerged into the light, and her eyes shot to my bare thumb where she'd once detected the blue-diamond ring.

"Dost thou keepeth the ring safe, my lady?" she said to me. Alice grabbed my arm and tugged me away from the girl in case she was carrying the dreaded pox.

The guards formed a wall that pushed the young villager outside into a bank of snow, cursing at her. She twisted her neck to meet my eyes as the heavy wooden door swung shut in her face.

"How troubling," said Alice as our bare feet padded back upstairs to the bedchamber, leaving the guards arguing over which one had allowed in the villager exposed to smallpox.

My bed was cushioned with blankets and furs, and yet I couldn't relax through the images of the girl checking for the blue-diamond ring on my finger. She was more than a witch—she had to be some sort of clairvoyant.

As Alice gently snored, I watched the strips of moonlight peeking through the window shutters. It was perilously cold outside, and somewhere out there was Nick—risking his life to defend our marriage that should technically never have occurred. Less than a mile away lived a girl who might know something that could help make sense of how I'd even come to be in this time. After the loss of Agnes Nightingale, I couldn't get past the fact that another witch had been dropped into my lap—almost like a miracle. *Like it's meant to be.*

I sat up, sweat seeping into my nightgown. Visiting a witch during the daytime was out of the question. But could I actually sneak out of Robin House at night without being seen? The snow wasn't a deal-breaker—I had a thick cloak warm enough to cook an egg in and fur-lined boots. Smallpox, on the other hand, wasn't a disease I was keen to catch, nor did I want to risk giving it to anyone at Robin House or —heaven forbid—reintroduce it to the twenty-first century. However, having a nurse for a mom had made me pretty savvy about avoiding viruses: if I didn't get close to anyone or anything in the village, and I washed my hands thoroughly as soon as I got back, the chances of getting sick were low. I was more at risk of giving Alice a panic attack if she woke before I returned. Sneaking out at night in midwinter was dicey, even for me, but it was also my best chance—maybe my only chance—to finally get some answers.

I made up my mind. I was going to attempt it.

Downstairs, the guard on night shift sat hunched over a book in the library. I slid into the pantry as silent as a cat, ready to declare the munchies as my excuse if he caught me. Beside the cellar door at the rear of the house, bundles of herbs were hanging upside down to dry. I tore off a few sprigs of each and slipped outside with two gold sovereign coins jingling in my cloak in case I needed to bribe the witch.

The air was arctic, and I didn't have a lantern, but the moon hung full and brilliant, and I took it as a sign to keep going. I found the pathway, kicking up powdery snow that spilled into the collar of my leather boots. I sank knee-deep into banks of snow as I descended the side of the hill, my cheeks already numb.

Down in the hamlet, the tiny house where Joseph Blackburn and I had come across the kids and the farmer was boarded up with hand-sawed planks of wood. Keeping away from it, I hastened along the dirt path toward the witch's cottage beside the alehouse, hugging my chest. Knifelike icicles hung from the home's thatched roof like monster's teeth. With my gloves protecting my skin, I banged on the decaying door, feeling no hesitation. More than anything right now, I had to get warm.

Time slowed before the narrow door parted from the frame a crack. The girl's eyes peeked out at me for a moment before the gnarled plank swung wide open. I rushed inside to where a gentle fire sizzled on a mound of stones in a central hearth.

"My lady," the girl stammered, falling to her knees.

"Please, you can get up," I said through chattering teeth. She stumbled upward and tightened her shawl while I took in the primitive space faintly lit by rushlights. The uneven ceiling of crudely cut wooden beams was so low in places that I had to duck.

"This was all I could find in a hurry," I said, pacing across the earthen floor to offer her stems of purple and green, careful not to make skin contact.

Her eyes flashed wide as she took them, her bony fingers skimming the foliage. "Lavender…mint…marjoram. Not any I 'ave asked for, but the lavender may help the head pains. I thank thee."

She separated them into bundles on an uneven beam of wood resting on two stumps. It was the closest thing she had to a table.

Hanging above her were charm-like knots of animal bones, snakeskin, herbs, and strips of hair.

"Is there smallpox in this house?" I said, unsure if I should move.

She shook her head, ebony braids flapping. "The pox plague is bound to the Blacke lodging at present. Down the street. Four did perish thus far."

"*Four?* I'm sorry to hear that." Man, I hoped that didn't include the little girls who'd been feeding the goat when Joseph Blackburn and I visited the village.

I looked for somewhere to rest my frozen legs, but the only vacant space was a bed made from a pile of straw with a wooden log for a pillow. The girl moved a bundle of knitting off a stool and dragged it over to me.

"May I speak plainly, my lady?" she asked as I sat down on my cloak.

"Please do." I shivered.

She crossed her legs on the dirt floor to sit beside me. "Thee came 'ere to seek answers. Let us speak them now. Thee may ask me anything."

For some reason, her frankness wasn't a surprise. My throat closed up as my eyes welled with tears. It wasn't easy to get the words out. "Can you please tell me if my husband is well? He's fighting a battle in the north."

The girl's eyes fell closed, and she sat there a while, rocking. "The king shall be nay more."

I gaped at her, waiting for more words, but was met by silence. "What do you mean the king shall be no more?" I stammered, hot tears burning my eyes.

Her gaze drifted to where my hand buried itself inside the heat of my cloak. "Thee has an enchanted ring. Yet I feel thee dost not understand it. And thee wishes to…most sorely."

My fingers shot out of the cloak, the blue-diamond ring glittering in full view. She already knew I was married to the king, by either snooping or magic, and I took it as a sign to waste no more time and speak freely. "You're right, this ring is enchanted, and I don't understand it at all. Can you tell me something…anything?" My voice shook with urgency.

The girl presented an upturned hand to me, her calloused skin so white it was nearly translucent. A lump grew in my throat. If I gave her the ring, she could refuse to hand it back, use it against me, or even disappear in time to the twenty-first century. I braced myself and dropped it into her palm, ready to fight tooth and nail at the first sign of trouble.

Her hand jerked as she brought the sparkling blue diamond to her eyes, her brow tightening. She glanced back at me with her lips agape. "Thee want the king dead."

"What?" My belly hit the floor. "I don't want the king dead!"

"This ring is under enchantment to take away King Nicholas," she explained, rolling it around her palm with the tip of her finger. "'Tis weak, though. 'Tis power shall last not long." The girl's voice was smooth, but disgust clouded her ageless face. "This be the devil's work. He shall come for thee. *Lex talionis,* mistress. Thee hast been up to nay good…changing things that should not be hath changed. *Lex talionis.*"

I was sure the phrase was Latin, but she didn't say what it meant. The heat of the flames from the fire licked my knees, but I couldn't stop shaking.

"Can you tell me where the ring came from?" I asked.

She nodded, a smirk creeping onto her face. "'Twas Joanie, I can see…cunning wench." The girl leaned forward so I could listen carefully. "Joanie hath passed on; she caught the deadly sweat. She was a cousin of mine. I met her but once, when I was a child and she came 'ere to visit. Joanie was the one who told me I had the sight in mine own eyes and hands." Her fingertips drummed lightly on her torn woolen kirtle. "Joanie lived up Cumberland way. She be a maidservant in the prison where Mary Stuart lodged, who thee calls the 'Queen of Scots'. Mary's eyes were nay good, and she did want Joanie to read to her, but nay one hath taught Joanie to read. Instead, Joanie did teach Mary Stuart all manner of alchemies, and they becometh cousins of heart. Mary Stuart had commanded Joanie to enchant this ring to curse the king." The girl touched my hand, her skin startlingly cold. "Before she came to Mary Stuart's prison, Joanie hast been a maidservant at the Palace of Whitehall, mistress. Joanie did love the king with all her heart. His Majesty was all Joanie hath spoken of when we met. Joanie was a defender of the true faith and despised Papists. If it be true that Mary Stuart gave Joanie a ring of the king's to curse, Joanie would 'ave made some trick to make it seem like the king was dead, but in fact *save* the king in secret."

She smirked with pride for her cousin's wit as I fought to decode her words. This witch believed that her cousin Joanie—who was also a witch—once worked at the Palace of Whitehall and adored King Nick. Joanie then moved to work in one of the castles where the treasonous Mary, Queen of Scots was imprisoned. Joanie became close to Mary, who learned about Joanie's powers of sorcery. Mary, Queen of Scots then commanded Joanie to curse King Nick's ring to destroy him. But instead of doing that, Joanie came up with an idea to curse her beloved king to disappear—literally—yet continue to live on elsewhere.

But even if that whacked-out theory was true, why was the ring cursed to send the king to Hatfield, Massachusetts, in the twentieth century? It was so random.

"Would thee take some pottage?" the girl offered, gesturing to a steaming pot hanging from an iron frame over the fire.

"No, I have to get back, but thank you," I said hoarsely, standing up. I opened my palm in a request for her to return the ring to me.

She slid the gold band further down her middle finger, sending panic quaking through me. But before I could react, she'd slipped it off again and passed it to me. "'Tis losing its power," she said again. "The ring was not meant to carry two persons, and for so many journeys, as thee hast done. My lady, this ring was enchanted for one use: to send the King of England so far from here that his person would be safe from harm, but of nay more threat to that vile Mary Stuart." Her wide-set eyes leveled with me. "The ring shall work nay longer soon, if not already. The ring will stop soon. I hope thee hast chosen well, Your Highness."

Her last two words were pointed, reinforcing that I'd taken my time-travel fortunes a little too far and written myself into sixteenth-century history as its queen. *Yup, that whole thing, Emmie.*

I psyched myself up to face the wintry night and fished out the two coins from my cloak.

"Thank you so much for this," I said, leaving the gleaming discs stamped with the king's insignia on the wooden beam beside her. She drew in a sharp breath before sinking to her knees in a deep bow.

I said goodbye and stepped outside into the bone-chilling blackness.

When I was a few paces away from the cottage, the girl called after me, her voice a faint line beneath the rising wind. "'Twas thee, Your Highness."

"I'm sorry?" I called back, lifting my fur collar over my mouth.

"Thee want to know why the ring would 'ave brought the king to thy time," she said from the door. "'Tis because of thee. It mattered not where the king went, as long as the place was far and as long as his heart was full and merry. The king would hast been most merry there, with *thee*, mistress." A smile of encouragement unfolded across her face before she swung the door closed.

He would have been most merry there…with you.

The meaning of the sentence replayed in my mind as I began the grueling climb through slushy snow back to Robin House. The reason why the ring was cursed to send Nick to my time—bringing Susanna Grey instead by accident—was because the witch Joanie wanted to send the king somewhere he'd be truly happy…which was with me.

It sounded side-splittingly bonkers, and yet, amid a myriad of unfathomable experiences this past year, something about it felt spot-on, like everything had finally fallen into place.

"*Lex talionis,*" the girl's singsong voice whispered on the curve of the wind. I still had to find out what that meant.

I rounded the final bend to Robin House—thirsting for the warmth of my bed—when I spotted a shiver of candlelight from the upstairs window. *Shit, I've been found out!* I rushed up the pathway that clung to the side of the manor. In the front yard, a huddle of guards clutching lanterns hovered around one of the watchmen who sat on a tree log beside the stables.

"The queen is here!" Alice yelped from behind me, and a guard separated himself from the pack to escort me to where she waited on the manor's front step.

"I'm *so* sorry," I said to Alice, who asked, "Where did you go?" at the same time.

"I–I just popped outside for a few minutes because I couldn't sleep, and I was so sweaty inside and couldn't get away from the heat of the fires," I said.

Her palm hit her open mouth. "Heavens, no…not you, Emmie."

"Not me, what?"

Alice's alarmed eyes darted to where the guards had gathered.

"What's happening over here?" I called, striding back to them, my boots crunching the dense snow. "It's the dead of night." Their lanterns bounced flickers of light as I approached.

"Step back, Your Highness!" snapped the young guard, blocking me from getting any closer. I could see that the seated guard was Joseph Blackburn. Why was his face covered with bees?

I gasped, nauseated, as the truth broke over me. They weren't bees: they were hundreds of pus-filled welts.

"He has smallpox," I said, clutching my sickened stomach. That's why he had been suffering from those awful headaches.

"You must take leave inside, Your Grace," said the guard. "We shall keep Mister Blackburn here for now."

"Outside? In this freezing weather—are you mad?"

"We cannot chance spreading the pox to your person, Your Highness. The servants' attic is above your chamber. Mister Blackburn may sleep in the stables."

I was so stunned that I couldn't speak properly. "Don't be insane! Alice and I will stay downstairs…or in the cabin outside."

Alice had appeared beside me, snow flurries landing on her cheeks. "Be calm, Emmie. I have sent word to my coachman to come for us in haste. The pox is terribly contagious, and it is no longer safe here. The guard is already riding to Hampton Court, and the coachman should be here by morning." She gently urged me toward the house.

"He is *not* staying out here," I said through worried tears. Joseph

Blackburn hunched forward, his head hanging into his knees. Inflamed blisters speckled the back of his neck. I'd learned enough about smallpox to know that the lesions didn't appear until the person had been exposed to the virus for weeks. He'd most likely caught it when I took him down to the infected village. It was my fault that he was sick.

Alice huffed at me, her face torn with distress. I didn't want to be difficult, and I was the queen now and had to be protected, even if I hated being put on a special pedestal above everyone else.

"Mistress Grey and I will sleep in the guest lodging this night," I said loudly enough for everyone to hear. "It's not likely to be contaminated, and there's a small fireplace in there. Mister Blackburn can come inside the house at once. If Alice and I are leaving the manor anyway, he can use my bedchamber."

"Clemence and I will make ready the guest lodging," said Alice. She scurried back into the manor.

"Please, somebody help him with food and water, or I'll do it myself," I ordered the guards. "If you wash your hands constantly and thoroughly—and stay well clear of any coughs or sneezes—I can't see why you wouldn't be fine. I'll send a doctor back here as soon as I can."

I hurried upstairs to scrub my hands and the blue-diamond ring in a pail of soapy water before changing into a fresh nightgown. I tossed every piece of fabric I'd worn to the village into the fireplace to be safe.

The moment I met Alice in the cabin out the back, she pressed a hand to my forehead. "Do you feel the heat even now?" she asked with a pinched brow.

"I'm not sick," I said in a reassuring tone. "I swear that it was just a hot flush. I get them sometimes."

You mean you were in the smallpox village, chatting with a witch about time travel and curses on the king. Things they kill people for around here.

I secured the blue-diamond ring inside the toe of one of my riding boots. Once Alice and I had built a fire, we both stretched out on the single mattress after I refused to let her sleep on the floor. There had been so much commotion that I hadn't really taken in that we were returning to Hampton Court Palace in the morning. It was hard to lie still and not disturb Alice through my overwhelming relief. I didn't give a toss that some of the men who wanted me dead might be at the palace, lying in wait. I was ready to go home, where I could call for doctors to help Mister Blackburn and I could be among the first to receive news about King Nick.

Nick, who wasn't meant to be in the north of England in the dead of winter, putting his life on the line for a twenty-first-century girl who'd muscled her way into his world. The witch had studied the ring and said it herself: Nick was supposed to be living in my time, with me —that was the point of the blue-diamond ring coming into his life.

The problem was that we'd already made our decision to stay in the sixteenth century, where we'd been in near-constant danger. The enchanted ring was nearly out of juice, Nick was at war with a murderous former duke, and the peaceful happiness that the witch Joanie had tried to bring Nick—and me—had slipped right through our fingers.

19

Given that the king was away battling a violent uprising, I braced myself for a spiritless and somber court. The moment we arrived back at Hampton Court Palace, however, it was clear I was way off the mark. A merry clash of lutes and oboes bled jubilantly from the stained-glass windows of the Great Hall as Alice Grey and I climbed the stairs in our traveling cloaks. With trestle tables stretching through the hall and into the neighboring Great Watching Chamber, men and ladies of the court sat giggling and chattering over jugs of ale and steaming platters of roasted halibut and turbot—as lively as I'd ever seen them.

That was until they saw me.

Lord and Lady Snell spied us first, followed by the Earl of Dorset, the sneering Ascots, and the remaining courtiers as a wave of awkward silence devoured the space. Nobody rose to bow to me—their new queen—and there was a severe shortage of smiles. I hadn't missed the glacial temperatures of the Tudor court, and I wasn't talking about the weather.

"It appears our arrival has made good time for supper," Alice said. "I could eat a swine."

Her comment barely registered over the ocean of accusing eyes still glaring at us. Alice made an unsettled murmur about the queen dining in private, and we continued through the Great Watching Chamber, nearly colliding with a servant boy grappling with a platter of fish from the servants' stairs.

We made our way down the stone stairwell in our bulky farthingales. "Such merriment while the king is at war," Alice castigated. "It would not please His Majesty."

I wanted to reply, but the words wouldn't form. In my eagerness to return to Hampton Court, I hadn't considered how the courtiers felt about my role in their king's troubles. The looks of hatred on their faces made their meaning plain: they blamed me for it. All at once, any excitement I had about returning to the palace evaporated.

Alice heaved open the doors to my chambers and shrieked with delight, nearly sending me out of my skin. Bridget and Lucinda glanced up from their shared platter of turbot, salmon, and pickled herrings with melted butter, yelping at the unexpected sight of us.

"We missed Your Highness above all things," Lucinda cried, leaping from her chair to curtsy at me.

"Oh, thank heavens, you are safe. We received no word of your person," said Bridget, dropping to her knees. She kissed both my hands.

"Alice and I were in hiding and couldn't write," I said apologetically.

Alice frowned, gripping her hip. "When I took my leave from court, I cautioned Mistresses Nightingale and Parker that I would be unable to write with news of the queen." She shook her head at Bridget's escaped memory, but her eyes shone with gladness that we were all back together.

"Well, we are surely pleased to see you both back and free from harm," Lucinda said, her cheeks glowing.

I'd actually missed Lucinda's bright company, and Bridget's hilarious sagas over the single guys at court, which she was already beginning as we sat down to eat. Their hair was plaited so intricately that they must've been bored senseless in our absence.

Their warm reaction to our arrival was enough to restore my appetite and distract me from my dark thoughts about Nick's safety—

at least for a few hours. His upper council chamber was visible from my courtyard, but the gilded window shutters remained fastened shut, intercepting any signs of life up there. I could've skewered Henry Howard myself for making so much trouble and putting my husband in danger. I wasn't sure I'd sleep again until Nick arrived home in one piece.

January continued to shroud the palace in clouds of chimney smoke, and the girls resumed my dance and music lessons to cheer me up. We received no status updates about Nick or Francis, but word reached me that the guard Joseph Blackburn had survived the smallpox virus—just not the unsightly scars. I could've screamed with relief. It'd be difficult to face him one day and see the cost of that in person, but I hoped I could apologize to him for my part in it.

The calendar welcomed February with a fresh dumping of snow, and claustrophobic courtiers had begun tattling on each other about petty things to keep themselves amused. Likely fearful of what might be said about him, the Earl of Dorset arranged a public swordfight between two renowned fencers in the Great Hall.

My ladies and I rushed in to the performance a few minutes late, my cheeks hot with embarrassment as we searched for seats at the rear. Four vacant stools sat beside the dreamy Earl of Surrey, and Bridget snorted into her fist with glee. The rest of us swallowed giggles as we settled in beside him. Sour-faced nobles twisted to glare at us from the front rows where the swashbucklers were already dueling. Lord Dorset scowled at me with those sugar-spoiled teeth of his that he was so proud of. He whispered to his neighbors, who curved around to shoot me death stares, before—one by one—the men rose to their feet. They tipped their hats to the swordsmen in apology before striding right past me and out of the hall. The exodus continued—row by row—until the only people left inside the Great Hall were me and my ladies, the swordfighters, the Earl of Surrey, and a handful of nobles who were permanently paranoid about the king's temper.

"Emmie, let us take our leave," Alice said quietly, her slender fingers touching my wrist.

"Did they all just walk out because I'm here?" I said, aghast.

"Heavens no, there must be some other cause," said Lucinda, but Alice's ashen face confirmed that I'd hit the bullseye on this one. The walkout was a public demonstration against me, the troublesome new Queen Emmeline.

"I bid you excuse me, my ladies," muttered the Earl of Surrey as he squeezed past us as modestly as possible. His athletic form sailed past our noses, but none of us were laughing now.

Alice gathered her skirts. "Come, let us take leave to Your Highness's chambers. We may make a note for the king and record the names of all who took part in this act of treason."

"His Majesty will be sorely vexed," added Bridget, but she could hardly look at me. I felt bad for her. It wasn't her fault she'd been aligned with a dud queen.

Feeling like the excluded kid at school again, I trailed the girls downstairs to my chambers, where nothing but embroidery hoops and sewing needles awaited me. A swell of dread erupted in my chest where it'd been festering since the coronation attack.

"I'm going to go over to my jewelry workshop," I said, halting. The swishing satin of our dresses fell silent beside a giant mural depicting the Battle of Bosworth. "Provided it's still there."

"Why would it be not there?" Alice said with a forced chuckle, moving closer to me. "We shall come with you."

"No, thank you…I just need a bit of alone time." I managed a reassuring smile, turning away as I blinked through the pressure of tears.

Three concerned faces watched me go. Alice, Bridget—and even Lucinda in recent months—had been nothing but loyal to a queen who was clearly going down and who'd dragged Alice's fiancé into a civil war. Had Henry the Eighth's ill-fated wives Anne Boleyn or Catherine Howard had such faithful friends when they were slated for the executioner's block?

With that grisly thought, I kept my head bowed so I wouldn't have to meet any more reproachful eyes and made a beeline for the work-shop where I could fall apart in private.

I hung around the studio until suppertime, putting the finishing touches on the hammered thumb ring for Nick. I'd just lit the candles when Alice, Bridget, and Lucinda arrived with a beef pie, a fragrant bowl of herby soup, and a generous slice of ginger cheesecake. I reas-sured them that I was doing okay and picked at the meal after they left, keen to polish the silver ring one more time.

The dimly lit palace courtyards were desolate by the time I slung on my cloak and headed back to my rooms, passing the stairwell leading to the king's Privy Chambers. It was unguarded—a sad reminder that the king was away from court. The square heels of my pumps scraped the hand-painted tiles as my feet turned right instead of left, scaling the stone staircase.

A chamber attendant spotted me inside the Withdrawing Cham-ber, tripping over his gangly feet. "Your Highness," he said with a bow, his cheeks colored scarlet. "May I be of help?"

"The king is away from court," I said, like Captain Obvious, "but I'd like to lodge in his chambers this night. I'd also appreciate it if you could get a message to my ladies that I am here and safely lodging alone."

The boy's bow was hesitant, but he led me through Nick's series of ornate rooms until we reached the king's private bedchamber. The sight of Nick's four-poster bed with its black quilted canopy was instantly pacifying. Despite every terror that had come our way, my love for Nick Tudor still felt absolute. I couldn't imagine that ever changing.

Tension began withdrawing from my bones as servants scampered through the space, lighting the fire and fluffing the silk pillows. The lanky attendant offered me food and wine, but I declined, thanking them all for their help. When the paneled doors finally closed, I stripped down to my smock and slunk beneath the fur-lined blankets. A glimpse of a smile touched my cheeks, and I rolled over, breathing in any traces of Nick's scent. I said my bedtime prayers like an exemplary Tudor wife, asking in earnest for my husband to be kept safe.

From that night on, I slept only in Nick's bed. The invaluable company of my ladies still filled my days, and Alice was the only one brave enough to bring up my change of sleeping habits. I could tell that it was more out of concern than anything else, and I explained that being in Nick's chambers was my only respite. There, I could still feel him all around me.

"I am certain our dear men shall return in haste," she reassured me for the zillionth time while stitching a serpent into the cuff of one of Francis's shirts. As she reached for more thread, her shoulder caught the corner of the hard-backed chair and she hissed through her teeth.

"Is that shoulder still bothering you?" I asked, my chest constricting.

"It troubles me only at certain angles." She offered me a don't-worry-about-it smile, but her eyes had that same sunken look that I'd seen in my own. The lack of news about Nick and Francis…Alice's shoulder injury that was my fault…the relentless snow…it'd become harder to get out of bed in the morning.

I was stitching the corner of a tablecloth for the poor when the doors swung open, inviting in a gust of wind and a pewter platter that smelled like a bakery at first light. Bridget and Lucinda had gone to the kitchens for some sweet snacks, which had become our mid-morning ritual.

"Heavens, at last!" said Alice. She rushed up to help them unpack the load. I reminded her of her bad shoulder and took over the task.

"Fresh macarons for our devoted queen," said Lucinda, biting into one. Her nose scrunched with exaggerated joy as she chewed.

I retorted with a playful scoff and appraised the spread of sweetened almonds, custard tarts, stewed cherries sprinkled with sugar, cookies with warmed dates, and my favorite: fluffy macarons. I reached for one, but Alice's hand snatched my arm to hold me back.

"Ouch," I said and then realized Lucinda was coughing. Her skin had paled in seconds, and her nails clawed at her neck. She hacked up a glob of chewed macaron, spitting it onto the rush matting. Strings of saliva dripped from her mouth as she hunched forward.

"Are you well?" I asked, the breath sucked out of me.

Bridget screamed as Lucinda slumped to the floor. I dropped to catch her at the same time as Alice. Our heads knocked together, but I felt no pain, my heart beating out of my throat.

"Touch no more food!" Alice ordered, as Lucinda rolled onto her back and vomited violently, almost choking. "I have seen this before now," said Alice, rolling Lucinda onto her side. "This is poison."

I couldn't speak, my eyes shifting between Lucinda's pallid cheeks and the clump of spewed-up dessert on the floor. Someone had poisoned the macarons, which were famous throughout the palace for being my favorite snack.

Alice was delivering instructions to Bridget, but I couldn't make out the words. Bridget nodded, hitched up her skirts, and ran outside to the courtyard.

Sweat poured from Lucinda's brow, and she kicked with agitation. Alice slipped two fingers inside Lucinda's mouth in an attempt to induce more vomiting.

I leaped forward. "Don't do that!" I cried. "That could make her worse." A girl from my school in Hatfield had overdosed at prom, and it's what the paramedic had said to the guy trying to make her throw up.

I crouched to feel Lucinda's pulse, asking her to look at me. Her eyes rolled backward, and both hands clutched her stomach. Her pulse felt weak.

Alice squeezed my shoulder, and I realized I was sobbing.

"It was supposed to be me." My voice slipped on the words. "It should've been me. They poisoned the macarons, and now Lucinda will—"

"Stop that," Alice snapped. "You are our blessed queen; we pray to God, day by day, for your health. Better any one of us takes our last breath than you, my lady. The king would never forgive us should any ill befall you."

"I'm no better than her; I'm just *Emmie!*" I said, shocking Alice. I scrambled to my feet, hunting for something, but I didn't know what.

"I don't want this...I didn't want any of this," I stammered. "First you...Blackburn...now Lucy. I–I can't hurt anyone else...I don't know what else to do." Tears spilled down my cheeks, and Alice rose to comfort me, but I shook her away. "We have to help Lucy," I said. "She *can't* die. None of this was supposed to happen."

Alice's face was grave as she crouched back down beside Lucinda.

Two hard knocks shook the doors, and I darted to open them. Doctor Norris was on the front step with Bridget, kicking snow off his slippers. He bowed to me from beneath his black hood.

"We think it's poison...please help her," was all I could get out.

Norris strode over to Lucinda and crouched. He dropped his nose to her mouth and cupped his hands around her lips, smelling her breath and then her puddle of vomit. Lucinda was beginning to shiver.

"Can we move her to the bed?" I said. Norris nodded and climbed off his knees with a groan. "She can have mine," I added in a don't-argue-with-me tone, opening the doors to my bedchamber.

Norris and Alice hoisted Lucinda up by the shoulders, and Bridget and I caught the weight of her hips and legs. Lucinda gasped painful breaths as we lugged her through the doorway and settled her onto the mattress. I dragged a stool to her side and pasted wet strips of linen over her forehead to cool her while Norris fussed over her. Not only did I want to help Lucy in any way I could, but what awaited me outside the safety of my chambers frightened me to my bones. I hadn't forgotten the sickening Tudor torture devices that I'd read about in history class. How much did the people here despise me that they would be driven to poison me? Were they so unafraid of Nick's wrath? Was it a member of Henry Howard's rebellion or just another rich courtier who detested me? How much further were they willing to go to get rid of me? Boiling people alive came to mind.

Bridget had begun hyperventilating and needed to lie down on her mattress. While Alice came and went from our chambers, monitoring the investigation that'd already begun, I stayed with Lucinda. I changed the sheets when she puked on them and offered her water, but she shivered so much that it was hard for her to ingest. Norris tried to catch her urine in a tin vessel, but few drops came. I had to bite away my frustration when he laid rows of leeches across her arms to "balance her humors". That had about as much effect as the weird gallstone-looking thing he kept dipping into water before making her take sips of it.

Shortly after dawn, a barber-surgeon arrived with a strong lisp and fierce eyebrows. He pulled a knife from his cloak that looked like a nail file and sank it into Lucinda's forearm, holding up a brass cup to catch the draining blood. I had to leave the room, maddened by the archaic treatments that surely had little benefit.

Bridget was trying to write a letter to Lucinda's mom, who was looking after little Ellie, but her dripping tears kept smudging the ink.

Soon after the barber-surgeon left, Lucinda stopped responding, and her breathing had turned shallow. Doctor Norris asked if we could have a word outside. I spooned a little water over Lucinda's lips before following him into the drawing-room. Alice and Bridget gathered behind me.

"Your Highness, I pray you forgive me," Norris said with his head bowed. "There is no more that can be done. Mistress Parker is likely in her last hours. May I send for a minister?"

"I'm sorry...what?" I mumbled. "She threw up this morning. Isn't that a sign that her body's still working through it?"

My words drew no relief to his face. "I regret that I am quite certain the lady is dying, my queen."

A cry spurted from Bridget's lips, tears brimming over her heavily made-up eyelashes. Alice's breathing was heavy with grief.

Miraculously, I didn't fall apart. In fact, I'd never felt so strong or sure of anything.

I knew what I had to do to try to save Lucinda Parker's life.

20

I swung my riding cloak over my shoulders while Alice chased me outside onto the front step.

"I'm going to go home and try to find some medicine to help Lucy," I said without looking at her. "My father, Doctor Grace, always had good remedies."

She returned a sympathetic frown. "Your father is with God, my lady."

"But he never threw anything out. The remedies will still be there."

Alice's lips parted. "Will there be time? It shall take days to reach Worthing." She grimaced at the silvery sky. "The streets will not be safe…there may be wicked men about. My lady, I cannot in good conscience let you do this."

"*Let* me? I'm going," I said, stronger than I intended. "There's no talking me out of it. I'll organize some guards to come with me. Please stay with Lucy while I'm gone. Can you do that? I don't want that barber-surgeon stabbing her with his scalpel again."

Alice dropped her head, her cheeks reddening. "Most certainly, Your Highness. God be with you—always. I will bid the grooms to make ready your horse."

I thanked her and hung there for a second, hating myself for using my position to intimidate Alice into submission. "I'll keep safe and be back as soon as I can," I said gently. "Please tell the grooms that I'll be at the stables soon."

The look on her face made clear that she didn't approve of my impromptu excursion, but I knew she'd obey.

Drawing my hood over my hair, I legged it toward Nick's chambers, bursting into the fire-warmed bedchamber where I'd left the blue-diamond ring inside his magnificent jewelry cabinet that was hand-carved from bone. I'd hardly slept all night as I sat beside Lucinda, so it was easy to fall asleep in the king's luxurious bed with the enchanted ring on my thumb. I didn't have time to panic about what the witch said about the ring being drained of power. Whether the time portal worked or not, I had to try. I couldn't let Lucinda take a bullet for me without doing everything I could to save her life.

I slept and roused at least three times, my drowsy eyelids letting in enough firelight each time to confirm I was still at Hampton Court Palace. I smacked a lump out of the pillow with the sort of irritation that only panic can inspire. Begging for sleep, I slowed and deepened my breaths.

Without warning, my butt plunged to the floor and slammed into cold linoleum. It took a minute for the contemporary room to materialize through my foggy brain...I was on the floor beside a vacant hospital-style bed. A familiar vinyl armchair sat empty in the corner. The number '23' hung lopsidedly on the peach door, and the toxic smell of disinfectant overcame my nose.

Shit, I'm at the Cedar Lake Rest Home! I left from here last time with Susanna Grey.

That meant I was in freaking Boston—not Hatfield, where my mom was a nurse and might have some medicine that could help Lucinda. A rush of nerves sent my stomach into free-fall as I flung the cupboard door open, stretching from my toes to reach for my cell phone. Polished metal met my fingers, and I exhaled with relief, sliding the phone down my bodice until it chilled my bare skin.

Bleary, starving, and looking like a period movie character in a sixteenth-century kirtle, I made it past a few stares from elderly residents to the front exit, mercifully escaping any sign of Ajay, the care worker who'd helped me last time, or any other staff in the home. Outside on the Boston streets, I paced down the road, dialing my mom's number from my cell phone and ignoring the eye rolls from people who caught sight of my period outfit.

Thank the stars, she answered, but her voice was hoarse. I must've woken her up after one of her night shifts.

"Emmie!" she said and cleared her throat. "Where are you?"

"In Boston. Sorry to wake you. How are you doing?"

She sighed deeply enough to inflate a hot air balloon. "I don't know. Surviving. I'm glad to hear your voice." She sounded exhausted.

"Yours, too. Mom, I need to ask you a medical question. If someone has been poisoned, what kind of medicine should I give them?"

"Who was poisoned?"

"No one you know…a friend. She can't get to a hospital, but I think she could be dying. Well, she is dying, apparently." The truth of that gripped my throat.

Mom sucked in a sharp breath. "What did she take?"

"I don't even know; it was something put into her food." I described Lucinda's symptoms from the ingestion of the macaron until now.

Another heavy sigh. "We'd have to know what toxin she ingested because the treatments vary. She'd need a toxicology report, possibly a ventilator if her respiratory system is depressed. Her liver or kidneys could be in trouble…I'm not a doctor, Emmie. Why can't she get to a hospital?"

"What about that black stuff—I forget what it's called. One of the girls at school had it when she OD'd at the prom."

"You mean activated charcoal? It can help for certain things, but it's usually given within hours of the poisoning. It sounds like your friend has been sick for a while."

"Less than two days. And I'm happy to try anything that might work."

Mom didn't reply. I heard her climb out of bed and a talk show playing in the background. She always slept with the television on.

"Well, do you think the activated charcoal's worth a try at least?" I pressed.

She sighed. "It's really unlikely to do anything. I've never seen it given after two days."

"*Less* than two days. Please, Mom, I have to try something."

Her television cut to silence. "You'd need hospital grade. Don't bother with the pharmacy. I should have some stored away at the rest home."

"Really?" I was already calculating. If I hopped on a bus to downtown and caught a connecting bus to Amherst, I could be in Hatfield before the day was out.

"I don't have any money on me," I realized out loud. It'd been so long since I'd had to think about my wallet.

Mom made a frustrated huff before swapping the phone to her other ear. "I'll get some of the charcoal and drive in to see you. Where in Boston are you?"

"Oh my gosh, Mom; are you even serious?"

"Emmie, one day, you'll learn what it's like to be a mother. Then everything I do might not surprise—or annoy—you so much."

Her words tore at my heart. In choosing a life with Nick in Tudor England, I'd all but abandoned my devoted mom. I wished that I'd never had to choose between them.

After she assured me that her car hadn't acted up in ages, I said I'd meet her at the library up the street. While reminding her of the time urgency, I asked her to chuck anything edible into her bag and to give our dog Ruby a massive cuddle from me.

It was a relief to enter the library, its warm atmosphere wrapping around me like a hug. I settled into a comfy armchair, flicking through a fashion magazine. *Holy smokes, I've missed fashion magazines.* When their garish colors and stories about celebrity spats became overwhelming, though, I dropped the dog-eared booklet back into the rack and scanned the nearest bookshelf.

It was the boring language section, and I went to move on until the thick spine of a lime-green tome caught my eye. It was a dictionary of Latin words and phrases, and I flicked through to the 'L' chapter, scanning for the phrase *Lex talionis.*

There it was, in black and white.

Lex talionis: the law of retaliation, e.g. 'an eye for an eye'.

An uncomfortable feeling slithered into my gut, settling there. An eye for an eye—why would the witch say that to me?

I tried to distract myself with an old crime novel that someone had left on the table, but three chapters in, I felt like I hadn't absorbed a word. I hadn't even turned twenty yet and I was married with a husband at war, my friend was dying, and here I was trying to read about a celebrity murderer who took out predatory men with her stilettos.

A middle-aged woman with scraggy blonde hair pushed through the library doors. It took me a second to recognize my mom. Her cheeks were sunken, and she'd lost weight. She hugged me without saying anything.

"I missed you," I said into her shoulder. She squeezed harder.

She shook her head at my billowy kirtle with bell sleeves but said nothing about it. I dragged two armchairs closer together, and Mom uncoiled a knitted scarf from her neck.

"I gather you don't have long," she said, handing me a crumpled shopping bag. Inside was a white plastic bottle labeled 'Activated Charcoal: Poison Antidote' alongside the directions for use and a bunch of medical jargon.

"Thanks so much for this," I said, the stiff plastic bottle unlike anything I'd seen in the sixteenth century. I should've brought an apothecary jar to transfer the contents into. "Unfortunately, I can't stay long," I added, my voice cracking. "My friend's really sick."

Mom had also brought me a packet of trail mix and two yogurt-coated granola bars. I downed the lot in a few bites, gulping water from her bottle. She tried to give me money, but I insisted that I didn't need it. US dollars didn't buy much in Tudor England.

"Is the charcoal for your friend Nick?" Mom said carefully. Her eyes were roaming all over me, searching for signs of injury or perhaps unhappiness.

"No, it's for a friend of ours…her name's Lucy." I left out the part about Lucinda having a baby daughter who'd just survived a form of tuberculosis.

Mom's hands twisted together, fidgeting. "If you take me to her, I can administer the medicine properly. It should really be given through a nasogastric tube, but I assume you don't have one of those."

"Yeah, we don't have one of those."

We do have leeches, though, and bloodletting. Oh, and that gallstone thing.

"It'll stain her teeth black if she drinks it," Mom warned. "Possibly permanently."

"It's okay. A lot of people where she lives have black teeth. It's actually kind of trendy there."

Mom frowned. "It's also critical that your friend doesn't aspirate this. That would make everything a heck of a lot worse. I also told you the charcoal will probably have absolutely no effect after this much time, right?"

"Yeah. But you never know…I have to try."

She paused, her fingers still fidgeting. "Can I come with you?"

My face fell. "You know you can't."

Mom wound her scarf back around her neck. "I know. Time travel and all that." Her posture stiffened.

My voice cracked with exhaustion, but—as usual—I had no time to lose. I stood up and gave Mom another hug that signaled it was already time for me to head off.

"Your dad wants to see you," she said as we pulled away, my hands sliding down to her bony wrists. "He asked me to call him as soon as you got back in touch."

"Is everything okay?"

She nodded, a blush creeping across her skin. "He just wants to catch up with you. It's a shame that it took all this for him to wake up, but I think he finally has. Can you believe it?"

My teeth dug into my bottom lip. After a decade of Dad being largely a no-show, I'd expected my mom to give the guy a tougher time about wanting a free pass back into my life. The problem was that Mom had zero sense when it came to my old man, and this time I wasn't here to help her handle his miraculous comeback.

You can always visit your mom now and then, Emmie. That's if you can find some medieval charger-cable thingy for the blue-diamond ring so it doesn't conk out.

"I have to go," I said tightly. Mom's hollow cheeks blurred through my tears.

She wrapped her arms around me again. I wasn't the only one crying. I reminded myself that college-aged kids across America were living apart from their parents. This was normal. If only Tudor England didn't feel so many centuries away—literally.

Mom brushed her nose with her knuckle. "Can I drop you off somewhere?"

"No, thanks…I'll just be here for a little bit longer." I eyed the quiet corner with the comfy armchairs that were out of view of the security cameras. With any luck, I could fall asleep there without ending up on a paranormal reality television show about mysterious vanishings.

Mom nodded at the blue-diamond ring on my thumb. "Ah, right. You have to disappear." She waved a hand magically.

I clutched her delicate fingers one last time. "Thank you so much for driving all this way. I know it was a big ask, and I'm *so* grateful."

"You didn't ask; I offered," Mom corrected. "And I'd do it again tomorrow if it meant I got to see you, even for a few minutes."

"Mom," I pleaded, reaching toward her as she stepped backward. She nodded like she was going to be okay, but her crumpled face betrayed the gesture.

I watched her stop at the book display by the entrance, grabbing a title that caught her eye. She held the book up in the air and smiled at me before returning it to the shelf. After blowing me a tear-stained kiss, Mom slipped away from me through the double doors.

I felt like the worst daughter who'd ever lived.

I crossed to the window display and picked up the hardcover text she'd waved at me. It was called *The Tudors: England's Most Notorious Royal Family*. My stomach wound into a painful ball. Mom was trying to connect with me on something she could never understand. I flicked to the section about Nicholas the Ironheart, deliberately squinting to blur my vision as I braved a few words, jittery at what I'd find.

The marriage of King Nicholas I and Princess Henriette of France was divisive and gave rise to civil conflicts that spilled across the border.

I snapped the book shut, every inch of my skin burning.

Why did it still say that King Nick married Princess Henriette and not me?

A woman bouncing a toddler on her knee kept scoping out my kirtle like I was some sort of matinee show. I blocked the offending book from my mind and hurried into the quiet corner of the library, relieved to find it vacant of prying eyes. After settling into a cushy armchair, I wedged the activated charcoal bottle beneath my arm and wriggled into a position comfortable enough to sleep in. Even if someone did see me vanish, at least it wouldn't be caught on camera. I jerked at the memory of the sleeping pill still sitting in the ring casing —I'd completely forgotten it last time! My fingers reached for the tiny latch, but the pill would make me groggy when I arrived back, and I needed to be fully charged to help Lucy. I decided to try to fall asleep without it first.

It turned out that I didn't need the pill: it took less than thirty minutes of meditating to send my shattered body into a power nap, but I woke back in the library in a disoriented spiral of nausea. I'd never regret pushing the ring's limits to try to save Lucinda's life, but if I never saw Nick Tudor again, I'd never get over it. The pattern of dozing off and waking in the library chair repeated on loop until the sky outside had darkened and the library had begun to empty. The woman with the toddler was long gone. If I didn't time travel soon, I'd be sleeping in a snowbank and probably waking up in a Boston emergency room.

I kissed the glassy tip of the table-cut diamond and slid my hand into the warmth of my bodice, my palm resting over my heart.

Come on…please. Take me home. I want to go home.

I smelled the sublime scent before I even saw him. My sluggish eyelids cracked open at the familiar aroma of rose oil and the heat of a crackling fire. I scrambled onto my elbows, searching the dim candlelight. It was nightfall at Hampton Court, and my husband, Nick Tudor, was sitting right across from me.

A gasp of shock shot from my throat like I'd been punched in the stomach. The love of my life was home safe!

But Nick didn't even move, let alone speak. He just sat in his gilded armchair, blinking at me with a lifeless expression. Something was terribly wrong—something even worse than Lucinda's poisoning.

21

"You're back," I said with a high-pitched cry. "You're okay." I rolled out of the bed, tripping over my skirts, which had twisted around me. My head ached from the malfunctioning time travel, and my balance was off.

Nick stayed frozen as I fell onto him. I folded my arms around his pearl-colored doublet, breathing him in. My skin throbbed with heat, and the world spun. *My Nick.*

He didn't respond—not so much as a flinch. I pulled back, searching his face. There were no signs of injury. "Oh, thank God," I said, pressing my forehead to his. "I was freaking out."

The bedchamber was as quiet as a graveyard, except for Nick's steady breathing.

"Babe?" I said, pressing my hands to his cheeks and angling his face to look at me. His seawater-colored eyes were blocks of ice. Was this PTSD? Or worse—had he come back from his war as the implacable Nicholas the Ironheart?

I climbed off him. "Why aren't you saying anything?"

He aimed a finger at the plastic bottle protruding from the bed sheets. "What is that?" he asked evenly.

All the air fled my body as I remembered. "It's for Mistress Parker." I reached for the bottle. "It's medicine from my time. She was poisoned."

"I am acquainted with Mistress Parker's condition."

"Is she still…is she alive?"

"To my knowledge."

His eyes flickered to mine, and our gazes fused together like magnets. After a moment, he looked away, climbing out of the chair to distance himself from me.

He poured himself a cup of wine and waved the flask at me, but I shook my head. When he took a long swig, still not showing any happiness or relief at seeing me, I felt like throwing the bottle of activated charcoal right at his head.

"Is something wrong?" I asked with deliberate terseness.

Nick didn't reply. He just turned toward the elaborately carved shutters shrouding the lattice window.

"Nick!" I snapped. He spun to me and glared. "What's wrong with you?" I said. "We haven't seen each other in months. I didn't even know if you were alive, and not a second has gone by that I haven't wished that you were standing here right now. And now that you are, the only thing you have to say is about this freaking bottle?" I shook it at him.

I expected fireworks in response, knowing my husband's temperament, but he just silently poured himself more wine, his jaw tight.

I exhaled through my teeth and reached for an empty cup. Nick watched me from the corner of his eye as I filled it to the brim. I took a giant sip of the sweet liquid before unscrewing the cap from the plastic bottle and emptying as much activated charcoal powder into the wine as the instructions directed.

Nick whirled to face me, both brows raised.

"Mistress Parker has to drink this immediately," I explained without looking at him. "It's a remedy for poison from my time, but it might not work. It's probably too late. Still, I'm going to try. It has to be better than bloodletting and leeches." I slid the plastic bottle beneath his bed, hiding it from the chamber attendants. We could get rid of it later. I grabbed the cup containing the medicine and headed for the doors. Nick seized my wrist to stop me, swiping away the cup of charcoal-infused wine with his other hand.

"You are my wife; you are not an apothecary," he said, dropping the cup onto the oak table. Before I could blink, he dug out the plastic bottle from beneath the bed and tossed it into the burning hearth.

"Nick!" I chastised, covering my mouth. It didn't take long for the licking flames to consume the plastic, sending up a disgusting, lethal stench.

He paced away, coughing into his armpit. When he'd settled his throat, he called for a page. A sweaty-faced boy arrived within seconds.

"See to it that Doctor Norris administers this remedy to Mistress Lucinda Parker without delay," Nick commanded with a rasp, handing the boy the cup containing the activated charcoal. "The queen is in need of supper," the king added while facing the carved stone mantel, swirling red wine in his cup. The page bowed and scampered away.

"I wanted to give that to Lucinda myself!" I exclaimed as Nick shut the bedchamber doors.

"I will have the linens made ready so you may wash," he said with his back to me. "You may then take supper."

A dumbfounded laugh spurted from my lips. Hundreds of words I could've shouted at him gathered on my tongue, but none fired. He picked up a scroll from a side table and began leisurely reading it. I couldn't stand being in this room another second. The smoke wasn't the only toxic thing.

"In case you didn't know, I missed you like crazy," I said without looking at him. "All I've done is wait for this day, longing to see you back home and safe. But, once again, this is not at all how I imagined it to be. I don't know what I was thinking."

I felt the heat of his eyes burning my back as I barged through the doors.

Smearing away tears with my fingertips, I power-walked to my chambers while looking any passersby dead-on in the face. I was officially over mentally apologizing for upsetting the nobles' ambitions by marrying the king. *Come at me, trolls! I wanted to shout. I've seen the fucking future, so yeah—I win.*

My chambers smelled like the stinky herbs my friend Mia's mom used to boil, but at least Lucinda wasn't alone. My crepe-pink bell sleeves brushed past the sunken cheeks of Alice, Bridget, and a few other well-wishers as I made my way through to Lucinda.

Doctor Norris was seated beside the bed, dabbing black liquid into the corners of her mouth. It pooled there before oozing down her chin. The gold wine cup beside him confirmed that the liquid was my wine-infused activated charcoal. I moved closer to appraise its effects, but there didn't seem to be any. Lucinda wasn't even able to swallow the stuff. Her eyes were closed, and her skin was an unearthly shade of gray.

Norris grunted as he straightened, a blackened cloth hanging by his side. "I shall call in the minister," he said, vacating the stool for me, but I felt too unsettled to even move.

Mom had warned me that the charcoal would be too late, and she was right. I'd had one chance to seek out help from the modern world and returned with something totally useless. Was there more I could've done?

I blinked away tears. Alice slid beside me, falling to her knees and clasping her hands together. Bridget slipped beside Alice, weeping again, and my legs buckled. I sank to the woven mat and joined them in prayer. I didn't come from a religious family, but as I sat there hearing nothing but Lucinda's shallow breaths, I outright begged for her life.

My eyes sprang open, meeting the silky edge of the bed sheet. This wasn't the first time I'd pleaded for the life of an innocent girl in this century. Nick's sister Kit had been destined to die in Tudor England until I manipulated things to stop it from happening. I'd literally inserted myself into a world where I didn't belong *and* saved the life of a girl who was fated to die at the age of eight.

My stomach crashed to the floor. Did *lex talionis*—an eye for an eye—mean that another life now had to be taken? Was Lucinda's life an exchange for Kit's?

Velvet slippers scuffed the matting behind us. The minister had stepped into the room, motioning for the rest of us to vacate the chamber.

"Are you wearied from your journey, my lady?" Bridget asked me in the drawing-room. Her eyes were so puffy from crying that it was a wonder she could see.

"Hungry?" added Alice, touching my sleeve.

I shook my head. I didn't know why they were so worried about me—all I could think about was the brilliance of Lucinda's smile...of her sitting on her usual stool across from me, stitching tiny butterflies with perfectly arched wings.

An abrupt stiffness swept over the chamber, everyone gasping and bowing.

I glanced behind me into Nick Tudor's heart-stopping stare. He towered in the doorway like the embodiment of kingly presence, a black coat elegantly draped over his doublet.

"Emmeline, will you share a walk with me?" he asked in his velvety voice. He'd never called me by my first name in front of so many people.

For a few moments, I didn't move. I was beyond pissed off with him.

His light eyes softened as they lured mine, his cheeks crimson where his dimples deepened. He felt guilty about earlier, I could tell. Plus, we had an audience, and publicly challenging the king in this world was a fast-track to even more disgrace.

I rose to accept his outstretched hand, my fingers folding into the tingly heat of his skin. We strode right past the guards with the untouchable authority that only the king enjoyed.

The snow had finally melted, but the air remained icy as we began to cross the courtyard. I dropped Nick's hand and folded my arms over my chest. He shrugged off his ebony coat embroidered with gold stars and crescent moons and laid it over my shoulders. I was too cold to resist, but I didn't let him see how much the touch of him soothed me. My heart still burned over how he'd treated me in his bedchamber after having being parted for months.

"Aren't you cold?" was all I said as we strolled in the direction of his private gardens.

He shook his head. "Here feels a great deal warmer after the wretched north."

While the days had become longer, I noticed a sandy-yellow light haloing the exterior palace walls, like extra torches had been lit tonight. Nick looked only at his feet.

"Where did you want to walk to?" I said flatly. I wanted him to know that I was still fuming.

"Perhaps you might tell me, Emmie; you appear to be in command nowadays."

I paused at the gatehouse leading to the privy garden. "Okay, you need to tell me what's wrong," I said, already trembling. "Because it's been pretty horrible here these past few months, and you being cranky with me about something is *not* helping."

He crossed his thick arms. "Cranky?"

"Pissed off," I explained. "Angry…mad…rude. That's it—the way you've been toward me today is *rude*. And I don't care if we're married or that you're the king—you don't treat me that way."

"You left me," he blurted, his voice carrying over the wind. He opened his mouth to say more, but his lips shut again. He looked away from me like he was too upset to speak.

"When?" I asked, dumbstruck. "All I've done is sit here and wait for you like a dutiful Tudor wife!"

He seemed to tower over me, a pillar of strength, but his face held the wounds of a child who'd been abandoned. "For many weeks, Emmie, I have suffered in ways you would believe not. The high north is a place of utter lawlessness, rife with savages who deny the will of their king and willingly seek the fate of high treason. The villages are infested with the pox and plague, and there were complaining soldiers and apostates at every turn. Then the traitor Henry Howard retreated, and I knew not where he was until he was sighted on the roads toward Robin House. All I could think of was you being there without me, and how Howard wishes us both dead. I made straight for Robin House until I received word of your return to Hampton Court. You cannot imagine my relief when I learned that you were safe here at the palace, and well—"

"Yes, actually, I *can* imagine that relief," I cut in.

"However, when I arrived here," Nick continued, "I found you to be gone entirely, with no letter or word of any kind and no sign of the enchanted ring. When my gentlemen informed me that you had been lodging in my bedchamber, I sat there in wait for countless hours, believing with every stroke of the clock that you would not ever return to me…and perhaps with my son and heir in your belly!"

My mouth hung open as I processed his barrage of words. "There's no son—or daughter—at least not yet. And that's why you're pissed off? Because I went back to my time to get medicine that could save Lucinda's life?"

He raised a finger. "You swore an oath to me that you would never take leave to your time without me unless your life was at stake. *Only together.* Did you forget our vow in such haste?" He looked like he might grab my shoulders and shake me, but he clenched his fists at his sides. "What if that ring, so utterly fickle, had failed in its enchantment and you could never return here? You wagered everything we have for a maiden that you do not even like!"

"No, I *do* like her," I said, stepping forward to find his face in the shadows of the courtyard. "All Lucinda Parker ever did to upset me was love you—the same way I do. How am I supposed to hate her for something I do myself as freely as breathing?" My breath shook, a quivery puff of ice. "The poison that Mistress Parker took was meant for me. So was the arrow that nearly killed Alice Grey. There was a fencing show at court while you were away, and almost everybody got up and left in protest when I showed up. The people hate me here!"

A blast fired somewhere west of the palace, chased by the muffled shouts of men, but Nick didn't move. He gripped his forehead with one hand, holding it there as we stood in a deadlock.

An alarming crunch behind me turned out to be the approaching boots of Doctor Norris. "Your Majesty," he said with a bow. "You may wish to be informed that, moments past, the queen's lady, Mistress Lucinda Parker, succumbed to death. The minister shall make preparations in haste, so the queen may return to her chambers."

"What?" I cried, tears obscuring my vision. "Mistress Parker died?"

The doctor's reply was an apologetic bow.

I should've gone to my chambers to comfort Alice and Bridget, but my feet burst into a stride toward the blackness of the Privy Garden—as far away from the death scene as I could get. It didn't matter that I was racing into ice-cold darkness; I couldn't get what the witch had told me out of my head. Her warning blazed through my brain, burning away every other thought.

"This be the devil's work...He shall come for thee...Thee hast been up to nay good...changing things that should not be hath changed. Lex talionis."

"Emmie!" Nick called behind me, but I kept going, chased by the bouncing light of his lantern.

When I reached the dragon fountain, I dropped onto the stone bench, searching for an end to the nausea choking my insides. My fingers were like icicles, but the blue-diamond ring burned hot on my thumb. I'd had no idea what saving Kit's life would do to this world, not to mention marrying its king, otherwise destined to wed Henriette of France. Now, because of my decisions, a kindhearted girl with a baby daughter would never open her eyes again and little Ellie would grow up without a mom.

"Why must you be out here in the chill?" Nick scolded when he caught up to me.

"It's an eye for an eye," I muttered, rocking back and forth to keep myself from freezing. "Lex talionis."

He sat beside me and wrapped an arm around my back. "Again?" he said, short of breath.

"Mistress Parker's death," I stammered. "It's payback for saving Kit's life when she was meant to die—or for me being here; I don't know. Maybe both."

"Payback?"

I searched for an older word. "Retribution."

Nick's arm slid off my back, his voice constricting. "You sound as if you are speaking of saving Kit's life with regret."

"I don't regret it," I admitted, tears dribbling down my cheeks. "The truth is, I'd make the same decisions all over again. But that doesn't mean what we did was right." I gripped my neck, feeling like I was choking, needing air. "You know as well as I do that none of this has been right."

Nick got up and crouched to face me. He collected my hands in his, his desperate eyes finding mine. "Emmie, no. No, you cannot do this. You cannot lose heart now. We have come too far."

I looked down at him through my swelling shame. How could I have ever believed that loving him this much would justify changing the path of history? How could I have been so selfish?

"I need to tell you something," I said to his stricken face. "I visited a soothsayer while you were in the north. There's one who lives near Robin House. She's poor and harmless; *please* don't do anything to hurt her. But I showed her the blue-diamond ring, and she recognized her cousin's work in the ring's magic. Her cousin was called Joanie—she worked for you once at Whitehall Palace as a maidservant." It didn't shock me that Nick demonstrated no recollection of the chambermaid, but his eyes hung on my every word. "This maid then went on to work for Mary, Queen of Scots when she was imprisoned. You know that Mary wants the English throne, and she made the witch Joanie curse the ring to get rid of you. What Joanie did, though, was curse the ring to take you far away from this world—not to kill you, but to save your life. She enchanted this ring to send you somewhere far away from here, where you'd not only be safe but happy. Do you get it? You would've been happy there...in my time...with me."

A flush drifted into his cheeks, and I wished there wasn't more of this story I had to tell.

"But Nick, the witch also said that we'd been up to no good... changing things that shouldn't have been changed. She said the phrase: Lex—"

"Oh Christ, may we have not a moment alone!" Nick interrupted, standing and spinning to where Francis Beaumont drew closer with four guards.

Beads of sweat gleamed from the earl's forehead, even though it had to be zero degrees. "Your Grace, the palace is...under siege," Francis stammered like he couldn't quite believe it. Nick and I gasped in unison. Francis continued his explanation, his voice dazed. "There is arrow fire beyond the west gatehouse. Horsemen in the hundreds have mounted an assault. They are armed with all manner of force and say hundreds more are at the ready. Henry Howard is leading them."

Nick's jaw hung open before he lurched forward and grabbed Francis's collar with both hands. "Are you damn certain?"

The earl nodded, his body rigid with fear.

Nick released him and pressed his palms together at his chin. "Go now and arrest every traitor that dares rebel against their king."

"But the numbers of m-men, Majesty. There are beyond—"

"Make haste!" Nick spat, and Francis hurried back toward the palace, trailed by the guards. I got up and leaned on my tiptoes to see over the hedges, my mouth hanging open. The glow of the lanterns had drawn nearer, and the air hummed with distant voices. Enraged men were attacking the palace, like something out of the French Revolution. I was shaking like a tree in a hurricane.

"You must be hidden," Nick said faintly, spinning in all directions like a cave might magically appear before us. "Perhaps in some place within the kitchens."

He went on, muttering about hiding spots and priest holes, but his voice drowned beneath the volume of my realization. The nobles' uprising was no longer against me; it was against the King of England himself and the Tudor dynasty as I knew it.

"No," I stated, my heart drumming through my ears. "Hiding isn't going to solve this."

"Only until it is over," Nick insisted, tugging me toward the path that wound past the sunken fishponds toward the kitchens.

I wrestled free. "This will never be over!" My breath was wild… jagged…but I kept speaking. "This is the end of the road, Nick." I couldn't see through the tears swelling in my eyes. "I've loved being with you, and even here in Tudor England—believe me, I have loved you more than I have ever loved anyone or anything in this life—but we can't do this to the world anymore. I have to leave and never come back."

He shuffled back a step like my words were bullets. He shook his head at me with a slow dread, his startled eyes pinned to mine. "No, Emmie."

"The world doesn't want me here," I pleaded, my tears spilling over. "I don't belong in this time, and the world knows it. It's like it's spitting me back out. People are dying."

"*I* will die without you!"

I stretched out a shaky hand, the blue-diamond ring like a light-bulb on my thumb. "Then come with me," I said. "It's what the curse wanted. I was never meant to be here; you were meant to come to my world. That's what was meant to happen." I gestured at the palace's stifling redbrick walls. "I *know* you want to escape all this pressure you constantly feel…it's why you love going to Robin House, where life feels safe and simple. It's why you chose to get married there!"

"Enough!" he hissed, folding an arm around his back like I might physically yank him into the future against his will. "You will not do this to me. We made our choice."

A cannon blast made us both jump. Nick gaped up at the palace wall, his forehead creased with distress. But when his eyes returned to mine, his expression had hardened with resolve.

"You will not dare give up on us, Emmie. You know I can never abandon my kingdom, leaving my sister to civil war and bloodshed. When I asked for your hand in marriage, you made a vow that you would never take leave of me again. I have wagered all I have for you and given you everything in return…I made you a queen! God willing, you will be the mother to a king—why is it not enough?"

"You still don't get it!" I implored. "I don't want the kingdom, the riches, the pressures. I didn't want to be a queen…I only came here for *you*. That's all I've ever wanted out of this."

"So, it is I who is now not enough," he observed, looking like I'd punched him in the heart.

"Nick, look at what's happening here!" I pointed toward the screams and shouts floating from the palace. The way he was looking at me—the absolute heartbreak in his face—hacked me to pieces. "Nothing lasts forever," I said, the agony in my chest making me curl forward.

"*We* do," Nick replied, struggling to speak. "We last forever." He reached forward and gripped the sleeve over my wrist, finding my bare skin with his fingers. "Do not let go," he pleaded. "Ne dimittas."

I plucked the gold wedding band off my finger and slapped it into his palm. I knew that Nick loved me, but not enough to trade his kingdom for it. He'd beg me to stay, but he'd never come with me and leave Tudor England…and every moment I stayed, I put him further in danger.

I wanted to freeze time so I could memorize every speck of him—a man I couldn't imagine living without—but he'd become a fuzzy silhouette through my weeping eyes.

When Nick lurched forward, begging me once again to hide with him, I exhaled with frustration and pressed my hands to his silky doublet, physically shoving him back toward the court.

"If you're not going to come with me, then *go away*," I ordered. "Go home. This is over now, do you understand? We tried, we really tried, but it's done, okay? Pretend I died…pretend I drowned in the river. You'll be free to marry again. Someone the people accept; someone right for you. Maybe you can still have Henriette."

I couldn't look at him but heard him crying—a sound I never wanted to hear again. I couldn't listen—I needed to leave before he broke my resolve.

"Just get away from me!" I screamed.

At that, Nick jerked back a step, shaking his head like he was flicking away flies. He brushed the heels of his hands beneath his eyes and cleared his throat, his tear-stained voice barely his own.

"If you wish to take leave of my heart so resolutely, Emmie, then so it shall be. May God be with you."

With those abrupt words, he spun around and headed back toward the palace, swallowed by the darkness like he'd only ever been a figment of my imagination.

I sank into the gravel and shuddered with sobs, hating myself for every mistake I'd made. How could I have ever thought I could be the fierce girl who became a queen and ruled the world like a badass. If only this was a fairytale instead of the real world, where girls like me didn't get to become Tudor queens.

With tears dripping from my eyes, I stepped over the knot gardens until I reached a patch of earth concealed by a row of manicured hedges. Grateful to be protected from the bitter wind, I lay on the freezing soil and pressed my eyes shut.

"I'm so sorry," I whispered, curling up into a fetal position. I lay there in a quivering ball, repeating my apology to Nick, Alice, Bridget, Kit, Lucinda—and everyone who meant something to me here. I begged for the oblivion of sleep to free me from the hideous ache in my heart and carry me home to where I truly belonged.

When footsteps neared, I froze, unable to breathe. Multiple pairs of boots were marching along the path nearest to where I lay.

"She hides here!" shouted a commanding voice that I knew too well.

My terrified gaze rolled upward to recognize Nick's broad silhouette through the glimmer of a lantern. The wobble of light moved, revealing a massive, familiar figure beside the king. I scrambled up, trying to edge away. Henry Howard stood beside Nick, a swarm of unkempt men gathered behind them waving pitchforks and hammers. My chest tightened with so much fear that it hurt to breathe.

Howard lifted his lamp to see me better. I crouched to escape it, but the light followed me. I was a mouse in a cage. Why was Nick just standing next to him like the two were old mates? Why weren't they tearing each other to shreds? Why wasn't Nick protecting me?

"Let the king speak!" spat Howard in his bullish tone. "Majesty, what say you? Will you persist in your offense of our gracious God by once more naming this heretic as our queen?"

My gaze flew to Nick, who looked down at me with a face absent of life. For the first time, he looked like the man in the terrifying portrait with the dead eyes and the cruel mouth. He was the embodiment of Nicholas the Ironheart.

"My lords," he said loudly, "I swear on my soul that this girl before me, who once bewitched your devoted king in a manner most vile and depraved, is a monstrous traitor to both king and God."

My head shook wildly, gratified men smirking down at me from all directions. Henry Howard glowed with smug victory, baring his teeth at me like the animal he was.

"By order of the king, bring her to the Tower to await trial on charges of heresy and high treason against the King's Majesty," the former duke bellowed.

"God save the king!" the men called in response.

"Nick, *please!*" I cried.

The sky blurred as my husband bent over me, the scent of fresh roses finding my nose. I searched for love in his eyes but found only storms of anger. He took hold of my thumb and yanked the blue-diamond ring right off it.

"No!" I shrieked.

"Take her to the Tower," Nick snarled without looking at me. "This witch dares enchant and humiliate the King of England. She has attempted to consort with the devil and extort from His Majesty a bastard child. She will stand trial to suffer a traitor's death."

"God save the king!" the orchestra of voices repeated. "God save His Grace!"

Their cries overwhelmed my screams as a hundred filthy fingers dug into my skin, stripping me of the rest of my jewelry and lifting me to the raven sky.

22

THE FURY TEARING THROUGH MY VEINS OBLITERATED ANY PHYSICAL pain as I was manhandled back across the gardens, through the snaking redbrick corridors, and into the gusty west courtyard. The shadowy square teemed with raging men brandishing homemade weapons, their shouts of treason striking me like gunfire from all directions. A subhuman scream cut through the noise, and when my throat burned from the pressure, I realized the roar was mine.

Nobody tried to help me as brutal hands shoved me through the battered gatehouse, across the windy moat bridge, and down the grassy slope leading to the River Thames.

"How could you do this to me!" I howled at the palace wall in the absurd hope that Nick might hear me.

Silence.

My teeth ground together, and my hands balled into fists. Was it possible that his public condemnation of me was just a trick? But it couldn't be. The chances of Nick openly accusing me of treason and heresy as part of some secret plan left me empty. If he cared about my safety, he would've just let me go back to my time. No, it was obvious to me what was happening here: Nick had aligned himself with Norfolk—allowing violent men to haul me away—because I'd wanted to end our relationship for good and leave him. He was never going to let me just walk away, leaving him brokenhearted and humiliated. I'd rejected the vengeful Nicholas the Ironheart one too many times, and now he wanted me to suffer for it. I'd been so stupid to think I was immune to his notoriously unforgiving nature.

"I hate you!" I screamed into the infuriatingly silent sky of stars.

The tides were too low for a barge to dock at the pier, so the rioters pushed me right onto the slippery mudflats. I covered my nose as they marched me across slimy mud soaked in sewage to reach the deeper water.

Somewhere inside the palace, Nick was probably sharing a flask of warmed wine with Henry Howard before an open fire, brown-nosing the former duke to win back the trust of the nobles. I'd been told how dangerous a dissenting duke can be to a king—especially when that duke had won the support of other aristocrats. Despite the risks he had taken for our relationship, Nick had always put his kingdom first, and now he'd handed me over to his enemies to save himself from being dethroned and dishonored. I hoped the guilt of that chewed holes in his insides for the rest of his life.

Another cry of anger burst from my lips as I lost my footing on the slick dirt and face-planted into the putrid sludge.

Two guards hoisted me up by my shoulders and threw me over the barge's edge, my legs tangling in my skirts caked in mud. As I clung to a bench seat, the barge glided away from the sparkling lanterns of Hampton Court Palace.

Away from Nick, and any hope I had of him intervening in my arrest.

Two guards sat between the oarsmen and me, gripping their swords with both hands. They shivered within their fur wraps. My adrenalin rush was fading, and the freezing air began to pierce through Nick's filthy coat.

"Ugh!" I grunted as I shook it off my shoulders like it was woven from the webs of spiders. I hurtled the slash of midnight velvet out into the middle of the river. Black water swallowed the costly fabric in seconds.

"Christ in heaven!" spat one of the guards. He reached out and smacked me on the back of my head. I swore at him, using all the modern curse words I could think of.

"Let her freeze," snarled the other one.

A guard wouldn't dare strike a queen unless he was sure her fate was already sealed. Whatever Henry Howard had done to poison the country against me was beyond repair, and now I didn't even have the blue-diamond ring so I could disappear. If only I'd told Nick what the witch had said about the enchanted ring losing all its power. Maybe then he wouldn't have bothered jerking it off my thumb, and I'd still have been able to escape.

I wrapped myself into a tight ball and shivered into my knees, praying that the journey would pass quickly. When the temperature dropped, the men on the boat ceased their chatter, leaving only the eerie soundtrack of oars cutting through the frosty river flow. My mind doubled back to the last time I'd been imprisoned at the Tower of London—the lecherous jailers and threats of torture—and I pushed each terrifying memory away.

One minute at a time, Emmie. Just live through this next minute.

I was so cold that I considered begging the guards for one of their furs. But determined to hold on to any dignity I had left, I instead refocused my mind by picturing a sun-swept beach speckled with palm trees. It got me through the time it took to reach the onion-shaped turrets of the Tower that dominated the skyscape. As if waiting for us, the Traitor's Gate portcullis stretched open its sharp teeth to swallow us whole. A single pigeon flew low, swooping past my ear. I envied the bird's freedom, its uncomplicated life. It'd never dream of trying to live four hundred years back in time with a capricious Tudor king predestined to become a tyrant. *Nicholas the Ironheart*—it wasn't like I'd never been warned about his vindictive nature.

"I need water," I grunted through my sticky throat as the boatmen tossed the ropes over the wooden posts. Ignoring my request, the guards shoved me onto the rotting deck that did little to improve the rancid, decomposing stink of the river.

I gazed up at the impossibly tall fortress of the Tower of London with its stone battlements, menacing slit windows, and double defensive walls. The death site of three sixteenth-century Queens of England.

You're not leaving here alive, Emmie.

The crippling terror in my body glued my short heels to the cobblestones, and the guards had to drag my weakened legs up the jagged slope. At the base of the stone stairs leading to the gardens, a man waited in a cap and black cloak with silver buttons. It was Master Carey, the Constable of the Tower, who'd handled my imprisonment here last time—back when this time-traveling mess began.

"Hello again," I said to him, followed by an abrupt chuckle. I was becoming delirious, which was probably a symptom of hypothermia.

Master Carey said little as he gravely escorted me upstairs to the royal lodgings inside the tower of St. Thomas, where Nick had pressed me against the windowpane on the night before my coronation. Shoving that memory out of my head, I hid my surprise—and relief—that I wasn't being led downstairs to a cell. I suddenly gasped at the thought Nick might be waiting in the royal apartments for me, ready to reveal that this was nothing more than an off-color joke—the worst prank ever played. But then I berated myself for giving him that much credit: the chambers were devoid of any kingly splendor, the priceless furnishings and wall tapestries stripped away, leaving only a barren, drafty space.

Instead of the spacious bedchamber I'd slept in last time, I was steered into a smaller room and left alone, the stark clang of an iron lock bolting shut behind me. Tugging on the rigid handle assured me that I was a prisoner here. I marked the length of the space with thirteen short paces along the tiled floor that reached a small fireplace. The rest of the modest room held only a single bed, an oak desk, and a standing candelabrum that I momentarily considered stabbing a guard with in an effort to escape.

I tugged the woolen blanket off the bed and wrapped it around me, crossing the tiles to peer through the two narrow stained-glass windows. So much had happened since I'd last seen this view of the River Thames from the neighboring bedchamber. The jumble of turreted buildings looked so short compared with twenty-first-century London—like a top layer had been sliced off the city. Despite the darkness of nightfall, ships and cargo vessels sat waiting for moorings near the north bank of the river. I swung open the window for some fresh air, but a freezing gust of wind slapped me in the face, bringing the fetid stench of the castle moat directly below, and I wrenched the windowpane shut again.

I wished for a fire, but there was no wood.

Another memory of Nick and I wrapped up in silk sheets at Robin House drifted into my vision, his breath hot against my ear as he pushed into me, and I forced the image away. As I lay down on the hard bed, my thoughts turned to the monster Henry Howard. During our first meeting at Hampton Court, he'd reminded me of the fate of Anne Boleyn—the girl that King Henry the Eighth had married for love, only to execute her when she upset him one too many times. My stomach twisted into a sickening knot. As hideous as Howard was, he'd seen this coming before anyone. I was ending up just like Anne Boleyn, except I'd been a Tudor queen less than a year.

I crawled beneath the blanket and tossed fitfully. Did Nick really have the stomach to put me through a grueling trial—let alone a beheading—out of pure anger and spite? Or was this all part of a terrible plan to scare me, to force me into following his command and staying in this century? He'd sprung our wedding day on me without so much as a conversation—that was proof of his tyrannical nature that I'd willingly overlooked. Or else, perhaps my arrest was a symbolic gesture to appease the raging Duke of Norfolk and his army, and Nick planned to release me once things had cooled down. If that were so, though, why wouldn't he have just let me escape using the blue-diamond ring? If he wanted me safe, why would he publicly condemn me and risk my life? There was no coming back from a king's damnation in a place like this.

The endless questions chased themselves through my mind until, in the early hours of the morning, I drifted off to sleep, but it was shallow. I jerked awake at every distant sound, my terrified mind convinced that each creak and clang was the executioner coming for me.

Counting blood-red sunsets told me that I spent an agonizing eleven days locked in that silent chamber with zero visitors or word from the king. At every waking moment, I was ready to fight in case someone burst in with a torture device or an executioner's axe. Meager bits of food were brought to me, but nothing else. There was too much time to think, too much time to cut open every moment of my relationship with Nick and dig through the tender wounds to unearth the mistakes I'd made.

Our love had exploded like a meteor that had fused us together so fast that I still hadn't caught my breath. He'd felt like home—like my *person* in the world—so incredibly quickly that it had colored every decision I'd made, even the one to try to save him from his dreadful fate as Nicholas the Ironheart. Before we met, I knew him only as the sixteenth-century king who ruthlessly ruled his nation. When I figured out that was because his little sister Kit had been murdered by one of his most trusted subjects, I'd had only one goal: to save Kit and to stop the boy I loved from becoming that tyrant.

Sunlight on the leaded windowpane reflected my stricken face like a mirror as I faced one truth after another: I adored Kit, but saving her life was perhaps the biggest mistake of all. I'd tried to change the path of history, Lucinda's life had been taken in exchange, and then I'd pushed Nick toward his hideous destiny anyway. I had been such an idiot to believe that I could insert myself into the past and live in it as a queen. It had proved almost impossible to convince the most accomplished people in the land that a twenty-first-century girl had the makings of a Tudor queen. Maybe the only chance Nick and I ever had was if he'd chosen to stay with me in my time and disappeared from the Tudor world. Surely life could've gone on here with Kit as the rightful new queen. For all this time, we'd been fighting an unwinnable battle, and while Kit may have been saved, Nick had been lost to darkness the way the books had always said.

I was still brooding over the timeline when, on the fifteenth day of my imprisonment, an unexpected tap sounded on the wooden door. I froze with fear as it opened slowly with an unnerving creak. Alice Grey looked so pasty and gaunt in the doorway that I almost didn't recognize her. She gaped at the sight of me, her brows drawn, and I realized I must have looked as unwell to her as she did to me. When we both recovered from our shock, we fell into each other, hugging, and I stifled the urge to sob into her soft hair that smelled like cinnamon cake.

"I was not permitted to come before now," she said, helping me to sit on the bed, treating me as if I was fragile. Tears pooled in her molten brown eyes as she searched my face. "My lady, are you greatly sore of heart?"

"I'm terrible," I replied honestly. "I've lost everything." Speaking the words aloud shattered my soul. It wasn't just my life here that was over. Unless Nick freed me, I'd never see the twenty-first century again: my mom, my friends—even Dad, with his stuffy Camry and boring public radio programs.

Alice was rubbing my shoulder, her other hand catching her escaping tears.

"What's happening at court?" I said faintly. I couldn't bring myself to ask about Nick.

She settled herself with a deep exhale. "The palace has calmed. The king has reformed his council, and Francis speaks in a manner most heartening. There have been feasts, and merriments, and the courtiers are making ready for the Easter celebrations."

I nodded, staring at my lap. Now that I'd been booted from the palace, the Tudor court was thriving again. I was right, I'd been nothing more than a parasite here, a plague. An alien from an incompatible world who did nothing but delay the king's malevolent, self-serving temperament by a year at best.

"Where's Bridget?" I asked.

Alice sighed. "Mistress Nightingale has taken leave to Buckinghamshire. I fear her heart has become much troubled these past weeks."

Shame crawled up my throat. When I'd met Bridget, she'd been so chirpy, so excited about becoming a maid of honour and meeting a rich husband. Another thing that had been lost because of me.

Alice placed a hand over mine, a cold band of polished gold surprising my skin.

She inhaled a breath. "Francis and I are married."

My mouth fell open. "Oh my gosh, that's amazing!" I hadn't smiled in so long that it nearly hurt my cheeks. "Where did you do it?"

"At court." The flush in her cheeks exposed the happiness that she was trying to hide from me. "My lady, that you could not be there has caused me much sorrow. After everything, Francis wished to wait not."

"No, of course not, it's brilliant news." I managed another smile of encouragement. At least Alice's life was falling into place, even if mine was crumbling to pieces.

The conversation dropped to silence before I summoned the courage to ask Alice if she knew anything about my fate.

Her lips trembled, her eyes meeting her lap. "Your trial will take place on the morrow."

All the blood fled my face. A sort of darkness overcame the room, and I lost all sense of myself, like I might pass out. Alice steadied me with both hands, and I could tell that she was fighting not to break down. "I wish I could help you," she stammered through a fresh swell of tears.

"I know," I said, leaning into her. The urge to tell her the truth about me—about where I came from—was so intense that it crawled onto my tongue, begging to be set free. This could be my last chance. But if I told Alice Grey that I was from the future, it'd put her at risk of being complicit in my alleged sorcery. I wanted her to enjoy her wedded bliss with Francis, not to have to testify against me at my trial. I had endangered too many people in this world already. So I sat there and clung to her hands, blessing her over and over in my heart for having been my one rock in this place.

She glanced up at me, sensing something.

"I love you, Alice," was all I managed through my choked voice. "You might be the best thing in this entire world. I will *never* forget you."

Her words were breathless whispers. "You are my queen and lady most dear, and I will love you forevermore."

The depth of her sobs as we hugged one last time made clear that she believed I didn't stand a chance at tomorrow's trial. I'd admired

Alice Grey for so many things: because she was spirited, feminist—for a Tudor, anyway—sharp as a tack...and almost always right.

I really was doomed.

With no hope of sleep that night, I lay awake, piecing together a plan. Surely Nick would be at the trial and would see how weak I'd become in just two weeks. He was a vengeful and merciless man—I knew that now better than anyone—but I still believed he'd loved me as completely as I'd loved him. It made me sick to my stomach to think that I could still imagine kissing him deeply—and even hunger for it. It was beyond shameful, like doting on a serial killer or the devil himself, but I guessed that love just didn't switch off that fast. And maybe I could use any feelings still between us to my advantage: at the trial, I would do whatever I could to convince Nick Tudor to set me free. I'd mouth the words "I love you" to him—even scream them if I had to.

I wasn't too proud to beg him for my life.

23

At first light, I was marched downstairs to the Tower of London's aging Great Hall, where hundreds of men jostled for space in their flat caps and showiest coats. I braced myself for the appearance of Nick, but I couldn't catch sight of him anywhere.

The guards ushered me up a short ladder and onto a wooden platform. On a table before me sat my three judges in somber black cloaks—the Baron of Wharton, the Earl of Dorset, and Henry fucking Howard. I wanted to hurl all over his infuriating smirk and dumbass ostrich-feather hat. He'd launched a rebellion against the king and queen—how was he judging *me* and not the other way around? However, Howard's presence confirmed that he and Nick had officially kissed and made up. Bile pooled in the back of my throat.

Late-arriving spectators shuffled in from the sides of the hall to watch the proceedings. I searched for Alice, but there wasn't a single female in the room apart from me. And still no sign of Nick.

Coward.

Lord Wharton's grating voice flooded the cavernous space. "Queen Emmeline, you are arraigned before this commission on charges of conspiring to procure the death and destruction of His

Majesty, the King of England, through means of malice, witchcraft, and adulterous incitations. How do you answer the charges?"

I pressed my lips together, trying to decide what to say. I'd been given no legal counsel or preparation of any kind.

"Not guilty," I said, clearing my hoarse throat. "I am innocent of the charges."

The baron then launched into a ridiculous story about me pursuing an adulterous affair with the Earl of Warwick—purely because I'd made a joke about him being in the king's disguise at the masquerade feast. It was the first of countless testimonies about how I'd bewitched the king without genuine love in my heart while secretly plotting against him. Hilariously, I was even accused of trying to seduce Mister Andrea Bon Compagni behind closed doors in my workshop, which was also the place where I apparently experimented with recipes of witchcraft. The young maidservant Clemence from Robin House was summoned as a witness and stood shaking before the jury. Unable to look at me, she testified that I'd regularly met with a village witch, and appalled cries exploded from the sidelines. I had no idea how she'd known about my visit to the witch in the hamlet, but I didn't blame her for her testimony. For all I knew, Clemence had been forced to speak out against me; plus, she was right—I had met with the witch, even if it was only once. More outrageous lies were outlined in excruciating and humiliating detail before the accusations turned to my family origins. With nobody able to verify the existence of the Grace family from Worthing, and Henry Howard arguing that I wasn't his niece and that I'd bewitched him to believe it so, the deceit became overwhelming. At no point was Nick implicated in anything; the all-powerful King of England was evidently so unimpeachable that he didn't even have to bother showing up for the trial. So much for begging him for my life.

I clenched my eyes until they were dry. There was no way these men would see me cry.

My thighs were aching after standing for so long before Lord Wharton finally called for silence. While his voice was grave, his eyes twinkled beside the equally as smug Henry Howard.

"This day, Queen Emmeline has made a plea of not guilty to the lords stood here as councilors to our sovereign lord and king, Nicholas of England, and the peers of the realm. After being examined here, each lord has said, one and all, that Queen Emmeline is guilty of all the charges brought against her."

An icy gust of wind blew through me, and I thought I might topple over.

Lord Wharton focused his fierce eyes on me. "Madam, as you have been found guilty, I shall proceed in judgment. You are hereby sentenced to die. From here, you will be taken to your prison in the tower of St. Thomas, and on the morrow at the strike of dawn, you will be executed by beheading, burning, or hanging as shall please His Majesty the King. Your marriage to King Nicholas of England is now null and void. You have no crown, no land or title, and you shall henceforth be known as Mistress Emmeline Grace."

A cough—or perhaps a chortle—burst from Henry Howard's haughty mouth. I wanted to drive my fist through his heart. Fortunately for him, I was swiftly escorted from the hall and back upstairs to my locked chamber. A stale cheese tart sat waiting for me on the table, but I could hardly breathe, let alone eat.

Nick didn't even come to the trial.

He couldn't pay me the freaking courtesy of turning up.

I smacked the pewter plate holding the cheese tart off the table, covering my ears at the brassy clanging. My fingertips slipped into my hair, and I grabbed the dirty clumps and tugged hard, wishing the pain would overwhelm my thoughts until I couldn't hear them anymore.

Why couldn't he have just let me go? Neither Nick nor I had to go through any of this—if he'd just let me travel back to my time and pretended that I'd drowned in the river, we'd both be safe. Did he really prefer the option of slicing off my head?

I fell onto the bed, lying flat and motionless like a corpse.

No matter how I tried to make sense of it all, my thoughts always circled back to the same place: this was my fault. Nick couldn't let me go because he believed that I'd abandoned him. I'd known about his monstrous vengeful streak since the beginning—what he was capable of if he felt betrayed—and I'd willingly walked right into the firing line.

Way to go, Emmeline Eleanor WTF-have-you-gotten-yourself-into Grace.

Now, because of my mistakes—and my deluded, naïve belief in love—the wrath of Nicholas the Ironheart would make sure that I wouldn't leave Tudor England alive.

Nightmares invaded any sleep I managed that night, filled with horrific sounds and images of wild spectators howling for my head at Tower Hill. If only it was still winter with a delayed sunrise to bless me with a few more hours of life. But spring had arrived and dawn would come quickly, bringing with it my execution.

As soon as the inky-black sky through the stained-glass window began to lighten, there was zero chance of more sleep. Frail with terror but determined not to be dragged outside in the nude, I tied on my plain, mint-colored kirtle and sat on the end of the bed. I lowered my head into a meditative position and tried to switch off my mind. I'd seen movies where criminals were in such a numb daze by the time they climbed the gallows that they didn't look afraid anymore.

No such luck. When a key twisted in the lock, and the wooden door swung heavily toward me, my anxious stomach surged and heaved, emptying bile onto the painted floor tiles.

"Wash that in haste," a velvety voice commanded the door guard.

I glanced up into the sunlit features of Nicholas the Ironheart. Immediately, I slid away as if looking directly at him would kill me right there. I felt his beautiful, deadly eyes assessing me.

"Go away…just go away," I whispered lifelessly. I resisted the urge to puke again as the guard scrambled in with a bucket and cloth. Nick stood with his arms crossed, glaring at the guard, who gave the spot a token cleaning before escaping again. The king charged at the door, heaving it shut before twisting a key in the lock.

I finally found my voice. "Get *OUT!*" I screamed. How dare he show his face to me? I was so physically livid that I could feel my skin burning and my teeth grinding.

Nick held out a shaky palm. "I bid you to be calm." The phrase shot me back in time to the similar words he'd said when we'd first met, when I was a prisoner in the Tower of London last time. *"Be calm,"* was the first thing he'd ever said to me. We'd officially come full circle.

I opened my mouth to reply, but the torrent of abusive things that I wanted to yell became confused in my throat. My jaw clenched until it hurt. Even if Nick had sorted out his messed-up head and was here to issue an eleventh-hour pardon, it was too late. I'd been publicly shamed and sentenced to die as a traitor, a witch, and an adulteress. Not even the king had the power to turn back the clock on that.

"How could you do this to me?" I eventually gasped. I wanted to shout the words, but my throat was too choked, my eyes too thick with tears, my chest too tight.

"I pray that you hear me," said Nick, sinking to his knees before me until our faces were level. "You must know the cause of mine actions." The regret filling his eyes flooded me with more rage.

"You *do* feel bad," I realized with horror. "You feel guilty about what you did to me in one of your insane tantrums, and now you want me to forgive you so you'll feel better after it's over. You're off your freaking rocker!"

When he opened his mouth again, I cut in first.

"Why didn't you just let me go?" I pleaded, my voice shredded. "No one would have looked for me in the gardens at night. I'd have just fallen asleep. I'd have disappeared. There were so many ways you could've swept my memory under the rug and moved on. I gave up everything for you—my entire life! *Why* would you punish me like this?" My face crumbled with more stinging tears. Worse than the punishment itself was the thought that Nick had instigated it...that had always been the most painful part.

"Forgive me...I bid you to cry not," he said throatily, reaching for me. I jerked away so violently that his hands shot up in defense.

"Don't you ever tell me what to do," I spat. "And don't you ever touch me again. Just get the hell away from me!" I crossed my arms over my knees, forming a tight ball. I'd stay that way until they dragged me down to the executioner's block. I was no longer human. I was ready to die.

A thundering of raging voices surged from a distance below, wafting through the window that was slightly ajar.

The crowds are already waiting for me. My nightmare is coming true.

I tried to shut out the hideous chants with my hands over my ears but to no avail.

Nick had moved to the window. "Do you hear that?" he asked me.

I threw him my most colorful foul-mouthed response.

Despite the modern language, I could tell he grasped the sentiment. He bit his lip and edged the windowpane further open with his elbow. "Listen closely," he said, watching me.

He actually wanted me to hear the bloodthirsty Emmie-haters crying for my head. What kind of sicko was he? Before I could reply, the drumming of feet from afar was chased by three cries of "God save the king!"

Nick swallowed tightly. "It is now done," he said.

"What's done?" I could've slapped him.

"The traitor, Henry Howard, has been beheaded."

My lips fell open. "*What?*"

I didn't think I'd heard right. The room was whirling in all directions.

Nick stepped closer to me, his voice thickening. "Last night, Henry Howard was tried, charged, and convicted of high treason against the King of England for launching a plot of rebellion and for plotting the poisoning of Mistress Lucinda Parker."

He took a shaky seat beside me on the bed. All I could do was gape at his ashen face, his soft scent of roses infuriatingly close to my nose. I hated myself for how much I still wanted to touch him, to run my fingers through his hair, to press my lips to his. *Why* couldn't I be free of that at least before he killed me?

A shimmer of tears coated Nick's eyes. "Emmie, I did not permit you to vanish from the garden the night of your arrest because I was in need of time. I had to make new a record of my last will and testament so I could make no error in naming the Princess Catherine

Tudor as my successor. Kit was plainly my heir apparent, but I needed to make the line of succession certain if I am to surrender my kingship. I was also in need of time to gather the evidence to ensure that Henry Howard would be convicted of treason." His distressed eyes could hardly meet mine. "I pray you will forgive me. You needed to believe it to be true as much as my subjects or their faithless army may have killed you in haste. I had to make certain there was no suspicion of any plotting between us."

I lowered the arm that had covered my eyes as if it could protect me from Nick's insane words. My voice was a faint line. "What on earth are you talking about?"

He glanced back at me, and our gazes seared together, drawing heat to my cheeks. Nick's breath wavered as he spoke. "The instant that I learned of Howard mounting his assault on the castle—meaning to take you from me—I was certain that I would boil alive every last one of them. Not only the men, but their brothers…their fathers…their sons." His cheeks reddened with shame. "I cannot bear to handle this beast I have inside me. You know there is true darkness in me. But the blacker the darkness, the brighter the light that shines upon it." He slid closer to me until our thighs rubbed together, his presence rattling me from the inside out. "I have tried to forget you, more than once. I did consider removing you from my world that night in the garden—bidding you to leave with my blessing—but all I see without you is intolerable darkness." His forehead tilted so close to mine that I could taste the mint on his breath. "Therefore, if you must take leave of this kingdom and I cannot bid you to stay, then—with your consent—I will leave with you."

He dug into the folds of his coat and presented a flash of brilliant blue. Both our fingers trembled as he gently glided the blue-diamond ring down my thumb.

Without letting go of my hand, Nick threaded his warm fingers with mine. "I bid you take me with you, Emmie. Can you forgive me for these past weeks? I have thought of naught else but the countless errors of my judgment through all of this. My lady, I beseech you to forgive me. The loss of your person would truly put an end to my heart. Forgive me for all my sins." His head bowed with shame and torment.

I could hardly speak through the boulder in my throat. The last few weeks had been the most chilling of my life. Nick's secret plan to condemn me so he could freely orchestrate his departure from Tudor England was shockingly dangerous, hideous for me, and thrown together in a moment of panic, but he'd done it all to save our relationship.

I'd been wrong. He never wanted me to die, he wanted to come with me...to give up his kingdom for my small life in modern-day America. That's why he didn't let me go when I was in the gardens; he needed time to defeat Henry Howard and ensure that his sister Kit was safe.

He wasn't Nicholas the Ironheart, he was just...Nick. He hadn't stopped loving me at all.

My head was spinning. "What about Kit?" I said in a breath. The thought of all this being another trick was too much to bear.

He squeezed my hand like he was terrified I'd let go. "Lord Warwick and his wife will heartily care for my sister, which I have made clear. Francis shall be a worthy Lord Protector, and when Kit is of age, I have full belief that she will be as gracious a queen as her mother Elizabeth."

"And you?" I added, tears dripping onto my cheeks. "What about all this? You said you could never leave this place." I shook my head at the Tudor world that surrounded us from all sides...his kingdom, his duty.

"I will learn to live without it," he replied in a strangled voice. He nodded at me with assurance, but I could feel his heart breaking.

"But Nick, I'm—I'm no royal." I thought of the decadence that followed him at every turn. "You've seen where I live. We eat cheese on toast; we—we clean our own houses. Well, unless you're my mom. Cleaning isn't her strong suit."

"Say not such things," he said, his hands finding my cheeks and pulling my face close to his. He wrapped both his legs around me in a protective circle. "You have you. You are my choice. *You.*" He dropped his forehead against mine, and I breathed him in.

Nick's heartfelt words roused my own flush of shame. At one time, he'd been *my* choice before things went south. I'd then tried to break off the relationship and go home. Surely he deserved the same chance: to try living in my time but be able to come back here if things didn't work out.

"I have to tell you something," I said as he pressed his lips to my tear-stained cheek. "The soothsayer that I saw also told me that the enchanted ring was never meant to be used more than once, especially by two people." Lines appeared in Nick's brow as I delivered the bad news. "The ring barely functioned when I went back to get medicine for Lucinda Parker. When I tried to use it in the garden the other day —before I was arrested—I already had a plan. If the ring failed, I was going to go back to that soothsayer to try to get her to re-curse it."

Nick's shoulders had stiffened. "What are you saying?"

My fingers curled tightly, preparing for the worst. "I'm saying that this ring might not work anymore. And if it does, and we travel to the modern world to live there, the chances of you getting back here could be *zero*. If you come with me now and you don't like it there...if you regret it and you want to come home—you might never be able to."

He leaned backward with a heavy sigh.

My mind was racing. "Could we just go to that soothsayer near Robin House now?" I suggested. "Maybe she can curse it again—like, recharge it—before we even try using it."

His fingertips tugged at his bottom lip in thought, but he soon shook his head. "I cannot reverse what occurred at your trial. I could assuredly pardon the execution in favor of another punishment, but I cannot be seen to be taking you from here. Men would believe it to be the makings of a plot between us. At such a troubled time, the Privy Council may move to depose the Tudor line. Kit would be imprisoned, or worse. It is too dangerous."

"So to disappear is a better option? You think it's better for the king to just *vanish* with the former queen on the day of her execution?"

"Not to vanish...to die."

I stared at him. "Come again?"

He nodded at the window. "I have the key to open the bars, and the Council will come to determine that we have willingly plunged to the bottom of the river. Kit will not suffer if I am thought to have taken my life, but she *will* pay for it if I abandon the throne and go into hiding with a queen convicted of treason and heresy. I have prepared a letter which declares that I could not live without you after all, and I will leave it in this room." He produced a folded piece of parchment from his coat. "The lords may wish to see our bodies to believe it completely," he added uneasily. "To that end, there shall remain suspicion over my fate, but I can think of no better alternative."

All the pieces slotted into place like a puzzle. Nick wanted us to feign a double suicide so the crown could pass to Kit.

I paced to the window, considering the plan. When the frame was open, the space was just wide enough for someone of Nick's size to slip through at an angle. The towering outside wall was impossible to scale. If we both disappeared from this locked chamber, and the window was left wide open, people would possibly believe that we jumped.

My heart thundered in my chest, my voice barely audible. "What are we waiting for then? If you're really sure."

Nick exhaled like he'd been holding his breath for a year and wrapped himself around me, squeezing so tightly that he had to loosen his grip. I ran my hands up and down his back, burying myself in his embrace as he used his free hand to unlock the window and swing the frame of bars out into the biting cold wind. There wasn't enough time for us to make up properly now. In my heart, I also knew it'd take time to get the image of Nicholas the Ironheart forsaking me out of my head. But in my world, we'd have plenty of time to talk through what had unfolded and set things right.

"We'll fix the ring," I assured, touching his forearm. "We'll find a soothsayer in my time, and we'll have it enchanted again. You *will* be able to get back here if you want."

A sad smile touched his lips. "Self-murder means the damnation of the soul, Emmie. If I am believed to have taken my life before God,

I can never return. Once I leave this way, I am finished with this world."

"And Kit?" I reminded him again, tightening my hold on his arm. After all that he'd done to protect his sister…could he really just abandon her?

He just shook his head at me, his despairing face shutting the question down. He couldn't talk about it. A new wave of pain engulfed my heart. Kit was going to be Nick's most difficult sacrifice of all. But the last few months had proven that he couldn't keep both her and me, and now he was choosing me. But unlike when I'd been given the same choice, Nick knew there was no way back. His sacrifice would be irreversible.

I folded my arms around his neck again and held him, his pounding heartbeat merging with mine. Surely becoming Queen of England would be a better fate for Kit than having married that French aristocrat. That had to be an upside.

I felt him melt into me, his fingertips stroking up and down my back. A flock of seagulls squawked as they glided over the Thames, signaling the full break of dawn. Through the window, the rallying calls of the Tower Hill spectators gathered in volume, ready for the second execution of the day…mine. We had to hurry.

Nick unfolded the note he'd written and placed it on the chipped floor tiles near the door.

"Come in haste," he said, climbing onto the bed and making space for me. I was curious to read what he'd written in the note, but we both had to fall asleep before the guards came knocking, and I didn't want to waste a moment of time. Plus, I'd come to Tudor England ready to make the most of it in every way I could, but now, I couldn't wait to get home to the modern world.

I lay beside Nick and slid into his waiting arms. He took one sniff of the blanket and pushed it away, removing his black leather coat and draping it over me instead.

We turned on our sides and he wrapped an arm around me from behind, clasping my hand wearing the blue-diamond ring and lacing our fingers so we were securely connected.

"What do we do if the ring doesn't work, and we can't get out of here?" I whispered into the linen pillow.

After a pause, Nick gestured to the window with our interlaced hands. "I suppose we will have to jump in truth."

Fear crushed my stomach like a soda can as he tightened his embrace. The heaviness of his arm soothed me like a weighted blanket, and I shut my eyes and prayed silently for sleep and for the ring to work.

My eyes popped open without effort. "I'm wide awake," I hissed with rising panic. The executioner was waiting for me, and if the guards came in and found us in bed together, both Nick and I could end up headless.

A sudden memory shot me upward like a bullet. I clicked open the enchanted ring's hidden compartment. "I forgot that I've got one sleeping pill left!" I said, wanting to kiss the little blue tablet. I snapped it into two halves.

"What is this?" Nick asked as I dropped one piece into his palm and swallowed the other half.

"It's medicine from my time that will help you go to sleep quickly."

He sat up and brought the pill closer to his face. "A sleep remedy such as the poppy-seed or lettuce in the milk of a lady?"

I tried not to chuckle at his old-school lactation therapies. "I'm not exactly sure what this pill is, but it will work...you can swallow it, it won't hurt you."

"I trust you with my life," he replied nervously before downing the pill and wincing at the aftertaste. We lay back down and he draped an arm over me and collected my fingers in his again.

After a few moments, he spoke quietly, the heat of his breath tickling my hair. "Emmie, you know I will have no manner of princely splendor in your world. I will have naught to give you: no jewels, no cloth, no horse, no feasts, no lands, no—"

I silenced him with a gentle shush. "I don't want those things," I said. "I want to make my own jewelry, with wire and pliers, just like I used to. I want to make dinners for us...to learn how to cook properly. I just want *you*."

I tugged his arm tighter over me, butterflies hatching in my stomach at the thought of having Nick Tudor all to myself in a regular house. Could we actually have a normal life?

To push away the terrifying thought that the ring might not work and we would have to jump to our deaths after all, I turned my head to look at his calming face. For a few endless breaths, he stared into my eyes, before he leaned forward and caught my lips with his. I ran my hand up the back of his neck and sighed, heat streaking up my spine when his tongue brushed mine. We both knew we couldn't let this escalate right now, but I shifted around to face him, and we rolled our tongues together and allowed ourselves a few minutes of hot, desperate kissing that had me gasping before he broke apart from me with a reluctant murmur.

I blinked back at him through slightly dazed eyes. "So what are your final words?" I stammered lightly. "In case the guards break in, or the ring fails and we have to jump…it's kind of morbid, but do you have any dying words, Your Majesty?"

We lay there for a quiet moment before he replied, his breath a soft kiss against my skin. "No matter where we shall travel, my lady— to the future or to God in heaven, I wish to be by your side. For I shall be a king no more, but merely a man, and I will worship and love you as such until the last breath of my immortal soul." He lowered his lips to the skin below my ear, sending a rush of sweet love through my veins. "Can you love me not as a king, Emmie, but as a man?"

My eyes watered with a rush of tears. "That's all I've ever done."

My stomach and my chest twisted with hopeful anticipation. Maybe now, I could finally prove to Nick that his wealth and power meant nothing to me, that all I wanted was an ordinary life with an ordinary Nick. Even though it made me uneasy to think what stealing him away from the sixteenth century would do to the Tudor dynasty as I knew it.

I twisted back around to face the window and cuddled into him. "Let's go to sleep," I whispered. "Ne dimittas. Don't you dare let go of me."

The last words I heard Nick Tudor say were a warm murmur against my neck. "As you love me, my lady, I wager my life and kingdom on it."

EMMIE
AND THE
TUDOR THRONE

BOOK THREE

Though fate frowned,
And now drowned
They in sorrow dwell,
It was the purest light of heaven for whose fair love they fell.

Icarus, Robert Jones' Second Book of Songs and Airs, 1601

THIRTEEN MONTHS LATER

1

THE SIGHT SHOULD'VE FLOODED ME WITH JOY, BUT IT DRIED MY throat to the bone. I pushed through the squeaky gate of my courtyard garden, meeting the broad back of my sixteenth-century boyfriend, Nick Tudor. He was standing over the trellis that was fastened to the wall, his muscular forearm hacking at a tangle of vines with a measly paring knife from our kitchen. No matter what time I arrived home from college—worryingly late or unusually early like today—this was where I always found Nick: alone, in our silent courtyard, tending to our garden.

My cumbersome art folder swung from my shoulder as I approached him, unease creeping up my neck. "Don't use that knife," I said. "It's for cutting vegetables."

"Vegetables are plants, are they not?" he replied without turning around. "Not unlike these vines." He didn't pause his assault on the clinging green tendrils. "You are early this day."

My folder slipped off my shoulder and slumped against my leg. "Yeah, they canceled face-to-face lessons this morning. The new virus strain isn't responding well to the vaccines."

Nick finally twisted to face me, the mid-morning sunlight setting the green flecks in his eyes ablaze. The constant war within himself to understand modern concepts like vaccines and viral strains was evident in his creased brow. Two chirping birds swooped past us in a violent mid-air battle and landed on our elderly neighbor Rosie's bird feeder, sending it swinging. A pair of crinkled eyes stared at us over the low brick wall separating our gardens.

"Morning, Rosie!" I called loudly, making my point.

"Oh gosh, I didn't see you there; good morning," she muttered before quickly shuffling away.

Nick barely registered the exchange, his eyes distant as his fingers gripped the paring knife.

"Are you hungry?" I asked him. "I can make us some sandwiches for lunch."

He shook his head. "I ought to complete my duties before the rain draws near."

"Fine."

The word hit with a clang—curter than I'd intended it—but I escaped inside our dimly lit terraced house without correcting myself. It wasn't Nick's fault that I hadn't pointed out to him what day of the year it was. It wasn't like a Tudor king would have a social media profile, or even a paper calendar, to remind him today was my birthday. I was unfairly testing him on something he could never pass—a strange, almost mean habit I'd developed in the past few months. Nick had been mostly patient with me when I'd packed my bags for Tudor England and attempted to make a life there, so now that we were living in my world, why couldn't I give him the same chance?

Because in the thirteen months that Nick has been living in the twenty-first century, he hasn't even tried to adjust to life here. He's not even really here at all.

The uncomfortable, daunting answer sank over me as I fixed myself a tuna-and-mayo sandwich with sliced spring onions from our thriving vegetable patch, courtesy of Nick's efforts.

My phone jingled from my satchel, and I fumbled to answer Mom's video call from Massachusetts before it rang out. I swallowed a peppery chunk of onion and grinned at the screen.

She sang me an off-key "Happy Birthday," her face shadowed by the bluish glow of dawn through the window behind her.

"Thanks," I forced brightly. "You're up early. Or are you just going to bed?" Her round-the-clock nursing shifts were difficult to keep track of.

"I just got up. Say hi to Ruby!" She waved our miniature schnauzer's fluffy gray paw at me, and my chest tugged. On days like today, the east coast of America felt even further away from our newly adopted town of Borehamwood in southern England. But the warmth in Mom's lined face rallied a spring to my voice. During the years I'd spent disappearing to Tudor England, she'd looked the opposite: tormented and gaunt. I still thanked the stars that all that was behind us.

As I washed the crumbs off my plate, I updated her on the latest developments at my jewelry college in London and how classes had been canceled until June. Instead, we'd been given a major assignment to work on from home.

"Well, you're safest at home, so I'm happy to hear that," she said through a yawn. "Where's Nick?"

I glanced at him through the gap in the back door that I'd left open for some air. He was crouched over in gray jeans and a navy T-shirt, tearing out weeds that had sprouted between the lettuce leaves.

"Gardening again," I said, facing the phone to him. "Did you expect anything less? He needs to have his own show."

"Wow, it does look like he's found his calling," Mom said with a smile. I didn't tell her that, to me, the impressive garden bursting with healthy tomatoes, peppers, cucumbers, and lettuce felt like the work of a madman. I also didn't mention that Nick had developed chronic headaches, that every day he rose before sunrise and was in bed at sunset, or that his little sister Kit—who we'd abandoned in the sixteenth century—had been appearing to him in his dreams as an angry ghost. As usual, I pretended everything was fine and blew kisses to Ruby before we hung up. Mom had been through so much with my relationship with Nick that I wasn't ready to share yet that things still weren't right between us.

I only had a couple of hours before I had to trek back into downtown London for my work shift, so I planted myself at our rummage-sale dining table—the only space large enough to accommodate my art supplies. A sane person would've just hung around the city and found somewhere to study before clocking on for work, but not me. The thought of leaving Nick alone for an entire day and night sent a shiver through me. He might start hallucinating again that the ghost of Kit was haunting him for leaving her in the sixteenth century, without a word of warning, to take over the Tudor throne at the age of nine. What he needed was years of therapy for what he'd been through—we both did—but, at the moment, he could barely get through breakfast without freaking out about the countless inventions and discoveries he had to get his head around.

An ordinary life with an ordinary Nick.

It was all I'd wanted when we'd escaped Tudor England to pursue a life together in the modern world. But this man was everything but ordinary. Now, when I gazed into those sea-colored eyes that owned full rights to my heart, only half a person looked back at me.

I stared at the blank sketchbook in front of me, my shoulders slumping. My major assignment for the break was to design a jewelry collection based on the concept of liberty. While I evidently had enough talent to gain admission to Central Saint Martins jewelry college in the first place, broad themes had never been my strong suit. In between twirls of my graphite pencil, I brainstormed abstract ideas on my sketchpad while trying really hard not to just draw the Statue of Liberty.

The back door knocked the wall as it swung further open, sending a jolt through me. Nick stepped in with his hands dripping from the outside tap. The slightest of smiles tugged at his lips as he passed me to dry his hands on the oven towel. I sensed that he was trying to make some sort of connection, and I tilted toward him eagerly.

"You say that you are to undertake your studies at home for a time?" he asked, running his fingers through his ruffled chestnut hair. A pang of longing rose high in my chest, and I pushed it back down.

"Indeed," I replied, mirroring his old-school speech. "But I still have to go in to work at the pub. Evidently, stale beer remains an essential service," I added with a smile.

He managed a faint smirk, and the conversation drizzled to a close.

I even pulled off a more heartfelt chat with my dad when he called to wish me a happy birthday—which was saying something given the fragility of our relationship after he'd been largely absent from my life. We actually chatted for so long that, when I hung up, I checked my watch and jumped.

"I have to go," I said, slipping my phone inside my satchel.

Nick was gaping at me from the couch, a sixteenth-century ruby bulging from his finger where he clutched the edge of a newspaper.

"This day is the anniversary of your birth?" he said, his eyes wide.

"It's okay," I muttered as I pulled on my canvas sneakers. "I don't expect you to know the date. I should have just told you, but I…I guess I forgot."

His voice had deepened. "But for you to say naught, Emmie; for what intention would you do such a thing?"

"There's no ulterior motive…it's just a dumb birthday."

He frowned. "Say not such things. We will mark the occasion with some manner of merriment."

I shrugged, silently acknowledging how awkward this was. "Maybe we can bake a cake this weekend or something. It's all good. I'll see you in the morning."

I stepped past him and into the earthy smell of rain without even attempting a goodbye kiss. The last time I'd done that, Nick had physically recoiled, ramming a knife into my heart.

I bit back the urge to cry as I hurried through sheets of rain to Elstree & Borehamwood train station, an onslaught of painful questions descending upon my brain: What if Nick's physical and emotional distance was because he regretted his decision to give up his kingdom for me? What if he desperately wished that he'd stayed as the glorious sixteenth-century King of England, where he'd wanted for nothing, was waited on hand and foot, and more importantly, had a purpose?

You seem so unhappy here.

But you chose this. You chose me.

The hour-long commute into central London brought with it an agonizing amount of time to contemplate how Nick and I had gone from moving to this world out of a powerful, irrepressible love to ending up so painfully distant from each other. For one, there were four hundred years of evolution that he had to get his head around—things like television, computers, cars, airplanes, and a powerless British monarchy were science fiction to him. There was no jousting here, no feasting, no Tudor dynasty—not even a Palace of Whitehall. Even hunting as a sport barely existed anymore.

As I crossed to the opposite side of the railway platform, I reminded myself to be fiercely grateful that we were even here: together, in my century, and living near London so I could attend my dream college. I hadn't gone to literally criminal lengths to get Nick identification papers for nothing. Hours spent trawling the dark web had turned into exchanging Nick's twelve-carat sapphire ring for a British passport and ended with a flight from Boston to London that had left us both crippled with anxiety. I hadn't slept through the night since, imagining the pounding on the door of fraud officers wanting to "ask me a few questions."

Our new life in the modern world was more than I ever thought we would have. Except, it didn't really feel like a life. Not with Nick keeping me—and the entire twenty-first century—at arm's length.

This isn't how it was supposed to be.

My chaotic shift at the Australian pub in Charing Cross mercifully silenced the angst in my brain for a while. I zipped up and down the bar pulling pints and wiping spills with my friend Alina, another jewelry student from Central Saint Martins.

"Happy Birthday, babe!" she said over the blaring AC/DC music, sliding something inside the back pocket of my black jeans.

"You didn't have to get me a card," I said, my cheeks lifting. "Thank you."

"It's more than a card." She scampered off, balancing two over-flowing pints. "Don't lose it!"

We didn't get a chance to speak again until our shifts ended. While the bar manager, Todd, locked up, I poured the three of us a beer—our usual after-work ritual.

Todd slid his bar stool so close to mine that our elbows grazed. "Cheers, birthday girl," he said, clinking our pint glasses.

"Thanks," I replied, avoiding his curious gaze, which I couldn't seem to hide from.

I tore open Alina's sage-green envelope. She smirked as I turned over the gift certificate and scanned the words:

To: Emmie Grace

From: Alina Popova

For: Joint Annual Membership to Historic Royal Palaces – Free entry to the Tower of London, Hampton Court Palace, Banqueting House, Kensington Palace, and Hillsborough Castle and Gardens.

Valid: 2 people, 12 months

"It's because you're always using history stuff in your designs," she said, blushing. "I thought you and your boy might like it."

"Thank you so much," I said, folding my arms around her perfumed neck. "That's really thoughtful." An alarm sounded deep in my stomach. Alina was right—my time in the sixteenth century had undeniably pervaded my jewelry design aesthetic—but it was on a subconscious level. The truth was, I'd done my best *not* to think about the Tudor world anymore. Sending my mind back there soaked my palms with sweat. There were so many harrowing memories attached to the sixteenth century that I hadn't even googled Nicholas the Ironheart and learned how the famed Tudor king's story had altered after our escape on the day of my execution. That part of my life was in the past—in more ways than one. And I was determined to keep it that way.

"Are you sure you can drag this mystery man of yours into town to visit all these places?" Todd quipped. "If not, I'll be your plus one."

I gave him a playful whack. "Nick will come. He'll love it."

The conversation fell to an awkward silence. My new friends in London knew I had a boyfriend named Nick that I lived with, but they'd never met him or even seen a photograph. My excuses that he was always too busy to come into town hadn't convinced them—especially Todd, who'd begun poking fun at the man in my life for being a people-hating recluse, which wasn't exactly off the mark.

Nick didn't like me "on the roads after dark," so when I worked the late shift, I usually crashed at Alina's downtown studio apartment, paid for by her property developer parents. It was past midnight when I collapsed onto her plush couch that smelled like scented candles and started swiping through my social media accounts. My high school bestie, Mia Fairbanks, had posted a gushy birthday message for me with a string of emojis from her college residence at MIT. I replied with matching fervor, but we both knew the online love-fest was mostly a performance. I'd only spoken to Mia a handful of times since moving back from Tudor England, all of which had happened over the phone. None of our stilted conversations had managed to adequately explain why I'd disappeared off the face of the Earth for the better part of three years without contacting her. For now, it was probably a good thing that we were living in different cities.

Alina's chic apartment had come to feel like a second home in only a few months, but a suffocating ball in my chest made it hard to sleep. Todd had pinched a nerve when he'd made fun of my hermit boyfriend. In the dead of the night, Nick's refusal to leave our cheap rental in Borehamwood felt despairing to me, like his inertia would never end. The Nick I'd met had literally ruled the world and been worshipped like a living god, dripping with jewels and authority. Now he was trapped in that tiny garden in Hertfordshire acting more like a caged animal. He was handling the transition to a different century much worse than I had, but I knew it wasn't fair to directly compare our experiences. Before I'd moved to Tudor England, learning about British history in school had given me a sense of where I was and what life was like. Nick had effectively relocated to a future planet where the only person he knew, or understood, was me. Why was I being so hard on him? I flipped onto my back, staring at the oddly shaped ceiling fan.

Because it's been over a year since he's been himself. You're living with a depressed stranger who hasn't even kissed you with any passion in months. This has to change, or you'll both go insane.

After managing a couple of restless hours of sleep, I woke to the distant honking of two city buses in a standoff and tossed back a coffee from Alina's espresso machine. I'd awakened with such an urgent need to talk to Nick about my fears that it clawed at my skin like insects. If he regretted his decision to give up his kingdom for me —if this was what his constant emo mood boiled down to—I couldn't wait another minute to know. I had to get home as soon as possible and have it out with him. The anxiety was eating me from the inside out.

It was early Saturday morning, and the streets were mostly empty, save for a few drowsy faces. I strolled briskly toward the Mansion House tube station, hiding my nose from a huddle of overflowing trash cans.

At the top of the hour, church bells clanged from St. Paul's Cathedral a few blocks behind me. The relentless sound of the ringing suffocated every cell in my body until I couldn't breathe, sending the remnants of coffee into my throat.

While Nick hadn't been in downtown London enough times to notice anything different about the city's historic cathedral, I'd been blindsided by the truth in my first week of college: St. Paul's Cathedral had always been an Anglican church—the mother church of the Diocese of London as part of the Church of England.

Until now.

Since Nick and I had reappeared in the twenty-first century like a magic trick, the iconic cathedral that dominated London's skyline was now the seat of the Catholic bishop of London in the *Roman Catholic* Church of England.

The brisk wind iced my cheeks as I descended the concrete steps leading to the underground tube station. By what felt like sheer luck, life had appeared to be mostly the same since Nick had given up the Tudor throne for me. The Earth hadn't swallowed itself whole, and the political landscape, the British monarchy, and the standard way of life were all as I remembered. Except for this one thing: The dominant Christian religion in England had changed from Anglican to Catholic overnight, like flipping a switch. It was a glaring tear in the fabric of history that I was sure was somehow our fault.

I couldn't get warm as I slipped into a seat in the furthest corner of the carriage, willing away the cold, ugly truth that wouldn't disappear, the way the cold, ugly truth never does.

I'd finally got what I wanted when Nick Tudor agreed to move to the modern world with me. But now, not only was my boyfriend broken, but so was history itself.

2

I sucked in a jittery breath and pushed through the door, nearly tripping over Nick's outstretched legs. He was sitting on the couch, a crumpled newspaper folded open over his thighs. If he wasn't so reluctant to be around other people in this world, I'd have suggested he try modeling as a job. With that brooding expression and those take-off-my-pants eyes, he'd be snapped up in an instant.

"What news?" he asked, scanning my face with alarm. "You appear wearied."

I wiped away the traces of mascara shadowing my eyes. Once I'd decided to confront Nick about his lingering anguish, I'd been preparing myself for the worst—that he really did regret his decision to give up his kingdom in exchange for me. If he said those words, they would become the worst words I'd ever heard, and I'd heard some truly terrible things in my time in Tudor England.

Putting off the inevitable, I raced into the kitchen for some water, nearly colliding with a magnificent bunch of fragrant wildflowers spilling from a glass jar. The carefully styled arrangement of deep-magenta, linen-white, and powder-blue blooms was right off the front cover of a home-decorating magazine.

"What's this?" I said, fingering the velvety petals of a cornflower.

Nick followed me into the kitchen, clearing his throat. "An offer most meager, but one from the heart to wish you a happy anniversary of your birth." The sense of him right behind me nearly knocked me over…his irresistible scent that evidently wasn't exclusive to his Tudor life. Just the sound of that man breathing melted me.

"I plucked the flowers from the roads in the village," he added.

I spun to face him, brightening. "You went into the village?"

His eyes shone with nervous pride. "More than that. I came upon a library with a great number of books and more of these newspaper things." He nodded at the heap of out-of-date newsprint on the coffee table. "I feel it is time to learn more of what has occurred in times past. What happened to the realm after we took our leave? Whom did my sister Catherine marry once she became queen? How many sons was she blessed with? Which one became king?"

My throat burned as he returned to his muddle of crumpled newspapers. The sight of him naively searching for news about his little sister Kit's transfer to power in 1581 drew a lump to my throat. Like that would be in the back pages of *The Times*.

It was the ideal moment to break the news about the nation morphing from Anglican to Roman Catholic since our return, and to press him about how he really felt about being here. If only the words would form in my mouth. A tightening wall of pressure grew behind my eyes.

"In truth, I wonder if we might journey into London this day, as you have proposed many a time," Nick said in a rush. "We may call on some manner of place that I knew in the past—it may be a merriment for your day of birth. However, we need not do so in haste; you have journeyed from London just this morning. Perhaps on the morrow."

My heart was beating into my ears. "No, I think it's a great idea. I'd love to go into the city with you." Instead of forcing a heavy, harrowing conversation, maybe what we needed was to get out of this stifling house. If Nick could just see some of his old stomping grounds, maybe he'd feel closer to home rather than further away. It might help break him out of these mental chains he was tied up in.

"Is there anywhere in particular you'd like to go?" I asked, sitting beside him. "You know my friend Alina? Just last night, she gave me an annual pass to visit some of the historic palaces of Britain for my birthday. Kind of amazing timing, actually."

"Truly?" He inhaled a deep breath. "Perhaps we may then call upon the Tower of London. You say it is in good repair."

My lips curled upward. "It looks almost the same as it did when I was a prisoner there." A memory pushed into my mind: my legs buckling on a rickety wooden platform inside the Tower's medieval Great Hall, nearly collapsing as I was sentenced to death by beheading. I steadied myself and reset my smile. "There's really cool stuff in there," I added lightly, "like the Crown Jewels, and some of the battle armor of your granddad, Henry the Eighth."

Okay, dating Henry the Eighth's grandson will never not be weird as hell.

A flash of warmth sparked in Nick's eyes as they met mine, our gazes clinging together. In an instant, I remembered why we'd gone through all this danger, pain, and adjustment. I imagined climbing into his lap and feeling his arms wrap tightly around me, his thighs firm beneath mine, his breath fanning over my lips. It had been so long since I'd known every part of Nick's body—his passion and strength, his red-hot attention to detail, the look in his eyes when he finally comes apart—that the thought of touching him made every cell in my body tingle with anticipation.

But as I sat there and looked into his ocean eyes, I saw half a man, a heartbroken one, who didn't reach for me.

"I'll just have a shower, and then we can get going, if you like," I said tightly, putting space between us so he wouldn't have to see the hurt swelling in my chest and crushing my face.

Our train ride into central London was charged with a fearful silence, like we were strapped to a rocket bound for another planet. Nick had seen twenty-first century London already, but his startled eyes still clung to every concrete building, cell tower, and semi-trailer that whizzed past the grimy windowpane. When the view was eaten up by the blackness of the underground tunnel system, his focus shifted to the strips of metal, blinking fluorescent lights, and stained upholstery inside the carriage. He jerked at every announcement grunted over the loudspeaker like it was the voice of God sounding from above.

He hovered close to me as we made two changes at Bank and Monument stations before finally emerging into blinding daylight at Tower Hill. I couldn't get my head around seeing him striding around without everyone else making space for their terrifying, glorious king, their heads bowed in deference. It was like seeing the world turned upside down.

While I'd been into the city a hundred times in the past six months for college and work, I hadn't come near the Tower of London—especially not with the king who'd once imprisoned his enemies inside the ancient fortress. As the historic monument's onion-shaped domes surfaced beyond a highway whizzing with cars, our two worlds smashed together, sending my mind into a spin. Nick trembled beside me as another flashback highjacked my vision: I was being dragged up the cobblestone slope from Traitor's Gate toward the Tower's menacing slit windows and battlement towers, faint with terror and certain of my impending death.

"Be calm, my lady," Nick said gently, but his voice was taut. He hadn't called me "my lady" since we'd left Tudor England. It settled my nerves a touch, and we paced down the noisy road leading to Tower Bridge, slightly dumbstruck and saying little more to each other. Pungent, fishy aromas drifted off the River Thames as we rounded the bend to meet the promenade that hugged the Tower's double defensive walls.

Even amid a pandemic, the promenade was scattered with tourists snapping selfies and chattering excitedly. I wasn't sure that Nick would ever relax around the short dresses, dreadlocks, and nose piercings that represented the diversity and expression of the modern world, but at that moment, he wouldn't unpin his eyes from the historic castle that would always be a hideous prison to me.

Together, we stared up at the high, paneled windows punched into the stone wall of St. Thomas's Tower that overlooked the olive-colored river. On the other side of those panes was the room in which I'd been imprisoned for more than two weeks…where Nick Tudor had begged me to feign a double suicide so we could escape Tudor England and move to the twenty-first century, never to return.

"No matter where we shall travel, my lady—to the future or to God in heaven —I wish to be by your side."

Did he still mean it?

The distant chimes of Big Ben stilled my restless mind, and I guided Nick toward the red flags signaling the ticket office where I could present my annual pass. The sight of a sixteenth-century king queuing to enter a castle that he'd expanded and fortified hundreds of years ago was another moment for my book of surreal experiences, which was already the size of *War and Peace*. How much thicker could it get?

A Yeoman Warder barked historical tidbits to tourists gathered at the arched entrance, which opened into a cobblestone pathway. Visitors buzzed about and chattered with local accents, rediscovering their city while international travel was still being limited.

"Are you well?" Nick asked me as we passed the chipped stone walls of the Bell Tower. I managed to nod through the iron fist in my gut, following his bewildered eyes as they sucked in every inch of the crumbling fortress. Being here was disorienting for us both, but it felt like a step forward.

"The Great Hall is gone," I noticed out loud, imagining the outline of the medieval structure that had housed my trial for treason, heresy, and adultery in 1581. As clear as day, I could still see the former Duke of Norfolk's smug face chortling at me as the Baron of Wharton read out my judgment from a scroll. I crossed my arms over myself, my pounding heart beneath my white cotton dress proving that I was still alive. I had survived, the Duke of Norfolk had lost his head, and Lord Wharton was no more than a pile of bones.

Be calm, Emmie.

We ventured inside the White Tower, and Nick's hands relaxed behind his back as he quietly explained the exhibits to me like a tour guide, including the uses of the weapons in the armory and the weakest spots in the battle armor of his infamous grandfather, Henry the Eighth. His detailed knowledge caught the attention of other visitors, and a couple of them leaned in closely, oblivious that they were being schooled on the Tudor era by Nicholas the Ironheart himself. Pride bloomed inside me. This project was working. We needed to visit Westminster Abbey, Hampton Court Palace…as many of his old haunts as we could. Places that hadn't seared terror into my heart the way the Tower of London had. When we stepped into a room marked The Stuart Gallery, Nick gently guided me right past it, his brows pulled together. He had no wish to see any exhibitions about the family of Mary, Queen of Scots—a sixteenth century relative of his who'd once conspired to bring the Tudor dynasty down.

Nick's mood drifted further south when we reached a painted sculpture of the face of his mother, Queen Elizabeth the First. He gasped at the portrait and then stared at it for a long time. When I finally coaxed him away from the haunting exhibit, he muttered more regrets that his mother Elizabeth had married her courtier Robert Dudley only because she had fallen pregnant with Nick, and had then died giving birth to his little sister, Kit. I'd always argued that Nick shouldn't blame himself for his mother's premature death, but he still believed it was his fault with every fiber of his being.

When we emerged into hazy sunlight at the top of a stairway, Nick's eyes were clouded. "To what end is there no mention of my kingship in the White Tower?" he asked me. "Or of my sister, Queen Catherine of England?"

"I have no idea," I replied as we headed down the oaken steps, a dart of alarm striking my stomach. Why weren't Nick or Kit featured in the Tudor exhibits when someone like Mary, Queen of Scots, and her family—the House of Stuart—had a dedicated gallery?

It wasn't until we bravely entered St. Thomas's Tower, edging the turbulent river, that we learned why there was so little memorabilia related to King Nick's reign inside the White Tower. The entire upstairs level of the old medieval palace had been turned into a Nicholas the Ironheart museum. Meandering along the creaky wooden floorboards, we found our way into the exact room of my imprisonment—the room we were alleged to have jumped from in our double suicide.

Nick looked like I felt: lightheaded and almost sick. Pinned to the largest wall was the entire story of our demise, illustrated with grisly paintings of a king and queen who looked nothing like us. The room also displayed a slice of embroidered carpet from Hampton Court Palace, a painting of Nick feasting with his privy councilors, a replica of his four-poster bed—even though the scarlet curtains were all wrong—and an ornate chest that was marked as once belonging to King Nicholas, although he whispered to me that he'd never seen the chest in his life. But it was the painting of Nick and I leaping to our deaths that sucked the color from my cheeks.

"This is crazy," I whispered to him. "I don't think I can stay in here any longer; it's freaking me out."

"I share your disquiet," he replied. "Besides, why is there still naught about my sister Catherine?"

I had no answer for that. Maybe Kit's reign as Queen Catherine of England had been far less dramatic than King Nick's. Perhaps there just wasn't much to say.

The only part of the Tower of London that we hadn't yet visited was the Royal Chapel, which Nick refused to skip, sending my stomach into a churn. How would he react if he noticed the Catholic liturgical objects inside the church? When was I going to break it to him that, since he'd abandoned his kingdom, England had erroneously swung from Anglican to Catholic?

My heart beat hard against my ribs as I trailed him inside the small chapel before balking at a shiny statue of the Virgin Mary ogling us from the right wall. I slid between Nick and the Catholic effigy, discreetly guiding him away from it. My stomach was in knots.

We paused before the altar, and Nick sank to his knees in prayer while my gaze snagged on a single red rose lying across one of the unmarked floor tiles. A hovering guide in a crisp uniform leaned into me.

"Somebody left that there for Anne Boleyn," she said quietly, nodding at the rose. "It's not marked, but that's Queen Anne's final resting place."

"Anne Boleyn is buried right there?" My eyes widened. "Wow."

Nick rose back to his imposing height, as taken aback as me by the words he'd just heard. Anne Boleyn had been his grandmother.

The mature guide lowered her croaky voice. "And about two feet to the right is where Lady Jane Grey is buried."

"The Nine Days' Queen," I said, remembering the poor young noble girl who'd been proclaimed Queen of England for nine days before Nick's aunt, Mary Tudor, had taken the throne in 1554, six years before he was born.

"God in heaven, yes, mine aunt had her beheaded," Nick recalled, forgetting himself.

My brows nearly hit my hairline, but the guide just tinkled a high-pitched laugh. "We must be quiet," she whispered. "But there are several tombs in here if you are interested. Of course, all of them were unluckily executed, otherwise they'd have been honored over at the Abbey. Queen Catherine Howard is buried in here, as well as Sir Thomas More, and right over there is the resting place of Queen Catherine the First. Just ten years old when she died." She pointed at a slate-colored slab of stone on the floor near the southern wall.

At first, the name didn't quite register the way it should have.

"You mean to say Catherine of Aragon," Nick said. "It is my belief that Queen Catherine was laid to rest in Peterborough."

"No, Catherine Tudor," the guide corrected in a hushed voice as another couple meandered past us. "She was the little sister of King Nicholas the First, who famously committed suicide. You don't know the story? After the king jumped from a window right here at the Tower of London and killed himself, his sister Catherine became the queen, even though she was only ten. She reigned for just a few months before Mary, Queen of Scots, invaded England, seized the throne, and beheaded Catherine. It's ghastly. That poor girl was just a child when she was executed. She was also the last Tudor monarch."

Everything around me was swimming, like I was underwater, and I'd lost the ability to breathe.

"This is...this is folly," Nick gasped. I mustered enough sense to take his arm.

"Are you feeling all right, sir?" the woman said, taking a step back. Nick was sweating through his T-shirt.

"He's okay...he's not sick...I'll just take him outside," I mumbled lamely. I thanked her and guided Nick toward the arch-shaped light streaming through the doorway. He managed a few paces before suddenly spinning back toward the stone slab. Moving in a hurried daze, he collided with a bald guy in a polo shirt who was trying to exit the chapel.

"Watch where you're going, mate," the guy warned. Nick's eyes flamed in a way that I hadn't seen in a year before he shoved the man backward with both hands. *Hello, King Nicholas, my old friend.*

"Nick!" I admonished. Everyone in the silent chapel was gaping at us.

Nick's hard shove had knocked the bald guy to his butt: the perfect incentive for a full-blown fistfight. But instead of retaliating, the man scurried backward, his eyes wide with fright. "He just assaulted me!" he cried shakily, keeping his distance from Nick.

The guide was speaking into her lapel microphone.

"She's calling security," I said to Nick. "And those Yeomen Warders are former military. Come on, we need to go."

Nick was standing over the slab of charcoal-colored stone in the ground, his face white. I inched closer to it, scanning the faded letters, my heart crawling into my mouth.

Queen Catherine Tudor, 1572–1582
Beheaded on Tower Hill and buried in this chapel in 1582

The earth fell out from under me, and all I could taste was bile.

There it was, literally carved into stone. Nick's beautiful, vibrant little sister Kit hadn't ruled England like we'd intended and imagined. Just a few months after we'd deserted her and the Tudor world, she'd had her head struck off her shoulders.

Nick's voice barely registered beside me. "For the love of God, what have we done?"

Inscribed into the wall above the tomb was a list of names with the heading *Buried in this chapel.* With a weight crushing my chest, I scanned for Kit's name and found it right after the Duke of Norfolk's, whom Nick had sentenced to death the day we'd escaped Tudor England.

1581 Henry Howard, Duke of Norfolk
1582 Queen Catherine Tudor
1582 Francis Beaumont, Earl of Warwick
1582 Alice Beaumont, Countess of Warwick

I sucked in a sharp breath, clutching my stomach. "Mary, Queen of Scots, killed them all," I choked out, barely able to utter the painful words. "She also executed Alice…Francis…the lot of them!" I recognized the names that followed Alice's as having belonged to Privy Council members in Nick's court.

"Emmie, what have we *done?*" Nick spurted again, a film of tears turning his eyes into bright-green crystals. Anguish cut up his face before he sank to his knees. At the edge of my vision, visitors were escaping through the chapel doorway, clearly afraid of this unhinged man with me.

I squatted beside him. "I'm so sorry," I said into his quivering shoulder. I was nauseous with shock. "But we have to get out of here."

Two guards in knee-length red coats strode into the chapel with searching eyes—not Yeomen Warders, but just as intimidating with their bearskin hats.

"He's fine; he's not dangerous," I said to them, holding out my hand like that could protect Nick from two of the Queen of England's bodyguards.

Nick was sitting listlessly with his back against the stone wall, his eyes glistening with tears. I crept into the space beside him, the stone floor ice-cold beneath my butt.

"What's wrong with him?" one of the guards asked me, crouching before us. The gold band under his chin that held his hat in place interfered with his speech.

"He just got some bad news," I said.

Nick met the guard's stare, his expression as lost as his voice. "Have mercy on my soul, my lord. For I have washed my hands in my sister's blood."

The guard glanced at me, frowning. "What are you talking about, man?"

Nick's gaze drifted to the list of executions on the wall—the names of everyone we'd ever loved in the Tudor world. The names of those who'd been brutally beheaded just so Nick and I could be together.

"In choosing light for myself, I have brought a great darkness upon the world," Nick said in a trembling voice. "I have denied the will of God—laughed in His face—and in doing so, I have damned my sister and all of Christendom to hell."

3

Getting Nick out of an open admission to using his sister's blood as a handwash gave me the focus I needed to escape the Tower of London and the horrifying discovery we'd just made. Stammering and pleading, I convinced the two guards that Nick was nothing more than a mentally unwell soul, but they took my contact details, just in case, and let us go.

We could barely drag our feet up the road leading to the Tower Hill tube station, too shellshocked to be of any comfort to the other. In a movie scene, we might've hugged and wept into each other's arms. But in reality, it was hard enough just trying to breathe.

This was just too dark. Out of the countless trials we'd faced—Lucinda Parker's poisoning, Alice Grey's shooting with an arrow, my near-execution—this was the most disturbing, the most incomprehensible. There was nowhere to turn, nowhere to hide from the stark hopelessness.

As our train careered through the tunnel of unrelenting blackness, all I could see was Kit's ivory skin and fiery red hair as she stood upon a wooden scaffold, shivering with the bone-chilling fear of a hunted child. The image mercifully disappeared, only to be replaced with my beautiful, selfless friend Alice Grey. She was crouching to place her head inside the wooden cradle of the bloodstained block, overcome by its metallic scent, knowing that her blood would be the next spilled.

All because of us.

A sharp cry burst from my throat, and Nick flinched beside me. Until now, he'd been a statue, staring into space. He pulled me into him with a heavy sigh, and my body erupted with convulsive sobs. Finally, my cheek was pressed to Nick Tudor's warmth, and I couldn't enjoy the moment. I was too busy fighting to breathe.

This was more my fault than Nick's. I was the one who'd refused to live in his world and fight for my place by his side as his chosen queen. I'd insisted that the only way for us to be together was to vanish to my time, spiriting away the King of England, which had cost Kit, Alice, and Francis their lives. They would never have known that Nick and I would still be alive, safe in the twenty-first century, while they rotted in the ground decades before they were meant to.

We didn't say anything to each other on the grueling commute home, nor while I fumbled to cook a tomato-and-basil pasta for dinner that neither of us had the stomach to eat. At least the meal brought us together at the dining table, even though the peppery scent of the basil leaves, fresh from our garden, made me want to puke. It was the oppressive silence, however, that triggered my swelling urge to scream.

"Nick, please say something!" My words bounced through the cool evening air as he picked at his pasta with his fork. Why was he always so freaking *silent* here? In the sixteenth century, it had been hard to get him to take a breath between his diatribes.

He'd avoided my gaze since the Tower of London, but our grief-stricken eyes finally met.

"What will you have me say, Emmie?" he said, his voice hollow. "I should have known that, if I quit my kingdom, that vile woman, Mary Stuart, the Queen of the Scots, would come for my sister. All through my reign, that devil was a thorn in my side, lying in wait for her chance to usurp the throne and declare herself the Queen of England, bringing ruin upon my family. Undoubtedly, she had the support of mine enemies, the cold-blooded Spanish and the deceitful French." His cheeks colored with shame. "A better king would have known this would come to pass. A better king would have known that, if you offend the will of God, you invite hell itself upon the Earth." He made a solemn pause. "Or perhaps I did know it all along."

The words hung in the air as we both processed them, our eyes lowered. "Is that why you've been so closed off since we came here?" I said eventually, sounding throttled. "You suspected that things didn't turn out well in your world after we left?"

Nick clutched his fork so tightly that his knuckles whitened. "All I know is that God chose me as his king, Emmie. I defied His will and, in following my heart, I willingly abandoned the realm and my sister. I betrayed my duty, I betrayed my countrymen; and in doing so, I handed the throne of England to a Papist heretic who murdered my sister and my subjects in cold blood." He went to say more, but his lips sealed shut, his face creased with distress.

We hunched over our bowls of barely touched pasta, my entire world collapsing around me like a fragile sandcastle being swept away by a rush of tide.

If Nick did regret his decision to surrender his kingdom for me, how could I blame him after what we'd just learned? People we both loved dearly had lost their lives because of us. The thick slime of guilt coated my insides, and I clenched away another urge to scream. Why couldn't things have gone the way we'd planned when we'd left the sixteenth century…with Kit becoming the greatest Tudor monarch of all? Why had that relentless, vicious woman, Mary, Queen of the Scots, been so power-hungry that she'd stripped away the life and future of a child with so much promise—so much love to give her people?

Why couldn't Nick and I just be allowed to be freaking happy? Why was the world always conspiring against us?

A tear bulged in the corner of my eye before dripping into a cherry-red swirl of pasta sauce.

You stole a king, Emmie. What did you think was going to happen?

Nick was up with the first glow of morning and back outside in our garden to meet the rising sun. I groggily sipped my steaming mug of coffee as I watched him through the living room window, unable to sleep any longer.

When he turned to grab the garden fork that was caked with dirt, I caught sight of his glistening cheeks. He was crying. My chest caved inward.

With a mournful sigh, I sat at the dining table and dragged out my college project, desperate for something to occupy my mind other than the death of a ten-year-old queen. I flipped open my sketchbook and slumped at the drawing of two gold earrings shaped like bird-cages, one of the cage doors stretched open with a bird escaping. I tossed my pencil. How juvenile and obvious. I needed to find a more impressive and original concept for "liberty" to meet the standards of Central Saint Martins.

After two more lousy ideas, I resorted to googling the concept on my laptop for inspiration. Swiping through pictures sent me down a rabbit hole of images that kept morphing into one of a young girl with blazing red hair, a mature face, and a cheeky smile with newly grown front teeth. It was impossible to concentrate with a planet-sized boulder in my heart. Ten-year-old Kit would never know the meaning of liberty.

I opened a new search window, sinking deeper into a pit of despair. I'd worked so hard to avoid looking up any information online about the past and how it might have changed because of Nick and me. I'd promised myself that I would focus only on our future. But, in the last twenty-four hours, I'd been upgraded from an absconder to a murderer. If I was going to survive this gruesome bombshell, I had to know *everything*.

My palms moistened with sweat as I typed the words.

Catherine Tudor death 1582

I braced myself and began reading the first article that popped up.

Fourteen months after the suicide of King Nicholas I, Mary, Queen of Scots, seized the throne of England on May 24, 1582. The following day, Mary had ten-year-old Queen Catherine executed for treason, along with several of Catherine's councilors and courtiers. While Mary, Queen of Scots, lost many supporters following this ruthless act, she managed to hold onto the throne, ending the House of Tudor and beginning the House of Stuart in England.

A chill wrapped around my neck as I reread the passage. The executions of Kit, Alice, and Francis had happened just over fourteen months after Nick and I had fled Tudor England. We'd been living in the twenty-first century for thirteen months. That meant, if we time traveled back to the sixteenth century right now, only thirteen months would've passed there too. Kit, Alice, and Francis would still be alive!

I snapped my laptop shut, a feeling of dread creeping up my spine. Nick had no idea how to use the internet, so he couldn't possibly know about this timeline. He couldn't know that, if we traveled back to the sixteenth century at this moment, his sister would have one month of life left…perhaps enough time to not only save her, Alice, and Francis, but the Tudor dynasty itself.

With my mind twisting in knots, I fixed us grilled cheese sandwiches, warring over what to say to Nick about what I'd just learned. By sunset, he was already in bed with the blinds drawn, and my mouth had stayed silent. I crawled into the bed beside him, trying not to wake him, but his eyes drifted open. After a while, he spoke.

"I had her," he said under his breath.

I sat up on my elbows, facing him. "What did you say?"

He heaved a sigh. "That plague on my people. Early in my reign as king, I had Mary Stuart imprisoned. When she made her claim as the rightful Queen of England, I had her arrested and sent to Tutbury Castle in Staffordshire." His drained eyes sank closed again. "Mary wrote countless letters to me declaring her love and affection for her dearly departed cousin Elizabeth, my mother—God keep her soul—and swore she wanted only to live her life in Scotland as the Queen of the Scots. I was but a foolish boy then, and so, against the counsel of Sir Thomas Grey, I granted Mary Stuart her freedom in Scotland."

My heart hurt for Nick's naive generosity, which Mary Stuart had turned around and spat on.

"You never told me that," I said, wanting to soothe the lines in his brow with my fingers.

He swept the heel of his hand over his forehead, a raspberry-sized ruby glinting from his fourth finger. "Had I known then that woman would steal the throne from my kin, I would never have let her out of my sight." With a deep sigh of regret, he rolled to face the wall.

I lay back down and let him rest, mulling over the fact that Nick seemed as upset about losing the Tudor throne as he was about the death of his sister. Years ago, I might've found that a bit bizarre, but I knew now how many men had died fighting for the English throne in the centuries before ours. The throne of England was God's seat on Earth…a direct line to the heavens. Losing the throne was like losing God's love.

Before long, Nick's lips were gently puffing breaths of sleep, and a frown was glued to his brow.

With anxiety tearing up my stomach, I climbed off the mattress and reached beneath my side of the bed until my fingertips brushed ice-cold metal. Nick's exhausted body didn't stir as I fished out our security box. With shaking fingers, I punched in the code and flipped open the metal door. Inside the safe sat Nick's fake passport and a small, navy-colored velvet box that squeaked when it opened.

It'd been so long since I'd stared at the blue table-cut diamond nestled within a halo of rosette rubies. The diamond had turned dull and milky, like a light had gone out inside. A witch had once warned me that the enchanted ring that had sent Nick and me through time was never meant to be used more than once, especially by two people.

For what felt like hours, but was likely only minutes, I sat and rolled the heavy ring around in my palm, my mouth like sandpaper.

Emmie Grace, you cannot be serious right now. The diamond is so dull that it's almost black. There's no way it would even work anymore.

I rested my forehead on the edge of the bed, my mind as torn up as my stomach. I was finally on the brink of having everything I ever wanted: my irreplaceable Nick, a spot at my dream college, a healthy relationship with my parents, new friends, and a job that suited my study hours. The thought of going back four hundred years into the past—where this unstable ring could leave us trapped forever...where I'd been sentenced to death and nearly lost my head—filled me with such terror that it almost made me catatonic. On top of all that, any attempt to stop Mary Stuart from snatching the throne of England would surely be a suicide mission, not least because Nick and I were both supposed to be dead. Turning up in the sixteenth century like our disappearance had been some sort of a sick prank could put the lot of us in the ground—not just Kit, Alice, and Francis.

But Nick had never forgiven himself for abandoning his little sister, and knowing now what that had cost her, he probably never would. What chance did he and I have of a normal, happy life with a weight like that on his shoulders? Would he ever forgive me if he knew there had still been time to save them, and I'd done nothing about it?

With the enchanted ring sitting on my thumb, I crept back into the bed and draped an arm over Nick, blowing through my lips to quell the butterfly storm in my stomach. I wouldn't wake him just yet. For one, I wasn't even close to sure if I wanted to go through with this, or if I was capable of going back there. But I was also almost certain that the dull, milky ring had finally been drained of its power. What if Nick got his hopes up that he could travel back through time, and the ring failed to transport us to Tudor England? Would that be the loss that finally destroyed any chance of peace in his heart?

My body felt heavier than a bag of sand, but my mind was exploding. Nick's heartbroken chest continued rising and falling beside me with the even rhythm of sleep.

Don't wake him, Emmie; don't get his hopes up. Just...see what happens when you fall asleep. See if this is even an option. Then you guys can decide if you'll stay.

I gently caressed his muscular forearm with my fingers. He didn't twitch, but the firm curves of his skin soothed my soul in ways that nothing else could.

Take the ring off, Emmie. You can't attempt something this huge without talking to Nick about it first. You have to take off the ring.

My fingertips brushed the cool ridges of the blue diamond. I wanted to pull the ring off, but a silent and overwhelming force stopped me. In fact, all I did was pull my satchel up into the bed with me, hooking its strap around my leg. It didn't make any sense, but it was a comfort…it held all my possessions: my asthma inhaler, my phone. I needed some sort of symbolic connection to the modern world if I was going to even consider going back there again.

This ring isn't even going to work anyway. And then at least you'll know. And you won't have to have that hideous conversation with Nick that maybe there'd been a chance to stop this. You won't have to break his shattered heart into even tinier pieces.

Curling my hand over his arm a little tighter, I shut out the torrent of confusing thoughts, closed my eyes, and waited for sleep to carry me into the darkness.

4

I DREAMED I WAS FREE FALLING, BEFORE A WOODEN PLANK SMASHED into my forehead. I cried out, clutching my head with pain. My eyes burst open to meet a brightly colored pattern of painted floor tiles. I sat up, the world sharpening around me through the blurred spinning. Paneled walls…a small fireplace…a standing candelabra that looked oddly familiar.

"What in the heavens?" Nick uttered in a strange voice beside me.

We were sprawled out beside the sharp corner of a carved oak desk, which had possibly collided with my head. A surreal feeling of recognition coated the pair of arched, stained-glass windows that peered at us from the opposite wall. I scrambled to my feet and dashed toward them. Through the latticed windowpanes, the sky was inky black, and the full moon shone a spotlight on a jumble of short black-and-white buildings with red roofs and smoking chimneys. Winding through the surreal landscape was a wide river, as dark as the night sky.

"Oh my God," I said, my voice not my own. I spun to face Nick.

"What is this? What is happening?" he said, his cheeks ashen, his eyes round with shock.

The blood drained from my face in a rush. "We're back in the sixteenth century. In the Tower of London, in St. Thomas's Tower, where we were supposed to have committed suicide." My eyes flashed all over the room, the puzzle pieces of my memory slotting together. "The bed's gone."

Nick was still on the floor where the single bed had once stood, his lips parted, his skin the color of milk.

"*What?*" he said in a breath.

I dashed toward him, crouching with trembling knees. "Nick, I can't believe it…it worked! I honestly didn't think it would. I thought too much time had passed, that the ring's power would be long gone, but it actually worked!"

He shook his head like flies were circling. "Again?"

"Nick, focus," I said, lifting my thumb, which held the enchanted ring, into his vision. "We've travelled back in time again to the sixteenth century. We're in the room that you rescued me from at the Tower of London. I'm so sorry that I didn't tell you, I…I honestly didn't think it would work. I didn't want to get your hopes up." The expression on his face had me afraid he'd pass out. "Nick, focus!" I said again, gripping his pallid cheeks.

A jolt from beyond the door sent my heart into my throat. Distant footsteps drew closer, like they were climbing a staircase. Nick blinked at me, eyes expanding, before he lurched to his feet.

"We must take leave of here," he said, looking more than out of place in his gray sleep T-shirt and black cotton pants.

"What about our clothes?" I said urgently, my forehead still burning from where it'd hit the desk.

"God's teeth!" Nick hissed, tugging open the oak desk's stiff drawers to find only old inkpots and blunt quills. Now that the bed had been removed from the room, there wasn't even a woolen blanket to cover ourselves with.

A heavy door thumped nearby, sending the both of us out of our skin.

"Should we just go back to sleep?" I whispered desperately, wiggling my ringed thumb at Nick.

He shook his head, grabbing the neck of the iron candelabra. "Too late," he replied. The candelabra was so heavy that it took him a moment to find the point of balance and grip it like a spear with both hands. "Wait here for my short return and remain out of sight," he commanded like the king he once was.

"What do you think you're doing?" I asked, my voice high.

"Saving you from yet another judgment of high treason," he said under his breath before kicking the door open with his bare foot.

Before I could stop him, Nick burst through the arched doorway with the speed of a knight on horseback. I crouched on the opposite side of the desk, my heart hammering a hole in my chest. Beyond the doorway, a man's voice shouted out, boots scuffed, and then someone gave a hideous grunt like they'd been punched in the gut. My forehead met my shaking knees. *Please, please, please, please.*

Nick reappeared in the doorway, draping a red coat with gold trim over his sleepwear. He tossed an embroidered coverlet at me that I recognized from the neighboring bedchamber that we'd stayed in on the night before my coronation. "Cover your person with this," he said quickly. "We must make haste."

"What happened?" I spurted, hooking my satchel over my shoulder before draping the silk coverlet around me like a cloak. Instead of answering, Nick took my wrist and hurried me into the corridor. I nearly stumbled over a young man in breeches, lying on the ground with blood spilling from his stomach. My gut heaved into my throat, but Nick tugged me away from him and down the stone staircase.

Oh my God, I think Nick just killed that guy...I'm back in the place of death.

I was gulping shallow breaths and unable to speak as I chased him outside onto a windy cobblestone path cloaked by nightfall. As silent as cats, we crept along the inner wall of the stone fortress until we reached the ominous black dome of Traitor's Gate. Murky water sloshed through the iron bars, carrying a putrid stench of sewage that made me heave. I'd forgotten how much Tudor England stank —literally.

"Make haste; there may be archers," Nick said, scanning the stone battlements high above us. The idea of ending up on death row again in this barbaric world was enough to send me chasing him down the steps that disappeared into water the color of mud. Gusts of wind blew off the surface of the river, as cold as snow flurries.

"We're going to *swim* out of here?" I gasped, taking a step back.

"The drawbridge will be guarded," Nick replied, slipping into the foamy water until he was waist deep. He cocked a finger for me to join him, his teeth already chattering.

You can't be serious! A seagull squawked as it swooped by in search of a place to roost as if answering my cry. I swore under my breath, dropping my silk coverlet onto the stone steps. I glided into the water in one movement, hissing through my teeth as ice-cold liquid enveloped my chest, stealing my breath.

Nick did a heroic job of trying to carry me and swim at the same time, but the instinct to stay afloat soon separated our bodies. My twenty-first-century satchel slipped off my shoulder, and I swiped underwater to catch it, but I couldn't—I was too busy trying not to drown. Mercifully, the blue-diamond ring was still on my thumb and not inside that bag. Losing our only ticket home was too black a thought to even consider.

Nick stayed close to me, and we kicked toward Traitor's Gate until we were clutching the iron bars like desperate prisoners. The gate was bolted shut. I tried to hold myself up out of the water to reduce the risk of hypothermia, but my muscles had frozen. Nick dived beneath the surface, and I screamed, but he re-emerged within seconds.

"The gate does not travel far down," he panted with relief, muddy water pouring off his hair. "However, the gate bears spikes, so you must be careful."

I nodded, and our alarmed gazes clung together in a moment of mutual support. I hadn't seen this much life in Nick's face in a year. "Just clear the gate and then swim upward toward heaven," he said steadily. "Hold the bars until I am with you, and together, we shall make our way to the river's edge."

The composure in his voice shot me back to when we were together in Tudor England last time. How was this the same man as the silent, lifeless gardener from our little terrace in Borehamwood?

Sucking in a deep breath, I dived underwater, saltwater pressing against the seam of my lips. I swam as fast as I could beneath the gate spikes and shot out of the water like a dolphin, gasping for breath. Nick was there waiting for me. He guided me along the gate until we had to let go of the bars and swim along the sand-colored wall toward the nearest wharf. The river felt like an ice bath without the sun to warm its surface, but at least the nighttime curfew kept people indoors and us out of view.

"I'm getting tired," I puffed.

"I'm here," Nick called behind me, a firm hand finding my waist and holding me steady. Inch by inch, we made our way along the stone wall and toward the wharf. When we reached the beams of decaying wood, I flung myself onto the deck and splayed out like a sunbather.

"We must move," Nick whispered, pulling me up.

I could barely sit up, and my voice was hoarse. "Can't we just stay here for a minute?"

"We must hide!" The fear in his tone shocked me to my feet. If someone recognized their beloved monarch, who had returned from the dead in a world rife with superstition, all hell could break loose.

Avoiding the glow of the street lanterns, we hurried westward past tangles of boats haphazardly moored along the sloshing river's edge. My senses returned, driving my face into my dripping-wet shoulder to mask the odors of garbage and human waste, but my pajamas reeked just as badly of fish and seaweed.

"Here," Nick said, ducking into a shadowy alcove between two thin buildings. Our little terraced rental on a quiet, tree-lined street felt light-years away.

He grabbed my hands with painful urgency.

"Ow!" I hissed.

"Do you have it?" he said before expelling a heavy exhale at the sight of the blue-diamond ring on my thumb. My fingers clung to his, but he pulled away, his face a brewing storm. "Emmie, what in Christ's name have you done? You cannot even consider the gravity of the danger you have put yourself in."

My throat closed up. "I was going to tell you," I stammered. "I'm as shocked as you are that the ring even worked!"

"*Going* to tell me? Did you think not of the ache it would bring to my heart to return to this realm that has put an end to my sister's life?"

"Not put an end," I cut in. "It hasn't happened yet—that's why I thought we should come back here. Nick, I looked up the timeline… Mary Stuart invaded England fourteen months after we left. We've only been back in my time *thirteen* months." Confusion flared in his eyes as he gaped at me. "We still have time to save Kit, and Alice, and Francis!" I explained.

For a moment, he looked dumbstruck, but then his face twisted. "By what means? I love my sister without end, and the thought of the fate that befell her is a torment to my soul. But while I may have been the king of this realm once, you forget that I abandoned my people by way of self-murder…I have taken my life before God. If I were to appear before my sister without warning, she would believe me to be a devil's phantom. Or worse still, as the brother who forsook her and fed her to Mary Stuart like a dog." Guilt dripped off his voice.

"It's not your fault that Mary Stuart stole the throne and had Kit and our friends murdered."

"It is entirely my fault!"

A passing shape beyond the alcove pierced the moonlight, sending my stomach into free fall. What if someone heard us? But Nick whispered that it was only a night watchman patrolling the streets.

When I was sure we were alone, I stepped closer to him and lowered my voice. "I get that you feel guilty about everything, and heaven knows, so do I. But we have two choices here: We can go to sleep right now with this ring on my thumb and wake up in the twenty-first century. I'd gladly hightail it home to a hot shower and a breakfast of bacon and eggs. Or, we can appreciate the fact that the blue-diamond ring had enough power to send us back here after all this time, to when and where your sister is *still alive*." Tears sprang to Nick's eyes as he blinked at me. "I think it's obvious what we have to do," I said, swallowing thickly.

He just stood there looking riddled with anguish until he pressed his palms over his eyes. "Christ, Emmie, why must it be such an impossible task to keep both the girls in my heart safe from harm?" He turned to rest his forehead against the wall.

Both the girls in my heart.

For a moment, I didn't speak; I was too busy fighting to not reach for him, to not run my fingers through his hair and pull his sweet mouth to mine, tasting every part of him that I missed so much it made me ache. But when I found my voice, I was resolute.

"I'm not leaving here without trying," I said. "It was me who insisted that the only way we could be together was to move to the twenty-first century. And I know you're not happy there." My voice slipped on the admission that Nick didn't jump in to deny. "I think part of that's because of the way you abandoned this world so suddenly. Your family...your throne. And while I know we can't go back on that now—and I don't want to—I want to do everything we can to try to fix the things that went wrong after we left."

His eyes fell on me as his throat tightened. "You know I killed that guard in the Tower. I took that boy's life with his own knife."

My stomach heaved. "I don't really want to know about that," I said quickly.

"It was him or you," he replied gravely. "And there may be more to come. Because I have not come back here to lose you to this place again. So, you must know what is at stake."

I just nodded at his warning, my chest burning.

A wearied exhale escaped his throat, and for a few moments, we stood silently, shivering in the blustery wind.

"What now?" I said, suppressing a pang for our warm bed in Borehamwood.

"We shall need to sleep a while." Nick kicked away dirt and leaves with his foot.

"*Here?*"

He shrugged off his coat, which had begun to dry, and laid it out on the ground. "I no longer have the key to the palace," he said with a straight face, and a bark of laughter burst from my throat. He returned a trace of a smile, and my tight chest loosened a little.

We lay down on Nick's damp cloak, which at least separated us from the grubby stones. To ensure that we didn't time travel back to the twenty-first century by accident, I slipped the blue-diamond ring off my thumb and placed it right beside my ear.

I'd forgotten how dark Tudor England was at night; how silent—even in downtown London. The few noises that penetrated the engulfing blackness made me shuffle closer to Nick: the squeaking of rats that could be carrying the black plague...the moans of a man wandering aimlessly...the haunting shrieks of wild cats mating.

"I'm sorry," I whispered into the soft cotton fabric of his T-shirt. "I should have been more careful. I should have told you that I wore the enchanted ring to bed. I was worried that it wouldn't work, and that you'd get your hopes up about coming back here to help Kit."

His eyes stayed closed as he sighed, his velvety voice sending a warm tingle through me.

"You know that I would follow you anywhere, Mistress Grace."

My chest filled with heat as I lifted my head to meet his eyes, but his were already closed.

5

LIGHT HEATED MY EYELIDS, DRAWING THEM OPEN. ABOVE ME, A huddle of slanted balconies interrupted the blanket of grayish sky.

Nick was already sitting up beside me. My fingers swept the rough stones for the enchanted ring, which was exactly where I'd left it. *Phew.*

"What time is it?" I asked drowsily, sniffing my pajamas. They smelled worse than a bucket of old fish bait.

While Nick had no idea of the time, of course, a distant hammering signaled that it was late enough for the blacksmiths and carpenters to be at work. A man in a walnut cloak and a flat cap strode across the gap beyond the alcove, and Nick pulled me into the shadows. He swore in a mix of old and modern English before tightening his coat so the only twenty-first century clothes that were visible were his black cotton pants. Still, the fire-engine red coat of a royal guard wasn't exactly discreet, especially paired with bare feet. He combed his fingers through his windswept hair, and I caught myself staring. Nick Tudor was the only guy I knew who could still look pants-dropping hot after spending the night sleeping on a street.

"I must buy some cloth...and shoes...and bread...and ale," he mumbled, making his list on the fly. "You should remain here out of sight."

"But we don't have any money." Two more men shuffled past the alcove, arguing over the price of something. Nick was fingering his ruby ring.

"You're not thinking of selling that," I said, my mouth falling open. "It's worth way too much. And I have two more years of college to pay for."

"Do not move," he said. "I shall make my short return."

My stomach curled in on itself as he slipped away into the most dangerous city I'd ever experienced. There was no police force in Tudor England and little law and order. Nick had never bought so much as a pair of shoes in his life—what if he was robbed for his expensive ring and stabbed before the next clanging of the bells of St. Paul's? What if someone recognized him as the former king?

I sank back into the alcove, crossing my arms over my pink-striped pajamas, like that would be enough to conceal my futuristic attire. The early-morning air chilled my cheeks and feet, and I scrunched myself into a ball, counting the minutes until Nick returned. Every time a person passed by the alcove at close range, I shrank further into the shadows, but none looked my way. When a drunken guy in a patched coat began shouting from the balcony above me in a slurred voice, I broke out in a cold sweat. But if he noticed me, he showed no signs of interest.

My stomach was an empty hole, my lips bone dry. When weakness began to overcome my limbs and my vision dimmed, I felt soft fingers scrambling to pull up my chin.

"Emmie!" Nick was leaning over me. "What are you doing? The ring is on your hand—you must take caution to not fall to sleep without me at your side!"

My eyes snapped open. "What? No, I'm not," I said, my throat sticky.

His face had whitened at the thought of me time traveling to the twenty-first century without him, which released some of the breath bottled up in my chest. He held a leather pouch to my mouth that smelled like sweat, but the refreshing taste of watered-down ale made me suck onto it like an infant. Nick dropped onto the stones beside me, tearing a grainy bread roll into two chunks and handing me one. The bread was dry and coarse, like chewing cardboard, but I wolfed it down. Beside him was a bundled-up linen sheet.

"Our fortune is favorable…we are merely a short walk from the market," he said, producing random items of clothing from the wrapped sheet.

Clutching the bread, my other hand dug through the clothes he'd purchased for me, relieved that the sizing looked about right.

"You should become a personal shopper," I said, pulling a linen smock right over my pajama top. I was too concerned about staying alive to worry about smelling like fish bait in front of my boyfriend. The smock only reached my knees, but the tawny-brown kirtle that I slipped over my shoulders hung to my ankles. I kicked off my pajama bottoms and stepped into a pair of gray woolen stockings, tying them on above my knees. "You thought of everything," I added, folding a white linen coif over my hair and fastening it at the base of my neck. I never thought I'd have to wear clothes as hot or uncomfortable as these again.

"The market seller was a woman," Nick explained. "She was help-ful." He'd swapped his gray cotton T-shirt with a white linen shirt, its strands hanging open at the neck. His muscled legs drew my gaze as he slipped out of his cotton pants and into a pair of leather trousers.

"No breeches?" I said.

"These are sailors' trousers," he explained, tying on a brown leather belt. "I have grown to admire some comforts of the modern world."

The leather boots he'd chosen for me were a touch large, but over my thick woolen stockings, they were wearable, especially after I laced them tightly. Nick clipped on a leather jerkin with hooks and eyelets before tying on a pair of leather ankle boots and flopping a dark knitted cap over his hair. He stood up, sweeping away a couple of wayward curls that escaped the hat. I could have grabbed his collar and tugged his infuriating, beautiful mouth to mine, but I swallowed the impulse. Wrapped in a square of linen was a sprig of mint, which he snapped in half and began chewing before passing me the other half. He'd also purchased a small prayer book, which he slid inside his leather jerkin, and he then gathered up a cloth bag that jingled with coins.

We tossed our modern pajamas onto a pile of trash and tied the remainder of our belongings inside the linen sheet so Nick could carry it over his shoulder. He tied the water pouch and coin purse to his leather belt.

"Next stop: Whitehall Palace for some oddball dancing?" I suggested jovially, wishing the mood would lighten.

He pressed his hands to his hips. "I have had the very same thought."

My brows flew up. "Seriously?"

"There is an inn near to the palace where we may lodge until we decide upon a course of action," he said. "The palace guards are known to frequent the inn and find trouble—it was a source of irritation of mine on many an occasion. It may be an opportunity to learn information about the queen that may help us."

"But what if the guards recognize you?"

"I do not even recognize myself." He indicated his poor-man's sailors' trousers and knitted cap.

I bit my lip, unconvinced, but at least it was a first step. We couldn't exactly waltz into the Palace of Whitehall and say "Ta-dah! We're alive!" to the queen after our supposed suicide. But to try to stop Mary Stuart and her army alone—without the help of Kit and the English cavalry—would be inviting the kiss of death.

We paced down the slope leading to the river's edge, dodging a cluster of wild pigs trotting out of the path of a rabid dog. Nearby, metal workers clanged their tools while men in hats hurried down to the water to catch a wherry. I'd already forgotten how small London was in this century, the open fields and pasturelands of the countryside visible just beyond the river. The smoke of hundreds of burning fireplaces sat heavy in my throat.

Nick complained of the rubbish and sewage all the way down to the wharves like a true twenty-first-century brat. I couldn't deny the comfort that brought to my chest. He'd undeniably perked back to life in the Tudor world, which left me a little uneasy. While he surely wouldn't choose this realm again over the marvels of the modern world, when it came time to return home, I didn't want him dragging his feet. That would make things painful for the both of us.

The easiest and fastest way to Whitehall Palace was to catch one of the countless wherries that rowed people up and down the river like it was a superhighway. I tugged the neckline of my kirtle up over my mouth, nauseated again by the fishy smells off the water. I trailed Nick to the closest wharf where wherries bobbed about like waiting taxi drivers. He called out to the nearest waterman, who agreed to take us to Whitehall Palace.

I hitched up my skirts and descended the small staircase that led to the rickety boat, then climbed aboard with a wobble while Nick paid the driver twopence for the trip.

We were fortunate to have the vessel to ourselves, and I sat close to Nick on the bench at the boat's rear while the experienced oarsman waited for the right moment to push off. A small wave rolled toward us and then we were away, headed for the shadows of London Bridge that towered over the wide, curvy river.

"Hold on tight," Nick said in my ear, and I clutched the wooden bench with both hands as our boat rocked and gushed over the turbulent tidal water beneath the bridge.

Once we were safely on the other side, the favorable tides made for a smoother ride, except for when we crossed paths with the larger sailboats transporting massive barrels and sacks.

A family of swans bobbed past us as the sandy-colored walls of the Palace of Whitehall took shape around the bend, sending Nick shrinking into his seat. Thank goodness his public portraits of an overweight, dour-faced king with a dark beard had looked nothing like the real man. Had social media existed in the sixteenth century, we'd have had zero chance of getting this far.

The palace seemed to move with the tides as our boat swung toward its disorderly jumble of roofs and buildings, the waterman rowing hard toward the closest public wharf.

"My sister is not here," Nick said under his breath, his brow puckered.

"How can you tell?"

"There is no Royal Standard raised."

I sat higher to survey the whipping flags atop the palace turrets. "Maybe the system's changed," I said as the waterman tossed a rope over the jetty's pillar. Nick's expression made it clear that, in this realm, royal traditions didn't change. He slung the knotted linen sheet over his shoulder and helped me climb onto the wharf.

Our boots had barely touched the decaying wood when a trio of men carrying scrolls pushed past us to catch the wherry before it departed. There was no transport schedule, no payment booth, no rhyme or reason. This whole world was freaking chaos.

It was strange—and sad—to witness the once-worshipped King of England practically shoved away by men waving to catch a ride. Nick spun and glared at them but, mercifully, held his tongue. If they'd known who he was, what he was capable of, they'd have died of fear on the spot.

Nick reset his nerves and quietly pointed out that his golden *NR* monograms had been removed from the palace gates and replaced with the royal cipher *CR*. *Catherine Regina. Catherine the Queen.*

"At least we know that Kit is still on the throne here," I said, my words returning a flicker of color to his cheeks. A burning urge to see Kit again tightened my chest. Nick's little sister and I had once been close—when I'd saved her life from Mathew Fox, one of the king's gentlemen who'd attempted to murder her. But when I'd become the Queen of England and nearly lost my head for it, Kit had been locked away at Kenilworth Castle and I'd barely seen her. I didn't just want her safe; I wanted to know her again. She was family to me…the little sister I'd never had.

Nick's touch on my arm broke the sting of my thoughts. "The inn should be in the lane beyond the palace," he said, keeping the brim of his cap low to mask his face. "We may find food and lodging there."

We meandered up the bustling public street that bisected the palace, brushing past men with scrolls wedged beneath their arms and women in bulging skirts and pearled hoods. It couldn't have been easy for Nick to be this close to the place he'd grown up in—he technically still owned Whitehall Palace—but as we passed beneath the covered walkway that connected the two sides of the court, he said nothing, his jaw tight.

"There," he blurted, pointing to a hanging sign lavishly painted with the words *The Golden Mermaid.*

The shadowy, timber-framed building squeezed between an alehouse and a cobbler's store didn't suit its grandiose name. A skinny boy in breeches a size too big for him met us inside the small inner courtyard. He offered to take our sack of belongings, but Nick tightened his grip on the sheet.

The innkeeper was a stout, red-faced man who'd seen either too much sun or too much ale—perhaps both. He demonstrated no signs of recognizing Nick, who negotiated a room on the third floor that overlooked the palace. We both brightened when the innkeeper threw in two free meals with our room price—that chunk of stale bread had disappeared quickly in my stomach.

Nick was tall for the Tudor era and had to duck his head as we entered our chamber.

"The room's quite nice," I said before the smell hit me in the face. I covered my nose as I leaned over the chamber pot to make sure it was empty.

Nick had bravely accepted our modest living conditions in the twenty-first century, but in his own time period, he raised an unsatisfied eyebrow at the damp, poky chamber with no fireplace. The double bed was more like a large single, but it had posts and curtains —practically a luxury in this century. He dumped the knotted linen sheet onto the chest and flipped open the window shutters, chilly air gushing through the glassless hole.

"Dimwitted huckster," he muttered. "This chamber has no view of the Whitehall gatehouse as the innkeeper promised."

"So, we won't be able to see who's coming and going from court," I said with disappointment, meeting him at the window. The most you could see of Whitehall Palace from here was a couple of turrets concealed by a high brick wall.

Distant church bells chimed from St. Paul's Cathedral.

"The dinner hour at last," Nick said, slipping his cap back over his head. "I could eat a swine."

I checked that my coif was still in place and followed him downstairs to the hall, which adjoined the neighboring alehouse.

Nick was right about this inn: a huddle of palace guards sat guzzling wooden tankards of ale at one of the two elongated trestle tables. Nick said he didn't recognize any of them, but would he really remember every face from his court? We kept a safe distance by sliding onto a bench at the opposite table.

Savory aromas wafted from a bulging cauldron hanging from an iron frame over the blazing fire. A servant boy dumped two tankards of ale on our table, and I gulped mine back like it was water. Nick finished his in two chugs.

"Another," he called to the boy, and reminded him that the innkeeper had included two meals with our booking, free of charge.

"Indeed, the pottage comes at no cost with every room, sir," the boy said before scampering away.

Nick blinked at me. "Dimwitted huckster," he repeated. "That innkeeper had me believe the dinner was some manner of special gift."

"It's good to see that dodgy salespeople aren't exclusive to the twenty-first century," I said, holding up my tankard in a "cheers."

Two steaming bowls of pea-and-ham stew were plonked in front of us. Nick pressed his hands together and whispered a few words of grace.

We sipped the thick, salty stew directly from the wooden bowls in famished silence, and I picked up on a confident fluidity to Nick's movements that hadn't been there in months. Was that because he was being fed in a dimly lit corner where no one would identify him, or was it because he was finally back in his own century?

The heel of my boot nervously nudged the rushes scattered on the earthen floor. "We need to come up with a plan," I said in a low voice. "I don't want to disappear from college for too long, or from my family, for that matter. My mom will go ballistic if she thinks I've gone missing again. Plus, my 'liberty' collection is also due in two months, and I haven't even got a concept yet."

Nick's face furrowed. "When you say, 'come up with a plan,' are you saying that you wish to devise a plot to stop Mary Stuart in her invasion of England, or a plot to return to your world so you may attend to your studies?"

I considered my answer. "Both."

"That is a great deal of plotting all at once." He tossed back the last of his stew.

"Who says it has to be all at once?" I placed a hand over his wrist, but he didn't react to the gesture.

Instead, he cupped his tankard with both hands, my fingers slipping off his warm skin. "I need to think upon it before making a plan," he said. "I need to call upon my conscience and make sure that mine actions bring no further bloodshed to the realm."

"There's a lot of *me* and *my* in those statements," I said. "Don't forget that there's two of us here."

"I do not doubt it."

His eyes were so striking—so intense—and so hard to read.

"Okay, well, you let me know when you want to discuss *our* plans," I said. "Because I don't think Mary Stuart's waiting around for you to figure out what *you* want to do."

The sarcasm in my tone pinched his face. "My lady, you know that our life is very little about what I want."

"What's that supposed to mean?" My mouth hung open. For a moment, we just stared at each other. "It's all right; you don't need to explain," I said, a tremble in my voice. "As I said before, I already know that you're not exactly turning cartwheels of joy in the modern world. But to be honest, I'm not sure you've tried hard enough to adjust to the twenty-first century. You need to get out there a bit more…make some friends…get to know the place."

He shot me a look that said I was speaking too loudly. I smacked down my tankard just to peeve him off, and it worked.

"Right. Well, it appears the lady has had enough ale," he said, pulling me up by my arm.

"Let go of me!" I hissed, shaking him off me and into the stare of every eye in the room, including the palace guards. As usual, we were making a complete spectacle of ourselves. The drama lasted all the way up the circular staircase.

Inside our chamber, I flopped onto the straw mattress, too drained mentally and physically to bother taking off my boots. The linen sheets were frayed, but they smelled clean, and I buried my face in them. It was only early afternoon, but we'd hardly slept on the ground in the alcove, and my eyelids felt weighed down by bricks.

It'd become obvious that Nick and I fought more in the Tudor world, but at least we were connecting again in some way. I peeked at him as he sat on the edge of the bed, fiddling with his boots. Good… we both needed to rest our brains before we made any concrete plans. But when he rose again, the laces in his boots had been tightened rather than untied. He grabbed his flat cap and flipped it over his ruffled hair.

I sat up. "Are you going somewhere?"

"Downstairs," he replied evenly. "Those guards may leave and take with them an opportunity to uncover information about the queen. I must know something of Kit—if she is well handled. Perhaps there is already a threat from the Queen of the Scots, which those men may have knowledge of." He sighed, tucking a stray curl behind his ear. "You are right, Emmie; time is passing, and we must take some measure of action."

My throat had dried up. "But what if the guards recognize you? Or wonder why you're asking so many questions?" I sat forward. "Let *me* go downstairs. I lived at Whitehall Palace for about five minutes. No one would ever guess who I am."

He made a small grunt. "You forget the vast differences between our worlds. A maiden, alone, asking questions of men she is not acquainted with? I will wager that is the surest way to find danger."

I knew he was right, so I didn't attempt to stop him as he escaped back downstairs.

With a heavy sigh, I slipped off the blue-diamond ring and dropped it into the tin of fragrant dried flowers beside the bed. Closing my eyes eased the burning of fatigue, and I willed myself to relax and not imagine the worst happening downstairs. Jerking at every muffled sound of raised voices from a distance, I let the feather pillow carry my restless mind away.

6

THE SHARP CLANGING OF BELLS THROUGH THE OPEN WINDOW SHOOK
me awake. I groaned into the hard-as-nails mattress, my wearied eyes
peeling open to find an empty space beside me.

I hobbled out of the bed with a stiff lower back and approached
the window. Dusk had fallen over the city, and men in hats and cloaks
were dispersing, heading home for the night. A young guy in an ankle-
length cloak strolled by on the street, calling, "Maids, hang out your
lights!"

Where the hell is Nick?

My heart rate tripled as I tied on my coif and smoothed down my
kirtle. I hurried downstairs, two at a time, bracing myself. What if
he'd been arrested and dragged away while I'd been dreaming about
liberty-themed jewelry and hamburgers?

I rushed into the hall and puffed an exhale of relief. Nick was
sitting with the guards we'd seen earlier, a tankard of ale locked in his
tanned fingers. A rowdy lutenist was theatrically plucking his strings in
a merry, silly tune, and the men were belly-laughing—including Nick.
Was he milking these guys for information or getting three sheets to
the wind?

Another party of men was crowding the other trestle table, their chattering and chortling turning the dining hall into the Tudor version of a rowdy pub on a Friday night.

Just as I was considering slipping back upstairs, one of the palace guards locked eyes with me. A shrill whistle shot through his gray beard.

"Such a pretty lass…come 'ere!" he called out. "You may sit on my lap." Nick squinted at me like he was having trouble focusing.

"Nay, the lass shall sit with me," chimed a younger guard with a mousy-brown ponytail. Nick didn't protest; he just joined the men in more obnoxious laughter. I leveled my stare at him. He was absolutely wasted. But at least he was alive. Servers whipped past me, carrying trays of tankards overflowing with ale like they couldn't keep up with the orders. I was the only woman in the hall, and I didn't like the attention it was attracting. But I also had no intention of leaving Nick down here in a drunken stupor. A hangover wasn't exactly going to help our day tomorrow either.

I marched over to him. "Return to our chamber," he grunted at me, a little slurry. "This is no place for a maiden."

"The lass is with you?" said the bearded man, exaggerating his surprise. Clearly, the heated exchange that Nick and I had shared earlier had been forgotten in the guard's intoxication. "Wife or strumpet?" he asked Nick, flicking his brows up and down provocatively.

I expected Nick to smash his fist into the guy's jaw. But instead, Nick tugged me down onto his lap, his thighs thick and heavy beneath me as I found my balance. The beer smelled twice as strong as I remembered. "This is my wife," he said, hiccuping in my ear. "Who ought to return to our chamber."

It was the first time Nick had referred to me as his wife since we'd swapped Tudor England for the modern world, but it brought me no joy. I was too busy fuming.

"Oh, I think it's you who ought to go back upstairs, husband," I said to him through a steely smile.

"Ooooh!" the guards rang in unison before breaking into laughter. "The lass is a frisky one," said the bearded guy. He leaned back on his stool to wave over a server, the side of his hand making deliberate contact with my chest.

I jerked away from him, my cheeks on fire. "Excuse me!" I said harshly, and the man's thick brows knitted together.

The last thing I wanted was for Nick to fly off the handle, but the last thing I expected was for him to sit there and let the man grope me. Nick said nothing; he was too busy gulping ale like it was water and he'd just spent ten years in the desert.

The roly-poly innkeeper pushed his way between two crowded tables. "Those not payin' to lodge for the night are to be on their way!" he called out, scooping up empty tankards.

The palace guards groaned. "Time to go home to the old duck," the ponytailed one said before discharging a belch laced with the smell of beer. I glanced at Nick, who appeared to have gotten nothing out of these men except for liver poisoning.

"Wait," I said to the guards, sliding onto the bench. "Did my husband tell you why we're here?" Nick's eyes flashed to me, but I barreled on before he could interrupt. "We heard that, on the morrow, the queen is going to hold a parade outside Whitehall Palace to meet some of the people. Is it true?"

The guards exchanged dumbfounded looks. "Who speaks such nonsense?" said the bearded one.

"The Queen's Majesty is lodging at the Castle of Windsor," explained the pony-tailed guard in an uncertain tone. Windsor was more than twenty miles away.

"Oh, really?" I feigned disappointment. "It must've just been a rumor. We'd love to meet the queen." I faked a smile at Nick, whose eyes had narrowed. "Do you think the queen will be at Windsor Castle for long?" I asked the guards, adopting an innocent expression.

"We cannot speak of that," said the bearded one.

"I suspect that you shall not catch sight of the queen before the festival of Christmas," said the ponytailed guard. "Not with the state of things."

"Make haste, you lot—you have no lodging here this night, so be on your way," barked the innkeeper, evidently unafraid of the royal guardsmen and their three-foot-long swords. Given that the queen wasn't in residence at the palace across the road, these boys were probably passing a bit too much time at The Golden Mermaid.

The other party of rowdy drinkers had begun filing out of the arched doorway. Nick was holding his forehead like the booze headache was already crawling in. He'd get no sympathy from me, but at least I'd uncovered that Kit was lodging at Windsor Castle—that was something.

A kind-faced server handed me a lit candle, and I practically stormed up the stairwell leading to our room with Nick stumbling behind me. Our window was still open, turning the chamber into an icebox, but fortunately the stink of used chamber pots had drifted outside.

Nick closed the shutters while I untied my coif and kirtle, every cell in my body aflame.

He sat on the edge of the bed and began unclipping his jerkin with deft, steady fingers.

I crossed my arms. "How's that head of yours? Has the hangover kicked in yet?"

He cleared his throat. "My head has never been better, but I heartily thank you for your care of it." His eyes met mine, as clear as water. The pungent smell of alcohol had also vanished.

"You're not drunk at all," I realized.

He raised a brow at me. "I had finally gotten somewhere with those men before you put yourself in such peril. I merely pretended to join the guards in their inebriation to make them comfortable enough to open up to me...so they would not suspect I was anything more than a curious drunkard who would not remember our exchange of words on the morrow."

My jaw hung. "But you were throwing back those pints like a total boozehound."

"I paid the innkeeper to water down mine ale." He leaned closer, his eyes catching the glow of the flickering candle. "And, my lady, the effort had its intended effect. I learned a great deal that may help us. Although I do admire you for what you were able to glean about Windsor."

I gasped, sitting beside him. "What did they say?"

"My sister, the Queen Catherine, is indeed lodging at the Castle of Windsor, and Lord Warwick is her Lord Protector and chief advisor."

My brows flew up. "Francis Beaumont." I had mixed feelings about the impulsive Earl of Warwick managing Kit's queenship, not to mention the country of England. He was reckless and irritable at the best of times, but he was also like a brother to Nick and Kit.

A worried thought flashed in Nick's eyes. "The reason why Kit is at Windsor is because there have been plots against her life, and Windsor can be more easily defended than our other lodgings."

"Plots against her life by Mary Stuart?"

He nodded, his brow pulled tight. "The men wished not to speak of it, despite their inebriation. It is a dangerous affair to be meddling in. But they spoke of Mary Stuart being in Carlisle Castle in the high north under imprisonment. Lord Warwick must have had Mary arrested this year past. I do not yet understand how Mary Stuart will be able to break free of that castle, but we know that she will invade England, so she must have an army lying in wait. I have my suspicions that the Papist earls in the north may be involved. The men also said that Kit is no longer betrothed to the French Duke of Anjou. This increases our troubles, because the French king may now choose to side with Mary Stuart in her assault on England. After all, Mary Stuart is a former queen of France, and Scotland and France are ancient allies." His knee was bouncing madly. "Did you read any such information in your history books about the French king joining Mary Stuart's army in her attack on England?"

I shook my head, pissed off with myself. I should've studied Mary Stuart's invasion like I was writing a thesis on it, but I hadn't had the chance. I knew little about the details of her invasion, which was a massive miss on my part.

Nick stood up and began pacing. "I suspect that the Queen of the Scots intends not only to kill the queen, but to restore the old religion in England. She has long been a believer of the Catholic faith. Perhaps she is intending to invade from the north while the French strike at the very same moment from the south of England. Christ, I wish we knew more of these troubles!"

My heart thrashed in my chest. "Nick, there's something I have to tell you."

His face paled. There had been so much bad news over the years.

I ripped the Band-Aid off. "England does return to the old religion. You haven't had a chance to notice yet, but in the future, England is now Catholic. And it wasn't like that before. I grew up with the Anglican Church of England, like you. Only after you gave up your kingship and pretended to commit suicide did the entire course of Christianity in England change."

He dropped onto the bed beside me, his fingers trembling as they gripped his thighs.

I wanted to hold my chest to stop it from cleaving open. My dumb college assignment felt so small and meaningless from this side of history.

Nick gazed up at the paneled ceiling as if conversing with God himself. For the first time in a year, I saw the steely, calculating face of the king I'd married. "How much time did you say we have until Mary Stuart comes for the throne?" he asked me.

My throat withered. "One month."

He nodded, engrossed in thought.

I tilted into his vision. "What about if you just reveal that you're still alive? I know that would be incredibly dangerous, but while Mary Stuart and her co-conspirators might be able to steal the throne from a little girl, they couldn't take it from Nicholas Tudor. The people here *loved* you as their king."

He made a slow, grim shake of his head. "The people would burn me for the disgrace I have shown to them and to God."

"Or they might weep with relief that you're still alive," I argued. "We could think up a reason why you disappeared. We could twist it to make it seem like you did it *for* the people."

"Emmie, you understand not what you are saying," he said gently. "If I were to do such a thing, and the people forgave me for it and were gladdened by my return as king, do you believe I could ever leave this realm again? If I am discovered to be still alive, and I am accepted back into their hearts, then I must remain in this world. Forevermore."

His words shot into my chest like a bullet.

I could do whatever I had to in order to help stop Mary Stuart. I would willingly put myself on the line to save the lives of Kit, Alice, and Francis. But I could not live out my entire life in Tudor England. With all the opportunities I had in the modern world—with everything I'd been through to get home—I could not spend the rest of my days in this dangerous, terrifying place that suppressed the voices and abilities of women. Not anymore.

Nick hunched forward, consumed with thought. "If we are to fight for this realm, we shall need a great deal of money, and horse, and cloth. Do you still keep that cloth of mine? In our modern home?"

My mind drifted to our wardrobe in Borehamwood, where I'd hung the clothes we'd been wearing when we left Tudor England last time.

"Are you saying you want to go back home…right now?" I asked, blood rushing to my cheeks at the thought of it.

He glanced at me. "If we do so, we may obtain the cloth, some manner of item to sell for money, and perhaps information that could be of value to our plight. The particulars of Mary Stuart's armies… where they are holed up…who else is involved in the makings of her plot."

I scooched onto my knees. "We could just go back for one day, and spend it reading everything we can about Mary Stuart's attack. We'd be twelve steps ahead of her every time."

Energized by the idea of seeing my home again—the safety and comforts of the twenty-first century—I scurried to slide the blue-diamond ring back onto my thumb. Nick untied his boots before flopping back onto the mattress, his arm falling over his eyes. He looked beyond exhausted.

I stripped down to my smock, my mind racing. Mary Stuart had no idea what was coming for her. All we needed was one day back in the twenty-first century to gather the most lethal ammunition of all —information.

I blew out the candle, sending the room into blackness, and snuggled beneath the woolen blankets. Nick shifted to face me, reaching for my hand so we could time travel together. His warm fingers threaded with mine and squeezed, sending a thrill of nerves from my heart down to the lowest part of my stomach. As I lay there caressing his fingers, it took physical effort not to lean forward and taste his lips again—his desire; his love.

But Nick didn't try to kiss me. He didn't even move.

With my heart stinging, I shut my eyes and let my memory carry me away to a less bewildering time.

My mind drifted back to when Nick and I had spent the night in the medieval tower of St. Thomas at the Tower of London before my coronation as queen.

My attempt to fall asleep early that night had been thwarted the moment Nick had draped his muscular arm around me from behind, his pelvis pressing against me and stealing any thoughts I'd had of sleep. With only one thing on my mind, I'd slid my backside up and down his thickening length, his breaths picking up speed against my ear as I ground my body against his.

He'd grabbed my wrists and flipped me onto my back, crawling over the top of me and yanking my smock over my head like it'd done something to offend him.

I hadn't forgotten the hunger in Nick's eyes as he'd pushed my thighs up and back until I was completely exposed and stretched open before him. He'd sat back on his thighs and wrapped his hand around his arousal like my own personal fantasy video while he gazed down at me, making me clench and beg for his touch.

That night, he'd driven himself into me so hard that the bed's wooden legs had begun bouncing against the tiles with every firm thrust, making me fear it would break beneath us.

"Worry not, my girl," Nick had said to me in a rough voice. "I would very much like to see you bent over that desk over there."

With those words, he'd scooped me up in his strong embrace, carried me over to the oak desk, and dropped me to my feet before it. A single swipe of his forearm had sent quills and inkpots tumbling to the floor before he'd pushed my chest down against the wood, holding me there with his palm. *God, yes.*

"I could come just looking at you like this," he'd said in a gravelly tone as he slid his length up and down the seam of my center, slicking my excitement for him all over it.

I'd wanted him so badly that it had made me throb, but he'd just brushed his soft tip back and forth over my perfect little spot, his sexy moans making my breath steam against the wooden desk. He'd rubbed my sensitive skin with the velvety head of his cock until I came in ripples of pleasure and then sank himself inside me, taking me so hard that the desk wasn't holding together any better than the bed.

After I'd exploded all over him for the second time, he'd withdrawn from me, his cock stretched tight. But instead of pushing back into me, he'd carried me to the window and pressed my palms against the lattice windowpanes before standing behind me. When I'd readied myself for him again with a renewed surge of arousal, he'd swept my matted hair to the side and brought his lips to my ear.

"I have the greatest view right now that I could ever imagine, so I felt it only fair that you be given something pleasing to look at too."

A giddy chuckle had rumbled out of me as I'd settled my gaze on the moonlit angles of the sixteenth-century London skyline while Nick returned his stare to my swollen flesh. I'd felt him watch his thick length disappear inside me as he pushed back in, his teeth clamping down on his lower lip as he hissed.

"This is where I belong, Emmie," he'd said in an aching voice as he ground his hips against mine, pressing himself as deeply inside as our bodies would allow. He'd stayed in there for several endless breaths, digging his pelvis into my ass like he'd go deeper if he could, before he dragged himself all the way out of me and then slammed himself back in.

I remembered a desperate, urgent want for this feeling to never end. I'd never wanted anything more than that man in that moment.

I still didn't.

When Nick's fingers had bit into my hips and he'd pounded himself into me until the cityscape had become no more than a blur, an entire universe of stars had formed before my eyes and then shattered into dizzying constellations as I came hard around him again.

He'd then slowed his movements while I fought to catch my breath and steady my heart that was thumping out of rhythm after three climaxes. But when Nick had turned me to face him and lifted my legs around his hips until I was straddling him, I'd guessed what his next move was. He was going to seat me on the mattress and thrust up into me while I rode him, probably until he erupted.

But this time, I'd had my own plans for my bossy-as-hell Tudor king.

After he'd lowered me onto the edge of the bed like I'd anticipated, I'd rolled over until I was sitting beside him rather than on top of him.

His brow had pinched while his lips curled up. "Where is it that you are going?" he'd said.

I'd then folded my legs beneath myself and pressed my palms against his toned chest, guiding him down so he was laying on his back. He'd crossed his arms behind his head, the action drawing my gaze to his tensing biceps as he'd looked up at me with expectation washed over his face. I'd squeezed the gorgeous muscles in his arms and then ran my tongue over them, the soft yet rigid flesh giving me an idea of how something else might taste.

"Sit on top of me," Nick had demanded in a throaty tone, but I'd never considered myself one of his subjects who would ever bow to his will.

"No," I'd replied firmly, pressing his arms into the mattress and swiping my tongue over the dips and swells of his muscular chest.

He'd tensed in my grip. "I need to be inside you, Emmie." His hand had reached down to palm his cock, his voice taking on a husky ache. "Feel how hard I am."

My response had been a murmur of approval as my tongue had continued to make wet circles on his skin that ran lower and lower as I shifted down the bed.

He'd ground out a few sensual grunts but had then collected his voice through his ragged breaths. "Emmie, I must feel your body wrapped around me or I will go mad."

My lips were hovering over his lower stomach, where I'd then paused and shaken my head at him. "Sorry, babe, no can do. Other things need to be wrapped around you right now."

He'd then made a sharp inhale when I enveloped his solid ridge in my hand and squeezed, savoring the sensation of his satiny skin that felt like iron beneath. He'd groaned as I'd slid my fist up and down with a snug grip before bringing my lips closer, swallowing hard with anticipation.

It had been my first time attempting this, and I was scared of hurting him. But when Nick sat up on his elbows and watched me with his pupils blown and his lips parted, it became clear that pain was the last thing he was worried about.

I'd steadied myself in his glassy-eyed gaze and swept my tongue over the soft crown of his cock, his abs clenching and his brows lowering with desire as I repeated the movement a few more times.

With a surge of confidence, I'd closed my whole mouth over him, drawing his beautiful tip inside and sucking on it.

Nick had breathed out my name before his head lolled back, driving me to take more of him into my mouth as I sank lower and lower over him, my cheeks hollowing as I sucked harder.

He'd then cursed and reached for the back of my neck, threading his fingers messily in my hair as he helped guide my mouth up and down. After that, he'd lifted up my hair to give him a clear view of my lips stretched tightly around him.

"That's it," he'd encouraged through shallow, raspy breaths. "*Yes*, that's good. You like that. So beautiful."

This. Was. Mind-blowing. It had been equal parts curiosity and wanting to pleasure Nick that had inspired me to do this, but I hadn't expected it to turn *me* on so much that I'd felt wetness dampening the flesh between my thighs. I'd moaned into his skin and continued working him with my mouth, up and down, up and down, as he grunted out needy murmurs that made me suck deeper.

"I will come if you do not stop," he'd said in a breath, but he was still gently driving my head up and down by my hair, and now that I knew how good he tasted, I had no intention of giving him back.

I'd hummed out sounds of satisfaction as I switched between tight sucks and gliding my tongue up and down the full length of him.

He'd kept gritting out my name between curses, his jaw clenched with pleasure and his fingers tight in my hair as I'd feasted on him like my only job in this world was to make him come harder than he ever had.

A sharp groan had then erupted out of him, and he'd pulled at my hair—a warning to move my mouth away before he exploded, but, no, that wasn't happening.

"*Emmie,*" he'd said through his teeth as he lifted his hips and thrust up into my mouth, but I'd kept my lips wrapped tightly around him, sweeping my tongue as I sucked.

He'd ground out a sexy-as-hell moan of pleasure and then sat up, digging his fingers in my hair and burying himself in my mouth until hot liquid spilled down my throat. With aching moans, I'd sucked him dry, my breath all but gone and my heart a thundering racehorse in my chest.

Immediately afterward, my cheeks had flushed hot with slight mortification when I realized how out of control I'd just become—how eagerly I'd sucked my husband off—but when he caught my cheeks in his palms and lifted my face to his, my shoulders instantly loosened.

The love that had burned in Nick's eyes as they gazed into mine—the devotion, the trust—had reminded me that all this was okay; that this was *right*. That, while Nick and I had proven to find it nearly impossible to keep our hands off each other, it was making us both ridiculously happy.

But when my eyes slowly drifted open inside that darkened bedchamber at The Golden Mermaid inn, they met the sight of Nick's furrowed face as he slept, almost fully clothed, with no part of his body touching mine except for his hand.

Heartache clenched my chest as I was reminded, once again, that the days like the one I'd just recalled were grievously, inexplicably gone. And so was the Nick Tudor I knew.

If only someone could tell me how to get him back.

7

A THIN FILM OF LIGHT PIERCED THE EDGES OF THE WOODEN WINDOW shutters. I opened my sticky eyes and rolled to face Nick on the stiff mattress, getting my bearings inside the inn's shadowy chamber.

He was sitting up on his elbows, his voice scratchy with sleep. "Why are we still at the inn? Why has the enchanted ring failed to bring us to your time?"

A surge of panic crashed into me. "How should I know?" I asked groggily, sitting up. Was that it? We were trapped in the sixteenth century forever?

My throat closed with dread as I looked at Nick, a memory swooping into my vision. "Remember the soothsayer that I visited in the hamlet village near Robin House, back when I was the queen?" I said. "She told me that the ring was almost drained of its power. Maybe there was enough magic left in it to get us here, but not home again." I hopped out of the bed and rubbed my clammy palms down my thighs. My mom would never forgive me if I disappeared on her again, this time never to return. I would never forgive myself!

Nick heaved a sigh and joined me at the window, flipping open the shutters to invite a gust of fresh, steadying air. "That soothsayer near to Robin House," he said. "She was able to understand the enchantment in the ring, true? How the magic first came to pass?"

"Yes. It was Mary, Queen of Scots, who had the ring cursed in the first place to get rid of you," I replied grimly. "It always comes back to Mary-freaking-Stuart."

He settled his gaze on the glimpse of lime-green pasturelands beyond the river. "We shall journey there and call upon her."

"You want to go to Carlisle Castle in the north and face Mary Stuart?" My voice was high. "Just us two?"

"The *soothsayer*," he corrected. "The hamlet is not far from here, and we have enough coins left to buy and keep a horse. We shall go to the soothsayer and bid her to curse the ring as before, so we have our means to journey home. We shall then return to our undertaking here to stop Mary Stuart, as we planned." He finally took a breath. "Clearly, there is no time to be lost." He grabbed his leather jerkin and began clipping it on.

I reached for my kirtle with reluctance. "But you need to stay hidden from sight. And now we're going to tell a witch that not only is the King of England still alive, but he's a time traveler who curses diamond rings? That's the plan?"

"Do you have a better one?" He finished the last hook of the fitted jacket and sighed. "My lady, I gave up everything to remove you from this wretched world so you could be safe and merry. If you believe I intend to lose you to this place again, then you know me not."

My lips fell open as he tied on his belt, his shoulders set. Nick was not only stressing out about the Tudor dynasty crumbling and the beheading of his sister and his closest friends, but he was also worried about letting *me* down. Guilt gripped my chest as I remembered pressuring him last night to return to the modern world—and to make the best of it—amid all this Tudor danger. But at the same time, didn't my needs count as much as his?

Silence chewed up the anxious air as we slipped into the last pieces of our clothing and tied on our boots. Not long after sunrise, a servant tapped on the door with a bowl of hot water, which we used to wash our faces and rub our teeth. Nick whispered his morning prayers while I folded our handful of belongings into the linen sheet and knotted it into a sack shape.

Despite the early hour, the streets downstairs were already buzzing with energy. Lawyers and clerks in billowy cloaks were making their way to work while wealthy gentlemen emerged from their well-located mansions to dodge wagons and pack horses on the move. Without the aggressive noises of car engines and beeping horns, the roads of Tudor England belonged to the pedestrians.

The air was especially cool for May, and I huddled in a corner out of the wind as Nick approached several men who lumbered past on horseback, offering each one money for his horse with his cap pulled low over his face. Nick's attempt at disguise probably wasn't even necessary: His cut-price, commoner clothes erased any suspicion that this could be the King of England who'd once worn diamonds in his hair and feasted on pies with birds flying out of them.

On his fifth try, he eagerly exchanged a handful of silver coins for the reins of a palfrey horse named Leo. I knew palfreys to be good traveling horses, but Leo was gaunt and underfed, with graying hair and sunken eyes. I suspected that Nick had paid more for the aging horse than it was worth, but this wasn't the usual location and protocol for purchasing animals, so we had to make do.

Leo flicked his tail lazily as Nick climbed up into his saddle in a single, swift movement before helping me up. I laced my arms around his waist from behind, breathing in the warm, comforting scent of buttery leather and Nick Tudor.

The clip-clopping of hooves on gravel soothed me as Nick steered Leo away from the palace, expertly dodging horses, carts, pedestrians, and potholes. Leo was a stubborn gelding, and Nick had to give him a firm nudge for him to make a right down a dusty lane about a mile away from the Palace of Whitehall. It didn't take long to reach the eighteen-foot-high city wall. Beyond the towering gatehouse that separated London from the countryside, the roads were quickly swallowed up by muddy grass paths bordered by wild fields, the traffic thinning and the medieval spire of St. Paul's Cathedral shrinking behind us.

Wind howled in my ears as we galloped across flowering meadowlands carpeted with golden buttercups, passing rustic cottages with smoke billowing from their chimneys, the air tasting fresh and vaguely of cattle. I'd forgotten how beautiful it was out here in the sixteenth-century English countryside; how peaceful.

My butt was beginning to ache from riding when we finally slowed to a trot as we approached a small hill blanketed with wild lavender in tangles of green and purple. A thatched roof peeked through a canopy of birch trees that rustled with chirping birds.

"I can't believe it," I said as Nick guided Leo to a stop some distance from Robin House.

Robin House was Nick's most private manor and the only place in Tudor England that had felt like home to me. It was the house in which we'd gotten married, where we'd spent our wedding night, where Nick had made love to me with such intensity and enthusiasm that I hadn't walked in a straight line for days.

My chest twisted tightly at the memory. "I wish we could go inside," I said.

He leaned into me, tripling my heart rate. "If only you knew how much I share that wish." My lips parted with surprise as he twisted toward me in the saddle, the growing stubble on his cheeks close enough to kiss, his hypnotic eyes inches from mine.

Oh my God. Nick, please. Just kiss me.

I'm so desperate to taste you, to touch you, to feel you.

I need you. I love you.

"Are you ready to visit the witch in the hamlet?" he asked me, blinking away.

My heart sank low into my stomach.

I managed a murmur of agreement, and Nick clicked his tongue for Leo to carry us down to the hamlet village nestled just beyond the hill. The terror of what we were about to do soon eclipsed any hurt I felt at his emotional distance.

Focusing on the task at hand, I reminded myself that the young witch had kept my dangerous secrets until now, as far as I knew. We had no choice but to trust her.

We'd already made our plan: I would approach the witch alone because she'd met me before. I wouldn't mention anything about the king being alive, and Nick would wait behind the small alehouse next door to her house and come for me at the first sound of trouble.

The hamlet was too small a village to be walled, so we approached it from the hillside and slowed Leo to a stop behind the crumbling alehouse. Nick helped me down onto the grass, and we reinforced the plan with our encouraging eyes, both too unsettled to speak.

With a pit opening up in my stomach, I rounded the corner of the wattle-and-daub cottage, my boots kicking up dust. Thick planks of hand-sawed wood had been hammered across the witch's square window. I sucked in a jittery breath and knocked on the rickety door that hung askew. A gentle wind swishing in a nearby tree was the only response. I banged harder before footsteps shuffled behind me.

I spun around to face a thin man with white tufts of hair standing outside the alehouse.

"Be careful if ye be touching that house," he called, clutching a wooden tankard. His voice was stronger than his body implied.

"Do you know where the girl is who lives 'ere?" I asked him, making a poor attempt to fake a rural Tudor accent.

His leathery brow crinkled. It was rare to meet someone this old in Tudor England. "Whatcha be wanting that witch for? We want nay more lasses bringing the devil's work to our village!" He shook his tankard at me, cloudy brown ale spilling out.

"I have no interest in witchcraft," I said quickly. "I'm just a friend of the girl's…barely even that…and I'm only passing through."

The man's expression softened. "Well, then I regret to pass on the bad news, lassie. The girl hast passed away some months ago. But she got herself into the devil's work, so she must pay the price."

"The girl *died?*" I said with dismay.

He nodded. "'Twas the queen's men who came for the witch before the winter. She had been into some dark arts with that Queen Emmeline. The one who jumped to her death. They burned the lass for her part in it."

I gaped at the man, who nodded a curt farewell as if he'd caught himself speaking out of turn. He slipped back inside the alehouse, leaving me to shiver in my thoughts. The young witch—whose name I'd unforgivably never known—had been burned to death for helping me understand more about the enchanted ring. And on Kit's command! I caught myself—Kit was only ten years old, so the order had to have come from her Lord Protector, Francis Beaumont. He was even more quick-tempered than my Tudor husband, which was saying something.

I hurried away to find Nick standing beside our horse, nervously rubbing his palms together.

"She's dead," I blurted through tears. "Francis had the witch burned because of what came out at my trial...how I'd been known to visit her for witchcraft." I wanted to bury myself in the smoky warmth of Nick's leather jerkin, but at the same time, I could've pushed him away with both hands. *Another death because of us...because of me!*

"What in the devil?" he said, his brow lining. At that moment, I hated this place more than I ever had; I'd have given anything to have been back in my century instead of facing another death in this brutal, primitive world.

Nick took hold of my arms, his eyes drilling into mine. "We will find another soothsayer. We will curse the ring again." When my eyes filled up, his voice cracked. "Emmie, forgive me. It overwhelms me with sorrow that you again face such despair because of me. Christ, what I have put you through."

"What you put me through?" I said, wiping my cheeks. "Nick, all this is because of *me*. I'm the one who brought us back here!"

He tightened his grip on me. "I am your husband! I am to look after you. I am the reason that you could not leave this realm in the first place, all those years ago when I fell in love with you and begged you to stay. From then until now, all you have faced is danger and death."

I grabbed the collar of his jacket and shook him. "Enough of this old-school, macho, chauvinistic crap! It is not your job to look after me—I am a grown woman, and I'm perfectly capable of looking after myself. I stayed in Tudor England because I wanted to...because I didn't want to be without you either. The reason we're even back here is because of *my* decision to wear the enchanted ring so we could try to save Kit and our friends. Okay? So now we just have to figure this out together. As equals."

A flush of emotion stained his cheeks pink. I didn't know where the pep talk had come from, but it was apparent that we both needed it.

He reached for me again, but when voices murmured from outside the tavern, we hurriedly climbed up onto Leo's worn saddle. Nick clicked his tongue and guided the horse into a canter over the grassy hill and deep into the countryside, putting distance between us and the hamlet.

After more than an hour of trotting in restless, aimless silence, Nick gave Leo's reins a tug near the bank of a trickling stream. Given that we were both prone to asthma, we had to be careful about riding too hard and fast.

Nick helped me off Leo's back before guiding the horse to the glistening ribbon of water to drink. Nick and I gulped water from our pouch and shared a roll of dry, grainy bread on the grass.

"I've been thinking," I said to him, swatting away a fly.

"As maidens tend to do so well."

I was pleased that he hadn't lost his sense of humor yet.

"We have to fix the ring, which means we need another soothsayer. Do you know if there are any in Windsor? Because the town can't be far away from here, and it's also where Kit is. We could kill two birds with one stone: get the ring re-cursed, and perhaps find a way to warn Kit about Mary Stuart's invasion without actually revealing ourselves to her. After all, that's what we came here for."

Nick stiffened before he blew through his lips, refocusing. "I know not of a soothsayer in Windsor; it is not as if I keep a register of the witches of the realm. However, Windsor will have food and lodging and, as a market town, it will be easy to blend in there."

I let out a long breath at the first concrete plan we'd agreed on. I was ready to collapse, but we still had hours of riding to do before we'd reach Windsor. Traveling by river boat would be faster, but that risked us coming into contact with more people, and we also didn't want to let go of our horse.

I refilled our leather pouch with fresh water from the stream before pushing up onto Leo's back and resting my cheek against Nick's shoulder. He had to tap my thigh to prevent me from falling asleep more than once as we rode across countless fields of grazing cattle, the unending blanket of green occasionally interrupted by a cottage, barn, or watermill. My butt had to be covered in bruises from the relentless clomping of Leo's hooves.

The sun was low in the sky when the gray, cylindrical battlement towers of Windsor Castle emerged in the distance. Nick slowed Leo to a walk as we approached the town walls, Nick's eyes glued to the stone turrets of the castle that housed his much-loved little sister.

Any warmth we felt over being this close to Kit—and Francis, which also meant his wife Alice Grey—evaporated into a noxious stink that sharpened as we neared the gatehouse.

"What on earth is that smell?" I asked, burying my nose in my sleeve.

"It is the midden," Nick replied, gesturing toward the heap of dung, animal carcasses, and fish guts edging the base of the wall. My stomach heaved as we passed by it and through the gatehouse.

Mud splashed the hem of my kirtle as we meandered on horseback past narrow, timber-framed houses with gables hanging crookedly over the street. Nick and I had visited Windsor before—during our tour of the country as the king and future queen—but I'd forgotten the extent of the poverty and filth in the townships outside London. A beggar held his blackened fingers up to me, but Nick swatted the man away.

The main thoroughfare had four inns to choose from, but The White Hart was the most secluded and therefore the obvious choice. There was no curtained bed in our room this time, just two straw mattresses side by side, a plain chest with a tattered cushion on top to fashion it into a seat, and a stained chamber pot. We were fortunate to have a window for some natural light, but the open hole was taped over with greased paper, blocking any view we might've had.

"Hungry?" Nick asked me, rubbing his shoulders like they were stiff and sore.

"I could eat," I said wryly, pressing my hollow stomach. "Are we dining in the castle tonight? I haven't had an entire roasted pig for a while, or any fresh macarons, for that matter. Sheesh, what kind of hospitality is this?"

He frowned at the joke that clearly stung, and I tried not to roll my eyes. When would Nick get it through his head that I didn't miss his princely riches? All I wanted was for us to be together in a world that was safe and, for the most part, free. All I wanted was to right the wrongs that we'd done so we could get back to the safety and comforts of the twenty-first century. All I wanted was for Nick to have an 'aha' moment that life was better there…so he could get out of that freaking vegetable garden and start living again…with me.

But, once again, he demonstrated no signs of such a realization.

With my chest heavy, we padded downstairs for a bowl of salty pottage served by the innkeeper's pregnant wife, who winced with pain at every turn. Every time she dug her ladle through the cauldron of stew above the crackling fire, I saw her arthritic hands as my hands and her wearied face as my face. When I imagined her having one of those horrific medieval births from movies, in which the women scream, sweat, and sometimes die, I saw myself dying in pools of blood while birthing Nick's baby in the Tudor world.

My heart sank deeper into my chest, chasing the last flame of hope that was flickering away into darkness. Since we'd left the inn outside the Palace of Whitehall, I'd been focused solely on finding the soothsayer, and then a warm bed to sleep in. But now that we were here, now that we'd stopped for a moment, reality crawled onto my face like a spider.

The enchanted ring hadn't worked last night, and the only soothsayer I knew or trusted here was dead. If the ring had conked out for good, that meant there would be no going home, whether Nick wanted to or not. Coming back here to fix the mistakes we'd made would be a one-way street…a road from which there would be no return.

Nick took quiet sips of pottage across from me, his exhausted head bowed. When I'd lived in this century as the Queen of England, I'd secretly begged for a simple life with him.

And now we were going to get it.

But it wouldn't be in the way I'd imagined. If we couldn't repair the blue-diamond ring, and if Nick refused to admit to being the former king because of his shame, then we were destined for lives like those of the innkeeper and his wife: boiling countless bowls of pottage, struggling to make ends meet, and trying to keep me from losing my life to childbirth. In escaping England out of an all-consuming, selfish love, we'd unchained the Queen of the Scots, and becoming a pair of poor sixteenth-century villagers would be our penance. Once again, history had proven that it didn't like to be messed with.

I downed a tankard of ale before ordering another, my thoughts spiraling into a roaring whirlpool.

I had him.

I had him…a Tudor king, living in the twenty-first century! I achieved the impossible. Which means I can achieve it again.

History could kick and scream all she wanted, but I wasn't giving up on our life in the modern world without the mother of all battles. I would turn up on the doorstep of every witch in England if that was what it took to get the enchanted ring re-cursed. I wasn't going to live in Tudor England until I breathed my last, and I wasn't going home without Nick.

History could bite me.

I chugged another gulp of ale, settling my gaze on the wooden cross nailed to the wall opposite me.

Then, out of nowhere, it hit me…the words in Latin once said to me by the witch from the hamlet.

"Lex tailionis…an eye for an eye."

The law of retaliation…the principle of reciprocal justice… measure for measure.

I still believed that this fundamental rule of the universe—an eye for an eye—was the reason why my former lady of the bedchamber, Lucinda Parker, had lost her life after I'd started messing with the path of history and saving the lives of those who'd been fated to die.

Since then, I'd stolen a king.

I sipped more ale, swallowing hard, like the action might also consume the dark thoughts that were choking me from the inside out.

Nick Tudor was never meant to be yours, Emmie. So, if you want to escape this world and return to your time again, what are you prepared to give up this time?

8

THE DESOLATE, SILENT BLACKNESS OF TUDOR ENGLAND AT NIGHT
summoned me into a sleep so deep that the shrill clanging of church
bells felt like a dream.

Nick was gently shaking my shoulder. "It is the Lord's Day," he
said sleepily. "We must attend the parish church."

"Is it okay if you go without me?" I murmured. "I need to sleep
more." I didn't want to be offensive, but my body was a lead truck.

"We enjoy the freedoms of your realm no longer, my lady. We are
commanded by the crown to attend the Lord's Day service. We
cannot be seen to upset the noblemen, or we risk arrest."

I sat up on my elbows. "We could be *arrested* if we don't go to
church on Sundays? Who came up with that rule?"

He cleared his throat. "As a matter of fact, I did."

Groaning, I kicked off the blankets, slipping the blue-diamond
ring off my thumb and hiding it inside the toe of my boot. I bit away
my disappointment that the ring had failed to work for the second
night in a row.

Outside, I wrapped my arms around myself to block the early-
morning air with ice on its breath, relieved to find the parish church
just a short stroll from our inn.

My empty stomach growled through the world's longest sermon, delivered by a young minister with spotty skin and a grating voice. Nick's imposing stature and rugged handsomeness drew the eyes of both women and men everywhere, but so far, there were no signs of recollection that he could be their deceased king. His greatest protection wasn't only the facial stubble he was growing, but the impossibility that such a low-born-looking man could be the infamous Nicholas Tudor—son of Queen Elizabeth the First, grandson of King Henry the Eighth.

By the time the service concluded, I was about ready to eat my coif. My stomach protested at the thought of more vegetable stew, so now that the sun had warmed the streets, I convinced Nick to stroll with me into the market square, where we could hunt down some Tudor-style fast food. The blue-diamond ring pressing against my toe was beginning to hurt, so he insisted I sit and wait on a tree stump nearby. Just ahead of me, merchants in knitted aprons were laying out everything from embroidered cloth to candle holders to chess sets to eggs and cheese, evidently permitted to make a living on the Lord's Day. A woman strode past with chickens hanging from a horizontal stick that balanced on her neck, the birds squawking and spraying feathers. Nick emerged through a cluster of shoppers carrying two salted beef pies and wearing a smirk of pride.

We found a quiet spot to eat, formulating our next plan with hushed voices. Nick was keen to scour the village doors for pagan markings that suggested a witch might be in residence, but after my public trial for engaging in the dark arts, we shared a concern that all the soothsayers had gone into hiding.

"We must do something!" he exclaimed suddenly, tossing his pie crust. "I am afeared that Mary Stuart draws nearer in her plot to snatch the crown by force, and we have done naught to stop it."

He wasn't wrong. If we still needed to find a witch, convince her to trust us and curse our ring to a century she knew nothing about, then travel forward in time to retrieve more information about Mary's plans, *and* travel back here again, we were off our freaking rockers.

"Forget the soothsayer for the moment," I said. "The idea of going to the modern world to get information on Mary was a good one, but there's no time for that now. Now that we're near the castle, we need to figure out how to slip a message to Kit and Francis without revealing our identities. We don't have a hope of stopping Mary Stuart without the involvement of the English army, especially if the French king is backing Mary as you thought."

I blinked at him, the words I'd just uttered settling in my whirring brain. We had to stay focused on Mission: Stop Mary Stuart, but as soon as that was over, the only thing on my mind would be re-cursing the blue-diamond ring so we could get the heck out of Tudor England.

Nick twisted to face the high battlement towers of Windsor Castle that speared the overcast sky. The distress in his eyes spoke volumes: Attempting contact with Kit and Francis was a massive gamble. If anyone suspected the King of England to be still alive, we'd have a bigger problem on our hands than Mary Stuart.

"I'll do it," I said, mentally preparing myself. "I'll be the one to get a message to them. If Francis is inside that castle, then so is Alice Grey. What I'm going to do is to try to get a message to Alice—I trust her as much as I trust you."

His brows flew up. "You intend to walk through the gates of Windsor Castle?"

"No, but I'm going to wait for some courtiers to walk out of them. All I need to do is find a lady of the court who's on her own, and then I'm going to bribe her to deliver a message to Alice." The thought of seeing my best friend in the Tudor world squeezed my chest, but I had to remain focused. "I'll say that I want to report an anonymous and imminent threat from Carlisle Castle in the north, and that's all," I continued. "If I don't mention the Queen of the Scots, it can't be taken as treason. Alice is smart enough to get it; she'll know that Mary Stuart is imprisoned at Carlisle Castle and that the threat is coming from her. You should stay here—away from Windsor Castle and anyone who might recognize you."

He touched my wrist. "My lady, I will not have you do my bidding, especially when it puts you in harm's way."

I didn't want to lose the heat of his touch that set my skin and heart ablaze, but I gently pulled away. "You haven't bid me to do anything. And this is not your responsibility alone."

He exhaled with visible reluctance as I made my way to the castle gatehouse, winding through a chaotic jumble of streets, past steaming piles of manure, flocks of geese, and carthorses that blocked the path before I headed up a muddy hill.

The drawbridge was down over the castle ditch, the spiked jaws of the portcullis stretched open. Courtiers were striding in and out of the castle like it was a shopping mall, chased down by market sellers offering their wares in baskets. The wealthy women claimed twice as much space as the commoners in their expensive farthingales, the pearls sewn into their hoods shining iridescently in the sunlight. There were at least twice as many men as women, their velvet doublets crossed with thick gold chains and their hats adorned with exotic feathers.

I searched for a young woman coming or going from court alone —someone too concerned about getting in trouble to interrogate me —but all I saw were imposing men carrying swords and the occasional middle-aged woman in a gabled hood, neither of which was my target. I'd had enough experience with the Duke of Norfolk and the Dowager Countess of Warwick to know that rubbing elbows with the older, more influential players at court rarely paid off. Nervous sweat beaded on my neck beneath my kirtle, and I shrank into the thin shadow of a balcony opposite the palace, slumping with defeat.

"There is a traitor against Her Majesty, our sovereign queen!" cried a raspy voice. A middle-aged man with wispy hair and a face like thunder rounded the corner, a small barrel wedged under his arm. His legs were grubby and bare—an unthinkable sight in Tudor England. He plonked the barrel down in front of me and climbed upon it, finding his balance. I covered my nose at the whiff of feces emanating from his blackened skin.

"The lord aligns with the queen falsely!" he called out to no one in particular.

"Be silent, you lunatic!" spat a passing courtier.

Sadly, I'd learned that mentally unwell folks weren't uncommon in the rural townships of Tudor England, but this guy was particularly rowdy. Spit flew from his lips as he shouted. "The Papist Earl of Warwick gathers an army with the treasonous Earls of Westmoreland and Northumberland to restore the old religion in England! The Earl of Warwick is seduced by the devil himself! He seeks to wed Mary Stuart, the Queen of the Scots, so she may claim an English husband! The Earl of Warwick will be king!"

Flashes of scarlet cut through the onlookers before a dull thud sent the dissenter into the dirt. He clutched the backs of his knees, crying out as two castle guards hauled him away by his arms. He'd surely be beaten within an inch of his life and probably executed for high treason.

But that wasn't the only reason I couldn't catch my breath. I raced away from the pit of danger, finding my way back to the market square with my stomach in my throat. Nick was where I'd left him, pacing back and forth, lines etched into his brow.

When he saw me, he sagged with relief. "Well? Did you find a lady of the court who could reach the Countess of Warwick?"

I shook my head. "There was too much commotion. There was a random guy outside the court who kept shouting at the top of his lungs before the guards took him away." I swallowed a jagged lump in my throat. "He said that the Earl of Warwick, Francis Beaumont, was planning to *marry* Mary, Queen of Scots, and become the King of England!"

Nick gaped at me. "What say you?"

"He was ranting that Francis Beaumont is working with the Earls of Westmoreland and Northumberland to gather a Catholic army, wed Mary Stuart, and become King of England with her as the queen."

Nick pressed a hand to his brow, his eyes flashing. "But we know that Mary Stuart has Francis die by the axe—am I wrong? It was written on the wall in the Tower of London."

"That's right," I said. "But maybe Mary Stuart uses Francis to get to the throne of England, and then has him executed so she doesn't have to share the throne—I don't know!" My voice had turned shrill. "What if this is true? What if Francis Beaumont is conspiring with Mary Stuart?"

A roar of frustration burst from Nick's throat before he spun around to kick a decaying barrel so hard that it smashed into a wall, breaking open. He turned away from me, his fists clenched. "It sickens me to think ill of Francis. That man is a brother to me."

"We don't know if this is true," I reasoned, desperately hoping that Francis wouldn't become yet another one of Nick's loved ones to betray him. "That guy looked pretty off his rocker."

"No, Emmie, I believe it is true," Nick said bleakly, his back falling against the white wall of a tailor's shop. "Francis is a Beaumont. His kin are of the old religion and have a direct line to King Henry the Eighth, my grandfather. Some have said that Francis should be next in the line of succession after my sister. By marrying Mary Stuart, he would become the King of Scotland without trouble, and in the course of time, the King of England. Why would he not seize such fortune? This feels clear to me."

The hurt in Nick's face pulled at my heart. "I can't imagine Francis betraying you," I said.

His knowing eyes met mine. "Not unless he believes his king to be dead."

I rested my depleted body against the wall beside him. This was all beginning to feel too big. Now Francis Beaumont was conspiring to take the crown? Nick and I had messed so much with the path of history that it was starting to resemble tangled Christmas lights.

"Let us return to the inn and rest awhile," Nick said with a wearied sigh, and I didn't argue. I needed him to stay strong and sane. His tendency to lose his cool and act out of vengeance rather than sense always felt dangerously near.

We fell asleep with ease and napped like jet-lagged travelers before we re-emerged before nightfall to find dinner somewhere other than the inn's poky dining hall. We risked running into thieves and trouble-makers after curfew, so we chose our street food quickly: boiled chicken legs with buttered bread.

I was dreading shutting ourselves back inside our chamber, with no television or books, when an explosion of music burst behind us. A pair of fiddlers had broken into a lively tune, encouraging random couples to dance spontaneously in the middle of the street. Four men in brightly painted costumes and makeup carried a sheet of wood past us and began constructing a makeshift stage.

"What's all this?" I asked Nick as villagers started congregating around us with delighted faces.

"I believe it is a traveling entertainment." He guided me back a few paces, keeping our distance.

I was frankly thrilled for some recreation and watched on my tiptoes while Nick scanned the expanding audience of spectators—all of them commoners and peasants in faded linen coifs and tattered, patchwork coats.

The actors leaped onto the stage like acrobats, scurrying into their roles, which appeared to be a king, two queens—played by men in gowns and makeup—and a court jester. I grimaced at the lousy acting...they were a far cry from Shakespeare's thespians.

Nick stiffened beside me as the storyline took shape. The play was about a king and queen returning from the dead to find that another queen had stolen the throne. The actor playing the jester tossed away his hat and cloak to reveal a devil's costume under-neath, complete with horns and a tail. The onlookers howled with juvenile laughter as the devil chased the king and queen around the stage.

A portly guy beside us, with ginger curls protruding from his woolen cap, made a crude snort-laugh. When Nick and I glanced at him, he poked his tongue out at us like a child.

"How dare you look upon your superiors with such offense!" Nick snapped at him. "You ought to lose your head!" The man's lips flat-tened, his eyes narrowing.

I grabbed Nick's arm and tugged him toward the street that led to our inn. The red-headed guy leaned into the glow of the street lantern, watching us go.

"Nick, that man's still looking at us!" I said through my teeth. "You spoke to him like you were the king! What if he recognized you?"

"Forgive me." Nick huffed a sound of frustration at the mistake he'd made. "However, if that man were to make a claim that the king was still alive, he would be hanged, drawn, and quartered. Still, it is no longer safe to remain here. We should take our leave from Windsor at first light."

When we reached the inn, he asked me to wait safely out of view in the stairwell while he arranged our early-morning departure with the innkeeper. The contents of my stomach rose into my throat. I hadn't stopped worrying about Nick being recognized since we'd arrived here, but this was the closest we'd come to that nightmare coming true. What if rumors broke out in Windsor that King Nicholas was still alive and hiding out like a recluse with his fugitive wife? Kit would never want to hurt him, but even the monarch couldn't thwart the wrath of the country's noblemen—my stint as the disgraced Queen of England had proven that. And now we couldn't even trust Francis Beaumont, the Lord Protector of the Realm, who was effectively running the country until Kit came of age.

Sleep felt like something we had to get through before we could escape this tainted town, but the aimless miles of countryside waiting for us offered little solace to look forward to. We still needed food and shelter, and we were no closer to finding a way out of Tudor England, let alone a solution to stop Mary Stuart.

After a fitful night's sleep, we headed downstairs to the stables, which were bathed in a pinkish, early-morning glow, and reunited with our horse, Leo. Nick suggested that we ride on to Maidenhead, another market town that might house a soothsayer that could help us re-curse the blue-diamond ring.

After trailing the curve of the river for five miles or so, we paused for a bite of bread somewhere around the village of Bray, keeping away from any smoking chimneys and other signs of life. Nick had once told me that he loathed the itch of beards, and he'd begun trimming his facial scruff with a small blade. As we stretched out on our cloaks beneath a sturdy birch tree that edged the rippling water, I ran a hand down my greasy hair. I wasn't sure the rugged look worked as well on me as it did on Nick.

He was scraping his blade against a smooth stone, sharpening it. "I vow to take better care of you in Maidenhead," he said without looking at me. "And to get you out of this dog's dinner that I have made of things."

My eyes rolled. "Oh God, this again." When would he catch on that it wasn't his job to look after me?

He sat forward. "You are indeed a marvel of a woman, my lady, but I am determined to be of some use to you." My brows flew up, but he barreled on. "As long as we remain in this realm, I am your husband, and I will take great pains to see you well and merry. We have plenty of coin, and at first light on the morrow, I shall search Maidenhead for a soothsayer who can help us. The moment the enchanted ring is in working order, I intend to bring you home."

My chest emptied of breath. "You want to leave Tudor England? Before we've done anything to stop Mary Stuart?"

His eyes softened as he looked at me. "Emmie, I will not put your life in peril for my kingdom. Not again."

The distant whinny of a horse stole our focus. About a hundred feet upstream, a young man with a bushy beard was tying a caramel-toned palfrey horse to a sturdy tree. The horse watched its owner stride into the river, fully clothed, until he was waist-deep in the murky water.

"Yikes, that guy's going for a swim," I said, shivering at the thought.

"Or a wash," said Nick. "Something we are both in need of."

"And that's no lie."

I was too afraid to give myself a sniff in front of the boy who I was desperate to kiss and undress, but who didn't seem to want to do those things to me.

Not yet ready to face more butt-aching horse-riding and squalid villages, I slid closer to Nick. His skin was lightly streaked with dirt, yet I couldn't get close enough to him.

"What is it?" he asked in a smooth, tentative voice. I could smell the mint sprig on his breath.

"Nothing," I replied, crawling right into his lap.

I was just so tired of holding back. He'd said it himself—we were married in this century, despite the jerk noblemen at my trial claiming that our marriage was invalid. Plus, hearing him say those things about bringing me home the first chance he could, about putting my life first...it reminded me of what we'd been through—what we'd given up—to be together. How on earth had we become so lost, in every sense of the word?

When I wrapped my arms around his neck in a persistent—almost desperate—hug, his strong arms folded around me, but I sensed hesitation. I pressed my face to his chest, feeling his heart beating against my mouth. Unmet desire tugged from deep within me, compelling my lips to kiss the soft linen of his shirt. He didn't move, but his heartbeat intensified as I continued kissing the fabric that separated my mouth from his body, unable to stop.

"Emmie," Nick said breathlessly before I clawed beneath his shirt to pull it out of his leather trousers, exposing his bare skin. He grabbed my wrist, trying to stop me for reasons I didn't understand, but I brought my lips directly to his skin, lightheaded with hunger for him. I slid my tongue across the rippled muscles that tightened in his stomach, the taste of salty sweetness sending an ache shuddering through me. I was prepared for Nick to bring this to a screaming halt, but when I licked a wet stripe across the skin beneath his belly button, a deep sigh rumbled in the back of his throat, and his grip on my wrist drew tight.

Please, let me do this. I need you.

My hands grasped his waist on both sides, keeping him in place, as I kissed and licked his stomach. When Nick's fingers slipped into my hair and his palm cupped the back of my neck, I moaned into his warm skin, wanting this to nearly the point of madness.

My cheek dropped against his taut stomach as I angled my head to stare down at the thick shape that was swelling in his trousers, stretching the fabric. My eyes turned heavy at the sight, and I lowered my hand and began a cautious but intent trail up the inside of his thigh. Nick's hand tightened against my neck as his breaths switched to ragged, and for a moment, it was happening…the man I was so attracted to that I couldn't see straight was returning to me…until a shout from afar shocked us apart.

The man who was swimming had drifted away from the shoreline and into a stronger current. He flapped his arms in our direction, his voice crying out in panic.

Nick shot to his feet, adjusting himself in his trousers. "Good God, that fellow will drown if he is not careful."

"I know," I said, loosening the ties on my boots so I could yank them off. The blue-diamond ring rolled out onto the grass, and I hurriedly slipped it inside the safety of our satchel.

"Surely you do not mean to go in after him," Nick said with disbelief.

"Of course I am," I said. "He's drowning!"

He chased me down to the water's edge. "What if *you* drown? And that water may not be pure!"

I called out to the man that I was coming to help. Nick made a frustrated huff behind me, and I could hear him kicking off his boots. Unable to wait for him, I strode into the river like lions were chasing me, yelping softly as the icy water blanketed my skin and stole my breath.

Nick splashed his way beside me and ordered me out of the water. I was too cold to argue, so I just shook my head with chattering teeth and powered forward toward the man. He was slipping under, and Nick plunged ahead of me until he caught the guy's arm. My numb fingers managed to clutch the soaked sleeve of the struggling man's other arm. Together, Nick and I tugged him toward the shoreline. When the sludgy river bottom met the soles of my feet, I relaxed, but I didn't let go of the man. He was panting, his balding head hanging forward like he might be sick.

"I thank thee, I thank thee, good sir and his missus; I shall pray for thee," he kept repeating through shivers. His eyes were a freaky ice-blue, almost translucent.

"You gave us quite a fright," Nick said, letting go of the guy when we reached knee-deep water. The moment Nick stepped away from him, my arm was yanked backward nearly out of its socket, my throat pinned with something sharp.

"Stop! What is this?!" Nick roared in a blur of splashing water as I was wrenched backward into the river.

"Stay back or I shall drown the wench!" a gruff voice barked into my ear, reeking of stale beer and fish. The man we'd just rescued gripped my neck painfully, his other hand pressing a blade to it.

Nick stood frozen in knee-deep water, a shocked look slapped on his face. "You godforsaken scum, let the lady go!" he bellowed. "What in the hell is it that you want?"

The man pressed his body against mine from behind, washing me with nausea.

"Mmm, I can bethink of one thing I want," he grunted in my ear. He smacked his hips against me so hard that I would've fallen forward had he not been holding onto me. My fists clenched at my sides, craving to fight this vile scumbag off me, but the knife at my throat pinched my skin.

Nick made a sound of fury and lunged at the man, who pulled me closer.

"Take one more step and I shall cut her throat," he said in my ear, his voice devoid of humanity.

"You will release the lady, or it is your throat that will be cut," Nick said through his teeth.

I was too choked to speak, but I pleaded with Nick with my eyes to be sensible. This was Tudor England—if this man slashed my throat, there would be no ambulances, no hospitals, and no chance of saving me.

The blade dropped from my neck just long enough to make a lightning-fast slice across my kirtle. One of my naked breasts fell out so quickly that it was obvious this pyscho had done this before—in one movement, he'd cut through both my dress and smock. I whimpered as he clutched my soft skin with his hand, making a sickening sound of pleasure as he squeezed.

Every inch of Nick's body tightened to barely contained fury, right through to his watery eyes. Any sense I had to protect myself was swallowed by a vacuum of rage.

"Let go of me! We risked our lives to help you!" I screamed, writhing and kicking backward at the man's legs. He shouted in my ear for me to stop, spraying my cheek with spit as he pushed the knife so hard against my throat that I gagged.

"Now give me everything thou owns before I defile this wench right in front of thee," he snapped at Nick with seething menace, still grasping my breast.

"We own very little," Nick stammered, paling. He dug into his pocket and produced a small handful of silver coins.

"Take the coins to my horse," the man ordered. "Keep a slow pace." His calloused hand finally released my breast to guide me back to the shore with the knife pressed to my neck. The bandit's muscular horse snorted as Nick flipped open the worn satchel tied to its saddle and tipped our coins inside.

"What else dost thou have?" the bandit grunted to Nick, gesturing to our horse down the river. My cheeks crumpled and I swallowed the urge to scream. Inside the cloth satchel tied to Leo was all the money we had left in this world. I wanted so badly to elbow this prick in the groin with all the strength I had, but my neck burned from the edge of the blade, and my survival instinct kept me still.

"Go and get thy sacks—all of them," the man said. "And thy horse. Bring them 'ere."

Nick reached his hand out in a plea. "I beseech you to call upon your good conscience; we shall have naught left!"

With a flick of his wrist, the man cut open the other side of my kirtle, gripping both of my bare breasts tightly in one scummy hand. His other hand held the blade to my neck. "Make haste!" he shouted at Nick, squeezing my breasts so hard that I cried out.

"God in heaven, I will gut you like a fish!" Nick spat as he backed away toward Leo so he could keep an eye on me.

"Go!" the bandit barked, pointing the knife between my thighs like he might cut the dress open there. Nick spun and ran for our things as the bandit clutched me from behind, murmuring with satisfaction while he kneaded my breasts. He didn't take his eyes off Nick, who was back with our satchel and horse within seconds. Tears spilled down my quivering cheeks.

Nick tossed our satchel at the bandit's feet, followed by Leo's reins. "Take it all, you useless, plague-sore peasant! Just let the lady go." Veins of fury rippled in Nick's neck, and he seemed to grow even taller.

I felt the bandit freeze behind me, calculating how he might get out of this. "Tie the horse to mine," he ordered shakily. "And the sack."

Nick hissed colorful insults as he knotted the two horses together before fastening our satchel to the larger horse's saddle. If this lowlife had known that he was robbing the former King of England, he'd have literally crapped his pants.

"Take the horses for a walk," the bandit said, still holding my breasts as collateral. He was no fool—Nick could have pretended to tie knots in the leather, so the two horses would come apart when the man rode away.

Nick gritted his teeth as he freed the bandit's horse from the tree and led the two animals around in a short, humiliating parade. The horses were firmly tied together, and so were the satchels.

"Stop there!" the bandit shouted when the horses were facing away from the river. "And get away from them."

Nick paced backward. The bandit dragged me with him to where the horses stood stomping their hoofs. He shoved me into the dirt and leaped onto his horse's back in one skilled movement, digging his heel into its blond coat. With a kick of his leg, he steered the chained-together horses into a gallop over the crest of a hill, unsettling the earth and leaving behind a billow of dust.

"Emmie." Nick's arms slid around me from behind, pulling me close. "Forgive me," he said into my neck, his voice thick with tears. "Vagabonds usually travel in numbers...I suspected him not. I beg your forgiveness. Oh God, Emmie, forgive me."

I didn't fall into him; I didn't even move. At that moment, the feeling of a man's arms around me—even Nick's—drew a surge of acid to my throat.

"We just wanted to help him," I said, my voice high and quivering. "I thought he was drowning."

"I know, I know," Nick said into my hair. "A deceit of the most wicked nature." When I pulled away from him, he gently turned me to face him, a plea burning in his eyes. "But we cannot lose heart. We have lost our coins, but we still have the enchanted ring." He nodded reassuringly at my boots sprawled out on the grass, where I'd been hiding the ring on our travels. "We are going to find a soothsayer and get you out of this godforsaken realm of horror, I swear it. No more of this, Emmie; no more."

My mind flashed back, a howl of despair rupturing from my mouth. I fell forward, clutching my skirts, my jaw clenching.

"What is it?" Nick said frantically.

I glanced up at him, my eyes expanding. "I put it in the bag. I—I put the blue-diamond ring in our satchel!"

His face jerked toward the empty horizon, his mouth hanging open.

An icy wind blew through the cuts in my dress as I stiffened to a statue, my heart clamping in my chest.

"That's it," I realized, tears blurring my vision. "The enchanted ring is gone. That fucking asshole took it...it's gone! We're stuck here...we're stuck in Tudor England...for the rest of our lives."

I shook my head, like I couldn't make sense of the words.

And now we've got nothing left.

9

Nick faced away from me, his haunted eyes focused on thoughts I couldn't read. His fingers were tightly curled and shaking.

"We must...we must find the robber," he said faintly.

The stark emptiness of the horizon chilled me to the bone. "How are we going to do that?" I asked. "We don't know which way he went, and even if we did, how are we supposed to catch up to him when he has our horse?"

Nick paced to the river's edge to scoop up his boots, his jaw tense. His lack of response said it all: Finding the bandit—and any hope we had of returning to the twenty-first century—would be like combing the surface of Mars for a single red hair.

Right now, we couldn't sit here and dwell. We had to get to Maidenhead before the sun set, and our only option now was to walk.

I trudged over to where my cloak lay on the rock and shook the dirt off it. Nick's cheeks colored as his eyes caught the gaping hole in my kirtle, and I quickly turned away from him. My fingers quivered as I tied on my cloak at the neck until it covered the slashes in the fabric.

My chest burned as we strolled along the grassy river's edge, keeping our distance from the few travelers we passed. As we walked in stunned silence, the sickening assault at the river faded into an even darker realization.

I was destined to become a missing person.

My mom, who'd only just recovered from my previous desertions, was about to have the light of hope switch off forever. She would never get her daughter back again. I'd never finish my degree at Central Saint Martins, never become a professional jewelry designer.

So many nevers.

The bleak thoughts poured into my brain with merciless force, weighing me down. I was too shaken up to speak, and evidently, so was Nick.

By the time we dragged our feet toward the crumbling gatehouse guarding the township of Maidenhead, the leather soles of my shoes were beginning to wear down. The fury in my body set my insides on fire. Without a coin to our names, we couldn't afford a piece of bread, let alone a pair of shoes, and I already had to find a needle and thread to sew up my kirtle. If I saw that bandit again, Nick would have to hold me back to stop me from choking him with my bare hands.

The entrance to Maidenhead smelled even fouler than Windsor, but at least the town gates were still open, despite the sinking sun. A beggar in a torn cloak that barely concealed his naked body bumped past me, and I flung my hands up, ready to fight.

"Be calm, Emmie," Nick said, gently guiding me away from the mentally unwell man who'd meant no harm. I searched the beggar's face the same way I had that of every other man we'd passed on the way, but none was the bandit with the ice-blue eyes who had my passport to the twenty-first century. My teeth ground together with rage.

"Oh my God," I blurted to Nick as we ambled toward the gatehouse. "What if that scumbag who stole the ring falls asleep wearing it? If the ring starts working again, he could wake up in our bed in the twenty-first century!"

Nick cast his gaze around to ensure no one was listening. "I share your fear," he said quietly. "A man like that with no manner of decency will surely be made mad in the New World. I believe that I would have met the very same fate if it were not for you, my lady."

Before I could respond to the unexpected comment, he

approached the two bearded gatekeepers and asked them where we might find a place to stay for the night in exchange for work instead of money.

The gatekeeper who barely fit into his doublet touched his sword handle like we were potentially dangerous. "There is a lodging for the destitute at the church…the first left turn and then make way to the wall," he muttered, waving us on like we were keeping him from something.

We followed the guard's instructions, meandering down a narrow street past sweaty-faced men hauling buckets of dirt on pulleys. A rabid dog lurched from the skeleton of a timber-framed house, barking and snarling, sending us to the opposite side of the road. I reminded myself that all of this was as eye-opening to the former King of England as it was to me.

"There it is," Nick said, pointing at a nondescript church. Three young boys huddled in the dirt outside, the smallest one scratching the pink scales on his hairless scalp. The other two didn't look much healthier.

The inns we'd been staying at until now hadn't exactly been the Four Seasons, but this home for the destitute made my skin crawl. Beyond the broken door hanging from a single hinge was a dank hall that served as an echo chamber for the poor man shouting at no one. Joined to the hall was a room scattered with piles of straw, some of them already claimed and others empty for the taking. Nick led me toward a vacant bed of straw in the farthest corner, but it was no escape from the stench of body odor and vomit that nearly made me retch. I gave the space a quick scan, noting a few people in extreme old age, some who seemed disabled, and others who showed signs of mental illness. No one made eye contact with me.

"We'll need another horse, Nick," I said, my breath shaking. "I don't want to stay here long; I want us to get another horse and start making our way to Carlisle Castle."

He drew back with surprise, assessing me. "You still wish to make a challenge against Mary Stuart?"

My nod was laced with sadness. "What other choice do we have? We can't go back home, so we may as well continue what we came here for. We know that we can't trust Francis Beaumont now, which means going to see Kit is even more risky than it was before. Plus, Mary Stuart was the one who had the blue-diamond ring enchanted in the first place—she was studying witchcraft. Maybe she's the one who can potentially get us out of this mess and back home to the modern world. Maybe we can kill two birds with one stone...try to stop Mary *and* try to find a way back home." The naivete of my comments wasn't lost on me, but if I didn't cling to a string of hope, I'd break down.

Nick fingered his jaw. "And what would you say to Mary Stuart if we were to stride into Carlisle Castle without incident? Are you to share with her our true identity, ask her to propose an enchantment of time travel for us, and, at the same time, bid her to refrain from her unfriendly invasion of England?"

"Pretty much," I said with a straight face. I wasn't in the mood to be condescended to or teased. Any attempts would be met with sarcasm.

"The high north is a place of utter lawlessness," he warned. "There are savages...the villages are infested with the pox and the plague."

"I can handle it," I replied, my shoulders tightening in readiness.

His face was a storm of thought. "If we become near enough to Mary Stuart to learn of the original enchantment spell to the twenty-first century, then there is only one way to ensure we escape her presence without losing our lives while also putting an end to her wicked plot. But you will not like it."

My breath lodged in my sticky throat. This wasn't my first sojourn in Tudor England. I knew what Nick—and this century—were capable of. "You think we should assassinate Mary, Queen of Scots," I said in a low voice, the shocking words bouncing off my ears. "You want to kill a queen."

He blinked at me, his gaze steady and unflinching. "I wish to stop a queen from taking the lives of those we love. Which we know for certain will occur. What's more, I have been thinking further upon Mary's plot. If she intends to subvert the course of religion in England and restore Catholicism, she may be working with more than the French. Mary Stuart may have the support of the Spanish and even the Pope in Rome. Those featherbrains would much sooner see Mary Stuart on the throne of England than my sister. What is to stop them all from invading England at one moment from every direction? That is what *I* would do. And the only way to prevent such a calamity from occurring is to take away their puppet, Mary. Not even the Pope in Rome can steal the throne of England from an anointed queen without another king or queen ready to sit upon it."

My stomach churned into a queasy mess. As much as I trusted Nick's judgment, I couldn't imagine adding murder to our list of crimes. But if it was just me and Nick alone, how else would we stop Mary Stuart? I also knew that Nick would never let me be the one to hold the knife. He'd executed innocents before—he would have nothing against ending the life of a woman who had plans to slice off his sister's head.

"How can we get money and a horse quickly?" I asked. "We don't have much time to lose." By my calculations, Mary Stuart would storm England in just under four weeks, and Carlisle Castle was hundreds of miles away.

He tapped his lips, thinking. "The fastest way to acquire more coin would be for me to wager a game of dice in the tavern. But I cannot play without some manner of bid to begin with."

I rubbed my ankles where the straw was tickling me. "You mean gambling? Is that even legal here? Plus, you could win some money, but you could also lose it all."

He stood up, straightening his jerkin. "My lady, I have never lost a game of dice, not once."

I winced. "That's because you were the king, babe. You get that, right? Everyone always let you win because they were terrified of you."

His confused frown was cute, and it softened the hardness that had lodged in my chest since the river attack. He grabbed his cloak, shaking it out. "I shall offer this cloth as my bid of entry. With any luck, I will win enough coin to buy a strong horse that will see us on our way to Carlisle Castle. The castle is a great many miles from here, so we shall have plenty of time to decide how to approach Mary Stuart."

I hadn't assumed he'd meant he'd go gambling this actual second, but he tilted his head at me in a polite farewell—so Tudor—before leaning so close that I could taste the mint sprig on his breath. "I bid you to remain in this chamber and keep to yourself. This is a house for vagabonds and strumpets—you must speak with no one. Do I have your word?"

Swallowing tightly, I made the promise and reluctantly watched Nick disappear through the archway. With nothing to do but sit on our pile of straw and wait, the memory of what had transpired at the river gnawed on my mind like a parasite. Why had I been so quick to believe that man was drowning? If I hadn't fallen for his dirty trick, he wouldn't have had his disgusting, stinking hands on my body, and we would still have the blue-diamond ring. I pressed my face into my knees and screamed without making a sound.

Why didn't I just elbow that scumbag in the groin? Why didn't I scratch his eyes out before I let him touch me like that?

For what felt like hours, my mind replayed the river incident to a relentless soundtrack of arguments, ramblings, and a baby crying. When the young girl beside me began knitting, I plucked up the courage to ask her to borrow a needle and thread so I could repair my kirtle. I needed something to focus on other than that pervert's filthy fingers on me. When she agreed with visible reluctance, I promised her that I would repay her for the thread if I could.

After I'd patched up my dress, a rumble of hunger sent me searching for the source of wafting aromas of garlic and chicken. I trailed the rich smells into the neighboring hall.

A cauldron bubbled away on the central stone hearth, which sizzled with fire, a stream of smoke puffing through the open hole in the ceiling. A woman with large ears poking from her coif scooped out a bowl of pottage and handed it to me without a word. I made a smile of thanks and tipped the bowl to inspect what emerged in the stew. Bits of radish, pumpkin, peas, beans, and a couple of bony chunks of chicken.

I sat on the nearest bench and drank from the bowl like I hadn't eaten in a year. A middle-aged man with missing front teeth plonked himself beside me, gesturing to the woman at the cauldron with some sort of sign language. She carried him over a bowl of soup, and I subtly edged away from him. The guy smelled putrid, but I didn't want to be rude.

"Thou hast not been here before," he said to me, pouring the soup into his mouth. His right thigh had spread too close to mine, but perhaps this guy knew the bandit who had our blue-diamond ring. By sight alone, the two of them wouldn't have made an unusual pair.

"We just got here today," I said in a tentative voice before coughing up a piece of chicken gristle.

He brought his face closer to mine, exposing a gaping hole in his earlobe. "*We*, is it? What brings ye to Maidenhead, then?"

How much longer would Nick be?

"My husband and I are just passing through," I said vaguely.

He nodded, sniffing. "Well, if it be true that I can be of any help, be sure to speak it. I know this town like the back of mine own hand. Pass through it from time to time doing work as a wheelwright."

He offered a doff of his grimy cap and I gave an awkward nod in response. But if he knew Maidenhead well…

"I don't suppose you've seen a man around here with two horses?" I stammered. "He has very light blue eyes."

The man stared at me strangely. "Plenty around 'ere with two horses. What business dost thou have with the fellow?"

My lips curled up in a slight smirk. "Well, that would be between him and me, wouldn't it?"

With his eyes dancing as they studied me, he slurped back his pottage, draining the bowl. "Can't say I know the man. Not without some manner of payment, at least."

"What kind of payment? My husband is just out…working."

He leaned closely enough for the choking stench of tooth decay to travel from his breath to mine. "What payment art thou offering?" A grimy finger traced its way up my arm. When he caught hold of the side of my shoulder and gently squeezed it, I shrieked.

"Get off me!" I cried, his dirt-streaked face morphing into that of the bandit's.

What followed were flashes: the guy with the hole in his earlobe lunging toward me; someone swiping past me to grab him with both hands; the cauldron of pottage crashing to the ground, spraying puke-like chunks of cooked vegetables across the earthen floor. When my vision cleared, Nick was chasing the man into the next room.

My enraged husband returned alone a few moments later, and the mute woman serving dinner shook her fists at him. With anger flaring in his eyes, Nick took my arm and hurried me outside onto the street.

"I said that I bid you to speak with no one!" he castigated in a harsh voice as we hastened away from the church like the police were on our tails.

"This isn't my fault," I shot back. "And last time I checked, you weren't my keeper, my dad, *or* my boss. You don't need to control my every move."

He spun around to block my path, his clear eyes burning with frustration. "There is still a great deal in this realm you do not understand. That man who held you had a hole in his ear; did you see it not?"

"I saw it yes." I bit my lip.

He waited until two laborers in muddied shirts passed by us. "That hole was burned through the man's ear with a hot iron—a marking to signify that he is an outlaw. In this realm, Emmie, you are the company you keep."

I tugged my collar higher, like I'd just escaped another brush with death. Nick exhaled and stepped toward me, softening his tone. "And we are now without lodging in which to pass the night. We cannot return to the church; that idiot may yet make trouble for us that we do not need."

"How much money did you win?" I asked, wrapping my arms around myself. The sinking sun had made the air bitingly cold.

His eyes darted away. "I wish for better fortune on the morrow. This night, I regret that we shall have to take shelter in a barn."

I swore under my breath. "I knew the gambling was a waste of time! Maybe we should just look for a job. Like some farmhand work or something...just for a couple of days. That guy with the hole in his ear said he'd been working as a wheelwright."

Nick just pulled a face and guided me away. We hurried along the patch of dirt leading to the outskirts of town before the last inch of sunlight disappeared. Sparse fields of forest green stretched beyond a spattering of whitewashed timber-framed houses with thatched roofs that belonged to the local farmers and yeomen. I pointed to a single-story house with darkened windows and no smoke drifting from its chimney.

"That one looks like no one's home," I said.

"And there is a barn close at hand," Nick added.

Scanning for any signs of life from the house, we crept toward the decaying barn, slipping past an overgrown vegetable garden, an empty henhouse, and a decomposing heap of rotting food and animal dung. The barn wasn't exactly a perfume store either, and Nick warned me to step around the scatterings of pig and horse poop.

"Up there," he said, pointing to a wooden loft sitting directly below the vaulted ceiling.

"It's cold in here," I said with a shiver as we climbed the crudely built ladder and crawled into the loft space, which was only about five feet high. We were in some sort of storage area for hay.

Nick began shaping a pile of the straw into a makeshift bed.

My stomach hollowed with nerves. "What if someone finds us up here?"

He kept his voice low. "We would be whipped for trespassing, or worse. We also have no papers, no kin to speak of…so let us make sure that does not occur." He paused his movements and slid a hand across his jaw. "It is time for us to think up some manner of an alias. We can say that we hail from a market town—one that is small in size and significance."

"What about Maidenhead?" I suggested. "We've seen the town now; we know what it looks like."

He shook his head. "The noblemen know Maidenhead well; it is a common place of rest for those traveling westward from London."

I slumped against the wooden wall. "Do you even know the names of any less-significant market towns?"

He rubbed his brow with his eyes closed. "I cannot tell you how many tedious petitions and papers I have read from such places.

Those that I can call to mind are…let me see…Thame…Royston… Banbury…Stratford."

I sat forward. "Stratford-upon-Avon?"

His brow lifted. "You know the place?"

I would've laughed if I hadn't been so terrified to make noise. Almost everyone knew that Stratford-upon-Avon was the birthplace of the world's most famous playwright, William Shakespeare.

"What is on your mind?" Nick said, trying to read my face.

My dry lips felt glued together. "Nothing." I was too thirsty, too exhausted, and too cold to explain the importance of William Shakespeare now to Nick—that slice of history could wait for another time. In 1582, Master Shakespeare was probably no more than a teenager, but he was most certainly alive. I had to be careful to not tangle ourselves with the real Shakespeares, but this was a fake identity that I wouldn't have any trouble remembering.

"I think Stratford-upon-Avon sounds good," I said as I helped him finish making us a bed. "How about we say your name is Master William Shakespeare? I can be Anne Shakespeare. We got married last Christmas, and we have a small farm on the outskirts of Stratford. You also enjoy writing poems and plays in your spare time."

Pride glinted in his eyes. "You speak like a natural of the realm. Very well, that sounds quite agreeable. Henceforth, I shall be Master William Shakespeare of Stratford."

I snort-laughed.

And I'll be Anne of Stratford.

I'd already been Emmeline, Queen of England, so this would be a cakewalk in comparison. I didn't want to make any trouble for the real William Shakespeare—or his wife—but Nick and I weren't exactly intending to blast their names from the rooftops. Quite the opposite: We were more interested in avoiding people and only using our false names if we had to. For now, it would do.

It wasn't easy to sleep in that icy pigeonhole without a blanket, pillow, or mattress. The freezing discomfort was fertile ground for my fears, which grew darker with every hour of the night. Nick and I were sleeping in a horse barn and pretending to be the Shakespeares, for crying out loud. We had no money, no home, no enchanted ring, and no way to stop Mary Stuart and her armies outside of plunging a knife into Mary's heart—if we could ever get that close to her.

But what was the alternative? If we marched into Windsor Castle, revealing to Kit and the realm that King Nicholas the First was still alive, it would mean torching my idea of convincing Mary Stuart to have us cursed back to the modern world. Nick would have to remain here forever, come rain or shine. It would also upset Francis Beaumont's plans to usurp the throne, and he had all the power in the world as the Lord Protector of the Realm. In a world of superstition and treason, coming out of hiding still felt fraught with danger. Our anonymity kept us safe, but it also kept us useless against the Queen of the Scots.

I rolled over to face the wall of moldy wood, the truth wrapping my heart in strips of ice.

No matter which way I approached it in my mind, no matter how hard I tried to worm our way out of this mess, Nick and I were done for.

I dreamed that Nick's face was buried between my thighs, the moans erupting from his lips sending delicious little vibrations through my core as he pushed his tongue inside me. I grunted out a deep sigh and tipped my head back, shamelessly lifting my hips up into his face and pressing myself against him.

"So greedy," he said with a groan, clutching my backside in his hands and pulling me even closer to his mouth. He swirled his tongue over my throbbing clit, sucking on it, and then burrowed his tongue inside me again, his heated eyes finding mine.

"*Come,*" he whispered needly against my glistening-wet flesh. "Come in my mouth, and then I will come so deep inside you."

Shivers of electricity ran from where his tongue worked me right down my legs and into my toes, my body writhing as Nick licked the life out of me. My moans escalated to gasping cries as my core clenched tightly and then suddenly burst in a river of warmth that poured pleasure into every corner of my body while he thrust his tongue in and out of me through my climax.

"*God,*" he said in a hungry voice as he sank two fingers inside me. "I wish to fuck you so hard this night."

A groan tore from the back of my throat as he twisted his fingers high up inside me.

"Yes?" he asked, his voice thick with need.

"*Yes,*" I said achingly.

"Emmie…*Emmie!*"

Nick was shaking me awake, his alarmed eyes inches from mine. "You must rise," he whispered quickly. "I hear the husbandman outside. He may come to fetch straw—we cannot remain here."

With my heart pounding and my body still clenching between my thighs, I scrambled to tie on my boots before we slipped down the ladder and through the barn's rear archway. Male and female voices drifted from the opposite end of the building. I didn't glance back as we bolted across the grass that glistened with morning dew, stopping only when we were halfway up the stretch of dirt leading to the town center.

"They didn't follow us," I said breathlessly.

Nick gave me a "that was too close for comfort" look. His facial hair would need another trim soon, and we were both in danger of smelling worse than a chamber pot if we didn't bathe soon. I was so thirsty and hungry that my head spun.

"I will find something to eat," Nick said, still groggy. "Wait here a moment, and speak to no man with a hole in his ear."

"God, no," I said. "Strictly fully fleshed ears only. Where will you find food without any money?"

He didn't answer, but I was too tired and faint to press him. He dashed toward the market square while I found a boulder to rest on and hugged my knees buried beneath my grimy skirts.

In less than fifteen minutes, Nick returned with two custard tarts slathered in lemon cream, and a brightness in his eyes that I hadn't seen since before the river attack. A smile grew on my face. "How on earth did you get these?" I bit into a warm, oozing tart before he could answer. I'd never tasted anything so sublime.

"I made a pact with the merchant," he replied, handing me a leather pouch of water.

I gulped the water so hard that my throat made an embarrassing glugging sound. "What kind of pact?"

He sat beside me on the rock, licking cream off his fingertips and sending a tingle through me that I had to ignore. "There is to be a wrestling tournament this day in the market square," he explained. "I have made my challenge and agreed to share my winnings with the merchant in exchange for the tarts and the water." He beamed with pride. "The merchant believes me to be a strong contender, purely by sight."

My eyes boggled. "You're going to wrestle? What if these guys are professionals? What if you get hurt? Or even recognized?"

His expression reminded me to keep my voice low. "The winner is to take three shillings. And this is a market town of little consequence, not the place where a king may be known by sight. What's more, I am a skilled wrestler, Emmie."

I expelled a jittery breath. Nick had once told me that he'd challenged the King of France to a friendly wrestling match, and he was undoubtedly built for the task.

"Be careful," was all I managed. "Emmie Grace doesn't do well in Tudor England without an actual Tudor. Preferably one named Nick."

His eyes turned soft and he blinked at me in a way that made my heart pick up speed. I wanted to reach for his hand, but my mind flashed to the bandit's calloused fingers on my skin, and my body seized up.

There was nearly an hour to wait until the tournament began, which I spent trying not to think about what we'd do if Nick lost the competition. I couldn't bear the thought of sleeping in that barn again and risking being arrested and whipped for trespassing.

A town crier called for the wrestling entrants to gather, and I trailed Nick toward a makeshift wrestling ring that had been drawn into the dirt with a rock. My palms were leaking sweat.

Three other men had gathered, stripped bare to their breeches. While Nick unclipped his jerkin and tugged off his shirt, I surveyed the competition. One guy was small but extremely beefy, one was closer to Nick's size, and the third could've been cast as Bigfoot in a movie.

"That guy is an actual giant!" I hissed, but Nick didn't reply. He was blowing through his lips, gearing himself up.

The first match, which was between the two smaller men, was called. I paced backward, joining the growing crowd of spectators. Within seconds, the little beefy guy had grabbed his opponent's upper body with both arms and flipped him onto the ground with surprising strength. I held my breath as he pinned him down.

The pale-faced referee called for "Goodman Shakespeare" next, and I pinched my nose to avoid giggling at the name. My smile vanished when Nick's opponent followed him into the ring—it was Bigfoot!

I turned away from the ring to face the other spectators, fixing my panicky gaze on a young woman with long black braids. When she grabbed her coif and winced like someone had been hurt, I spun back around with my heart thrashing.

Nick had Bigfoot pinned to the dirt, muscles rippling through Nick's back as he held him there with sweat dripping from the unruly curls of his hair. Approving murmurs swept through the audience as my Goodman Shakespeare, with his breathtaking smile, was proclaimed the winner.

I darted toward him, ready to celebrate, but he whispered to me that the tournament wasn't over yet. He now had to wrestle that beefy little guy.

Piece of cake, I said to myself.

A male spectator wolf-whistled as Nick and his final opponent circled each other, Nick teasing him with his sparkling eyes.

Nick made a jerky move and then halted, confusing the guy, before snapping forward with lightning speed and tripping him to the ground. I thought he had him, but the little guy roared and rolled away, flicking himself back up onto his feet in one lithe movement.

Nick ducked forward, and they grabbed each other's forearms, their legs tangling in attempts to drag each other down. Nick managed to hook the guy by the shoulder and flip him onto his back, but his opponent was so fast. The little beefy guy hooked both his legs around Nick's, tripping him. Nick slammed into the dirt on his side, swearing as the little guy grabbed his arm and yanked it backward, immobilizing him. When Nick failed to free himself in time, his opponent—Goodman Cooper—was declared the winner. Three silver shillings glinted in the mid-morning sun as Cooper held them up to the sky to a few measly cheers. Nick had been the spectators' favorite.

A streak of blood trickled from Nick's eyebrow, seizing my breath. A simple cut could turn lethal in Tudor England if it became infected. He approached me with a sheepish look on his face before the organizer grabbed his shoulder and pressed something into his palm.

"Are you okay?" I asked as Nick wiped the blood from his eye. I tried to gauge whether the cut was bad enough to need stitches, but he was leaning over his palm, counting.

"Four pennies for second place," he announced with relief.

"Which you'll have to split with that merchant, right?" I dabbed his cut brow with the cleanest part of my sleeve. "So, that's two pennies. Wow, we're rolling in it."

Nick winced at my sarcasm, but at least the cut didn't look too bad. "Two pennies will buy us perhaps one or two nights in an inn if we are able to find lodging at a small cost."

"One or two nights?" I tried not to sound dismayed. "We need to get money through something other than violence and gambling. You're lucky you didn't lose an eye or worse."

He slipped the coins into the pocket of his leather trousers. "Most certainly a wise thought. I shall be greatly sore on the morrow."

A girl around my age with white-blond hair strolled past us, carrying a basket of folded linens. She handed a pile of fabric to a waiting man in exchange for a coin.

"Why don't I see if I can pick up some casual work washing sheets and clothes in the river?" I suggested, my shoulders lifting. "I'll work around the clock if I have to until we have enough money to buy another horse so we can keep making our way north. I bet the towns on the way also have work for a washerwoman."

"Emmie, you are not able to work," Nick said like he was stating the obvious. "You forget that we are now Mr. and Mrs. William

Shakespeare of Stratford. As my wife, you are expected only to do your duty to serve and obey me. If a mistress is to be seen working, it means her husband has run off and left her destitute. Yet, to say we are wedded not, but are lodging together, would see us arrested for obscenity." He rubbed his jaw, deciding. "I shall find work in haste. Perhaps some manner of labor, as you suggested."

My heel tapped a rock, disappointment sliding into my chest. Not only did I have to watch the former king of this realm reduced to manual labor for reasons I felt responsible for, but I'd have to sit around and twiddle my thumbs while he did it.

"It's ridiculous that I can't work," I said for good measure. "We could be earning twice as much money."

Nick shrugged like he didn't make the rules. He'd been the one to set the standard when he was the monarch of this old-school, chauvinistic place—but I didn't remind him of that.

After paying the merchant his two pennies, we traipsed up and down the streets, knocking on doors until the sky darkened to a deep shade of purple. But after the poor season for crops due to a frosty start to spring, nobody was interested in hiring Nick, despite his size and strength. We purchased a night at the cheapest inn in town and two bowls of pottage before suffering through a hellish sleep in a single cot bed infested with bedbugs.

The next morning, we downed two bowls of oatmeal with sour milk, provided by the innkeeper, and emerged to a larger gathering than usual in the market square. News had reached the town from as far as Windsor: The Lord Protector of the Realm, the Earl of Warwick, had been sent to Tilbury in the country's east to deal with a rumored threat from Spanish warships.

Blood drained from my face as I met Nick's startled expression. He'd already suspected the Spaniards to be involved in Mary Stuart's plot to restore Catholicism in England. Now the Spanish Armada was on our doorstep, and for all we knew, Francis was heading there to cement his secret, treasonous involvement in Mary Stuart's plot. All he needed was to be granted a divorce from his wife, Alice Grey, to marry the Queen of the Scots, which would be taken as a declaration of war against Queen Catherine.

My mind raced, calculating. We'd been back in the sixteenth century for around a week, which meant the Tudor throne would be seized in a violent uprising in close to three weeks. We were taking too long!

My pulse sped up as Nick led me away from the square to where we could speak in private.

"We must remain determined, my lady," he said, his eyes steadying me. "We will continue to make our way north through Coventry. It would be wise to avoid the marshlands and their pestilence. I have also put my mind to how Mary Stuart will escape the Castle of Carlisle to make her assault on England, and the answer is that she must not only be working with the Papist earls in the north, but also with traitorous lords across the country. There are a number of lords loyal to the old religion in the midlands, around the county of Nottinghamshire—they were a pest during my reign. To such men, Mary Stuart's presence in England is all the encouragement they will need to pursue a rebellion, if she is able to ensure support from the French and the Spanish. During our journey north, we must be more than careful about what we say openly, especially when we reach Nottinghamshire."

I expelled air from my lungs, refocusing. Nick and I agreed that there was no point in staying in Maidenhead any longer. We'd exhausted all the employment options, and wrestling was no longer on the table now that the tournament had moved southwest toward Reading. Our best option was to cut our losses in this dried-up town, use our last coin to buy a cheap horse, and continue farther north. As long as we got to Mary Stuart before her invasion on the twenty-fourth of May, we'd still have a chance of blowing up her evil scheme.

Before scouring the animal market, we took a bath in the icy river outside town and attempted to clean our wet hair by rubbing it vigorously with strips of our clothes. The memory of a sharp blade digging into my neck in knee-deep water sent me splashing back to the shore. The flashbacks of the bandit unfolded like scenes from a horror movie, but I didn't share them with Nick. The last thing I needed was to have him think I was traumatized by an event he blamed himself for—it was something I was going to need to deal with later. When he emerged from the water, bare-legged, bare-chested, and as jaw-droppingly beautiful as a Renaissance sculpture, I found myself looking away like I was invading his privacy. He toweled off while I turned away from him, and we awkwardly dressed like we were two strangers.

The truth cut deep. It wasn't only my life in the modern world that had slipped away from me. While hiding out in Tudor England as a presumed-dead king was surely no life worth living for Nick, I couldn't deny that he understood the mechanics and nuances of this world far better than he could ever understand the twenty-first century. And every time he was physically near to me, but made the decision not to touch me, he felt further and further away.

Even if—by way of a miracle—we saved our family and friends here, restored the Tudor dynasty and the future Church of England, and found a way back to the twenty-first century...would Nick still choose me? At the river near Bray, he'd said that he wanted to take me home and out of harm's way, but he'd said nothing about staying in my century with me...about giving up his homeland all over again in exchange for that quiet inertia he'd slipped into in the modern world. Did he still want us to have a future together that looked far more like my life than his? Did he still even want me at all?

I was no longer sure that I knew the answer.

10

THERE WAS ONLY ONE HORSE AT THE MAIDENHEAD ANIMAL MARKET available for one penny—a female rouncey that snorted at us with her nostrils flared and the whites of her eyes showing strangely. Still, we gladly handed over the measly coin to the sour-faced dealer.

"I am afeared this horse is frantic," Nick said to me as he wrestled with the reins to stop the horse from rearing.

"And now we know why she cost all of one penny," I said, keeping my distance until Nick reached down to help me climb onto her back.

While the smoky-gray horse was erratic to ride and frightening to make eye contact with, she did a valiant job of getting us to the town of Aylesbury after a day of riding hard. Nick had a manor there that we'd lodged in before, so we found a church at the opposite end of town and kept quiet in the darkened chamber that was reserved for the destitute, there only to sleep and hide. The footsteps of prostitutes coming and going at all hours and drunken arguments in the dead of night made for a sluggish dawn when Nick roused me to be on our way.

I christened our mad-as-a-hornet horse "Ophelia" in keeping with our Shakespeare theme, and Nick didn't query the suggestion. He'd slept so poorly on the thin smattering of straw that he could barely stay awake, let alone manage any decent conversation.

After a bite of grainy bread and some water, we continued north to Buckingham, where the churches were too overcrowded with outcasts and vagrants to have any space for us. I didn't want to risk arrest by hiding out in another barn, so I convinced Nick to spend the night in the countryside beneath a shaggy tree fringed with soft grass. Using my riding cloak as a blanket, we shivered through the night and woke up to insect bites and headaches from a lack of sleep.

With Ophelia swishing her tail and stomping fitfully through episodes of blind panic, we made it through the medieval villages of Hardingstone, Enderby, and Loughborough, sleeping in churches on the way and becoming progressively more irritable with hunger and fatigue.

The sinking sun had turned the wattle-and-daub cottages on the hillside a shade of honeycomb when poor Ophelia dragged her hooves toward the township of Nottingham in the East Midlands. The crumbling stone walls of Nottingham Castle rose up out of the town's haphazard jumble of thatched roofs shrouded in woodsmoke.

"I don't suppose you have the keys to the castle?" I said, only half-joking, as Nick slowed Ophelia to a walk. After so many days lost to the lonely countryside, the murmur of voices that wafted from the other side of the town wall felt comforting.

"I regret that this castle has fallen to ruin," he replied. "I have had not much need to repair it; I could never bear being this great a distance from London."

Ophelia stomped her hooves through the slushy mud. "Does that mean the castle is empty?" I said into the curve of his shoulder. "We could sleep in there, couldn't we?"

"There most certainly remains a constable of the castle and some manner of garrison," he replied. "We shall be more safe finding another church that will lodge us. And Emmie, now that we have reached Nottingham, forget not my caution that we may now be near the company of men involved in Mary Stuart's plot."

"I get it," I said. "We need to keep our ears open and our mouths shut." I swallowed my disappointment at the thought of another night spent on the floor of an overcrowded halfway house.

Nick guided Ophelia around the curve of the city wall to meet the town's gatehouse, and my heart slumped into my hollow stomach. Nightfall had descended over the town, and the high wooden gates were already bolted shut.

A curse escaped my parched lips, and Nick assured me that we would easily find a barn in which to hide in a rural community like this one. Ophelia was being uncharacteristically obedient, and Nick steered her back down the hillside toward a scattering of farming properties marked with rustic clusters of stables, cart houses, and animal pens.

When we neared an expansive property housing a number of old, crumbling structures and barns, Nick slowed Ophelia to a stop and helped me down onto the squelchy earth without making a sound. It was one thing to hide in a barn when it was just the two of us; it was another to do it with a maniacal horse as our pet.

We crept toward the barn that was nestled the farthest away from the main house, and found it mercifully empty aside from a scrapheap of rusted farming tools. Nick quietly tied Ophelia to a hook in the wall while I climbed up the rungs of the ladder leading to the loft. The space was larger than the one in Maidenhead, and for once, I didn't feel cold.

"I shall find some manner of crop to eat," Nick said under his breath, and I gave him a thankful nod. I sipped water from our pouch and twisted around in search of the source of a strange, gentle buzzing sound, but found no obvious cause for it.

Nick soon returned with a handful of meaty carrots that he'd yanked from the earth, plonking himself beside me and passing me half. From the shadows of the loft, I watched his handsome profile savor each meager bite, like a deprived beggar.

I forced a smile, the carrot fresh and sweet on my lips. "We're nearly there. We're going to make it to Carlisle Castle."

The dirt coating his face had darkened his skin and brightened his eyes. "That may be true," he said somberly, "but we do not yet know how to approach that devil of a woman in order to be close enough to drive a knife through her heart. For one, I feel as if I could not wrestle a bird, let alone an army."

"Babe, are you okay?" I leaned forward to gently cup the back of his neck. "Nick, you have a fever!"

His eyelids drooped. "I do not feel at all well."

I helped him lie down on a bed of straw, my heart shooting into my throat. A fever wasn't just a fever in Tudor England. It could mean death.

"What do you think caused this?" I asked, feeling his burning forehead again.

He shrugged. "We did not ride near the marshlands, so it is unlikely to be the marsh fever."

"What are the symptoms of marsh fever?" I wouldn't put anything past this medically dangerous place.

He sighed, his voice a little gravelly. "Fever, a sore head, a frantic mind, a vexed stomach…I am not entirely sure."

I wanted to shrink into myself. If I'd brought Nick back to this world only to watch him die of marsh fever—whatever that was—or some other hideous disease, I'd never, ever recover.

His fiery hand patted mine. "It is not marsh fever, my lady. Be calm. However, it would do you well to keep your distance until I am recovered. With any luck, this is no more than a passing fever."

Clutching myself tightly, I sat vigil while he dozed in and out of a restless sleep, my mind fighting off bouts of panic. In the early hours of the morning, I poured the last few drops of water from our pouch onto my coif to make a compress and draped it over his forehead. At first light, his skin was a furnace, and he shook through his chills.

My catastrophic thoughts chewed up my insides. I couldn't watch Nick slip away and leave me in Tudor England alone and shattered with heartbreak; it would be a fate worse than death. My mom was a nurse—what would she say to do? Above all, he had to stay hydrated and rest.

After scampering down the ladder, I carried a wooden bucket outside and placed it beside the barn door to catch some rainwater for our pouch. I could've screamed at the stretch of cloudless sky that was streaked pink by the breaking dawn. Why couldn't rainy England have rained on the one day I needed fresh water the most? There would be wells of water closer to the town, and something to eat if I dug through the scrapheaps, but the thought of leaving Nick here alone left me faint. What if the farming family woke up and discovered a potentially infectious invalid squatting in their barn? What if his sickness worsened?

My breath was a nervous puff of steam in the frosty air as I sneaked along the edge of the barn toward the vegetable crops. The only signs of life were the squawking chickens and the robins swallowing beak-fills of morning dew.

Something I'd seen on a survival television show clicked in my memory. If I sopped up the morning dew with the fabric of my dress, I could squeeze some droplets into Nick's mouth. I didn't want to think about the grime clinging to my clothes, but this had to be better than the risk of dehydration. I hurried toward a bed of crisp lettuce and wiped the hem of my kirtle across the leaves until the fabric felt damp.

Back inside the barn loft, I woke Nick up enough for him to tilt his head forward and swallow the few droplets of water that trickled from my hemline as I squeezed.

I settled him back into some semblance of comfort on the straw before slipping back outside. My success with the dew experiment had charged my confidence, so I ventured a little further into the vegetable patch. The mounds of earth closest to the barn were plugged with root vegetables like radishes, carrots, and turnips, before meeting strips of spinach, peas, and cucumbers in neat, well-farmed rows. The healthy green of the leaves sent my mind back to our little terrace garden in Borehamwood. Despite being waited on hand and foot when he'd been the King of England, it was undeniable that Nick had a talent for growing vegetables. I should've appreciated it more; been less afraid of it being the behavior of someone who'd lost the plot.

My stomach growled, and I crouched to snap off some peas and cucumbers, bundling them into my skirts. The root vegetables would be the most filling, so I abandoned the lettuce and spinach crops and headed back for the carrots, which could also be eaten raw.

"What displeases you about the lettuce? I believe them to be my finest work," said a voice behind me.

All the air fled my body as I spun to face a young man in a linen shirt with the sleeves rolled up, his shirt tucked loosely into a pair of leather breeches. His flat cap barely contained his sandy-colored curls, and his blinking, hazel eyes held mine for a moment. I needed to explain, but my mouth wouldn't catch up with my galloping heart. Where had he come from? He'd crept up on me as silently as a cat.

"Why are you thieving from my crops, my goodwoman?" he asked in a calm voice. A golden-blond ringlet fell over his eye, and he flicked it away.

"I'm sorry," I fumbled, still clutching my skirt of peas and cucumbers. "I'll put them back."

He crossed his arms. "After you have cut their stems with your dirty, street-urchin hands?"

My face heated. "I can pay you for them," I said quickly. "I'm so sorry…as soon as I find some work around here, I will pay you right away, plus extra for your trouble. I'm a…I'm a washerwoman." I decided against mentioning my husband squatting in the nearby barn. Not only was Nick feverish, but he'd told me that married women couldn't work in this century without attracting unwelcome attention. It was better if this guy believed I was here alone.

"Do you know the punishment for theft in this county?" he said, not unkindly. "Hanging, but I may be persuaded to agree upon a whipping."

"I said I'll pay for them."

With his arms still crossed, he scanned me from head to toe. "You say you are a washerwoman in search of work. How are you with the duties of a common maidservant? It just so happens that I am in need of another maidservant for my household; I take it that you are trained?"

"Very well trained," I replied without thinking. "I can clean, make beds, wash clothes; that sort of thing."

He shifted on his calf-high boots, which were caked with dirt. "Do you hail from Nottinghamshire? How may I address you?"

My throat was a desert. "My name is Anne Shakespeare of Stratford. I'm on my way to Cumberland in the north to visit my...my aunt, but I was robbed on the roads near Maidenhead, which is why I don't have any money on me."

His perfectly shaped lips fell open. "Did they catch the ruffian?"

I shook my head and glanced at the barn, making silent pleas that Nick wouldn't materialize in search of me. It was an act of mercy that this guy appeared to be the forgiving type rather than malicious, and if he was gracious enough to offer me some work at the farm, I could earn some money while Nick recovered from his fever. I could slip Nick food, and the moment he was well, we would be on our way to Carlisle Castle with coins jiggling in our pockets. While we didn't exactly have time to lose, this felt like the first lucky break we'd had.

"Is that your horse?" the man asked with a trace of amusement, pointing to Ophelia's swishing tail poking out from the side of the barn. My brows flew up.

"You need not fear me, mistress," he said. "I shall have the horse brought to the stables for food and water."

"Thank you," I replied tightly. I couldn't quite believe this yeoman's kindness; it rendered me a little mute.

He held a hand out to me—a peace offering, perhaps. "My name is Mister Hugh Wynter. If you accept mine offer of work, you may begin this day and pay off your debts to me for the crops you stole."

I accepted his fingers, and something shifted inside me at the soft warmth of a young man's touch. Our hands quickly separated, his eyes blinking fast. "Have a care to avoid that barn," he said, gesturing to the building housing Ophelia and Nick. "It is beset with bees from the hives, and we are yet to rid the place of them."

The buzzing sound I'd heard in the barn loft...the place is infested with bees.

He gestured toward the main house like I should follow him. "Bring the peas and cucumbers to make a pottage with," he said over his shoulder, and I chased after him across the mud, struck with alarm over the cooking I'd be expected to do as this man's maidservant. I was hardly a master chef in the modern world, let alone in Tudor England with its oddball recipes.

We passed by a small building that smelled like a bakehouse before reaching the two-story timbered home with a thatched roof. We had to climb through a pen of hissing geese to reach the house's rear door, where a girl who looked a little younger than me waved the geese away to make space for us.

"Phoebe, may I present Anne Shakespeare of Stratford," Hugh said to her. "Anne will be joining the household."

"May God save you, mistress," the girl said with a curtsy. Her skin was porcelain-white beneath her tattered coif.

"May God save you," I replied awkwardly, mirroring her curtsy. Peas and cucumbers tumbled out of my dress into the mud. I cursed under my breath, crouching to collect them. Phoebe squatted to help me, and I gave her a grateful smile.

"I trust that you will show Anne what is to be done," Hugh said to Phoebe before pacing up the few creaky steps leading to the house's rear door. I appreciated that he didn't reveal my attempt at thievery to my new colleague.

I was desperate to get back to Nick, and he needed to eat something, so when Phoebe asked if I wanted to help her in the kitchen, I nodded vigorously.

The house's rickety rear door opened into a kitchen filled with pungent aromas of spices, garlic, and ginger. Pewter cookware hung from iron bars hammered into the low ceiling beside bunches of drying herbs that dangled over a wooden bench. Phoebe hurried over to the fireplace, where an iron cooking pot was hanging over the flames. She gave its contents a stir, releasing clouds of fragrant steam.

"The name of my kin is Brooke," she said to me in a shy voice.
Phoebe Brooke.

She tossed the peas I'd attempted to steal into the pot. "Dost thou like gingerbread? I made it fresh this morning." She wiped her petite hands on her apron.

"Wow, you get up early," I said lightly. "And I would love some, thank you."

We chatted a little bit while I chewed half of the buttery gingerbread, which was still warm and soft. Phoebe was only sixteen years old and hailed from the local township of Nottingham. For someone so young, she tended to the pottage over the fire like she'd been cooking her entire life. She didn't say how she'd come to be in

Hugh Wynter's service at such a young age, but she commented that we were fortunate because Mister Hugh was a kind and well-mannered person. I relaxed a little as I helped her slice up the cucumbers.

When her back was turned, I slipped the other half of the ginger-bread inside the bodice of my kirtle. "Would it be agreeable if I did one walk around the property outside before I start working?" I asked in a rush. "Just to get my bearings and learn the lay of the land?"

She shrugged, confused by my language, but she got the gist. "I should think so. We likely shall not see Mister Hugh again until supper at best—he most often spends the day in his bedchamber." I must've looked surprised because she went on to explain. "Mister Hugh is not unwell; the master simply prefers to work in his chamber rather than the downstairs hall. It may be that he finds the solitude pleasing."

I thanked her again for the gingerbread before venturing back outside into the misty morning air, its scent laced with manure. Evidently, as servants, Phoebe and I were to come and go only through the house's rear door. I strolled past the geese and along the paddocks with purpose, as if I was studying the place, in case anyone was watching me. When I finally reached the barn that edged the border of the property, I slipped inside and hurried up the ladder to where Nick lay.

His drooping eyes blinked at me through the shadows of the loft. "What in the devil, Emmie—where have you been? I was on the brink of coming to search for you."

I pressed my hand to his brow. His skin was still warm, but not quite as hot as before. *Thank God.* I handed him the gingerbread.

"Where did you get this?" he asked, snapping off a piece for me.

"No, it's for you; I already ate some," I said, biting away a smile. "I got caught this morning stealing vegetables from the farm—but don't freak out. Instead of arresting me, the yeoman offered me a job! Can you believe that? I'm going to work here as a maidservant just for a few days, although he doesn't know that. The moment you're better, we're getting back on the road to Carlisle. I know we're in a hurry, but you can't go anywhere until you're better, and this is a way to make some money in the meantime."

Nick's mouth hung open. "You accepted a position of work in the yeoman's household? Does the yeoman know of me?"

"No, but it's better that way, isn't it? You said that married women don't usually work, so it's better if he thinks I'm flying solo. Plus, he forgave me for the vegetables, but he might not be so accepting of the two of us having squatted in his barn—especially when you're sick with a fever. I think it's best if you just stay here out of sight for now, and—"

"Emmie!" he cut in. "Do you know what shall be expected of you as a maidservant to the yeoman? Is there a lady of the household?"

"Do you mean is he married? Um, I don't think so. No one's mentioned a wife."

Nick was staring at me but seeing something else. "Emmie, the yeoman may wish to lie with you, and it will be your duty to oblige."

"Lie with me?"

"Take you to his bed!" He gripped his stomach like he might be sick.

My breath lodged in my throat. This world was primitive and sexist, but it was also ultra-pious and conservative. Was I really expected to get my kit off for my boss like some sort of sex slave? I was too aghast to speak.

He sat forward, clutching his forehead like he was woozy. "We must take leave of this place and find another lodging until I am well enough to work."

"No," I said firmly. "You need to rest and get yourself better before we do anything. Plus, where would we even go? You haven't met Mister Hugh, but he's nice—he forgave me for the theft like it was nothing."

"Mister Hugh?" Nick's gaze clung to mine for a long moment. "You already think well of him."

I tilted my head at him. "Nick. I am not going to sleep with the master of the house. He'd have to force himself on me, and let's just say that it wouldn't be the first time something like that happened to me, but it would certainly be the last for *him* by the time I was done with him."

My words sent a flush of shame to his cheeks. "Make no mistake, I feel endless horror for what occurred at the river near to Maiden-head," he said, his face darkening. "If I ever see that devil's spawn again, I will kill that man with my bare hands."

I shook the topic away, choosing not to remind him about the time I was also nearly raped at the Tower of London when I'd been impris-oned there. I was well versed in the brutalities of this world, and I'd had enough of running from them. If I had my time at the river again, I'd knee that bandit in the crown jewels with all my might.

Nick was blinking at me with wary eyes.

"There's a sweet young girl who works in the house called Phoebe," I reassured him gently. "It's not like it'll just be Hugh and me in there. Plus, as soon as I work up the courage, I plan to tell him that I have a brother here as well, in case he finds you here. If he thinks you're my brother rather than my husband, then I can still work. The fact is that we need money urgently to keep moving north to Carlisle Castle, and if he's offering it, then I'm taking the job. We've lost too much time already."

Nick's head dropped back into the straw, an arm falling over his face. "Do what you must, my lady. I am too weakened this day to fight you on it."

After filling him in on our horse Ophelia's upgrade from the barn to the stables, I reluctantly left Nick alone and resurfaced outside into the rising sun, which had tinted the ripples of crops into a shade of caramel. As I climbed over sticky mud and animal droppings to reach the main house, a face appeared in the upstairs window before hastily shrinking from my view.

Hugh Wynter had been watching me.

11

PHOEBE'S POTTAGE WAS SIMMERING OVER THE FIRE IN THE EMPTY kitchen, flooding the house with fragrant, rich aromas that tortured my empty stomach. I'd told Hugh I was well trained as a maidservant, so I set to work wiping up the food scraps left on the bench, sneaking the occasional bite into my mouth. With no idea where Phoebe was, I heated one of the pails of water over the fire and used the steaming liquid to clean a pile of dirty pewter dishes before setting them to dry upon the bench.

A chest set against the wall contained exactly what I'd hoped was inside: strips of linen cloth for cleaning. I dipped a cloth into the washing water and wandered into the main hall, holding my breath like a trespasser. A glint of light moved through the small window. It was Phoebe's coif catching the sunlight outside; she was crouched over a patch of earth, sprinkling seeds.

After swiping the damp cloth across the mantel above the fireplace, I leaned in to inspect a trio of miniature portraits in tiny frames. One was of a young boy that might've been Hugh Wynter as a child, and the adult portrait beside it was unmistakably him. No one would deny that he was attractive, with soulful, greenish-gold eyes, and a halo of sandy-blond curls. The third portrait was of a young woman with olive skin and a peek of dark hair beneath a white coif. Could she be Hugh's wife or sister?

The windows were latticed but unglazed, and a pleasant wind rustled through them, interrupted by a murmur of voices. A moment later, the kitchen door banged shut, and a male voice moaned.

I crept closer to the kitchen, still feeling like an intruder in this house. Through the arched doorway, I saw that Phoebe was hunched over a teenage boy with long legs who sat on a stool.

"I bid thee to be still," she said to him. The boy's response was muffled. When I stepped closer, making my presence known, his mocha eyes flashed up at me, startled.

Phoebe spun around. "Oh, it is just Anne, the new housemaid," she said with relief. "Anne, thou did frighten us." She was sticking a small iron tool inside the poor boy's mouth. "Be still," she ordered and then snapped her arm back with a hard jolt.

The boy's hand flew to his mouth, his eyes scrunching as he groaned.

Phoebe held up a pair of pliers that gripped a blackened tooth coated in blood and spit. "Anne Shakespeare, may I present Jasper Blacke. This tooth hath kept him up all the night."

The offending tooth made a hollow ping as she dropped it into a dish. I gave Jasper a brave smile, and he nodded his greeting with his palm still pressed to his mouth.

I didn't know how Jasper fit in around here, but he moved around the kitchen with casual familiarity, his chocolate ponytail swinging from the nape of his neck. Either he was standing funnily, or his posture was slightly lopsided, like one leg was shorter than the other.

"I best make my return to the stables," he said, grabbing an apple from a pile on the counter and tossing it into the air. "It is a pleasure to make thine acquaintance, mistress," he said to me. What was left of his teeth crunched into the apple as he nudged the door open with his knee and escaped outside.

"Does he work here?" I asked Phoebe, and she nodded.

"Jasper hast been in Mister Hugh's service longer than I. He tends mainly to the horses."

"Well, now I know who to come to when I've got a toothache," I said with a chuckle. "Yikes."

Footsteps clomped down the staircase in the adjacent hall, and Phoebe stiffened like a soldier. Hugh appeared in the kitchen, looking nothing like a tough-talking sergeant with his restrained but warm smile.

"Are you traveling well thus far, Anne?" he said to me.

"Absolutely; thank you," I said. I made sure the linen cloth in my hand was in his view. "I've cleaned the kitchen, and I was just dusting inside the hall."

"I am grateful for it." He looked at Phoebe. "I favor a chicken for supper this day. Will you make the preparations?"

"Most certainly," she replied with a small curtsy.

"I neglected to mention earlier that the two of you may share a lodging in the servants' chamber," Hugh added. "I trust there is room?" he asked Phoebe, who nodded.

Hugh settled his shy gaze on me. "Perhaps I may offer a tour of the house, where I may instruct you on how I prefer things to be done. Phoebe usually attends to the cookery, so to that end, I wish to direct your person to other tasks of the household."

Phoebe stepped forward. "Allow me, Mister."

He shook away the suggestion. "It is really no trouble. An excuse to escape the pile of papers requiring my attention upstairs," he added with a smile.

I followed Hugh into the hall, registering a pleasant scent of cloves that trailed him everywhere. The hall was by far the largest room in the house, but Hugh explained that he rarely used it because he received few visitors.

"If I may speak plainly, do you enjoy a great number of kin?" he asked as we passed by the trestle table lined with bench seats.

"No, we're not a big family," I said, stiffening at the unexpected question about my life. "What about you?" I diverted.

"I am regretfully quite alone," he replied without looking at me.

He pointed at a clutter of tools beside the fireplace, explaining how he liked them ordered. A wooden cupboard stood beside the mantel, displaying shelves of serving platters and bowls that Hugh assured me would only be needed once in a blue moon. The only items that looked remotely flashy were a pair of silver spoons and a silver saltshaker.

"And here is where you may find the linens," he said, nudging his leg against an oaken chest beside the staircase. "Be sure to press the cloth tightly to suffocate any fleas when you change the bedding."

He faced me with his hands pressed to his thighs. "I feel that is enough now, for fear of overwhelming you." He looked at me for a moment before averting his gaze. "I bid you a pleasant day."

"Actually, Mister Hugh, I wanted to mention something about my family," I blurted out before he could leave. "I'm so appreciative of the work you've offered me and for your forgiveness for the vegetables. You've been more than kind. But…" My throat locked.

"What is it?" He stepped closer with a furrowed brow. "You may speak your conscience."

My heart was a racehorse. "It's not just me who came to your farm to seek refuge. I have an older brother, William, he—he traveled with me from Stratford, and he caught a fever on the roads, so I've been looking after him."

Hugh tilted back with surprise. "Where is the fellow now?"

"In the barn at the back of the property," I said in a nervous rush. "The one that you said was infested with bees and not to go near. I'm so sorry; we really didn't know where else to go."

I couldn't lift my gaze from my scuffed boots. When I finally looked up, Hugh's eyes were pinned to mine. They quickly lowered.

"You have courage," he said. "I admire you for it. But I cannot have an infectious man lodging on my property. It would be a peril to us all."

I felt my skin turn crimson. "I understand. I'm so sorry. I promise you: We'll be gone within the hour."

When I turned to leave, hiding my disappointment, he reached his hand out to stop me, catching the fabric of my kirtle. "Forgive me," he said, whipping his hand back like he'd forgotten himself. "I intend not for *you* to take your leave from here."

"If my brother leaves, then I leave," I said like that should have been obvious.

He gripped his hip, his eyes searching. "What affliction is it that troubles your brother?"

"I think it's just a passing fever," I said quickly, trying to ease the concern on Hugh's face. "He's had no other symptoms, and this morning, he seemed a little better."

He sighed. "Very well. Your brother may continue to lodge in my barn on the condition that he is not to leave that place until he is unquestionably well. I will instruct the servants to avoid the barn, and you may bring him food and broth, but you are otherwise to keep away for fear of infection."

Relief filled my lungs with air. I could've hugged Hugh for his kindness.

He brushed a hand over his tangle of curls. "If you forgive me for saying so, it has altogether been too long since I have shared the company of a maiden of such grace. I feel it does me good." He blushed a smile, and I couldn't help but smile back.

"Thank you," was all I could think to say.

He tipped his head in a polite nod. "Inform your brother that I look forward to making his acquaintance the moment he is well. God willing, we may then discuss the matter of work for the both of you. I could also use a laborer who can tend to the farm."

The thought of Nick Tudor, the former King of England, being subordinate to this young man as his farmhand was enough to make me shudder, but I held Hugh's attentive gaze. "That's an amazing offer; thank you. I'll tell him."

Nick slept the most of that day away and the next. I was beginning to feel headachy and lethargic, but I suspected it was caused by lack of sleep rather than whatever illness Nick had. The straw mattress beside Phoebe's bed in the poky servants' chamber wasn't much more comfortable than the barn floor, and Phoebe roused me before dawn each morning so I could light the fireplaces while she prepared Hugh's breakfast.

On the third day of my employment at Hugh Wynter's farm, I

woke to the roosters' crows with itchy red bites dotting my ankles and shins. I tossed my woolen blanket outside, hoping some direct sun would burn away the fleas, and then wrapped up a chunk of buttered bread with two apples and threw my cloak over my shoulders. Hugh had told Phoebe and Jasper about my brother lodging in the barn, so I was able to openly bring Nick food and water. The onset of spring had taken the bite out of the air, and I traipsed over the silvery dew to the barn, stifling yawns.

I climbed the ladder to the loft and found an empty patch of straw where Nick should have been. My stomach collapsed into free fall.

"Good morrow, my lady."

He strode out of the shadows at the opposite end of the barn, looking up at me with a stick in his hand.

"You're up!" I cried, hopping back down the ladder. "And you look good." I rushed to feel his forehead. The fever was gone. I could've wept with relief.

"I feel quite well," he said, his dimpled smile quickening my heart-beat. He cocked his finger for me to follow him to the other end of the barn. There, scrawled into the dirt, was a series of squiggles with dates beside them.

"I have drawn a map from here to Carlisle Castle," he said, pointing with the stick. "This is where we are now in Notting-hamshire; we are to ride through the north and west of Yorkshire, through Durham, and then on to Cumberland. I make it to be a journey of nine or ten days to the castle. If Mary Stuart is to invade England in two and a half weeks, we must take our leave from this place no later than the morrow or we risk running out of time."

"Tomorrow?" I stared at the map, willing the dates to change, even though I knew they wouldn't. "How much money do you think we'll need to get to Carlisle Castle without having to do any more squatting?" I said. "The next yeoman who finds us hiding in his barn might not be as forgiving as Hugh Wynter."

Nick tapped his lips, calculating. "How many coins have you earned thus far?"

"I have no idea. We've never even spoken about my wages."

He made a tsk sound. "That is because you are a maiden." He

leaned against the wall, crossing his thick arms. "Has this Hugh fellow been kind to you? Well-mannered?" He scanned my face.

"Well, he only kissed me the one time."

Nick's jaw fell open, and I rushed forward, guilty but smiling. "I'm kidding, I'm kidding, I'm sorry. That was a bad joke."

"Good God, woman, are you making an effort to return me to a fever?"

He ran his fingers through his mussed hair, forever the most handsome man to ever exist, even when compared against the dashing Hugh Wynter. "Now, as your *brother*, my lady," Nick said, "I am to speak for you. I shall accompany you to the house to request reasonable payment for your time and labor, and we will then be on our way."

"Wait," I said as Nick swirled his boot around the dirt to destroy the map evidence. "You were still sick only yesterday. If you stride into Hugh's house without his permission, he might have a panic attack, and we'll lose his favor. I haven't told you yet, but he's offered you work here as a laborer."

Nick grunted. "I have not the time to be a laborer. I am to stop a war against my countrymen by the Queen of the Scots. What's more, I have yet to contrive a reasonable plot on how to become near enough to Mary Stuart's person to fulfill our plot of assassination, and there is still a great deal of thinking that must be done."

My chest tightened with a familiar feeling of dread.

"You're right; we need to get going," I said glumly, reminding myself that Nick and I weren't two villagers looking to wash sheets and cut firewood in exchange for honest wages. We were the former king and queen of this realm that was on the brink of civil war and bloodshed because of the decisions we'd made.

"Hopefully, I've made at least enough money by now to keep us going if we live on the cheap," I said. "But I will be the one to talk to Hugh this morning. I'll come back as soon as I can fill you in on what he said."

Nick looked wary at the idea of me negotiating my own wages, but I reminded him that women weren't the feeble creatures he'd grown up to believe we were. I unpacked the bread and apples for him and hurried back to the house to help Phoebe prepare Hugh's breakfast omelet of eggs, butter, sugar, and currants.

As I rounded the rear of the house through the goose pen, I nearly crashed into Phoebe's back legs. She was crouched over, vomiting into a mass of watery, greenish goose poop.

"Oh no, are you okay?" I said, forgetting that she'd have no idea what the word "okay" meant.

Jasper dashed down the house steps clutching an earthenware mug. "This here is ale with some egg yolk and honey," he said, crouching beside her.

Phoebe puked again, and Jasper gave me a sympathetic pout. My eyes zeroed in on the gaping hole in his left earlobe. A trace of alarm met my chest. Nick had said that criminals were marked by a hole burned through their left earlobe.

Phoebe thanked him for the mug and managed a small sip. "Forgive me," she said to us. "I mean not to be of any trouble."

"Perhaps thou shouldst take some rest," Jasper said.

"Yes, I can do your duties this morning," I added. "You usually get the water from the well before making the breakfast, right?" I scooped up the empty bucket by her side. "I'll get it."

Phoebe clutched her lower stomach, her cheeks colorless. "I thank thee. The affliction oft passes by noon hour."

"Go lie down," I encouraged. "When I see Mister Hugh, I'll tell him you're not well."

"And I shall attend to the master's breakfast," said Jasper. For a kid of his age, he had a sweet, responsible nature. I decided I wasn't going to judge him by that hole in his ear.

Phoebe thanked us both repeatedly before wiping her mouth with her apron and heading back inside with Jasper chasing after her. I hoped that whatever illness Nick had suffered hadn't spread to Phoebe, but he hadn't left the barn, nor had he been sick to his stomach.

Before I broke it to Hugh that I was quitting my job five minutes after he'd hired me, I had to help Phoebe with her tasks.

The well was a short stroll from the house, past the stables and through the orchards. After tying Phoebe's bucket to the rope, I sat on the stone wall circling the well shaft. I used both hands to turn the stiff wooden handle, lowering the bucket. When I leaned forward to see how far the bucket had traveled, the ground broke from under me, sending the world spinning and flying upside down. For a split-second I was in free fall before a wave of ice-cold water splashed my face, a teeth-chattering jolt sending searing pain through my thigh.

It took a second for the scrambled scene to straighten around me. I was sitting in a pool of freezing, waist-deep water, and a vast, black tunnel stretched high above me. A circle of light beamed from the top, and I reached for it in a hopeless moment of disorientation.

"Help!" I shouted, my voice bouncing off the stone walls.

Water sloshed around me as I stood up. How had I managed to fall into the freaking well? *Emmie, you idiot!* The walls had to be twenty feet deep, but at least the lack of rain had left the water shallow. This could have been the end of me.

"Help!" I cried again, this time at the top of my voice.

Silence. I snatched the swinging rope and threw myself onto it like a monkey. I was no gymnast, and the attempt at scaling the rope burned my palms. I'd barely made any progress when the old rope frayed and snapped, sending me plummeting backward. I coughed up water, clutching my throbbing thigh that had caught my fall earlier. The empty bucket floated in the water beside me, and I smacked it away with irritation.

"Help!" I shouted again to the echoing silence. I repeated the cry countless times before searching the murky water for something else that might help, like a twenty-foot ladder might suddenly emerge. Cursing at myself, I shouted for help over and over until my throat burned.

A black shape flashed across the circle of light, and I shot to my feet, calling out. It was just a blackbird that hopped around the surface of the well with a mellow whistle, and a sort of manic energy flooded my limbs as I realized how truly alone I was. I stupidly tried to climb the mossy stone walls like a spider before smashing my fists into the water with frustration at myself.

At least Jasper had heard me say that I was going to the well for water on behalf of Phoebe. When I was discovered to be missing, surely this would be the first place they'd look for me. But people mostly kept to themselves on the farm, attending to their tasks. It could be hours before anyone noticed my absence, and I'd promised Nick that I'd report back to him about retrieving my wages so we could resume our journey to Carlisle Castle. What if he came looking for me at the house and got into a squabble with Hugh? Nick was hotheaded and uncontrollable at the best of times.

My legs were turning numb, and I was beginning to shiver. If I ended up catching some horrible disease from this water, delaying our departure further, I'd blame myself until the end of time! My cries for help continued until my throat was raw.

I sat with my head hunched over my wet knees for what felt like hours before the light above me dimmed like a cloud had passed over the sun.

"Anne!" gasped a man from high above.

My head snapped up to meet a silhouette of a figure peering over the top of the well, crowned with a mop of curls. It was Hugh Wynter.

"Help me! I've fallen in!" I cried stupidly.

"Are you wounded?" he called back.

"I don't think so!" I gave my sore thigh a squeeze to make sure, but any pain I felt was bearable.

He disappeared from the circle of light for a painfully long minute before returning to dangle a fresh line of thick rope down the well.

"Place your foot inside the loop!" he called as I caught the rope. He'd tied the end into the shape of a noose. I stepped into it like a stirrup and awkwardly clutched the rope above it with both arms.

"I'm in; you can pull!" I called, holding on for dear life.

Hugh made grunts of effort as he hauled me up, each hard tug lifting me another foot higher. When I was halfway up the well shaft, I stopped looking down.

My eyes were pressed shut when a pair of hands grabbed me by the shoulders and heaved me upward. Any impropriety of touching a man in the Tudor world went out the window as I folded my arms around Hugh's neck, clutching tightly. He hefted me over the stone wall, and I didn't let go as we tumbled in one mass onto the lush grass, our legs tangling together.

"Are you well?" he asked, his mouth so close to my neck that his breath tickled my skin. I could smell cloves again, and woodsmoke.

"Thank you; I'm fine." I took a moment to catch my breath before breaking away from him. My voice was hoarse from shouting. "Thank you, thank you, *thank you,*" I repeated, climbing to my feet.

"There is truly no need to thank me." His cheeks were flushed, and for a moment, we didn't speak as the past few seconds sank in.

I'd held onto him for too long.

It had been forever since I'd felt a man's arms around me, and I'd held on for a moment too long. It made my stomach feel concave and jittery.

Hugh moved close to me again, inspecting me for injury.

"I'm really fine," I said, putting distance between us. My boots were soaked sponges, and my wet dress clung to my legs. "But I should change."

"Of course." He made a polite step back so I could head for the house.

"Thank you so much again," I said, unable to make eye contact with him without feeling weirdly flustered.

"Not at all," he insisted. "I beg your forgiveness for the state of ruin of the well that led to your fall. I shall have the wall mended at once. If anything had happened to you…"

Before he could look at me that way any longer, I offered another "Thank you" and made a beeline for the house, his gaze burning a hole in my back.

Phoebe was resting on her straw mattress with an arm over her face. I attempted to change my clothes in silence without disturbing her, but as I peeled the wet hose off my feet, she sat up.

"Anne! What mischief hast befallen thee?"

I explained why I was so wet, and she apologized profusely for being so unwell that I'd had to take over her tasks. After I drummed home that my fall wasn't her fault, the conversation shifted to my rescuer, Hugh Wynter, and an adoring glow crept into Phoebe's cheeks. That was when it hit me: She was crushing hard on her cute boss. I didn't know her well enough to tease her about it, so I took a different tack.

"So, is there a Mrs. Hugh?" I asked with a slight smile playing around my lips.

Phoebe's face dropped. "Why dost thou ask that?"

"I'm not interested in him," I clarified. "I'm just curious. He's a nice guy, and obviously handsome. But he seems lonely to me."

Her face turned somber. "There was a Mrs. Wynter…a Mistress Audrey Wynter. Before I came into Mister Hugh's service, the two were already wedded, but the mistress died a year past."

"His wife died? That's terrible." *Poor Hugh.*

A bell tinkled from the hall, and Phoebe sat up straight. "Mister Hugh is calling for our assistance."

"I'm coming!" I sang out and hurriedly finished tying on a clean kirtle over my linen smock. Phoebe got up and smoothed her apron before trailing me into the hall. Hugh stood by the fireplace, the portrait of his deceased wife staring me down from the mantel.

His eyes made a quick slide down my body. "Do you remain well after your incident?"

"Yes, I'm fine," I replied, relieved that my thigh sported only a bad bruise.

"Wonderful. I am to receive a gentleman guest this afternoon, a Mister Holborne, and we shall have matters to discuss in private. I bid that you attend to my chamber and ensure that all is clean and tidy."

"Of course," I said without thinking. I still needed to resign from my job, collect my wages, and be on my way. But after this morning, I couldn't just walk out on Hugh when he had things for me to do. He'd practically saved my life.

He asked Phoebe to prepare a cooked lamb and chicken, a baked fruit tart, and some fresh bread with strawberry preserves. She curt-sied before dashing into the kitchen, leaving Hugh and me alone.

A moment of awkward silence stretched between us. "May I inquire after your brother's health?" he asked before I could escape upstairs to clean.

"Oh, he's doing much better today, thank you," I said with genuine gratitude. "Actually, I wanted to talk to you about that." I ran my clammy hands down my dress. "My brother and I so appreciate your offer of work for the both of us—we really do—but now that he's better, we have to be on our way. I'm so sorry to have wasted your time, but we were only passing through on our way to Cumberland."

He didn't try to hide his dismay. "Oh, truly? Well, yes of course, but…I will admit that I am sorely disappointed. In a short time, you have proven to be a fine maidservant."

An embarrassed chuckle slipped from my mouth. We both knew that wasn't true. "Thank you for everything," I said, strangely a little tongue-tied. "Would it be acceptable for me to get my wages off you?"

His face fell. "You mean to leave this day?"

"Not until I've tidied your bedchamber like you asked," I said quickly.

He sighed. "Very well. I shall make ready your wages. Will you and your brother take some dinner here at the house before you depart? I would like to make the acquaintance of the fellow who has taken up lodging in my barn."

"Yes, of course…thank you."

Hugh headed outside for some air, his shoulders slumping. A rock grew in my stomach at the thought of Nick and Hugh meeting face to face. Hugh was poor by a nobleman's standards, but he was a richer man than those we'd encountered so far. For all we knew, he'd seen the former king's portrait before.

The surge of adrenaline sparked by my fall down the well had sucked some of my strength. Feeling a little woozy, I ventured upstairs into Hugh's bedchamber, tingling with nerves I couldn't switch off. I loved Nick more than I'd ever believed was possible, but something about Hugh Wynter upset my equilibrium.

Hugh was evidently wealthy enough to own a four-poster bed, but its craftsmanship was plain, and the curtains were missing. After dusting the wooden pillars with a linen cloth, I moved to the table piled with papers and messy pots of ink. I dusted the candlesticks and attempted to scratch some of the old wax off the wood. There were two chests lined against the wall, and I wiped down their lids before glancing at the door to make sure I was alone.

If someone had caught me opening the chest, I'd have said I was just doing a thorough cleaning job, but the truth was that I was curious. What sorts of things did a mysterious man like Hugh Wynter store in his room? He was so different from Nick.

Only one of the two chests was unlocked. It held mostly papers with confusing lists and numbers, some pewter jugs and plates, and a small woven pouch. When I peeked inside the pouch like a shameless snoop, I gasped. Inside was a coiled-up chain of wooden balls tied to a crucifix. I dropped the pouch back into the chest like it was covered in mice. The last time I'd encountered a wooden chain of Catholic rosary beads in this Protestant realm, they'd been around my neck, choking me. Was Hugh Wynter a clandestine Catholic?

Keeping my ears pricked for footsteps on the stairs, I dug a little deeper into the chest and recovered a picture frame. Inside was a portrait of an attractive woman with deep-set eyes and reddish-brown hair. Was she Hugh's wife? I squinted to read the tiny inscription beneath the portrait:

Mary, the Quene of the Scots

My chest emptied of breath.

My fingers froze over the image before I turned it around. Folded into the back of the frame was a tiny, rolled-up piece of parchment scrawled with a series of random symbols that resembled Egyptian hieroglyphs. The note was signed with a single letter I understood: *M.*

I slipped the note inside my dress and returned the portrait to the chest. My heart thumped in my ears as I hurriedly finished cleaning so I could get back to Nick before he ran into Hugh first and confirmed our departure.

When I was finished upstairs, I bolted across the field of vegetable crops, nearly colliding with Nick at the entrance to the barn.

"Good God, Emmie, where have you—"

"Nick, we can't leave here just yet," I cut in, breathless. "I think you need to take that job as the laborer here. Even if it's just for a couple of days…even if it's just for one day."

His brows lifted. "To what end? We must make haste for Carlisle Castle."

"To the end that Hugh Wynter, the yeoman, has a portrait of *Mary Stuart* in his bedroom, as well as a set of Catholic rosary beads, *and* this coded letter signed with the letter 'M.' It was with the portrait." My fingers shook as I handed Nick the note.

The frown didn't leave his face as he scanned the parchment.

"What do you think?" I asked, my chest high in my throat. "Do you think the letter could be from Mary Stuart? You said that there were dissenters loyal to the old religion living in Nottingham. I think Hugh might be one of them!"

He looked at me, his lips falling open. "Could we be so fortunate as to come upon the home of one of Mary's very conspirators while we are on a quest to stop her?"

"You said that this area is a hot spot for lords planning Catholic rebellions," I maintained in a hushed voice. "Hugh Wynter could be involved with those guys; he could be part of their army. Plus, the fact that Mary Stuart is successful in her mission to overthrow the queen says to me that the secret army she's building is big. There could be thousands of Hughs ready to support Mary Stuart...they could be everywhere!"

Nick's eyes were flashing. "Perhaps you are right. I have been thinking upon how to approach Mary Stuart at Carlisle Castle with any success, and I have come up with naught. Perhaps this is a gift from God. After the losses we have endured, this may be our chance. If you can leave this letter with me, I will make every effort to solve its riddle this night. If it is indeed a manner of communication with Mary Stuart, we should remain here and learn everything we can about her plot. But Emmie, we have little time if we are yet to ride north. We may spare a day at best."

My mind was buzzing with the first breakthrough we'd had in weeks. "If we stay here, you'll have to meet Hugh," I said, "but after that, you should keep as far away from him as possible. If Hugh Wynter is connected to Mary Stuart, he might actually recognize you."

Nick's frown deepened. "But if I am to keep away from the man, how am I to obtain any information about Mary's plot, and in such haste?"

My mind darted to the glowy look in Hugh's eyes when our limbs had been entwined beside the well. "Leave that part to me," I said. "I'll get whatever I can out of Hugh, and I'll do it quickly. We may even learn something that stops us from needing to go all the way to Carlisle Castle. You never know—maybe Mary Stuart is going to journey south."

Nick's jaw set as he nodded, the decision made: We would stay here for another day while we uncovered what Hugh Wynter knew about Mary Stuart's planned invasion.

We hung there in silence for a moment before Nick looked at me, his voice tensing. "This is the closest we may come to saving the realm and the life of my sister, Emmie. Therefore, I urge you to take any opportunity in your power to learn what is in that man's heart. Do you understand?" he added, his face tightening. "I bid you to do whatever it is you must."

12

I TROD CAREFULLY OVER THE VEGETABLE CROPS ON MY WAY BACK TO the main house, seeing only Nick's grave, emotional expression as he'd said the words.

I bid you to do whatever it is you must.

What did he mean by that? Surely he wasn't suggesting that I *seduce* Hugh Wynter to milk him for information? I should've just asked Nick outright, but his potential answer sent a sickening ripple through my stomach. He hadn't made love to me in more than a year now. Had I officially fallen into the friend zone, and now he wanted to pimp me out for intel about Mary Stuart?

I swallowed my dark thoughts, unable to even consider that possibility.

Phoebe was chasing rats away from the goose pen with a broom, and I offered her a look of sympathy as I inhaled a steadying breath and headed inside. Hugh Wynter was going to think I'd lost my marbles when I told him that my brother and I had decided to stay and work on his farm after all.

I found him sitting at the trestle table in the hall, fiddling with a small cloth pouch.

"Mister Holborne has been held up on the roads," he said to me, standing up. "But, I have your wages." He slid the pouch to me.

"Thank you so much, but I'm wondering if it's too late to change my mind," I said with a wince. "My brother would like to stay here and do some work on the farm after all, if you'll have us. I know…I'm sorry, we're a bit all over the place." My brow creased with apology.

His lips fell open a little before a boyish smile crept onto his cheeks. "Well, as I said, I should like that very much. However, I am beginning to fear that your brother is no more than an apparition. May I make his acquaintance at once?"

"Sure, I'll go get him," I said, trying not to feel guilty that, after only a day, I'd likely be quitting my job again.

"No, your brother may yet have a contagion," Hugh said, grabbing his flat cap. "I shall meet him at the barn, where he may continue lodging if that pleases him."

I gulped and followed Hugh outside, trying to get my head around Nick Tudor playing second fiddle to this younger, infinitely poorer, and less powerful man.

As Hugh passed into the barn ahead of me, my heart drummed in my throat. Why was I so worried about these two meeting?

Nick was sitting on the ground in the corner and jumped to his feet, shoving the coded note from Hugh's room into his pocket. He stood nearly a head taller than Hugh, who offered him a polite doff of his cap, but Nick barely broke a smile.

"Is something amiss with your knees, fellow?" Hugh asked a little tersely. I gathered that Nick was supposed to bow to Hugh, as his inferior.

Nick didn't so much as flinch. "I have been told I have excellent legs for all manner of sports and pleasures," he said, staring Hugh down, a strange sort of challenge on his face.

Behave, Nick.

Hugh's brow furrowed, but he didn't bite back. "You appear strong," he agreed, scanning Nick's arms. "If you are indeed willing to accept mine offer of work, you may begin at once. The wall of the well is in need of repair. Your sister may show you where it is."

The smile on Nick's face didn't touch his eyes. "That would please me, my good man. I regret that I was not in better health sooner, so I could complete the repairs before my sister nearly lost her life to her master's broken well."

Hugh stared blankly at Nick, tension eating up the air between them.

"Come on, I'll show you where the well is," I cut in, taking Nick's arm.

"I shall return to the house in wait of Mister Holborne," Hugh said to me. "There is a clear view of the well from there," he added, making clear to Nick that he'd be watching him.

Nick made cutting remarks about Hugh all the way to the well, but I was reluctant to criticize the man who'd been so kind to me, despite his possible connection to Mary Stuart. Before Nick and I could speak any further, Jasper called me back to help with Hugh's guest, Mister Holborne, who'd just trotted in on horseback. I hoped that Hugh and his friend would catch up downstairs, or even outside in the sun, so I could search his bedchamber for more clues about Mary Stuart. But Hugh invited Holborne upstairs to share a jug of wine served with fresh bread and strawberry preserves, and I swore under my breath.

While Jasper sat by the kitchen fire, turning the chicken and lamb on a spit, Phoebe taught me how to make Hugh's favorite sauce. We mixed the yolks of two raw eggs with the pressed juices of unripe grapes and a few scoops of sugar. *Gag.*

I made an excuse that I needed to sweep the front deck, in case Mister Holborne wanted to sit outside, so I could keep an eye on Nick. For someone who hadn't had to lift a finger all his life, Nick had worked surprisingly hard repairing the well and had moved on to inspecting a broken plow. It was the sort of outdoor work he'd embraced in Borehamwood, and something clicked inside me. *He likes this stuff. And he's good at it.*

After Phoebe and I served the sliced lamb and chicken to Hugh and his dour-faced mate, I told Phoebe that I was going to check on my brother, almost forgetting to call him "William" instead of "Nick."

My heels sank into the mud as I trudged through the pasture, holding my hand up to block the glare of the sun. Nick rested on the handle of the plow. "Any luck with our quest?"

I shook my head. "I can't imagine Hugh keeping seditious material anywhere other than his chamber, and he's been in there all afternoon, chatting with his guest. I'm actually surprised he didn't do a better job of hiding that note."

"I have not yet had time to make heads or tails of the note," Nick said, rubbing his brow, which was streaked with dirt. "I intend to undertake the task this night. If you are able to search the master's bedchamber, be sure to look beneath the mattress."

"I'll try," I said. "I'm generally not in Hugh's bedroom a whole lot." I meant it lightly, but he didn't smile.

He blinked at me for a moment, searching my face. "You did not mention that Mister Wynter is quite a handsome man."

"Do you want me to get you his phone number?" I asked with mock seriousness.

He rolled his eyes. "You may first get that man a comb for that frightful muddle of hair."

It was my chance to ask him outright what he'd meant by his "do whatever it is you must" comment, but a shout from behind us stole the moment.

Jasper was bounding over to us from the house.

"Phoebe is bleeding...there is too much blood...the maiden is bleeding!" he said.

"What? Where?" I said, my heart racing.

Jasper just hunched forward like he might be sick.

"I'll come and get you if we need any help," I said to Nick before chasing Jasper back to the main house. Phoebe lay in the servants' chamber in a cold sweat, clutching the fabric of her kirtle, which was soaked in blood.

"What happened?" I asked. "Where are you bleeding from? Have you called for a doctor?"

"The doctor shall want payment," Jasper said helplessly.

"What about Hugh?" I asked, but Phoebe rolled over and clutched my wrist with surprising strength. "Nay, I beseech thee... Mister Hugh must not know about the baby."

My hand flew to my mouth. "You're pregnant?"

I should have suspected it after her morning barf session, but Phoebe was only sixteen. That said, people did have babies much younger in Tudor times than in my world. Was Jasper the father?

She hitched up her dress, revealing the source of the bleeding, which was worse than I thought.

"I'll pay for a doctor," I blurted to Jasper. My pouch of wages was in the barn. Surely I had more than enough coins in there for a single visit.

"Anne," Phoebe protested, but I turned to Jasper.

"Take our horse Ophelia if you need to," I said to him. "Just get a doctor, please!"

I took a clean cloth from the chest in the kitchen and asked Phoebe if it was okay if I used it to try to stop the bleeding. She nodded, her eyes cast down and her cheeks pallid.

I had absolutely no idea if what I was doing would have any effect, but I pressed the cloth between her legs, applying pressure in an effort to slow the hemorrhaging.

"Can thou bring me to the barn?" she asked me in a shaky voice. "The doctor may attend to me there, and the master need not know."

Unease prickled my skin. Phoebe was unmarried, and I understood that her pregnancy could cost her her job in this century, but how on earth could we hide something like this from Hugh? The look on her face broke my resolve. Plus, it was her body and her decision.

"Do you think you can walk?" I said, helping her up. She steadied herself and began gathering up the bloodied sheets so Hugh wouldn't see them, but I stopped her with my hand.

"I'll do that. Let's just get you lying down again—quickly."

I helped her down the back steps before Hugh could emerge from upstairs.

Nick was still over at the plow, his eyes widening at the sight of Phoebe's weak stance and bloodstained skirts. I gestured for him to keep his distance, not wanting to freak her out.

Inside the barn, I scrambled up the ladder and grabbed my pouch of coins before tossing down some fresh straw for Phoebe to lie on.

"Is it alright if I leave you here for a few minutes?" I asked, wishing I'd thought to bring water. "I'll go and soak the sheets, so Mister Hugh doesn't see the blood."

She nodded, holding her lower stomach with both hands. "Wilt thou be so kind as to bring me some cloth to change into?"

"Of course." I patted her clammy fingers, and she gave mine a frail squeeze.

On my way back to the house, Nick met me near the goose pen. I explained what had happened, even though it made me uncomfortable to share something so private about Phoebe. He promised to keep the barn in his view while he worked in case she reappeared, and I darted inside to strip the mattress of the soiled sheets.

I submerged them in a bucket of water and pressed down a few times until the water turned a light shade of pink.

After running a clean smock and kirtle down to Phoebe, I returned to the house to meet a dull pounding of approaching horse hooves. I hitched my skirts and hurried up to the road to meet Jasper and a second man on horseback.

"She's down the back in the barn," I said quickly.

A stout man in a billowy black coat jumped off his horse and gave me a curt nod. He made a beeline for the barn in the distance, leaving Jasper to tie up the horses.

"Can you go to Phoebe?" I asked him. "I'm worried Hugh will come downstairs and find the place empty." I pressed my pouch of coins into Jasper's hand. "You can pay the doctor from this."

He thanked me and set off with the horses, his legs almost buckling beneath him.

I kept myself busy by wiping up the kitchen benches and scrubbing chunks of roasted meat off the spit. Hugh usually liked a pottage for supper after a big dinner, so I heated some water over the fire and tossed in chunks of carrots, onions, and turnips, along with the leftover strips of chicken.

The stew was bubbling when Jasper pushed through the door, his hair matted with sweat.

I could barely get the words out. "What happened?"

"The doctor hath said that Phoebe will be well," he said faintly. "But the baby did not live."

My gaze dropped to my feet. *Poor Phoebe.*

Jasper was intent on caring for her, so I poured him a bowl of the pottage to bring to the barn. We agreed that she should come back to the house and lie down in her own bed like she was sick rather than hide out in the barn and risk having Hugh suspect there was more to this situation.

Jasper gratefully swapped the bowl of pottage for my cloth pouch, which was empty of coins.

"The doctor took *all* of it?" I said with dismay.

He nodded, his face flooded with apology, but it wasn't his fault the doctor was greedy. I chewed my bottom lip, reminding myself that Nick and I still needed to be paid for today's work—that was something, at least.

The sky was dimming when the fading sound of horse hooves battering the earth announced that Hugh's visitor, Mister Holborne, had finally left. With Hugh insisting that Phoebe remain confined to her chamber in case she was infectious with a disease, it was up to me to serve the pottage, knead the dough for the morning bread, feed the animals, and empty the chamber pots while I held my nose to block out the stink.

Soon after nightfall, I returned to the barn to bring Nick some leftover chicken for dinner with a slice of buttered bread and a cup of homemade ale. He rested against the wooden wall in the upstairs loft, his sleepy, greenish eyes gazing at me. I had to drag myself away from him to return to the house so I could undertake another of Phoebe's tasks: preparing Hugh's bedchamber for his sleep.

Hugh asked if I would pour him a bath and waited politely downstairs until it was ready. Inside his bedchamber stood a wooden tub behind a thin curtain, where I found two large buckets of water from the well. I hung the buckets over the fireplace to heat the water and quietly lifted the lid of the chest that held the Mary Stuart portrait, keeping one eye on the closed door. I dug through the chest, but there was nothing new to find, and the second chest was, frustratingly, still bolted shut. If he kept treasonous material in the unlocked chest, what on earth was he hiding in the other one?

Footsteps creaked on the stairs, and I carefully flipped the chest closed and lurched away from it.

"May I inquire whether the bath is yet ready?" Hugh said from the other side of the door.

"One minute!" I called, using a cloth mitten to unhook the steaming buckets of water from the fireplace. I emptied them into the bath, scalding water splashing my arm.

After blowing the red spots on my skin and silently cursing myself, I straightened my coif and opened the door. Hugh was leaning against the wall in a white linen shirt untied at the collar. I warned him that the bath might be a bit hot.

"Worry not; I take pleasure in the heat," he said, his eyes entangling with mine for just a moment.

With a yawn, he grabbed his shirt with one hand and tore it over his head. Catching a flash of muscles, I spun to face the wall, my cheeks burning. I heard the privacy curtain pull closed, followed by the splashing of water as he sank into the bath.

"God's wounds!" he said through his teeth.

"Too hot?" I said with a wince. It was the first Tudor bath I'd ever drawn.

"It shall cool in haste," he said kindly, but the jerking of his limbs gave away his discomfort. "Will you stay and make ready the chamber?" he asked from behind the wall of fabric.

"Of course." Being in the room while Hugh bathed was beyond awkward, but the curtain was opaque enough that neither of us could see through it. Given he rarely left his bedchamber, and that Nick and I had to be on our way, this could be the best chance I had to continue poking through his belongings.

There was more gentle splashing, and I crouched beside the bed like I was straightening the sheets.

"Were you born in Stratford?" Hugh called out.

"I was," I said, searching beneath the mattress like Nick had suggested.

"What is the trade of your kin?"

My breath caught in my throat. "My family has a farm…kind of like this one."

There was nothing hidden on this side of the mattress, so I shifted to the opposite side of the bed.

"Did you say that you have an aunt in the north?" Hugh continued. "You appear rather eager to be received there."

"Yes, um, my aunt moved up there, and she has a young daughter who we want to visit. My cousin."

Back to lying like it's a sport.

This side of the mattress also turned up nothing strange.

"What was it that brought your aunt such a distance from Stratford?" he said.

I pressed my lips together. What was with the twenty questions?

"Love," I blurted, fluffing up the feather pillows and folding open the sheets. "My aunt met a man closer to Stratford, but it turned out that he was from Cumberland. They fell in love, so she married him and moved up there."

"How pleasing," Hugh said, shifting in the bath. I couldn't believe that he was stark naked on the other side of that curtain.

He was silent for a moment. I crept toward his desk for a closer scan of his jumble of papers.

"And what of you?" he eventually said, his voice deepening a little. "Can it be true that a maiden so bewitching as you is without a love so tender like that which stole your aunt away to the north?"

My searching hands froze, and I sensed that Hugh wasn't moving either. It was an extremely forward question for the sixteenth century, but he said nothing to backtrack.

"I guess I haven't met the right person yet," I lied, my breath short. "And I'm pretty happy with life the way it is at the moment."

"You are?"

I gently guided open the drawer of his desk, cringing when it creaked. The drawer held only stacks of candles lying on their sides, blank pages of parchment, and unopened ink pots.

Hugh's voice had tightened. "What if you were to meet a man of honor—the *right* man of honor—who also made his fortune far away from your home? Would you leave the company of your kin for a love so true, as did your aunt?"

Do you mean like moving four centuries in time to an entirely different era?

"I believe I would," I said, surreptitiously closing the desk drawer.

He shifted in the bath, triggering another splash. I was running out of time. Hugh's questions about love were also drawing sweat to my palms.

"What about you?" I asked, commandeering the role of interviewer. "You said that you don't have a lot of family around here?"

"I was born in Nottingham," he said, "but I regret that both my father and my mother have gone to God; may their souls rest in peace."

"I'm sorry to hear that."

He cleared his throat. "The truth is that I am no stranger to loss. Mine own wife was lost to the deadly sweat. Before she could bear me a son."

I tried to sound like I didn't already know about the fate of Hugh's wife. "I'm so sorry...that's terrible."

"I am grateful for your kindness. I confess that it has been difficult to take pleasure in anything without my wife by my side, but one must seek to find a purpose higher than oneself; would you agree?"

As I rummaged as furtively as I could through Hugh's papers, a page at the bottom caught my eye. The paper was unsigned, but half of it was scribbled with the same strange symbols as the other note I'd found.

A purpose higher than oneself.

"Are you still there?" he asked.

"Yes," I replied, slipping the note inside my bodice. "Sorry, yes...a higher purpose, you said. What do you mean by that?"

He sighed. "A life of meaning...one of more consequence than that of personal inclination and desire. Doing the work of the Lord, I suppose. Mistress, is the room yet prepared?"

I glanced at the bed, with its sheets folded neatly open and its pillows fluffed. Everything looked tidy.

"I think so."

"May you pass me a warmed cloth?"

A warmed cloth? Shit.

"Just a moment." I grabbed a linen cloth from the chest and held it over the fire with the tongs until the fabric felt warm to the touch.

"It's ready," I said. The vigorous swishing of water must've been Hugh climbing out of the bath. I reached around the curtain to pass him the cloth, and my fingertips brushed the damp skin of his hand.

"I heartily thank you," he said a little tightly, and my feet felt glued to the rushes on the floor. I tried not to imagine Hugh rubbing the cloth over those toned muscles I'd glimpsed earlier.

A moment later, he was standing in front of me, blond curls dripping. His athletic torso gleamed bare; the thin cloth wrapped around his lower body like a towel. He raked both hands through his wet hair like this was perfectly normal and studied the room.

"All appears well. Phoebe should be pleased that you stood in for her duties this day."

"It was nothing." My sticky throat made it hard to speak.

His brow lined. "What do you believe ails Phoebe? That is two times this week last that she has fallen ill."

Were we really doing this? Having a conversation with Hugh wearing no more than a thin cloth around his waist?

"Gosh, I'm not sure," I said, protecting Phoebe's secret like I'd promised. "Hopefully it's just a little virus that will go away quickly."

"A what?"

"A malady," I corrected, trying to avoid his eyes. And his everything else.

He crossed his arms and watched me until I couldn't help but look at him flush in the face. "May I speak plainly?" he asked, a slight tremble in his voice. When I nodded, he inched a step closer. "I feel there is something altogether different about you," he said, his eyes raking over my face. "Something rather rare and captivating. I understand that you are close with your kin—close enough to steal for your brother when he was taken ill, and to travel hundreds of miles to call upon your aunt. I understand that the thought of being parted from them would bring pain to your heart. But, if you will allow it, I feel that I must speak my feelings."

Every inch of my body seized up as he closed the remaining space between us.

"Anne," he said softly, his caramel eyes caressing my face, his cheeks coloring pink. "I wonder if you might…allow me the pleasure of pursuing you."

"Pursuing me?" I stammered.

"I will ask your brother for his permission, of course. At first light, if you shall allow it."

Hugh Wynter asking Nick Tudor if he can date the wife that he sacrificed his kingdom for? I'm not sure that Hugh would live past sunrise.

He took my silence as a sign to plead harder. "It has been too long since I have shared the company of someone who brings a flutter to my heart. Someone I may wish to share my dreams with…my secrets. I understand that you are without means; without a dowry. Yet I feel that, were I to spend some time with you, I may grow to adore you. And so, I ask you now…Anne." His eyes had turned soft. "Do you feel that you could, with time, come to find in your heart a place for me?"

The world had stilled around me.

Someone I may wish to share my dreams with…my secrets. Was this my chance to find out what he knew about Mary Stuart's plans? But at what cost?

As if he'd heard my question, he leaned closer until our lips were inches apart and held them there until I tasted the sweet heat of his breath. And then his lips were touching mine, softly and gently, and flooding me with warmth. Before I could stop myself, my fingers were in Hugh's damp curls, and I was kissing a man again who wanted me. His mouth tasted like strawberries, and I pulled him a little deeper, my sigh echoing his, until my eyes flashed open, meeting a face that wasn't Nick's. A lightning bolt shot through my lips and down my arms, sending me staggering away.

"I have to go," I said, my lips on fire.

"No, no…do not go," he whispered, his hands cupping my cheeks, his eyes slipping down to my mouth. "I'm sorry."

I wriggled away from him and escaped the room, smearing away tears with my fingertips.

13

THAT NIGHT, I HARDLY SLEPT BENEATH THE STIFLING, SICKENING blanket of guilt. I'd tasted another man's mouth while my Tudor husband had lain less than thirty feet away.

I hadn't asked Hugh Wynter to kiss me.

But you didn't stop him immediately, Emmie. You let him kiss you, and in those few moments, there was a betrayal.

I focused my panic-stricken mind on making sure that Phoebe was still snoring lightly beside me and hadn't taken a turn for the worse. The other lifeline that I clung to was the second coded note still hidden in my dress. There were more important things to think about than a five-second kiss with Hugh Wynter.

Five long seconds, your fingers in Hugh's wet curls, strawberries on your tongue.

I rolled to face the crudely cut beam of black wood that stretched horizontally through the white wall, tugging the wool blanket to my chin. How would I feel if Nick had kissed another girl? How would I feel knowing that, in the five seconds he'd kissed her back, his knees had turned a little weak?

My face crushed in the darkness, along with my heart. It was too painful a thought to even consider.

I didn't want to wake Phoebe with my sniffling, but once the tears swelled up and spilled over, I couldn't stop them. The noose of shame tightened around my neck, choking me, and leaving me with only one option: I had to confess to Nick what had happened, or the pressure and guilt would become unbearable.

But Nick and I were already hanging on by a thread. What if I lost him because of this? Plus, he'd said to me: *Do whatever it is you must.* Right before kissing me, Hugh had mentioned wanting to invite me into his secrets. Would Nick have even encouraged the kiss because of that—wanted me to pursue Hugh's affections further?

Confusion and indecision ate me alive that night. At the first rooster's crow, I got up with my eyes burning from a lack of sleep. Before Phoebe could wake, I tied on my knee-high woolen tights and kirtle and fastened my coif over my unwashed hair.

I had to tell Nick about what had transpired in Hugh's bedchamber, regardless of what it cost me. A lie like that was too heavy, too sinister to carry around on my back. I'd also once caught Nick kissing one of my ladies of the bedchamber, Lucinda Parker, and I'd forgiven him for the transgression, despite his protestations that the kiss was chaste. We could get through this. We would have to get through this. Because losing Nick Tudor was not an option I was willing to consider.

My chest felt filled with cement as I tied on my boots, silently rehearsing my confession.

Hugh Wynter kissed me, and I kissed him back, for just a moment. But you're the one I love.

Phoebe moaned from her mattress.

"Phoebe? Are you well?" I leaned over her. Her face twisted like she was in pain, and her forehead beaded with sweat. I'd thought she was doing better!

I whispered soothing words and gently lifted her smock. There was no bleeding, but the linen sheet wrapped around her straw mattress was drenched with sweat.

"I'll ask Jasper to get the doctor back," I said quickly.

Phoebe shivered and clutched the side of her neck like it was sore.

An angry, red lump bulged from her pale skin there, possibly a swollen lymph node.

"It's going to be fine," I reassured her. "I'm going to get you some water and a doctor."

I raced into Jasper's tiny chamber beside ours. His cot bed was already empty and neatly made. I darted outside into the brisk morning air and found him in the stables, shoveling horse manure into a wheelbarrow.

"I bid thee good morrow," he said with a bright smile. "How goes Phoebe?"

"Not good," I said. "She's got a fever and has a big lump on her neck that looks sore."

"A lump?" He pinched his throat with alarm before hurrying toward the house with me at his heels.

At the entrance to our bedchamber, he stopped dead in his tracks, and I banged into his back. "Take not another step!" he snapped at me.

"Why? What is it?"

Jasper guided me back into the kitchen, his voice a shallow breath. "I shall…I shall call for the doctor." His eyes were round with terror.

"Why can't we go in there?"

"'Tis the pestilence!" He rested against the wall to hold up his quivering body. "It must be what took her child."

"What's the pestilence?" My mind fought through all the illnesses I'd heard of in the Tudor world, none of them inspiring as much fear as… "Oh no," I said, clutching my chest. "You mean the plague." Jasper didn't answer, but his stricken face told me I was right. All I knew of the black plague was what I'd seen in movies set in the medieval period, with thousands upon thousands of deaths.

"We have been cursed by God," Jasper moaned, almost panting. "I shall ride to the village for a doctor. Thou ought to wake the master and inform him without delay."

My throat was stitched closed. I didn't want to venture into Hugh's bedroom again, even to bear urgent news. "What should I do to help Phoebe?" I asked.

He shook his head fiercely. "Thou must stay away from her. The pestilence is what took my mother and father from this mortal world. I would not wish its terror upon my worst foe."

Outside, my pulse raced as I watched him ride away in a trail of dust, wishing that Nick would emerge from the barn to tell me everything was going to be okay. Not that I'd let him anywhere near the house with the black plague inside it.

Overwhelming helplessness washed over me, sending me to my knees on the rickety back step. Would it be selfish to ask Hugh for our wages so that Nick and I could leave this diseased house right away? But what if it was already too late and I'd caught the plague? I'd slept next to Phoebe the entire night.

A dreadful feeling of impending doom weighed down my insides. Just when we thought we were winning, Tudor England was smacking us back down. Right on schedule.

Monitoring myself for any signs of illness, I headed up the staircase and found Hugh's bedchamber door shut. A light tap on the wood roused a muffled response before the door creaked open. He stood in a loose nightshirt that reached his thighs, his hair a tangle of curls beneath his linen cap.

Before he could assume I was here for another kiss, I curtsied. "I'm sorry to disturb you, but I have some bad news," I said in a rush. "Phoebe isn't well again, and Jasper thinks it's the plague…the pestilence." Hugh gasped, his hand flying to his chest. "Jasper has ridden into town to find a doctor," I added gravely.

Hugh had every right to board himself up in his bedroom, but he threw a cloak over his shoulders and bounded past me and down the stairs. I chased him to Phoebe's door, where he paused, his brow glistening with sweat.

"Phoebe?" he said through the small gap in the doorway.

"It is I," she said in a weak voice.

"It brings me sorrow to learn of your suffering," he said hoarsely. "Jasper is calling for a doctor, and I heartily pray that the light of God shall shine upon you. We shall bring some broth to the door." He nodded at me in a silent command, and I darted into the kitchen. As I warmed a pot of chicken bones over the fire and seasoned it with sugar, some of the tension eased in my shoulders. If Hugh could remain calm in the face of death, so would I.

I searched my mind for a memory of how the black plague was transmitted, but the disease barely existed in the twenty-first century. The safest thing to do would be to steer clear of Phoebe and to keep washing my hands well.

Madly checking my neck for lumps, I placed a steaming bowl of broth outside Phoebe's door and gently let her know it was there. A banging drew my attention to the hall, where Hugh was hammering planks of wood from the fireplace across the window, boarding up the house from the inside. I didn't like the thought of not being able to see outside, but I obediently handed him plank after plank while he hammered, the escaping daylight slowly shrouding the room in darkness. Hugh's skin had turned ashen, and his fingers trembled. But I was the one who'd shared a room with Phoebe and touched her blanket when I'd checked her for blood. If anyone was going to get the black plague, it would be me.

"My God, was it your brother who brought the pestilence to this place?" Hugh said suddenly. "You said that the fellow was not well—"

"No," I said quickly. "He never had any lumps or anything; just a fever that went away as fast as it came. And he's been absolutely fine since then."

Hugh nodded and turned away, making no further argument about it. But if he was silently pointing the finger at Nick, I couldn't blame him.

"Do you want me to ride into the town to get any supplies?" I stammered to his shaded face. The boarded-up window was making me claustrophobic and panicky.

"You cannot take your leave," he said like I should know that. "There is the pestilence in the household. To that end, we are bound by law to remain within these walls for weeks no fewer than six. Once Jasper makes our troubles known in the town, I expect a watchman will be appointed before the day's end."

"We can't leave this house for *six weeks?*" I said, aghast.

Mary Stuart will own England by then.

"If the pestilence spreads to the town, many thousands will be lost to it," Hugh said with irritation. The look on my face softened his eyes. "Fear not, Anne; our watchman may bring remedies and food if we are in need of it."

I gripped the edge of the trestle table to hold myself up, shaking my head. "But...I don't want to be trapped in here. I'll do what I can to help, but my brother and I...we have to be going."

"Thank the Lord that your brother has been lodging beyond the house," Hugh said like he was thinking out loud. "If the fellow is willing, he may serve as watchman and bring us our food and remedies."

The orders that Hugh issued next left me lightheaded. If Phoebe died, she would have to be burned along with her bedding and mattress. Hugh would also hunt for some red paint to smear a large cross over the doors—a signal that the house was cursed with the plague.

A clopping of approaching horse hooves drew us both to the strips of light between the window boards.

"It's Nick," I said without thinking. I had no idea why he was out riding at this early hour, but it was the least of my troubles.

Hugh peeked harder. "What fellow is Nick?"

"Not him," I said, correcting myself. "It's just my brother. I thought it was Nick—this peddler we met in the village that said he'd bring us some cloth to buy. We've had a flea infestation, and he said he'd bring the cloth to the farm." I was rambling to hide my stupid mistake.

"Goodman Shakespeare!" Hugh called through the gap.

Nick's face fell at the sight of us peering creepily through a boarded-up window. He jumped off his horse and tossed the reins aside. "Oh no...no, no, no," he said, darting toward us. "What mischief is this? Surely not—"

"The pestilence," Hugh confirmed shakily. "We have been cursed by God."

"Emmie!" Nick called without thinking, and I could've smacked him, despite having just made the same error.

"It's just your sister and Mister Wynter!" I called out. "Are you feeling well?" I asked him through the wooden planks, desperately trying to conceal his slip-up as possible delirium. Hugh was looking at me a little strangely.

"I feel fine," Nick said, pressing his bright eyes to the gap. "Who is it that suffers the dreaded pestilence?" His voice was choked with panic.

"Phoebe," I replied. "So far, she's the only one showing any symptoms, and Jasper has ridden into town to find a doctor."

"Allow me inside," Nick said, blinking rapidly. "I can be of help."

Hugh moved closer to Nick's voice at the window. "It must be troubling to be parted from your sister at such a time," he said, "but you know that is not to be thought of. What would be of help is if you were to serve as watchman. You may bring us remedies and food, and meet with the town magistrates to report on the progress of the pestilence. Is that agreeable to you?"

Nick pressed his fingers to the boards and nodded at the man who'd had his tongue in my mouth the night before. My throat closed up.

"I shall protect your dear sister," Hugh said to him. He pulled me away from the window, and the last thing I saw was Nick gritting his teeth at Hugh. The days in which he'd sat on a gilded throne and called the shots felt like lifetimes ago.

Lighting candles in the gloomy house did nothing to improve the mood, and neither did Hugh's well-meaning instructions that I knew would have little effect. I was to light bits of leather in the fireplace and air each room with smoke to choke any disease. All the process achieved was pushing my sensitive lungs toward an asthma attack. I pressed my nose to the earthen floor in the kitchen, gasping for fresh air to breathe.

Watching Hugh dig through a chest of homemade remedies for some snakeskin drove home how hopeless this situation was. Snakeskin had about as much effect against the black plague as the olive oil, sheep's fat, and parsley juice that he left at Phoebe's door. I reminded myself that I wasn't this man's captive: If I wanted to walk out the door, I could. What kept me inside the house was my conscience. What made me so special that the rules of quarantine didn't apply to me? After all, I'd just been through a pandemic in the modern world.

After checking on Phoebe from a distance, I set to work tidying the kitchen and washing Hugh's and Jasper's sheets in case of any infection. With Phoebe's bedchamber off-limits and my mattress squeezed beside hers, where was I to sleep for the next six weeks? My stomach hollowed with nervous discomfort. I had to talk to Hugh…to make it clear to him that I wasn't going to share his bed. But maybe he'd back off now that death had arrived on our doorstep.

Jasper had experience with the pestilence and encouraged me to keep changing my clothes like it was a sport, so I grabbed a fresh outfit from the chest in the hall and hid inside the kitchen to change. I crossed my arms around myself to tug off my kirtle, touching a crinkly edge of parchment. My fingers stiffened over the coded note that I'd found last night in Hugh's bedroom, minutes before he'd kissed me. In all the turmoil, I'd forgotten it!

With Hugh back upstairs in his bedchamber, I peered through the window gaps every minute, waiting for Nick to reappear. It didn't take long. He was keeping close to the house, anxiety tearing up his face. When I hissed his name, he lurched toward the boarded-up window.

His eyes were watery and red-rimmed. "Do you remain well?" he asked.

"I'm fine," I said, wishing I could reach out and touch him. "What about you? You don't think it was the plague that you had last week, do you?"

"I have thought on it, but not at all," he said. "I had not the terrible sores, nor the thirst, and I did not become frantic."

"That's good."

He exhaled with a hand to his brow. "If I have brought you back to this godforsaken world to lose you to its maladies, that shall be a fate worse than death for me." His voice broke open, and I sensed he would've reached for me if he could. "Do you understand?" he said. "I *cannot* lose you, Emmie."

"It's okay," I reassured him, pressing my fingertips to his. "First of all, I'm the one who brought us back here, remember? Plus, we've been through worse than this. We're going to be fine. As soon as Phoebe is better, we're going to get out of here. We'll find another way to stop Mary Stuart—if it's not too late by then." My heart sank, too aware of Mary's timeline. In sixteen days, England would be hers.

Nick's expression leveled with me. "Phoebe will not recover. You understand that, right? The pestilence is a wicked, merciless disease."

I bit back tears and changed the subject. "Come closer so I can whisper."

He leaned in so closely that I could've kissed his eyelashes through the gap in the boards.

"I found another note," I said under my breath. After checking over my shoulder that we were still alone, I pushed the crumpled parchment through the gap.

He opened the note, scanning the text.

"Did you manage to decode the other note that I found?" I asked before a thump sounded behind me.

"Hide that!" I hissed, spinning to where Hugh stood at the bottom of the stairs.

"Jasper has made his return with the doctor," he said, bounding past me. I trailed him into the kitchen, where the back door swung open, inviting a shock of cold air.

I shrank into myself as a monster of a man in a floor-length cloak stepped into the space like a creature from a horror movie. His entire face was covered by a mask of jet-black leather that was shaped into a long, curved beak, with tiny glass holes for his eyes. He tipped his wide-brimmed hat at Hugh.

"Where is the patient?" The leather mask muffled the man's rural accent.

Hugh indicated the door to Phoebe's room, and the doctor used his cane to push it open.

Jasper and Hugh had a quick chat, and I learned that the man's name was George Baker, and he wasn't a licensed physician at all—he was a local tailor who moonlighted as a plague doctor on the side.

Great. A total quack.

I hung near the entrance to Phoebe's room and watched George Baker sniff a pomander of herbs hanging from his neck before approaching her resting body. He retrieved a small vial from his leather satchel and pressed it to Phoebe's lips before tapping a few drops of the liquid onto her neck lump.

"What is that stuff?" I whispered to Jasper, who appeared behind me.

"'Tis likely to be dragon water. And that may be mithridatium," he said as the plague doctor dropped a bean-sized knob of goo into Phoebe's mouth. When she began coughing, I had to hold my tongue. I had no idea what mithridatium was, but given that bloodletting and the alignment of the stars were among the top cures in this century, George Baker's goo didn't exactly flood me with confidence. And what the hell was dragon water?

"Keep the patient warm and be certain to avoid eating any onions," the plague doctor ordered when the three of us were back inside the kitchen. He held out a gloved palm to Hugh. "The sum is to be one half-pound."

It felt like a total cash grab by this tailor, but it wasn't my place to judge the mechanisms of an earlier century—and he'd risked his life by being here—so I stayed silent. While Hugh paid the bill, Phoebe's coughing fit escalated. What if this man's "medicine" had made her worse?

I covered my mouth with a handkerchief and ducked into her bedchamber. The smell of urine and sickness from her mattress nearly made me heave.

I blanched at her sallow skin that shivered with fever. Her eyes were pressed shut, and she was chanting prayers under her breath. After trickling some water onto her cracked lips, I escaped the room so she couldn't catch sight of my grief. Tears burst through my eyelids, and I choked on silent sobs. I barely knew Phoebe, but she was so sweet and *young*. I hated this world; I hated how hopeless and primitive it was. I hated it so badly that I could've screamed.

"Anne?" Jasper had been saying my fake name, and I hadn't responded.

"Yes?" I sniffled and wiped my eyes. "Sorry…I'm just upset about Phoebe."

His features tightened with sympathy. "Thy brother is asking for thee."

"Thank you."

Wiping my damp cheeks, I found Nick waiting at our usual spot by the boarded-up window.

"Are you alone?" he asked me.

I double-checked. Hugh was back upstairs, and I could hear Jasper faintly reciting prayers outside Phoebe's door. "What is it?" I said.

He kept his voice barely above a whisper. "This night last, I met with success in making sense of the riddles of the first note you discovered. Each symbol appears to correspond with one letter of the alphabet. The very same cipher applies to the next letter you gave me this morning."

All the air fled my lungs. "And? What do the notes say?"

His low voice was barely audible. "You were right in your suspicions. The first note is a letter of sedition from Mary Stuart. The Queen of the Scots has made contact with the Papists and commoners alike in the counties by way of a secret faction of Catholic priests. There is a priest lodging in Nottinghamshire named Mister Holborne."

"Hugh's friend that was over the other day," I remembered with disbelief. "His name was Mister Holborne."

"Mary Stuart has called upon the believers of the old religion to support her as the rightful Queen of England," Nick continued. "Together with these many hundreds—or even thousands—of Papists, she will prepare a great army to fight by her side on the day she proclaims herself as queen, with promises of support from the kingdoms of France and Spain. Once she has the throne, Mary Stuart then intends to restore the old religion in England with every expedition." He took a breath so the words could sink in. "The second note is a letter of reply from Mister Wynter. He says that he will help the Queen of the Scots in any way he can and is preparing an armory of weapons. He names himself by way of a number: seventy-seven."

An urgent voice shouted out from upstairs. I left Nick and dashed up the stairs two at a time. Jasper was in the hallway, clasping the back of his head with both hands. He looked like he'd seen a ghost.

"The master has it," he stumbled. "He has the pestilence!"

"*What?*" I rushed into Hugh's bedchamber. He was lying on his bed in a shiver, his head of curls soaking the mattress with sweat.

"Come no closer!" Hugh ordered before moaning at the ceiling. "Oh, why have you cursed me, God?"

Jasper was shaking. "We need the Doctor Baker to make his return," he said to me. "But we should not take our leave from here. Can thy brother ride to the town?"

"No," I said. "That man isn't even a doctor and is a waste of time; please believe me on that."

"Then what are we to do?" Jasper's eyes bulged with fear.

I shook my head, panic rushing up my neck. "I don't think there's anything we can do. We just need to look after them and keep our distance. There's nothing else we can do to stop this. I'm so sorry."

His face contorted with distress, and he sank to his boots, crying into the wall. And then my own tears spilled, unrestrained and sodden and hopeless.

For three days, I attended to Phoebe and Hugh while Jasper did his best to help but mostly hid inside his room. I couldn't blame him for that. Watching Phoebe and Hugh get eaten alive by the black plague was something that I knew would haunt me for the rest of my life if I was lucky enough to survive this. They cried, and screamed, and sweated, and prayed, and shouted at things that weren't there. Furious, painful lumps sprouted from their necks and armpits, and I wanted to soothe the sores with balm, but Jasper pleaded with me not to touch the sick at all. I think he was paranoid about me being the next to perish, leaving him alone in this house of death.

Nick sat vigil outside the boarded-up window and relentlessly begged me to let him through the locked door, but I was unshakeable. Not only did we need him to continue bringing us food, water, and firewood, but if both Nick and I succumbed to the black death, there would be no one left to stop Mary Stuart.

Do you really think there's any chance of that happening now, Emmie? Wake up! Mary is coming for you all unless the black plague gets you first.

Phoebe died on day four. She passed away in a state of fevered madness that put the fear of God into me. I was now washing my hands in hot water every ten minutes and changing my clothes three times a day. I slept on the floor in the hall beneath the window, as close to fresh air and Nick as I could get.

I reluctantly left the reassuring sound of his voice to help Jasper carry Phoebe's body, swollen with buboes, to the door with gloves covering our hands. Two men from the village, sent by the magistrate, met us on the steps in Tudor-style hazmat suits and wheeled her away to be burned along with her clothes and bedding. Nick and I caught a stricken glimpse of each other through the gap in the doorway before Jasper locked us back inside on the magistrate's orders. Hugh Wynter was still upstairs, writhing and moaning in hellish discomfort, but so far, the disease hadn't spread beyond the farm.

Jasper and I were locked in a terrifying game of Russian roulette, taking silent bets on who was to be cursed first with this hideous death sentence.

That night, Nick made more urgent pleas from the window.

"Emmie, we do not belong here!" he said, his fingers pressed to the boards. "We must be thankful that it is God's will that you remain well, and take our leave of this purgatory of torment before our fortunes change."

The temptation to leave was fierce, but I kept my composure. "I can't leave Jasper alone here to tend to Hugh; he's just a kid, and Hugh's in a terrible way. Plus, if I have the plague, Nick, I can't risk giving it to you."

"Speak not such words!" He drove his fist into the wall, sending a jolt through it. "I can remain idle no longer, my lady." He rested his forehead against the wood. "You cannot ask it of me to remain on the other side of this wall while you live among the deadly pestilence. I mean to pull you out of that house with my bare hands and carry you out on my back!"

"No, you will *not*," I said, repeating the conversation we'd had almost hourly since this had begun. "If you come into this house, not only will I never speak to you again, but you will have to drag me out kicking and screaming so badly that we'll probably both end up dead from the plague. Nick, please be patient and think positively. I'm being really careful."

He puffed an exasperated exhale, and I rested my head on the boards that separated us.

A sudden thud from the ceiling made me jump out of my skin. I asked Nick to be quiet and listened for more noise, but the upstairs returned only a deathly silence. Jasper hadn't budged from where he slept in his chamber.

"Oh no," was all I could get out before I scampered up the staircase.

By the time I used a set of iron tongs resting against the wall to inch open Hugh's door, I was shivering with fear.

He lay on the floor beside his bed, his sweaty blankets tangled around him. I crept closer, my stomach high in my throat. Curls of gold sprouted from his head like an angel's crown.

"Forgive me," he mumbled, his eyes barely open. My hand caught my chest with relief that he was alive.

"Can you get back into the bed?" I asked, keeping my distance.

"I can make every effort to try." He sat up woozily and caught his forehead like his head was fiery with pain.

"Come no closer," he warned as he gathered himself to stand. He toppled, and I moved on instinct, darting to catch him. He weighed a ton, and I nearly collapsed beneath him.

"What are you doing? Get away!" he said with horror, but it was too late. I'd already touched him, and he was clearly incapable of handling himself.

"Just let me help you into bed," I said, attempting to guide him back into the linen sheets without touching his body or the bedding with my bare hands. The heaviness of dread made my movements sluggish. Had I just infected myself with this hideous disease?

Olive-green eyes gazed into mine as he sank into his pillow. "I fear I am on my deathbed," he said through shivering lips.

"That's not true; you are going to make it through this," I lied, fiddling with the blanket until it covered him properly.

He smiled, still undeniably cute despite his pallid skin. "Would this be a terrible time to ask you if you had considered my proposition of a courtship?" he said through cracked lips.

I couldn't help but chuckle, and he tilted his head at me.

"If I were not beset with this dreaded pestilence, mistress, of what nature would your reply have been?" When I withdrew at the question, he pressed me. "I beseech you to humor a dying man. If I were to be well and strong, do you believe that you could love me truly?"

I inhaled deeply, unsure whether honesty was the best policy at a time like this. "You're a kind man," I said eventually. "You're also very charming, and I can see why your wife chose you. I'm so sorry about what happened to her, and I can't even imagine how big a hole that has left in your life. But…Hugh, I'm not the answer. I'm sorry."

For a few moments, he just lay there, his ailing eyes hard to read.

"What an enigma of a woman you are," he finally murmured. "I admit that I cannot make sense of you. One moment, you appear to be the most shrewd, cunning woman upon whom I have ever laid mine eyes. The next, you demonstrate such childish ignorance. Or is that, too, a part of the treachery you commit?"

Treachery?

He was clearly having delusions, so I gave him a comforting look and topped up his water from his jug. But the way he was staring at me sent a chill across my skin.

"The question that plagues me…" Hugh said, like he was continuing a sentence, "is why in God's name would you do it? To what end would a king and a queen exchange their throne and kingdom for a life of servitude, poverty, and disease?"

The room collapsed over me as Hugh sat up on his elbows.

"I am truly at a loss, Queen Emmeline Tudor. For what gain are you and His Majesty, Nicholas of England, hiding away on my land?"

I couldn't swallow, nor could I breathe.

"What on earth are you talking about?" I stammered, my lungs fighting for air and my cheeks on fire. But Hugh's shrewd eyes were impossible to escape.

"Queen Emmeline, I may be a sick man, but I am no man's fool," he said evenly. "I feel I have been kind to you most resolutely, and I have little time left. I heartily ask that we waste it not on lies."

My chin fell to my chest, where my heart was battering my ribcage.

"How did you know?" was all I could say.

14

THE EXPRESSION ON HUGH'S FACE SPOKE VOLUMES. WHILE HE'D suspected my alleged brother William and me to be the presumed-dead King and Queen of England, he hadn't been sure of his suspicions until I'd just confirmed them—and to a man who had a direct line to Mary Stuart. All shame aside, I could've prayed right then that he died of the plague, taking our secret with him.

"How did you know?" I repeated faintly.

A flush of color returned to his cheeks. "There was a number of occurrences. The first was when I became acquainted with your brother, whom we both know is not truly your brother. He did not seem the vagabond type at all, and I know a nobleman when I see one. The both of you, in truth—your good teeth, your manner of speech, your lack of knowledge of household duties. What's more, I felt not the bond of blood between you both, but more the flame of desire." He expelled a sudden, throaty cough, but I was too stiff to duck away from it. "When I asked you about your kin, I too felt a degree of deceit," he continued hoarsely. "Then, I made as good as an offer of marriage to you, and you made no answer. It seemed so unlikely that an unmarried woman of your age and standing would refuse a man of my position, choosing a life of destitution and shame in its stead."

I shuffled back a step. "So, you kissed me just to test me."

His eyes flickered to mine, sending a message. No, there had been more to the kiss than just a test.

He sighed and continued. "When I met the man you claimed to be your brother, I noticed a scar on his cheek. As a child, I heard tales of the scar of King Nicholas as we played games of jousting and war. But I did not connect the scar to the king until the telling words we shared this day past. In a time of terror, you called your brother William 'Nick,' and he called you 'Emmie.' Short for Nicholas and Emmeline, of course."

My heart sank. So, those slip-ups hadn't been lost on Hugh. And he was evidently no fool.

He seemed to shrink into the sheets as his breaths became shorter. "I am at the door of death, mistress. So, I bid you to tell me: Why on God's green earth are you here? What plot could the king possibly have in mind that would make him dishonor his holy self and choose to perpetuate a claim of self-murder?"

I could've collapsed into the floor and slept for a hundred years. I was so utterly tired of holding everything in and hiding from the truth. I barely knew Hugh Wynter, yet I felt a burning need to confess everything to him: the time travel, the decision to give up this century for the modern world, the secret battle we were in with Mary Stuart. It wasn't like Nick and I were ever escaping the sixteenth century again. That bandit from the river was long gone with our enchanted ring.

But, once more, the Tudor throne had to come first.

"If I tell you why we're here," I said carefully, "I want you to tell me something too." Hugh raised his brows. "I know you have some involvement with the Queen of the Scots, Mary Stuart," I said. "I know she is planning a revolt and that you've promised to join her army and have been stockpiling weapons, which I believe are inside that locked chest of yours over there. I know that you are Number Seventy-Seven. And I want you to tell me everything you know about Mary Stuart's plot. How will she break out of Carlisle Castle? Where are her armies holed up? What other countries are involved, and where will they attack from? Tell me what you know, and then I'll tell you why the king and I are here."

His eyes were wide, his chapped lips parted. "How is it that you know of the plot of Queen Mary? You have been prying through my bedchamber!"

A rumble of laughter rose in my chest, but I suppressed it. If Hugh knew the extent of what Nick and I had knowledge of, and the things we'd seen, he would lose his mind.

"Tell me what you know, and I'll tell you why we're here," I repeated.

He dropped back into the pillow like his head was sore, his tongue tracing his dry lips. I held his cup of water to his mouth so he could drink. His fatigued eyes sank closed, and I tensed. What if he died here and now? But then he began speaking in a weakened voice.

"My true queen, Mary Stuart, has raised an army bigger than you can even believe. Every Papist across the realm is planning to take up arms in just a few weeks and join the queen's rebellion to restore the true religion in England. The French and the Spanish are gathering armies, and the Pope in Rome has issued a papal bull calling upon the followers of God's true word to dispose of the last heretic Tudor, the child Queen Catherine. I am merely one of these many hundreds of Papists, and that is all I know. I know not the particulars of where the other armies will strike from or where they lie in wait. All I know is that I cannot stand the Tudors, and I am as impatient as any to see Mary Stuart on the throne of England as its rightful queen." His dry throat clacked as he swallowed.

"How does she plan to break out of Carlisle Castle?" I asked him again. "Are the English nobles up there planning to storm the castle?"

He tittered a light laugh. "What makes you so sure to believe that Mary Stuart is in the high north? No, mistress; the Queen of the Scots is presently residing in Sheffield Castle, not fifty miles from here. If it had not been for the pestilence, I would have been granted a secret audience with Her Grace this week to learn more of the role of the Nottinghamshire army in her revolt. You would have done better to seek my counsel after that meeting, but for now, I have told you all I know."

Mary Stuart was in *Sheffield?* That was the very next county.

Hugh's woozy eyes focused on me. "So now it is your turn, my lady. Confess to me why our king and queen are hiding away like peasants in a lowly yeoman's cottage in Nottinghamshire…in a house of the pestilence, no less."

I rubbed the back of my neck. Why couldn't I just tell Hugh the truth? He'd most likely die within hours and—by all accounts—had been fearlessly honest with me. But of all the people I'd lied to that I loved, Hugh Wynter didn't even register on the scale.

"We never planned to come to this farm," I stammered, searching for words. "After I was sentenced to die at my trial, the king decided at the last minute to leave the throne rather than lose me. So we went on the run and have been hiding out ever since, looking for a quiet place where we can be together. I know it doesn't make a lot of sense, but it does to us."

Hugh's brow crumpled, his chuckle disbelieving. "You mean to convince me that the King of England forsook his crown, his country-men, and his God, for *you?*"

My jaw hardened, and I pulled back a little. He moved his pale hand closer to mine, and I sensed that he would have touched my skin if it had been safe.

"One more question, *Emmeline*," he said faintly. "You must know that Nicholas Tudor is as good as dead. That snake shall never return to the throne of England, and if he were to be discovered alive, he would be beheaded for his treachery before you could say 'Amen.' When I made an offer of courtship to you, my lady, I was well and with some means. I offered you a future. So, why did you forsake me? That man out there is not a king; he is a traitor to God and country; he is worth less than a devil; he has nothing!"

My chest heated and swelled to the point of bursting. "No. He still has me."

Hugh's expression steeled before he rolled to face away from me, a groan escaping his lips. When I asked if he was okay, he didn't respond.

I sat beside him for a while, pressing a wet compress to his forehead and keeping his lips hydrated with drops of water. Nick must've been panicking after I'd left him so abruptly at the window, but I couldn't abandon Hugh in this state. With each hour that passed, he grew more and more delirious, shouting random passages from the Bible, accusations of treason and heresy, and orders for strange foods like herons and minced salmon. A little while after sunrise, with the candle burning low by the bedside, Hugh begged me for the king that he'd just described as "worth less than a devil" to come and heal him with one touch.

"I'm sorry," I whispered. "I can't."

His cracked lips parted grotesquely, and he failed to take another breath.

My body was numb as I inched down the creaky stairwell with bile burning the back of my throat. The downstairs was silent and cold. Jasper had been sleeping late since this nightmare had begun, and I couldn't blame him.

Unless he's got the black plague too. Panic punched me in the gut. The thought of being the only person left alive in this forsaken house made me shake with terror.

"Jasper!" I called out, hastening into the kitchen that led to his bedchamber. So that was why it was so chilly in here—the back door was ajar. Voices were speaking outside in heated conversation. A second later, Nick pushed his way through the doorway, his aquamarine eyes flaming.

"My lady!" he said breathlessly, rushing in to hug me. "You vanished for a time too long—do you even know the state of my heart?"

"Don't touch me!" I cried, pushing him off me. He looked stunned. "I might have the pestilence; I've been tending to Hugh," I said, my voice breaking. I was so exhausted that I could barely stand.

"If you have the pestilence, then *I* have the pestilence," he said, closing the space between us again. His gaze leveled with me as he took my wrists. "I have had quite enough of this mischief, my lady. We are to take our leave of this place and without further ado."

"Jasper," I said, noticing him standing in the doorway. He looked frustrated with Nick but otherwise healthy, despite the red rings around his eyes. Thank goodness.

"What news of the master?" he asked me.

My brow crumpled. "I'm sorry," I said tightly. "He's gone." Nick's mouth fell open, and he rushed forward to cup the back of my neck. His fingers were like ice. "I feel no heat," he said, releasing a huge breath. "Do you feel well, even now?"

"I feel okay," I said, hoping I wasn't imagining things. While I was knackered enough to fall asleep standing up, I didn't feel sick or feverish.

"I shall inform the magistrate of the master's passing, and then we are to be rid of this house of horrors," Nick said. He asked Jasper to prepare the horses for riding, like the natural commander he was.

"Our wages," I blurted, remembering that we hadn't been paid yet. I'd spent everything I had on the doctor for Phoebe. "Jasper, do you know where Hugh keeps his coins?"

He shook his head.

We made a plan that Jasper and Nick would go and sort out the magistrate, and I would search for the wages that all of us were owed.

The chests and shelves in the downstairs hall turned up nothing, so I had no choice but to search Hugh's bedchamber. Keeping my eyes away from the shape that lay motionless on the bed, I rummaged through his desk. Seizing the opportunity to learn anything else I could about Mary Stuart, I grabbed every document and map I could find and stuffed as many as would fit inside my bodice. But there was no sign of any coins.

I swore under my breath. The last thing I wanted was to stay inside this house of bad memories, but without any money to travel with, Nick and I were back where we started.

Then, it hit me. I dashed downstairs to the cupboard housing the silver spoons and saltshaker and collected them inside the pouch of my apron. Thank goodness Jasper wasn't here to witness me looting the home of a dead man.

Sunlight warmed my face and hands as I sat on the back step, waiting for them to return. After what felt like hours, the geese clucked and scattered as two horses trotted up the dirt path, and my cheeks lifted into a relieved smile. Nick could've taken any horse of Hugh's, but his strong legs were cradling our crazy Ophelia.

He reached his hand out and hauled me upward onto her sturdy back. I clasped his waist from behind, breathing in his soothing, leathery scent. He reached around to squeeze my thigh, sending a rush of warmth to my chest.

The darkness of dread sank over me as my mind traveled back upstairs to the night before the pestilence had arrived. After everything Nick and I had been through, I'd let Hugh kiss me. All I wanted was for the throbbing truth of that to sink to the bottom of the ocean, but it kept surging back to the surface, ready to slam me in the gut.

I pulled out the silver spoons and saltshaker and showed them to Nick in an effort to divert my mind. "All I could get were these," I said. He just leaned into me like he'd missed me, the curls growing around his neck tickling my cheek. I resisted the urge to sweep his hair to the side and press my lips to his warm skin.

Jasper was fighting to steady his overzealous horse beside us. "May I ride with thee into the town?" he asked, blushing shyly.

"Of course," I said. "Jasper, how old are you?"

"I am thirteen, mistress."

"*Thirteen?* But you're…"

"Tall for my years," he said with a sheepish smile. Jasper wasn't much more than a child, but he had a maturity beyond his age, and years of physical labor had grown muscles on his young body.

"You're coming with us," I said firmly, so Nick would know not to argue. "At least until we can get you on the road back home to your family."

"I have no kin, mistress," he said matter-of-factly. "My kin were all lost to the pestilence. Mister Wynter found me in a home for the destitute two winters past and kindly offered me work and shelter."

Nick tensed in front of me. If Jasper rode on with us, it would be hard to hide our true selves and talk openly about Mary Stuart and our plans to assassinate her. I also hadn't had a chance to tell Nick yet that Mary was much closer than we thought. But I couldn't leave Jasper alone when he wanted to stay with us, so we'd have to figure things out later.

Together, our horses rode toward the crumbling castle on the hill overlooking the walled township of Nottingham. I rested my head against Nick's back, comforted by his warmth and the gentle rocking. Every time Ophelia jerked, kicking up dust, the documents I'd shoved inside my bodice crinkled.

We were lucky that Hugh lived so close to the town, and within twenty minutes, our horses trotted through the gatehouse and into the main lane of Nottingham. After dodging bundles of firewood and the contents of a chamber pot that had been emptied from a window, Nick slowed Ophelia outside a sign colorfully painted with the words *The Bell Inn*. He smoothly dismounted before helping me off her back and onto the dirt path.

He handed me her reins and disappeared through the inn's gate-house with Hugh's silverware in his pocket. I hadn't missed the rotten-egg stench and mangy dogs of the Tudor towns, but finally being free of Hugh Wynter's farm made me weak with relief.

Nick re-emerged from the shadows, his scruff of facial hair bleached blond by the sunlight.

"Come; we have two chambers and dinner at the ready," he said, taking Ophelia's reins from me and tossing them to a stable boy. I hadn't realized how much I'd missed him taking control of things I knew little about. In my world, it had been the opposite: I was the commander and Nick the follower.

Jasper thanked us repeatedly, especially for his private room, which was a luxury in this time period. Renting two rooms cost us more silver, but Nick's game plan was evident: If we had our privacy, we could talk freely about our next steps. Mary Stuart's invasion was now less than two weeks away.

After devouring two bowls each of pottage loaded with bacon chunks, lentils, and leeks, Jasper bid us goodnight, even though it was only midday. The events of the past few days had turned the three of us into ninety-year-old zombies. We agreed to meet back downstairs at first light.

The room that Nick and I shared was small but clean, and I could've kissed the fireplace.

I ached for a hot shower, but I had to make do with a bucket of cold water and a stained linen cloth that had been placed outside our door. At least that was better than a swim in a stream infested with sewage where strange men thought they had the right to cut your dress open and squeeze the softest parts of your body. I shook the repulsive memory away.

Nick used the tinder box to light the fire, and I hung the water bucket over the iron frame so we could wash without freezing to death. He sat on the bed behind me as I untied my apron, my breath becoming shallow. We were technically married and had more than consummated our union. So why did it feel so strange and dizzying to undress in front of him? I considered suggesting that we leave each other alone while we wash, but the corridor was damp and tight, and we were a couple, so why make this weird?

Because you haven't been naked in front of him for more than a year.

Nick quietly cleared his throat as I unlaced the bodice of my kirtle, the rolled-up maps and pages of parchment falling into my hands in a crumpled heap.

"Good God, what is all that?" he said behind me.

"Papers from Hugh's desk," I replied, dropping the pile onto the chest. "I grabbed them before we left, but I have no idea what they are. I thought maybe there'd be something in there about Mary Stuart. Have a look if you like."

He didn't move from the bed as I tugged my kirtle down to my knees and stepped out of it. Leaving my linen smock and tights on for now, I dipped the cloth into the steaming water and wrung it out. Hot water trickled down my arm as I wiped the cloth down my face, melting into its warmth.

"Gosh, that feels good," I said, sweeping the cloth across my neck and down my forearms. Nick didn't speak, but I felt his eyes on me as I peeled my tights off my aching legs. I rubbed the damp cloth down my skin, wiping the dirt and memories of Hugh Wynter's farm away. Feeling Nick's steady gaze from behind made me tremble and scramble for something to say.

"I still need to tell you what Hugh said about Mary Stuart," I said with my back to him, dipping the towel back into the water and twisting it. "Just before he passed away, I confronted him about it."

Nick sat forward, creaking the bed. "You did?" he said urgently. "Go on."

"We were right. Mary Stuart is raising an army of secret Catholics across England. The French and Spanish are getting ready to strike, and the Pope in Rome is also involved. He's written to Catholic priests across the country to take up arms against Queen Catherine. Hugh said he didn't know where the other armies will attack from, but together, they're all going to invade England. Presumably with the help of some of her co-conspirators, Hugh was going to have a secret meeting with Mary Stuart this week to learn more details about the revolt, but then he fell sick."

Nick made a grave, angry exhale. "That woman is unworthy of a kingdom. This country will never be free as long as she lives."

I tugged the linen smock up over my head, cool air sprinkling goosebumps across my skin. With my body bare down to the underwear I'd made from a coif, I swept the wet cloth over my chest and around my stomach. The air had become sticky and warm, and Nick's breathing had changed. I wanted to turn around and expose myself to him, to bring my bare breasts into his view to see what he would do with that sight, but I was almost faint with nerves.

"What we didn't know is that Mary Stuart isn't in Carlisle Castle at all," I continued through a quiver. "Hugh said she is less than fifty miles from here, in Sheffield Castle." Nick gasped.

I sucked in a brave inhale and turned to face him, holding the damp washcloth across my chest, covering my breasts. "I think we should go back to your plan to assassinate Mary," I said. "If she's so close to here, then we still have time."

Nick averted his eyes from me and moved to the chest, sifting through the pile of papers and maps. "Do we have proof that Mary Stuart is in Sheffield Castle?" he said, his voice sounding thick. "It could be a plot."

"Not yet." I toyed with telling him now or later that Hugh Wynter had also figured out our true identities. That wasn't going to go down well with my paranoid Tudor king.

"This is an inventory of the household," he said, swapping one page of parchment for another. "This appears to be some manner of plan for a new bakehouse. And this is a map of the farmlands of Nottinghamshire."

"I just grabbed everything on his desk," I reminded him, slipping my smock back over my head. Disappointment slid into my chest, piercing it. I'd been half naked in front of Nick, and he'd turned away.

With my heart splintering, I watched him speed-read another page. "Oh, good God."

"What?" My face paled.

"This is a letter by the hand of Mister Wynter. It seeks advice for a delicate matter involving a servant girl. In the letter, Mister Wynter says he believes the servant girl to be with child...with *his* child. He seeks a doctor who can make an arrangement. The letter is dated two weeks past."

My fingers flew to my mouth. "Phoebe was pregnant! Are you saying that Hugh was the father?"

"It appears to be so," he replied somberly. "It brings me no pleasure to say that Phoebe was fortunate to lose that child. I have known of men to commit murder against their maidservants who are with child rather than be accused of rape."

"Oh my God," I said faintly, resting on the edge of the bed. I'd suspected Jasper to be the young father of Phoebe's baby, but it'd been Hugh Wynter all along. He'd put the moves on her like he had me. It was probably why he'd caught the pestilence from Phoebe while Jasper and I hadn't. "I don't think he raped her," I said, remembering Phoebe's fawning crush and Hugh's smooth words. "He seduced her."

Nick made a small grunt. "As you well know, I had concerns about the yeoman's manner toward the maidservants. I regret not to say that I am relieved that lecher of a man turned to Phoebe rather than you."

The words floated out of my mouth like air. I just couldn't keep them in anymore.

"He kissed me."

At first, Nick paused, like he hadn't heard right. Then all the color in his cheeks died away. "Come again?"

I could taste my thumping heart. "When I was with Hugh in his bedchamber—before the pestilence arrived—he kissed me."

Nick's eyes clouded like he was confused before he barked a strange laugh. "You made a jest about this before."

My voice was a faint line. "I'm not joking this time."

Two lines deepened in his brow. "He *attacked* you?"

"No. He was…attracted to me. He asked if he could 'pursue' me, and of course, he didn't know that you and I were a couple."

Nick got up and paced toward the fire, his back to me. A torturous silence stretched out between us before he finally spoke, his voice not his own. "And how did you feel about him? Did you…did you intend to have a dalliance with him? Had the pestilence not arrived?"

"No!" I said. "I didn't feel anything for him."

He turned to face me, his features pulled tight as he asked the one question I'd been dreading more than any other. "Did you kiss him in return?"

My breath lodged in my throat, my lips too dry to form a reply.

My fingers in Hugh's curls…him naked under a towel…strawberries.

Nick's brow creased, and he fell into the chest like he could no longer stand. "Oh my God."

"Nothing happened," I said, my voice wobbling. "Hugh said he wanted to pursue me, and then he kissed me out of the blue, and I pulled away. That's all."

Nick sighed heavily and looked up at me, the candlelight turning his beautiful features into a stunning but sorrowful painting. His fingers were quivering. "Emmie, I can tell by your face that there is more to this. Do not lie to me."

"There isn't!" My tears finally burst free, spilling onto the wool blanket.

"No, there is." Nick shook his head before slumping forward. "I have felt it," he said, choking on the words. "I knew that man meant to come between us."

I couldn't think of what to say. Nick knew me. He knew that I'd kissed Hugh Wynter back, even if it was for a few seconds. Nick Tudor was the one person I'd never been able to hide from.

"I love *you*," I said, my voice breaking open. "I feel nothing for Hugh Wynter."

He sighed bleakly. "But not the way I love you."

"That's not true!"

His cheeks were ablaze as his face flashed back up. "I would never even dream of letting a maiden close enough to kiss me for fear of what it would do to your heart. Do you have any idea how this makes me feel? You and I are more than a common couple, Emmie. All our troubles…everything we have given up to be sure we are never parted." He pressed a hand to his heart, his face tightening with pain. "This breaks me."

A bark of mirthless laughter burst from my throat. "Are you kidding me? Nick, I *saw* you kiss another woman once. Lucinda Parker at the masquerade ball, or have you conveniently forgotten about that? That didn't exactly feel like Christmas to me either."

He shook the memory away with a flick of his hand. "I swore on my life to you that was a chaste kiss as a gesture of gratitude for the help I offered Mistress Parker's child."

"A child that might be yours," I reminded him.

He lurched to his feet. "I swore it to you then, and I will swear it to you now on mine own life: *That* kiss was chaste. Can you do the same?" He crossed his broad arms, his face so torn up that I could barely look at it. "As you say you love me, Emmie, you will speak only the truth. Did you kiss that man in return? Mister Wynter?"

Fresh tears swelled in my heartbroken eyes. "Only for a moment."

He just stood there nodding, blinking fast, before turning away from me. He dug his fingers into his chestnut curls, his breaths coming out short. How could I have ever even considered kissing another man? Nothing had changed in years of life-and-death danger…Nick Tudor still owned every beat of my heart.

I scooched onto my knees, my eyes dribbling tears. "You said to do whatever it is I must!" I said defensively. "You wanted me to get information out of Hugh at any cost."

His brows flung upward. "You believe that I intended for you to enter into an affair of the heart with that man? An affair of the flesh?" He smacked his fist into Hugh's papers, sending them flying.

"How can you even think that of me? After all we have been through!"

"You haven't so much as kissed me—not with any passion—for a *year*," I argued, my anger over that fact raging to the surface. "You have no idea how much I have missed that…missed you!"

Don't you have any idea how much I fucking miss you! I wanted to shout. *Touching me, wanting me, loving me.*

He leaned into my vision, his eyes filled with shock. "You doubt me? That is why you have forsaken me?"

My voice was as tight as a fist. "You haven't acted like you love me for a long time. Not in that way."

He gestured around the room like I was insane. "What in God's name do you call all this? I am here with you, living like a peasant, without my throne or my family. I betrayed God for you, Emmie—I could not be more devoted!"

"Nick, you have not been happy since the day we left the Tower of London, and you know it." His stunned face blurred through my tears. "In my world, you seemed so…*lost*," I said. "You hung out in that tiny garden all day; you didn't want to meet anyone or get to know the place. You hardly ever smiled. And you never wanted to touch me."

A sheen of tears coated his seawater eyes, and he sank back onto the chest.

When he spoke, his voice sounded ripped in two. "I know that I have not done well by you. You must understand, I was born a prince…I became a king when I was twelve years old. I know naught of your world. I know naught of how to provide for you there."

"And that's why you haven't touched me in a year?" I said with a bewildered shake of my head. "Because you can't *provide* for me?"

"No," he said like I wasn't getting it. "Emmie, I made love to you when we were wedded in the eyes of God and living in my kingdom. If we were to be blessed with a child then, I would have given our son or daughter not only a most tender love, but lands and titles. Until I am able to provide for you, how am I to lie with you? If you become with child, I will have naught to offer you both."

I sat and gaped at him, gobsmacked. "You haven't come near me because you don't want me to get pregnant?"

He pressed his lips together. "You know not how difficult it has been for me to control myself around you. At times, I have felt I could not bear the torture of it. This past year, I have touched you again and again in my dreams, Emmie, only to wake and find myself in this unbearable agony."

I sat higher on the bed, trying to meet his gaze, but he wouldn't look at me. His face had turned dazed and tight, like he was seeing something that wasn't there. The look in his eyes had me worried that he was visualizing the kiss between me and Hugh, but I didn't dare ask.

And why on earth hadn't he just told me the reason why he'd been avoiding my touch?

But one look at Nick's hunched shoulders, his strained brow, his wearied gaze, and the truth crystallized. As a man born and raised in the sixteenth century, he was deeply ashamed that he hadn't found a way to look after me the way he had when he'd sat on the throne. It was another sharp difference in our two mindsets.

"I don't need you to provide for me," I said shakily. "I keep telling you this, and I need you understand it or its going to ruin us. I don't want *things* from you. All I want from you is *you*. And don't say you have naught to offer me. What you give me is love—that's *everything*." My voice was throttled. "But you have to be happy, too, Nick. No matter which world we live in...you have to trust in us."

He just threw me a look that I one hundred percent deserved. I shrank into my shame. How could I ask him for trust after what I'd just confessed about Hugh Wynter?

I wanted so badly to touch him, but I gave him space, letting him sit with his crushed gaze pinned to the floor. When I couldn't hold back anymore and shifted near him, he got up and reached for his boots.

"What are you doing?" I said, wiping my cheeks, which was a pointless exercise. My tears refused to stop falling.

"I shall return by morning."

I sat forward. "The *morning?* What do you mean? Where are you going? You can't leave me here all alone!"

The pull of his laces being tied was his only response.

"You're seriously leaving me here without any explanation?" I said, my voice turning accusing. "Where are you planning on going all day and night? Where will you sleep?"

When he grabbed his hat without answering, I smacked my head onto the pillow. "Fine. You want to punish me for Hugh Wynter? Go ahead. It's not like you and I haven't been through enough shit!"

He stood in the low archway of the door, his voice as desolate as his face. "Be sure to latch the door behind me. And make certain to listen for my knock upon my return. I bid you goodnight, Emmeline."

The door closed hard behind him. I buried my face into the sheets, sharpened blades spearing my heart until it was full of holes as I wept.

15

I was in a fog of exhaustion and fury when Nick and I met Jasper in the shadowy corridor just after sunrise. Nick had arrived back at our room only an hour earlier, bringing the sooty stench of heavy smoke and red rings around his eyes. Where the heck had he been the entire afternoon and night? I knew he had every reason to be mad at me, but I still glared at him.

"Anne and I shall be riding on to Yorkshire this day," Nick said to Jasper without even consulting me. "We have matters to attend to in Sheffield."

"I know the place," Jasper said as we padded, single file, down the narrow staircase leading to the downstairs hall. "A cousin of mine is a cutler there. He is famed for his skill at making knives."

Nick and I shared a glance. If we were still planning to assassinate Mary Stuart at Sheffield Castle, we'd need a good knife.

Were we still planning to assassinate Mary together? At this point, Nick didn't seem to want to be anywhere near me.

Baskets of bread and tankards of watered-down ale were waiting on the trestle tables for early-bird guests like us. We sat and chewed the coarse bread in groggy silence, my eyes, swollen from crying, drifting to Nick across the table. How was he even functioning after being out all night? Why were tufts of his hair blackened with smoke? Where had he been, and who had he been with? Had he been with one of the multiple girls that I'd noticed giving him a flirtatious glance on the streets of Tudor England? My heart made an aching twist.

"Will you tell us where we may find your cousin in Sheffield?" Nick asked Jasper. "I should like to make his acquaintance."

Jasper's face brightened. "I shall come with thee and take thee to his person, if thou agrees to it." The poor kid was desperate for company. Surprisingly, Nick looked at me for approval.

"Of course," I said, placing a hand on Jasper's forearm. "That would be great; thank you." I felt Nick's eyes cling to me, but I kept my gaze lowered.

In exchange for the expensive saltshaker that Nick had used to pay for our rooms, I convinced the innkeeper to let us take a basket of grainy bread rolls with us, and an old leather pouch for water. Whether Nick still wanted to be with me or not, we had to stay focused and not lose sight of why we'd come here in the first place.

While Jasper wandered outside in search of a well for water, Nick and I assessed our belongings over the hall table. We had two silver spoons left, a wooden comb, a couple of toothpicks, a linen cloth, a tinderbox that he'd pinched from the room upstairs, a few spare clothes, and a bedsheet to hold everything in.

"Where were you last night?" I asked under my breath before Jasper could return.

He took a moment to answer, his eyes glued to the sheet he was tying. "I made my return to the farm."

"Hugh Wynter's farm?" My brow pinched. "Why would you go back there?"

His voice was as hard as slate. "I burned it to the ground."

I sucked in air. "You did what?"

"That place was infested with the pestilence." He slung the knotted sheet of belongings over his shoulder and strode out of the hall, his jaw set.

I chased him into the sunlit stables where a yawning boy was resaddling our horses. "But it's up to the local magistrates to decide what to do with that house," I said. "Why would you do that?"

His lack of reply nearly made me boil over. What about Hugh's animals? What if Nick had been caught? Arson was as much a crime in this century as it was in my own. What if he'd set fire to himself while torching a house made almost entirely of scraps of wood?

"You could have killed yourself," I said through my teeth. "Or been arrested. You still might be if they come after you! What if someone saw you?"

He roughly tied our bundled-up sheet to Ophelia's saddle, his lips pressed tightly together.

"That was beyond reckless," I said. "And it wasn't your property to burn down."

"No, I suppose it was not," he said, twisting to meet my gaze. "Yet that man saw no reason not to burn my house to the ground."

We stood there blinking at each other, his face as tormented as mine.

Jasper bounded through the archway from the street, holding up the ballooning water pouch with a grin. Was Nick planning to tell him that he'd reduced his master's house to a pile of ashes in the dead of the night?

We mounted our horses, and I loosely held Nick's waist from behind, my mouth turned down, still grappling with what he'd done. At that moment, I would've given anything to be strolling into my morning class at Central Saint Martins, a takeout coffee in hand, instead of bracing for a butt covered in bruises from riding, followed by a life-threatening plot to murder a queen. Nick burning down Hugh Wynter's house paled in comparison to what lay ahead of us. If our plan to assassinate Mary Stuart went as we intended, how would I live with myself, knowing I'd had a hand in someone's death? I pushed the unhelpful thought away, reminding myself that this wasn't the modern world, and we were engaged in a battle to the death, like it or not. I also had to appreciate the fact that Mary Stuart wasn't in Carlisle in the high north after all; had she not been as close as she was, our chances of stopping her attack would have been finished.

The distance to Sheffield Castle was probably no more than thirty minutes as the crow flies, but on horseback, through dense pockets of forestland and winding rivers with few bridges, the journey took the entire day. For someone who hadn't slept for more than an hour, Nick powered through the ride with fearless strength.

The shroud of nightfall edged closer as the turrets of Sheffield Castle emerged in the distance, stealing my breath and my confidence in one fell swoop.

Mary Stuart is inside those walls, ready to kill or be killed.

I was reluctant to let go of the last pieces of our silver when we needed them to buy food and a knife, so Nick suggested we make a fire and camp the night outside the town walls. Now that I'd seen the castle's steep battlement towers, formidable stone walls, and wide moat with a menacing drawbridge, I was lost as to how we could ever get close enough to the imprisoned queen to plunge a knife into her heart.

We slowed our horses inside a grass clearing, close to the castle wall, that was flanked by thick trees on all sides—the perfect hideout. Nick kept glancing up at the castle turrets peeking over the treetops, nervously fingering his hair. Everything that had happened in the past few weeks—the black plague, the loss of Phoebe and Hugh, telling Nick about the kiss and feeling the distance between us multiply immeasurably—had been a distraction.

This was it. This was our chance to put an end to Mary Stuart's monstrous plans, protect the lives of the people we loved, and save the Tudor throne.

"Jasper, do you think you could help find some firewood while I set up a camp?" I asked, pointing through the trees. "That stuff over there looks dry."

"Most certainly, mistress," he said obediently, scaling a log and cracking his way through shrubs.

When his dark ponytail disappeared, I drew close to Nick.

"How are we going to do this?" I said quietly, my stomach flipping like pancakes. "How on earth are we going to get inside that fortress of a castle?" Now that we were here, it felt like a suicide mission.

"Hugh Wynter," he replied, his teeth clenching at the name. "We know that Mister Wynter was set to meet with the Queen of the Scots this very week. We also know that he is Number Seventy-Seven. On the morrow, I will approach the castle and present myself as Mister

Wynter, sent by a Mister Holborne—the priest you spoke of. Should the name fail to draw out the queen, I shall pass on a message that I am Number Seventy-Seven." His brows drew together. "The trouble we face is how to acquire a good knife before then. I may need to ride with Jasper this very night to meet with his cousin, the cutler."

My breath was shallow. "But you can't be the one to meet Mary; you're the former king! There's no way you can just turn up at the castle and show your face." Bile rose into my throat, but I pushed it back down. "I will go to the castle. You can give me the knife."

"Emmie, there is no choice to be made," he said without looking at me. "Not by any means can your person make the pretense of being a yeoman by the name of Mister Wynter."

"Then we'll go together," I said. "You'll be Mister Wynter, and I'll be your companion."

Before he could respond, Jasper tramped through the bush, hugging a pile of firewood. He dumped the logs onto the dirt before Nick gestured to our restless horse.

"Would it trouble you to ride to the town with us before the curfew?" he said to Jasper. "I should like to purchase a slab of meat for the fire and a knife from your good cousin to cut it with."

Jasper frowned at the dimming sky but nodded, forever the people-pleaser. Nick assumed I'd join them, but I insisted I'd wait at the camp. They'd be an hour at best, and my butt was burning from the long day of riding. The scars of the river bandit lingered closely, but I didn't want to become incapable of being alone. Plus, I needed time to work myself up to the confrontation with Mary Stuart. If there was an opportunity to kill her, I couldn't fall apart. I had to stay tough in this unforgiving world.

"I'll be fine," I reassured Nick's wary eyes.

They left before the sun could set, and I kicked away sticks and leaves to make space for the fire. With the flint, steel, and tinder, I lit a spark and blew on the flame until it flared healthily. Feeling pretty proud of myself, I sat on a log and toasted a chunk of bread over the crackling fire until Nick and Jasper returned with two plucked chickens and a double-edged dagger.

"The best we could do," Nick said, flopping the pink, rubbery chickens onto a rock.

We strung them onto the long dagger, and Nick turned it over the flames like a spit, the stillness of nightfall sending the three of us into fits of yawns. Nick and I still needed to discuss when we would approach the castle, but Jasper stayed within earshot. That conversation—and my anxious stomach—would have to wait until morning.

There was a flat stone right beside me, but Nick chewed his dinner on the opposite side of the smoldering fire, his brow set with lines that had been glued there since I'd told him about the kiss.

The long curls of hair that clung to his neck and the scruffy bristles on his jaw had disguised him as a different person, but all I saw was the man that I physically ached to be close to. The fire kept my body warm, but a block of ice grew where my heart had been.

When he couldn't keep his eyes open any longer, he stretched out on the ground far away from me, cementing the space between us and leaving a black hole in my chest. It was devastating, having him choose to keep such a distance, but I was so drained of energy that I lay down where I was, pulled my cloak over me, and slept through the night.

The sky blushed early at this time of year, and when my eyes drifted open, Nick's patch of earth was empty. Jasper was sitting up, nibbling on a leftover chicken wing.

"Where is my brother?" I asked him.

"The fellow rode out early," he said, tossing the wing bones into the fire.

I scrambled to my feet, breaking into a cold sweat. "Did he say where he was going?" Jasper shook his head. The castle turrets loomed threateningly in the overcast sky.

He went to the castle without me.

Once the images appeared, I could see nothing else.

Guards brandishing thick swords, dragging Nick away by his shoulders.

A nobleman, recognizing Nick and exposing him as the treasonous king.

My beautiful Nick, resting his neck on an executioner's bloodstained block.

"Who goes there?" Jasper's tense voice cut through my dark imaginings. He took a shaky step toward the cracks in the bushes. "God's teeth, it is thee, Goodman Shakespeare," he said with a heavy exhale.

Nick stepped through the tangle of vines, and my legs buckled with relief.

"She is not there," he said, his distressed eyes on mine. "The information you had is false."

"What?" I said, moving closer to him. "Are you sure? Maybe the guards just didn't tell you—of course they'd want to keep her presence a secret."

Jasper's confused gaze darted between us like he was watching a tennis match.

Nick flung the dagger into the dirt at his feet. "I paid the guard with the leather jerkin off my back to make certain of the knowledge, and I have known enough dimwitted guards to know when they speak the truth. The man said the person we seek had been at the castle this month last but has since escaped and was last seen on the roads to Scotland."

"What person dost thou speak of?" Jasper said tentatively. "May I be of any help?"

My hand pressed my swirling stomach. I was so sick of this feeling, this panic-stricken loss of control. "There was just someone we wanted to visit in the castle," I mumbled to Jasper. My vague reply didn't soften the lines on his confused brow, but I didn't have the energy to make any further explanation.

She is not there.

We were too late. Mary Stuart had escaped the clutches of the English at Sheffield Castle, was probably halfway to a safe haven in Scotland, and would invade England in just over a week. She would likely strike from the north, and the French and Spanish would come from the east and the south. Her plan was coming into effect, right before our eyes.

I gnashed my teeth, fighting the urge to fling every swear word I knew at the gloomy sky. We'd come so close, but we'd lost…wasted too much time at Hugh Wynter's farm, where I'd let that lecher kiss me and break the fragile bond I'd had with Nick. All for nothing.

Nick slumped onto a rock and breathed heavily at his muddied boots. A dense silence weighed down the air, and Jasper shuffled on his feet, visibly uncomfortable at the sharp change in mood.

He grabbed his woolen cap. "Thy company hast been a kindness to me, my goodsir and my goodwoman," he said. "But I feel it is time for us to part. Thou have some important business, and I shall only be in thy way."

"You're heading off?" I said, stepping closer to him.

"I should begin to make my way south before the onset of the harvest season." He pointed to the hole in his ear, his cheeks pink. "'Tis not easy for me to find work with this, mistress, so I must take my time."

"I'll miss you," I said, touching his sleeve. His face flushed hot before he pulled me into a short but heartfelt hug. When we parted, his smile was slightly woozy. When Jasper Blacke grew up, he was going to make someone feel very lucky.

A defeated-looking Nick rose to shake Jasper's hand. I dug into our sheet and held out our last silver spoon, offering it to Jasper. Nick didn't try to stop me; in fact, when Jasper protested, he encouraged him to take it. The boy pressed his hat to his chest with gratitude before leaving us with a sad smile, a thickness forming in my throat.

I sank onto a rock and cupped my chin, my head a deadweight. Back to the burning reality: Mary Stuart had already escaped Sheffield Castle, and Nick and I were done for.

My mind was still scrambling desperately for ideas. "What about if we send an anonymous letter to Kit, letting her know about the threat?" I said. "Maybe that's what we should have done all along."

"Such a letter would be read by the Earl of Warwick before it ever reached the queen," Nick said, staring into the remnants of the fire.

"And we can't trust Francis," I remembered with a sinking feeling. "Wherever Mary Stuart is, maybe she's already with the Earl of Warwick, plotting their romantic overthrow of the throne. Yay for them."

Silence consumed the air.

"I guess it's over, then," I said in a thin voice.

Nick played with a stick, his shoulders as stiff as his tone. "So where does this leave us, Emmie?"

A cool wind stroked the back of my neck. "What do you mean, 'Where does this leave us?'"

He wouldn't look at me. "I know not how to get past this. In truth, I am not sure that I can."

A terrible feeling of dread crawled into my stomach. "Are we still talking about Mary Stuart?"

He puffed a long, weary sigh before sitting on the rock opposite me, his face struck with heartache. "Every time I close mine eyes, I imagine the events of that kiss."

The pain in his eyes crushed me, and I had to look away. "I'm so sorry that I hurt you," I said, blinking through the burning pressure of tears.

He rose again, pacing restlessly. "I know you feel that you and I have grown apart since the events of a year past, but the truth is, Emmie, that I feel the opposite. Since the day I met you, at every moment, I have felt close to you. Like I might turn, and you would be standing there, even when you were not. Your hold over my heart knows no end." His voice cracked. "And now my heart is greatly sore. I am sore of heart that I am not a calm and reasonable man. I am sore of heart that I have been unable to make you happy. I am sore of heart that I had to follow you out of this world and into one where I am of no use and unable to provide for you the way I should. And I am filled with devastation knowing that you are trapped in this barbaric place again without a hope because of me. How could I have willingly pursued such a life for you?" A rush of color filled his face. "And then I remember that *you* found *me*, my lady. Before we met, I was a king as good as betrothed to the princess of France. And then you appeared in my garden, too suddenly for me to hide. Like a bolt of lightning. Tell me—how does one outrun a bolt of lightning?"

I stood up, every part of me trembling. "I don't ever want you to run away from me."

I paced toward him, my chest hot with love, but all I saw in his face was hesitation and mistrust that had never been there before.

I know not how to get past this. In truth, I am not sure that I can.

When I turned away with a sting in my heart, he clutched my

hand to stop me. "Emmie, I know that I handled it poorly. Forgive me."

"Handled what poorly?"

His cheeks were flushed. "The kiss you shared with Mister Wynter. If I am honest, I could have killed that man with my bare hands if he were not already dead. But burning his house to the ground was not the right response either."

The kiss still tasted sour in my mouth. "It's okay. It's not like there's a good response for something like that."

His eyes held mine, liquid green and clouded with emotion. "No, there is indeed something else that I should have done."

I inhaled, preparing myself. "And what's that?"

His warm hand reached for the back of my neck and tugged me forward. I gasped as his mouth caught mine and held on, his soft lips bleeding into my own. My knees gave way, and time and place disappeared as Nick cupped my cheeks and held me up with his lips on mine. There was no danger anymore—no fear—just the sweet, heavenly warmth of Nick Tudor's mouth as it devoured mine like it was the first time we'd ever kissed. *Oh my God…* His tongue nestled into my mouth like it belonged there, and I melted into his sweet sighs, my lips and my body responding to his with a deep, urgent need. I pressed my hands to the back of his neck and held him tightly against me so he wouldn't leave. Now that our mouths were fused like this again, I couldn't bear to be anywhere else; I couldn't endure a return to that world in which I wasn't allowed to kiss him, to taste him, to love him the way my heart begged to. But nothing about Nick's actions suggested he wanted this to end any more than I did. He wrapped his arms around my back and squeezed as he kissed and kissed and kissed me like he'd been drowning and finally found air.

With our tongues twisting through our ragged breaths, he slid his hands down my lower back and I groaned, pressing my hips hard against his. He pushed his thigh between my legs and stepped between them, his rock-hard ridge burrowing against me through our clothes. When I lowered my hand and gripped his length over his trousers before running my palm up and down it, he moaned a sound into my mouth that just about undid me.

A noise cut through the trees, and we broke apart, panting heavily.

"Do you hear something?" Nick said without letting go of me.

"If someone finds us here, this could look pretty dodgy," I said, my lips tingling and my voice breathless. "A man and a woman hiding out near the castle? Talk about suspicious."

"We should ride to the village," he agreed, his hands still cupping my face, his eyes glazed-over as they stared into mine.

God. I needed so much more of him. But we reluctantly separated, and I hurriedly kicked dirt over the fire while Nick tied our belongings and the dagger to Ophelia's side. I gripped a leather strap to mount her, still reeling from that mind-blowing kiss, when the bushes behind me cracked and snapped. Before I could turn around, hard fingers dug into my shoulders.

"Nick!" I screamed as the world turned black.

I clawed at the fabric hood covering my face before I was yanked backward through thorny bushes and tree branches that whipped my skin. Nick was shouting my name from a few feet away.

"Let me go!" I cried, thrashing and flailing my limbs in an effort to break free of the hands that tugged me, but they were too strong.

Nick was also going crazy nearby, but his shouts were a comfort. Wherever I was being taken, so was he.

The pulling and dragging finally stopped, and then I was violently yanked upward into a confined space that smelled like leather and dried flowers. A heavy body half fell on top of me.

"Emmie?" Nick said frantically into my face before he was heaved off me. A distant voice made a "Hah!" sound, and the floor beneath my boots rumbled and shook.

It clicked: *We're inside a coach.*

I'd spent enough time in Tudor England to know that captives weren't usually transported in coaches, which were a luxury reserved for the exceptionally wealthy. I felt for the velvet seat before someone smacked my hand away.

"Be still," said a gruff voice.

"Touch her not!" Nick barked from the opposite bench, and I sensed him kicking, but he must've been pinned down like me.

Shivering with fear, I tried to note the changes in direction so I could map our route in my mind, but with my head covered, I was too disoriented. We'd been moving only for about ten minutes when the coach made a sudden lurch before it stopped. We were still very close to the town of Sheffield.

A moment later, I heard the coach door fling open and a man's voice from below say, "Follow me."

My captor roughly pulled me down the steps and onto smooth stones—the sort of structured ground that also meant money. I sensed Nick's presence ahead of me as we were led into a building that felt slick beneath my boots, like the floors were tiled. After a left turn followed by a right, I was jerked to a halt.

"Enough of this," Nick spat beside me, his voice muffled by his hood. "Show yourself and make your complaint, or I make no promise for your safety. I assure you that I am in no mood for mischief."

"He is noble," said a young, high-pitched voice. "I can tell by his manner of speech." After a pause of sharp silence, she spoke again. "You may remove the hoods."

A moment later, the stifling fabric was tugged off my head, flooding my eyes with intense light and blowing cold air onto my cheeks. Sunlight streamed through giant stained-glass windows behind a small shape standing in silhouette several feet away. I held a hand to my brow, tapestries and armor on the walls taking shape in my vision. We were in some sort of Great Hall, but one too small to be within a palace; this was more like a manor.

The petite figure took a step closer as my eyes adjusted to the light, and the blood drained from my face in a rush.

"Dear God," Nick breathed.

Before us stood the Queen of England, Nick's little sister, Kit.

16

Nick sank into a bow beside me, and I mirrored the action, my heart belting in my ears.

Kit knows we're alive, Kit knows we're alive, Kit knows we're alive.

She paced forward, a Renaissance painting in her cone-shaped gown of apple-green satin encased with a linen-colored waistcoat. She was a year older since I'd last seen her, but a decade more mature in her expression and stature. She stopped at Nick, standing on her toes as her sky-blue eyes inspected his face. His gaze stayed fixed to a carved fireplace lining the back wall, his shoulders rigid.

"This man is not my brother," she said in an even voice that betrayed her age. I tried to maintain my poker face, but it was hard. Even with Nick's facial scruff, longish hair, grimy skin, and homeless-guy outfit, surely Kit would recognize her own brother. Especially when he was standing beside me—another face that Kit was more than familiar with.

Her eyes flashed past mine before returning to Nick.

"Are you quite certain, Your Majesty?" said the same man's voice that I'd heard outside the coach. The Earl of Warwick, Francis Beaumont, curled around to face Nick and me. He'd been standing behind us. My eyes immediately swept the room for his wife, my beloved friend Alice Grey, but she wasn't here.

Kit turned to Francis, exposing a stunning display of elaborate braids beneath her pearled hood. "He is not the true king," she said firmly. "A true king would never abandon his kingdom." My heart broke a little for Nick beside me.

All of this was jaw-droppingly preposterous. Clearly, these two knew our faces! Unless it was so unbelievable to them that we were alive, and in such a state, that it created a smokescreen that they couldn't see past.

"May I?" Francis asked, offering the ten-year-old queen a short bow.

She made a regal nod, and I felt a stab of sympathy for the Kit I knew, who loved to play with toy animals and read adventure stories about knights and damsels. Francis sauntered closer to us in his shining, ivory-colored doublet with a faint gray pinstripe, bringing with him traces of musk and cherries. Nick didn't meet the eyes of his former best mate while Francis scrutinized his face.

So, the duplicitous Earl of Warwick hasn't yet left Kit for Mary Stuart. He's still playing her and all of us.

"Enough!" said Kit, and Francis quickly backed away with submission. "My brother would never have abandoned his kingdom or survived that jump from the Tower," she said. "And that maiden is much too thin and dirty to be Emmeline." She glared at me. I hadn't realized until then how much weight I'd lost since we'd arrived in Tudor England. "You may remove these vagabonds from my sight," Kit said. She'd matured ten years in just thirteen months.

"As Your Majesty desires," said Francis. "The matter of why this peasant was asking after a most secretive prisoner at the Castle of Sheffield shall be handled by the sheriff of the town."

My throat bulged with a tight swallow. So that's why we were here —Nick's brazen attempt to see Mary Stuart at Sheffield castle hadn't gone unnoticed. What didn't make sense was why the Queen of England was this far from London, and why she'd even considered that this man could possibly be her dead brother. Had someone recognized Nick, other than Hugh Wynter?

"I ask thee to spare the maiden," said Nick in a heavy rural accent. "The maiden hath naught to do with my business at the castle."

Francis darted toward him. "Hold your tongue, you driveling idiot!" he snapped. "You are before the Queen's Majesty—you have not been given permission to speak!" I'd forgotten how easily Francis Beaumont lost his cool. He launched into a rant about the prisoners deserving a traitor's death, and my heart pulsed through my ears. Our only way out of this danger was evident. I stole a sideways glance at Nick, sending him a silent message.

This is our chance. Let's just admit who we are so we can all make a plan to stop Mary Stuart before it's too late!

But he remained frustratingly rigid beside me, and I didn't want to unmask us without his consent. The room fell silent save for the rain gently drumming the stained-glass windows.

"I am weary," Kit said, sinking into a hard-backed wooden chair dressed with a fringed cushion.

"Her Majesty the Queen is weary," Francis repeated like we hadn't heard. "Take the prisoners to the jail in York," he ordered the two guards.

"No!" Kit called. "I hear the rains and wish not to distress the horses. The prisoners will lodge this night in the manor with the other prisoner, and you may transport them on the morrow. Now I bid you goodnight."

She rose and strode out of the room in her doll-like gown that glittered with jewels, her lacy bell sleeves crinkling as her tiny arms swung.

Francis snapped his fingers at the guards, and they lurched forward to escort Nick and me back through the archway. The knob of a sword handle against my back pushed me down a dim corridor until we reached a nondescript door at the end.

One of the guards unlocked the door, and we were shoved inside a poky room, my knees banging against a bed frame. The boy sitting on the mattress shot to his feet, a hand flying to his chest.

"Goodman and Goodwoman Shakespeare!" said Jasper Blacke

like he didn't know whether to laugh or cry. The guards slammed the door and latched it from the opposite side.

"What are *you* doing here?" said Nick. His protective hand squeezed my shoulder and I leaned into him without making it obvious to Jasper that we were a couple.

"I met with trouble not five miles out of Sheffield," Jasper replied with a flush of embarrassment. "I met a child on the road who said a thief hath stolen her locket. When I made an offer to help the lass find the lout, she stole my silver spoon! So, I chased the lass—right onto lands belonging to a justice of the peace. When the sir made inquiry after my master, I gave the name of Mister Hugh Wynter, and the next thing I knew, I was brought to this place! I know not where I am, but it seems not at all like a jail."

"It's not a jail," I confirmed, unsure whether I should ask Jasper if he knew that the Queen of England was lodging in this same manor.

"This is more than strange," Nick said uneasily, breaking away from me to rest on the edge of the bed.

The room was the size of a closet and housed only a single bed, a small oak table without any drawers, and a lattice window facing a wall of red bricks.

I was pleased to see Jasper's sweet face—albeit under chilling circumstances—but once again, his company meant I couldn't raise questions with Nick, like why he insisted on keeping up this charade. If we just admitted the truth to Kit, she could help us, and more importantly, we could help her save the kingdom. I understood Nick's crippling guilt about staging a suicide in a deeply religious time, leaving behind his sister and his country, but hiding out like fugitives had gotten us nowhere.

"Has anyone told you why you are here?" Nick asked Jasper. "Perhaps it is because of your mention of the name Hugh Wynter to the justice of the peace. Your master was deeply involved in an intrigue."

The door clicked and swung open, and a bearded guard pointed at Nick and me. "Come with me," he grunted.

"Where?" I replied, but it was back to the grabbing hands and the pushing. This had to be killing a guy like Nick, who'd spent the first twenty-three years of his life doing the shoving.

Nick and I were led through the drafty Great Hall that we'd been inside earlier and into a richly decorated drawing-room. I twisted around to take in the ornate cupboards displaying gleaming silver plates, a long table draped with an expensive embroidered carpet, and wrought-iron candle stands that flickered with lit candles. The loose rushes strewn across the floor perfumed the air, which was gently warmed by the fireplace.

The moment we were alone, I rushed to Nick. "It's time to tell Kit the truth," I said. He averted his eyes. "I know you're scared to; I know there are risks."

"If I am known to be the king once more, I may be tried and executed for high treason," he reminded me, his cheeks ashen.

"She's your *sister*. She'd never do that to you."

"Emmie, you are of a different time," he said by way of explanation.

"What if we just tell Kit alone?" I said under my breath. "Brother to sister. If we explain everything to her, she'll understand why you did what you did. She can let us help her save this kingdom, and no one else has to even know that you were here."

"My sister is ten years old!" he said like I wasn't thinking this through. "What understanding can she have of all this? The heresy of a journey through time…of my betrayal of God and country? Kings marry for alliances, Emmie, not love. I have told you this before."

The door broke open, sending aromas of perfume and roses seeping into the air. Kit's steps were light in her silk slippers, and her teeth chewed her bottom lip.

"Leave us," she said to the guard, and he quickly obeyed. She'd come alone.

Kit paced toward Nick. She dropped to one knee and pressed her pink lips to his hand.

"Your Majesty," she said in a soft, trembling voice.

A gasp escaped Nick's throat before he tugged her to her feet, wrapping his arms around her little body. Tears sprang to my eyes as her fiery red hair disappeared into his embrace.

"You know me," he said as he pulled back, his eyes glittering with a film of tears.

Kit was shaking. "Indeed, I know you, my brother." Her eyes darted to mine, but any affection Kit had once held for me had vanished. While she physically clung to her brother, she looked only frightened of me.

"It's so good to see you," I said to her in a whisper.

Her reply was a shy nod, and she turned back to Nick. "Why are you not dead?" she asked him with the point-blank honesty of a child. "Are you here to plan a rebellion against me and take back the throne?"

He looked so crushed that he could hardly speak. "No...no," was all he could get out.

I wanted to give him a moment to collect himself. "Earlier in the hall, you pretended not to know us," I cut in gently.

Kit looked up at me. "I wished not to make trouble for you. That is why I made the journey from Windsor and without my ladies or courtiers. I wished not to become the subject of hearsay."

"But what made you even think we were alive?" I asked her. "Why did you come all this way?"

"One of my courtiers received a letter from an acquaintance in Nottinghamshire; a local yeoman. The yeoman said that a man and his sister were living on his farm, and he suspected them to be the king and the queen, believed dead."

"And you accepted this claim of treason?" Nick said.

"Something about that letter and how the man described your person...it gave me hope that the story was true," she said. "That my brother was still of this realm." Her voice broke on the words, and her eyes filled with tears.

I collapsed inside, wanting to put an arm around Nick—and her —but I couldn't move.

I also couldn't believe that Hugh Wynter had ratted us out to the queen, even before I'd confirmed his suspicions about our identities. And what advantage would it have given him to do so? All I could think of was that it would be like dropping a bomb on the Tudor dynasty. If Kit and Nick began fighting over the throne, it would give Mary Stuart the perfect opportunity to parade into England and seize the country for herself. But that idiot of a man had been out of his depth. Nick had never hungered for war, and he would *never* put the throne of England before his sister. I wiped my mouth where Hugh's lips had once been.

Nick brushed a tear from his eye. "It warms my heart to see you," he said to Kit.

Her face softened for only a moment. She stepped away from him.

"You must both feel hungry," she said. "And I am tired."

"Kit, we must talk more," Nick said urgently. "There is much to discuss."

She wouldn't look at me. "Do you mean to explain why it is that you abandoned me?" she asked him. "And all of Christendom?"

An uncomfortable silence swallowed the air. Nick had no simple answer for that.

"Was it for her?" Kit pointed at me.

"No, no, it was not for her," he lied without even thinking, and a part of me died inside. "But we must talk, and most certainly behind closed doors."

She blinked at him, now keeping her distance. "Then let us take supper together this night. But there is one other who I wish to join us."

"The Earl of Warwick," Nick guessed, his voice tightening.

"I trust the earl with my life," Kit said pointedly, and Nick's gaze dropped to his boots. "And he is the Lord Protector of the Realm."

Nick and I shared a look. If only Kit knew what Francis Beaumont was planning behind her back.

Before we could say anything, she turned for the door. "I shall have you both brought to my dining chamber within the hour," she said.

Her tiny fist knocked on the oaken doors, and they flung open. She slipped through them, and the doors rattled shut as the guards closed us back in.

Nick's hands slid into his hair, his eyes clouding with torment. "My sister is greatly displeased with me."

"But she's also so happy to see you," I said softly. "I can tell."

He just shook his head, his hand pressed to his brow. I made a sorrowful exhale and rubbed his trembling back, but there was little time to wallow. We were to soon join Kit and Francis for a Tudor-style feast, where they'd undoubtedly have a zillion questions for us. And what about Jasper? He had to be sweating bullets over where we'd been dragged off to by the guards.

That conversation would have to happen later. Rather than being escorted back to our cupboard of a room to change, a stony-faced guard wheeled in a small chest of folded clothes.

"I wonder who these belong to," I said to Nick as he helped me tie on the pieces of a lilac-colored gown with cut sleeves. "This fabric isn't cheap."

He didn't reply. Creases lined his brow as he clipped on his velvet doublet and pulled on his breeches. Seeing Kit again—and what she'd said to him—had kicked him in the gut.

A guard led us up a creaky staircase, his subordinate gaze pinned to the floorboards. It was a blessing that no one made eye contact around the queen or her companions—the fewer eyes scrutinizing Nick, the better.

As we padded nervously along a gallery of paintings, I reminded myself that, if word broke out around the manor that Nick was the former king, returned from the dead, that didn't mean his cover would be blown countrywide. Rumors could easily be contained in a place with no photographs, internet, or national newspapers. It would also be considered high treason to start whispers that the king was still alive. These lowly guards would have to be off their rockers to risk being hanged, drawn, and quartered.

The queen's dining chamber was a small, pleasant room containing only a linen-covered table lined with cushioned benches and a stone fireplace that blazed with a comforting glow. Nick and I were alone, so I stole a peek through the stained-glass windows overlooking a courtyard garden that housed a pelican fountain. A high brick wall blocked any view of what was beyond the manor.

"My lady," Nick said with surprise.

I spun around to meet the shell-shocked, toffee-colored eyes of Alice Grey in the doorway.

"Alice!" I said, rushing toward her without thinking. I ached to hug her, but her protruding belly stopped me in my tracks.

My palm hit my mouth. "You're pregnant," I said, losing all sense and decorum.

She held her belly through the mulberry-colored satin of her gown. "M-my queen, I know not what words to say," she stuttered like she'd seen a ghost. And the ghost was me.

"I know. I'm so sorry," was all I could manage past my stinging heart. If I'd known that Alice Grey was here, I'd have planned something better to say—some form of explanation as to how I'd returned from the dead. I sucked in her features. Now that she was married, her lovely, long hair was twisted up beneath a stylish French hood.

A trumpet blasted from the hallway, sending me out of my skin. Alice darted sideways so Francis Beaumont could stride through the archway with his confident gait and perfectly styled black hair.

"Her Majesty, the Queen," he announced stiffly, without looking at Nick or me. Had he also pretended not to recognize us downstairs when we'd arrived? Francis Beaumont had never been an easy book to read.

The four of us shuffled to stand around the dining table and bowed our heads as Kit entered the room. She was so small and light that her footsteps barely made a sound. I wasn't even sure she was at the head of the table until she commanded us to sit in a soft voice.

I'd expected an instant interrogation about why on earth Nick and I had faked our own deaths and turned up a year later in Sheffield, but the room was eerily quiet while a parade of steaming dishes was carried in and presented to the queen. There was no live musician to soften the stark silence, probably because Kit had traveled here with a skeleton crew to keep her visit discreet.

Nick and Francis sat opposite each other, their breathing heavy and their hands clenched. A pendant of the queen's image hung from a thick gold chain around Francis's neck, and I tried not to send him a silent, glaring message that we were onto his dirty dealings with Mary Stuart. Kit was speaking to Nick quietly under her breath, and he bit his lip so hard that I thought it would bleed. This was officially the most uncomfortable dinner that I'd ever attended, and I'd lived in the Tudor court.

Pregnancy had only exacerbated Alice's notorious appetite, and she devoured a thick slice of salted seal opposite me without looking up. She had to be consumed with curiosity about where Nick and I had disappeared to and why, but she knew better than to ask something so bold before the queen and former king.

I leaned a little closer to her over the table. "Congratulations on your happy news," I said. Startled at my addressing her, she touched her rounded belly before Francis raised his voice.

"The Queen's Majesty intends to speak," he announced.

Kit's cheeks matched the salmon on her plate. "I fear that I am in a dream," she said simply. "But mine eyes heed that my brother is yet among the living." She blushed with emotion, and Nick blinked painfully. "I have brought you to this supper so we may learn how and why this miracle has come to pass." She looked at Nick flush in the face. "Why are you alive? Why do you look the way you do? And what trouble are you in that you should be having dealings with mine enemy, the Queen of the Scots?"

"Say it now," Francis finally burst, his fingers clenching his soup spoon. "Say now why in God's name you would choose a pretense of self-murder to conspire and plot against us with that devil of a woman, Mary Stuart!"

"I have done nothing of the sort!" Nick said sharply, paling with shock. "Perhaps I should be asking you the same question, Lord Warwick."

Francis gasped before lurching forward as if to grab Nick by the neck.

"Enough!" shouted Kit.

Alice panted frightened breaths and gripped Francis's forearm, holding him back.

"I ask you again: Why were you at Sheffield Castle?" Francis barked at Nick. "Discovered to be not only alive after falsifying your own death, but caught in an attempt to meet with our enemy?"

Nick rose to his imposing height, his hands clutching the edge of the table. "Because your enemy is making a plot against you as we speak," he said through his teeth. Kit shrank back in her seat. "You should have very grave concerns about what that vile woman is up to."

"The devil you say," Francis spat.

"Did you know that Mary Stuart is at Sheffield Castle no longer?" Nick said to him, his eyes ablaze.

"I do know, as a matter of fact," the earl snapped. "The Scottish queen had a conspirator at the castle who killed three of my guards. Mary Stuart made her escape and is believed to be already in Scotland, in the Castle of Cessford."

"Close to the border of England, then," Nick said pointedly. "That is because Mary Stuart has raised an army of supporters across England. She has the favor of the King of France, the Spanish Armada, and the Pope in Rome. Tell them, Emmie," he said to me, and my cheeks flamed hot. "Tell them what else it is that you have learned."

I tried to clear my sticky throat. "Mary Stuart is going to invade England with her army, along with the armies of France and Spain," I stammered. "The day after she invades, she's going to execute the queen and take the throne of England."

For a moment, nobody spoke.

"*How?*" Francis eventually blurted like none of this was making sense. "How could I know not of such a plot?"

Because you're involved in it, that's how.

More thick, torturous silence devoured the room before Francis spoke again, his voice faint. "And you know this for certain?"

"We know this for certain," Nick said.

We've been to the future. We've seen your graves.

"When?" Kit said in a frightened voice. Her heart-shaped face was the color of milk, her eyes widening into two blue plates.

"In nine days," I said.

17

EVERY PERSON AROUND THE TABLE GAPED AT ME, WITH THE EXCEPTION of Nick. Like me, he'd had time to process the news about Mary Stuart's invasion of England.

"To speak of the death of the queen is to speak words of high treason," Francis said darkly.

"My wife speaks the truth," Nick shot back.

"And how do you know all of this?" Francis snapped, his charcoal eyes on fire. "Unless this is no more than part of your plot of conspiracy with the Queen of the Scots."

"Francis," Alice cautioned, albeit in a hesitant voice.

"We're not part of any plot," I said, glancing at Kit. The poor thing had frozen into a ten-year-old ice sculpture. "But we do have inside information, which is why we're here. We came back here to warn you; to help you. You could all end up in the Tower of London within days if you don't take this seriously."

"Came back from where?" Francis said to me. "The land of the fairies?"

"Control your temper, husband," Alice said, a little louder than before. Her eyes then moved to Nick and me, sharing the same look of expectation as Francis and Kit's. The moment of truth had arrived.

"What say you?" Kit said, leaning forward. "Where is it that you have been, my brother?"

Three dumbfounded faces blinked at us.

Nick's bottom lip disappeared between his teeth. "Emmie and I have been lodging in Hertfordshire for the thirteen months past. We have a small house and keep to ourselves. We have been the cause of no suspicion there." His eyes lifted to Kit, bleeding a silent apology.

"A small house?" Francis said incredulously, like he was talking about a nest of snakes.

"But why on earth?" said Kit, her trembling lips parted.

Nick sucked in air but couldn't seem to catch his breath. "When Emmie was convicted of treason and heresy and sentenced to die, it was the only way to save her life. I wished not for Kit to suffer for my judgments, so I felt this was the best course of action for us all."

Francis, Kit, and Alice exchanged looks of utter bewilderment. Sixteenth-century kings did not willingly walk away from their thrones.

"So, you did do it for her," Kit said, revisiting Nick's denial earlier.

"You gave up the throne of England...for Emmie," Francis clarified like it was the most horrifying, strange thing he'd ever heard.

Nick's cheeks scorched red. "I suppose that I did. I do not expect you to understand."

"You love her that much," Alice said breathlessly.

Francis's accusing eyes shot to me. "You let the King of England do such a thing?"

"Not exactly," I replied, trying not to quiver. "More like I made him do it."

"Emmie," Nick cut in.

"No, they should know." I pressed my hand over his thigh beneath the table. "The truth is that, when I was the queen, I couldn't handle it," I said shakily. "The dislike and distrust by the nobles...the attempts on my life that nearly got Alice killed and did get one of my ladies killed...the Duke of Norfolk's rebellion...it was all too much;

too dangerous." I felt Alice's soft gaze on my face. "So, even before I was arrested and sentenced to die, I told Nick that I was out." His face dropped down beside mine. "I told him that I couldn't live this life, and that I was escaping, and he chose to come with me. I really didn't give him any other option if he wanted us to be together." A tear escaped my eye and landed on my silver plate. "And I'm sorry that I took him away from you. I'm *so* incredibly sorry." I wanted to look at Kit, but I couldn't.

Nick rested his hand over mine, his thumb brushing back and forth over my skin.

"But why did you not speak the truth to me?" Kit said to Nick. "You left a letter in which you said you intended to commit self-murder."

The remorse that eclipsed Nick's face was gut-wrenching. "Sister, believe me, I wanted to with all my heart...but I feared that to do so would have brought you into my treasonous, faithless act."

Alice was looking at me like I'd just fallen off an alien planet, like she didn't know me at all.

"And have you returned to take your place as king once more?" Francis asked, blinking nervously.

My eyes shot to Nick, who shook his head. "You know that I cannot do that now. And that no one other than those in this room must ever know of this. What we need now is stability for the throne, not more unrest."

"And if my brother and Emmie are to be believed, Mary Stuart means to make an assault on England," said Kit, her alarmed eyes turning to Francis. "So, what is to be done about it?"

With our desserts of baked fig tarts and spiced fruit cake left mostly untouched, the five of us shifted into the more spacious drawing-room. The fire had been stoked and the ornate chamber was dressed with flasks of wine and platters of snacks that the guards would end up polishing off later. Upon the queen's orders, we were left alone— no guards or servants to overhear our conversations.

The Mary Stuart subject had been dropped for the moment so Francis could think on it, and Kit had her tiny hand pressed to Alice's belly, an eager smile painted on Alice's face. I topped up my wine and caught sight of Nick and Francis in yet another heated exchange. I hurried over to them.

"Before I took leave of the throne," Nick said to Francis, "the French king and I had agreed upon a marriage treaty for Kit to be betrothed to the Duke of Anjou."

"That treaty is now null and void," Francis replied coolly.

The look Nick gave him was pure steel. "And might I ask why?"

A chill curled around my neck as the two men stepped closer together, their fingers curling tightly at their sides. "The Duke of Anjou is old enough to be Kit's grandfather," Francis exaggerated. "But more so, your own disgrace in committing an act of self-murder led the French king to put an end to the betrothal."

Nick's eyes were two sharpened daggers. "So, you did not break off the marriage treaty so that you could divorce your wife and make an offer of marriage to the Queen of the Scots in her stead? And then take your place on the throne of England?"

My mouth dropped open.

I expected Francis to fly off the handle, but he just stood there in a sort of dazed silence. After a few moments, he swallowed tightly. "You wound me," he said in a choked voice. "And you forget all too easily that I am a Beaumont, a descendent of kings. I would need not a foreign queen to make a claim to the throne of England."

"Is that your admission?" Nick said darkly. "Now that my person is aside, you intend to align yourself with Mary Stuart and to make a claim of high treason as the rightful King of England?"

Francis paced backward, shaking his head. He didn't look guilty or cornered at all; he looked...devastated. "When *ever* have I demonstrated anything other than my boundless devotion to you and your family?" he said, his cheeks empty of color. "When?!" he shouted, stunning the room into silence.

Nick twisted to glance at me, but I had no answer for this.

"What made you believe this of me?" Francis persisted, his eyes popping with anger.

"It was something I heard," I cut in shakily. "A man in Windsor announced it on the street. He said that you were planning to wed Mary, Queen of Scots."

Francis gasped a bewildered laugh. "A man on the street? A man on the *street!*" He grabbed Nick by his velvet collar, but Nick didn't fight back. "How could you believe this of me!" Francis demanded. "You are not only my king, you are a brother to me! Your sister is my sister! And you are to believe the blathering of a man on the street?"

The truth slid into my chest.

We were wrong. Francis isn't in cahoots with Mary Stuart. It was just mind-less Tudor gossip. The reason he didn't know about Mary Stuart's plot isn't because he's involved in it, but because he's clueless. If only Alice Grey's brilliant dad, Sir Thomas Grey, was still the chief advisor to the monarch. He'd never have let Mary Stuart get this far.

Francis had let Nick go and was standing with a hand to his brow.

"Forgive me, my brother," Nick said to him. "I believe now that I was wrong."

"You, too, forget that I am wedded to my heart's deepest desire," Francis added, shaking his head. "To even think I could leave my wife and child destitute! You believe I mean to set a torch to mine own heart. This leaves me sorely wounded."

"I'm sorry, Francis," I said, touching his embroidered sleeve.

Alice knew better than to make any comment, but I could tell that she was hanging on our every word, her cheeks reddened. Kit was also watching the interaction with anxious eyes, and I offered her a look of reassurance, despite feeling as lost as she was.

Nick put his hand on Francis's shoulder, and Francis didn't wriggle away. "I beg you for your forgiveness, my brother," Nick said to him. "I should not have been so quick to believe a falsehood about a gentleman that I have known for so long."

Francis stood there nodding, his throat bulging tightly.

Nick shifted on his feet, still looking at Francis. "You speak as if you could not imagine being parted from Alice for any reason at all, even the fate of the realm," he said carefully. "So, now you under-stand why I could not let mine own wife go."

Francis's coal-colored eyes blinked at Nick, his lips parting.

"Good God," he said like something had just clicked into place. "I believe I do understand. I understand you. Christ, perhaps for the first time."

Nick slumped like he might fall, physically overcome with relief. He then lurched forward and grabbed Francis by the scruff of his neck in a manly hug.

"Make no drama of it!" Francis cried, embarrassed.

I beamed as the two best friends shared boyish smirks of mutual affection. The flush in Francis's cheeks said it all: He was as relieved as Kit was to have the irreplaceable Nick Tudor back.

"How about a game of chess?" Alice said to them, breaking the tension. "I always enjoyed watching you two play."

"My dear, we have matters to discuss of great importance," Francis said, his face tightening again.

"That is a good idea," Kit cut in brightly. "I will take pleasure in watching you play chess." I didn't blame her for latching onto something other than talk of her death, especially at her age. She hitched her satin skirts and hurried across to the chess table beside the fireplace, sinking into a cushioned chair.

For a blissful few minutes, we silently watched Nick and Francis make their expert opening chess moves. The game had barely begun when Kit started stifling yawns.

"Your Grace, would you permit me to accompany you to your bedchamber?" Alice asked her. "The hour is late."

Kit looked at Francis through drowsy eyes. "My lord, would you counsel me on the morrow about what it is that you intend to do about the Queen of the Scots?"

I averted my gaze, still guilty about being so quick to believe the gossip we'd heard about Francis. He was evidently already running the country; he didn't need to wed Mary Stuart for that.

"Most certainly, my blessed queen," he said with a bow of his head. I watched Nick's affectionate eyes follow Kit out of the room with Alice at her heels.

Francis moved his knight out of harm's way. "I meant to ask you: Who is the boy?" he said to Nick. "The cripple."

"You mean Jasper Blacke," Nick said. "He has naught to do with any of this." He captured a pawn with his bishop, and Francis grimaced.

"But you and the cripple were both known to this Wynter fellow, the yeoman traitor," Francis said, brazenly dragging his queen to the middle of the chessboard.

"Jasper worked at Mister Wynter's farm," I explained as Nick scrutinized his chess pieces. "He left along with us after the pestilence outbreak, and we became separated in Sheffield, but he really doesn't have anything to do with any of this. He has no idea who we really are. And he's not a cripple…one of his legs is just a bit shorter than the other."

Francis grunted. "The boy shall be freed at first light. We need not have any more mouths to feed."

I glanced at the gigantic, uneaten platters of sliced eggs and poached pears sprinkled with almonds, raising a brow.

"On this issue of the Queen of the Scots," Francis said to Nick, "you know it is a matter for the Privy Council."

"There is no time for that," Nick said gravely.

"We must raise an army if we are to fight that beast of a woman," Francis argued. "We are presently low on numbers, armor, and skilled captains after Norfolk's rebellion this year past, and the pestilence has brought devastation to the west. But if we summon Parliament and request more money—"

"The Scottish queen means to invade in *nine days*," Nick reminded him.

Francis smacked his hand across the chessboard, sending the pieces flying. "Tell me why did you not bring this matter of perilous urgency to me sooner?"

"Because we believed you to be one of the conspirators."

"Ah, yes, that man on the street," said Francis, and he chugged his wine. "You also know the French and the Spanish ambassadors must have had a part in this. Christ, we are done for." He sighed into his cup. "The hour draws late, and I cannot away to bed without some course of action to present to the queen on the morrow. If we are indeed too late to involve the council, then this rests solely with you and me," he said to Nick. "We need a plot, and we need it this night."

"You, me, and Emmie," Nick said, reaching to cup my knee. "Emmie is as much a part of this as I am."

"Certainly," Francis said politely, but this wasn't exactly a world in which women's opinions were encouraged. Once again, I'd have to prove myself to Francis Beaumont.

"We need to arrange a meeting with Mary Stuart," I said calmly. "Face to face."

Francis made an incredulous sound.

"Hear me out," I said. "The man we stayed with who was conspiring with Mary, Hugh Wynter, was one of hundreds or even thousands of Catholic dissidents in England. He'd been writing to her in secret, using coded messages, under the number 'seventy-seven.' It's how Mary has been communicating with her supporters. We should write a letter to Mary from Number Seventy-Seven saying that he wants to meet her urgently at Cessford Castle. We can include something that convinces her the meeting will be worth it. Except it won't be Mister Wynter who turns up at the meeting, it will be us."

Francis tilted back in his chair like he'd seen me for the first time. "You mean to assassinate the Queen of the Scots," he said to me.

"But Mister Wynter had a go-between with himself and Mary Stuart," Nick cautioned. "That priest who visited him—Mister Holborne. What if that man knows that Mister Wynter, Number Seventy-Seven, has passed, and he has already reported the matter to Mary? She shall know that the offer of the meeting is the makings of a plot."

"We could walk right into a trap," Francis finished. He tapped his lips with his ringed fingers and looked at Nick. "No, I have a better idea. Tell me…why were you so ready to believe that I was involved in a plot of conspiracy with Mary Stuart?"

When a flush of guilt found Nick's cheeks, I answered for him.

"It's because of your claim to the throne," I said. "And you're from a famously Catholic family. It just made sense that you would have so much to gain if you teamed up with the Scottish queen. It could make you the King of Scotland and England."

"Quite," he said to me. "Which is why I shall write the letter to Mary Stuart from my person. We are all aware of the sad history of my family's devotion to papistry. I will make a pretense to Mary Stuart that I desire for the throne of England to be returned to a Catholic prince. With my royal blood, I can make an offer of marriage to Mary Stuart and say that, together, we can overwhelm the Tudor child-queen with greater ease than she might achieve on her own."

"To what end?" Nick asked, tensing with uncertainty.

"To the end of securing the meeting," Francis clarified. "Do not believe for a moment that I intend to leave my wife and child for a plot."

"I think it's a good idea," I said, but Nick's wary expression held.

"To put such words on paper would put you in great peril, my lord," he said to Francis. "It is an open admission to high treason, even if it is false."

"But we would tell Kit, who is the queen, so where's the risk?" I asked him. "She's the top of the totem pole."

Nick's brows gathered as he looked at me. "You forget, my lady, your own fate when you were suspected of high treason a year or so past. The Privy Council...the noblemen...they have enormous power in the realm. Enough power to force a king to abdicate and feign self-murder in order to have his way."

I slumped with a defeated exhale. Nothing was ever easy in the sixteenth century.

Francis rose from his stool. "With respect, it is not your decision to make, my lord," he said to Nick. "It is mine, and I choose to write the letter to Mary Stuart. Kit will agree with my counsel; I know she will. I shall inform the queen at first light. For now, however, I need only parchment and a quill."

He dragged his stool to the beautifully painted oak desk beside the set of virginals.

"Are you certain about this?" Nick asked as Francis flipped open a carved writing box.

"How will Mary Stuart know the letter is really from you?" I added. "It could be a forgery."

Francis dipped his feather quill into an inkpot. "The way around that, my lady, is to include in the letter information that only someone of my circumstance could have knowledge of. My traitor of an uncle was once racked and executed for his involvement in a Papist plot with Mary Stuart. I will make reference of a personal nature to it... perhaps share the words mine uncle spoke to me before his arrest."

As Francis began scraping words across the parchment, I caught Nick's face in the firelight. His eyes were shining with something I hadn't seen in thirteen months...hope.

18

THE GILDED CLOCK HAD TICKED PAST MIDNIGHT WHEN NICK AND I BID Francis goodnight. The plan was for Francis to send the letter with a messenger overnight who'd know nothing about its contents. Francis's red wax seal also ensured that Mary Stuart would take the letter seriously—if it got to her in time.

The night guard led Nick and me up a spiral staircase to a different bedchamber than the cramped room we'd been locked inside earlier. I hoped that poor Jasper was fast asleep in that single bed downstairs and not freaking out about his fate and ours. When Phoebe had fallen ill at Hugh Wynter's house, Jasper had nearly fallen apart.

The guard bid us goodnight and my eyes swept the spacious bedchamber with a stained-glass window, a four-poster bed, and a gently crackling fire.

"We are alone at last," Nick said, blowing through his lips with relief. He sat on the bed and cocked his finger for me to join him.

"We are," I said, sitting beside him on the edge of the feathered mattress. My fingertips traced the silk coverlet embroidered with swirls of gold thread stitched into animal shapes. "I don't think I ever want to leave this room," I said. "It's lovely."

And safe. And has no queens to kill.

Nick shifted behind me, his warm hands finding my shoulders. I expelled a sigh as he massaged my aching muscles. "You mean to say that you prefer this place to hiding in a barn and sleeping on dirty straw?" he said with mock surprise.

"Well, when you put it that way..." I was turning to liquid beneath his touch. "Although the best part was the pestilence. God, I miss that."

His forehead rested against the back of my hair, and I breathed in his scent that I could never get enough of.

Nick dropped his soft lips into the crevice of my neck. "We have faced a great many troubles over the years, have we not?" he said, placing a featherlight kiss on my trembling skin.

"Let me see..." I said breathlessly. "There was the time Mathew Fox tried to kill me."

I felt his frown, but the kisses didn't stop. I murmured a sigh, my fingers finding the thick curls of his hair behind me.

"And that one-day fever thing, when I was hallucinating," I added. "That was almost as bad as the time you told me you were marrying Henriette of France and asked me to be your concubine."

"What about the occasion you told me you were a heretic time traveler, and I made threats to arrest you?" Nick said, his breath hot near my ear.

I chuckled. "Well, there was the time you *did* arrest me, and I was sentenced to be beheaded."

He skated his hands down my arms, making me tingle.

"We speak much of your pain, but what of mine, Mistress Grace? You have been most troublesome to me too." His fingers continued down to the sides of my waist, where he held me through my gown, gently but firmly.

"I don't recall *you* ever being sentenced to die," I said, becoming a little short of breath.

"On the contrary...every time you left me, leaving my heart in pieces," Nick said, guiding me to turn around and face him. "Believe me, that torment was equal to an execution."

My legs naturally parted, and he shifted his hips between them, close enough that our faces were inches apart. Something that I hadn't seen for a long time swelled in the shallow sea of his eyes.

Desire crept into my cheeks, hot and tight.

"Tell me…what am I to do with you?" he asked lightly, tucking a wisp of hair behind my ear.

"Do you mean in general or right now?" I said brazenly.

His face flushed, his eyes becoming more dazed. More needy.

I pulled his muscular thighs closer until his body was flush against mine, my throat locking. I couldn't resist a downward glance, a warm ache building between my legs at the sight of the thick shape pressing against his breeches. After so many months of keeping me at arm's length, the hot kiss we'd shared near Sheffield Castle had unlocked something in him. Something I missed to the point of physical pain.

My voice came out strained. "I need to introduce you to something called *contraception*," I said, returning my gaze to his face. "It's not for everyone, but it's for me. It allows you to make love, but not make a baby."

His brows drew together, and I kissed the space between them. He was too cute. "I know," I said in a gentle voice. "It's probably against your beliefs." He was, after all, from one of the most devoutly Christian periods in history.

"How does such a remedy work?" he offered, watching my face as he pressed his hard ridge against me through my dress, holding himself there for a moment. My head tilted back and I clutched his forearms, a plea for him to stop taunting me.

I sucked in air and found my voice, tracing my finger down the slight curve of his nose. "There are a number of ways, but for me, it's just a little white pill. Taken once a day."

"Little white pills that are in the twenty-first century," he reminded me, his hips loosening a little against mine.

My shoulders sagged. "Of course," I said, feeling the wind leave my sails. "Of course, we can't have any of that anymore." My mind drifted to the bandit who'd stolen our ring…our future. That asshole had taken everything from us.

Nick reached out to gently stroke my face, his fingertips caressing my cheek. "And so, again, I ask. What am I to do with you, Mistress

Grace? When all this is over. If we are fortunate enough to put an end to Mary Stuart's plot, what are you and I to do?"

"I wish I knew," I said, refocusing my breath and allowing my mind to consider the sickening prospect of being trapped in Tudor England forever. "Maybe we could just live in this house," I said, wrapping my legs around him with affection. "Like I said—we'd never have to leave this room. One thing I'm very happy about," I added sincerely, "is that you now have your sister back."

The relief and tenderness in his smile filled my chest with warmth.

Mention of Kit and Mary Stuart had managed to ice down the room for a few moments, but our groins were still fused together, and Nick's erection wasn't getting any smaller. In fact, the shape in his breeches had only swelled and tightened, and he shifted a little, straining.

"Emmie?" he said thickly, his hands sliding back down to cup my waist again.

"Yes?"

"May I put an end to my suffering, just once? If we are careful." I hadn't seen Nick's face pucker with need like this in more than a year; hadn't heard his voice take on the raspy edge of arousal. A gush of warm wetness pooled between my thighs.

"Do you know how long I've been waiting to hear you say that?" I asked, my voice a shaky breath.

With clear, determined purpose this time, he cupped my hips and grinded himself against me through the fabric of our clothes, the feeling of his thick hardness rubbing against my core making me expel a small cry. When he pulled back a little, I cupped his ass and tugged him back against me with one rough movement, my aching flesh smacking against the velvet that stretched over his erection.

"God, woman, you mean to torture me," he said as he roughly untied and tugged down my kirtle, his hand searching under my smock. The tips of his fingers brushed the underwear I'd made from a coif, and a breathless moan escaped my lips as he grazed two fingers across my folds through the fabric. Just as I went to beg him to touch me bare, he peeled the damp linen off me, and a moment of cold air hit my swollen skin.

I tipped back onto the bed as he lifted my smock to my waist, a sound of pleasure leaking from his lips as he looked down at me, exposed and glistening for him.

His fingers slid through my slick flesh, touching and feeling and gathering wetness that he used to stroke my most sensitive spot. My head lolled back onto the mattress, and my legs parted further for him —a plea for him to keep caressing me, his exquisite touch stealing all the oxygen from the room.

"God, Emmie," he breathed in a taut voice before he slid down the bed with his fingers still teasing me until his face was so close to my throbbing, pink skin that I could feel his breath. His hands spread my thighs apart, opening me up, and for a moment, he just stared at my heated, wet flesh.

"How have I resisted this for a time so long?" he said, looking up at me, his incredible eyes turned foggy with desire. "I must have the restraint of a saint."

He scooped up more wetness and used it to gently circle and tease that perfect spot between my thighs. I moaned, watching him.

With both his hands, he parted my flesh again and closed his mouth over me, licking and sucking and making little moans of pleasure.

"Ohmygod," I said in one breath, my head hitting the mattress as I tilted my hips upward and let him devour me. His tongue was like rough velvet, dragging up and down my flesh with broad, hungry strokes before sinking deep into me, swirling and sucking like he was making out with me.

With a guttural sound, he pushed the backs of my knees up into the air, and I opened myself up to him almost obscenely, so he could swirl that talented tongue of his all over me until I was virtually shuddering from the sensation. The sight of him eating me like I was his last meal on Earth ignited a fireball inside me that threatened to explode and set the room on fire.

"I have missed this sorely," he said, throaty and deprived, before he lowered his mouth to burrow his tongue inside me again, as far as it would go. My eyes rolled back into my head, and I grabbed the thick curls of his hair like that could steady me…like it would save me from the burning fire of his thrusting, sucking, lapping tongue.

"You know you can't get pregnant by doing this, right?" I managed to pant as I clutched the silk coverlet, fisting it. "We could have been doing this all along." I was still annoyed that Nick had kept all this from me for more than a year.

His breathless mouth unlocked from me, and he soothed the frustration of that by quickly returning his deft fingers to my slick, slippery flesh.

"But, Emmie, I have told you before…taking my mouth to you leads to needing to be inside you," he said as he sank two fingers into my core, twisting them up and deep. I cried out as his fingertips found the spot inside me that was like lighting a match and gently rubbed it, his soft moans giving away the extent of his own arousal.

"Is that good?" he asked, his breath shallow, his lips parted.

I could barely nod, let alone speak.

"Look at you," he whispered hotly, his eyes locked to where my body clenched around his fingers. "So tight and warm and wet."

I'd forgotten how good it felt to have Nick Tudor touching me, but right now, I needed him naked…I needed to see and feel him bare, the way he was with me. He was much too sexy to be sitting here in a freaking doublet and breeches.

Taking charge, I sat up and scrambled to free his beautiful body from the fabric hiding it, a frenzy of unclipping and untying until I'd peeled the doublet and shirt off his skin. After he tugged my smock over my head, I ran my fingers down the ripples of his muscles, drinking in the sight of him, before I untied his breeches and slid my hand inside the gap, searching for the rigid flesh beneath. His parted lips breathed the most delicious, needful sigh as I felt him bare…thick and tight, hard yet satiny, all at once. I pulled him out until he was in my hand, so hot and engorged, and I closed my fist tight around him. His head lolled back, his eyes fell closed, and I had to kiss that sensual mouth of his.

Our kiss was wet and hot, all swirling, entwined tongues and aching moans. He gripped the back of my neck as I slid my slick fist up and down his length, brushing my thumb over the velvety head that leaked from the tip. I glided my hand up and down a few more times, rubbing and stroking, while I watched his face contort with pleasure. I wanted to taste him the way he had me, but his hands were all over me again, his fingers sinking deep inside me as he brought one of my breasts to his mouth and sucked on my puckered nipple like it was giving him life.

The physical need was too much, and seconds later, we were scrambling for the only sort of physical contact that could make the pain go away. Nick was panting as he scooped me up with one arm and sat me on top of him, his other hand brushing the crown of his cock against my slick folds. I couldn't stop moaning—it was embarrassing—but he didn't seem at all put off; in fact, every time I made that sound, his face creased like I was driving him crazy with desire.

We both watched as the tight head of his cock disappeared inside me, and a moment later, my body filled with blinding, thick heat as I sank down into heaven. My eyes fell closed, and my chest arched as Nick caught my breasts with his hands, bringing my nipples to his mouth and tonguing them until they glistened wet.

We were both sweating and moaning like out-of-control teenagers, but I was just so utterly full of him. White-hot need set every cell of my body alight as he guided my hips up and down his rigid length, my eyes glued to the sexiest sight in the world: Nick's face clenched with pleasure. He breathed a moan as his eyes met mine, and a hot flush of love flashed up my cheeks. I leaned forward to kiss him and taste his sweet sighs, his tongue twining deeply with mine. I couldn't imagine another man ever tasting this good, smelling this good, feeling this good.

His strong arms gripped me as I moved my body up and down his length, his hips thrusting to meet mine with hard, intent smacks. Then the bed, the floor, the world fell out from under me, and there was only Nick Tudor…deep and hard and stretching me tight. He looked at me; his intense, glittering eyes holding mine, his face so flushed and pretty in this state.

"I love you," he said in a breath.

An aching heat bloomed in my chest. "I love you so much," I said.

He reached to cup my face, his eyes soft. "You must know my heart aches for you," he whispered.

I clutched the sides of his face, his brow slick with sweat, and kissed his full lips. "I love you," I said again, and his response was to take me more urgently; our foreheads pressed together, our lips wet and kissing, and our hearts mirroring each other's galloping beats.

"Does this please you?" he said, gripping my ass with both hands and rocking his hips against me until there was nothing visible of his length, it was buried so deep. For a moment, he didn't move; he just stayed in there, like my body was an extension of his.

I couldn't make any words.

"Do you like that, Emmie?" he repeated, his eyes dark now and full of hunger. He began pulling out and pushing in again, and the friction was almost unbearable.

When I managed to speak, all I could get out was, "*Yes*...don't stop."

He looked down, his glazed-over eyes focusing on the sight of him sliding in and out of me as my body gripped his cock, his darkened shaft glistening with my need for him. And then his tongue glided up the side of my neck and across to my mouth. My head tipped back with each deep thrust of his hips, but he wouldn't let my mouth go, his lips holding mine and gently biting down, his tongue lolling around my mouth with firm, lustful movements.

"God, Nick, you feel so good," I bit out, my fingers digging into his muscular shoulders and holding on as he drove himself into me. My eyes were so heavy now that I couldn't lift the lids.

When I felt on the edge of explosion, he turned me onto my back and lifted one of my legs over his shoulder, his other hand pressing my chest down into the mattress. It gave me the perfect view of his toned body as he took me so hard that the headboard behind us was striking the wall with every thrust, merging with the moans that burst from my lips. At that moment, I couldn't have cared less if the guards in the hallway heard us...all I wanted was more of him.

"You like that," Nick said, looking down at me, and it wasn't a question.

"I do...it's too...it's too much," I breathed, almost in agony from the euphoria. His hips pulled back until I was unbearably empty before he slammed them back against me until I was stuffed entirely full of Nick Tudor. His pace and intensity accelerated again until I was close to the edge, and he knew it.

"I want you to look at me when you come," he said, almost begging the words.

He was all strength and depth and fire as he pounded himself into me, my leg still hooked over his shoulder, the rest of me becoming floppy beneath the overwhelming weight of the ecstasy he was giving me.

"That's it, Emmie," he said, his eyes on mine. "Look at me when you come on me."

My aching pleasure edged the crest of a wave and then suddenly exploded into a gushing torrent of melting, liquid heat that clenched around his cock and squeezed all the strength from my body, leaving me lightheaded and shuddering.

He pulled me up and hugged me breathlessly, and I clutched his damp hair as we held each other in a panting hug. Moving as one shape, we fell sideways onto the ruffled coverlet and lay together in a huddle of exhaustion, whispering breathless murmurs of love and appreciation. We'd burned the room down, and yet the tug of arousal sounded within me again, almost instantly. I slid my hand down Nick's chest and rubbed his taut stomach before I let my fingers track lower. He hadn't come yet, and his cock felt rigid and stretched in my hand. For a few moments, he let me stroke him, one of his arms draped over his face like he couldn't bear the pleasure of it, before he sat up and held my wrist.

"Do not feel that you ought to," he said with his infuriating Tudor politeness, and I smacked his hand off me. My response was to move further down the bed and bring my face to his thighs.

"Where is it that you are you going?" he said, a dimple deepening in his blushing cheek as he gazed down at me.

"I want to look at you," I whispered.

My face was inches from where he lay bare and heavy in my hand, a damp ache building between my legs again as I slid my fist up his length before stroking the soft curves of his tip. He was breathing beautiful little moans again, driving me to keep going, to squeeze him tighter.

"Did you touch yourself often?" I asked, pressing my lips to the inside of his thigh, kissing the sweet skin there. "For all those months that you wouldn't be close with me?"

His fingers were now in my hair that had come undone, playing with the disheveled strands. He took a moment to answer.

"Not often enough," he admitted. "I wished not to encourage those thoughts for fear of feeling only more tortured around you."

"Poor baby," I said, looking up at him, my cheeks flushed with desire. I stroked and squeezed his length. "Want me to kiss it better?"

It was one of the most confident things I'd ever said to Nick between the sheets, but this was what thirteen months of abstinence had done to me. I was ravenous for him.

"God, Emmie," was all he said as his fingers slid through my hair to cup the back of my neck.

I brought my mouth to the engorged head of his cock, which at that moment was like looking at cake when I hadn't eaten in a year.

"You must be so full of come," I said, my voice a hoarse whisper. Before he could reply, I closed my mouth over his soft tip.

The look that eclipsed his face as I sucked on him was the ultimate turn-on. He hardened further in my mouth—if that was even possible —and I filled my mouth with him, sliding down, as deeply as I could take him, his sweet, sighing moans coaxing me on and wetting the flesh between my legs. He was in my hands, my mouth, as I sucked and licked him, devouring and needing, his chest rising to sit up so he could watch me. He bunched my hair in his hands and studied my mouth as I bobbed up and down over him, catching sight of how vulnerable he looked at that moment. This Tudor king, divine and powerful, was made utterly helpless by my mouth. It only made me suck him harder, loving him with my lips and tongue, showing him how safe he was with me.

I wanted him to come, but he reached for my shoulders and guided me up his body again, catching my panting mouth with his and laying a kiss on me that stopped my breath. His tongue lolled with mine so sexily, and I was caught up in it when I suddenly felt myself being lifted into his arms and carried.

Cool air sent a sweep of goosebumps across my bare skin as he dropped me to my feet beside the stained glass window, turning me around until my hands were pressed to the fogged glass panes.

"What are you doing?" I said with a smile, although the thrill of him taking a step back to look at me, naked before him, stole away any more words.

"I wish to see the moonlight kiss your body," he said hotly, and I could sense his head tilting to look at me. I was so slick between my legs that my flesh must have glistened in his view. He made a tsk sound, like I was too much to bear, before he sank to his knees behind me and gripped the backs of my thighs.

I grunted out the world's longest, most shameful moan as he dragged his tongue up and down my flesh again before closing over my clit and sucking it. After he'd drank that up, he brought his mouth back to my opening and buried his tongue inside me.

I was falling into the window...if those brightly colored glass panes hadn't been there, I'd have been in the garden bed below.

"Nick, please," I begged as he swirled his tongue up and down my folds, making indulgent little groans as he feasted on me. As good as it felt, he was opening up a cavernous void inside me that almost felt intolerable.

"What is it, Emmie?" he asked, his mouth still locked to me.

"I'm so..."

God, that tongue of his.

"What is it that troubles you?" His voice was a hot whisper against my flesh.

"I'm so...I'm so *empty*," I gritted out.

His lips left me, but his mouth was still close, breathing warm air against my skin. "What is it that you need?" he said, sinking one of his fingers deep inside me. I moaned and arched. When I didn't answer, he added another finger and twisted it up inside. "You need to be full?" he asked thickly.

"Yes," I panted.

Two of his fingers were now buried inside me to the knuckles of his hand, and he reached around to press on my lower stomach with his other hand. "Like this?" he said behind me.

More embarrassing Emmie moans escaped my lips, but I didn't have a hope of suppressing them. Nick's fingers felt incredible, but it wasn't enough...I needed to be stretched full with him again. I turned around and reached between his thighs.

He pulled his hips away from me, teasingly. And then his fingers were gone too, and the sudden emptiness made me ache.

"What is it that you need?" he repeated, taking a step back and watching me with those gorgeous, glittering eyes of his. He actually crossed his arms at me like a complete smart-ass, all pretend innocence. He was going to make me ask for it, and I was far too desperate for him to play games.

"I need you...I need you to make love to me," I managed to get out.

His hungry gaze dropped to the slippery flesh between my legs that was now throbbing, begging for his relief.

"What else?" he said with a throaty rasp. "What was that word we used to say—"

"*Fuck*," I ground out, my core clenching with need for him. "I want you to fuck me. Now."

His eyes flickered up to mine again, his face so flushed and beautiful that it could steal a girl's breath. "But I thought I made it clear, Emmie, that I wished not to fuck you—on the bed, up against that wall, bent over the desk over there—for fear of putting a child in your belly."

He still had his arms crossed! And he'd already taken me tonight.

"*Nick*," I said, my voice carrying a warning. "If you don't give your wife what she needs right now—on the bed, up against that wall, or bent over the desk over there—she's going to get up and walk out that door right now. Naked."

Of course, I had no intention of being anywhere other than physically joined to Nick Tudor's incredible body for as long as he would allow it, but he didn't have to know that.

Before I could say another word, I was scooped up again and carried. He dropped me onto the oak desk, my bare butt meeting polished wood as he swept his arm across the desk's surface, ridding it of its contents.

He grabbed my thighs and tugged me toward him with one firm movement, the crest of his cock brushing against my slick folds. I expected him to sink himself into me, but all he did was inch the velvety tip inside, his eyes, weighted by lust, holding mine.

"What is it?" he said. "You wish not to wait a little longer until I fuck you, Emmie? Perhaps we may pour some wine first?"

My jaw clenched with frustration. "Nick Tudor, do you know how infuriate...ahhhhh."

He plunged himself deep inside me mid-sentence, his eyes pinned to my face, watching my reaction. And then he pulled out again and leaned back a little, giving himself a clear view of himself entering me.

He made a low, guttural noise. "That looks so good," he said, his face doing that sexy-as-hell contorted thing again. His strong hand guided my chest back until I was lying on the desk, and he stayed standing, our hips meeting with hard, wet thrusts. Just when I thought I was going to come again, he flipped me over, and my feet slid to the floor, the backs of my thighs pressed to his. He pulled my shoulders up until I was vertical and wrapped his arms around me from behind, cradling me.

"I love you," he said into my ear again, and I breathed the words back to him, clutching his tensing biceps as he smacked himself into me over and over and over and over, whispering the sexiest things in my ear that I'd ever heard. His movements became wilder and more out of control until he suddenly groaned and drew out of me. I turned around, and he spurted his warm liquid across my stomach instead of inside me where a baby might be made. I brought my mouth to the puckered lines in his brow and soothed his breathless pants with my kisses.

A moment later, he'd steadied himself and wiped my stomach clean with a cloth, but his eyes were still hazy.

"And now, you are to come again, my lady, but this time in my mouth," he said before dropping to his knees again. Clearly, I wasn't the only one who'd become insatiable during our thirteen months of abstinence. My elbows fell back against the desk, holding me up.

"I don't feel much like a lady right now," I said with Nick's head between my legs.

An adorable laugh fled his lips, blowing a rush of air onto my tingling, puffy flesh.

"Then, you are to come in my mouth, my *miracle girl*," he corrected, the hot rasp in his voice making me grab his hair and press my hips into his greedy tongue.

And so it went on, as each hour of the night was swallowed up by our physical and emotional reunion that wouldn't be sated. It had to be close to daylight when we finally exhausted ourselves and collapsed into a bundle of intertwined legs and arms, awash with love.

"I am yours," Nick breathed, his voice a kiss on my shuddering skin. My reply was a yearning, loving murmur.

And then, without warning, it rushed into me, like a flash flood... an overwhelming darkness...a crippling sense of impending doom.

And I knew.

This was the calm before the storm.

19

MY EYELIDS PEELED OPEN TO FIND NICK SLEEPING PEACEFULLY BESIDE me, the peach glow of sunrise lining the edges of the wooden window shutters. I snuggled into him, suppressing the pang of desire that tugged deep within me whenever my body rubbed against his. But our profound exhaustion had finally caught up with us, and we continued to doze through breakfast and lunch. It had to be mid-afternoon when he crawled on top of me again, heavy and warm as we made love once more, his face flushed with lust and longing.

Panting, I rolled onto my back with an arm over my head, battered and sore but tingling with fulfillment. How I could feel more in love with this man than I had before was beyond me, but I was almost drunk on his touch, his scent, his steady gaze.

Nick lay beside me, his eyes locked on my pink nipples before his gaze made a slow slide down my body, hovering between my thighs. He lay a hand there and gently guided one of my legs to the side, opening me up.

He groaned. "It is enough for me to just sit and look at you," he said with fresh hunger in his eyes.

"Oh no," I said through a laugh, making a show of covering myself with my hands. "What this body needs now is food."

He sighed and sat up. "It pains me to say that you are right. We must eat and also learn whether Lord Warwick has yet informed Kit about the letter to Mary Stuart."

I muttered a sound of protest at the mention of Mary's name and covered my eyes.

Nick got up to carry a pot of water to the fireplace so we could wash. We scrubbed our skin with damp cloths and vigorously rubbed the dirt out of each other's hair. Nick used a small blade to shave, and when he was finished, I ran my hand down his satin cheek before pressing three needy kisses to his lips, one after the other.

Once we were dressed and I'd braided my hair, we descended the spiral staircase to a distant trill of girlish laughter. The tension that had lived in my shoulders since we'd arrived back in Tudor England loosened a little. Kit sounded happy, which at that moment, was the best sound in the world. We found her in the drawing-room, playing dice with—

"Jasper!" I blurted with surprise.

"Good morrow, Your Majesty, and may God save you," Nick said to Kit with a bow, and I sheepishly copied.

With the formalities out of the way, Nick patted Jasper on the back in greeting before sharing a brief but warm hug with Kit.

"How are you?" I asked Jasper quietly, and his eyes popped with wonder.

"Thou told me not that thou art acquainted with the queen!" he said under his breath. He showed no signs of also knowing that Nick was the former king, and I his wife, so I just smiled.

"It's a long story, and maybe one better for another day," I said vaguely, hoping he wouldn't press me for more of an explanation.

But evidently, I wasn't the person on Jasper's mind. He spun back to Kit and returned to their dice game, her eyes lively and doting.

Oh no. Be careful with that little heart of yours, Catherine Tudor.

I watched Kit and Jasper play for a few minutes, fighting a smirk. They were just kids, but they both seemed high on energy around each other. My heart pinched when it hit me that, even if they came of age, Kit and Jasper would never be able to be friends, let alone anything more. But when Nick brushed past me, giving my shoulder an affectionate squeeze, the pity diminished a little. If Nick could love a commoner like me, why not his sister?

Kit called for some food to be brought in and invited me into the game of dice she and Jasper were playing, while Nick picked up a lute and began a gentle strum. When I inquired after the others, Kit explained that Alice was upstairs resting, and Francis was writing letters to the lords of the council on matters unrelated to Mary Stuart.

Had Francis briefed Kit yet on our plan to request a secret meeting with Mary? I didn't dare ask in case he hadn't. We nibbled on chunks of fluffy manchet bread with salted fish before Nick returned to the lute, and we all watched him play for a while.

Inch by inch, the knot inside me began to loosen and unravel. Now that we'd reunited with our friends and family in Tudor England, and now that Nick and I had reconnected in every way possible, being stuck here forever wouldn't be so bad. Maybe we'd be allowed to live in this beautiful manor tucked away in Sheffield, where Kit and Alice could visit us without attracting the attention of the nobles and courtiers.

I'd relaxed in the comfortable setting, finally able to exhale, when Alice strolled in after her lie-down. She was pleasant to me, but emotionally miles away from where we'd once been. Once again, I'd have to earn back Alice Grey's trust, which was a task I completely deserved.

While Kit, Alice, and I played endless rounds of a card game that resembled poker, Nick taught Jasper how to play the basic chords of "Greensleeves," the song he'd written for me, on the lute. Whenever his eyes tangled with mine from across the room, I lost track of where I was. As long as Nick and I were in a good place, I could handle being here. I could handle a life in Tudor England.

Francis joined us in time for supper, and the six of us dined with significantly less tension than we'd experienced the day before. I said a little prayer for poor Jasper, who fumbled his way through what must've been a terrifying first dinner with the Queen of England. Despite knowing less than me about the protocols, he practically inhaled the fried sturgeon bathed in olive oil, the smoked herring sprinkled with sugar, and the roasted pheasant dressed with sliced onions. I assumed that Jasper was free to go after what Francis had said the night before, but no one had asked him to leave the manor, and he was, unsurprisingly, in no hurry. Jasper still had no clue that Nick and I were the former king and queen, and because the others referred to us only as "my lord" and "my lady," he still believed us to be William and Anne Shakespeare from Stratford.

Over dinner, I overheard Francis and Kit quietly discussing the letter to Mary Stuart, which eased some of my jitters. As long as Kit knew about our plan, we were on track.

After our dessert plates were cleared, we all headed upstairs into the long gallery for a stroll past brightly colored biblical paintings and busts of Roman emperors.

Jasper sidled up beside me, his voice low. "If I may speak plainly, mistress, how is it that thou and Mister Shakespeare know the queen? Am I mixed up in some manner of plot?"

My nails dug into my palms. Unless I'd misheard, Jasper had just switched from calling Nick "Goodman Shakespeare" to the more deferential "Mister Shakespeare." He'd figured out that we weren't two peasants from Stratford.

"You're not part of any plot," I assured him. "It's honestly a mistake that you were even brought here, and you know you're free to go now. But I hope you'll stay," I added with a friendly wink.

Jasper's espresso eyes burned a hole in my cheek as we walked several paces behind Nick and Kit. "So, thou—*you*," he corrected, adopting the formal phrase, "wilt not tell me how it is you knowest the queen?" he said with a smirk. "I mean not to pry," he added quickly. "But I now see as plain as day that you and Mister Shakespeare are highborn. Maybe one day you will make known to me why a nobleman and a noblewoman came to work upon the farm of a lowly yeoman."

"One day, I'll tell you," I confirmed with an apologetic glance. "But not until I've spoken to Mister Shakespeare about it first. I'm sorry, Jasper; I don't mean to be a closed book."

We'd reached the stained-glass windows at the tip of the gallery, so we turned around to amble back the way we'd come. "One more thing, if I may," Jasper said, clearing his throat. "I would very much like to remain in the company of Mister Shakespeare and your person as your manservant. I shall do any task you dost desire, and I ask for little in return. Food and lodging are enough for me."

"Oh, Jasper, that's so nice of you to offer," I said. "Let me talk to Mister Shakespeare about it, and, of course, we would pay you on top of food and shelter." I shook my head at him with a smile.

Later that night in bed, when Nick and I lay breathless and entwined, I told him about Jasper's questions and his offer. We agreed that Jasper should be kept out of the loop on both our identities and the Mary Stuart issue for as long as possible. But we were both quite taken with the kid—he was so kind and hard-working—and Nick said we would need some servants in this realm. We agreed to accept his offer and retain our identities as the Shakespeares for now, but with two adjustments: We would admit our first names to be Nicholas and Emmeline and confess ourselves as a married couple instead of brother and sister. Jasper would surely begin to work out the truth for himself, and when he eventually asked about it, we would tell him as much as we could.

After Nick poured his love into me again, I was fast asleep when his velvety-soft lips kissed my arm. My groggy eyes drifted open. The patches of sky lining the window shutters were still black.

"The messenger has already made his return from Scotland," Nick said, his voice husky with sleep. "Francis says there is a letter."

In an instant, I was wide awake. "What does it say?"

"I know not. We are to meet Francis downstairs."

I wrapped my cloak over my linen smock like a bathrobe and tugged out the braid that fell down my back. Nick and I hurried down the stairwell in our bare feet and found Francis standing by the fireplace in the drawing-room. He was chewing his thumbnail and looking at us with anxious eyes, his other hand clutching a folded piece of parchment.

"Well? What news of the letter?" Nick asked. My stomach was high in my chest.

"I have not yet opened it," Francis said stiffly. "It is a task we should share."

Nick nodded. "Go ahead."

The fire gently hissed and popped as Francis broke open the wax seal. I could see the letter was not coded and was written in French. Francis's eyes flew down the page. "Mary Stuart accepts the meeting!"

A sound of relief burst from Nick's mouth, and I fell against his shoulder, barely able to stand. I could've kissed Francis for the words he was saying.

"The letter says we may meet Mary Stuart at Cessford Castle, on the border of Scotland, as soon as we are able. She encourages a hasty journey."

"She took the bait," I said with shaky laughter. "I can't believe it."

"Do we believe it?" Nick cautioned. "This is indeed a most hasty response."

Francis nodded. "The messenger said that he rode hard through the night. I offered him a rich reward. And I trust the man; he is a fine fellow."

Nick released a heavy exhale and sank onto a stool. "So, we are to journey to Scotland."

"At once," Francis said. "The roads in the wretched north bring their own troubles, and we know not what mischief we may encounter."

"Agreed," said Nick. "Let us take our leave this very day. Mary Stuart will make her assault within the week, and there is no time to be lost." He reached for my hand and laced our fingers together, and I rested my head against his muscular shoulder.

Francis ordered the night guard to wake the servants to prepare us an early breakfast. As the inky streaks of sky between the window shutters began to lighten, the three of us made a plan. We'd leave the coach here and ride on horseback to avoid drawing attention to ourselves. Rather than taking a guard along and risking word leaking out about our secret rendezvous with England's sworn enemy, we would also invite Jasper. He was strong for his age, and streetwise, and Nick and I trusted him. Francis had more than enough money to secure our food and lodging, and we'd share the coins among us in case one of us was robbed on the roads.

"What if we are all robbed together?" I asked as we sat down to sweet omelets and watered-down wine that I could barely stomach through my growing unease. The river incident with the bandit was scorched in my memory.

"Let us hope that does not occur," Francis said. He reached for the saltshaker. "And what of the queen?"

"The queen cannot accompany us," Nick said immediately. "It is much too dangerous."

"There is no doubt of it," Francis agreed. "But shall her person remain here or return to Windsor, perhaps?"

"Shall who remain here?" said a sweet voice.

Kit swished toward us like a Renaissance doll in mint-colored satin, the sleeves of her gown slashed open to reveal slices of pale-pink silk underneath.

"Good morrow to you all," Alice said with a smile, trailing Kit into the room. I could have sworn that her pregnant belly looked a little larger each day. A flash of warmth radiated through my chest. I was so happy for Alice.

"We were discussing the letter we received overnight from Scotland," Francis said, glancing around to make sure the five of us were alone in the room.

Alice went straight for the manchet bread while Kit sat beside Nick, blinking fast. "How goes the letter?"

Nick and Francis talked Kit and Alice through the contents of Mary Stuart's message of response and the details of our plan to travel to Cessford. Alice's skin paled while Kit's eyes expanded.

"I shall go to Cessford with you," Kit said.

Nick shook his head. "My dear, you know that it is much too dangerous for the queen to ride high into the north, much less to enter Scotland."

"Your brother speaks the truth, my most beloved and gracious Majesty," Francis added. "It is plainly out of the question."

"Out of the question?" Kit cried. "I am the queen, and I shall go!" She turned to Nick, her azure eyes filling with tears. "You are the keeper of my person no longer. For years and years, you would lock me up in castles and order me to be away from you. Then you left me altogether, making me believe you to be dead!" Nick's face fell, but Kit didn't stop. "I may be a child yet, but I am still the Queen of England. This is my kingdom now, and if you are to undertake a journey to save it, then I shall journey with you. And I would sooner command your imprisonment, dear brother, than have you lock me away in a castle. If you do not consent, I *will* have you taken to the Tower!"

The room shrank into silence. Nick looked stunned and flustered, his palms rubbing anxiously together.

I knew my husband. He would absolutely loathe the idea of taking Kit on a death-defying mission like this. At the same time, however, his remorse over abandoning her when we'd escaped Tudor England was a torment to his soul. He had something enormous to atone for, and he knew it.

When he finally spoke, his voice sagged with defeat. "Very well. The wish of the queen is my command. I place myself at your feet, Your Grace."

Kit's eyes popped with surprise that was quickly swallowed by determination. Before Nick could change his mind, she launched into a plan about how she would be able to travel with us safely. She would dress like a commoner and hide her Elizabethan red hair.

Francis leaned toward her. "My queen, most beloved and adored, as your Lord Protector, I must counsel you against this."

"It is concluded," Kit snapped, and Nick gave him a commanding nod to accept the decision. Francis sighed and chugged a cup of morning wine. He knew better than to attempt to argue with two Tudors united.

"What about Alice?" I asked, and she glanced at me. "You're so close to having your baby," I said to her.

She smiled bravely. "I shall do as my queen and my husband desire."

I didn't let my sadness over her submissive comment show on my face. Alice was about as feminist as a sixteenth-century woman could get, but she had still been born into a different time. She was trained to do only as the men and the superiors in her life instructed.

"My wife should be making preparations for her childbed,"

Francis said, reaching for Alice's hand. "We have made an agreement to have the child at our estate in Warwickshire."

"Yes, you should do that," Kit said. "Birthing a baby is a most perilous business. Alice and the baby might die."

Tension chewed up the air, but Kit was too young to be aware of the effect of her blunt words. Francis's cheeks had turned a shade of gray.

"The four of us will journey to Scotland," Kit announced, her petite hands clasped in her lap. "My person, my brother, my brother's wife Emmie, and Jasper Blacke. Lord Warwick, you shall journey with your wife to Warwickshire and see to it that your baby is born without harm." Francis's lips parted with surprise. "It will draw even less attention to have four of us on the road rather than five, will it not?" she asked Nick.

He gave her a nod, a blush of pride in his cheeks for her smarts. "The smaller the party to journey to Scotland, the better," he agreed.

Francis shifted uncomfortably in his seat, his fingers still grasping Alice's. "Make no mistake, I am grateful without end for the queen's kindness in allowing my person to be close at hand for the birth of our child," he said in earnest. My heart squeezed for Alice, who adored her hotheaded earl. "But I am the one who wrote the letter to the Scottish queen," he added, his brows pulled together. "Should I not be the one to greet her person?"

"The meeting is to be between only Mary Stuart and myself," Nick said in his naturally authoritative tone. "I shall make a pretense to be the Earl of Warwick, and Mary will have no cause to disbelieve it. I am the cause of this calamity and therefore shall be the one to put an end to it. What's more, I am considered quite dead already in this realm, so should some ill befall me, it will be no great loss."

All four of us expelled appalled huffs, mine loudest of all.

"Nick, nobody here is losing you," I said, closing my hand over his wrist. "And I am going in with you to meet with Mary Stuart, whether you like it or not. That's not up for debate."

Our companions lowered their eyes as Nick and I stared each other down. When he sighed and sucked back a cup of wine, I knew that I'd won this one.

Kit's eyes sparkled. "While my brother and Emmie meet with that traitor, I shall remain close at hand with Jasper Blacke," she said. "It is concluded."

I did wonder whether she would have pressed harder to attend the meeting with Mary Stuart if her minder had been anyone other than the older boy with the ponytail and the cute smile.

As we finalized the arrangements, including which horses we'd take and where we'd make our overnight stops, Francis gnawed on his bottom lip. It wouldn't be easy for a man like him to sit this one out, but I was so pleased for Alice that he wouldn't miss the birth of their baby.

A thought crossed Francis's eyes, and he leaned forward. "There is one more caution I wish to make, my lord," he said to Nick. "Mary Stuart may be the spawn of the devil, but she has a reputation for being a most bewitching, charming woman. So much so, that few English gentlemen were even permitted to meet with her during her imprisonment for fear of her persuading them toward her cause. Never forget what that woman is," Francis drummed home. "A traitor and a conspirator."

I glanced at my Tudor husband, the most charming and bewitching person I'd ever known. Mary Stuart was about to meet her match.

"I have heard this about the Scottish queen, and I take it to be rather useful," Nick said with a glint in his eye. "Let Mary Stuart use her charms and believe that she has come to bewitch my person. For that will make it easier to become close to her, and then I am going to pluck out that thorn from my side once and for all."

"What do you mean?" Kit asked, biting her fingernail.

A hush came over the room before Nick collected her little hands in his, blinking at her. "My dear, I mean to kill Mary Stuart."

Kit's face froze before she glanced at Francis and then at Nick. "I don't want to be the queen anymore," she blurted in a small voice.

Francis's mouth fell open and Nick squeezed her hand, drilling his gaze into hers. "I know," was all he said.

Nick was tasked with inviting Jasper into our plans, and I made him promise not to do anything to force the kid against his will.

"Always so kind of heart," Nick said, bringing his lips to my forehead and holding them there for a few moments. The spot tingled long after he left, and I set about choosing some better clothes to take with us than the rags we'd arrived in. Nick was to borrow a couple of Francis's amazing outfits, and Alice loaned me two of her maternity gowns—a massive stroke of luck with their loose comfort.

She helped me tie on a satin kirtle and gown the color of boysenberries, apologizing that there hadn't been enough time for the queen's cook to prepare me some fresh macarons. Her recollection of my favorite snack at court made it even harder for me to look at her tender-hearted face.

What if things didn't go the way we planned with Mary Stuart, and this was the last time I'd be close enough to Alice Grey to smell the cinnamon in her hair? Or what if a miracle occurred and Nick and I found a way to have Mary Stuart enchant us back to the twenty-first century, and I never saw Alice again? With my heart pressed in a vise, I reminded myself that I'd been in this situation more than once, and somehow Alice and I had always found a way back to each other.

She sank onto a bench draped with a Persian carpet. "I must say that I do feel quite useless with this big lump," she said in a light-hearted but apologetic tone. "I do wish that I could journey with you and help you with your plight. I also wish that my husband could ride with you. Although I could not promise he would be calm in a crisis." She made a face and I chuckled.

"Alice, you have something much more important to do," I said, sitting beside her.

"Than saving the realm?" She raised her brows.

"You are bringing a new life into the realm. There's nothing more important than that."

She smiled, running a hand over her bump. "Do you feel the baby will be a 'he' or a 'she'?"

I inhaled deeply, searching my intuition for the answer. "I think it's a 'he.'"

"Heavens, with Francis's temper?" she said, alarmed, and we both laughed.

"With you as his mother, Alice, that baby is going to be utter perfection."

"Bless you, Emmie." She patted my hand.

I swallowed the concrete in my throat. I couldn't bear leaving Alice Grey one more time without a warning. "Alice," I stumbled, "I need to tell you that…after this trip to Scotland…I'm not sure if we're going to see each other again."

The look on her face broke me. "Emmie, say not such things! If you feel the journey to be one of such peril, then I beseech you not to go!"

"No, it's not that," I said quickly.

There was so much more that I wanted to say to Alice, but I'd trained myself to be unflinchingly silent over the years. My mouth wouldn't unlock.

"There is more to this than you say," she realized, her wide eyes searching mine. "More to all of this." Her voice dropped low, and she spoke fast. "Emmie, I know there are things you are not telling me. Why you vanished this year past, choosing to live in hiding, like a peasant, rather than be with your kin and share your plight with us… leaving behind the comforts and riches you deserve as the wife of Nicholas Tudor. I cannot make any sense of it. If I may speak plainly, I believe not a word of it."

Panic rushed into my ears, circling my chest and pulsing through my veins. Alice Grey had always been able to read me like a book.

"Oh Emmie, I beseech you to tell me the truth," she pleaded. "You and the king have not been lodging in a small house in Hertfordshire; I know it. Where is it that you have been? What drove you to make a false claim of something so vile as self-murder? What is it about you that I do not know, that I feel as if I have never known?"

I could have chewed a hole through my lip. How would Alice ever be able to make sense of any of this mess without me telling her the truth? But to do that would be to expose Nick and me as heretics. Alice's husband Francis had boasted to me about burning heretics in the past. Plus, I didn't have the enchanted ring anymore to prove my bonkers story the way I had with Nick. When I'd first told him that I was a time traveler from the future, I'd had to literally drag him through time to get him to believe it.

But if I was going to live in Tudor England for the rest of my life with Alice Grey as my best friend, I couldn't keep lying to her. It was making me feel diseased inside.

I clasped her trembling fingers in mine.

"Alice, I'm going to make you a promise. If I make it back from Scotland—*when* I make it back from Scotland—I'm going to tell you some things. Some things that I'm hoping will explain a lot." I swallowed hard, choking on my own voice. "But not before then, okay? We're about to leave, and this one is going to be a long conversation."

She sat and stared at me like she was seeing me for the first time. "So, there is more to this story," she said in a whisper.

"A little more."

Alice, I know everything that is going to happen in the world for the next four hundred years.

A sheen of tears coated her eyes. "I shall count the days until then. For I love you as dearly as a sister, Emmie, and yet I feel there are things about you that I have never understood."

"You will," I said, my throat constricting. "I promise."

I hugged her as tightly as I could without hurting her precious baby. Unlike during our previous goodbyes, however, my heart ached a little less this time because I was finally going to confess the truth about me to Alice. I just had to do it in a way that kept Nick and me safe, and I had to let him know about my decision first.

"I love you eternally, Alice Grey," I said into her shoulder. "You bring that baby into the world safely, you hear me?"

I felt her tight swallow. "I shall. For my baby boy will need to meet his dear aunt, Emmie."

I pulled back, wiping my cheeks.

"Before you go," she said, reaching into an embroidered pouch tied to her jeweled belt. "I made this for you."

She handed me a small brass pendant dangling from a gold chain.

"A pomander," I said, breaking into a smile. "Thank you so

much." I brought the pendant's tiny casing to my nose, inhaling the aromatic herbs and spices that were intended to ward off bad air outside the safety of the manor.

"And this," she added, pressing something cold into my palm. I opened my fingers and was nearly blinded by the glittering sapphire the size of a postage stamp.

"Alice!"

"Keep it within your gown at all times," she said. "In case you are to find yourself in any trouble, heaven forbid, I want you to have this. I thought of a coin purse, but it would be too heavy."

My fingers curled around the stone's hard ridges. "That is incredibly thoughtful, but what if I lose it? I'd never be able to give it back to you."

"I care not if I ever see that jewel again," she said. "What I do want is to see *you* again." She pressed her lips together, her eyes watering. "My word, Emmie, I have missed you so."

My eyes suddenly let loose a waterfall of tears. Alice caught me in another hug, gently patting my back, even though her little shudders gave away that she was crying too.

I tried to thank her again for the jewel, but I couldn't speak. All I could do was hold her.

20

"Ophelia!" I cried, my boots crunching against gravel as I strode toward the skinny gray horse madly swishing her tail. "I thought I'd never see her again."

"When you were both arrested outside the Castle of Sheffield, we also took the horse," Francis explained a little sheepishly as I ran my silk glove down Ophelia's wiry mane. She snorted and stomped her hoof.

"I want to ride her instead of the mare you had planned for me," I said to Francis.

He glanced at Nick like I'd lost it. "This horse is frantic, my lady, and she is not yet saddled for riding."

Jasper stood clutching a sack of daggers given to him by Francis to distribute amongst ourselves. Kit was beside him in her traveling cloak, her eyes drifting down Jasper's mocha ponytail. *Earth to Kit,* I thought with a smile.

"We shall keep to the agreed horse," Nick said to Francis. He paced toward me, cupping my disappointed cheeks. "Ophelia has put in more than enough miles for us these past weeks, Emmie. Let us allow her some rest and ride a horse that is not raving mad."

"Okay, fine," I said with a pout. I'd become attached to Ophelia the same way I'd once become devoted to Stella, the Florentine mare I'd ridden in Nick's court.

Francis's hands fell against his thighs, the pressure of time closing in. "You saved our lives," he said to Nick, his cheeks taut. "You saved England. I am at a loss for how to thank you."

"Do not thank us yet," Nick said, curling his arm around Francis's shoulder. Arm in arm, they wandered through the archway and out into the sunlight, sharing a brotherly goodbye that would've softened even the hardest of hearts. When I turned away to give them some privacy, I caught sight of Alice's face in an upstairs window. She pressed her fingers to the latticed glass and I held up my hand in a farewell, my throat choked with tears.

Several minutes later, our three horses trotted through the manor's towering gatehouse, a cool, ominous wind whipping my skin through my traveling cloak, which concealed two of Francis's daggers. Kit was sharing a horse with Nick, leaving me to ride alone behind them, which I didn't mind. Concentrating on controlling my female palfrey and keeping up with my more experienced riding companions served as a helpful distraction from the terror of what we were setting out to do.

To kill a queen in cold blood.

As our horses galloped across the sodden grasslands, kicking up splatters of mud, I yearned for the warmth and comforts of the guarded manor back in Sheffield and its four-poster bed occupied by my delicious, softly sighing Tudor king. Now Nick was just a broad shape up ahead of me, with a little girl in a velvet traveling hat clutching him from behind.

The further north we rode, the colder the air grew that penetrated the silk scarf tied over my face, and the more consumed with loneliness I became. I was sure the reason why Kit had insisted on coming along was her penchant for adventure, but none of this felt like a fun road trip. With the grim purpose of our mission shadowing us like a thundercloud, nobody was in a talking mood during our overnight breaks in the rustic villages of Yorkshire and Durham. Nick slept between me and Kit, his mood souring as much as my own with every passing hour.

Every time a stranger on horseback galloped up behind us on the open roads, my gloves squeezed the leather reins, and my heart leaped in my chest. Mercifully, however, nobody attempted to rob us, and we purposefully avoided the dense forestlands for fear of thieves. I searched passing faces for the ice-colored eyes of the river bandit who'd stolen our blue-diamond ring, but I knew that finding him was a hopeless wish in a country this big. Swallowing the bitterness of disappointment, I forced myself to accept that I'd never see that ticket home again.

As we rode closer to the border of Scotland, the grazing cattle and English timber cottages gradually became replaced with uninhabited lime-green hills, jagged rock formations, and glassy lakes that provided water for the horses. We rode like robots until late into the night, and in just a few days, we reached Northumberland, a freezing wasteland of unforgiving wilderness. My back ached from riding, and my eyes burned with fatigue, but we had to keep going—we had to reach Mary Stuart before her invasion on the twenty-fourth of May. If our messenger had made it to Cessford Castle at lightning speed, so could we.

"Now is when we must be vigilant of the border clans," Nick said over a smoky fire at our campsite near the village of Otterburn. "I am afraid that none speak highly of their ways."

Kit sat on the opposite side of the fire from me, her hollow eyes staring into the amber flames that snapped the air. Nick and Francis had been right: This was no trip for a ten-year-old, let alone a ten-year-old queen. She was so exhausted and overwhelmed that she'd even stopped paying attention to Jasper. But the way she hovered close to Nick—the same way she had in the manor—clarified why she'd insisted on coming on this wretched journey. It wasn't just because of the adventure…now that Nick had returned from the dead, Kit didn't want to be apart from her brother, even for a moment.

Jasper tossed the remnants of his chicken bone into the fire. "How are we to get past the border clans?" he asked Nick.

"We shall bribe them," he replied matter-of-factly, and my hand brushed my side, where Alice's sapphire was still safely lodged in my bodice.

"But we are English," said Jasper. "Will the Scots be bribed by the likes of us?"

Nick gave a mocking laugh. "The border clans know no allegiance other than to what is most favorable to them on each day." He tapped the pouch of coins roped to his belt. "It ought to take no more than a gold sovereign or two. And forget not, it will be Emmie and I alone who will pass through the clan territories, so you need not feel afeared."

Kit gaped at Nick. "Surely you do not mean to leave Jasper and me here."

Nick calmly reached for another chicken leg. "We already agreed that only Emmie and I are to meet with the Queen of the Scots."

"No!" Kit said, springing back to life. She wiped an unwashed clump of tangerine hair from her eyes. "I want to come with you."

"Kit, you cannot," Nick said.

I met Jasper's knowing eyes. This was about to become another Tudor-style blow-up.

"You never allow me to do anything at all!" Kit cried, crossing her arms over her chest, her brows slanted.

Nick laughed lightly. "And what do you call this, Your Grace? No man but me would dare bring the Queen of England to such a forlorn, miserable place as this."

"Then why bring me here at all?"

He gave her an incredulous look. "My queen, it is you who said that you wished to make this journey. You insisted upon it—threatened mine imprisonment in the Tower!"

"Well, now I am insisting that you take me to Cessford Castle with you to meet mine enemy."

Nick huffed. "No, Kit."

"Yes!" She threw a stone at him, and he ducked it. Something whizzed past my ear and landed in the fire, sending embers flying in a shower of sparks. I yelped with shock and shuffled out of their path.

"What in the devil?" Nick cried before a second arrow flew into the fire, spearing the ground and swinging upright.

I gasped, scrambling farther backward into Nick's soft doublet. He wrapped an arm around me and pulled me protectively into him, his other arm shrouding Kit.

His chest rattled against my ear as he spoke to someone. "What is it that you want? Say it now!"

Clutching Nick tightly, I tilted my face to see who he was talking to, my heartbeat practically exploding out of my chest.

A group of four men was hovering on horseback, three of them aiming sharpened arrows at us from their longbows. The fourth was giving us an unpleasant stare, his arms crossed over his tartan tunic with long, draping sleeves. "What is thy business here?" he barked at Nick in a thick Scottish lilt. His eyes drifted across Nick's luxurious velvet doublet.

"We are on our way to Cessford in Roxburghshire," Nick said, a little too quickly. "We ask for safe passage."

The man's furry black brows met in the middle. "Cessford near to Jedburgh? What be thy business there?"

Kit's clammy fingers found mine beneath Nick's cloak and clutched them tightly. I gave her hand a reassuring squeeze. The other riders had shifted to form a perimeter around our group, their bows pointed at us from all angles.

"I have a meeting to attend with Mary, the Queen of the Scots," Nick said bluntly, which drew a gasp from Jasper's throat. "The meeting is one of great import."

A moment later, a pair of strong hands seized me from behind and wrenched me backward into the humid smell of mud. I wrestled free and clambered to reset my balance, holding back a scream. The guy in the tartan tunic was pressing a dagger to Nick's throat.

"And why would a pompous English gentleman have cause to meet with our queen?" he grunted at Nick.

This knob had no idea that he was talking to the former King of England, or that the Queen of England sat a few feet to his left. Kit was now clutching Jasper, hiding her head against his trembling shoulder. The clansman who'd hauled us off Nick had returned to his horse and his bow.

"One moment; I have a letter to present," said Nick. His fingers shook a little as he slowly retrieved a crumpled piece of parchment from his doublet, the blade still held to his throat, and handed it to the man. "This is a letter from your queen," Nick said. "You may read the letter and inspect the seal; it confirms the meeting."

The guy drove a menacing look at Nick's determined eyes before pacing backward, releasing the blade. Nick rubbed his neck and I slid back in under his arm. He held me tightly and pressed his lips to my hair. We waited in agonizing silence as the clansman squinted at the letter for far longer than he should have needed to. He turned the parchment over a few times, brushing his grubby fingertips over Mary Stuart's broken wax seal. The other three clansmen kept their horses steady without lowering their pointed arrows.

The one holding the letter turned to them. "These English braggarts claim to have a meeting with our queen," he scoffed.

The men finally dropped their arrows and guided their clomping horses back a few paces to share a muffled conversation.

"Be calm, my lady," Nick whispered into my ear. "This was certain to occur. It is impossible to enter Scotland without the permission of the clans."

The guy with the eyebrows and the letter bounded back toward us. "We shall bring thee to Cessford Castle on the morrow." He tossed the letter down to Nick.

"I thank you for your kindness," Nick said, slipping the note back into his doublet.

"For a fee of protection," the man added. He grinned, exposing a top row of decaying teeth.

Nick nodded, keeping his cool, as he dug into his cloth pouch. "I believe that a sovereign would be more than fair for safe passage, would it not?" A gold coin bearing the Queen of England's insignia gleamed from his open palm.

The clansman inched closer with a hand on his sheathed dagger, his bulging eyes drifting from the shining gold disc down to Nick's sagging pouch.

"I tell you what: Why not make it two coins?" Nick suggested with a careful smile. "But not one more. My kin still need to eat." He retrieved another gold sovereign and handed it to the speechless clansman. Jasper and Kit looked like I felt, like their lungs were searching for air but finding none. What was to stop these men from robbing us blind?

The clansman pocketed the two coins in the sleeveless cloak draped over his tunic, his face twisted into an uncertain grimace. After sweeping a threatening gaze across all four of us around the disturbed campfire, he spun around and swiftly mounted his horse.

"We shall make our return at first light," he said gruffly. With a "Hah!" he turned his horse and pounded away toward the rolling hills of the highlands with the other men giving chase, the horses' hooves sending a spatter of muck across my dress.

I crumpled forward, hugging my knees with a bowed head. Kit unhooked her arms from Jasper's neck and crawled back against Nick's side. She burst into tears and Nick rubbed his jaw against her hair. "Fear not, my dear girl," he said. "Those men will seem not so frightening on the morrow in the light of day. Come...we should all try to get some sleep."

Her delicate fingers clutched the edge of his doublet, hanging on like he was a life raft. "Please...do not leave me alone on the morrow," she wept. "I beseech you. I am too afeared."

Nick's eyes softened, meeting mine. I gave him a sympathetic nod of encouragement. We couldn't leave Kit alone in a place like this with thirteen-year-old Jasper. It wasn't safe.

Nick ran his hand down her blazing red hair. "Very well," he said. "We shall journey to Cessford together on the morrow. All four of us."

Jasper puffed a sigh of relief, and Kit's expression lifted as she pulled back to read Nick's face. "Do you mean it truly?" she asked. When he nodded, she flung her arms around his neck, squeezing so tightly that I thought she might crush him.

Over her shoulder, Nick gave me a small, helpless smile, and I smiled back, resting my sore muscles against our linen bundle of belongings. At that moment, Nick and Kit had never looked less like two Tudor royals and more like what they were above all else: two orphaned siblings who adored each other.

The rough-talking clansmen made good on their promise, and not long after sunrise, we were riding across the rugged Scottish border-lands with our four local escorts.

When Cessford Castle materialized over a desolate hill, my break-fast of buttered bread returned to the back of my throat. It was small for a castle, with only one turret and defensive tower, but the walls of stone looked ancient and thick—the sort of walls that would be impossible to escape if one was caught attempting to murder the castle's resident royal.

With my stomach churning, I replayed our plan in my mind. The four of us would band together and go in to meet with Mary Stuart. Nick and Jasper would carry two daggers each, so the guards could find them and take them away. I would hide one more dagger in my bodice—a small, thin blade that resembled our paring knife back in the modern world. After we were past the guards, Jasper would distract anyone surveying the meeting and I would discreetly pass Nick the dagger for him to hide in his sleeve. With my blessing, Nick would use his heartthrob face and smooth, sophisticated tone to charm the Queen of the Scots. From what he'd been told about Mary, she'd be all too keen to flirt back in a playful exchange. If Nick could just get physically close enough to Mary, he would drive his hidden dagger into her chest.

The thought of murdering the woman burned my throat until I had to spit into the dirt, but I reset my nerves. For the thousandth time, I reminded myself that this was the only way out of our situa-tion—the only way to save the people we loved and the Tudor throne.

Escaping the castle after killing the queen would be the trickiest part. Our solution sent a swell of nausea to my stomach, but it was the best idea we'd had. Late last night, I'd sewn our final three daggers into the lining of Kit's cloak, giving us easy access if we made a grab for them. Female children were so insignificant in the Tudor world that Nick assured me the guards wouldn't even think to search his little sister. It saddened me to use ten-year-old Kit as an armory, but she was thrilled to be given a purpose. Her eyes gleamed as we approached the castle gatehouse, her bright-red braids of hair care-fully hidden beneath a white coif.

The clansmen had left us about a mile out of Cessford, so the four of us rode alone over the castle ditch, our breath short and our bodies stiffening.

Showtime.

I slowed my horse and patted its wiry neck with sweaty palms while Nick greeted the castle guards up ahead, handing them his crumpled letter. After inspecting the queen's seal, they waved us on to ride inside the castle with three guards trailing us. After our horses were led away, we were ushered on foot into a gusty inner courtyard. I wrapped my arms around myself to keep the icy wind from piercing my core. A pleasant-faced attendant carried in cups of warmed wine on a tray, and I tossed mine back, wishing I could have another. Every minute we stood there in unbearable silence, waiting for instructions, the gnawing pit in my stomach expanded.

Kit hung off Nick like a fifth limb, and he gave me the faintest hint of a reassuring smile, which said, *Be calm, Emmie.* Jasper's stoicism in the face of possible peril was surprising, but I'd slowly started figuring the kid out: He was terrified of disease, which made sense after the black plague had stolen his parents from the world, but other battles didn't seem to faze him nearly as much. He made small talk with one of the guards, maintaining his composure, while my fingertips rubbed madly together, my throat bone dry.

Be calm, be calm, be calm, I told myself on loop.

Heavy and purposeful footsteps marched through the nearest archway before a man in a stunning coat of midnight-blue velvet emerged from the shadows. Nick greeted him with a polite bow.

"Lord Warwick, I believe?" the man said to him in a Scottish accent, tipping his feathered cap. "It is a pleasure to make your acquaintance. I understand that you have undertaken quite a journey in request of an audience with Her Grace."

I noticed that he didn't refer to Mary Stuart as "Her Majesty the Queen" now that she had technically renounced the Scottish throne in favor of her son James. Nobody seemed to know what to do with Mary Stuart.

"The audience has already been granted, my lord," Nick said to him, handing over Mary Stuart's letter. "May I present my sisters, the

Mistresses Beaumont," he added, gesturing to Kit and me, "and my manservant, Nicholas Grace. We are all here to meet with the queen, if it should please Her Grace."

I almost snickered. In choosing an alias for Jasper Blacke, Nick had combined his first name with my last name, which had made it easy to remember. And, for today, Kit and I really were sisters.

The man in the lovely cloak made a curt nod before scanning Mary's letter. No person of his station would dare question a royal in this century, so he demonstrated no curiosity or judgment about what Mary was up to.

"The queen and I came to no agreement about the date or hour of our meeting," Nick said calmly. "Therefore, I ask that you forgive our unexpected arrival. Is the queen likely to give an audience on this day?"

"The queen may," the man said coolly before handing the letter back to Nick. "Follow me, my lord."

We quickly chased him through the archway that opened into a drafty corridor. Was that it? Mary Stuart was going to see us right now? Equal parts relief and fear crashed into me with such ferocious speed that I nearly collapsed into the stone wall.

With two brawny guards trailing us like gangsters, we shuffled up a spiral staircase, along a long gallery hung with fading tapestries of mythical sea creatures, and into a plain, square-shaped room with two benches lining the walls. Hampton Court Palace in England made this castle look like a run-down shack. Now that we were here, the lengths Mary Stuart had taken to steal the glorious throne of England were making even more sense.

"The guards will need to search your persons," the man in the cloak cautioned.

"Certainly," said Nick, holding out his arms.

The guards set to work patting down Nick and Jasper, relieving them of their daggers as planned, while the well-spoken man disappeared through a pair of guarded wooden doors. My nervous palms were slick with sweat and I rubbed them against my dress.

The guards didn't even look at Kit, but one casually pointed his thumb at me. "What of 'er?" he said to the shortest guard, who appeared to be the one in charge.

My chest caved inward as my mind flew to the thin dagger stuffed inside my bodice. The short guard grunted his approval, and I was yanked forward, two calloused hands brushing down my legs and arms. I shut my eyes and tried to block out the memory of the bandit at the river. The guard stepped away from me and my eyes opened, meeting Nick's concerned gaze. I passed him a subtle look of relief. The guard hadn't found the dagger, nor had he touched me inappropriately.

The pikes held by the door guards clanged as they uncrossed and the man in the cloak paced back through.

"Her Grace will see you now," he said smoothly.

My knees buckled. Nick took Kit's delicate hand in his, and I wished he could take mine, but I held my nerve. I inhaled a deep, calming breath and followed them through the paneled doors to where Mary Stuart, the Queen of the Scots, was waiting for us.

21

MARY STUART'S PRESENCE CHAMBER WAS STARK AND COLD, WITH NO throne or canopy of estate. She sat rather plainly in a carved chair by a small fireplace, folds of partially stitched fabric rippling from her hands down to the tiled floor. On a cushion at her feet rested a young maid with strawberry-blond braids clutching an embroidery hoop. A long-haired, sausage-shaped dog stretched lazily across Mary's silk slippers.

"Your Grace," Nick said with a deep bow. Before I could get a good look at the Queen of the Scots' face, I copied him and folded forward, my heart drumming through my ears.

"I bid you good morrow, Lord Warwick," Mary said with a gentle smile and a French accent, her voice light and musical. Not at all threatening. The young maid stared up at Nick, her round eyes visibly struck by his handsome face.

"At last, we meet," Nick said to Mary Stuart, oozing charm. "I must speak plainly and say that it greatly pleased me to receive your favorable response to my letter."

Mary's deep-set eyes swept across Jasper and me before settling on Kit. Panic gripped my chest. Kit was the queen that Mary Stuart was plotting to bring down. It suddenly seemed preposterous that she wouldn't recognize her.

But Mary's eyes drifted away from Kit with no hint of recollection. "You brought friends with you," she said to Nick, demanding an explanation, as I took in her features. She was long-limbed, like a model, and almost sickly pale but quite breathtaking. She could certainly be described as beautiful.

"I brought two of my kin and a manservant," Nick said like that wasn't important.

"To such a meeting as this?" Mary replied delicately.

Nick gave a dismissive flick of his hand. "My manservant goes where I go. As for my sisters, they begged to accompany me so they might meet such a fine and gracious queen as Your Grace. The Beaumont family has long admired the Stuarts." He sounded so sincere; he was doing brilliantly. The young maid pinned her gaze to her embroidery, but her cheeks had colored pink.

Mary slowly shook her head and momentarily stuck her needle between her teeth so she could reset her fabric. "Rather an extraordinary declaration for an English courtier to make."

Nick gripped his hat in his hands. "And yet, I make it all the same." His tone deepened. "Your Grace, I have come a long way to offer myself to you."

Mary's brows raised like he'd said something provocative, but her copper eyes danced. Nick smiled at his "poor" choice of words, with his off-the-charts magnetism, and she blushed.

Good. She finds Nick Tudor as irresistible as I do. That'll make things easier when he has to get close enough to kill her.

Were we really going to kill this soft-spoken woman? My throat felt pierced with needles.

"I have come a long way to demonstrate my support for you, my true queen," Nick clarified, bowing his head like she was a deity. Jasper and Kit had become two frozen mannequins beside me. "As you are aware, my countrymen have suffered a great deal at the hands of the Tudors," Nick continued smoothly. "Since Queen Elizabeth, the Tudors have refused to even consider restoring the old and true religion in

England. They speak of the Pope as if His Holiness is the devil himself. And after King Nicholas took such vile action as to commit self-murder in the betrayal of God, leaving the realm to no more than a *child*—well, if I may speak plainly, Your Grace, I have had quite enough." He stepped closer to her, dropping to one knee like he was proposing.

Mary's fingers paused on her thread, her chest rising and falling a little faster. The maid, now at eye level with Nick, looked like she could eat him up like ice cream.

"Mary, my most gracious and truest queen," Nick said earnestly, "I would sooner die a traitor's death than live a life in which your person does not occupy the throne of England, of which you are most deserving as the true, Catholic heir of King Henry Tudor. Our country is weak; our lords of the council are at war with each other. The rebellion with the Duke of Norfolk a year past left our army in tatters. I have the ear of the ambassadors to France and Spain, and there has never been a more opportune time to strike. Your Grace, it would gladden my heart without end to lead an army for you against Queen Catherine, if you will have me."

For several moments, Mary gazed down at him while I continued to gawk at this woman who had caused so much trouble in my life. Her auburn hair was plaited beneath a plain hood; the collar of her ruff was sewn with seed pearls. The lace that edged her crimson bell sleeves was fraying, and her slender fingers were bare of gemstones. Mary Stuart was not a queen with much money.

She made a slow, steady inhale before unhurriedly folding up her sewing and handing it to the maid at her feet.

Nick was still on one knee, poor thing, and Mary glanced at the rest of us over his shoulder. "I wish to speak without the company of your kin, Lord Warwick."

Nick rose back up, nervously rubbing his thigh. "Your Grace, if it pleases you, I beseech you to allow my sisters to stay."

"So that they may act as witness when you report my treasonous words to Queen Catherine?" she quipped.

"Not at all," Nick replied, shrugging off the comment. "The more eyes and ears you have in the English court, the better, even if they belong to a feeble woman and a child."

Feeble woman? I had to let that one pass.

"So now there is to be a plot?" Mary asked, her eyes daring. The young maid's breathing had intensified, but she kept her eyes lowered.

Nick smiled and tilted his head at Mary like she was making things difficult for him. "Believe me when I say that my sisters feel the same way as I do about the state of affairs in England, or they would not have made such a perilous journey here," he said. "In fact, I wish to present mine eldest sister, the Lady Anne Beaumont, as a match for your illustrious son, His Royal Highness, King James." Nick lifted his hand at me, and I cowered inside. We hadn't discussed this, but he was clearly improvising—finding a way to keep Kit and me in the room so he could access our hidden daggers.

I glanced at the two burly guards standing beside the door.

"Good gracious, you do keep a high opinion of yourself," Mary said, tugging her shawl tighter. "Very well, but at least have your companions sit down; all these *faces* looking at me," she added like that was a horror.

Nick turned and nodded a command, and Kit, Jasper, and I stepped over to the wooden bench beneath the window. I sat on the edge, poised to move quickly when Nick was ready for the dagger. Would he give me a signal? What about the young maid? Would she lurch up in defense of Mary and try to wrestle him for the knife? Would he have to stab her too? How on earth would we pull any of this off with those door guards just a few feet away?

Mary was now complaining to Nick of the drafty accommodations at the castle, and he was sitting in the chair beside hers, the young maid leaning a little too close to his leg. The shaggy-haired dog hopped onto its bony paws and disappeared beneath Mary's billowy skirts.

I stole a sideways glance at Kit and Jasper. Kit was sliding her little fingers up and down the outside of her cloak, feeling for the daggers. I placed a hand on her knee and gave her the subtlest of headshakes. She was so young to be put in this position.

Nick was hunched forward, listening intently to Mary, who'd confusingly switched their language to French.

With no clue what they were saying, all the air in the musty room evaporated. I rubbed my sweaty neck, riddled with anxiety, and watched Nick like a hawk. Mary was speaking gravely, but it was Nick's reaction to her words that turned my blood to icy water. He jerked backward like he wanted to get away from her, startling the maid at his feet. When he turned to look at me, the horror in his eyes shot me back to when he'd learned about Kit's death in the Tower of London chapel. *Oh no.*

Mary said something more in French before Nick rose and approached our bench, his face washed of color.

"My good man," he said to Jasper. "I bid you take the young Mistress Beaumont outside for a time."

"Me?" Kit said with dismay.

Nick offered his hand to me. "Lady Anne, will you please join me in the company of the queen?"

"Of course," I said in an unsure voice, my panicked heart thumping against the dagger in my bodice. Why would Nick kick Kit and Jasper out of the room? They were an essential part of our plan!

Not one to argue, Jasper took Kit's hand and gingerly guided her through the doors crossed with pikes.

Mary Stuart sat and watched me with unreadable eyes while I dragged a stool over to her. The young maid shifted away from Nick with visible reluctance, making space for me. My mouth was drier than a desert at high noon. Why had Nick called me over? I sucked in a deep breath, trying to sense the heaviness of the dagger strapped to my chest, but I couldn't get any air.

Mary dismissed the guards with a flick of her wrist, leaving Nick and me alone with her and the maid. The heavy doors banged shut, making me jump.

Nick placed a hand on my knee. "Emmie," he said thickly.

"What are you saying?" I replied, my breath a rush in my ears. "It's Lady Anne Beaumont."

He shook his head. "She knows, Emmie. The queen knows who we are."

Every inch of the room slipped away into darkness, like it had been swallowed up by the earth.

My jaw hung as I dragged my eyes to Mary. Her smug, stiff smile said it all: She'd figured us out. She knew who we were—and most likely knew that we were here to kill her. A deathlike coldness gripped my body.

"I admire your courage," Mary said to me in a steady voice. "I especially admire such courage when it comes from the heart of a woman."

Flustered, I turned to Nick, but he'd become mute.

"How did you know it was us?" I stammered to Mary, not wanting to believe it. My eyes darted down to the maid, who was clearly doing her level best not to stare, but how could she not after what she'd heard?

"There is a great deal that I know," the queen said obscurely, fingering a thick, gold signet ring circling her middle finger. When she brought the ring to her lips and began whispering into it, Nick reached his arm out as if to protect me.

"Tread lightly, Emmie. This is witchcraft."

"*Witchcraft?*"

Mary smiled and lowered her wrist, allowing me a clear view of the face of the ring. It was shaped like a flower within a circle, an image I'd seen before—carved into the cheek of the witch, Agnes Nightingale, that Nick had once hanged for heresy.

My stool scraped the tiled floor as I lurched backward.

"Be not alarmed," Mary said in a gentle tone. "It is a simple watching spell. I was merely seeing how the young Queen Catherine occupies her time outside. She appears to do no more than wait for her brother and with a troubled heart." Nick looked away, his eyes storm clouds.

"Okay, fine, we get it," I snapped at Mary. "You're one talented bitch...sorry, I meant witch. I guess you saw this all coming, then, but allowed us to travel all the way here in any case. Was that so you can kill us right now? Because that would make things so easy for you, wouldn't it? No need to invade or start a war. And you'll finally have the throne of England, which doesn't belong to you and never will, no matter where you park your butt." My words seethed through my teeth. With the exception of Nick, I'd lost everything because of this woman. Mary's young maid was gaping up at me.

"The queen is not intending to kill us," Nick said, his quivering hand back on my knee. "Or I would not have let Kit out of my sight."

"Then what the hell is going on?" I said, wishing I could untie my stifling bodice and toss it at the wall.

Mary leaned toward me, the sun streaming through the window casting light upon her bronze eyes. "I wish to make a bargain with you. I have shared my proposal already with King Nicholas." Nick tensed beside me. "I am aware that you have made up your mind about me, but you are misguided," Mary said to me. "I have no desire to kill an anointed king or an anointed queen, especially one so young as Catherine. But I cannot put an end to what has already begun. The throne of England does belong to me and always has. I have thousands of men, from England to Spain to Rome, ready to take up arms in my name and restore the true religion in England. Make no mistake, I will take your throne, but I am prepared to offer something in return."

I inhaled a sharp breath, bracing myself.

"If you surrender the throne to me without incident," Mary said, "in exchange, I offer King Nicholas and Queen Catherine their lives."

My eyes swept to Nick, my mouth falling open. Keeping Nick and Kit alive was all I wanted. But, to him, losing the Tudor throne would be as unimaginable as losing Kit. It was his family's legacy, their birthright. He was holding his head in his hands.

"But how will you guarantee their lives?" I asked Mary. "And what sort of a life would it be if you kicked them off the throne and sent them into hiding? I don't understand—are you talking banishment?" Surely Mary wouldn't be that stupid. King Nick was already believed dead, but if Queen Catherine was banished by a foreign queen, she'd still have countless English supporters who'd want to fight for her.

Mary's eyes gleamed unnervingly. "You believe I know not the blasphemous actions of you and your Tudor king these past years? You forget that I was there when the king's coronation ring was enchanted by a most powerful soothsayer. You forget that I have the powers of the sight. My dear, with mine own eyes, I have already seen the journeys you have taken with that enchanted ring to places that one cannot begin to believe." She was playing with her signet ring again while her young maid panted unsteady breaths like this was all too much. "And now I offer something to you that is much more valuable than banishment," Mary continued. "If you give me the throne of England now, I will allow King Nicholas and Queen Catherine to use the ring's enchantment to take leave of this realm. I will not stop you," she added to Nick. "You may use the enchanted ring to make your return to the future. But if you ever return to this realm, I *will* kill you."

My chest was torn open and set on fire. Mary Stuart wanted to send us all forward in time, where we would be safe and together—even Kit! My soul flashed and seared with blinding, beautiful light before it was devoured by a despairing darkness.

"There's something you didn't see with your magical little ring there," I said painfully. "The blue-diamond ring is gone. A bandit stole it from us near Maidenhead in England. He's probably in the twenty-first century right now, wondering what the hell he's been smoking."

Mary brushed the comment aside. "You place altogether too much importance on the ring," she said. "What matters, my dear, is the *spell*. And I remember the words of that enchantment as clear as day. All I need to do is to cast the very same enchantment."

A gasp burst from my throat. "Are you serious?" I grabbed Nick's hand, his fingers curling into mine.

Mary had her eyes set on the wall behind me, seeing something that wasn't there. "The king's coronation ring that you say was stolen by a bandit...I can see that its enchantment has come to an end. Had that ring been yet in your possession, it would have taken you nowhere."

I sucked in a steadying breath. So, the blue-diamond ring had contained enough magic to bring Nick and me here in the first place, but it would never have gotten us home. That was some relief. While that disgusting bandit now had a multimillion-dollar royal ring that he didn't deserve, at least he couldn't use it to travel through time and attack women in my century.

Nick's body was tilted toward mine, and I wanted to crawl into his lap and weep with relief. Could we really be on our way home?

"I will provide another enchantment," Mary restated, "but there will be some difference. For one, I cannot take the chance that a Tudor will return to this realm once I am the Queen of England. That is not part of the bargain. Your departure will be permanent, and therefore, the spell will be for one journey only." My throat tightened as she looked at Nick. "Mine enchantment will bring you to when and whence you last had the blue-diamond ring in the twenty-first century; I can make that come to pass. But the spell will never bring you back to this world."

Nick's fingers had tightened in mine. I was more than okay with that arrangement, but what would he think of it?

"There is one more condition," Mary added, and for the first time, her voice carried a tremble. "This particular enchantment is intended for one person only. As you have seen, it can work for two souls, but never three." She paused so the information would sink in. "Only two persons may take the journey through time."

I slowly shook my head, trying to catch sense of what she was saying. If Mary could only send Nick and me home to the twenty-first century, what would happen to Kit?

She expelled a heavy, pointed sigh. "I hope I am clear when I say that this bargain is to exchange the lives of *two* Tudor royals for the throne of England. Therefore, King Nicholas and Queen Catherine should take the journey through time. Not Mistress Grace. Or you may all choose to remain here, and none of you will ever set foot outside of this castle," she finished, her eyes shining strangely.

"You cannot in good conscience mean to send my sister and me to the future alone!" Nick snapped hoarsely.

"Why not just cast the spell twice?" I asked, my heart crawling into my throat. "You can send two of us, and then the other one."

Mary offered me a sympathetic smile that I wanted to slap off her face. "If only the enchantment had that sort of power, Mistress Grace.

For an enchantment of this size, only one may be cast. It can take many years for such a spell to wear away."

Nick hunched forward and breathed into his knees.

"No!" I said to Mary, rubbing his trembling back. "There has to be some other way!"

When Nick sat up again, he looked like he might be sick all over the floor. "Be calm, Emmie," he said to me, his voice a thin line. "I know what we shall do." He drove a look of pure venom into Mary, but his expression was resolute. "You will send Mistress Grace and my sister Catherine to the twenty-first century without further delay, and then I will offer you my neck freely. Do with me what you will, you heartless devil, and have your blasted throne. As long as Emmie and Catherine are safe."

"Absolutely not!" I cried. "No, send Nick and Catherine like you said," I said to Mary before she could accept his offer. Her stunned features blurred through my tears. "I will be the one to stay here," I pleaded. "You can let me live. I'm a nobody…I'm no threat to you. Just stick me on a farm somewhere, and I'll never cause you any trouble. *Please.*"

"No!" Nick's face was a burning-red firestorm. "I will never consent to that."

Mary's maid gasped a small sob, and Mary shot her down with a look sharper than a blade before settling her gaze on Nick.

"I accept your offer," she said to him. "If you wish to send Queen Catherine and Mistress Grace to the future and remain here in their stead, I can promise you a clean death by the sword."

A cry burst from my throat.

Mary spurted a huff, like she was fed up, and rose to her imposing height, embroidered satin falling over the tips of her silk slippers. Her maid jumped to her feet and scooped up the wriggling dog, her cheeks splotchy like she might cry.

"It seems as if you need a moment alone," Mary said to Nick and me. "I need not bear witness to this eruption of sentiment. I shall take my leave for you to think upon it, but I will make my return shortly. Take not too long, Your Grace," she warned Nick, like there would be consequences for becoming a nuisance to her.

Mary and her pink-faced maid disappeared through the double doors, the clanging of crossed pikes making it clear that we were still being guarded.

Nick turned to me, his eyes bleeding pain. "Emmie, I beseech you. Not in any way would I agree to this unthinkable bargain if I did not believe it to be the only solution that will keep you and Kit safe."

"You can't let that woman do this…you *can't*," I said in a low, desperate voice. "She's going to win!"

I'd never seen my larger-than-life husband look so defeated. "Mary has already won, do not doubt it," he said grimly. "I was a prince for one and twenty years, Emmie; a king for nine. I know when I have my back against the wall. That woman will never allow us to walk out of this castle alive."

My eyes flashed down to where the dagger was still concealed inside my bodice.

He shook his head at me. "We have lost the element of surprise. To attempt that now would be folly."

My stomach hardened into a sheet of rock. "But we could still get the English army to fight! We don't have to accept her offer!"

"You know it is too late for that. The invasion we learned of in the future is set to occur in two days, and with the support of France, Spain, and Rome, no less. If we push Mary's bargain aside, she will kill us all in a moment."

"So, we walked right into her trap," I said thickly, my eyes stinging.

He nodded, catching my escaping tear with his knuckle. "We did. We thought too much of Mary's treason and too little of her interest in the dark arts. That woman has indeed become powerful."

"And now you're going to lose the Tudor throne to that witch," I said, my voice breaking on the rancid words.

His despairing eyes fell closed. "All my family has worked for…the bloody battles we have fought…to see the dignity and title of the Queen of England pass to that treasonous heretic." His teeth clenched. "At least, if I am dead, I will not see that horror come to pass."

I pulled him close. "Don't even say those words!"

He folded his arms around my neck, his wet eyes dampening my skin. His voice was in pieces. "Emmie, you must know that I would never take that journey with Kit to the future without you."

I could hardly speak, my chest hurt so much. "But Mary will kill you if you don't."

She'd been adamant that both Nick and Kit had to disappear, one way or the other. The only way she'd allow me to take Nick's place and escape to the future with Kit would be if she had Nick executed.

If you wish to send Queen Catherine and Mistress Grace to the future and remain here in their stead, I can promise you a clean death by the sword.

"In truth, Mary Stuart could have killed us all the moment we set foot in Scotland," he said into my shoulder. "We must consider ourselves fortunate that the woman has enough humanity left to allow two of us to take leave of this place." He pulled back, his red-rimmed eyes leveling with me. "And that is to be you and Kit—the only persons I truly care for in this world or any other. You know that I cannot let that child die. It is what we came here for—to save her life."

"But not at the cost of yours!" I couldn't see through my tears. The fact that we were even having this conversation made the room spin of control, like I was on a horrible, nauseating ride that I couldn't escape.

"Nick, I'm the one who caused all of this," I said in a breathless whisper. "*I* came to your time. *I* fell in love with you. *I* allowed you to abandon your throne and let Mary Stuart through the door. I hate the fact that the only way that you and Kit can leave this castle is to take a one-way trip through time to a world that you don't understand." My voice broke open. "But this is what Mary wants—for you and Kit to go—and that's what's going to happen."

I couldn't look at his beautiful face; my eyes were drowning in tears. The thought of sending him to the future on a one-way ticket without me was unthinkable...I couldn't think it. I couldn't even believe it.

I would just have to live it.

I would have to find a way to survive in this world without him. If Mary Stuart let me live, I'd devote my life to finding a soothsayer who could perform the same enchantment as Mary and bring me back to Nick. I clung to the smallest inkling of hope that thought inspired.

He cupped my face and brushed his thumbs across my soaked cheeks. "Emmie, please cry not," he said, but he was crying too. "This is not your fault," he whispered. "It is Mary's. It was Mary Stuart who had that ring cursed in the first place. And I cannot regret what has since come to pass; how could I?" He pressed his soft lips to my forehead, holding them there. "The ring brought me to you. I felt a love so deep that everything else fell away. It gave me a reason for breathing on this earthly plane. From the moment I was born, all I was told was that there was no place more beautiful in this world than heaven. But then I met you, and the only place I ever wanted to be was here, by your side. How could anything be more beautiful than a life with you? God made me a king, Emmie, but you made me a man. And that means more to me than you will ever know."

I sobbed into him, a repulsive, gut-wrenching truth collapsing over me like a rotten cloak that I couldn't take off: I was going to lose Nick. After today, I would never see him again. At that moment, I could've plunged my dagger into Mary Stuart's heart without a second thought.

Low voices chattered on the other side of the doors, and we snapped upward, sniffling and wiping our eyes.

"So, let's tell her," I said with determination. "It's going to be you and Kit, like she wanted. I'm going to stay here."

Nick shook his head slowly at me, his hands curling so tightly over mine that he almost crushed my fingers. "Emmie, you cannot take this away from me. You *must* let me do this, please. I am begging you with all my heart."

"Take what away from you?"

His shattered eyes filled with tears. "My chance to do what is right. I could not save my mother, Emmie, when she went to God. I could not save Kit when Mathew Fox made his attempt to steal her life away. Had you not been there, Kit would have died, plain and simple." His lips trembled, his face a heartfelt, urgent plea for mercy. "Please, let me save the girls I love. I have no interest in being in a world in which you are not. Besides, what life could Kit and I have in a realm in which we understand naught?"

"But at least you'll be alive," I said, my chest heaving with painful, piercing breaths.

His voice was a whisper. "My lady, I will live on through Kit. That girl has my blood and my heart." He reached for my hand and placed it on his hammering chest. "*You* and Kit have my heart." He could scarcely get the words out. "Let me die for you both, Emmie, please. This is what is right; this is what I want. All I wish for now is for you and Kit to be safe. She will become a sister to you; you can show her the future in all its comforts and pleasures. You know that girl adores adventure." His gorgeous, devastated smile broke me.

"But it won't be the same without you." My chest erupted with breathless, convulsing sobs. I didn't want to accept...I could never accept...but Nick Tudor had always had a way of undoing me.

He took me in his arms, and we wrapped tightly together, squeezing until we became one body and one beating heart.

"You have given me so much more than this world ever could," he said through gasps. His lips, salty with tears, kissed every inch of my face until my trembling mouth found his. We kissed deeply and with frenzied desperation, tasting each other's tears, and whispering breathless words of love.

"You have always provided for me," I cried into his lips. "You have changed my life...my heart...and I am going to pray to your God each and every day that I will see you again, in this world or the next. And I promise you, then you'll really know heaven."

He brushed away his tears that wouldn't stop pouring and took my hands, his fingers shuddering almost as much as his voice. "And I will thank God that my girls are alive, and free, and happy." He tried to smile through his crushing heartbreak. "Be *happy*, my miracle girl." He tucked a lock of hair behind my ear. "Be happy knowing how loved you are."

22

My aching eyes pulled open for only a moment. I moaned and clutched my head, which throbbed at the temples, and rolled onto my stomach. All I could smell was oral-scented laundry liquid, the scent so strong it was almost toxic.

I dragged my deadweight of a body to sit up, the room falling into place around me as my vision gradually cleared. My eyes, red and swollen, blinked up at the paint-chipped ceiling. There was no smell of woodsmoke or gentle crackling of a dying fire, just the deathlike silence of the queen-size bed and two bedside tables, hand-painted in a cheap powder blue. Beside me, a pair of tiny leather boots poked through folds of striped cotton sheets, the dainty body that wore them lying upside down.

"Kit!" I blurted, my voice a throaty whisper.

When I touched her arm, she didn't flinch. Her skin was ghostly pale, and her eyes were shut. I wasn't sure she was even breathing. I gently clutched her shoulders, so small and frail in my fingers, and tugged her upward. She expelled a shuddery sigh before her eyes drifted open, staring into mine.

Thank goodness. Her white coif had fallen askew over her tangerine braids.

"Emmie?" she said in her sweet voice, and I pulled her close to hug her tightly. The scent of roses and lavender on her skin hurtled my mind back to just a few hours ago.

Kit and I are sitting on ice-cold tiles, our arms and legs threaded together, rocking back and forth as the world rises and swirls all around us with a terrible, howling wind.

"It's okay," I mumbled, tears blurring my eyes. "We're safe."

She twisted to gawk at the room like it was an alien landscape, her gaze locking onto the ceiling fan. Her clammy hand squeezed mine so hard that I thought her fingers might break. "I believe the enchantment worked, Emmie," she said shakily.

"Yes," was all I could get out, my back resting against the wooden headboard so it could hold me up. Mary Stuart's terrifying spell—her chants rising in volume until she was screaming—had worked exactly as she'd said it would. Kit and I had woken up inside my bedroom in my Borehamwood terrace—the exact place in which Nick and I had fallen asleep weeks ago when we'd time traveled to Tudor England. An intolerable, searing pain drilled into my chest and rose up into my neck, choking me.

I could still see him—a flash of chestnut curls and weeping eyes as he was dragged from the room by two stony-faced guards while Mary strode toward Kit and me, whispering into her signet ring.

My vision wobbled again with a fresh swell of tears, my chest bursting, my mouth wanting to scream like a wild animal's, but Kit was trembling beside me, crawling into my side. I wrapped an arm around her and bit into my lower lip, willing my eyes to stay dry. *Don't cry, don't cry, don't fucking cry.*

I could break down later. When I was alone, I could allow the tidal wave of unthinkable despair to crash over me and drown me. I would cry for Nick then. I didn't know how my body was going to make it through that many tears. But right now, I had to think with a level head. Taking my bag to Tudor England with me had been one of the dumbest decisions I'd ever made. Now I had no money, no identification, and no phone. Everything had been left behind in the sixteenth century.

Including the man that I loved more than anything else on this Earth.

My chest compressed with violent, crushing pain again, and I silently berated myself to hold it together in front of Kit. Her little body was quivering into my side.

The waves of loss kept breaking over me with relentless force as my mind tore backward. I hadn't even had a chance to tell Alice Grey the truth about who I really was. Had Mary Stuart executed Alice and Francis—even their new baby—for their loyalties to the Tudors and his connections to the English throne? Or had she let them live thanks to the same crumb of compassion that had allowed Kit and me to go free?

One person that I was sure I would never learn the fate of was Jasper Blacke. There would be nothing on the internet about a commoner like him. Had Mary Stuart allowed Jasper to ride out of that castle and back across the borderlands into England, or had she executed him like she had my beautiful husband?

I was desperate not to burst into tears in front of Kit, but I couldn't wrench my mind away from my selfless Nick. The man who'd turned out to be *nothing* like his infamous epithet, Nicholas the Iron-heart. All that man had wanted was for the people he loved to be safe, and he'd done everything he could to make that happen, including give up his life.

"I need to get up," I said to Kit in a shuddering voice. If I didn't stand and move, I was going to break apart at the seams.

As we climbed out of the bed, Kit's awestruck eyes swept every inch of the space and its strange articles: the teal-green metal lamp, the dresser stacked with old magazines that I used for design inspiration, the electric radiator lining the wall.

"I have so much to explain to you about this world," I said, taking her fingers in mine. "And I promise I will."

What did Nick always say to me?

Be calm, Emmie.

I gasped an agonized sob, and when Kit flinched, I bore down on my pain, pushing it beneath the surface with all my might.

She trailed me into the hallway while I deliberately faced away from her, hiding the grief that twisted my features. The house was dark and musty, and I made a mental note to open all the windows in the morning. But it brought me some relief to find the place exactly as we'd left it, given I was now several weeks behind on rental payments.

What time was it? The sky was a blanket of ink through the living room window. As I turned toward the wall clock in the kitchen, my eyes caught the back door that led to our courtyard garden. I spun away from it, my chest full to bursting. The thought of seeing Nick out there, tending to the plants, nearly sent me to my knees.

"This is your home?" Kit asked, her feet nervously locked to the worn carpet.

"Yes. I lived here with your brother," I said, attempting a smile, but my cheeks were filled with lead.

Her face and shoulders fell, and I rushed forward to catch her in a hug.

"It's okay, Kit," I whispered into her sweet-smelling braids of hair. "I promise we're going to be okay."

She sniffled, and I crouched to my knees, her broken face deepening the pain in my heart.

"I want you to know something." I smoothed down a loosened string on her kirtle. "This world is very, very different from yours, I know," I said carefully. "But I promise you that it is absolutely *amazing*."

Her wet cheeks lifted a little.

"It's going to take a lot of getting used to, but I think you're going to be very happy here, Catherine Tudor. I really mean that."

Her teary eyes held mine for a moment before she blurted a question that made her breath quiver. "Emmie, what do you believe happened to my brother?"

My cheeks tightened, the tidal wave of grief swelling behind my shoulders again, ready to engulf me and drag me under.

"Why don't we have a look and find out?" I replied in a barely audible whisper. Nick's grisly death at the hands of the Queen of the Scots was surely burned into every history article and book on the sixteenth-century Tudors.

But I couldn't face it yet. I wasn't ready to see it written in black and white like it meant nothing. It would kill me.

"Tomorrow," I said to her. "We'll look at everything tomorrow."

Her voice wobbled. "How will you know? Do you have a library?"

"Kind of." I hoped my laptop would still turn on after having been switched off for more than four weeks straight.

"Am I still the queen?" she asked naively, her voice a bewildered breath.

I wrapped an arm around her. "No, my love," I said softly. "But what you are here is totally free. No one is coming to hurt you, ever again. No one is going to expect things of you or put the fate of the world on your shoulders."

She blinked up at me.

"We're going to get through this," I said, as much for my benefit as hers. "We're going to get through this together, and I'm going to show you some things in this world that you will *love*."

Her eyes expanded as I tried to smile, imagining introducing Kit to things like ice cream, chocolate, movies, and theme parks. A faint trickle of hope leaked into my hollow chest. With whatever little money I had, I would give Kit the best childhood imaginable. The kind of childhood she would never have had as a sixteenth-century Queen of England.

She hovered there on the carpet, thin with grief and clearly frightened to take a step further inside my futuristic home.

"I have a lot to show you, but how about a nice, warm bath first?" I suggested. "Baths haven't changed much in four hundred years, except we all have taps with running water now, not just the queen," I added with a wink. "While you have a bath, I'll make you something yummy to eat and then tuck you back into bed and read to you. How does that sound?"

She nodded vigorously, her eyes drying up.

Once Kit was inside a steaming cloud of bath bubbles, I left the bathroom door open and dashed into the kitchen to fling open my freezer. I sagged with relief to discover a cardboard box of stuffed-crust pepperoni pizza. It would be the perfect thing to serve Kit until I could figure out how I was going to restock the refrigerator. Not only would that mean introducing her to the grocery's store's fluorescent lights and aisles of junk food, but my wallet had surely rotted by now at the bottom of the River Thames.

As I slid the frostbitten pizza inside the oven, a memory of handing Nick a plate piled with greasy slices of overcooked pepperoni latched onto my back.

Let me die for you both, Emmie, please.

A gust of heat blasted my face as I shut the oven door.

How could anything be more beautiful than a life with you? God made me a king, Emmie, but you made me a man.

I slumped to my knees and clutched my chest with both hands, heaving silent sobs into the linoleum floor that left me gasping.

Kit and I curled up beside each other in the bed I'd once shared with Nick. She was scrubbed clean and back in her sixteenth-century linen smock, her spirits a little higher since she'd tasted pizza while I'd done my best to explain the science behind electricity and lights.

She closed her eyes while I read to her from Nick's Bible, her jaw stretching open with yawns on loop. Within minutes, her little body was lost to the peaceful arms of sleep.

I lay there in the darkness with an arm stretched behind my head, a mountain higher than Everest growing tall over me and breaking through the ceiling. The climb to the top of that mountain, where some sense of happiness and purpose awaited me again, felt insurmountable. How would I ever get all the way up there? How would I get out of bed each morning knowing that I would never look into his mesmeric eyes again; never hear his steadying voice or feel his protective arms around me? How would I raise Kit on my own? She didn't even have any identification papers. How could I go to college classes if I had Kit to look after? How on earth would a ten-year-old Tudor queen handle something like school?

I rolled onto my side, Nick's words crashing into me like waves breaking against a gloomy dock.

All I wish for now is for you and Kit to be safe. You can show her the future in all its comforts and pleasures.

Easier said than done, Nick Tudor, I thought, a flash of fury charging through me. Now that I was back here, his decision to stay behind in Tudor England and die by the sword made perfect sense. It was the easier option. It was the option without the mountain of inconsolable grief to climb. He would never have to learn to go on without me.

My lady, I will live on through Kit. That girl has my blood and my heart.

My cheeks crumpled into painful folds, my choked tears dampening the pillowcase. I pressed my lips tightly together so Kit wouldn't wake to the sound of me crying, my arms crossed over my aching chest.

Why did he leave me? Why did he have to die? Why did he send me away to climb the world's highest mountain when I can't even walk?

Sleep granted me only two hours of blissful oblivion before the early-morning light filtering through the bedroom blinds slapped me in the face.

Nick is dead.

Nick is dead, but you're still here, in the twenty-first century, with his ten-year-old sister to look after.

Facing away from Kit, my body shuddered as I wept silently until my eyes burned. Finally, I forced myself out of bed. Staying focused on anything unrelated to Nick Tudor would keep my eyes dry and my heart from shrinking further—it had to, or I was going to sink into a deep, black hole of depression.

Keeping an ear out for Kit, I sat at the dining table over a mug of bitterly strong coffee without any milk to weaken it and flipped open my laptop. I nearly threw up my own heart as I navigated to my emails, the temptation to search Nick's fate on the internet agonizingly near.

Instead, I chewed my lip until it bled and scrolled through my emails, replying to my mom's sequence of messages, which had become progressively more concerned. My fingers raced across the keyboard as I typed that I was fine and that I'd lost my phone, which was why I was emailing instead of calling. I said that Nick and I had been on a road trip for the last few weeks and, when my phone had disappeared, I'd had no way of contacting her. It was a dumb excuse and did nothing to explain his disappearance, which she would eventually notice, but it was all I could manage for now. I promised to call her as soon as I got a new phone. But to do that, I'd need to order a new bankcard so I could access my money. Did I still have a job at the pub downtown after skipping so many shifts without a word of explanation?

Intense, glittering eyes drilled into me, and I spun to face the bedroom doorway where Kit stood, her hand pressed to the doorframe.

Intense, glittering eyes that weren't his.

"Morning," I said, forcing a smile. "How are you feeling?" Her tiny shoulders shrugged beneath her smock, and I led her to the dining table, wishing I had the ingredients to make her something fun for breakfast.

"We need to go and get some food," I said, my voice thin. "I actually do have some cash here that I used to leave for your brother, but what I don't have is a house key. It sank to the bottom of the river with everything else. This isn't really the sort of neighborhood where people leave their doors unlocked; I've heard too many dodgy stories." I was thinking out loud…rambling. Kit just blinked at me with confusion.

My lips parted as I remembered. "Oh wait, my neighbor has a key! She asked to swap house keys awhile back, and she's as nosy as all hell, so I didn't really want to, but Nick thought it was a good idea, so we did. Thank goodness; I really didn't want to have to pay for a locksmith."

A touch energized by the sliver of a plan to focus on, I tore open a packet of crackers and lamely arranged some on a plate for Kit to tide her hungry stomach over before we braved the grocery store.

Half an hour later, we were dressed and tapping on my neighbor Rosie's front door. Kit was playing with her rolled-up sleeves behind me. My smallest shirt hung on her, making her look even smaller than she was, but it would draw less attention than a sixteenth-century kirtle with bell sleeves. Once we'd sorted out food, our next visit would be to the local thrift store for some clothes in her size.

It took a few minutes for Rosie to shuffle her way to the front door from her rear courtyard, which she rarely tore herself away from. Calling to her over the brick wall that separated our two gardens would have been easier, but I couldn't even look at our back door, let alone set foot in that courtyard. How could I have wasted so many months wishing that Nick would separate himself from our garden? The ache to have him back there again, hacking at the vines with his muscular forearms and determined brow, reached inside me and gripped my bones, rattling them from the inside out. My eyes were red and raw, but the tears kept spilling, like a tap that wouldn't switch off. I faced away from Kit and wiped my cheeks, silently begging that she wouldn't see me crying.

Rosie's door swung open. My hand stayed tightly clasped to Kit's. "Oh, good morning," she said to me. "I thought you'd gone away."

"Morning, Rosie," I replied weakly. "Yes, we were away for a few weeks."

We were in Tudor England, trying to stop an invasion by Mary, Queen of Scots. I nearly caught the black plague! Oh, and then the man I love more than I will ever love anything in this life was beheaded. How have you been?

Rosie's curious gaze lowered to Kit with her oversized shirt and intricately braided hair.

I introduced her as my younger sister, and Rosie didn't press me for more information, although a moment of surprise crossed her face.

"I'm just wondering if you still have my spare house key," I said. "I'm so sorry to bother you, but I've lost my bag. It had my wallet and my phone in it."

"Oh no! Yes, of course. Just wait here, dear." She withdrew into her dark hallway, and I whispered the names of strange objects to Kit as her eyes flashed across Rosie's rusty letterbox, her metal drainpipe, and her boxy red car.

"I didn't know you have a sister," Rosie said, reappearing. She smiled at Kit with wrinkly eyes, and Kit buried her face in my arm.

"Does Little Miss live nearby, or is she from America too? Is she moving in with you? Perhaps attending the school up the street? What year will she be in?"

My teeth bit the inside of my mouth. Why couldn't Rosie ever mind her own business? But these questions were bound to come up again—especially if Kit was going to be living with me—so I could use the practice. Lying had become my second language, so I calmly explained that Kit was my half-sister from London who I hadn't seen for a few years. For reasons I didn't reveal, I said that she'd come to live with me for a while. At some point soon, I'd need to sit down with Kit and explain why she could *never* tell anyone the truth about where she'd come from.

"And where is Nicholas?" Rosie asked me point-blank, oblivious to the effect his name had on me. I just stood there and blinked. The mountain grew tall over me again—too high, too formidable—even though I knew I would have no choice but to try to climb it.

"Are you all right, Emmeline?" Rosie's brow folded, and she reached out like I might collapse.

"I'm okay," I managed, stifling the urge to be sick all over her fraying doormat. "Just a bit tired." I couldn't answer her question about where Nick was; my mouth wouldn't go there. Instead, I took Kit's frail arm in mine and turned away.

"Don't forget what you came for," Rosie said, lurching forward to press my spare house key into my hand. My skin connected with cold metal, and a memory blazed from my fingers. An icy, thick band of solid gold, a table-cut diamond of deep blue, a halo of rosette rubies.

The ring brought me to you. I felt a love so deep that everything else fell away.

"Thank you, Rosie," I said, nearly choking on my own voice.

Be happy, my miracle girl. Be happy knowing how loved you are.

With Rosie's curious eyes burning a hole into my back, I took Kit's fingers and led her toward the street, forcing my drained feet to keep going, willing my devastated, despairing body to climb.

Kit and I had been out of the grocery store for less than three minutes when she had what I suspected to be a panic attack. The towering building of glass; the beeping cars; the nattering, multicultural passersby in modern outfits—it was all too much for my informally adopted ten-year-old sister from sixteenth-century England. Despite my best efforts to shield her at my side and explain everything with calm, careful words, she had frozen, whitened, and then collapsed. I gently walked her over to a low brick wall that edged the parking lot until she was able to breathe steadily again.

The stroll home was long, my wrists burning from where the heavy grocery bags hung, but the entire way, I kept Kit's mind distracted with funny and soothing stories about Nick's introduction to the twenty-first century. I told her about when he began eating a packet of bread rolls in the middle of the grocery store because he thought everything in there was free, and the time he emptied our bag of stinking garbage into the public street, which was definitely not the done thing in the modern world.

By the time we reached the house, she was still short of breath and her eyes were red.

"How about another one of those lovely, warm baths?" I said with a brave smile that barely lifted my cheeks as I dumped the grocery bags onto the counter.

"I think I would like to sleep," she said, rubbing her eyes. I glanced at the clock. It was only mid-morning, but Kit looked spent.

"Sure, you can have a nap," I said, pulling out a packet of breakfast muffins. "How about something to eat first?"

She shook her head, and my heart sank. Kit would never get her energy back if she didn't eat something. But when she slunk away into the bedroom, I didn't try to stop her. Instead, I made a mental note to ask her what her favorite foods were. I'd do whatever I could to get her to eat, even if that meant cooking some of those oddball Tudor recipes. I had to make Kit well...I had to make her happy. Not only for her, but for *him*.

With my heart sucked into a black hole, I pulled three boxes of frozen pizza out of the bag and crouched in front of the freezer, finding room. A muffled voice sounded from a distance and my head shot up.

"Kit?" I called out. "Are you okay?"

Silence.

The voice sounded again…male, and too far away to be coming from inside the house. The tightness in my stomach loosened a little, and I returned to the grocery bags, digging through them.

Thump, thump.

My stomach hit the roof of my mouth as I glanced at the noise coming from the back door and froze. With my heart beating in my ears, I rose to my feet and inched toward the door's frosted glass panels.

"Who's there?" I asked with a threat in my tone. There was no way into our back garden without a key. What if it was one of those local ratbag teenagers who'd been robbing houses on our street? What would I do?

I'd fight like freaking hell, that's what I'd do. No one else is taking anything from me, ever again.

"Emmie?" said a man's voice that sent me spiraling into a downward funnel of shock.

The voice murmured again, this time at a lower volume like it was speaking with someone else.

"Emmie?" the voice said again, more persistent. Another thump. "Emmie, it is I! Are you there?"

Thump, thump.

My body was an ice sculpture, my lips frozen open, my breath glued to my throat. I'd lost the ability to speak.

The tall shape beyond the frosted glass hovered there for a moment before disappearing backward, leaving nothing but blurry sunlight.

I lurched forward and gripped the door handle, my hands struggling with the lock. My fingers shook with maddening urgency until I managed to unlock the door and fling it open.

Nick Tudor stood beside the trellis of vines, his sea-colored eyes wide, his skin pale with shock.

For a moment, we just stood there, wordless and gaping at each other.

"*What?*" I heard myself breathe.

He expelled a strained cry before dashing toward me, wrapping himself around my shuddering body and holding me up until I couldn't feel the ground beneath me. The soft curls of his hair tickled my neck as he pressed himself into me, and all I could smell was leather and roses. All I could smell was Nick. All I could smell was life, and love. And, in an instant, I was at the top of the mountain.

There was no breath left in me, let alone words.

Beyond his trembling shoulder, another long-legged shape approached with a small, cautious smile. It was Jasper Blacke.

I pulled away from Nick, my fingers finding his cheeks, which glistened with tears. His skin was warm and wet from crying.

"You're here," I whispered, my chest heaving with a convulsive sob. "You're here, you're here, you're here." I shook my head, light-headed and almost sick. Was I imagining this? "*How?*" I said, reaching forward to press my hand to the silky doublet cloaking his chest, his heart pounding against my shaking fingers. "*How?*"

His hand reached to take mine, but I couldn't let go. I would never let go.

His forehead collapsed against me like he could hardly hold himself up before he pulled back again, his dumbfounded eyes sucking me in. "I truly believed that I would never lay mine eyes upon you again," he said, a painful, disbelieving laugh bursting from his throat. He smiled—a smile so heartfelt, so beautiful, so thick with relief—that I began laughing, too, through my tears.

"Oh my God," I cried, drawing him into me again, burying myself in the soothing warmth of his embrace. "Are you really here? How is this even possible?"

His voice rattled against my breathless chest. "I am truly here, my lady. I made it home to you." He touched my chin and lifted my face, emotion pouring from his eyes into mine. "And I beseech you, with all my heart, Emmeline. Please—never take me away from here again."

23

My eyes couldn't accept what they were seeing. While Kit lay sleeping, Nick Tudor was sitting beside me at our dining table, rehashing the events of the last day while Jasper half listened and half gawked at the room of oddities. They'd both arrived back in our bed while Kit and I had been at the grocery store, and when Nick took the dizzyingly confused Jasper outside for some air, they'd become locked in our courtyard garden. My cheeks hurt from smiling, my heart was a mess, and my breath was all but gone. I'd offered to wake Kit straight away, but, as desperate as he was to see her, Nick wanted to let her sleep.

His fingers stroked mine, his clear eyes fused to me like I might disappear, while he told me what had happened. After he'd been dragged away from Mary Stuart's drawing-room while she performed the spell on Kit and me, he'd been taken to a locked chamber shared by Jasper. Nick, overcome with grief, had confessed everything to Jasper, including about the time travel. At that moment, he'd felt there was nothing left for him to lose, and Jasper seemed like the kind of person who could handle the truth, despite his young age. They were left alone without food or water until the next morning, when the chamber door unlocked. Believing it to be Mary's guards coming for them, Nick and Jasper made an agreement to fight to the death rather than be taken willingly to their executions. But it wasn't the guards who entered the room; it was Mary Stuart's young maid. She was weeping and confessed her hatred of the Scottish queen, whom she'd once loved, but who'd been seduced by the dark arts and had been forever changed by its irresistible power. The maid had grown up with stories about King Nicholas of England and had been dumbstruck to discover him still alive. At enormous risk to her life, she offered to help Nick and Jasper escape from Mary's castle so they could return to England, proposing to conceal them inside a wagon of laundry.

My breath was lodged inside my burning chest. "So, what happened then?"

Nick's fingers gripped mine tightly. "I told the maid that I did not wish to accept her offer of escape to England," he said, a flash of guilt reddening his cheeks. "Forgive me, Jasper," he added.

Jasper just shook his head. "When I think of it now, it seems a truly impossible quest," he said. "But I will always thank that maid for her courage."

Nick swallowed hard, his thumb brushing back and forth over my hand. "I told the maid that what I wanted was to journey forward in time, just as you and Kit had done. And Jasper made the same bid, for fear that to remain behind would be to lose his life."

The words sank in, holding my heart. "You asked to come back here. Rather than to be set free in your own country...in your own time."

He tilted into me, his eyes locked to mine. "Of course, Emmie. *Of course.*" He shook his head, utterly bewildered. "You still doubt me?"

He caught my tears with his knuckles, gently wiping them away.

"But how on earth did the maid manage to send you forward in time?" I said, still worried that my eyes were playing tricks on me.

He inhaled deeply, his mind drifting back. "That young maid turned out to have the heart of a lion. Show her, Jasper."

Jasper reached into the pocket of his breeches and produced a gleaming band of solid gold. It was Mary Stuart's signet ring.

"I am too afeared to wear it on mine own hand," he said, dropping the ring onto the table like it was diseased. "Who knows what wickedness that woman hath been up to with this ring?"

"You wore Mary Stuart's ring to travel through time?" I said, holding my brow with confusion.

"That maid was at the hand of Mary Stuart since she was a child," Nick explained. "She said that Mary's ring holds all her enchantments. After performing a spell, Mary would not wear the ring for days on end because the ring holds the core of the spell. If Mary wore the ring afterward, she would go on to meet the same fate of the spell that she had just cast. Therefore, after performing the spell on you and Kit, Mary removed the ring from her hand, which is how the maid was able to steal the ring that same night."

I glanced at Jasper and then at Nick. "But Mary said the spell would only work for two people!"

Nick made a slow, sad shake of his head. "The maid said that was folly. All along, that witch could have sent the three of us to the future without trouble...the four of us, in truth," he added, looking at Jasper. "Can you believe the cruelty of that woman's heart?"

My eyes and mouth were stitched open. "I–I can't believe it. That maid...she saved your lives. She saved my life; she...Mary must have killed her for what she did."

Nick's lips pressed together grimly. "We can only hope that Mary did not suspect the maid to have had a hand in our disappearance."

His soft fingers were back in mine, squeezing and caressing like he couldn't let go.

"Emmie, what transpired with Mary Stuart after we took our leave?" he said, his face clouding. "How much blood was spilled when she made her claim for the throne of England? What does it say happened to us all? Do our subjects believe that Catherine and I abandoned them? For how long did the House of Stuart reign?"

I shook my head, swallowing the rock in my throat. "I don't know. I've been too scared to look. But let's give it a go, shall we?"

My laptop was plugged in to charge on the kitchen counter. I grabbed it and flipped it open. Jasper gaped at the brightening screen, his brows hitting his hairline. Even Nick still knew little about computers and the internet, and he kept his distance.

"I'm going to have to run you guys through this magical little device later," I said, my fingers whirring across the keyboard. "Trust me: You'll never look back."

Mary, Queen of Scots. *Click.*

I opened the first article and began reading. About halfway down the page, my brow scrunched. "Oh my God."

"What is it?" Nick said quickly.

"It says here that Mary Stuart died in 1587—that's only five years after we left. Her son, James, inherited the throne of England, but not until 1603, so who was in between?" My eyes hurriedly scanned the text, expanding. "It says that Mary Stuart was taken captive by Queen Elizabeth in 1568 and was imprisoned in England for nineteen years. In 1586, she was found guilty of plotting against Queen Elizabeth to take the throne of England and was beheaded for treason in 1587." I stared at the screen like I didn't recognize it. "This can't be right…it's all so different!"

"My *mother*, Elizabeth?" Nick said, shaking his head. "No, my mother died in 1572—the year Kit was born."

I backed up to the search window and typed in a different name.

Queen Elizabeth I. *Click.*

My eyes couldn't keep up with the insane words that flooded the page. When my jaw fell open with a sharp gasp, Nick scrambled behind me, reading over my shoulder.

My stomach was in my mouth. "Nick, it says here that your mother didn't die in 1572. She died in 1603—that's the year that Mary's son, James Stuart, became the King of England!"

Nick gripped the edge of the dining table, his knuckles whitening.

Jasper leaned forward. "Are you…are you saying we changed the future?" His mouth was agape.

I was still reading. "Nick, your family *did* get rid of Mary Stuart, eventually. Your mother, Queen Elizabeth, executed Mary Stuart in 1587 for her plots to steal the Tudor throne. Mary never succeeded in her quest to become the Queen of England." Tears swelled in my eyes, thickening my throat. "Instead, your mother ruled England for *forty-five* years. She became known as Gloriana, a symbol of English independence and national pride. The people adored her, and she made an enormous sacrifice for her nation by never marrying."

"Never marrying?" Nick's voice was an astounded breath. "What of my father, Lord Dudley?"

I clicked through to a different article, but the information was the same. "It says here that Queen Elizabeth never married. She was also known as 'the Virgin Queen.'"

Nick's knees buckled, and I slid his chair closer. "You should really sit down," I said, touching his forearm to hold him steady.

His eyes were swimming, his brow a mess of lines. I was afraid he'd pass out. "But what of…what of Kit and me?" he said.

I spun back to enter another search, my fingers quivering so badly that I could barely type.

King Nicholas I. *Click.*

There were millions of results. My eyes skimmed over links to websites about rulers of Montenegro and Russia, but there was nothing at all about my Nick.

Nicholas Tudor, 1500s. *Click.*

A courtier from the reign of Henry the Eighth. A bishop of London. No princes; no kings.

"Oh my God." My skin tightened like I might faint.

"What? What does it say?" Nick's eyes were flaming jewels that burned into me, like I had all the answers.

"You and Kit…" I stammered, my voice rising in pitch. "It says here that…it says that you were never born."

He blinked slowly like he hadn't heard right. "What did you just say?"

I had no answers for him. Jasper ran both hands through his hair while Nick gaped at me like I'd just told him that he didn't exist. Which I more or less had.

I twisted back to my laptop and clicked through to an image of Queen Elizabeth the First at the age of forty-two. The woman in the painting was the embodiment of regal poise, with porcelain skin and crimson hair the exact shade of Kit's. The caption beneath the image read *England's Virgin Queen*. I spun the screen toward Nick to show him.

"You didn't lose the Tudor throne," I said, my heart in my mouth. "When you left the sixteenth century—forever, this time, according to Mary Stuart's enchantment—it must've altered the path of history more than we even thought possible." The words I was saying felt unbelievable. "Nick, you and Kit no longer exist in the past—you never did!"

He blanched and clutched the side of his satin doublet. "Then how am I here now, in this place, in the flesh?!"

A cold wind blew into my chest, and I jerked forward to cup his cheek again. He was real; he was warm.

"I don't know," I said, still spinning. "Somehow, the spell removed you from the timeline of history, yet it still brought your body and soul here. So it didn't kill you, but it altered the course of your life—I don't know; it doesn't make sense. Do you still have the same memories?"

His eyes were flashing and unfocused. "I still have the very same memories."

"Perhaps it was a parting gift from Mary Stuart," said Jasper. "Perhaps the queen did want you to be together after all, in her own twisted way. She hath proven herself to be most powerful."

"Or maybe there was something off about that spell," I said, holding Nick's paling face, worried he'd disappear.

"Your Grace?" said a small, astonished voice.

Kit was standing in the doorway, her mouth open, her muscles rigid.

"Your Grace!" she cried again, running to Nick. He caught her in his arms, that desperate, disbelieving laughter returning to his mouth as he pressed his lips to her rust-colored hair.

She stared at him in a daze before grabbing a chunk of his hair. "Are you really here, or are you a phantom?" she said, and he laughed.

He took in her face, his eyes wet and gleaming. "My dear, I am here; I am here. Oh, my heart is so merry." He freed one hand from Kit to pull me close until he was hugging us both at once, unbridled happiness radiating from his eyes. In all the years I'd seen him rule as the King of England, he'd never looked so resplendent, so full of life…so unlike Nicholas the Ironheart.

"Oh, my gracious, and it is Jasper Blacke!" Kit blurted with surprise.

Jasper blushed at her, and Kit's lips curled up with delight.

"I never did get to say farewell to you, Your Grace," he said with a smile. "I felt that a bit ill-mannered."

As the three of them caught up over more breathless explanations, a twisting unease slithered into my stomach. How could the Tudor family tree have changed so dramatically? What impact would Nick and Kit's disappearance from the dynasty have on the path of history as I'd known it?

I turned to my laptop and typed another quick search.

What is the state religion in England? *Click.*

The established religion of England is the Anglican Church of England, although religions of all sorts are found throughout the United Kingdom, including Catholicism, Islam, Hinduism, Judaism, and Buddhism.

I flopped back into my chair, inhaling a breath. While Nick and Kit had bizarrely disappeared from the Tudor lineage, at least the course of religion in England had corrected itself to that which I'd known. The timeline of British monarchies still led to the House of Windsor, so apart from Nick and Kit's vanishing from the Tudor timeline, things were right where they were supposed to be. How I'd managed to steal two members of one of history's most famous royal families—and seemingly get away with it—was beyond my comprehension, but I wasn't about to question my luck after everything we'd been through.

As I closed off each internet window that was still open, the solemn eyes of Queen Elizabeth Tudor locked with mine through the screen. A gush of silent words poured into my mouth.

Queen Elizabeth…I don't know how I will ever be able to thank you. How will I ever cope with my heartache—my guilt—for the children you lost? You would have been so proud of Nicholas and Catherine, your heroic, selfless son and your brave, magnificent daughter. The truth is that I don't understand how it is that I have them now and that you don't, but I promise you that they are loved. They are loved as much as love allows. Their lives will be anything but lost, anything but meaningless, and I will never let any harm come to them ever again.

I caught Nick's steady gaze across the table as he looked at me, his eyes soft at the edges, the message clear.

"I love you too," I mouthed through my tears.

"Christ, that is like ice."

"Don't move," I said, my graphite pencil between my teeth. "Twenty-three years as a Tudor royal and you're scared of a little cold metal on your skin?"

He made a playful scowl as I adjusted the thick chain draped around his neck. "I never said I was afeared," he replied defensively.

"There." I took a step back. Nick was leaning against the wall beside our dining table, his hands tucked into the pockets of his gray jeans. His muscular chest was bare, and a masculine, gunmetal-silver chain hung undone around his neck, one side dangling lower than the other.

"You look like a male supermodel," I said without a trace of surprise, clicking a few photos with my new phone. "You've really got to get on that; we could make a killing pimping you out to fashion brands."

I showed him the photos, and he grimaced at himself like he was embarrassed.

"It's totally different to sixteenth-century jewelry, I know, but trust me," I said. "This is good stuff." I unhooked the chain from his neck and sat back over my sketchbook, flipping through my ideas for the concept of liberty.

There was the thick, undone chain draped around a man's neck that I'd just demonstrated with Nick. Another page held a sketch of a stiff, ruff-style necklace of white lace that was broke open at the neck. The third image was of a golden crown melting off the wearer's head and down their forehead.

"I think this might be my best collection yet," I said to Nick. "Just in time for classes to start up again next week." I pretended to wipe sweat off my forehead.

"I am greatly proud of you, Emmie," he said with a smile that made my heart jump. "Should I make us something to eat for lunch?" His use of contemporary phrasing and his attempt to behave in a modern way made me squeeze his tanned forearm.

"Actually, I have a bit of a surprise for you today for lunch." My stomach hollowed with a nervous flutter.

"You do?" He frowned and smiled simultaneously.

"We've got somewhere to go today," I said cagily. "Kit and Jasper know; they're going to stay here." I gestured to the living room window facing the garden. Through the glass, Kit was painting a portrait of Jasper Blacke, who was being more than patient, sitting on a plastic stool with his hands resting on his knees.

I collected Nick's fingers in mine and tugged him toward the bedroom. He made a suggestive murmur of interest, but my jacket and shoes made clear that my plan involved getting more dressed than undressed. As I sat on the edge of the bed and tied on my low-top sneakers, my mind drifted down to the security box beneath the mattress, which housed Mary Stuart's signet ring.

Nick and I had agreed to wait twelve months for any remnants of her spell to wear off before we would hand the ring in to the British Museum. Journeying back and forth to the sixteenth century like time-traveling tourists had brought Nick and me together, but it had also cost people their lives and caused two Tudor monarchs to vanish from the path of history. We both knew there was no going back anymore.

"To where are we going?" Nick asked as he slipped on his worn leather boots. "It is not the Tower of London, is it? I feel the wounds yet of our last ordeal there." He winced.

"It's about an hour's drive from here, so if you're hungry, you'd better hurry with those laces," was all I said. I checked the rideshare app on my phone. Our car was a few minutes away.

Nick quizzed me all the way along the congested motorway about where we were headed and what was inside my bulging rucksack, but I kept my lips sealed shut, breathing through my anxiety. It wasn't until our car was inching through traffic on Hampton Court Road, fifty minutes into our journey, that Nick pressed his face to the window, gasping.

"Good God, is that…? It is! It's Hampton Court Palace!"

"In living color," I said with a bright smile, sitting higher in my seat to catch sight of the palace's jumble of redbrick chimneys. A memory of strolling down the avenue of clipped yew trees in the Privy Garden with Alice Grey giggling beside me speared my heart.

"But that's not where we're going," I said as the palace walls shrank in the rearview mirror. Nick's pout was too cute. "We're almost there," I reassured him, patting his hand.

After only three more minutes of steering down quieter, more suburban streets, our driver pulled up beside a high iron fence caught in a tangle of overgrown vines. I was almost faint with nerves as we stepped out of the car.

"Welcome to Thames Ditton," I said, finding my composure, as Nick surveyed the quiet street lined with leafy trees that offered glimpses of impressive, well-kept houses.

He smiled at me, his hands in his pockets. "Very well, I give up. What is this place?" he asked, his speech becoming more modern by the day.

I pretended to zip my lips and retrieved a rusty key from my hand-bag. "Come on." I unlocked the ornate gate and pushed it open with a heavy, dragging scrape.

With our hands entwined, we headed along a twisting pathway of flat stones enveloped with lush, uncut grass. At the tip of the path emerged a sprawling, two-story house with steeply pitched gable roofs, lattice windows, and white walls dramatically striped with vertical planks of black timber.

"Goodness," Nick breathed beside me. While he'd grown up in the likes of Hampton Court Palace and Whitehall, he'd spent enough time as a commoner in my world by now to appreciate the value of a home like this one in Greater London.

I silently collected his warm fingers in mine again and led him around the side of the house, where a private courtyard opened into a grassy clearing flanked with thick, lofty trees rustling with chirping birds.

I paused on the courtyard stones and turned to face Nick, my calm smile betraying the butterfly storm in my stomach.

"Welcome home," I said.

His mouth fell open, his eyes returning to the stately building behind his shoulder. "*Home?*"

"We bought this house a few days ago," I said, pleased at how healthy the garden looked…at how much space there was for Nick and his green thumbs to go nuts out here. "I know I should have told you," I stammered quickly, "but the house came up for sale so fast, and you were spending all that time helping Kit and Jasper with their adjusting, and…I guess I just knew you would love it, and I *really* wanted to surprise you."

His stunned eyes shifted between the house, the garden, and me, his lips on the verge of laughing. "Good God, Emmie, is this a jest?" He took my shoulders, lifting me off the ground for a moment.

"Of course not. This is home!"

He gasped again, unable to take his eyes off the house. "It is…it looks like…"

"It's a Tudor house," I said. "With a big enough garden for you to start your organic food business with Jasper that we talked about. It's also only a few miles from Hampton Court Palace if you ever want to go there and feel a bit more at home. It's so perfect that I didn't even sleep the night before I made the offer; I was so worried that someone else would buy it."

He reached for my hands, trembling and dazed. "But how on earth did you pay for this, my lady? This is positively a manor; a country estate!"

I blinked at him. "Actually, it was Alice Grey who paid for it."

His brows drew together. "Alice, the wife of Lord Warwick? I do not follow."

My throat thickened, the memory still raw. "When I last saw Alice, before we left for Scotland, she gave me a gigantic sapphire to carry with me in case we ran into any trouble on the roads." I clutched the tiny brass casing of the pomander hanging from my neck that Alice had made for me—a much more personal keepsake that I would never part with. "Remember the first day I went into London to start work again at the pub? That same day, I had the sapphire valued by an auction house, which offered to buy it on the spot. Let's just say the jewel paid for this house, the rest of my college fees, and then some."

I shuffled on my feet, the smile falling off my face as I registered what I was saying.

Nick tilted into me. "Is something amiss?"

I was suddenly unable to meet his eyes. "Are you upset with me?" I said. "For doing all this without telling you? For selling Alice Grey's jewel behind your back?"

He lowered his face to mine, his scent of soap and springtime teasing my nose. "I am not *at all* upset with you for acquiring a home that I shall never wish to leave, nor for parting with Mistress Grey's jewel in order to pay for it." His eyes were soft. "Emmie, we both know that Alice would have desired this very much. That dear girl loved you nearly as much as I do."

I nodded, biting the inside of my cheek. I reminded myself that, by all accounts we'd read, Alice Grey had lived a long life in the court of Queen Elizabeth the First and had married Francis Beaumont and borne him two sons. The difficult part was that changing the path of history, and removing Nick and Kit from the Tudor timeline, meant that Alice had never known me at all, even if I'd bizarrely retained my memories and keepsakes. But perhaps that was for the best, given that I had never been able to confess the truth about myself to her the way

I had promised. A ball of sadness grew in my chest and I did my best to push it away.

"So, Mistress Grace, what is inside that sack of yours?" Nick asked, tapping my rucksack with his boot. "I do hope it is some manner of food. I could eat a swine."

Grateful for the distraction, I scooped up my bag before stepping into the grassy clearing with a smirk on my face. Nick hovered nearby, inspecting the stems of a rose bush, as I unzipped the bag and pulled out a picnic blanket, a box of berries and grapes, a container of soft cheeses and sliced ham, a loaf of sourdough bread, a packet of fresh macarons from the bakery, and a flask of wine painted in a metallic-gold shade.

"What is all this?" Nick said with a smile as I laid everything out on the blanket.

"You don't recognize it?" I challenged.

He sat down opposite me, surveying the spread of snacks before a flush drifted into his cheeks. "It is the very same meal we shared at Robin House on the grass. The first time we were alone together. Before you fell ill with the one-day fever."

I popped a grape into my mouth, heat pouring into my chest. He'd remembered. "Not the very same meal," I said, "but close. I don't actually have a wine flask made out of solid gold."

"Oh, Emmie," he said, sliding toward me, his thick legs wrapping around mine. "That was the day I asked you if I should marry Princess Henriette of France." He grimaced. I clutched my heart in pain, and he chuckled with sympathy, taking my hand and pressing his lips to my wrist.

"I think of that picnic like it was our first date," I said shyly. "Man, I wanted to kiss you that day. Badly."

His cheeks flushed. "As did I. As clear as day, I remember...I wished to kiss every inch of you on that carpet." My thigh rubbed against his as he leaned forward and brought his soft lips to mine, sending streams of syrupy warmth down my arms and legs. The kiss could so easily have escalated in that secluded garden, and it was never easy to stop with him, but my mind was locked on something else. I pulled away and expelled an anxious, shuddery exhale. His eyes were already glazed over with desire.

"I still need to show you inside the house," I said, stalling. "You're going to love it; it's beautiful in there."

He reached for the sourdough. "Tell me of it."

"Well, it has four big bedrooms. One for us…one for Kit…one for Jasper, and…one for the baby."

His brows flung upward as he slid a wedge of cheese into his mouth. "A baby? Ha. A sweet thought indeed. But why stop at one?"

I sat and watched him chew, my heart thumping into my mouth. My hand slid down and pressed my lower stomach.

Nick's jaw froze, his voice a breath. "Good God."

"That's right," I said softly. "The house was just the warm-up. This is the real surprise."

He sat up on his knees, his mouth hanging open. "Emmie! You are with child?"

I nodded, my throat drying up. While giving birth at the age of twenty-one would make me a younger mother than I'd have ever intended, to Nick Tudor, we were the perfect age for this—if not a little late. I'd accepted long ago that our timeline would probably always be a little different to other people's.

"It happened during one of the nights in the manor at Sheffield; I'm sure of it," I said. "So much for being careful," I added with a wry smile.

A stunned cry burst from his lips before he slid close to me, holding his hands out like he wanted to hug me but wasn't sure if he should.

"It's okay; I'm not going to break, and neither is the baby," I said, guiding his arms around my waist. I melted into his hug, his breath trembling so sweetly against my ear that I turned and kissed his cheek.

When his shoulders suddenly seized up, I pulled back. "Everything okay?" I asked.

His brow was a tangle of lines. "Emmie, a baby…with you. My God, I wish for nothing more. But how am I to provide for the child? We have been back in your time not yet five weeks."

I tried not to roll my eyes at the reason Nick had spent a year keeping me at arm's length, making me pine and ache for his body to the point of physical pain. Instead, I pointed at the corner of a white brick wall peeking through a cluster of trees at the opposite side of the garden. "Do you see that little cottage over there? It's our gorgeous little guesthouse. We can rent it out to people visiting Hampton Court Palace, which will bring in some money for a while. A house and garden like this are also going to need a ton of maintenance. Why don't you be the one to manage the property and the guesthouse while you set up your organic vegetables business with Jasper?"

His brow pinched with thought before his lips curled up. "I believe I would find that most agreeable."

My smile nearly reached my ears. "That's great!" I crawled into his lap, and he slipped a pale-pink macaron into my mouth before kissing the crumbs off my lips. "I can't wait to show all this to Kit and Jasper," I said, savoring the taste of heaven—a Nick Tudor-and-macaron-flavored cocktail. "My mom also wants to visit, and she'll be the first one on a plane when I tell her about the baby. Although she's going to think I'm on crack for having one so young. But I bet she'll want to stick around for a while so I can figure out college. There's no way I'm dropping out, and I know she'll be happy to help us."

"It will greatly please me to see your dear mother again," he said, unscrewing the wine flask. Leaving the wine and soft cheeses to Nick, I nibbled on bread and macarons to the gentle rustling of wind in the trees and the occasional whistle of a sparrow. I couldn't believe this was our home.

Thank you, Alice.

My eyelids fell closed as a breath of wind tickled my cheeks, my body sinking into Nick's—so happy, so at peace.

He ran a soft finger down my cheek. Warm lips touched mine, and I mumbled a murmur of encouragement. He cupped the back of my neck and pressed me closer until all I could taste was sweetness and wine through his delicious, breathtaking sighs. I was lost in his mouth, craving more, when he pulled back, his brows lifted with alarm. "Emmie...we are not wedded in this century."

I sat up on my elbows, panting from the kiss. "And?"

"*And?* We cannot have a bastard child!"

He sprang to his feet like the idea was abhorrent, and I sucked in a breath and rose to meet him. No matter what century we lived in, no matter how much he mimicked my modern speech, Nick would always think like a Tudor.

"I thought you might feel this way about it," I said with a knowing smile. "Although, in this century, there is absolutely nothing wrong with having a baby out of wedlock."

He shook his head at me. "No, Emmie, no, I beseech you…that is a step too far. I will not make my child a bastard. Especially when his mother is so much beloved by me."

"*His* mother?" I said with a hand on my lower stomach. "I think the baby is going to be a girl, and we're totally calling her Alice."

Nick teetered on his heels, his eyes swimming with thought before he inhaled a deep breath. I could see where this was going.

"No," I said, flinging my hand up. "No, you don't get to do it this time."

He blinked with surprise. "Of what do you speak?"

I smoothed down my white shirt that wasn't going to fit me for much longer. "I was actually planning to do this later, but what the hell. We'll do it now."

He just looked at me with his heart-stopping stare. "Emmie, what are you doing?"

I sank to one knee, relieved that I wasn't in my third trimester of pregnancy. I'd never get up again.

Nick's lips parted as I took his trembling fingers in mine.

I searched for the right words as I gazed up at him, his cheeks flushing pink, his saltwater eyes glistening in the sunlight.

"Nick Tudor," I said softly, "you gave up a kingdom for me. You gave up your birthright…your entire history. I will never know the true weight of that, and I will *never* be able to repay you for it. But I want you to know something: You are so much more than a king to me. You're the single most important person in my life…my soulmate…the first person I think of when literally anything happens to me. You're the first person I think of at all. And you matter in this world as much as you did in the past. In fact, from where I'm standing, you matter more." I took his hand and pressed it to my lower stomach. "I know that you feel like you abandoned your duty when you left the throne of England, but all you did was love your family more. There is no shame in that. There never was. And while I will never be able to give you a kingdom, I do give you my life. Every beat of my heart. And I know that it's not the same as the hearts of millions of your subjects, but it is *all* yours. Without end."

I gently guided him down to his knees, his chest rising and falling with each breath.

"Nicholas Henry Edward Tudor," I said into his watery eyes. "Will you marry me? Again?"

He laughed through his smile, a tear slipping from the corner of his eye before he pulled me into the heat of his embrace. "Do not doubt it, my miracle girl. I will marry you in this world, and I will marry you in the next." He laughed again, burying himself in my neck. "I knew not that a woman could ask such a question in this time."

I rolled my eyes at that, but the smile didn't leave my face. I rested my chin on his shoulder. "Can you believe we've made it this far? Can you believe what we've been through since that first picnic at Robin House?"

He sucked in a weary breath. "This indeed has been a battle hard won."

"You can say that again."

He pulled away, sliding his hands down my arms as we folded our legs together on the blanket. "But we won, didn't we?" he said, his eyes gleaming.

I laughed with disbelief. "We did. We really did."

We were crying, smiling, laughing, all at once. And then he slid close to me again, his legs and arms wrapped around me, until our eyes were locked together, inches apart.

"Emmie, by now you must know that there are only two hearts that I have ever truly wanted."

I exaggerated my gape of horror. "You have another woman on the side? Already?"

He chuckled, pressing his brow to mine. "Stop that. Do not even say such things."

I smiled. "Mine and Kit's," I said simply.

He kept his forehead pressed to mine, heating my skin with his own. "*Three* hearts," he corrected with a smile, placing his fingers on my lower stomach.

I cupped my hand over his. "How did we get so lucky?" I asked softly.

He jerked his head back, grimacing. "You call this lucky? I have never worked so hard for anything in all my life."

"Well, you are a Tudor king," I said with a heavy sigh. "Do you even know how to work?"

He gave me a gentle, playful whack on my backside, and I murmured my appreciation, wriggling even closer.

Without separating our bodies, he lowered his mouth to mine, his voice a sweet breath. "Will you show me inside the house? Where we may have a moment alone, before Kit and Jasper learn of this place?" The look in his eyes sent a hot flush through me.

"Of course," I said, collecting his fingers in mine. He helped me rise, and the moment I was at eye level with his shoulder, it crashed into me like a memory breaking free: our first picnic at Robin House —our first date—when I'd teased him about his princely riches.

"You have a wonderful life," I admitted softly.

He side-eyed me. "That depends on what you find wonderful."

"Riding horses to secret picnics…eating pies with birds flying out. Is that flask solid gold?"

He made a dismissive grunt. "You believe my life is all recreation?"

I held my hand up to my eyes to block the glare of the sun. Would he remember?

"We have a wonderful life," was all I said.

His eyes flashed, something within him unlocking. "You believe our life is all recreation?" he said with a pretend scoff, not missing a beat.

I beamed at him, my heart growing in my chest. "I most certainly do," I said. "You were right. There is nothing more beautiful than a life with you."

He just made a sound like I was too much for his heart and pulled me into him. My head rested on his shoulder as he led me toward the house.

"I just thought of another name for our baby," I whispered.

He turned to me, his lips on my cheek. "And what is that, my lady?"

"Elizabeth."

HISTORICAL TIMELINE

THE HOUSE OF TUDOR

England

1485   Henry Tudor defeats King Richard III at the Battle of Bosworth to end the Wars of the Roses. He founds the Tudor dynasty and becomes King Henry VII, before dying of tuberculosis at age fifty-two.

1509   Henry VII's second son is crowned King Henry VIII. He marries six times and executes two of his wives. During his reign, Henry VIII breaks from the Catholic Church and declares England Protestant so he can marry Anne Boleyn.

1547   Henry VIII's longed-for son becomes King Edward VI at age nine and rules England for six years. Aged just sixteen, he dies of disputed causes.

1553   In a Protestant plot to prevent the throne passing to Edward's Catholic sister Mary Tudor, Henry VIII's distant relative Lady Jane Grey is proclaimed queen for nine days and is never crowned. She is executed along with her conspirators.

1553   Mary Tudor wins succession to become Queen Mary I. Her persecution of English Protestants earns her the nickname 'Bloody Mary'. She dies childless, aged forty-two.

1558   Mary's half-sister Elizabeth fights off succession claims by her Catholic cousin Mary, Queen of Scots, and is crowned Queen Elizabeth I. Elizabeth cements Protestantism in England and rules the nation for forty-five years before her death in 1603. Choosing to never marry, she becomes known as 'the Virgin Queen' and earns her place as one of the longest-reigning and most-loved monarchs in British history.

Elizabeth Tudor never has any children.

THE
END

ACKNOWLEDGMENTS

The first person I must thank is *you* for reading this book. To every excited reader who messaged me after finishing Emmie and the Tudor King, asking for more—and more spice!—I humbly offer this work to you. Thank you, thank you, thank you for your support. It means everything to me.

To Jenny Hickman, Elle Beaumont, and the entire Midnight Tide Publishing family: I will be forever grateful that my kingly kissing stories have found such a wonderful home. Jenny, this omnibus would simply not be here if it weren't for you and your encouragement. It also looks so beautiful—*thank you*. I value you and your incredible talent so very much. P.S. All the books!

To Kim, Tanja, and the team at Deranged Doctor Design—thank you for kicking butt with another stunning cover!

Thank you so much to my editors, Arielle Bailey and Emma Savant, for beating this series into shape and for guiding Emmie and Nick onto the path they deserve. I am forever in awe of your story-making and wordsmith skills. As always, your input has taken this book to higher, deeper, and graver places.

To the magical Chelsey Flood, who read an early version of this story that now makes me cringe: Without your support and guidance, I wouldn't be writing these words now. Thank you.

I owe so much gratitude to Martha Wells, the medical whizz, whose abundant and sage advice about arrow wounds, extreme shock, corpses, and oozing bed sores that didn't make the final cut, changed so much of this series. Without your guidance, Emmie would have bled out shortly after her arrival in Tudor England. Thank you for saving her life, and my novel. Hugs.

Thank you to the beautiful souls Jeanine Hsu from niin, and Nathalie Melville and Jan Preece from Hatton Jewellery Institute, for teaching me everything Emmie knows about designing and crafting jewelry. I loved being in your creative world, if only for a few days.

Thank you to the divine Kathleen Pasqualini for being my beta reader, my Australian slang fielder, my source for random US facts, and for thwarting Emmie and Nick's attempts to wake up in the library without their kit on, LOL.

I couldn't believe that I had to fly to England to visit Hampton Court Palace, Windsor Castle, and Kenilworth Castle—among others —for this series (such a drag!), and said research trip wouldn't have been the same without my Tudor tour partner-in-crime, Darren Waters. Thanks for keeping me company, Mr. Waters, and where are we researching next?

Thank you to the brilliant British historian Dr. Tracy Borman for your random facts about Tudor England: I'm still fangirling that you even answered my email.

A gush of thanks beyond words to Mum, Dad, Thom, Tania, and the rest of my extended family, including all the much-loved Canadians. I'm so grateful for all of you, and the most enjoyable times of my life are spent with you.

Speaking of my people: Brent, Brady, and Aubrey, while I feel like I disappear into another world every time I write a novel, if there was even a hint that I might never be able to get back to you, I would toss that part of my life into a fire. You come first, always.

I would like to wholeheartedly thank Emmie Grace and Nick Tudor for choosing me to tell this story. Wherever you are—and I know you are somewhere, living as quiet a life as you so wished for—I promise to leave you alone now. Except, wait...what if there's still some power left in Mary Stuart's signet ring? *cue dramatic music*

Last, but never least (especially if we're talking pounds— sorry, had to get that one in) I want to thank the Tudors themselves, particularly King Henry VIII. I joke about Henry, but the truth is that I like him, even though he made such appalling decisions at times. Without Henry's face-palming shenanigans that changed Britain forever, I'd never have fallen for this dramatic slice of history that has captivated people for centuries. The Tudor dynasty is ultimately what inspired me to write stories about charismatic kings stricken with the dart of love (Henry's words, not mine). So, without further ado, I wish to thank Henry VIII, Katherine of Aragon, Anne Boleyn, Jane Seymour, Anne of Cleves, Catherine Howard, Catherine Parr, Mary I, Elizabeth I, and Edward VI. Wherever you are, broken family, I hope your hearts are mended (and your necks, gulp!) and please know that—nearly five hundred years into the future—we still speak your names.

ABOUT THE AUTHOR

Natalie Murray is the author of Emmie and the Tudor King (2021), Emmie and the Tudor Queen (2021), Emmie and the Tudor Throne (2022), and the Emmie and the Tudor King Special Edition New Adult Omnibus (2022) from Midnight Tide Publishing. The time travel romance series follows a high school graduate to a reimagined Tudor England where she meets a doomed, but utterly dreamy, Tudor king. The series has received acclaim from Foreword Reviews, InD'-Tale Magazine, YA Books Central, and popular YA authors Brigid Kemmerer (A Curse So Dark and Lonely) and CJ Flood (Infinite Sky), among others. Emmie and the Tudor King was an award-winning finalist in the 14th Annual National Indie® Excellence Awards in the New Adult Fiction category. Natalie is currently penning a series of adult contemporary romance novels from beautiful Lake Macquarie on Australia's east coast, where she lives with her husband, two children, and pet snake, Reggie.

You can find Natalie Murray forgetting to update her website or procrastinating on social media at:

nataliemurrayauthor.com
instagram.com/nataliemurrayauthor
facebook.com/nataliemurrayauthor
tiktok.com/@nataliemurrayauthor

MORE BOOKS YOU'LL LOVE

If you enjoyed this story, please consider leaving a review! Then check out more books from Midnight Tide Publishing!

www.midnighttidepublishing.com

A CURSED KISS

By Jenny Hickman

Living on an island plagued by magic and mythical monsters isn't a fairy tale...it's a nightmare.

After Keelynn witnesses her sister's murder at the hands of the legendary Gancanagh, an immortal creature who seduces women and kills them with a cursed kiss, she realizes there's nothing she wouldn't do to get her back. With the help of a vengeful witch, she's given everything she needs to resurrect the person she loves most.

But first, she must slay the Gancanagh.

Tadhg, a devilishly handsome half-fae who has no patience for high society—or propriety—would rather spend his time in the company of loose women and dark creatures than help a human kill one of his own.

That is until Keelynn makes him an offer he can't refuse.

Together, they embark on a cross-country curse-breaking mission that promises life but ends in death.

THE CASTLE OF THORNS
By Elle Beaumont

To end the murders, she must live with the beast of the forest.

After surviving years with a debilitating illness that leaves her weak, Princess Gisela must prove that she is more than her ailment. She discovers her father, King Werner, has been growing desperate for the herbs that have been her survival. So much so, that he's willing to cross paths with a deadly legend of Todesfall Forest to retrieve her remedy.

Knorren is the demon of the forest, one who slaughters anyone who trespasses into his land. When King Werner steps into his territory, desperately pleading for the herbs that control his beloved daughter's illness, Knorren toys with the idea. However, not without a cost. King Werner must deliver his beloved Gisela to Knorren or suer dire consequences.

With unrest spreading through the kingdom, and its people growing tired of a king who won't put an end to the demon of Todesfall Forest, Gisela must make a choice. To become Knorren's prisoner forever, or risk the lives of her beloved people.